THE ZOMBIE BIBLE

Stant Litore

FICTION BY STANT LITORE

THE ZOMBIE BIBLE

Death Has Come Up into Our Windows
What Our Eyes Have Witnessed
Strangers in the Land
No Lasting Burial
I Will Hold My Death Close
By a Slender Thread (forthcoming)

THE ANSIBLE STORIES

Ansible: Season One
Ansible: Season Two

and

The Running of the Tyrannosaurs

Dante's Heart

The Dark Need (The Dead Man, #20)
with Lee Goldberg and William Rabkin

NONFICTION BY STANT LITORE

Write Characters Your Readers Won't Forget
Lives of Unstoppable Hope

THE ZOMBIE BIBLE

BOOKS 1 - 5
THE SILVER EDITION

DEATH HAS COME UP INTO OUR WINDOWS
WHAT OUR EYES HAVE WITNESSED
STRANGERS IN THE LAND
NO LASTING BURIAL
I WILL HOLD MY DEATH CLOSE

STANT LITORE

A Westmarch Publishing release.

ISBN 978-1942458203

Previous editions published by 47North, an imprint of Amazon Publishing.

You can reach Stant Litore at:
http://stantlitore.com
zombiebible@gmail.com
http://www.facebook.com/stant.litore
@thezombiebible

PRAISE FOR STANT LITORE'S
THE ZOMBIE BIBLE

"Heartbreaking and wonderful." – *Conflictium*

"I find myself riveted to Stant's prose, not only because I'm eager to find out the characters' fate but because his words are so beautiful. The story has stayed with me days after reading it. I highly recommend." – Denise Grover Swank, author of *The Curse Keepers*

"Stant Litore has been doing fascinating phantasmagorical things with zombies in biblical times." – Jeff Vandermeer, author of *Annihilation*

"Beautifully composed and frighteningly well-researched... Well worth the read... Beyond the rich historical background and the desperate fight for survival, *Strangers in the Land* is a story about otherness, what it means to be a 'stranger'... Far from being 'just another zombie book', it is a remarkably clear look at what it means to impose a system of inequality among a culture." – *Examiner.com*

"To say I loved this book would be an understatement. I could not put it down." – *The Seattle Post-Intelligencer*

"*The Zombie Bible* is philosophy played out in bleak landscapes. It's psychology set to the harsh strains of Prokofiev. Litore's prose is lean and hungry; his characters are faceted all-round like various colored stones; his scenes pulse with blood and life, ring with metal or reek of sweat and undeath." – Marc McDermott

"Like Cormac McCarthy's novels, *I Will Hold My Death Close* does not pull its punches. A beautiful, brilliant tale, it offers a pretty bleak picture of the human condition and the human struggle against the terrors of this world." – Andrew Hallam, Ph.D., Metropolitan State University of Denver

"Litore's vibrant writing . . . rips the lid off of the King James version and reveals to us a world of intense human hopes, dreams and pathos, with a liberal dose of horror seething in the shadows. You've never seen anything like this before." – Richard Ellis Preston, Jr., author of *Romulus Buckle and the City of the Founders*

"If I could write a one-word review, it would be *Wow*. I still can't get over the beautiful horror of Litore's writing. Regina was a breathtaking character who stole the show for me. Even as I write this review, my eyes mist over. Highly recommended." – Jennifer Bielman, *Reading and Writing Urban Fantasy*

"Intensely troubling and sharply beautiful. I highly anticipate the opportunity to reread it." – Timothy Widman, *Wandering Paths*

"Gruesome and human and lyrical and horrible, *The Zombie Bible* is like nothing you have ever read. Once you're in, you'll stay."
– S.G. Redling, author of *Flowertown* and *Damocles*

"Stant rebuilds the zombie mythology from the ground up."
– Rob Kroese, author of *Mercury Falls* and *Schrodinger's Gat*

"What Litore has done ... I call it the de-sanitisation of the gospel: a visceral, messy, human take on a message of a visceral and tangible hope."
– Siku, creator of *The Manga Bible* and *Drink It!*

"A good novel should go for the throat; *Death Has Come up into Our Windows* goes for your heart, rips it out and eats it before your eyes." – Lucinda Rose, *Rose Reads*

"This book is one of those things that you run across and immediately know it will be either amazing or awful - and nowhere in between. The author did an incredible job of bringing his characters to life - you could taste their fear, ache with their grief and rage with them. This is the most life-like and empathetic portrait of a prophet I've ever read." – *Burgundy Damsel*

"Stant Litore's retelling of biblical stories as episodes in the age-old battle of humanity against the rise of the undead ... is fantastically good. The mashup more than 'just works' at about every level. Whether it's Old Testament prophets battling zombies from within a Babylonian-besieged Jerusalem or Rome during the rise of Christianity, Litore has found a compelling voice and style and approach." – *The AudioBookaneers*

"Nothing about this novel was phoned-in. Even parts of the story that we already knew by heart were revealed brilliantly with the gentle hand of a master surgeon. And Litore told the story his way. I found it refreshing, respectful, and loving."
– James Garcia, Jr., author of *Seeing Ghosts*

CONTENTS

DEATH HAS COME UP INTO OUR WINDOWS

BASED LOOSELY ON
THE EVENTS OF JEREMIAH

587 BC

---

*for all our forebears who labored
in pursuit of a better world*

HISTORIAN'S NOTE

THE CRISIS CREATED by an outbreak of the walking dead offers a telling diagnostic of those flaws in the human condition that resurface, century upon century: our tendency to let problems fester untended until they become crises, our frequent inability to work together for a common good, our quickness to forget the lessons our grandparents learned at the cost of much sweat and blood, and the extent to which our privileged classes ignore and deny responsibility for the plight of the impoverished and the disinherited. Our ancestors often described the attacks of the hungry dead as acts of either divine retribution for human sins or divine abandonment in utter grief at human evil, and in at least one sense they may have been correct: the rapid rise of an outbreak is nearly always a consequence of our own failings.

Even across a gap of millennia, those scrolls attributed to the prophet Yirmiyahu (whose name we anglicize as "Jeremiah") retain their power both to evoke the memory of one of history's most tragic outbreaks of the zombie plague and to move our hearts with one of history's most eloquent appeals for social justice. A minimum of historical context may suffice to set the stage for our narrative. As a levite's son, Yirmiyahu was a member of the privileged class of the priesthood, though he was born in a small village; moving early in his life to the more urban center of Yerushalayim, Yirmiyahu was apparently appalled at the level of poverty he witnessed there. Taking up the role of a prophet—a navi, or bringer of words from God—he began to preach in the streets and on the Temple steps, demanding that the city dwellers return to the terms of their ancestors' Covenant with their deity—specifically, communal provision for orphans and widows, monotheism, abstention from human sacrifice, clean burial for the dead, and the observing of a periodic year of yovel in which all slaves and indentured workers would be released from their bondage or their debts.

At about the same time, the youthful king of the Hebrews, Tsidkiyyahu ("Zedekiah"), ceased paying tribute to Babylon in the east—and then used the savings in large part to garrison the city against a possible invasion. That invasion came swiftly, and Babylon established a lengthy and debilitating siege. Food stores within the city ran low, and in the overcrowded conditions created by the hurried evacuation of the surrounding countryside prior to the siege, an outbreak of the dead (who had never fully been cleaned out of the city's back alleys) surged unchecked. Yirmiyahu believed that this situation, taken together with the injustice and corruption of Yerushalayim's leaders, made holding the city untenable—and that the only course of action that would merit God's favor and forgiveness would be to surrender the gates of the city and beseech the aid of the Babylonians in cleansing the city of the dead and feeding its famished populace. Yirmiyahu's very public voicing of this opinion did not make him popular with the king and the merchant class, who in a surrender would lose everything.

In this crisis there was a terrible irony, one likely not lost on the prophet. A century earlier, Yerushalayim had faced a similar siege and its population had been similarly outnumbered and locked within the city's narrow walls; yet the earlier siege had crumbled when the pestilence raged through the enemy camp, so that the enemy turned and devoured one another. The walls of Yerushalayim had sufficed to keep out the enemy, both living and dead. In the generations since, these events had become a bedside story of divine deliverance that mothers related to their children.

Doubtless, the king and the merchant class in Yirmiyahu's time trusted that this story would be repeated, but to Yirmiyahu two factors in the current emergency must have appeared strikingly and appallingly different.

First, the king of a century earlier, unlike the current monarch, had been one who maintained programs caring for the city's poor and who outlawed religious practices of foreign origin.

Second, this time the dead were not outside but inside the walls. The living and the dead, both starving, were locked in together.

***

One personal note before we begin. The scrolls of Yirmiyahu are often treated as the first jeremiad, an outpouring of rage and gnashing of teeth against a city's injustice and decay. But there is a lake of emotion, cold and dark, beneath those quick bursts of anger. These scrolls are a lamentation (to me, a poignant one), a wrestling with the likelihood of despair. Historians know that the city fell after a bitter and protracted siege and that the few survivors were led away in chains, their temples looted and burned, their abandoned homes loud with the moans of the dead. Yirmiyahu's recorded sayings come to us as cries in the dark; pleas for justice that fell, at the time, on deaf or frightened ears. His story confronts us with the horror that our greatest efforts to heal and preserve our communities may not be enough. In the end, there may only be hunger, illness, and a slow death that brings neither peace nor rest.

The horror of what Yirmiyahu saw and what he endured is nearly too much for me. In reencountering his words, we can do one of two things. We can flinch away—turn our back on the suffering and eat, drink, and be merry, leaving death until tomorrow. Or we can gaze on the horror with unblinking eyes and listen with shuddering hearts, and make the choice Yirmiyahu demands, searching within ourselves or asking of God whether we have the courage to live lives of hope and action even when faced with almost certain failure, letting our efforts burn hot as a sun in a universe that appears governed (though we hope and trust that it isn't) only by the law of entropy.

FIRST DAY: TRUTH AT THE BOTTOM OF THE WELL

BY THE TIME they lowered Yirmiyahu into the old well behind the king's house, the city around them was already dying. Neither the king nor the priests would admit it, but there were more dead every day, and some of those dead were walking.

It was an empty well, nearly dry; yet when Yirmiyahu reached the bottom he found mud, and for a moment he panicked, his throat seizing up—he didn't know how deep the mud might be; his legs sank into it. Then there was solid earth under his feet. The mud was higher than his knees, a cold, wet suck around his legs. He shivered and shrank against one of the cistern's stone walls as the guards pulled the rope back up. He thought about clutching it, realized it would be useless. They would only lower him back in— or haul him halfway up and drop him, claiming an "accident."

The men above were laughing as they left; he could hear echoes of it, distorted in the long shaft of the well. He gazed up. A circle of sunlight, pale and distant, far above him, a reminder that somewhere above this hole in the ground there was light and deity. He lifted his hand, shaking a little. Even if he could not reach that light, he could perhaps be heard. "God!" he cried. "Help me out of here. Don't let me perish like this."

The echoes of the guards' mockery had faded, and no voice of God or man answered Yirmiyahu from that high circle. His heart quailed; he drew a shuddering breath and stilled the shaking of his hands.

Well. He was here.

He forced his gaze down. The mud lay quiet in these shadows unless he moved. He'd smuggled half a crust of bread into his loincloth—the only clothing they'd left him. His back and arms were scraped and sore from the times he had swung against the stones as they lowered him. His hair and beard had not been cut in long months, while he'd been locked in the cellar of the king's house; he must look like a nazarite, like Samson of old, who slew a thousand walking corpses with only a donkey's jawbone.

The stones against his back were cold so he stood in the middle for a while, his legs trembling. He'd almost forgotten how to stand in the last dark months. Closing his eyes, he felt the still air, listened, listened. He might yet hear God's voice again—he might hear her even in this dark well. He might. That silence above him was as terrifying as the darkness in which he stood—this clinging, tangible *hoshekh*, a darkness that touched both body and spirit. For once, no divine words welled up within him. Perhaps God had already turned away from her decaying city, and from Yirmiyahu within it.

He tried to slow the beating of his heart. Tried to remember how to think. He was a levite; though others of the priestly caste disowned him as a troublemaker and a rabble-rouser, he was still a levite, a dedicate; a levite must have the deepest commitment to God and to the Covenant (that he'd learned from his father) and to the People (that he'd learned from his wife). They might throw him in a well; still, he was a levite and a prophet. In the street or in a well, he would hold to his covenant with God.

He hungered but did not eat. He didn't know whether Tsidkiyyahu the king had ordered him into the well for only a day or for two days or three, or if he'd been left here to die. He didn't know how long he'd already stood here in the mud. The light above looked more pale than before. Besides that far circle, he saw where there was light on one side of the well below it; the sun had been above him when they lowered him into this place, but now it must have swung across the sky. I will know how many days pass, he thought.

The chill crept inside him, making him shake. He might not last the night without clothing to cover him. Up there, the heat baked every hint of favor and life out of the city, but down here it was cold as dream country. His lips felt dry. "We are People of the Covenant," he whispered. "Each of us made in the likeness of God." He repeated it, words that comforted though they did not warm him. In the silence of God, Yirmiyahu murmured the words she had given him before, words whispered to him in the dark, over the past few years. The words that mattered. "We are People of the Covenant. We are the spouse of our God."

He thought of the city, the heat making the air over its walls ripple. He thought of its quiet gardens with their dry beds where once there had been pools of quiet water, its stone paths, its treasure-houses. The palace of the king, with this deep well in one of its lower courtyards. And the crowded back streets, where Yirmiyahu had taken to living these past months, after sending his wife away from the city before the siege. These were the dry streets of an unreplenished city relying on dried or drying wells, where bands of orphans hunted for scraps or broke into smaller houses to tear food from the larders. He had seen a young child dying in one street, her skin stretched too tight over her ribs, her eyes wide and unseeing. In the next street, mothers who could still afford bread baked cakes for Astarte, the most popular of Yerushalayim's foreign goddesses, and pretended they could not hear others' children begging for food at the door or crying in the night.

"I know your ways," he whispered, reciting the words God had found for him, words she'd sent, through him, to priests who didn't wish to hear. He trailed his fingers through the mud. It had been a season since he had felt the ground wet. There was a sheen of dirt over his body. "I know your ways. You've relied on broken and dried cisterns rather than the well that nourishes. God says: *You were my branches, beautiful with good fruit, well watered and tall. But drought comes with a roar from the desert, and the branches are withering.*"

How strange, this cold mud under his fingers, earth that had become full of water yet grew nothing. Yirmiyahu lifted his hand toward his eyes but could no longer see his fingers. Everything was dark. He looked up again. There were stars there, beautiful though faint, too far away to give him light. His stomach snarled like a lion, and he took the bread crust from his loincloth, lifted it to his mouth. It was hard and dry and had no flavor. It hurt his teeth to chew it; he thought of dipping it in the mud to moisten it, decided not to. He kept chewing slowly and at last swallowed a little bit of it. That made him thirsty, which was worse. He kept eating.

Something moved against his leg and he jumped, almost dropping the bread. With a sob he leaned back against the wall and finished the crust. Only a worm, or some snake. He was not alone in this mud, then; some other living creature God had birthed into the world was here with him. He tried to calm his breathing, take comfort from that. He looked at the stars again. Other people in the city, and in the land, were perhaps gazing up at those same remote stars. Even his wife might be standing at this moment at the door or the window of a house in the village he'd sent her back to, her face tilted up and bathed in starlight.

Beneath those same stars, an army was camped about the city, keeping its people trapped inside the walls, in narrow streets between buildings of stone or dried mud with sunbaked white roofs; and, inside the walls where food and water were already short, the plague. A few unclean dead, or many (their number grew so fast), were hunting in the alleys: the shambling corpses, their hands scratching at doors, pulling at the fragile wood. A few months ago, he had seen two—one had been a priest, *a priest*, one of his own caste, still clad in the simple white robes of the levites who kept the Temple—he'd seen those two tear down a door and drag a woman out into the street. He had run at them, crushed one's head with a shovel he'd taken from a worker at the wall. But the other—the priest—had sunk its teeth deep into the woman's shoulder. He remembered her cry of pain, the wildness of her eyes, her terror. He remembered the way the walking corpse that fed on her looked up at him when he came at it, its eyes with nothing in them but hunger and animal hostility. He remembered its wavering moan.

After the priest lay unmoving in the dust, Yirmiyahu killed the woman. Gasping, he leaned over the shovel, gazing down at her broken body. No one else came. He stood there a long time, shaking, gazing in horror at the woman he'd killed. The body would otherwise have risen to hunger and eat in the dark—yet this had been a woman's body, a sacred and life-giving body, shaped in the likeness of God herself. Yirmiyahu gazed at the woman's eyes, glazing already in death. It was too terrible for tears; he just stood and shook.

***

Now, in the well, he wrapped his arms around himself and stumbled in slow circles through the mud, trying to stay on his feet, trying to keep warm. He was so weary. In this darkness he felt as though his mind might come apart as easily as a bread crust soaked in mud. "We are the People of the Covenant, of God," he said hoarsely in the dark, "each of us made in her likeness." He kept saying it; it was good to hear words, though speaking made his throat more dry.

He had barely been a man when he'd first heard those words, newly come to Yerushalayim from his father's village, a few short years past, with a small pack of white clothing and gifts from his grandmother, and a lovely and laughing wife walking beside him. He'd just secured a small house in the city with the coin his father had sent with him. Intending to study with the levites, he meant to go to them at the Temple steps in the morning, the long lines of them with their austere faces.

Then God had spoken in a voice that made the hot night air tremble. Yirmiyahu had been dressed in a loincloth then, as now, for it had been the middle of the night. He'd stepped out of his new house into the street and listened, while Miriam dreamed in their bed. The stars had been as far away then as they were now, but all around him had been the looming presence of the lives of the people of that new city, in their hundreds of stone houses.

Yirmiyahu, the voice called. *My Yirmiyahu.*

"Are you calling me, *adonai*?" he whispered.

There was a silence. Then the voice was at his ear. *Before you were in your mother's womb, I knew you.* The voice became a whisper, as though sharing a secret between the two of them. *Before you were born, I set you apart, called you as my* navi, *my prophet.*

That word rushed through Yirmiyahu like a sudden wind through the door of a house, knocking aside his carefully placed furniture and pulling curtains and veils aside from the openings to inner rooms. The *navi*, the prophet, the bringer of *niv sefatayim*, the fruit from God. There had been many in the history of the land, men and women who could hear God and who carried her words to the People, words as full and round and fertile as apricots or pomegranates. But Yirmiyahu didn't know of any who now spoke or did healing in the land. *Navi, navi*: he trembled.

"Yes, *adonai*," he breathed, his eyes wide. He knew there could be no other answer, not to her. He knelt, there in the street, his heart shaking within him. "But *adonai*, I am young, I am—"

There was a soft pressure against his lips—like a woman's fingers hushing him—a touch cool and soft, a touch of divine fingers. He trembled, his heart beating within the well of his chest. All about him in the air, he sensed God quivering, vitally present, like a vast tree invisible in the night, a deep and inexhaustible well beneath its roots, water drawn upward, cool and quiet, to the full fruit that clung to all God's branches.

Do not go to the priests in the morning, the voice said, and the invisible branches moved gently in the air. *Go to the people, my* navi. *Look in the streets, look at how my People live, how they keep the Covenant, see what they do in this city. Then, when it is nearly dusk and wind is in the olives, go to the priests. Take my words, Yirmiyahu. Take them to the Temple. I have set you tonight against those who lead nations and cities, to pluck up and to break down, to destroy and to overthrow, to build and to plant. Go, Yirmiyahu.* That small, small whisper in his ear, soft as wind in trees yet firm with command. *Prepare yourself. Take my words and speak them. I make you this day a fortified city, a rooted cedar, a wall. They will fight against you, my* navi, *they will throw themselves against you, but they will not prevail against you, for I am with you, to keep you and deliver you, nourish you and strengthen you.*

***

A rustle above him broke his thoughts as abruptly as a man breaks a twig; glancing up, Yirmiyahu saw shapes silhouetted coldly against the stars. He called hoarsely for help, heard an echo of laughter again. His tormentors were back. They threw something out over that hole of sky, and it fell. For an instant his heart surged with hope at the thought of food, a bundle of food; then he felt the rush of air and the mass of it hit the mud beside him in the terrible dark. He heard the cracking of bone, and his belly heaved at the sweet and overpowering stench of the rotting dead. The thing stirred, and he saw two glints of starlight—eyes in the dark. A low, shuddering moan filled his ears, surrounding him, echoing in the narrow well.

Yirmiyahu lurched back with a cry. Stumbling, he fell into the mud. Kicking out with his feet, he scrambled away until he felt the stone wall cold against his shoulders.

The glints of light were coming at him. A loud slurping of mud as the thing moved, dragging its broken body through the muck. The creature's moan went on and on. He could not see it in the dark, but he knew it was reaching for him, fingers groping to seize his leg and pull him toward its teeth. He kept kicking, his heart wild with beating, his breath coming fast. Light-headed with fear. He felt the brush of its fingertips against his skin and shuddered with loathing, as though maggots had touched him in the mud. With a low cry he got his knees under him, the mud cool around his thighs; reaching down, he seized the creature's hair near the roots and hauled the thing's head away from his leg. It hissed and twisted, trying to bite at his arm; its strength was terrible. With his other hand he snatched his loincloth from about his hips, wadded it swiftly, and shoved it into the creature's mouth, muffling its low growl.

Yirmiyahu forced its head down into the mud. He panted, his arms straining, his muscles screaming with the effort of holding down the corpse. Though the mud closing over its head silenced it, it did not grow still, nor did its limbs flail in panic. It was not a living man. It was an incarnation of raw hunger and need, and it required no air to live; its hands were beneath it, pushing. The creature strained to force its reeking body out of the mud, even as Yirmiyahu strained to keep it submerged. With a gasp of panic, Yirmiyahu felt his arms trembling; in another moment or two they would give out, and the hungering creature would be on him. Leaning his back against the wall for leverage, he lifted his leg with a wild shriek and brought his heel slamming down on the thing's head.

The blow pressed the thing deeper into the mud, but still it strained to rise. Screaming, Yirmiyahu brought his heel down again and again, with all the force he could, hard blows to the back of the thing's head. For a few moments, it kept fighting him; then Yirmiyahu felt something hard give beneath his heel, and the thing went limp. He smashed his heel into it twice more before falling back against the wall, moaning with horror. Before him in the dark, he saw the lumpy shape of the corpse's back above the mud. Yirmiyahu slammed his palms wildly against the stone wall at his sides, screaming through clenched teeth, trying to control his panic.

Dimly, he heard laughter somewhere far above him.

That sobered him. He fell silent, simply leaned against the wall, breathing hard. He didn't bother to look up; he didn't care to see the silhouettes of his tormenters leaning in, looking down into the dark, mocking his fight for survival. He growled low in his throat, anger bubbling on the rim of his mind. What people were they up there, joying in the torment of their prisoner? How could *these* be People of the Covenant, people who shared his city and his God?

His heart began to slow down. He dragged his hand across his eyes, wiping away dirt and muck and sweat. The laughter had stopped; one of them called down something, but the echoes of the well distorted the words. He did not plan to beg them for water or food, or even let them know whether he'd been bitten or not; doubtless they would grow bored in a few moments and go their way. His anger started to fade as fatigue crept over him again. They tormented him, he realized, because they were men without hope for the future. They grabbed at what small-hearted pleasures they could, because they were increasingly certain, somewhere deep in their spirit, that the next morning, or the morning after that, or some morning soon would find them cold and dead—or perhaps lurching, mindless, through a deserted city in search of meat. They had chosen not to hope.

He began to think, using this moment of cold clarity to hold off his fatigue and horror.

His loincloth was likely irrecoverable—but he could not last this night naked. He was certain of that. Hissing through his teeth, he bent quickly to do what had to be done. He began stripping the creature of its clothes, fighting not to retch at the scent, muttering a Hebrew psalm under his breath—one of Dawid's—to distract his mind from what he was doing. He could feel the thing's cold skin beneath his hands, not hard but terribly soft. He gagged, leaned into the wall a moment, fought for air. That touch—that *touch*—on his hands. On his heel, on his shin. He moaned. Unclean. He was unclean. He was a levite, and his hands had touched *the dead*. The words of the Covenant and the Law rang within him, demanding atonement, words of purpose and command that had been established centuries past, when the People were still tent dwellers in the desert, lying awake in their wool bedding and listening for the moan of the dead in the hills:

You shall bury the flesh of the dead, and raise above it a cairn of stones, a warning to any that see.

You shall not touch the flesh of the dead, for the dead body is unclean. If a man touches the flesh of the dead, you shall put him from your camp, and watch him. Seven days you shall put him from your camp.

Those were *mitzvot*, commandments for keeping the People clean and vital and free of the clinging, hungering dead. Yirmiyahu's palms stung where his fingernails dug into his skin.

He drew in ragged breaths. Unclean. He should be cast from the People. He had touched the dead. Yet—he was already cast out, already isolated. He glanced up at that circle high above him, with its faint promise of starlight. He was in the dark, he was alone, he was cold, and his uncleanness in this well would harm no others of the People. Unclenching his hands, he returned to his work. He would *not* die here. He had been called to God's service, and there *was* still a city to preserve, to call back to its Covenant.

He'd seen so many broken covenants. The priesthood had broken faith with the people, hoarding grain while children starved in the streets and condoning the defilements at Tophet. The king had broken covenant with the people, delighting in wealth rather than in the health and feeding of the city. The people themselves had broken covenant, binding themselves to other deities, who demanded less and promised more than they could indeed offer. Yirmiyahu hissed through his teeth as he peeled cloth away from flesh. Even *he* had broken covenant—with his wife. He'd sent Miriam away as the city grew violent. He squeezed his eyes shut against the anguish of that memory.

But clean or unclean, he would not break covenant with *God*. He was God's prophet, her *navi*. His task was to speak for her, to bring her words like water-rich fruit to a people who insisted they were content with dried crusts. He must do that; he must stay ready to do that, whatever came; he must last the night. He must keep trying. He had been thrown in here, unwilling to be silent; if the king ever let him out, he would not be silent then. But first he must live. The rhythmic phrases of the old Hebrew prayer soared from his lips, the prayer of Dawid, louder and still louder, until the sound of his voice filled the well. Lifting one of the corpse's arms, he pulled its tunic free, then dropped the naked arm into the sucking mud and staggered back. The fabric he clutched was torn and filthy with blood and viscous fluid and muck; but if he could make it through this night, the next day might dry it. The tunic might be unclean, but it was clothing, it was life. He wrung out what dampness he could, then draped it over his shoulders. It was not warm but it was heavy, and perhaps that would make some difference.

***

For a while he sank to his knees, the mud around his waist. He shivered in his improvised shawl, fitfully moving from sleep to quiet sobbing, and back to sleep again. He woke in starts from half dreams in which he had felt the cutting of teeth into his arm or his leg, certain the corpse had risen from the mud, that it was groping for him. He tried to force himself to move, to reach for it and feel whether it lay still, there in the dark. He reached out his trembling hand, felt cold flesh, jerked it back. He was sweating. His hands kept shaking. He tried to reach out again, but he couldn't, he couldn't. It was coming for him, it was coming in the dark. He shrank against the wall and listened, listened for that terrible moan. Heard only his quick heartbeats. Shaking. Unable to sleep, he knelt sobbing, leaning his back against the wall, his own wrenching, human moans repeating one word, the name of his wife. Over half a year since he'd seen her. "Miriam," he groaned, "Miriam. Miriam—"

Then he called the darkness by its name: *hoshekh*. Naming it, knowing it, might at least keep it from choking him: *hoshekh*. The darkness that is darkest of all darknesses, the darkness that hides in the back of caves. The darkness that fills the mind of one who refuses to hear the cries in the street, the darkness that hides behind the ribs of a man or a woman, that eats at everything that is real and true inside them. *Hoshekh*. Once, the Lawgiver had called a plague of *hoshekh* upon the people of the cities of the Nile, who had not heard the cries of their slave workers or their wives, the cries when soldiers took their infants and drowned them in the river. And when those unhearing people yawned and lay themselves down for sleep, the *hoshekh* poured from their mouths like dark milk until their houses and all their land was filled with it. When they woke in the morning, they were blind and could not even move from their beds, for the *hoshekh* was heavy on them as they lay, and heavy inside them, as though they were at the bottom of a pool of dark mud. For three days and three nights they lay moaning in the *hoshekh*, while the people of Israel ate and sang in the hovels of the slave encampments, where there was light and, for once, no work.

Hoshekh, Yirmiyahu called this darkness in the well that pressed on his skin. The whole city above must be filled with it, this night. Darker than dark, the city. Only the dead could move through it with their slow feet, their leaning bodies scraping against the walls of houses and shops, their fingers reaching over the stone, hungering.

***

When he opened his eyes again, it was still dark. He did not know whether it was the same night or another, or how long he'd slept. His stomach growled like a wild beast fighting to gnaw open his belly. He trembled in his rags and cried out wordlessly. Passing his hand before his face, he saw only its outline. His lips were terribly dry, his tongue and throat more so. The stench of death in the well was strong, too strong to become used to, and he retched into the mud in great heaves, though little came up, for he had already retched up the bread and water he had in him. He was still on his knees, and when he moved them a little he found his legs were numb and stiff; when he moved them a little more, they went violent with pain. Clenching his teeth, he waited for the pain to pass. Tears ran from the corners of his eyes, hot against his cheeks.

He had awakened from another evil dream; frayed tatters of it still clung to him like the clothes he wore, clothes he'd taken from the dead. Waking, he still saw the faces of children, the whites around their eyes, heard the shrieks from their open mouths. Saw the rotting flesh of the hands that gripped them, pulling them down into the pit. Standing in a circle about the pit, men and women with pale faces and their arms at their sides. The pit atop the hill of Tophet. In his dream he screamed at them. "I see the blood of children on your skirts!" he cried, extending his arms toward the women, but he couldn't reach them.

For just one moment, he thought maybe—maybe—that hill, all of it, had been only a dream. Maybe it had only ever been night terrors and nothing more. Maybe he had dreamed it all, here at the bottom of this cold well. But no: it had been real, terribly real.

***

In the tense months before the siege began, Yirmiyahu had still lived with Miriam his wife in their little house near the gates of the city. It had been his habit in the afternoons to urge the men at the city gates to petition the priests for bread and grain to feed Yerushalayim's forgotten children; many times he'd lifted his eyes to the hill while he spoke and seen the haze of smoke above its ridge. From its position in the hot air, Yirmiyahu could tell the smoke came from the old shrine on the hill's far slope—a sign that some of the People had resumed sacrifices to Chemosh, the heathen god who lived at the shrine. Sometimes Yirmiyahu would fall silent in the midst of a heated conversation with a merchant at the gates and stare for a long time at that smoke. Eventually the merchant would turn to look, too. Some of the merchants scowled then and made a sign against evil with their fingers; others took on a thoughtful look. Other times the merchant's face would darken with shame, and he'd turn quickly and strike up a conversation with some other man who was near, eager for a reason to hide his face from the *navi*.

The hill troubled Yirmiyahu. For the *navi*, monotheism was a fiercely ethical matter, in a way that later men in later centuries would rarely understand or remember. To Yirmiyahu's mind, being covenanted to one woman and to one God taught a man steadiness, the steadiness needed to stand in a strong wind. To have many women or many deities was to be buffeted by winds from many

STANT LITORE

directions; it meant not knowing who one was called upon to protect and worship. It meant being accustomed to a degree of faithlessness, to offering merely a conditional devotion to both God and woman. It meant the ease of distraction, of picking and choosing from one's responsibilities and relationships, laying down those that were most difficult at a particular moment and devoting more of oneself instead to those that required less work and less truth.

Other tribes saw these things differently, quite differently, but Yirmiyahu was the descendant of generations of levites, and he was watching the city of his People die. His unease with seductive, heathen deities was hot in his chest. Gazing at the smoke on the hill's summit, Yirmiyahu almost thought he could hear, faint in the day's heat, the calling of those hungry gods and goddesses whom his People had not brought with them out of the desert long ago but had found waiting for them in this land. Deities who spread their arms wide and moaned: *Come to me, I will give you wealth or security or love, or what you desire, only feed me, feed me. I am so hungry; don't you want to feed me?*

Sometimes the cries of those other gods, who had established no abiding Covenant with the People, rose from a faint moan on the hill to a shriek of urgent, demanding need; at those times he would look away from the summit, shivering even in the day heat as the merchants chattered and argued around him. And all the while, Yirmiyahu's God murmured from behind the veil in her Temple, *I am here. If you want me, you must be faithful to me, and you must nourish my children. You must work hard to provide for them. Then I will let you take me in your arms and I will delight you and nourish you.* A God of Covenant for a People of the Covenant, a divine spouse and not only a divine lover. That is how the *navi* saw it.

It would be an easy thing, perhaps, to keep his eyes from straying to that hill. To not ask what sacrifices Chemosh received up there. Yet Yirmiyahu couldn't stop looking. The sight of that haze gnawed at him. Of all the People's lovers, he *feared* Chemosh. Chemosh was a god apart. Astarte's love was playful and vitalizing; Baal's was stern and demanding; Dagon's was tempestuous, overwhelming, and fickle as the sea in which he swam with his fish; but Chemosh—that was a god who would beat his lovers and batter them. And Chemosh would only grin darkly in the knowledge that such treatment would just convince his worshippers all the more of his power and his strength to provide for them, keep them, and shield them: that the more he beat his worshippers, the more they would fall to the earth, kiss his feet, and beg for the privilege of feeding him.

In bed at night, with the soft breathing of his wife beside him, Yirmiyahu would wake sometimes, thinking of that hill, trying to persuade himself that those sons and daughters of the People who visited the shrine were bringing only fruit or sheaves of barley to the god. Yet his heart told him it wasn't so.

Once he came awake with a start, thinking he'd heard weeping. He bolted upright and gazed into the dark, but the sound faded from hearing as swiftly as any dream sound might. Miriam stirred beside him. "What is it, husband?" Her voice heavy with sleep.

Yirmiyahu was breathing hard, the sheets sweaty beneath him. He didn't look at her; he kept gazing in the direction from which the sound had come, if there had actually been a sound. His ears strained to hear it. With a dryness in his throat, he realized he was staring in the direction of the Temple.

"Yirmiyahu?" A little fear in her voice. There were dead now in some of the alleys of the city. A noise in the night was something to fear.

Yirmiyahu let out his breath slowly. He didn't wish to frighten her with what was likely only a dream. Turning to her, he saw her eyes soft and liquid in the dark. Her soft form on the bed caught at his heart; he set his hand on her thigh.

"A bad dream," he murmured.

After a moment he felt her small hands take his, drawing his palm to her lips. He let his heartbeat slow; if God was weeping for something done on that hill—if she needed him—she would call for him. But right now his wife needed him. This had not been an easy year for her, and she was more often the one who woke with bad dreams. The moist warmth of her lips pressed his hand, and he tried to smile in the dark but couldn't. Couldn't shake the feeling that something was terribly, terribly wrong.

"Come back to sleep," Miriam whispered.

He lay beside her and took her firmly in his arms, feeling the warmth of her; the hard bite of his anxiety eased.

Miriam pressed herself to him, kissing his neck once, and stroked his back with her fingers. After a while her hands slowed and were still; her breathing slowed. He kissed her hair and held her, wakeful, while she slept. He kept listening in the dark, waiting to hear that sound of weeping a second time.

Yirmiyahu didn't close his eyes again that night.

***

God did call for him—the next day.

As noon approached and Yirmiyahu wended through the narrow streets toward the gates, God whispered to him. There was pleading in her voice. *There are things I need you to see,* she whispered. *There are things you need to know, my* navi. *Up on the hill. Go to the hill, my* navi.

If he had known just how terrible those things would be, what God would ask him to endure, perhaps he wouldn't have had the courage to climb that hill. As it was, Yirmiyahu climbed slowly, reluctantly. He glanced over his shoulder once at the roofs of the city within its walls, wooden roofs and roofs of brick clay, mixed patches of bright and dark in the afternoon glare of the sun. Then, turning his back, he went to see what he must see, a grimness in his face. He met no one else on the slope; whatever worshippers had been here were not here now. It was a long climb, and when he reached the summit under its brooding oaks, he was nearly out of breath.

There he found the altar, and behind it, the massive statue of the god, a thing of gold under the trees. Yirmiyahu's eyes took in its distended belly, its bloated, grasping hands, its gaping mouth. The god's lower jaw hung down to its feet, and through it, Yirmiyahu could see the sacrificial pit, a hole opened in the earth. On the god's golden lips—the lips of the pit—Yirmiyahu could see stains. He shrank back, turned from the pit a moment to touch the ashes on the altar. Still warm. And two great lamps yet burned at either side of the god, their oil sending up a heavy-scented smoke.

He swallowed. Some of the People had been here, feeding the god, even earlier that very day, though they were now gone. He glanced again at the god's face. Chemosh's eyes were small, just tiny notches in the gold statue, and Yirmiyahu did not feel watched. The god was fed, content, and in any case this was not a god of seeing or hearing. This god was all mouth and belly.

Who had been here, feeding it? Olive farmers from the slopes of the Mount on the other side of the city, where olive trees, beloved of the People, swayed in the wind? Or tanners and potters and anxious craftsmen come out from within the city walls? What people were feeding this god? And what was the god eating? A levite who had been raised hearing all the lore of his People, Yirmiyahu knew enough about the hungers of the heathen gods for horror to paralyze his heart. Seeing those stains on the golden lips, he could hardly breathe.

Get a torch. The voice of his own God came in a whisper through the leaves overhead. *See what your own People, my People, are doing.*

Yirmiyahu refused for a moment, hanging back, dread chilling his body.

Get a torch, my navi. The voice in the air was insistent.

Yirmiyahu cast about, found a fallen oak branch, gasped even as he reached for it—for there, caught on a jagged root of the oak, a tattered strip of white wool lay dirtied on the earth. No doubt it had been torn loose from the hem of someone's garment. The sight of it tore through Yirmiyahu. He crouched, touched the wool gently, lifted a bit of it between his fingers. He began to tremble. The oak had torn this wool from a *levite*'s garment; he was certain of it. The weave was fine, and his fingers could detect the pattern that was woven into the hems of the robes worn by every male of the priestly caste. His own hem was woven in the same pattern. His hand shook, and he fell back on his rear, breathing hard.

A levite had been here. His heart grappled with this; perhaps the priest had come only as he himself had, to spy out the doings on the hill. Perhaps it had only been that. But the cold horror that gripped him, tightening his throat, told him otherwise. The levite had been here as a participant. With irrevocable and wrenching certainty, Yirmiyahu *knew* this.

Getting to his feet and returning, shaking, to the altar, he lit the branch he carried from one of the lamps. He lifted the branch high over the pit, dread closing his throat; a circle of firelight lit the earthen floor below—a floor near enough to leap down but too far to climb back. There were bones there, many of them. Small ones, so small, the bones of children of the People—femurs and ribs, and at least two skulls within the reach of the torchlight. And that stench, rising from the bowels of the god. The horror licked at the bottom of his throat, bile rising in him. He covered his mouth and nose with his hand and kept looking, feeling the presence of his God at his shoulders, like a great terebinth with her branches leaning over him, shading him.

The whisper of God's voice came to him, soft yet irresistible as wind in the branches. *My People try to drink from dried and broken cisterns*, the voice whispered, *and forsake the well that nourishes; they forsake me. Instead of replenishment, desiccation. Instead of birth and growth, the withering of the young. Instead of my womb, this grave in a god's belly.*

Yirmiyahu peered down at the bones in the flickering light. The reek dismayed him, and the nearness of the god's statue dismayed him, too. Those bones, bits of digested people in the god's belly, made him cry out without sound, his mouth open, his insides heaving. He retched at the lip of the pit.

Long ago his own ancestors had sacrificed their firstborn at altars, even as other peoples in the farther parts of the land still did. But one of his People's oldest stories told of the Akedah, the binding of the firstborn, when God had placed her hand at Abraham's chest and stopped him from drawing his knife across his son's throat. When Yirmiyahu had been a small boy, his father had told the tale with horror and panache, and young Yirmiyahu had shivered to think of the upraised hand, the flash of the knife, the cry of the boy.

Abraham had taught this to all his children, and they to their children: We do not feed God, God feeds us. God is sufficient to feed herself and us. To honor her, give back some of the food she has given—fruit of the orchard or the first of the flock—but do not give your own young, for that is an abomination before God who brings all births.

Now Yirmiyahu gazed down into the foreign god's dark belly, and his insides grew cold. He wondered how many of the People had come to worship here, how many had come to feed the god. Was it easier to covenant with a god you'd fed, one you hoped would owe you gratitude, however cruel that god might be, than it was to covenant with a God who fed you?

As the initial bite of his horror dulled (though the stench of the pit remained intense), he tried to understand those remains. Some of the bones were cracked, as though a great beast had broken them to suck out the marrow. A fresh chill took Yirmiyahu. Gods did not need to break bones to feed. Something mortal had *fed* on those children the People had tossed into the god's belly.

The need to understand this horror—the need to know, to see what his God wanted him to witness—that need steeled his heart and limbs. He stared down at those bones in the torchlight, thinking quickly of how he might make a rope—perhaps tearing up his own robe and braiding the strips—to get down there for a closer look. There were just those bones and their terrible riddle, down there. Nothing else. He waited a long moment, trying not to retch. Then—then—

A shambling, leaning figure lurched across the circle of light below. A small figure, no larger than a boy of eight, its head turned to the ground, unaware of the watcher above it. Moving slowly, dragging one leg, but without any apparent pain. It simply limped across his view and disappeared again into the dark beyond the torch's reach.

With a sharp gasp, Yirmiyahu flung himself back, away from the pit, falling onto his side in the twigs and leaves beneath the oaks. His torch, fallen, clattered over the lip of the hole and disappeared. A breath afterward, a long, low wail from beneath the earth. A shuddering moan. Even the oak branches above appeared to tremble at it. Yirmiyahu threw an arm across his eyes and pressed himself to the earth, unable to breathe. His body tensed in wild denial.

The moan faltered. There were a few more after it, several together. There were dead in the pit: walking, hungering dead. He felt the scream building inside him, a scream that caught behind his tonsils and would not come out, would never come out. He felt like choking.

Perhaps one of the dead had fallen into the pit, then fed on the children who were brought to the god—children who then rose to moan and stumble about the pit themselves. Or perhaps one of the child sacrifices had been bitten before the child was brought to the hill, the bite concealed beneath a ceremonial vesture so that the child's parents might not be dishonored or declared unclean. Perhaps that child had been feverish when brought to the altar and had risen afterward in the earth—to feed later on the other sacrifices. Whatever horror had occurred, the pit was now full of the unclean dead.

The thought struck Yirmiyahu with a clarity as bracing and impossible to ignore as ice water poured, stabbing, at his face. The People, his People, his God's People, were not on this hill feeding Chemosh, eater of children and protector of cities; they were feeding *the dead*. The unburied dead.

He couldn't understand this.

It bewildered him and tore at him and shattered him; he lay on the ground shaking.

He lay there through most of the evening, caught between panic and prayer, tossing in a sickness that was not of the body. A wind stirred the oak leaves above, and there was a quiet creaking of branches. Sometimes, in it, he heard the soothing whispers of his God. Whenever the wind was still he could smell the dead, and he waited for the wind to come back.

***

Returning to the city before dusk, Yirmiyahu strode in wrath to the levites' houses in the street of the Temple. He burst into the home of the high priest, shattering the door from its jamb, as furious in his need to get in as though he himself were one of the dead. A woman inside had been slicing roots with an iron knife; now she shrieked at the apparition of this man in priestly robes with his hair flying and his eyes hot with rage.

At the breaking of the door and the scream, the high priest came from the back room, in his prayer shawl. Yirmiyahu seized him by the throat and slammed him into the wall; the priest was not a small man, but Yirmiyahu's speed and ferocity shocked him into stillness.

"*What have you done?*" Yirmiyahu roared.

"What?" the priest gasped. "What?"

"You are the head of our caste in the city, you *must* know about it! What have you done on Tophet?"

The priest's eyes glanced to the side.

"Don't." Yirmiyahu squeezed slightly, his chest heaving. "Truth, I want truth."

The priest wetted his lips; his hand clutched Yirmiyahu's wrist, but the *navi* did not let him go.

"The People believe if we feed the dead—" The priest's voice was hoarse from the prophet's grip on his throat; "—they will not hunger so much for us. Then they can perhaps rest again."

The words speared Yirmiyahu. Now it was clear—the moaning in the pit, the bones of children, all clear. All terribly clear. The People were tossing a few of their firstborn into the pit at Tophet to suffer there in place of their other children, those they prayed would now be safe in the streets of their city, the hunger of the dead abated and mollified.

Yirmiyahu stared at this priest, the high priest of the People, as at some animal that had lifted up onto two legs and drawn about itself the skin of a man. Always before, in Yirmiyahu's crying out of God's words on the Temple steps, he'd thought the high priest a familiar, comprehensible thing, a priest drunk with comfort and prestige, neglectful of People and Covenant. But now the priest seemed to Yirmiyahu's eyes not merely something far worse but also something unexpected and alien. Yirmiyahu found it difficult to breathe.

"Abomination," Yirmiyahu snarled. "This is *not* how we serve God in Anathoth."

"You're not *in* Anathoth." The priest's eyes were dark.

Yirmiyahu stood panting, his hand still gripping the priest's throat, holding him to the wall but without squeezing. He felt eyes on his back—the woman who had been cutting roots. Suddenly he felt closed in, locked in this house with mad people. "I will make sure *every* levite knows about this," he hissed.

"Most of them know already," the priest said.

Yirmiyahu could see the truth of it in the priest's eyes, hear it in his own ears. In his heart, he reeled. The levites of the city were defiled! The caste was defiled: it had broken Covenant. The very robes Yirmiyahu wore on his body were defiled. "Unclean," he hissed, his hand trembling at the man's throat, everything in him shaking, wanting for one wild instant to squeeze and cut off the other man's breath. "Unclean!"

"You are a fool, Yirmiyahu," the priest rasped, his throat moving beneath Yirmiyahu's hand. "A fool who thinks he hears God. God stopped speaking to us generations ago. God no longer hears; God has left the land, and I do not believe there is any *navi*. The space above the Ark is empty. What is important now is to keep the People calm, make them unafraid. King and People tithe to the Temple and know they will have peace from living enemies. And they bring offerings to Chemosh on his hill, knowing they will have peace from the dead. Why should we object to what happens on that hill? Going there, people don't have to be afraid. These are small sacrifices, young man."

"I will *find* someone to tell," Yirmiyahu roared.

"Do that," the priest wheezed. "Spit on your own caste, if you will. Just get out of my house."

"I will *raise* this city against you!" Yirmiyahu hissed. He threw the man to the floor and stood over him, his chest heaving; the woman watching from the other room screamed and came at him with the knife, but Yirmiyahu dodged it and then rushed out the broken door and into the street. There was a cry behind him but no pursuit; he ran wildly through the streets, hurrying toward the small house where he lived with Miriam. As he ran, he tore the robes from his back and dropped them into the dust, until he was bolting through the night street in his loincloth, his hair streaming behind him. Window slats clacked shut as he passed. His side burned, but he didn't slow; he had to run, he had to run, or he would collapse crying again in the dust.

***

From that day, Yirmiyahu wore no wool that had the patterns of his caste woven into it. Those patterns had been defiled and he could not wear them, not until the caste was redeemed, the tomb at Tophet filled with earth, and the city fed and healed. Instead he took up the brown garments of a common day laborer each morning, then went to the Temple to cry out the words God had whispered to his heart when he'd risen at dawn from the bed he shared with his wife.

"I know your ways!" he shouted on the wide Temple steps to a gathering crowd of levites in their white robes, merchants in red, a few laborers in brown, and, in the back of the crowd, a few veiled women in the shade of the sunbaked brick houses of the priests that lined both sides of the street. Many of the levites frowned darkly; some of the merchants looked pale with fear. Some were listening, some looked troubled.

Sometimes as Yirmiyahu spoke a shudder would pass through the crowd, as though a cold wind had swept down the street. None of them spoke or murmured or whispered while the prophet pleaded with them, this man who said he was a *navi*, his voice sharp in the silence, echoing from the walls of the priests' houses. His listeners were tense; all the city was tense. There were rumors of trouble with Babylon, bad trouble, perhaps even an army on the way. A siege might mean a long time without wares coming or going from the markets. Those merchants in the crowd, when they walked to the city gates to converse with other men of trade, had only to glance up to see the armed men the king had paid to stand on the walls of the city.

So most of them did not look up when they went to the gates.

And all they had to do was glance down the back streets as they passed by to see the hunger of the city's poor and to hear, from time to time, a moan from one of the city's dead, hungering and eating in the city's narrowest, darkest streets.

So most of them did not look down those alleys.

"These are the words I bring you from God!" Yirmiyahu cried. Though he had stood twice a week on these steps since coming to the city, today his eyes were dark with the knowledge of what he'd seen on high Tophet. He spoke with more suffering and fury than he ever had before. "God says: *I know your ways! You say to each other, Peace, there will be peace, for look! The Temple, the Temple of God, the Temple of God is here! All of you are deceived.*"

His nostrils flared—it seemed to Yirmiyahu in that moment that a reek of decay was rising from the street, the same reek he had smelled above the pit on the hill. It was thick; it nauseated him. Even his own skin stank of it. "There is no peace, do not *talk* about peace!" he cried. "We are People of *the Covenant!* If the least of us falls on the desert road, we are to turn back and lift him onto our shoulders before we walk on. If any women hunger in the field, we are to leave some food behind for them to glean. Yet in our city, this very city where our God consents to dwell with us, you don't look outside your windows. You hear the scream of a woman violated in the alley and you cover your ears. No man is taken and stoned for that defilement. You hear a child crying from an empty belly and you go to your inner room and eat, humming to yourself to shut out the noise. You don't look outside your windows. And now death, death has come up into our windows! Why can't you hear it? Our pact with God is rent and torn, a rending made terribly visible to us in the tearing of flesh by the teeth of the unclean dead."

He raged now, and the merchants' faces were white. The priests listened with dark, furious faces; he met their eyes, screaming out his words, challenging them, demanding that they respond, that they act. What veil did they wear over their eyes? How could the city's suffering and peril be so hidden from the eyes of these sightless men?

"Levites!" he cried. "Men of my caste! How can you wear those garments? God's garments, given to our father's fathers when they vowed to bring the suffering of the People before God and bring God's mercy and nurturing back to her People. To reach one hand to our God and with the other lift our People from the dirt—that is our calling! You care only for collecting tithes, and keeping the People quiet and unafraid. They should *be* afraid! Don't you understand the things we do here will drive God from the city?

"How dare you come to this Temple in those garments! How can you not stand naked before us today, forbearing such clothing while any one of our People in the city is naked? For every woman and child stripped in some street or alcove, God in whose likeness they were born is stripped and bruised. For every child taken up the hill to the pit, you throw God, too, into the hole. You stand by while she is defiled and beaten and thrown to the dust, and you stand here about these steps wearing her clothes! Hooting like owls in the ruins of this covenanted city: Peace, peace, we have peace! We have God's clothing; we wrap ourselves in it and look holy. We have God's Temple; we dwell in God's house that we've taken. We are satisfied. We have everything we want from God; let her cry in the street, for we have what we want from her. We are secure. We are safe. We have peace." Yirmiyahu screamed: "*What is this peace?*"

That was when one of them—he did not see who—hefted a rock from the dusty ground and hurled it at him. Other stones soon followed, hard and brutal.

***

Fear is a sickness.

To treat it, Yirmiyahu kept wandering alone and unsteady through the wide streets of his memory, only sometimes noticing the reek of the corpse or the wet, clammy mud around his legs. It was still dark at the bottom of the well, but he could sense the lumpy shape of the dead body rotting beside him in the mud. His feet were swollen and numb, his tongue large inside his dry mouth.

He rested against the wall and had conversations with people who weren't there, though his lips barely moved.

Sometimes, smelling the dead in the well, he thought he was smelling decay from the pit on Tophet. He shuddered in the dark. Once he pressed clenched fists to his temples and moaned.

His own efforts at the gates and at the Temple steps had not stopped the smoke from rising above that hill. After his flight through the streets, pelted by stones, and after sending his wife safely from the city the next day, Yirmiyahu had begun talking with the guardsmen at the walls, the younger ones, hoping to recruit some of them for a raid on the summit. If his cries at the Temple could not put an end to the sacrifices, perhaps a few swords might suffice. He was desperate; the anguish of what he had seen clutched at him, making it difficult to breathe when he thought of it.

Most of the guardsmen wouldn't listen to him, some because they were afraid of the priests. Others because there was no threat to their own children, and they did not want to see the need. Still others because they had seen dead in the streets and the way of appeasement appealed to their minds. But a few were beginning to hear him, he thought.

Three weeks passed. Then one morning, even as the sun rose over the wall, something happened that drove Tophet utterly from his mind.

Yirmiyahu woke to the sound of clinking metal and shouts from the wall. When he wrapped a brown cloak about himself and stepped out into the street, people were screaming; there were many, many people in the streets, the olive farmers from the Mount and the barley farmers from the river valley, all rushing into the city. "They're shutting the gates!" the refugees cried. "The king's men are shutting the gates!"

Babylon had come.

Yirmiyahu stood on the edge of the street by the gate as the people streamed past, his hair lank and unwashed about his face, and terror took hold of his heart and squeezed it, so that he sank back against the wall of a house. A vision filled his mind, sights of what might be, of what evils the actions of this day might bring. Terrible images of the restless dead gnawing on bodies, many, many of them in the streets. Then God's words came, rushing wildly through him, a river, a torrent, a flash flood of speech, of warning and outcry. He screamed the words, right where he stood, even as the people flowed past.

At last he stepped out into the middle of the street, fighting the people who buffeted him, clawing his way toward the city's main gates, screaming in a fever of horror, desperate to be heard by the king's men, the armed men slamming heavy beams across the gates. "Death, death has come up into our windows!" he cried, as he tried in vain to force his way through the crowd. "We must yield the city! We must yield the city! Or the horses of the east will trample beneath their hooves only the bones of the dead! Open the gates! *Open the gates!* Do not lock the People in with the dead! Do not do this thing! God will leave the city! She'll flee the city!"

***

The siege shut about the city; small camps of tents sprung up to watch each of its gates, the sun bright on so many helmets and shields. Bowmen moved in and out of the tents and their horses whickered, so many horses, more perhaps than the land had ever seen. In the city for long months, people hungered while the priests rationed out grain to those who could afford it. There were famished, slouching dead in so many streets and ill-lit corners. Yirmiyahu heard their moaning through the boarded-up windows of the scribe's shop where he'd taken to living, having sold the house where he'd lived with his wife as soon as he sent her away.

There was rarely a day during the siege when Yirmiyahu could hold silence for long; the words came so fast and so forcefully that he was like a twig in a river. It was as though God was weeping behind her veil in the Temple, rocking in sorrow over the Ark while the dead ate in the streets. Wherever Yirmiyahu stood in the city he could hear her. In the scribe's shop, he would stir at times from a trancelike state to find that he'd been spilling God's mourning, desperate words from his mouth for hours. He would reach up to touch his cheeks and find them wet.

If Yirmiyahu had been like the Temple levites, a man of the city rather than a man of the country—if he'd seen God as a masculine and potent deity rather than a bringer of fruits, if he'd seen God as one who protects the People rather than one whom the People protect, if Yirmiyahu had not heard her weeping, if he'd been as a deaf man, if he hadn't been her *navi*, he might have been embittered toward his God. He might have blamed her. He might have shrieked at the irony of Babylon's arrival—as though God had taken action where her People refused to, closing the tomb at Tophet by encamping an army between the hill and the city. If the men and women of Yerushalayim wanted to feed the dead now, they would have to offer their own flesh.

But Yirmiyahu could hear God's keening in the Temple, and he knew that her People had abandoned God and not God her People. It was the king's greed, and the complacency of the priests and merchants who advised him, that had kindled the wrath of the great cities in the east. Perhaps God who sobbed now in her Temple had been as alarmed at their coming as anyone in the city. Yirmiyahu didn't know; he only knew that God's lament for her People was violent and overpowering, and it wrenched his heart.

When he rose in the mornings and washed his hands and arms up to the elbows, then his face—in those early mornings of the siege while there was still much water in the city's wells—he comforted himself with the thought that he'd been right to send his wife away, that the anguish in her eyes when he broke covenant with her was atoned for by her distance from their beleaguered city, by her safety in her parents' home in Anathoth in its quiet river valley, days from this starving place, this place of tears.

***

"The granaries are emptied. You know this. There is no food left, and only the dead are eating. Surrender is the only way to preserve the lives in this city." Yirmiyahu pleaded with Tsidkiyyahu the king. Long months had passed, and terror had grown in the city. Still Yirmiyahu had beseeched the priests and the guardsmen, had begged outside the doors of the king's house for the gates of the city to be thrown open. The guardsmen had exchanged pale glances at their posts.

Perhaps thinking that so many feet of earth might serve to silence the *navi* where threats seemed not to, the king finally tossed the prophet into a cell beneath his house. There, in the dim light, as weeks passed, Yirmiyahu learned for the first time what *hunger* really was, how there could be a hole in the belly, a hole with teeth around it, threatening to chew up your insides into one great empty place, one that your mind might fall into and never come back.

When the king came to visit his cell one night, it took such effort even to speak, to do anything but groan. "You have known me a long time now, Tsidkiyyahu. You know that I do not lie to you, though you don't want to hear me, though you wish to believe I'm mad. Please. There is so little time left." He tugged at his bonds. "Let me free. Let me speak to the people of the city at your side. We can still change what is coming."

"What is coming, what is coming!" Tsidkiyyahu began to pace. The whites around his eyes showed. "Why do you always bring *these* words, *navi*? You weaken the hearts of my men on the walls. They need to hear words of victory, not your talk of futility and disaster."

"The city will die if you don't yield the gates," Yirmiyahu groaned. "Why won't you understand?" He gazed at the king with sunken, weary eyes. He was a young king, a rash young man who must have still been a boy not long before. His face was strong with his will, but his eyes were filled always with fear. Fear lived in Tsidkiyyahu's skin. Regarding him, Yirmiyahu was certain that whether the king sat or stood, walked or lay down, he must feel the bite of that fear at all times.

With cold dread, Yirmiyahu thought of what was occurring outside the king's house. How the guards now stayed on the city walls, slept and ate there without coming down, or if they did, descending only into the walled, secure courtyard of the king's house. The same courtyard that held a well that was no longer giving water. Outside that walled courtyard, the people of the city locked themselves in their own homes, or went through the streets armed with whatever implements they could find: a shovel, or a tailor's stick, or even the beam from a weaver's loom—Yirmiyahu had seen two men carrying one of those, with a veiled woman following them through the streets, as though they expected to swing the massive beam together and crush the heads of any lurking corpses that stumbled into their path.

"I will not give up this city," Tsidkiyyahu shouted. "This is my father's city, and his father's. It is the greatest city in the world. I will not give it up. Beseech your God to protect us!"

"She will not," Yirmiyahu whispered. "You have broken Covenant with her."

The young king hissed. "I have given *monthly* sacrifices at the Temple. The levites fatten on my tithes. Why *shouldn't* God defend us?"

"Sacrifices," Yirmiyahu murmured, sweat stinging his eyes. "She is so weary of sacrifices."

Tsidkiyyahu thrust his pale face into Yirmiyahu's. "Listen to me, you fool," he breathed. "Ours is a strong and prosperous city; we have trade routes with every nation of the earth. I *will not* let it fall." Tsidkiyyahu's voice shook. "Our fathers' fathers lived in tents, Yirmiyahu. In *tents*. Wearing coarse wool and living off milk and gathered roots, like animals. Look at us now, look at all our fathers built. In my palace there are purple fabrics from Tyre and Sidon, ointments from Kemet. We have markets, scribes, educated men who chatter in the evening at our gates. We have strong men on the walls and strong gods to protect us. I have three sons and I will leave this city to them intact. With its walls standing. And you, *navi* or no, you are going to rot in this cell where your words can make no man's heart quail, until Babylon marches home."

Yirmiyahu was silent a moment, weariness heavy on his shoulders. "Purple fabrics," he murmured. "Men who talk at the gates. The Pharaoh of Kemet said such things as these to our Lawgiver, about the cities of Kemet. Yet Kemet was not given the Covenant and the Law. We were. No nation, though it have decorated tombs taller than mountains and all the world's perfumes—no nation can be called great if some of its people starve, or are sold to beds in other cities, or are forgotten, or sacrificed to the dead to make a few men feel safe."

And then words, God's words, filled Yirmiyahu's ears and his chest, as though God had heard the king and was crying out her reply, until her *navi* gave in and murmured her words aloud:

> *What use to me are perfumes from Sheba,*
> *or sweet cane from far countries?*
> *Your burnt offerings are not acceptable,*
> *Your sacrifices do not please me.*

He caught the king's gaze with his. Tsidkiyyahu's eyes were pale with restrained fear, Yirmiyahu's were bloodshot, exhausted. "God is leaving the city," the *navi* said. "She cannot stay—the Covenant is shattered; God's ears are violated with the screams of her People."

He closed his eyes, leaned back against the wall, as a vision—a terrible witnessing of the future—poured into his mind with the words. "This is no great city, O king. And I—I have seen—I have seen with my eyes—how your resistance will end. God sees what will happen; it is before her eyes day and night. So many deaths. So many. And as many nights as the gates are closed against Babylon, closing all of us inside, those many nights the dead gather in your streets. You must—*must*—lie down, let the king of Babylon place his foot on your neck. Otherwise, what is left of the city when he takes it will be burned with fire, its walls broken like the walls of Yeriho, our People felled like an oak or a terebinth, leaving only a stump behind." He opened his eyes, saw Tsidkiyyahu's horrified face, the king's hand making the sign against evil. "Your wife will be put to death after the soldiers of that foreign land touch her. Your sons, Tsidkiyyahu, your three sons will be killed as you watch, knives to their bellies. And the king of Babylon will cut out your eyes, wanting your sons' deaths to be the last sight you remember in your long life as a captive."

"*Be silent!*"

Yirmiyahu laughed bitterly and felt the laughter would break him apart. "Do you think I haven't tried to be? I am silent and my bones groan within me, I cannot sleep all the night for the roaring of the words rushing through me. I cannot be silent."

***

Though his eyes were open in the shadow at the bottom of the well, Yirmiyahu lay in an exhaustion that resembled sleep, his body shivering in his improvised coat of defiled and tattered cloth. His mind moved, slow as kelp in the Middle Sea to the west, into other dreams of the past.

For Yirmiyahu, that year of the siege had been a bitter struggle, one fought over men's hearts and with no weapons keener than words. When he was not in a cell, he spent the year at Baruch's shop. The sunlight through Baruch's boarded windows had been a blessing, as had been the silent way Baruch cared for him and took down the prophecies and warnings he spoke. In Yirmiyahu's memory, clear as a lake bed seen through unrippled water, Baruch the scribe sat behind his desk with a papyrus scroll spread before him. Baruch: his name meant "blessed," and he was: a man who could afford bread and who knew how to read and write Hebrew with a speed and facility Yirmiyahu himself lacked. Baruch was bald, so that the sunlight shone on his head as on a warrior's shield. His little shop sat against the northern wall and the light came through a window on the south, at the shop's front. Baruch slept in a little room upstairs, and Yirmiyahu slept on a few blankets before the desk, ever since he'd sent his wife away and sold his small house.

Often in the hour before the sun dropped beneath the south wall and cast them into night, Yirmiyahu would pace across the shop—four strides each way—and pour words from his mouth like water from a ewer. When God sent the words like a river, the *navi* could not dam or channel them; they rushed through him. At times he nearly shattered apart with the force of the emotions *sweeping through his body:*

> *A voice is heard in Rama*
> *cries and bitter weeping*

God is weeping for her children
she refuses to be comforted
for they are gone

Baruch's hand moved with speed and certainty, sketching with his stylus the angular shapes of letters, the gift God had given to the Lawgiver many generations before, that her words might be heard whenever the Lawgiver's scroll was read.

Yirmiyahu wept as her words, terrible words, rushed through him. Ever since the gates closed, those words had been words of horror and dismay, of warning and of pleading, words telling of the death that was already creeping within the city. The recitation would end before the sun fell; Yirmiyahu would collapse in grief and lie on the floor, fighting for breath. Then Baruch would set his stylus quietly aside, stopper the flask of blueberry ink, and breathe slowly over the scroll to dry it. He would roll up the scroll and bind it with a yellow string, then kneel beside Yirmiyahu and sit with him, not speaking, with his head bent in prayer. Sometimes, Baruch just watched his friend's face. Baruch sat with him through the long watches, listening to the occasional scream in the streets. He would sigh and settle his legs more comfortably, set his hand on the *navi*'s shoulder, and wait for his grief to pass.

Some days the words came early, and Yirmiyahu would lie for long hours in a stupor on his pallet below the window as the words of God tore through his body like shrieks. On those days, as Yirmiyahu lay twitching on the pallet, Baruch paid an assistant to take the scroll of Yirmiyahu's words and read it aloud at the Temple steps or at the gates, pleading for the gates to open and the people to be fed—even if this meant they were fed bread and meat out of the hands of Babylonian soldiers. Baruch even paid for a guard to protect the assistant, in case the priests' anger should turn violent as the words were read. Baruch did this to honor the *navi*, who'd told him on the first day he entered his shop of his private covenant with God, a covenant he'd made the day the gates shut. Yirmiyahu had promised her he would speak to the priests at the Temple steps and to the guards at the wall each day without fail.

One evening Yirmiyahu opened his eyes and saw the day's last faint light through the cracks in the wood barring the shop's window. Baruch sat beside him, but Yirmiyahu ignored the scribe, gazed at the cracks of sunlight—for a little while he did not recognize the shop's window, and for some reason those broken pieces of light terrified him. He whispered:

How lonely is the city that was full of people,
How like a widow.
She weeps bitterly in the night,
with tears on her cheeks;
she has none to comfort her.

He saw the dead gnawing on crippled children in the shadow of the broken wall. He saw soldiers marching through the ashen ruins of the city's houses, their conical helmets and their spears with shining bronze heads, and they were not soldiers of the People.

A sharp slap across his cheek. He turned and blinked, saw Baruch there. Slowly he felt the cool floor under his body, the air on his skin, the sting in his face. Baruch was frowning. His lips moved, and Yirmiyahu focused and heard the scribe's words: "Enough, friend. Where is your hope? Where is your conviction that the words a *navi* brings can change hearts? That the city can be restored? Where is your hope, huh?"

Yirmiyahu's lips were dry, his eyes also. A soreness in his muscles. "I am thirsty," he whispered.

Then Baruch grinned and grasped his friend's arms, pulling him up from the floor.

"Why do you fight the priesthood so?" Baruch demanded after he'd filled a clay bowl with water and held it to Yirmiyahu's lips for a while. The priests had begun threatening Baruch for harboring one they'd cast from their number, but Baruch was known and honored by the merchants and professed to fear the priests little. In any case, a few of the younger levites, a very few, had begun coming in secret to his shop during the evening dark to listen, and to ask questions of "the mad *navi.*"

Now the scribe gently set the emptied bowl aside, and Yirmiyahu leaned against Baruch's desk a moment, recovering his breath. "Until there is justice in the city," he rasped, "we are as a dry well that waters no growth. We are as parched earth, from which even God's skillful hands can grow only withered and sickly things."

"They're going to kill you, you know." Baruch's voice was very quiet. "Someday soon."

Yirmiyahu reached with trembling fingers and tapped the scroll with his fingertips. "They cannot kill these. They cannot kill or silence the words of God." He caught Baruch's eyes. "And it is these, and not I, that will nourish our starving people and open the gates of the city before everything is lost."

"Huh," Baruch grunted, and bent back to the work. "I fear you are wrong, friend," the scribe muttered after a moment, his hand moving swiftly across the dry papyrus. "The scrolls are fragile, too. A mere splash of water and they crumble apart. They are more mortal than men."

***

Hoshekh filled the well as wine fills a cup.

Yirmiyahu's skin was burning a little. He slept fitfully and woke finally with sweat cold on his face and back. A fever had broken. He breathed shallowly for a while, watching the stars, praying. Then slipped back into a half sleep.

"Fear is a sickness." He could hear her, hear Miriam's voice. He slipped, eager as a fish into water, a fish released from a hand over the side of a boat, into a dream of that night, their last night together. She had dampened his brow with a cloth and then cleaned his wounds; it was the day he had spoken against Tophet, before the siege, the day the levites at the Temple had pelted him with rocks, pursuing him through the street before he'd been able to get to the door of his house. And when he'd reached the house at last, they had almost torn down the door before leaving. At least they *had* left.

Miriam's hands on his face and limbs were soothing. "Fear is a very great sickness. It makes them weak, husband. It's like a fever. They toss in their beds with it. They'll give anything up, or hurt anyone, to feel safe again." She whispered, "This might hurt, husband," and touched the cloth to a gash in Yirmiyahu's leg. He hissed and stiffened as she cleaned grit out of the tear in his skin. His leg all about that gash was bruised and swollen, but the rock had not broken it. By some miracle, nothing had broken.

"They're like the gleaner in Anathoth," Miriam said softly as she dabbed the wound. "Hannah. Do you remember her?"

Yirmiyahu forced himself to breathe deeply, easily. "The girl with the dreams?"

"Yes, the girl with the dreams." Miriam sighed. "She was afraid, too."

The girl Hannah had been one of the poorest in that little farming village; her father and brother had died in a fever. They had not risen from the ground afterward; it had been an ordinary fever. But it had left Hannah without resources. In Anathoth, Yirmiyahu recalled bitterly, the Law was still followed, the Covenant still kept. As required by the Covenant with the God who nourishes, the reapers of the fields left any grain that fell and did not stoop to pick it up; they left it for any who needed it. Joining other women who were without husbands or fathers, Hannah walked the fields each harvest, following the reapers, gathering up the grain that fell, taking it back to her tiny house to feed herself during the cold months.

Thinking of those fields, Yirmiyahu was taken suddenly by a fierce longing for Anathoth, for a quieter life studying the Law and preparing for the priesthood, back before he had ever heard any voice calling him in the night. Before he had lived in this sweltering, populous city, where the streets were noisy and most people did not hear God.

The village of Anathoth had pitied Hannah, yet most people tried not to think about her—not because she was poor, but because of what she did about her dreams. At first, night after night, terrors took her in her sleep and made her scream within her house. The village's wise woman brought herbs and tried to calm her sleep, but the herbs didn't work very well. "She is too sick with her fear, I cannot cure it," the woman confessed to the town's elders, her eyes moist with tears.

In time Hannah found her own way of coping with her dreams. She began taking the town's young men into her house by night; they would come to her at first in the fields at harvest as she carried grain back home, and out of sight of the reapers they would walk with her. Then they began slipping furtively into her house by night, or on hot afternoons while most of the town slept. Hannah was very quiet, and though some of the town's women stared hard at her closed door, they heard no moans or cries within. Yet they stopped talking with her—even the other gleaners did, and Hannah would walk a little behind the others at harvest, gathering what she might, a lonely ghost of the past, hungry and silent.

One evening, shortly after he married Miriam but before they began packing for the move to Yerushalayim, Yirmiyahu came home from talking with the elders about all the things he must remember when he came before the Temple priests and asked to be one of them. Yirmiyahu came in through the door into the little rooms of his house humming, and then stopped, startled. There were Miriam and Hannah, sitting together by the cookpot, making dinner. Miriam glanced over her shoulder at him and her smile caught at his heart. "I asked Hannah to eat with us, husband," she said. "I hope you aren't displeased?"

Another man in Anathoth might have raged at not having been asked first. But Yirmiyahu was newly married and drunk as with wine on Miriam's kisses and her laughter and her voice. So he simply sat across the cookpot from them, looking bewildered. Miriam finished their stew, then instructed Hannah on where to find a half loaf of bread in one of the baskets at the room's corner. As they ate, Miriam talked, sharing stories of her childhood or asking Yirmiyahu's opinions on matters of discussion in the town; she listened to his replies attentively with soft, laughing eyes. Though Hannah was mostly silent, she smiled warmly when Miriam broke off a piece of bread and gave it to her, and once she reached out and gripped Miriam's hand so tightly that Miriam winced.

"Why did we have a guest?" Yirmiyahu asked his wife later that night, holding her in his arms in their bed, panting softly after their love.

Miriam gazed at him, looking very serious, though her face was still flushed, strands of her hair sweaty across her face. "She has no one to hear her, husband. It hurt to see how lonely she was."

"Hear her? She was very quiet—I don't remember her saying much."

"Yes, she did," Miriam said, and Yirmiyahu remembered the smiles and the grip on Miriam's hand. He had often seen women communicating across a street with a look or a turn of their shoulder. Perhaps women had a language that didn't need words.

"Miriam, I am not sure," Yirmiyahu murmured, "that she is a good woman to have in my house."

"Because she invites men," Miriam said quietly, her tone still serious. "But no one has tried to stone her for it, and no one has made her leave. And the women of Anathoth ignore it and get their husbands to ignore it, as long as she doesn't invite a man who is married." Miriam's eyes were soft in the dark. "We all heard her screams, husband. Something happened to her as a child. Something her father did to her. She's very afraid to sleep without someone else near her or holding her."

***

As Miriam tended him with the cloth and with her soft hands, Yirmiyahu tried again to understand what his wife was telling him. Always she seemed to have something worth listening to, but it was not always easy to understand what she meant. He thought of the white-robed men chasing him through the streets with their rocks, their round, furious, terrified eyes. He thought of the way Hannah's eyes had often been round like that, showing their whites.

"The gleaner," Yirmiyahu murmured. "I need to pity the men at the Temple steps. That's what you're saying."

"I'm saying they're afraid and ill, husband," Miriam said quietly. "I don't pity them. They hurt you." Her voice caught, and Yirmiyahu closed his hand around her fingers for a moment. He eyes searched Miriam's face and saw something he'd missed before, in the year since they'd settled into this little house. A little wrinkling around her eyes. Yirmiyahu felt a pang of regret. In taking her to this city, he had removed her from all the women she knew. His wife was lonely here. And when she had suffered a terrible loss earlier that year, the most terrible of losses, she had shut herself within this little house, and no women had come to see her. Her husband had stayed home more of the time for a while, and had held her in his arms, but had been at a loss as to how to comfort her. Those lines around her eyes—were those loss or were they loneliness, with no one to hear her?

"I am sorry," he whispered. "Sorry we are here."

He tried to lift himself, groaning at the pain of his bruises. Her gentle hand on his chest pressed him down. Her eyes deepened with worry in the light of the tiny oil lamp on the table. His vision had gone blurry for a moment. He saw in his mind, so clearly, the shambling dead beneath the altar at Tophet. He hadn't told Miriam of it; he didn't know if he could speak of it to her yet without weeping.

Miriam's lips brushed his cheek. "Lie still, my husband." He heard the plop of the cloth in the ewer, then the drip of water as she lifted it. His vision cleared, and he saw her lift the cloth to his face. It was cool and moist against his cheek. As she looked down at his eyes, a smile awoke in hers, and he warmed to see it. "I've changed my mind. On your belly, my husband."

He rolled over with a groan and a violent ache of his muscles. She helped him, then took her hands away, and when they came back and settled on his shoulders, they were moist with oil. Her hands moved over the muscles of his shoulders and back, rubbing in an ointment that flickered with heat along his skin, then cooled after her hands passed, making him gasp. "Where did you get that?"

"From the widow who keeps her booth by the Sheep Gate." She spoke softly, her lips not far from his ear. "I overpaid her. She looks so thin."

"It's wonderful, my wife." He started to breathe more deeply, the pain in his back dulling, though the aches in his arms—where stones had struck him as he shielded his head—still burned. But then Miriam brought more oil and gently ran her hands up his arms, and her lips placed slow kisses on his back. He shivered. "That feels even better," he murmured.

"And this?" she whispered, catching his earlobe gently in her lips, her breath moist and soft.

Before long he found himself on his back again, holding her in his arms, ignoring the aches that remained. The night had turned suddenly gentle and soft in their home, and he parted her garments, whispering to her from the People's most ancient song of love, a song of laughter and tears, a song of the sweetness of a man's union with a woman and a God's union with a People who had captured her heart: "Oh my beloved, you are to me as the lily among the thorns."

"As the apple tree among the trees of the wood," she whispered back, "is my love among the sons." She kissed him lightly, and when she drew away her eyes were heated. "And his fruit is sweet to my taste." She laughed, clear as a bell, and touched him. "Make haste, my love, make haste, and be like a gazelle or a young stag on the mountains of spices."

And he moved within her, slowly, for he was still terribly sore.

He woke now, still caught in the joy of it, the touch of her skin on his, the way she held him tightly, warmly inside her. And as he drew in a shuddering breath, his eyes open but unseeing, he was suddenly back in the stench of the dead and the aloneness of his cistern tomb. The darkness around him, so different from that gentle night, was as a stab in the belly. He yearned for her. He yearned now for fresh water and sunlight on his skin and for every sweet thing he had ever known, but especially for her.

SECOND DAY: IF ALL HER PEOPLE WERE PROPHETS

LAUGHTER FAR OVERHEAD; living men stood up there, staring down into the well. Yirmiyahu looked up at them, their silhouettes against the circle of starlight. "Let me out!" he began to beg, his rasping voice echoing in the cold throat of the well.

More laughter and muffled talk. Another bundle shoved over the brink of the well, smaller than the last. He tensed as it dropped.

This one had a gaping wound in its side and its wrists were bound. The fall broke its legs and split open its belly. Still it struggled to get on its knees in the dim light, its intestines spilling from its abdomen in a rush of guts and viscous fluid. Its eyes were wide, its jaws snapping as it toppled over and rolled toward him in the mud.

For a few breaths, as the broken creature moaned and wallowed, Yirmiyahu just leaned against the stones of the wall, watching it. His body felt heavy and cold. I have turned to stone, he thought, I am part of the wall.

This creature had been a girl, perhaps twelve winters old. Maybe less.

For a long moment Yirmiyahu hesitated, stunned.

It had been a girl, a little girl.

The creature's milky eyes were fixed on him; its mouth opened in a long growl. His heart hammered in his chest.

"I'm sorry," the prophet whispered, "I'm so sorry."

He stumbled to his feet on weak and aching legs as it snapped its jaws and fought to get close to him. He took its head in his hands, holding it tightly at arm's length—the creature was very strong—and dragged the corpse to the wall. He slammed the head into the wall, hearing a crack of bone. The creature kept writhing and kicking, trying to twist its head in his hands to bite him; he slammed it into the stones again and again. He kept hitting the creature's head into the wall until it was still at last. Then he stood over it numbly, gazing down at that shattered body, the likeness of God broken and defaced. His hands hung limply at his sides. He moaned, a sound not unlike the moan of the dead but voicing anguish and horror that the dead could never know.

He saw bits of flesh in the mud and on his clothes but no blood. No blood. The girl's chest had torn further open; a few ribs now jabbed out through the skin and the torn garment she wore. Yirmiyahu glanced up at the circle of night over his head. They would drop other dead in after him. If he was to survive, he would need more than clothing; he would need some weapon or tool with which to put an end to these unclean corpses. He cried out the name of his God, begging her forgiveness for the violation he intended to commit.

Sweating, he reached down and took hold of one of the dead girl's ribs and wrenched it free, snapping it away from the rib cage. He held the rib before him like a long, white knife, while the body sank slowly into the mud. Yirmiyahu wished he might murmur the Words of Going, but his throat closed and he couldn't get them out. What right had he to wish her rest after tearing at her body, and when none of his deeds and none of his words had sufficed to protect her, or any of the city's children?

"Death has come up into our windows," Yirmiyahu whispered as he held the gleaming rib in his hand. He gazed at its jagged end and everything it portended: the wrecking of the bodies of children and women, and in them the very body of God, kicked aside and left shaking in the street by the levites and the merchants and all who ignored the hungering of famished bodies outside their houses or the bleeding of raped bodies in the alleys behind. He thought of the defiled bodies of the dead lurching between sleeping houses, some with ribs like this one exposed amid torn and gaping flesh, glinting in the light of the moon and the stars.

How the impoverished men and women in the city had hastened to find wood to bar the one window in their home . . . In the early nights of the siege, when the plague was really just beginning, their houses had been open to the night air, and in the quiet hours, dark shapes had appeared in the windows, a glint of eyes in the starlight, hands clutching the sills. They had crawled through, reaching for the warm life within. Grabbing the leg or the arm of whoever slept inside the house and pulling that flesh to their waiting mouths. Men and women would wake to the shock of teeth cutting into their bodies. They would wrestle with their attackers in the dark, but it was too late. Some would be devoured while they writhed and cried out; those in the next house would cover their ears and pretend they heard nothing. Others lay feverish with terrible wounds once the dead were sated and wandered out, until they fell into a sleep without breathing and then woke with a hunger as intense as that of a dry well for rain.

Yirmiyahu ran his fingertip across the broken edge of the rib, feeling the sharpness without cutting his skin. For a moment, even in his horror, he marveled at it. He held it up, gazing at the long, graceful curve of the bone. The first woman had been made from one of these. It was a marvel. He remembered suddenly how, in the early part of the siege, he had knocked on the door of the widow's shop near the Sheep Gate in the hot morning—for no reason other than that she had been a friend of his wife's. He'd heard someone moving inside the booth, but no answer came to his call. Then a thump, like a body fallen. Uneasily, he forced the door and slipped into the dark booth. Something moved near him, then he saw the widow's silhouette and knew by its movement that it was not her. He leapt backward through the door, into the sunlight, and it followed him out. It was terrible. It had the widow's face, except that the nose had been chewed away, and one eye was gone. One arm hung broken at its side; the other reached for him.

That a body made to bear life into the world could be turned into *that*.

***

Each time he woke, dozens of times, clutching the rib, the world was still dark. And so cold. A levite, Yirmiyahu had always had a roof over his head—even if this past year it had only been the roof of Baruch's shop—and a rug to wrap himself in. He hadn't understood the cold before, the way your hands could clench up and stop working, the way your body shook as though coming apart. He breathed through his teeth, for his nose burned. He tried to remember the sun, the day heat that beat on his arms. Thought of the day, months before, when he'd led the children to break the granaries behind the Temple. Their bodies had run with sweat; by the time they reached the tall, tomb-like shapes of the grain silos, each of the children (and he himself) had been covered in a layer of brown dust that stuck to them. Children made of earth.

Yirmiyahu had leapt up the sod ramp to the first silo, stripped away his shirt, taken up a great shovel, and broken apart the locks. A heave of his arms and the door to the silo shot open. Grain came running out, a rush of golden beads. Priests tried to stop them, rushing at them from the courtyard, and there was a bitter fight behind the Temple grounds, a more brutal fight than Yirmiyahu had ever imagined. The children kicked and bit at the priests who grabbed them, and gouged at their eyes with reaching fingers; Yirmiyahu saw a white-robed priest knock down a small boy with a blow to the head. With a scream, Yirmiyahu threw himself bodily into the priest and bore him to the ground, clouting the man's head with his fists. There were the high shrieks of children, the curses of grown men, and the thickening cloud of dust that so many wrestling feet kicked up into the air. In that haze, an anger took Yirmiyahu that burned hotter than any he'd ever known. He lifted the shovel in both hands and swung it, slamming its blunt blade into men's bodies. His chest was soon damp with spatters of blood. He could hardly see anything; he just swung whenever he came upon a man-sized shape, screaming words in Hebrew and other loud cries that were not words. "Elohim adonai!" he howled, "Elohi, Elohi, my God, my God!"

At last they routed the priests. The children who could filled the bowls and jars they'd brought with grain, then ran away into the streets, disappearing. Yirmiyahu leaned a moment on his shovel, fighting to breathe against the tightness in his chest. Then he staggered to where one of the girls lay moaning in the dust, her head bleeding. He tore strips from his clothes and tried to bind wounds; the dust settled slowly, the shapes of grain silos and Temple walls and bodies gradually becoming more distinct and real in the haze around him. One child died in his arms, choking on blood, trying to speak and unable to make any sounds but that horrible sucking sound of blood going into the lungs. Then the child shuddered and was still, and later the king's guards found the *navi* like that, still holding that broken body.

They took Yirmiyahu, bound his wrists to a pole in the courtyard of the king's house, and beat him. He cursed them each time a fist or a foot struck his ribs, and the blows kept coming until he hung from his wrists, something broken. He hung there and rasped. Blood dripped from his lower lip, sweat from his brow and hair. And gradually, amid the roar of his body and the desperate wheezing of his breath, he realized someone was talking to him and had been for a while. He turned his head, clenching his teeth against the pain. One eye was too swollen, but through the other he saw a thin man with a lean face and many rings on his fingers. His clothes were finely made and rich in hue, something maybe from the Sea People. He had the newness of a first-growth beard, trimmed carefully and braided. His green eyes watched the prophet warily.

"Tsidkiyyahu," Yirmiyahu breathed. He had never seen this youth before. But he was certain who the man was.

The king stopped what he'd been saying and smiled faintly. "So you *are* listening to me," he said.

Yirmiyahu just looked at him. A rage burned just beneath his skin, but it took too much effort even to breathe. He hung there and kept his eye on the young king.

"If it's grain you want," the king said quietly, "you can buy it."

Yirmiyahu fought for breath to speak. "Half those children . . . are orphans. The other half . . . bond slaves. The city's children . . . suffer . . . for your pride. You revoked . . . the *yovel* . . . the year . . . of God's favor." It took so much out of him, the effort of speech, and the last word fell into a sharp groan.

The king crouched, like a boy looking into a pool, and his face was only a breath from Yirmiyahu's. His eyes were intent, but the *navi* could see the fear in them. "Babylon crouches on the Mount of Olives watching us, like an old crow. Like a *flock* of old crows—all those bowmen with their feathered shafts. This is no time for the *yovel*," he hissed. "I will not destroy you—you are a holy man, *navi*. But why do you stir up the people of the street?"

Yirmiyahu began to laugh slowly, then his body shook with it. Tsidkiyyahu leaned back on his heels, his face aghast; the prophet laughed, his mouth open, his body heaving painfully where he hung. Yirmiyahu felt moisture on his cheeks, knew that he was crying. He stopped laughing, panted for breath. He gasped out the words of God that poured through him in a sudden wild rush:

The snorting of their horses has been heard in Dan,
at the neighing of their stallions all the land shakes.
They come, they devour the land and all that fills it,
The city, and all who dwell in it.
My joy is gone, my grief gnaws at me,
My heart is sick within me.
Listen, the cry of the daughter of my People
Fills the north and the south of my land.
On your garments I see the blood of your sons and your daughters.
Now listen.
Now look, Tsidkiyyahu.
The dead will fill your city, and the sky is filling with crows,
None can scare them away.
And they will silence in the cities of Yehuda and in the streets of Yerushalayim
the voice of mirth and the voice of gladness,
the voice of the bridegroom and the voice of the bride,
for this land will become a desert.

As the last words fell from Yirmiyahu's lips, he lowered his head, looking only at the bruises on his legs and the hard pebbles and dirt of the courtyard of the king's house. He was empty now, and he felt a breeze pass over his skin and then through him, as though there were holes in his body. He just breathed.

"You're mad," Tsidkiyyahu whispered.

The prophet made no answer. After a while there was the rustle of the young king's clothes and his steps passing quickly away across the courtyard. The whisper of fine linens brushed back from where they hung across a door. Then nothing. Yirmiyahu was aware of the sounds but gave them little thought. He lifted his head wearily and felt the sun on his face. His wrists ached where they were bound, but that hardly mattered to him, for all of him was an ache except for the cool empty space inside him where the words had passed through and then gone. From his one eye he watched the wide and uninhabited sky. Somewhere he heard the howl of a jackal. When the king's men came to untie his wrists and set him free in the city, they found him sleeping.

***

Yirmiyahu found a new reserve of strength when the hole in his sky lightened again. He climbed unsteadily to his feet, his hands grasping the stones of the cistern wall; then, with slow steps, he began to circle the well, always with his hands on the wall before him. It was calming, these slow circles, his legs wading through the wet mud. He felt very warm and did not know why. Lifting his fingers to his lips, he found them hot to the touch. Thirst made a desert of his throat until it hurt to breathe. Still he walked in his circles, each one tracing the edges of his world. The stench in the well was terrible, and his eyes watered. At one point he stopped and gazed up at the faraway circle in his sky and screamed for help or mercy. He called out many times. He called Tsidkiyyahu's name, and the name of one of his guards that he remembered, and Baruch's name, and Miriam's. Many times. His throat ached. He could not tell how loud he was calling; his voice sounded distant to him, detached from his own lips and throat.

He realized that he'd fallen silent for some time, and that the mud was sucking hungrily at his thighs as he forced his way through it in his slow circles. Without halting his steps, he closed his eyes. He kept walking. Kept walking.

***

On an evening very early in the siege, Yirmiyahu had burst into Baruch's shop, his hair flying wildly about his face. The Sabbath was coming. "Quickly!" he called to Baruch, who was sitting at his scribe's desk. "Before the sun sets— write down these words. These words, my friend!"

> *The days are coming when I will make a new Covenant with my People, who have broken our old one. They will hear my Law in their hearts, and I will be their God, and they will be my People. There will be no need of priest or teacher or for one to say to his brother, Know these ways of our God, for they will all know me, from the smallest child to the richest man. I will forgive them, and clasp them to me, and nourish them, and no longer remember their darkness.*

"A fantasy," Baruch told him later as he shut and barred the shop's one window. "The world will always be inhabited by the eaters and the eaten. It is how things are."

"But it breaks her heart." Yirmiyahu had washed his face and elbows ritually, preparing for the day's last meal—a meager one it would be, a bowl of grains. Baruch sat and made his stylus dance across the papyrus, writing down the words Yirmiyahu had brought. Yirmiyahu glanced at him, at the speed and evenness with which his hands moved, a speed he could never match. Something full welled up inside him. The words the *navi* brought *would* save the city—they had to—and there would be so much work to do to mend the torn Covenant and make the city once again a place to which God might be welcomed, the way a man might welcome his bride to a peaceful and wholesome house, swept clean. With bowls of stew and loaves of bread readied for passing around a wide circle of kin seated on their banquet cushions. A place to feast together, a place where God might laugh with her People, even as a bride and her husband might laugh together in a good house and eat with their family before her husband swept her into his arms and carried her to bed for a night soft with their loving.

There was so much to be done. The city *would* be saved. Surely the city would be saved. Did not God's words about a new Covenant promise it? Yirmiyahu clung to that, and his blood thrilled within him, demanding action. The mending must begin now, this evening—it couldn't wait for the accord of priests or king.

"Baruch! You must call the children into the shop, the children in those streets, who are without fathers. Teach them to write as you do. Then they will not be hungry."

Baruch looked up, startled. "Who is to pay for it?"

"No one." Yirmiyahu smiled, this sudden hope within him as heady as spiced wine. "But you have an hour after dark, between when we eat and when we sleep—we spend it now in idle talk, or sometimes I just sit silently recovering from the words of God while you write. But this is more important than talking, more important even than the scroll."

"More important than the words of God?"

Yirmiyahu dried his hands on a ragged cloth and spoke with passion: "Obeying the words of God is always more important than talking about them."

"Huh," Baruch grunted. "Huh." His brow wrinkled in thought, his eyes glinting. "If you bring those orphans, Yirmiyahu, and if I do not need to feed them, and if they do not shit on my floor, then in the hour before bed, I will teach them the aleph-bet."

"You are a warrior for God, my friend." Yirmiyahu clasped Baruch's arm, grinning. But Baruch pushed him away hastily: "Your hair is dripping on my scrolls!"

Yirmiyahu stepped back. "Where you see a child who may shit on your floor, I see a child who will one day be a great scribe, or a man of business, or a secretary to the king."

"Huh."

"And one day you will see the man that child became, and I will hear you laugh."

Then they prayed and sang in hoarse voices a welcome to the Sabbath. And when the Sabbath was past, Yirmiyahu ran from the shop and went to gather up children. And of course Baruch *did* give the children grain to eat and water to drink, as he taught them those stark Hebrew letters that had been designed centuries ago to be chiseled into tablets of rock and not scrawled into scrolls of papyrus. Baruch could not look at their thin bodies and then hold back his grain. But often after that, he and Yirmiyahu were hungrier.

***

Sometimes Baruch told the children stories afterward, tales he had heard or read, tales of heroes, of Dawid and his Mighty Men when they lived in the Cave in the wilderness. Of Benayahu, who on a day of snow leapt into a narrow canyon and fought one of the dead with his bare hands, tearing its head from its shoulders. And Eleazar the Ahohite, who stood with Dawid, just the two of them in a field of barley, with the dead in a circle closing round them. Eleazar and Dawid fought long into the dusk, their spearheads flashing in the dim light, while the dead pressed in on them, hands clutching at them, mouths open in long moans. But as the moon rose, both warriors walked away victorious through a field of still corpses.

And there was the time that Dawid had encamped in the hills near Bet Lechem, when the town had been infested with the wakeful dead. Looking down at the little houses and the shambling figures in the streets, Dawid had laughed. "Oh, if someone would only bring me water to drink from the well of Bet Lechem by that gate!" And three of his men heard and fought their way into the town, felling the dead with their spears. Two of them held off the dead while a third pulled up a bucket from the well. Then they ran back into the hills, the bronze heads of their spears dripping with gore. When they brought Dawid the water, his face went very still, in shock at what they had tried, what they had done. He rose and took the bucket in his hands. He would not drink from it, but poured it out in a libation to God. "Far be it from me before God that I should drink the blood of my men," he said. "At the risk of their lives they brought me this water."

The children sat on the floor and gazed up at Baruch with hungry eyes as they devoured his stories of their People, that nourishment they needed as desperately as they needed grain. Yirmiyahu, too. He felt like a child again, listening to the wild stories of their ancestors. Some evenings Yirmiyahu wondered if Baruch, too, was a kind of *navi*, and if the fruit of God might come to the People through the scribe's tales, as much as through Yirmiyahu's messages. He would have to ask Baruch to write some of these stories on the scroll.

Those evenings spent in the People's remembrances of Dawid and Benayahu and Eleazar were the only moments of peace and wholeness in Yirmiyahu's life since Miriam had gone. At these moments he felt something like happiness again.

Yet there would still be mornings when he woke shuddering from dreams filled with God's quiet sobs, and as he lay breathing, he'd find himself whispering Miriam's name, his face wet with tears.

***

He had sent her away. It was something he didn't want to think about, but the memory of pain in her eyes came to him when he wasn't wary, in the moments before sleep or after waking, or worse—in the quiet hours between, when his dreaming self would walk through a wood of cedars, tall and dark, some forest of Lebanon in the north, a wild place. All through those trees he would hear her weeping, a sound that tore at him until he was frantic, his hair flying about his face as he darted through the trees and underbrush but could never find her. A few times he thought he caught a glimpse of her from behind, a figure with long, unveiled hair and a dress the color of the sand; he would run for her, calling out, then awake before he reached her, his eyes opening at the very moment she turned to face him.

Now, in the well, where there were no mouths to feed, no kings to battle, no holy work that kept grief at bay, that memory found him and fastened to him like a great leech in the mud, and he lay against the wall as it drank from him.

On that last day together, as dawn slipped into his house with the sound of voices in the street, Yirmiyahu had lain beside his wife in their bed, his body sore and stiff, the wounds on his legs aching from the previous day's stoning, though much relieved by Miriam's ointment. The *navi* had watched her sleeping, her soft body, her graceful eyelids, the delicate curve of her jaw. He thought how beautifully she was made, how God, who had birthed her into the world, must have meant for the whole world to look like that, like her. At peace, glowing with beauty. Yirmiyahu smelled her hair and caressed the long strands of it. Surely the *navi*'s task was to call the People to be worthy of God, and worthy of such a woman as his wife, made in God's likeness.

The first time he'd seen her, she was dancing in the barley during the Feast of Tents, with all about her the pavilions and booths of the People, and above her a night filled with stars. He had danced with her, and asked her name and her mother's, and she had laughed when he told her he was a levite by birth, like her, for she did not believe him. After they danced they had kissed, and the touch of her lips on his left him dizzy, and when he stumbled back to his father's tent he'd realized how sharp, how bright in color were the tents and the people and the wild thyme growing by the path.

The wedding bowl had cracked beneath their feet. He remembered how she had hummed as she moved about their first home in Anathoth, and the way she cried softly a few months later as she packed his levite's robes and her green linen gown—a gift of her mother's—for the long walk into the hills to Yerushalayim. The words they'd spoken together when he came into the room to hold her. The soft warmth of her beside him as they finished the packing together.

They had gone in the summer, and on the first night of their journey, as they laid out their bedding beneath a stand of terebinths, the cicadas in the branches made a roar with their wings that drowned out all the world's other sounds, wrapping husband and wife in a hum of privacy, the two of them alone together in the summer night. He remembered the gentleness of her kisses on his throat, the soft noises they had made together, the way she lay in his arms afterward and dreamed with him of children.

But they had also lost a child in this house, in this bed. That time Miriam had wakened in the chill hour before dawn to a flow of blood between her thighs, and her scream had awakened him. He'd held her, too numb for words, too shattered by the sight to rise and light the lamp; they wept together in the darkness of their small house. Everything in him had felt crushed and beaten by the sight of that blood. In this city the very bodies of women were desecrated; their very God was violated, and the uncleanness and disease of the People had become so great that no house in Yerushalayim could now be safe from its touch—even his own house, even his own bed.

At last he rose stiffly, gathered up the defiled sheets, and comforted his wife, though his breast felt hollow and empty as a dry well.

Things had been different after that. There had been a fierceness to her kisses, and a sorrow that welled up in both of them at times, so that they sat quietly by the cookpot some evenings without speaking. Some *hoshekh* had crept into their house.

Miriam didn't conceive again, though she asked often for her husband's touch and sometimes wept afterward; he, for his part, felt an anxiety creeping upon him, fierce and bitter: a need to protect her. When he went out into the city with that grief behind his eyes, and when he went to the Temple to speak, haranguing the priests on the white-baked stone steps, he felt keenly around him all the lives he was not doing enough for, but especially hers.

***

On that last morning, Yirmiyahu lay beside her, his body bruised and battered, and thought of what must come. Those who had beaten him would seek her out as well. The night before, they had pursued him even to the door of this house. He flinched at the thought of Miriam cast to the earth, bloodied and stoned. His heart pounded within him, his hands made fists around the bedding, and she stirred beside him at the movement. Yirmiyahu was breathing harshly. He searched inside his mind, frantic, maddened, like a man rushing about within a house with no windows and a lion barring the door, throwing himself bodily into one wall, then another, searching for some other exit. But there was no other. There was only one.

"What is wrong?" Her voice beside him was soft with sleep.

He relaxed his hands, and calm came over him, cold as winter. There was only one door in this house. He accepted it. He had to, because he was not strong enough to bear seeing her body broken in the dust, beaten and torn by jagged stones. He rolled to his side and then got to his feet, not looking at her. He couldn't, not yet. "Get dressed," he said, his voice cool and distant.

"Yirmiyahu?" Worry in her voice.

He moved about the small, lovely house, slowly but with purpose. He took out the little wooden box in which he kept his coin and spread a woolen cloak beside it, a winter garment he hadn't needed to wear in months. He opened the box and emptied it out, all of it. A music of metal, coins clacking against each other and then thudding into soft, heavy wool. He let his hand rest for a moment on the empty box; his eyes traced its ornate carvings. It was a rich little thing, a parting gift from his grandmother when he left Anathoth. It had been in the family, she'd said. "Your mother's mother's mother's mother's mother kept her little wooden gods inside it." The skin around her eyes had crinkled with amusement. "If my parents had not betrothed me to a levite," she said, "I might still be keeping little wooden gods inside it. But it has been consecrated for other uses now."

Yirmiyahu trailed his fingers across the little coins. Few enough, yet more than many in the city had. Keeping them in the box—was that another idolatry? Had there been moments when these coins had been to him like small metal gods? Governing his life, choosing his paths for him? Had he prized comfort and this little house with his wife more than his responsibility as *navi*? If the *navi* was to urge the People to become worthy of such a woman as his wife, he must throw himself even in the path of stones. But he could *not* do that here, in this house, where some stones might fly past him and strike his wife.

For the briefest moment, his hand stilled over the coins. His heart raced. He thought of bowing before the priests, wearing again the white robes. Residing in safety in this home with Miriam, until their lives were blessed at last with children. This would mean refusing to be *navi*, turning a deaf ear to God's cries in the night for the lovers who'd forsaken her. Yet even if he *could* do that thing, even if it were possible to shut out the voice of God, he could not do that and remain himself, remain true. Uprooted from truth and Covenant, he would be a man he reviled, a man who disgusted him, a man who could ignore the bruises on the thighs of children and the screams at the summit of Tophet. In time, even Miriam would revile him if he broke Covenant with God, if he became that man.

His lips thinned, and he wrapped the wool around the coins and knotted the cloak tightly to keep them from spilling. He did not need them. He would leave that box empty and let God fill it with her *shekinah*, her invisible but fertile presence, as she did the Ark in the Temple, leaving no space for other things. Compared with what else Yirmiyahu was giving up this day, these little coins were trivial, quaint objects—curiosities that others had attached importance to, as he himself once had—but in the final measure of little worth.

He felt a touch on his shoulder, a soft hand. He drew in a shuddering breath and blinked back hot tears. He didn't turn to look at her, and his voice was gruff. "I am hated here." His rough hand closed over her smaller one, gripped for a moment, one warm squeeze, and then he removed her hand from his shoulder and got to his feet. His body ached with soreness. "I cannot have you killed with stones in my place, and I cannot say what things God will need me to do, what angers I will provoke in the city." He left the cloak full of coins at his feet and moved to the urn of water that stood near their bedding; he felt her gaze on him as he took up a waterskin—the large goatskin bag he used when he had a long walk to make—and dipped it in the urn, filling it. In the dim light, the reflection of his face was just a shadow on the water; the water was cool and wet on his hands. He stood bent over the urn for a long moment, just breathing. Unwilling yet to lift his head and face her.

"My husband?" That quiver in her voice caught at him. "You are frightening me."

He couldn't delay this. "The coins are for you," he said, his voice rough. "You must go. I will sell the house and send the money after you." He straightened and took up the waterskin. "I am going out to hire a few guardsmen to keep you safe on the road to Anathoth."

"Anathoth?" The word was almost a scream. Suddenly he felt her touch at his waist, her arms moving to hold him; he shrugged her off and strode toward the door, halted at her cry.

"But you cannot send me away! I am your wife!"

Swiftly, she came before him and knelt; in her eyes burned a panic too fierce for words. "Please," she wept. "Please, do not put me away, Yirmiyahu. Husband! I have been with you—in everything—suffering with you. Does it mean nothing to you?"

Yirmiyahu groaned and bent swiftly, taking her arms and pulling her to her feet. He had never seen her so helpless before, not even when she'd lost the child. Never seen her kneel or seen her eyes overfill so openly with tears.

Something inside him choked off all words, all explanations. None of them were sufficient or could ever be. None of them could speak his heart to her. He held her eyes with his. "I have to keep you safe."

"Not like this," she whispered. Her eyes flickered with understanding and with terrible grief.

"It will be all right. Miriam." His hands trembled where they grasped her arms. He forced the words out: "I free you of your bond to me, though there is no priest here to affirm it or record it. Go where you will. Be safe, my beloved."

She just gazed at him; it was as though she'd been struck across the face and was now holding terribly still. He gripped her arms once, then released her, turned from her. He felt the burn in his eyes and feared he would weep, too. If he did, he would not be able to refrain from embracing her, from begging her forgiveness for this thing he had to do, this thing he *must* do to keep her safe.

Anger roared up inside him, a lion turned loose; he went to the door, threw it open, and strode through. She did not move or cry out his name, but he felt her watching him. He walked out into the street and then on into the tangle of the city, uncaring of where his feet might take him, leaving the house behind. His heart burned within him. He could not keep her here. He *could* not.

But how he'd *wounded* her!

As the lily among the thorns, his love, and he'd—

With a snarl, he quickened his pace until he was almost running. There were curses hurled after him as he jostled his way through the people in the street— the sweaty, reeking river of the living who made the rough stones of the street smooth with their hundreds of feet. He needed to find guardsmen he could hire, but first he craved only a moment alone, to breathe, to—

He threw himself into a side alley and against the shaded clay wall of a shop. Slammed his open palms against it. "*God!*" he shrieked. "*God!*"

Sobs grabbed hold of his chest and squeezed his breath and his life into something as small and tense as a wrung towel; he cried and beat at the wall; he fought for breath in small gasps. When he could he screamed again: "*God!*"

A hot wind blew down the street; he didn't heed the glances of passersby who covered their faces with their hoods or street veils, if they were women, and hurried past. For a moment he felt the warm breath of the air on his skin and at his ear, like God's breath. *I am with you always*, the breath whispered. *Even now, even now, Yirmiyahu.*

"I have broken covenant with my wife," Yirmiyahu replied, a moan rising in his throat. "I have broken covenant with my wife."

The wind brought no answer to his ears or to his heart.

Yirmiyahu slid to his knees and leaned his head against the wall, pressing the side of his face against the cool clay. His shoulders shook, and he spent the rest of the day there.

***

Yirmiyahu's head jerked up. With terrible lucidity, he saw the mud in the well, the cold walls, felt the thirst in his throat. Panic seized him. He was going to die here.

With a cry, he forced himself to his feet, though the exertion threw him into such dizziness that he thought he'd vomit. His stomach heaving, he faced the wall, searching with his fingers. Stone, mortared and polished smooth by long years of holding water. His fingertips found small cracks, tiny ledges; gasping, he gripped them. Wrenched his foot from the mud with a sound like something spewed from the stomach of a sea creature. His numb toes slid along the stones. Whimpering and muttering, he tried to pull himself up by his fingertips, thinking his toes might find some higher purchase.

Nothing. He lost his grip and slid into the mud, his fingers badly scraped. He moaned and beat the wall with his hands. Bent his head, his forehead against smooth stone. Breathing hard, he muttered a quick, urgent prayer. He'd been taught that God was to be found in all the depths of the earth, in every place. She must be here, too. Though one of his eyes was swollen too dry to make tears, Yirmiyahu wept and begged.

Why had God let him be cast in here? How terribly had he failed as her *navi*? Had she utterly left the city, driven from it by the desecration of her children?

He quieted, listened. He heard only his own panting in the horrible silence of the well.

Roaring hoarsely, he lurched to his feet again, scrambled at the wall, fighting it in a panic, reaching for holds, anything. He got his toes into a crevice no wider than a coin, reached for a higher handhold, pressing his fingertips against the stone, wheezing as he searched. Nothing—nothing! His calf trembled from the strength it took to keep gripping the rock with his toes. He reached farther over his head, then groped far to the left, then to the right along the smooth stone. He found shallow impressions in the rock, nothing he could use to pull himself up. He gazed at the circle of daylight far above him. Almost more than anything else, more than water or food, he wanted that light. He wanted to stand in an open place, tilt back his head, and feel the sun's heat on his eyelids. He howled, a bestial cry of need that echoed in the well but brought no answer.

His leg gave out; he collapsed, fell over one of the corpses, shoved himself off it in horror. Losing his balance, he tumbled to the side, plunging his face into the dark, sucking mud. A moment of desperate terror, then he lifted his head, got to a crouch, and pressed his back to the stone wall, his knees drawn up. Frantic, he scrubbed mud from his face with the heels of his hands. His eyes stung. The rot in the well assailed his nostrils anew; he beat at his face with his hands, moaning. He was alone, alone. He would die here. He drew his knees close and shut his eyes, praying again, muttering. "We are the People of the Covenant," he rasped. "Made in the likeness of God." Tapped the back of his head against the wall, as a child does when frustrated, a child who is too young to speak. "We are the People of the Covenant," he groaned, "the spouse of the Giver of Life. None of us lost, none of us forgotten. We are her own."

He fell silent, listened for some trace of that small whisper of God. Then prayed again. He kept tapping his head against the stone.

***

Darkness again.

He blinked his eyes but could not see. He tried to cry out—*adonai, adonai, my God, my God*—but his throat was too parched. He was shivering, though he felt hot as an iron blade set too near a fire. He touched his skin with fingers caked with mud; he burned. He became aware of wetness about his belly and sides; he was sitting slumped in the mud, leaning forward over his knees with his feet planted on what must be sound earth under the muck. Only that position and the cramped immobility of his bent legs was keeping him upright.

For a long, long time he wept. He sat in a world of wet and shadow, of *hoshekh* that clung to the skin and seeped inside him. *Miriam*, he croaked. *Miriam*.

He would never forget his last sight of her. Those eyes overfull with tears. She had always been overfull with love; in loving her and then leaving her, he had taken hold of her and crushed that love from her, until her tears came out at the eyes like that, a terrible wound he had given her, whom he loved.

His lips formed, almost soundlessly, the words his throat could not make. *Adonai, oh adonai. Giver of Life, Sacred Womb, Maker of all that lives and moves. The kings have failed the People. The prophets, too. I failed Miriam. I failed you. I am dying in a dry well. It is over. Who will take responsibility for this People? What* navi *will be there to preserve whatever can be preserved of the city and the land?*

Whether in echo of his own despairing thoughts or in answer to them, remembered words sounded in his heart: *Would that all her People were prophets.*

That was Miriam. Miriam had said that. She'd been quoting Moseh, the Lawgiver who'd led their ancestors out of the desert with many wonders, and given them the *mitzvot* to keep justice among their tribes and keep the People clean of the dead.

Would that all her People were prophets. Spoken as Miriam crouched over a pot making a stew. Yirmiyahu had seated himself across from her that night. He was talking of—things. The walking dead that had begun to appear. The famishing of widows and children in the city. It was months yet before the start of the siege. "People do not feel safe," he was telling her. He'd been younger then, bewildered but confident that the city would be saved, the People brought back to the Covenant. He'd been sure even the levites would listen, if he just went often enough to the Temple steps.

He had not yet seen the hill of Tophet.

"People do not feel safe in their own city. Miriam, my Miriam, there are children starving, alone. Easy prey for the dead. And I think there are more dead in the city than we think." He chewed on his knuckles a moment—a nervous trait he'd later drop entirely after Tophet, after sending Miriam away, after his heart became smaller and harder inside him.

On the other side of the cookpot, Miriam's face was aglow, not only with the sweat of laboring over the stew but also, as Yirmiyahu would later know, with the pregnancy she'd just become aware of, the pregnancy she would tell her husband about later that night—a blessing and a joy that, like Yirmiyahu's faith that the priests could be won over, would be all too brief.

But a the time he was barely aware of the brightness in her eyes, so occupied was he with his doubts. He had been *navi* only a few short months. God's words still came rarely to him, and still only at night. In truth, Yirmiyahu felt alone. "Miriam," he murmured, "this is not like the old days. I am not like the old prophets. Eliyahu called fire from heaven to cleanse the land; the undead withered and crumbled to ash. And Devora the Old—though no fire fell from the sky, she razed half the vineyards of Israel before the land was cleansed. She did it, though. And there were—healings."

He shook his head. These tales had been passed down from grandfather to grandson and from grandmother to granddaughter through centuries of levites. Now, for the first time, he wondered whether all of that had really happened, if the *neviim* in the past had ever truly stood before the People or against the dead with anything other than words from God. "Healings, Miriam," he said, his eyes on the stew, on the bubbling, on something that was certain and could be trusted: when you put hot fluid over coals, it bubbled and a pleasant scent went up. It needed no story from your grandfather for you to trust *that*. Like God's voice in the night, the boiling in the pot was *there*, evident, something a man's own eyes and ears could know.

Yirmiyahu continued reciting the stories, searching for comfort in the names and acts of each previous *navi* who'd mended the Covenant and preserved the People from the ravenous dead. "Yarobham's hand was bitten, his arm gray—a prophet healed him, calling on the name of God. And a Syrian came to Elisa asking to be healed; he was already shaking with it. And Elisa sent him to the river and washed away the bite as though it were only dirt on his skin. And when Menahem the Mad repented and the prophetess Hadassah instructed him to take every walking corpse he could find in the city and impale them on the walls, every last one, until there were eighty-seven in all, writhing and moaning in the morning sun—" Yirmiyahu's voice grew softer as he imagined the horror of it. "*When that was done,*" he whispered, "*all in the city who'd been bitten but had not succumbed grew hale again.*"

"My husband." Miriam touched his hand with hers.

He barely noticed; his eyes saw other things. "I am no prophet like Elisa or Hadassah," he said. "I have only words and no other gift, no power to heal the bitten or feed the starving. When I pray—" He bit, and a little blood ran from his knuckles. "When I pray, God only sends more words. What good are words when we need a gift like Elisa's?" He pressed his fingers to his temples. "What kind of *navi* am I, Miriam?"

"A dutiful one," she said after a moment, "a man who keeps Covenant and asks others to, a man the People need right now, a man I love." Miriam gripped his fingers, squeezed them. "You don't have to contend with eighty-seven dead, as Hadassah did, or with hordes out of the northern cedars, as Devora did. There are only a few dead, and there is grain behind the Temple to feed the city, or most of it," Miriam offered. "If all the priests and all the merchants in this city were men like my husband, all would be well. What the People need is the gift you *do* bring from God, Yirmiyahu—the gift of words that are true, when everyone else fills their ears with words that are not. Would that all God's people were prophets!"

Her voice was soft, and Yirmiyahu found himself drawn from his doubts to listen; he saw the way her eyes shone. Her gaze held him, catching at his heart.

"If only we all heard the words you hear," she said. "If only we all listened as passionately, with such suffering, as you do, husband. But most of us can't, and many don't want to." She paused a moment. "I think I feel God in the house sometimes, in the mornings—but I never hear words. Only you do. As a woman," she added softly, "I know how important it is for someone to hear you, and how hard it is. There are so many places where I cannot speak, even if I had a lot to say; it wouldn't be permitted, and you as my husband must speak for me. I cannot stand in the street like a man and cry out what is in my heart. God can't do this either, I think. She needs you to speak for her. Without your words, the priests would keep her shut away behind that veil in the Temple, the way some husbands shut away their wives, or locked into the Ark; no one would hear her." Her eyes shone above the glow of the coals.

"Until all her people are prophets, your words are all we have, Yirmiyahu."

THIRD DAY: WIND IN THE DARK

HE STARTLED, his body lurching out of a sleep that had been deep but of unknown duration. The hiss was near him in the dark and very loud. His vision was blurred, but he could *hear* it. If it was really there. His hands tightened, and in one of them he felt the slender rib he'd torn from the girl's corpse. A life gift from a man's body to a woman's, that rib could now be converted in the brutality of this well into a weapon. His unclean hand grasping the rib, he again felt feverish with shame, complicit in all the defilements of his city. He hacked from his scorched throat and rolled onto his knees, almost falling into the mud.

That hiss!

The thing had not seized him yet; perhaps it was less mobile even than the last had been. A desire to live roared up inside his chest like a monster bursting into life, fierce and undeniable, though it had not been there a moment before. He blinked desperately, could see a dark form only an arm's length away. He threw himself at it, certain he would feel teeth cutting into his arm but just as certain that if he delayed but a moment he would find himself half-conscious again, helpless food for the broken thing that would eventually crawl or wriggle near enough to feed.

This was the most terrible of his struggles in the well.

It was a scuffling, a wrestling without sight or even clarity of mind; just two human bodies, one dehydrated and shaking, the other too broken to permit the use of more than one limb—just two bodies tumbling and tearing at each other in the mud and the dark. Brutal, silent, except for Yirmiyahu's labored breathing and the other thing's hissing and biting on air. Yirmiyahu stabbed again and again with the sharp rib, piercing perhaps the creature's neck, upper chest, or even face, but whatever demon gave it the semblance of life did not perish. For one instant that jolted through him like a silent scream, Yirmiyahu felt the thing's teeth scrape across his bare shoulder, but he was rolling with it on top of him, and a knee pressed up into its belly sent it tumbling to the side into the mud. A wordless, rasping cry, and the *navi* threw himself back on top of it, driving the rib down like a spear. One dry, cold hand clutched at his arm, pulling his wrist toward snapping teeth; Yirmiyahu caught a reflection of the distant sun in two gray, scratched eyes. That was enough to orient him. With his other hand he grasped the thing's hair, holding its head still. Its strength was terrible, but he forced his arm up above its jaws and twisted and drove the rib hard between its eyes. The thing bucked under him.

Then it was still. No last rattle of breath in the throat. Only stillness. Yirmiyahu collapsed over it like a spent lover, and for a while everything—the corpse, the mud, the well, the city outside, God—everything simply stopped existing. He did not even dream.

***

He woke as dry as though he'd swallowed the sun and it had caught in his throat. For a long stretch of uncounted and unaccountable time, he gazed up the sheer sides of the well. It was difficult to conceive of any world but the cracked stone walls and the still, cold form beneath him and the distant circle of sunlight and heat, as untouchable as a bird and silent as a mirage in the desert.

Yirmiyahu wanted to call out to God, but his body was spent, and in weary dread he felt sure his prayers would only echo unheard in the hollowness of the well. Surely God was leaving her city as it became defiled and uninhabitable, leaving to the desert the People she'd once called from it.

He lay on the corpse; he could feel the hard stillness of it keeping him half-propped out of the mud. The touch of its breast against him was like the touch of a stone in winter. He was shivering, though he only just now realized it. He thought about that for a while, tried to muster the strength of will to lift himself.

He wondered whether the guards who'd come for him had let Baruch go. And what might have become of the children? Baruch had been teaching them when the guards came in the evening; the children had let out cries of dismay. Baruch had just risen to his feet, silent and impassive, a man carved out of a cliff wall. Seizing Yirmiyahu by the arms, the guards had pulled him out the door, not even bothering to bind him. The *navi*'s last glance over his shoulder had been at Baruch and the children framed in the doorway: so many eyes on him.

What would become of them all? He had seen dead shuffling along in the alleys they passed as the guards pulled him toward the king's house. How many were there now? And how long would the city's walls stand? Would there be only dead within when the Babylonians finally breached Yerushalayim's towers of stone?

He lifted himself up on his hands, sobbing with the effort. He needed to get away from this body. It reeked; everything reeked of death. There was too much death, too much. He wanted only to hurl himself into the cool mud, and if he died there and the slithering things beneath it ate him, it was enough: he would be content. So long as he did not have to look with his own eyes on any more unclean death.

Breathing hard, he glanced down at the corpse.

His breath caught. Everything in him stilled.

For a long, long time, he just stared at the torn, defiled face.

A terrible sound came from his throat, a sound he had never heard a living being make. A low keen, a moan as heavy with yearning as the wailing of the dead. It was like the scream a hare makes when a farmer has caught it and is beating it with a great stick to kill it. That madness scream before the hare falls into the burrow that has no bottom, the burrow that keeps plummeting all the way down to death. Yirmiyahu lifted mud-caked fingers, cupped the dead face in his palm, the flesh of it so cold it sucked the heat from his hand; it was as though a hole had been punched right through him, and now wind was rushing through the dark in his belly. The moan in his throat rose to a shriek that tore up everything in his chest and left only jagged streamers of flesh and spirit.

It was her face. Hers. Miriam. His wife. It was *her* face.

It was shattered, it was distorted, the eyes emptied of everything and flesh torn from her, but it was her; he knew that face, he couldn't be mistaken. It was her.

She'd come back, then. Somehow, before the siege began. She'd come back to the city, or had never actually left—she'd come to find him, perhaps come even to their old house.

But she hadn't found him; somewhere within the city, the dead had found her.

Yirmiyahu screamed until his throat was raw with it. He fell to his side, his hands cupping her head, pressed his face into her shoulder, unable to look at those dead eyes. He kept screaming, and then he could make no sound at all; and still he screamed, his mouth open without any sound but the rasp of escaping breath.

THIRD NIGHT: AS PAPYRUS BURNS

AT THE WELL'S BOTTOM, Yirmiyahu lay without waking, his body racked with cold and dryness. In the city above, the walking corpses fed and felt no remorse for the cries or the panic of the living. This was a night of the dead, in a city of the dead. He knew it, he knew it. *Hoshekh.* Surely everything above him was dead.

To wake fully would be unbearable. Yet what dream or words out of the past could aid him in this moment? His mind fled through memories that were recent but held no comfort.

***

Tsidkiyyahu had held the scroll in his own hand and let it burn. The fire licked and chewed at the edges as he unrolled it slowly over the candle he'd brought to Yirmiyahu's cell, letting the flame spread a shadow of crackling darkness across the tiny lines of black text.

It took three men to restrain Yirmiyahu. He screamed and kicked, throwing his torso from side to side as though to wrench his arms loose of their bindings by brute strength, like Samson of old, whom no cords could restrain unless he'd first been held and gentled in a woman's arms.

Yirmiyahu threw back his head and howled; still the men held him. Still the little scroll burned; the young king unrolled it a little at a time, watching the slow creep of the flames, inexorable and destructive as pestilence. In desperation, the prophet turned his head and seized on the throat of one of the guards, biting, digging in hard with his teeth. His mouth filled with the taste and scent of human blood; the guard cried out shrilly, and in a moment the others had torn Yirmiyahu loose and cast him to the earthen floor. A sandaled foot slammed between his shoulder blades, holding him still. He growled and spat until a guard shoved the butt of a spear into the back of his head.

Then he lay still, his eyes open, the room unsteady to his gaze. In a kind of stupor, he watched the king feed Baruch's scroll to the flame, one column of ink at a time. The fire's hunger was too hot now for the candle's thin wick; the flame was too high. The candle melted even as Yirmiyahu watched, wax streaming down its sides. It shortened and shrank even as the flames fed upon the scroll, for fire is the only one of God's creatures that eventually grows thinner and smaller the more it devours.

In the end Tsidkiyyahu flicked his fingers, dropping the last crinkling bit of ash onto the earthen floor. Yirmiyahu watched a few flakes of it drift on the air.

The earth was cool against his cheek.

Sandaled feet stepped into his vision—fine sandals, studded with tiny gems, so that they startled the eyes. He heard the king's voice above him.

"I want you to make me a vow, Yirmiyahu. I want you to vow you will never again make such a scroll. On pain of death—not for you but for the scribe you hire."

Without lifting his head, Yirmiyahu wetted his lips and spat on the sandaled feet. Then the hard weight of a spear slammed into the back of his head again, and he fell off the floor and into a dark place.

***

Baruch had tried to warn him. Scrolls, those children of God's lips and men's hands, were as fragile as the children of women's bodies. They might be devoured as easily, lost as easily, forgotten as easily. If a people could forget the pain in the eyes of children, they could forget God. And if a people could forget God, they could forget the words she gave. If they could forget the words she gave, they could forget the pain in the eyes of children.

***

"We must make a new scroll." His lips were parched and cracked. Savage pain in the back of his head where the spear had struck him. "Miriam, we have to tell Baruch. Miriam, tell Baruch."

The hand that had been dabbing his brow with a damp cloth paused. The voice near his ear was deep and resonant. Baruch's voice. "Miriam isn't here, friend. You sent her away."

Yirmiyahu coughed once. "Why would I do that?"

The cloth dabbed again, now at his eyelids. It felt very cool, very soothing, though only when it touched his closed eyes did he realize how hot, how seared they had been. "Hush, friend. Rest now; you were beaten badly. We can talk later."

***

In his sleep, Yirmiyahu heard a woman humming, somewhere near—a soft sound, very beautiful. It made him think of his grandmother, in his father's house at Anathoth, and how as a child he'd wakened often to the sound of her humming as she worked at her loom by the window, bright threads of dyed wool moving through her fingers. She was always humming lullabies, even when it was morning and the world was waking; perhaps she felt the world was too much awake and ought to doze more of the time. He remembered sometimes sitting in her lap as a small child while she hummed, while his father, her son, was away, sacrificing a white bull or an unblemished goat in atonement for the uncleanness of the people or in honor of the blessings given him by the Giver of Life. Yirmiyahu remembered his grandmother's scent of dried rosemary, and the way her humming sometimes bloomed like a sunflower and became her voice, a soft voice unroughened by age.

Sleep, my child, sleep,
And I will sing to thee
Of the sun and the rain
And the sycamore tree
And the ships that walk on the sea.

Yirmiyahu opened his eyes, found himself staring up at stout rafters of cedar, warm with sunlight. A white butterfly, no larger than his thumbnail, hovered about one of the rafters, its wings opening and closing like a child's hands. Yirmiyahu felt a wool blanket gentle and warm under his fingertips. He drew in breath slowly, then breathed out. Sore, he sat up; he was in a little wooden room with a high window. This wasn't the house of Baruch the scribe. And it wasn't the house he'd shared with Miriam his wife in Yerushalayim before the siege, or the house he'd shared with her for a short time in Anathoth. This was *his* room, his own room in the home of his childhood, in that sturdy old house of cedar, his father's house, a place of safety and surety. At the table in the next room, he'd learned to read, tracing his fingertip gently over the lines of hard, angular letters in his father's scroll of the Law, the only scroll the town possessed. Though his writing had always been slow and halting, he could read more swiftly even than his father, or any of the other levites in his father's town. He used to stand at the doorstep of this house after dark, looking out over the fields by moonlight and reciting the *mitzvot*, the many rules of the Law, in a rumbling Hebrew dialect that was now centuries old but very beautiful.

He flung the blanket aside; he was in his loincloth. He slid his legs from the low bed; his feet hit the cool wood floor. He sucked in his breath; the firmness of that wood was strange to him. How long had it been since he'd slept above a wooden floor rather than an earthen one?

He could still hear a woman humming faintly; his grandmother must be at her loom. He pressed his hands to the thin mattress and pushed himself to his feet. The rafters were just above his head; his hair brushed them—this room was smaller than he recalled. He swayed a moment, caught at one of the beams with his hand. He stood there sweating—why was his body so weary?—and listened, listened. The humming became song, and his eyes widened. The sound wasn't coming from within the house. It was coming through the window, from outside. And it was a voice he knew.

His heart raced. "Not grandmother," he whispered. "Miriam."

Without losing another moment, he hurried from the room and darted through the dining chamber, his hip colliding with the table in his haste. He reached the door, hurled it open, threw himself out into sunlight so bright it seared his eyes and left him standing, blinking, in the grass.

He heard her laughter, high-pitched and sweet, and in a moment felt her warm, small hand take his, and another hand pressed over his eyelids; afterimages still danced hot and white against the dark of his lids. He moaned with the pain of it.

"You'll be all right, husband." Her voice, near his ear. "But how funny you looked, leaping from the house in your loincloth, like you were on fire!"

"I *am* on fire," he murmured.

She laughed again, and he felt the softness of her lips pressed to his. It overwhelmed him, so that tears stung against his eyelids—or perhaps that was the pain from the sun against his brow. They would need to find shade. But for this moment he simply relished the touch of her smooth hand against his eyelids and the taste of her mouth.

When she took her hand from his eyes and he opened them, blinking, they were seated together on a cool white stone in the shade of a tall terebinth with branches that seemed to spread a roof of leaves across half the sky. He remembered that tree; his father used to read passages from the Law to him beneath it.

He looked at his wife. She was young; she looked as she had when they first met. Her hair was dark in the shade, her eyes darker; he couldn't stop gazing at them. His lips were parted; he was rapt. Her small hand he held in his. Somewhere across the fields that stretched wide and free about his father's house and the nearby village of Anathoth, he could hear a herdsman singing, a sound faint and lovely.

The leaves of the terebinth above them moved without any breeze, and he was speared by the cold certainty that he was asleep and dreaming—and that this wasn't any night dream but a *true* dream. There was a vividness to it, a reality to the ache in his hip where he'd hit the table, the warmth of Miriam's hand in his. His heart beat within him. He felt, with that utter and complete certainty that only comes in dreams, that Miriam was truly visiting him—to say good-bye—and that when he woke he would not see her again.

"Miriam," he whispered.

She smiled, her eyes moist; then her face crumpled. "I missed you."

Almost shyly, he reached out, touched her hair, then caressed it. "Forgive me," he whispered.

"You wanted me to go." Her eyes were deep. "I—I couldn't. I got as far as the gate, then dismissed the man you sent with me. I went back into the city. I went to find you." Her face flushed, and Yirmiyahu could feel her anger like lightning in the air. "You had no right to send me away. I am not a dog, Yirmiyahu, or a donkey, or a packet of dried herbs you can return to my mother because you're afraid you'll only lose it."

"I know." He took one of her hands in his, gripped it, his face contorted with the violence of his grief, the strain of trying to pour into words something that mere physical, animal sounds could never contain or convey. "I was afraid for you—"

"In all that city, what could you need more than me at your side?" Her eyes flashed. "And what could I need more than your arms around me and your heart listening to me? Yirmiyahu! We were going to have *children* together—if we could."

"I know," he whispered again.

The terebinth faded from sight; everything became a featureless gray. There was only her, and in a moment she would be gone, too. Yirmiyahu cried out and pulled her to him, held her tight, felt her tense. Then her body relaxed and she shook with silent sobs. He breathed raggedly himself, unable to bear the sweetness and the pain of this moment. Everything tight, painfully tight, in his chest. He crushed her to him, breathed in the scent of her hair, felt her warmth in his arms, whispered her name again and again.

"I love you," he said hoarsely.

"And I you," she wept. "I you, my husband."

***

Sunlight came through the cracks in the boards over the window, sharp splinters of light that made his eyes sting. He lifted his hand but could still see the light through his fingers. He drew in breath slowly, the loss of her a violence in his chest. His head turned from the window; Baruch was sitting there beside the blanket on which he lay. When their eyes met, Baruch nodded once, though his face showed no other expression.

Yirmiyahu moved his lips to speak, but his throat was too dry.

"We are under house arrest, friend," Baruch said quietly. "The king is merciful." His lip twisted.

Yirmiyahu shut his eyes a moment. Already the dream was slipping from his mind, like bright foliage torn away and riding the wind into the distance. The ache in his chest. He swallowed once. He had to put away thoughts of her. The memory of the past days—the burning of the scroll—it all came back. There was work to do. There was always work to do. More now than before.

He was *navi*.

Yirmiyahu tried to get up; the room spun. Baruch's gentle hand on his breast pushed him back. "Lie still," his friend murmured.

"Have to"—a hoarse croak—"another scroll—and copies—many as we can—"

"You do that, my friend, and they will bury you somewhere. That young king will drop you into some dry well and leave you there until this city is nothing but ash." Baruch's voice was firm, as uncompromising as the hand that kept Yirmiyahu down. Yirmiyahu clutched at his friend's wrist, though his fingers seemed weak as twigs. He had to get up. He had to speak the words God had spoken to him—for this he had given up Miriam, sending her away while he remained here. He had to keep going. Had to—

"Help me," he rasped.

Baruch didn't move his hand. His voice was intense, more impassioned than Yirmiyahu had ever heard him speak. "It is only a miracle of your God that you are alive—God, and my begging at the king's door. It is over, Yirmiyahu."

Yirmiyahu's lip curved grimly; he felt consciousness slipping from him and fought it. "Only when I'm dead," he growled as he fell.

***

He woke abruptly. It was dark, utterly dark. He threw out his hands, felt cold stone around him, hard and immovable. The well. He was in the well. The burning of the scroll, waking in Baruch's house, that conversation with the scribe—all of it many weeks past. His heart pounded. In the midst of those memory dreams, he'd been sent a true dream beneath the waving branches of the terebinth: he was certain of it. Miriam had visited him in his sleep. Coughing clawed into his throat and he bent over, hacking into the mud, his insides trying to hurl themselves up his throat and out into the well.

When he could breathe again, wheezing in the dark, he felt around slowly; his hand found the cold chest of one of the corpses, which lay almost against his side in the mud. He needed no light to tell him which it was; his heart told him. Shaking, breathing in great rasps, he lay over the body. His hands moved up the still form, remembering her, until they found her face, which was slick with mud; he gripped her head but could not turn it. His fingers found her still, hard eyes and traced the large roundness of her nose, which he had always loved and which by some marvel had survived her death intact. He ran his hands up over her brow and found her head shattered, punctured, and tears burned his eyes. He found her lips with his thumb and traced them; they were no longer soft as they had been in life. Weeping, he kissed her. Taking her lower lip between his, he kissed her gently, tasting mud and old blood. The reek of her was sickeningly sweet in his nostrils; he ignored it and kissed her as lovingly, as yearningly, as he had on their first night. Until his next coughing fit seized him and shook him like a rabbit in a jackal's jaws.

He hadn't been there when she perished. That was the only thought that could grip the slick, sliding surface of his mind. With the same clarity and certainty with which he'd seen her in the true dream, beneath the terebinth—a *navi*'s clarity in seeing what had been or what would be—he now saw her walking in the city, her eyes swollen from tears. Saw how Miriam had returned to find him, unwilling to leave him, the man she had suffered with and loved, the man she was covenanted to. She'd found their house dark and empty, its new owner not yet moved in; from the door she'd called out her husband's name. There'd been a noise, a clatter in the other room, a thump against the wall. "Yirmiyahu?" she'd called. She'd stepped carefully through the dark, looking for him. She'd approached the door to their bedchamber, where they'd made love so many nights, and other nights simply fallen asleep holding each other, and still other nights gone to sleep with their backs to each other, their hearts pierced by anger or guilt from some fight left unfinished. Her small fingers had touched the wood of the door, nudged it open. With a creak it had swung inward. She peered through it, in the dim light from the room's small window, light torn by the broken, snapped, violated slats of wood that had half barred that opening; something had smashed through it. Beneath the window, in its faint, shredded light, she could glimpse a shape crouching.

"Yirmiyahu?" Her voice softer, with fear.

The shape had straightened slowly, its eyes glinting in the dim light. Its hands lifted. A low groan in the dark as it took an unsteady step toward her.

Yirmiyahu couldn't see the rest. Perhaps Miriam had frozen in terror, seeing that hulking figure move toward her; perhaps she'd bolted, darting into the other room only to crack her hip against the table and tumble with a shriek to the floor. The vision passed from him, slipping away as swiftly as had the true dream beneath the terebinth.

Yirmiyahu groaned through clenched teeth and twined his fingers into her hair. He kissed her again as he wept, leaving tears and mucus on her nose and cheek.

He hadn't been there.

And with a jagged rib, he'd completed the desecration of her body, the defiling of a body holy and beautiful, her body, his wife's body. How completely he had failed her and betrayed her.

She'd needed him, she had come for him, she'd come back to find him. And when that corpse had torn into her, he hadn't been there.

That knowledge roared through him, and in its passing the last certainties inside him lit and cracked like papyrus on fire; everything in him simply burned away. He kissed her until the remnants in his chest crumbled into ash; then he lay still, clasping her, half lying in the mud that remained as mute testimony that the empty husk of the well had once been a body filled with water and life.

***

A slow crawl of time that could not be tasted or touched. The three corpses grew colder, the reek of them thicker. Harsh coughing in the well in between those stretches of fitful sleep in which the only sound was the rasp of labored breathing. Then more coughing.

***

Perhaps in the city above—if it were not already lost to the lurching dead—perhaps the new scrolls, the copies Baruch had made, though reluctantly, had found a few voices to recite them on the Temple steps; perhaps some of the younger levites gathered in quiet rooms even now, drawing the slats over the windows, then speaking in hushed whispers of Yirmiyahu's words. It was possible. But in the well Yirmiyahu was bereaved of words. His grief had torn so much out of his chest that he simply lay, unlistening, like a corpse waiting to be stirred.

It was possible that in an hour, or a day, or a week, if he still breathed, the guards might pull him out, shivering like a child from the womb. Perhaps God would speak then; perhaps she would gift him with new words, words that would cup him as a woman's warm hands might cup an infant, holding him, words of such promise and hope that they could replenish both his heart and this drying and dying city. Or perhaps, though no words should come, were he to be pulled into the brightness of the day above and into the fierce light of God's presence, he might yet emerge from the well with a primal scream, a raw shriek capable of conveying the horror and loss of every severing of bond and covenant that men or women had suffered since the first birth. This was possible. The silence in the well might be the silence of utter bereavement or the silence before birth. In the fertility of her heart, God's capacity for giving birth and loving rebirth might still be greater than any death—if she hadn't left the city entirely. Or if she had but might yet come back, even as Miriam had come back from the gate, and if she survived her return, as Miriam hadn't. Yirmiyahu didn't know. He could no longer hear God weeping behind her veil. He could no longer hear anything but his own labored breathing.

***

Yirmiyahu lay over his dead wife. The well filled with death as with dark water and with darkness that filled the mouth and nostrils until he lay completely still, the fire in his ribs snuffed out. His body almost forgot to breathe. In this hole in the city there was neither pain nor sorrow nor regret nor memory of joy. The world was cold and filled with the hungry and the dead, and in the numb *hoshekh* of time everything was lost and nothing recovered. In the lethal, irremediable quiet, Yirmiyahu waited without thought or movement for the whisper of God's voice or the rattle of a dying breath in his throat. Waiting in the silence, waiting in the silence.

.

WHAT OUR EYES HAVE WITNESSED

BASED LOOSELY ON THE EVENTS
OF THE MARTYRIUM POLYCARPI

ANCIENT ROME

To my wife, Jessica, for her love and her laughter
and
To my daughters, River and Inara—
may we strive to our last breath
to leave you a better world

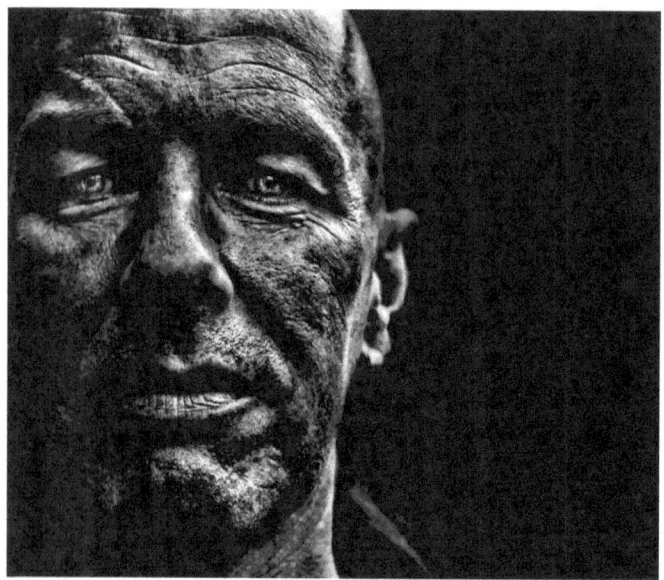

Polycarp's gaze

HISTORIAN'S NOTE

WHAT YOU ARE READING is one installment of *The Zombie Bible*, a series of narratives based on certain well-known records of humanity's enduring struggle with the undead. The original records are a mixture of poetic texts, lyrics to ancient songs set to drum and lyre, works of prophecy, legal testimonies, and chronicles both historical and hagiographical. Originally inscribed in Hebrew, Greek, Aramaic, and Latin on substances as varied as papyrus scrolls, chiseled rock, animal skins, and thin parchment, these records speak eloquently to us of one of history's few constants:

Hunger.

The persistence of hunger as a defining factor in the human condition has never been more clear to us than today, as we face the resurgence of the old pestilence in several parts of our globe. In those regions of the world already broken by earthquakes and famine, where men and women no less noble or intelligent than you and I (though considerably more impoverished) each day face the menacing threat of the walking dead, the greater horror is the brutal reality that the dead represent: the reality that people devour people, and that when our dead rise, they look like us.

If we can learn anything from retelling the stories of our spiritual ancestors—whether Polycarp the martyr, David the lover, Devora the prophetess, Samson the warrior, Simon the fisherman, or any of a hundred others—we can perhaps learn again how to face a rapidly decomposing world with a wild and conquering hope, an impossible hope.

I do not know if hope can be stronger than hunger. But I know that they believed it so.

***

Few episodes in European history have left such a lingering impact on Western consciousness as the outbreak of the living dead in ancient Rome and the subsequent persecutions of the early Church and its sister sects. It's important to know that these outbreaks didn't occur until late in Rome's history. While it lasted, the Roman Republic had seen only a few isolated encounters with the undead—the loss of an embassy in Pontus, the discovery of an infected island in the Middle Sea during Pompey's campaign against the corsairs, and that terrible winter that left one of Julius Caesar's forts in Gaul surrounded by a forest filled with moaning and ravenous dead.

It wasn't until the time of the Emperors that an outbreak occurred within the Eternal City itself. At first, a few reports of cannibalism in the riverside ghetto known as the Subura were largely ignored or dismissed as the primitivism of the immigrants who in that century were already flooding into Rome in great numbers from the East. But in Rome under Nero, conditions in the swollen belly of the Subura became so crowded and so unpoliced that the pestilence grew to an epidemic that threatened to consume Rome itself. Nero in his madness and panic torched the city, then blamed both the plague and the fire on an obscure Eastern cult that had taken hold in the Subura. The cult, who called themselves Brothers and Sisters of the Fish, had seen enormous gains in membership during the year of the plague, as their apostles offered both a promised cure for the walking death and a vision of a more egalitarian city in which no crowded and hungering Subura would exist.

The fire ended the outbreak, but Nero's persecutions afterward did more to secure him a place in history than either the dead or their elimination. Tacitus's Histories record the lurid details of what occurred in a tone so objective and documentary that its power to shock the reader is magnified. Pointing to the cultists' communion rite, which on the surface appeared to resemble acts of cannibalism, and to their talk of the "Gift" of a cure that involved touching and absolving the restless dead, Nero apparently adopted an extreme "punishment shall fit the crime" approach to extinguishing their gathering. The few walking corpses that had been rounded up and chained were loosed in Roman arenas on hundreds of captive Christians, and Roman crowds cheered to see those who had (presumably) brought the plague to Rome devoured by it.

Mindful of how fire had cleansed the city, Nero made living torches of the cult's leaders, both men and women, burning them on trees in the Emperor's gardens. Senators and patricians of Rome walked through the gardens while the captives burned around them; they talked of the latest scandals, or affairs of state, or how to replace members of the Senate and the People that had perished in the epidemic. They did not glance for more than a moment at the human torches that lit the garden paths, nor listen too closely to the muffled screams from their gagged mouths. In this way, Rome balanced its accounts and banished from its streets both the memory of the plague and (they believed) the presence of those they blamed for it.

***

Modern readers are often astounded by the crumbling of Rome; everything we know about the Roman military (its discipline, its encouragement of innovation and creative problem-solving, and its adherence to a rigid code of duty and patriotism) appears well suited to the task of quarantining and eliminating an epidemic of the undead. Yet everything about Roman culture and religion conspired to leave the Roman civilization helpless against the actual occurrence of that plague within their own city. Three cultural norms made this the case: sanitation, caste, and ancestor worship.

First, the Romans placed an unprecedented importance on sanitation; as the river was badly polluted, nine vast aqueducts carried clean water to the hillside homes of the wealthy and to public fountains throughout the city. Additionally, the more affluent classes spent several hours a day bathing and oiling their bodies. The Romans invented the world's most advanced sewage system up until that time. The wealthy housed their dead in marble mausoleums, houses of dignity and silence; the poor housed theirs in catacombs beneath the city— in both cases, out of sight. This concern with cleanliness translated too easily into an aversion to contact with the lower classes.

That brings us to caste. In the days of the Republic, an enterprising man could raise caste on the basis of merit and money. By the time of the Emperors, the caste system had become much more rigid. The ghetto dwellers in the Subura, in particular, were ignored unless they began to riot during a grain shortage—a circumstance that Rome's upper castes feared more than any other horror. Pestilence along the riverside tenements and insulae—unless it spread to the wealthy villas on the Palatine Hill—represented only the loss of so many hungry mouths. This meant both that the majority of residents in the Eternal City lived out their lives in almost unspeakable poverty and hopelessness, and that the Roman government paid little if any attention to outbreaks. The Roman military, barred by law and ancient custom from crossing within the boundaries of the city, had its eyes on the distant borders, not on the slums at home.

Third, ancestor worship. The Romans looked to their entombed fathers for religious guidance and for intercession with the gods. When high-caste Romans found their fathers, brothers, wives, husbands, and slaves rising from their deathbeds and hungering after their flesh, this crisis was a negation of everything they lived by, everything they'd known to be true. The realization that their honored dead could not be called upon to aid them in their crisis—that the dead were the crisis—shattered them.

***

When the dead walked the streets, Romans shut their doors—but the type of refuge one took depended on caste. The patricians on the Palatine Hill lived in vast, one-story villas with no outward-facing windows; all windows looked inward, on a shrine about the hearth and on a garden atrium spacious enough to walk about and take pleasure in. Before the rising of the dead, this lack of outer windows served to prevent the inconvenience of looking at one's neighbor; a high-caste villa (inhabited by a single family) was its own unit, inviolable and inviting no interference in its own governance.

The multistoried and crowded apartment complex one encountered in the slums, known as the insula, was a very different type of shelter. While there were no outward windows on the first story (originally a precaution against thieves), the upper stories had windows looking both inward on the narrow atrium and outward on the streets and the other buildings that loomed near. In the insula, it was impossible to ignore one's neighbors. You could hear them through the wall. You could smell them. You could hear the splash as the next-door tenant tossed his offal into the street. If you stepped to your window, you could see the daily traffic of the Subura, and once the plague began, you could see the dead hunting.

This fierce proximity likely contributed to the persistence of the forbidden religion, despite the persecutions of Nero. The early Christians insisted that all human beings smelled the same, hungered the same, suffered the same; their message of the essential value of every Brother and Sister of the Fish, regardless of caste or sex, was one that resonated with the riverside tenants and eventually even with some youths in the high-caste residences on the hills. The stories they told also offered a fresh way to understand the loathsome rising of the dead, in their emphasis on a break from a tragic past (whether a communal past or an individual one), absolution rather than personal responsibility for atonement, and the promise of an eventual restoration and recovery of everything that had been or would be lost.

It is perhaps one of history's great ironies that the Church of later centuries fell so often into the same cultural dead ends that the early apostles abhorred, permitting reverence for the dead to take precedence over compassion for the living. My own hope is that this narrative, an account of the acts of Polycarp, might hold for us an admonition and pause for thought, even here in the towns and cities of our own time.

Our story opens several generations after the reign of Nero. Though barely recognized as such on the Palatine Hill, Rome's second outbreak was already well underway.

THE DAY BEFORE THE IDES OF AUGUSTUS

CAIUS CROUCHED AND LIFTED a bit of the creature's gown between his thumb and fingertip, then used the fabric to wipe away the gray, viscous matter from his dagger. The corpse was *distorted*, a nightmare version of a woman. Perhaps a woman as demons of the underworld might imagine her, if they had never seen one. Its face drained of all pigment except where it had been gnawed and chewed, between the woman's lip and her right ear; half her upper lip had been bitten away, exposing the long roots of her teeth. A mangled cavity where the woman's nose had been, and pale eyes that were like the eyes of dead fish. A few moments before this thing had torn through the door of Caius's official station, hands lifted to grasp at him, its mouth emitting a low cry of hunger that Caius could still hear, loud in his ears, even now that this thing lay still on the floor.

For a while Caius stayed crouching, his heart racing, waiting for that cry to fade from his mind. He found it difficult to breathe; the walls of his little office were very close. Struggling for calm, he took note of details about the corpse. One arm was broken and twisted at a terrible angle. Much of its left leg was chewed, and across its lower belly, the white garment it still wore was torn. The flesh beneath it was ripped open too. When this thing had been a woman, when she'd died, something had been *eating* her. Numb, he drew his eyes from the thing's wounds, scanned the rest of its body. Hair done up in what must have been an elegant coiffure. Blood matted in it now. Traces of cream on the thing's one remaining cheek, some expensive cosmetic. The smaller two fingers on its right hand were missing. On its left, a silver ring graced the third finger. That held his attention a moment; he swallowed. The ring was familiar, and though he tried, he couldn't recall where he'd seen it before.

He drew a slow breath, pressed the back of his hand to his lips, tried to recover. One thing was clear. The corpse that'd smashed into his office wore a white gown of the finest fabric, though much of it was now in tatters. A patrician's gown. When this creature had been a woman, screaming as other lurching dead fed on her, she'd been a *patrician* woman, a daughter of Rome's highest families.

"Where did you come from?" Caius whispered. Sweat on his palms.

"I'll try to find out, dominus," a thin voice said behind him.

With care, Caius set aside on the floor the knife he'd driven into the thing's head. Gradually, the world around him began to exist: the guttering of the oil lamp, the breeze through the broken door lifting tiny bumps on his skin; the warmth of his dagger's hilt in his hand, slick with his sweat; the sweet, nauseous reek of decay; the too-fast breathing of his aide who stood behind him. Uneasy, he lifted his eyes toward the shattered cypress wood of the door, catching a glimpse through the broken wood of the sunlit public square beyond and his lictors moving to guard the exits into the nearby streets. His lictors were not really guards—just a ceremonial entourage accorded to the city's highest-ranking official. No doubt taking up station around the square made them feel useful. The actual guardsmen stood somewhere outside near the prisoners' sheds; he'd hired those with coin.

There was no one else in the square; at the cry of the dead, Romans did not come to look—they shut their doors.

The corpse beside him had filled the office with its stench. "Burn it," Caius growled without looking from the door. "And bring me the old man."

He heard his aide retreat farther into the building. With an almost silent groan, Caius got to his feet, retreated behind his desk, and stood there, splaying his hands on the wooden surface and leaning forward. The grain of the desk was fine cedar from Gaul. The luxury of it brought him little comfort. Nothing he owned brought comfort or solace anymore. This desk, the military medals on the wall behind him, the sword that rusted in its sheath in his study at home—they were only tokens of failure. He had stopped looking at them.

Caius measured his days now solely by the slow walk from his high villa down to the baths, a few streets below on the slope. There he sat in long silences while dutiful slaves scrubbed his back and other men, young and old, chattered at the other end of the shallow pool about politics or scandals or heroic ambitions, or other things that were dry and constant as dust. They had learned not to interrupt his silences. Caius would let the water lap at his thighs and breathe in the steam, then stand while the slaves clothed him in a toga immaculate and perfect in its summons to duty. After that, the walk back up the hill to the temple of revered Justitia, defender of the wronged—a walled, marble complex of vast size on the opposite slope of the Palatine from his villa, with his small official station an annex just outside the wall, like a barnacle on a ship's hull, and beside it a row of wooden sheds for the temporary holding of the accused. He walked with firm, quick steps and without any slouch to his shoulders, though his insides were hollow and empty. The small clump of official lictors carrying their bound rods of office trailed behind him, signaling to any who looked up as they passed that here walked one of the senior magistrates of Rome, in whom was invested the hopes and the keeping of the Eternal City.

The walk always ended here, at his office.

Caius didn't watch the two slaves who entered the room from the inner door, though he listened to the slide of the corpse across the floor. "Scrub that floor," he called without glancing up, and heard them stop by the door. "I want no trace of that thing left, not a drop of blood, not a flake of skin, not a strand of hair. You hear?"

"Yes, dominus," one of them murmured, and when Caius remained silent, the slide of the body resumed. Caius heard the crack of the door being kicked the rest of the way open, a wooden rain of splinters. That walking, hungering corpse had made kindling of his door. Always before, when someone had come to that door, they had come not as a visitor nor a passerby nor a client but as the accused, as shattered Romans driven by hunger to sometimes extravagant crimes. Often men had been forced through that door, trembling. Caius had seen their heads jerk when they heard it click shut behind them.

Until today. This ravenous corpse had burst through like an accusation itself. And what strength these dead had, to break a door! The dead could use *all* their strength, uncaring; they would break themselves in breaking through a door to get at the living, in the desperation of their hunger. This one had broken its arm doing it. The accursed thing had worn a patrician's gown and a ring of considerable price. This hadn't been some wretch come crawling uphill from that rats' nest of the Subura—that throng of riverside tenements and crowded insulae that smothered the banks of the Tiber. That river ran brown, having taken within itself all the sewage and offal of the Eternal City. The midstreet ditches carried refuse downhill from the quiet villas and gardens of Rome's upper castes, and in the entrails of the Subura, men and women who lived like animals chucked their own vomit and dung in after it. Caius's lips thinned. All filth, both Rome's offal and Rome's human dregs, drained down into the Subura—where, a year ago, those dregs had overwhelmed and drowned his son. His only son. Now all that filth was backing up; the diseased dead were stumbling up the long slopes. A few packs of dead stalked even the Palatine Hill, and Caius's hired guardsmen were kept busy thinning their numbers. Men said in the streets that the statue of Roma in the Forum Romani had been heard crying out Rome's secret name in the dark watch before dawn—the name that once uttered must bring about Rome's fall.

But that loathsome corpse that had shattered his door—that was no thief or whore from the Subura. It was not even a merchant's wife who had lurched free of her tomb after being bitten by a thief. This was one from the *old* families. What, by the *gods,* was it doing here? He leaned harder on his hands, sucking in breath and trying to think past the roil of emotion in his chest. The walls *were* very close. One fact was a cold, clear light in his mind: he had the old man, the Greek, who led those who disturbed the dead. He glanced up, noted the trail of slime left behind by the slide of that corpse. As with the dead, so with the rotten among the living: cut into the head and the body dies.

"Dominus." It was his aide, speaking from the inner door. Caius raised his head and looked past his aide to see the old man standing in the doorway. A man preternaturally tall, his head bald and his wrists manacled before him.

"Polycarp," Caius said curtly, an identification not a greeting. He gestured to the space of floor in front of the desk. A smear of viscous fluid led from that space to the hole that had been the outer door. The aide remained by the inner door, and the old man came forward and stood before the desk. His eyes were calm, though they held weariness like the stress of an old house in a high wind. He stood straight, exuding confidence, though the creases about his eyes told of physical pain—possibly his joints, judging from how gingerly he held his manacled hands and how slowly he had moved. It was not the slowness of reluctance but the slowness of one in pain who takes great care with where he places his body, which muscles he chooses to move and when.

"Good day." The old man's voice rasped a little with age, but there was strength in it.

"You know who I am?" Caius fixed his eyes on the man.

Polycarp looked back without blinking. Or answering.

"I am Caius Lucius Justus, the praetor urbanus. You are arraigned for sedition and treason, Polycarp. My guardsmen took hold of you because they were informed that you lead the new atheists."

"We are not godless," Polycarp murmured. "We simply devote ourselves to a different God."

Caius waited a moment, getting his emotions under control. "I will not insult you by asking you to explain that *we*." His voice had grown icy. "I know you have followers throughout Rome, probably many. Nevertheless, I have you, and others from your insula. It is enough. I mean to put a swift end to this infection in the belly of our City."

Polycarp glanced over his shoulder at the brown smear across the marble tiles. "It seems you have other infections to worry about," he offered dryly.

Caius flexed one hand, feeling the grain of the wood beneath his palm, resisting the urge to beat the desktop with his hand, driving his anger into the wood. Then he stiffened. Out of nowhere, the thought hit him of where he had seen that ring before. That little silver ring on the dead hand. It was a betrothal ring, bearing no device or gem—an ostentation of the Aemilii, who considered themselves too famed to need any device and thought their family name an adornment richer than any other they might offer. That dead, half-eaten girl had been Flavius's daughter, who would have wed Drusus Aemilius in another year. Caius couldn't recall whether he'd ever met her, but he knew her father, and he knew that ring. His hand shook slightly. Flavius's daughter. Gods. Not just any patrician girl. The daughter of a senator, and not a quiet backbencher at that—one of the first men in the city.

"This thing is devouring Rome," he muttered. Across from him, Polycarp was watching him as though to peer into his heart. Something in Caius's chest constricted and hardened into a tight, enraged knot. "This is your doing." He gave Polycarp a cold, assessing look. "Even youths on the Hill neglect the rites and the obligations to our honored fathers." Once, the festivals for the honored fathers had been lush, extravagant affairs—*magnificent* affairs. Now . . . "Because of your teachings, too many youths no longer bring offerings of fruit or bread or wine to the shrines of our fathers, who hunger now and cannot rest. And whom they devour—" He blanched. "Those cannot rest either," he muttered after a moment.

A crawl of silence. That terrible stain on the floor.

Polycarp was watching him with an intensity in his gaze that Caius found unsettling. He struggled to hold his temper, distracted himself by shuffling through the sheaf of parchment on his desk—notes from his informants and reports from various minor officials on this movement that had taken hold in so many border towns and now in Rome itself. "Polycarp the Greek," he said, his tone clipped. "You were in Smyrna for a while among the Christians there. Then you came here, to Rome, where in the past we have put your leaders to death. Why?"

"I am most needed here."

"I might not agree with that," Caius muttered. "But certainly the filth of the Subura has proven fertile ground for you."

"Yes," Polycarp said softly. "I know you think that. Probably you imagine me to be some parasite fastened to Rome's belly. But you've found the gathering here on the hill, and it frightens you. My calling has been to feed all of Rome, Caius, not only the Subura."

Caius sucked in a breath, his hand pausing over the papers. "What do you mean by that?" His hand trembled slightly, almost too slightly to be seen; yet Polycarp's gaze flicked to his hand and then back to the praetor's face.

"We share bread," Polycarp said. "An act of remembrance and purpose in this city where both the living and the dead hunger. We have shared bread with slaves and with their masters in the Subura. We have shared it with merchants of the lower slopes. And we have shared bread with sons of the Palatine Hill."

Caius's eyes burned with the thought of his own son. His hand kept shaking.

"You intend to put me to death," Polycarp continued. "This seems certain to me. But it will do you no good, Caius, and even if you succeeded in suppressing the teaching and the sharing of bread, it would only do Rome harm. But you will not succeed, for it will not end with me. You have the wrong man." Polycarp smiled wearily.

"Who is the man I need to execute, then?"

"He is not here. Though he is, I trust, in all places."

"Speak plainly, you abominable Greek!"

Polycarp gazed at him a moment and his smile faded. There were lines about his eyes, but they were lines of fatigue, not fear. "Your mind is very Roman, Caius, and very literal," he said after a moment. "Perhaps you think the only way to deal with the dead or the living is with a sword cut, as though all ailments are of the body only. But however many heads you cut, the dead keep rising—because you have not understood why they hunger, why they find it necessary to rise and eat. You make the same mistake with the living who are discontented in this city. There are other ways, Caius, to give the living and the dead rest—"

"So I've heard," Caius cut in. "You *touch* the dead." He glanced at the grain of the wood beneath his hands, struggled for calm, composure, *dignitas*. "Some magic from the East, the informant tells me. The most debased kind of superstition."

"I might call *yours* debased, praetor urbanus. You try to feed the dead with wine and bread and fruit, carrying bowls of it to your mausoleum, while your brothers and sisters in the Subura live famished and ravenous lives without bread or wine or fruit or hope. In your literal-mindedness, you give the dead the food they don't need and keep the living starving for the food they do need. You are the highest officer of Roman justice. I ask you, Caius Lucius Justus: what justice is this?"

"Your words twist everything," Caius said. "But I know everything you have done in Rome, Polycarp. I have questioned Julia and others my guardsmen took from your insula. I know about your sharing of bread. I know about the rites where your followers pass around a cup of warm blood and a handful of flesh. I know how you meet in the tombs and Catacombs, disturbing the dead in your obscene belief that you can satisfy the wrath of our ancestors with no more than a wish and a hope and a mumbling of platitudes brought here out of the East." He took a shuddering breath. "And you have the gall to tell me you are not troubling our dead, that you are not spreading this desecration in Rome."

"I am not spreading this desecration in Rome," Polycarp said softly.

"Don't mock me."

"What do you wish me to say?" Now there was an edge of anger in the old man's voice, and his eyes burned. "The dead hunger and walk. You need someone to blame, and it's clear you've brought me here to make an example of me. Yet I am a Roman citizen—"

"Then you will be tried as one!" Caius roared, his face livid. "Tomorrow! I have witnesses against you, Polycarp. We will satisfy Justitia, whose temple this station serves, and then you will burn!"

"Why even a trial?" Polycarp asked. "I am condemned already; your words confirm it. Why not burn me today?"

"Don't tempt me."

That smile, that self-affirmed smile, returned to Polycarp's lips. That smile that said, You do not shake me. I know who I am, and you cannot bend me.

"You wish to silence me," Polycarp said, "so you will give me a jury of ears to hear me."

Caius leaned forward, enunciating each word. "Some on that jury will have lost someone to the dead. They are furious. They want someone to suffer for what has been done in Rome. So do I. You will burn, Polycarp. I promise you that."

Polycarp's eyes darkened. After a moment he said, "The shed I'm kept in is dark and quiet, and a good place for prayer. I am growing fond of it. May I go?"

His voice was so calm and clear. He did not sound as though he were asking for permission. He sounded more like he was *dismissing* the praetor.

Caius bit back the words he wished to speak, words that would diminish him and the dignity of his office. After a moment he gestured for his aide, who quickly took hold of Polycarp and led him out of the room, taking him down the hall toward the other door that led out to the sheds. Polycarp left without a glance over his shoulder at the praetor. Alone again, Caius drew in a deep breath, then slammed his hand on the desk.

That detestable Greek and his followers—the dregs of Rome—had taken Caius's son from him. Had destroyed him. Had destroyed his house. Caius heard the sound of a door opening and shutting elsewhere in the building: Polycarp being put away. *Burn* him.

His gaze lifted to the shattered door; his slaves were there, waiting permission to enter. One held a cloth, the other a pail of water. Caius's gaze settled on the brown smear across his floor, and he ignored the slaves.

Flavius's daughter. Gods.

He was alone here, alone with those medals on the wall, mute reminders that whatever his fortune in past battles on far borders, he had lacked the strength to protect or preserve his own. Even here within the walls of his own city. In his way he had failed Rome as surely as the old Greek had; the heat in his breast flickered out as quickly as it had come, leaving only cold hollowness in its place. It was often so. He would stand in his toga behind his cedar desk and prepare judgments, yet inside that toga and inside his skin, he was only the husk of a man. He was alone. No living members of his family. If not for dignity and duty, he would have thrown himself on his sword months past.

It was a powerful thing, that Roman dignity. It must be observed not only in word and deed but in the posture of his body, in the stillness of his hands when he spoke, in the fashion of the draping of his toga after the baths, in his gait, in the austerity of his face.

His forehead ached; he opened his eyes, realized he was leaning over his desk like a woman grieving. Angrily he lifted his head, stood like a man. He stood there, breathing, just breathing.

A tap at the door, and his aide's voice. "She came right from her villa, dominus."

"What?"

"The dead girl. She must have come from her own home. The guardsmen saw her stumbling down the street from the uphill villas."

Caius turned on the aide. "Why didn't they bloody stop her, then?" He gestured furiously at the splintered door, then strode to it, his aide following. He shoved the broken door out of his way and stepped into the sun.

The sky was blinding after the close dimness of the station office; he stood and let his eyes adjust. A guardsman, armed with a stout pole, leaned against one of the sheds along the wall of the temple compound, ten strides away—the sheds where the prisoners were kept. The man looked pale. Caius gave him a cold look. Why hadn't his guardsmen stopped the corpse of the patrician girl? The sight of her stumbling toward them, reeking like a thing on the wrong side of the grave and hissing at them, had terrified them. That was why. Nearer at hand, Caius's entourage of lictors waited faithfully, togate men carrying bundles of rods bound with cords, emblems that he whom they walked behind carried power to discipline and correct the Roman people.

Caius glanced down at the grit and dust of the station's doorstep. Perhaps there had been footprints there, mute records of the coming of the dead; now there was only a long, smudged swath through the dust where the body had been dragged back out. He grimaced and squinted uphill against the sun. Flavius's villa was ten streets above them on an offshoot of the Via Sacra and was significantly larger than any villa around it; it was right near the hilltop, below the Palatine House where the Emperor would reside during the colder months. The Flavii were an old and wealthy family, much older than the Emperor's.

Everything was still on the hilltop. In the afternoon heat, none of the living were stirring; no slaves were in the streets and would not be, perhaps, for another hour. Caius imagined the dead girl lurching along in the street, making her way on shuffling feet to his door, her arms lifted in accusation. She had come to *his* door. He cursed softly and shaded his eyes.

"Are you going to ask the Senate to convene?" his aide asked.

"Why?" Caius murmured. "So they can sit around and argue while this gets worse? The Senate can go to oblivion before I let them waste my time." He looked out over the city, listening. There—he could hear it now. Moaning, carried to him on the wind: the cries of the dead. Somewhere in the city. He glanced uphill toward the villas of Rome's high families and clasped his hands behind him to keep them from shaking. *Flavius's* daughter. The dead were not just a few lurching shapes in the lower gardens of the Palatine; they were bursting into villas now, or perhaps seizing and ingesting good citizens from the street. He didn't know. But they were here. They were breaking through his door. And he was left alone to deal with them; the Imperial Family, and the Praetorian Guard with them, had left the city at the start of the summer. No doubt they were in one of their expensive country villas, where opulent pleasure gardens to arouse the envy even of the princes of Susa were enclosed within walls within walls within walls. The Imperial Family had walled out the dead and all the living who were of lower classes than themselves—indeed, all of the City of Rome. The only real power in Rome now was his—the keys to what remained of the state treasury, the authority to hire armed men, to convene treason courts, and to order executions. The Emperor…Caius grimaced and counted the days. Tomorrow was the Ides. On the Kalends, fifteen days ahead, the Emperor would be starting back to Rome. He would have to write to warn him against returning before the pestilence was better contained.

Caius's face darkened. He should have had that cesspool, the Subura, burned to the ground last winter, when the pestilence first began to cause real trouble. But he had not understood the extent of the threat. How could he? Rome Mighty and Eternal had survived everything: riots, grain shortages, screaming Celts leaping over the walls, axes in hand. No doubt it could survive this too. And the use of fire to stop pestilence was no small thing. In a city as crowded as Rome, fires could be ill afforded because it might prove impossible to put them out.

Coldly he took stock. He had guardsmen. He had Polycarp in custody. And a few others of his kind, minnows he'd netted with the whales. The wench he'd interviewed earlier that day, the former slave, Dora Syriacae, with the proud look in her eyes and her bearing; his heart troubled him at the memory of her words. And the youth, that *boy*, a patrician boy, one of the Caelii, hardly older than his son had been. *Another* patrician sneaking into the Subura to worship with the desecrators. But tomorrow, a trial, and Rome would be cleansed by fire of that foreign vine in their city whose growth so entangled their youth and starved their dead fathers.

"One hundred eighteen," he murmured.

"Dominus?" His aide sounded uncertain. Well, this day would rattle anyone.

"One hundred eighteen," he repeated. "Guardsmen."

"One hundred twelve, dominus."

"One hundred twelve," he repeated.

"Yes, dominus. A century and twelve. Six didn't return from the Subura last night, when they took Polycarp."

"Why wasn't I told?"

His aide paled. "I only received the report an hour ago, dominus. They ran into some dead in the alleys, and I take it the encounter was harrowing. The captain got himself drunk and didn't come in this morning."

"I'm not paying him to drink," Caius muttered. He should see the man, reprimand him, but he hadn't the energy. "Dismiss him. Find his lieutenant and have every man posted on this hill. They are to patrol these streets."

"*These* streets, dominus? The streets of the upper Palatine?"

"That's what I said. I don't want any more shattered doors." He glanced at his own door, what was left of it. "Have that one replaced. Reinforce it with iron. No, have Decius do it. You get to the villa of the Flavii. Find out if they know what has happened and if all is well there. Then find me and report."

"Yes, dominus."

"Dismissed."

His aide hurried up the street, and Caius stood in the sun, resisting an urge to rub at his temples. He stared at that splintered door and whispered a prayer to Janus, the two-headed keeper of doors both visible and invisible. Caius's hands shook even as he clasped them more tightly. With a shudder, Caius thought of the cracking of Rome's invisible doors: the doors between the patrician hills and the plebeian sewage of the Subura; the doors between life and death; the doors between the open Forum of the present and the cluttered, private chambers of the past. Could nothing be held closed? Would there be no order and health in Rome's house?

One locked door, in particular, stood in his mind, with fresh horror after his day's encounter with the gowned dead. His son's door.

He wanted to see his son.

Nodding curtly to his lictors, he began to take measured steps out into the street, walking with anxiety and dread back to his own villa and the door to his son's room. The lictors filed behind him, duty-bound to escort him to the doorstep of his home.

***

All about the bed in his son's room hung the masks of his ancestors, their masks for public occasions, dried now, some of them cracked, some of them faded in color and as hideous themselves as the faces of the dead; but they were his ancestors. Only the *di parentes* of his family could watch over his son.

The thing on the bed snapped its teeth in the air and twisted and bucked, writhing, its face contorted with terrible hunger and rage, its eyes blind, like small, scratched gray coins. Caius sagged back against the door and watched, just watched. Beyond that door and all about him, this villa high on the Palatine Hill was silent; the slaves tiptoed when their master was with his son.

Caius recalled the first time he'd seen his son like this, back at the end of the winter when the dead first appeared in the Subura. Caius hadn't known the dead were rising at the time, hadn't believed the reports he'd heard. He'd only known there was violence, a riot, on one street in the slum. In most seasons the Subura was best ignored, but a *riot* could not be tolerated. Riots left unchecked became very dangerous. Caius had sent guardsmen in.

When the guardsmen came back—their numbers diminished—they had brought with them, chained and gagged with bloodied cloth, the praetor's son.

Seeing him, Caius had crumpled to his knees—he, a Roman, on his *knees!*— and it seemed hours before he could move or speak. His lictors stood silently by, shifting their feet, nervous at the nearness of the chained, animate corpse. The captain of the guardsmen who had brought him stood by as well. Waiting. They seemed to understand that the regular rules and expectations of *dignitas* did not apply here, under these conditions. Dignity operated by entirely new and different rules, when Rome's highest public official saw his son so devoured by the dead and so changed.

At last Caius had beckoned one of the guardsmen near with his hand, asked the questions he had to ask. Briefly, giving his report in quick, clipped phrases, the hired man described what he had seen on that street.

"How did it happen to *him?*" Caius interrupted, his voice hoarse and choked.

"We found him at an insula. The Christian women they call 'holy widows' were there, and there were dead coming at them out of the alley. Eight of them, growling and hissing like beasts. Your son was with four or five men holding the door of the insula against them, unarmed. The dead broke through. My own cohort was close behind, and we encircled the entire district, five or six insulae. Several riverside tenements. I lost three men getting your son out of there. The women were—screaming. Inside the building." Sweat broke out on the man's brow. "After what we witnessed in there, praetor—we burned everything. All of it. A few dead came lurching toward us out of the fire—they were still walking, still moaning, even as they burned. We made sure to destroy all of them, all the bodies." The guardsman swallowed. "Your son. Those bites on his arms. He died of fever even while we were burning the street. We'd seen what would happen. We—we expected it, praetor. He was dead. Not breathing. Yet he opened his eyes as we carried him uphill, chained, on a litter. He opened his eyes. And he was like this." He gestured at the gagged, growling corpse.

It had been too much to take in; the effort of it had shattered him. He had clung to the few facts he could grasp: the rising of the bitten dead, his son's destruction, and his son's inexplicable presence in an insula in the Subura, defending the lives of some meaningless community of women. "I didn't know he was part of that—that cult." His shoulders shook; in a moment he would be sobbing.

"Get out of here," he whispered. "Let me be alone with my son."

***

Now, watched over by all the great men of his ancestry, Caius's son fought his chains on the bed. Looking on, Caius refused to weep. A magistrate of Rome should weep for Rome only and not for kin or companions lost.

Yet he was also a father.

He'd had his slaves nail the bed to the floor after the third time the corpse overturned it, wrenching hard enough that the bed flipped and came down on top of it. Such things only happened when someone was present with his son in the room. When his son was alone and the door was shut, as far as Caius could tell, his son lay silently on the bed, limp in his chains—until he heard someone move about or speak near the door, in which case he would thrash into wild motion again.

At first Caius had ordered his house slaves to feed his son and bring him drink, though he'd had to threaten his slaves with beatings, then with crucifixion, to make them approach the corpse. The first man with the courage to do it had lost two fingers to the snapping teeth when he tried to feed biscuits into the corpse's mouth. Knowing the pestilence would take him, Caius had his throat slit and had commanded the body burned.

Then he had one of the house's female slaves try; the slave women were less costly to replace. But the same thing happened; when she poured water into the corpse's throat, it was spewed back at her. With a hissing scream the creature lurched, almost upending the bed, and fastened its teeth deep into the woman's arm.

Her screams had been terrible to hear.

Only by cutting away a large chunk of her arm were the other house slaves able to get her loose from the ravenous, growling thing in the bed.

After giving orders for what was to be done with her, Caius had stormed from his chamber and raged into the atrium under the open sky. Standing there in the garden at the heart of his villa, he'd turned in circles, screaming at the windows of the rooms of his house: "What is *wrong* with you insects? Can't you even feed one boy! One bleeding boy! *What is wrong with you?*"

For an hour he'd shouted obscenities, the veins standing out in his neck. At last he collapsed and lay on his belly in the garden, weeping into the dirt. He stayed there all night. The earth felt cool against his cheek; in the end it was a comfort, something real, something he could trust.

The next day, he did not have anyone attempt to bring his son food or water.

Now Caius leaned against the door of his son's room, his chest tight. Though he had no cup in his hands to make a libation, and though he was not standing beside any fresh sacrifice in a temple, he prayed. He prayed first to his ancestors, staring fixedly at their masks of clay or woven grass where they hung high on their wall above the bed. He spoke with them for a long time, explaining the crisis and pleading with them. Then he prayed to the unseen *lares* of his house—the old, old gods of home and hearth, who have no names.

All the while, his son roared and snarled and spat, and tore at the tattered mattress with his nails. After praying, Caius stared down at his son, everything inside him gone empty and cold. He should end it. He knew that. He should have his son's body burned. But that was no way to give a Roman citizen rest. And this was *his boy*. He'd had only one son. Only one. His wife Scipia had died in childbirth; when the midwives had sent for Caius, he had come quickly, but not quickly enough. After hastily accepting the newborn son as his own and then handing the child to one of the women, Caius had stood silently by Scipia's bed, gazing down at the stillness in her eyes. For all that night, he gave no thought to his son (for whom the midwives quickly found a wet nurse), nor to the family hearth, nor to any of his responsibilities as *paterfamilias* of his house. He simply gazed down at his wife as her body cooled and hardened.

When he'd risen stiffly at last, in the chill hours, and went, half-aware, to tend the hearth, he had found it as cold as she. He'd reeled back in horror; the cold hearth was a sacrilege. A Roman patrician must never let the fire in his home go out; he, and he only, no slave or servant, must tend it, honoring *his* fathers who'd passed the fire down to him. In that one night, Caius had failed both his wife and the *di parentes*, his ancestors.

That was really when everything had gone wrong. The world had tipped on its side, and he had been sliding off ever since, his fingertips scrabbling for purchase. Since that day, everyone else he cared about *had* slid away. Only he was left, the last player clinging to a tilted stage.

When the boy's time came to greet the gods in person, Livius his son should have awaited them in a great stone mausoleum, high on the hills of Rome, with inscriptions of honor carved into the cool marble on which he lay. Now Livius reeked of decay rather than burial spices, and leapt in his bonds. And when Caius himself died, no son would tend the hearth for him or perform the rites to remember him and honor him. Caius Lucius would become a wandering shade, restless, hungry, homeless. An eater in the dark.

Shutting the horror of it away into some dim compartment far from his heart, Caius set his hand upon the door.

"*Vale*, Livius." *Be well.* The greeting seemed a terrible joke, yet Caius could never leave the room without speaking some word of parting. This was his boy.

He left, shutting the door quietly behind him. The growling of the thing could be heard too clearly, even through the barrier of stout cypress wood. Refusing to hear it, Caius strode down the hall and out into the atrium, crossing the garden toward his study. He walked blindly, by habit, his eyes noting neither the eyes of the slaves watching him carefully from the windows about the atrium, nor the last summer blossoms on the cherry tree, nor the vines that had twined about a neglected marble Cupid (not because of a neglectful gardener, but because the gardener had fled the villa the same day Livius was brought home to his bed; since that day Caius had attended little to the affairs of his house and had not bothered to replace him).

When he reached the study, Caius seated himself in his chair, keeping his back very straight. There was no need for public *dignitas* here, no need for posture—not even his slaves were permitted to enter the study—but *dignitas* was the one raiment left to him; otherwise he was stripped and bared to the icy rain of a malicious world, one that had already cut from him his wife and his son, a world where the ancestors no longer interceded or cared. So even in the extremity of his grief, he sat like a Roman.

There came a knock at his door.

Caius took slow, slow breaths until he felt capable of answering. "You may open the door," he said.

The door swung open. The slave there—one of the females—knelt swiftly at the threshold, without entering.

Caius glanced at her briefly, indifferently. "What is it?"

"Your aide is at the door with a message, dominus."

Caius looked more closely at her. Her face was white, and the hands she held clasped in her lap were trembling. She kept her eyes lowered dutifully. Whatever the aide had said had scared her. A hard stone of dread settled in Caius's belly. "Well? What is the message?"

"He said to tell you he'd been to Flavius's villa, dominus. There was no answer at the door, but he heard moaning within. He—he heard—the dead, dominus. Inside. He went to the nearest villa, where Cassius Tertius and Portia live, dominus. Domina Portia told him that Flavius is away on business, touring Transalpine Gaul. His wife and daughter had the keeping of the villa. She said the moaning had started the night before, and they'd been too scared to go to Flavius's door."

Caius cursed. "Is my man still at the door?"

"Yes, dominus."

"Tell him to send guardsmen to the villa and to make sure the men don't speak of it to anyone. The hill is anxious enough after the past few days. We don't need a panic."

"Yes, dominus."

"And you tell the other slaves this. If anyone in *my* villa speaks of what they've heard, I'll have every woman in this villa *flayed*. And the left ear cut from the head of every man. Am I clear?"

"Yes, dominus." She was shaking.

"Leave."

"Yes, dominus!" She sprang to her feet and shut the door. Caius could hear her quick footsteps running down the hall.

Then silence.

Gods.

He sat in the silence, thinking of that enclosed villa farther up the slope. And thinking of the body of Flavius's wife, shuffling about its dim rooms. Were her slaves diseased and hungering as well—or had they fled? How had the daughter gotten out into the streets, and not the mother?

He shook his head, reached for his stylus and parchment and for a little bottle of ink. He uncorked the bottle, dipped the stylus, paused. He sat there awhile, the stylus held poised over the bottle, a great drop of blue ink clinging to its tip.

What was he to write?

What *could* he write?

Flavius was another man who had lost a wife and a child, even as Caius had, though he did not yet know of his loss. What was there to say?

Blinking the weariness from his eyes, Caius began to ink words into the parchment, in hard Latin capitals. *To Flaccus Flavius Germanicus, in Transalpine Gaul,* he wrote. *Caius Lucius Justus, praetor urbanus, Rome. Vale.* He dipped the stylus again, then began to write with a furious haste, barely making the letters legible. This infuriated him—a letter, as everything else, needed discipline and poise—but he did not slow his speed. He must write this quickly or not at all.

I must express my dismay in informing you that a tragedy has befallen your family in Rome. The nature of it is of such horror that I can only write of it because I am able to reassure myself that you will receive it with that same dignity with which you once received word of the tenth cohort's defeat along the Rhine when we campaigned together in Germania, so many years ago. I know that in you the blood of the ancients is strong and that you are well able to receive news of terrible misfortune. I must inform you, Flaccus Flavius, that your wife and daughter are deceased. They became afflicted with that unmentionable plague that appeared in Rome during the last winter. I know that it will bring you some comfort to learn that I have made arrangements to ensure that their suffering will be brief. The ashes will be held in a silver urn under the care of the Vestal Virgins and under the watchful eyes of the gods until your return to the Eternal City.

A dutiful and patrician wife, and a daughter of grace, beauty, and intelligence, betrothed to a fine house: Rome is lessened by their loss, and all Rome continues to hold the ancient, eminent family of the Flavii in the highest respect and reverence.

Si vales, valeo, amico meo.

He set the parchment aside to let the ink dry. Then he wrote, less hastily, a missive to the Emperor in his pleasure gardens.

There are wakeful dead within the city and they are many. Your Divinity would be best advised by his appointed magistrates and by the people of Rome to prolong the time of Your pleasure and rest. Though we know Your sense of duty to the Senate and People of Rome is matched only by the wisdom of Your governance, the preservation of Your life is of great priority; I will make Rome safe for Your return if You but delay that return to the next Ides.

Finishing the message and placing it aside with the other letter, his face grim, Caius reached for another page.

There was one more thing that needed doing. He had known it, perhaps, from the moment that patrician girl had burst through his door. Dipping the stylus again, he began to pen the order, the last order he intended to give as praetor urbanus. He could pass the small parchment to his lictors after Polycarp's trial.

By this order, he would atone for his failure and for that of his family. He would atone for not having raised Livius a good Roman worthy of his fathers and for not having been there when he died. He would atone even for Flavius's absence when *his* daughter died, and for the shortcomings of all the fathers of Rome who had not kept the city clean and secure. He would not allow the next generation of Romans to let the hearth fires go out, misled by Polycarp's cult until all the patrician dead returned, even as the Subura's impoverished dead had returned already to wander empty Rome, neglected and ravenous. Caius would do more than simply put Polycarp to death. He would do Rome one great service: he would end the plague, regardless of the cost, regardless of any death toll needed to achieve it. His hand trembled as he inked the first words of the order.

AN ETHICS OF HUNGER

Earlier that week in the Subura.

DAWN

ROME, EVEN THEN, was an old city—ancient and vast. Its great bulk sprawled over the slopes of seven hills, with the river Tiber winding between them, its banks choked by the crumbling insulae of the Subura. Each morning, the Subura's residents woke to the reek of diseased fish pulled from the river and human urine and goose shit, and to the honking of geese on the water—there were always many near the river. The birds were sacred; six centuries ago when the Celts invaded, axes in hand, the warriors had startled a flock of geese on the Tiber. The birds had risen into the air with their loud voices, waking the people in time to defend themselves. Today the geese often clogged some narrow street, but when this happened, people stood by and waited for the geese to clear the way. To harm or show disrespect to a goose was one of Rome's oldest taboos. It was also treason, though the praetor's hired guardsmen rarely bothered with arrests in the Subura.

Lately, the birds were a comfort. Where the foot traffic of the Subura was halted by slow-moving geese, one at least knew there were no walking dead on that street.

Each morning, the geese woke Rome. Then the men of the Subura hurried to market to buy the day's produce or sent out slaves if they owned any, and hurried themselves to whatever shop they'd found work at. The free women cleaned house or knitted fresh patches onto clothing that was already a patchwork of faded fabrics. The slave women were kicked from their masters' beds and sent to prepare baths. And while the streets were still shadowed—the sun blocked out by the looming buildings—lines of slumped-shouldered, weary women, both slave and free, could be seen trudging toward the nearest public fountain with lidded jars on their shoulders.

With them walked Regina, empty water jar on one shoulder, her arm around an old woman whose steps stumbled more often than not. Both she and old Flora wore wide-brimmed hats, gifts from Father Polycarp, a precaution against the emptying of chamber pots from sixth story insula windows. Urine brought a fair price from the fullers who used it in the cleaning of togas, but to the ill or those weary of life, hauling pots down from a fifth- or sixth-story apartment and then up the steep, cracked streets to the fullers' shops near the Forum seemed too much for the day. Regina was used to the splashes of offal into the street; they were the least of the Subura's indignities. Yet she was grateful for the hat.

Each morning, Regina slipped out of Father Polycarp's insula, paused a moment at the doorstep until she heard Marcus Antonius slam the bolt shut behind her. She tugged the wide hat securely over her hair and looked around quickly at the morning grimness of the alley. Sometimes there'd be a smear of blood on the wall across, or a silent body in the street, or a not-silent body that she would watch carefully. Once she was sure it was safe, she hurried down the Via Noctis to Flora's insula—one considerably larger but in far worse repair than Polycarp's.

Flora's grandson brought in some food by working from before dawn to after dusk as a fuller's assistant, but as he had neither the coin to purchase a slave nor the meal to maintain one, it fell to old Flora to clean the apartment, prepare the morning and evening meals, and trudge down to the fountain and back. Regina had seen the grandson at the meetings in the Catacombs; she knew he was one of theirs. So each dawn, Regina came to the door of Flora's insula to take the water jar from the grandmother's trembling hands and carry it for her. Each time, Flora kissed Regina's cheek and smiled at her, with eyes that were beautiful and old, and then walked with slow, exhausted steps beside her.

Fetching water was not safe. The brotherhoods guarding the fountains at the crossroads might molest them. Or there might be too many women at the fountain and it might take too long to return: for some women, that would mean a beating. Worse still, the women had to cast uneasy glances down each alley they passed. When there was movement in the alley—a dark shape, a dull sheen of eyes—Regina pulled Flora past as quickly as she could and hastened on with her head low, her heart pounding.

That silhouette might have been only a street thief or a beggar rising from his night's bed in the alley's refuse.

Or it might have been one of the dead.

Earlier in the year, it had been common to encounter one or two of those a week. But the last month had been bad; quite a few mornings, wary residents had emerged from their insulae to see dead feeding in the street, sometimes not just one but two or even three. And there had been the matter of the potter's shop in the fourth insula on the Via Borealis. The potter had lived with his two sisters in a second-floor apartment and had just taken in his brother's family of six after an eviction. The newcomers squeezed together into the potter's bedchamber, while the potter and his sisters slept on the shop floor by the wheel and the clay bowls. One of the brother's small boys was suffering from a fever that night.

When the potter's rent wasn't paid on time, the landowner had finally pounded on the door, then unlocked it to venture inside, his face dark with the kind of wrath only men who own property can show. But when he threw open the door, a terrible stench spilled out, and with the reek came nine hissing dead.

After eating the landlord, the dead had wandered moaning in the atrium for a few hours. The other tenants had slammed shut their doors at the man's screams, and they kept them shut. Toward midday, an infant in one of the first-floor apartments started to wail in hunger; the dead clustered at that door and pummeled on it until they finally broke through and devoured the family inside.

Before dark, one of the crossroads fraternities appeared at the outer door of the insula, en masse, eight armed men, self-appointed keepers of the winding streets and servants of the old gods of the Roman crossroads, men who called themselves the Subura's honored caste, though the rest of the Subura considered them thugs. Some were military veterans whose pay hadn't quite emerged from tightly locked state coffers (or had been squandered on drink). Some were manumitted slaves who'd once served as bodyguards, some were former assassins who'd been discredited and could find little work in the Forum. These men had in common wounded lives and a hunger for coin. They had taken to hunting the "risen fathers" and demanding protection fees from insulae near their crossroads. The brothers traveled in pairs, or three or four together, and so far had kept the numbers of dead thinned.

These eight were hired by the landlord's widow, at a price that would almost certainly bankrupt the insula. Arriving, the men found the widow hiding in the alley just outside. They threatened to kill her if she couldn't pay inside of two months, forced from her a promise that she would sell the building if she had to. In tears, she unlocked the insula for them, and the brothers went in.

Only four walked back out.

That had happened last week. Word of it had spread through the Subura. Father Polycarp in his insula had begun making nightly rounds, knocking on each tenant's door before dark and waiting for the tenant to call out that all was well. And the last few days, when Regina had gone to the fountains or to the market, she'd taken to glancing up at the dark windows in the high buildings, fearful that she might see a gray, torn face peering back.

When someone in the Subura was bitten, most of the time they concealed it, went home, locked their doors. Fever and death followed a few hours later or during the night. If others were locked in with them—family or others sharing rent or squatting along with them—these unfortunates might be wakened later by grasping hands and devoured. If the person lived alone, they woke mindless, hungry, shambling about the room, locked in until kin came to look for them, or the insula's owner came for rent, or some thief picked the lock on the door, or until they broke through the door themselves. There might be many such rooms in the Subura now, people locked in with their hunger, awaiting release.

***

Regina and the other women filed down a narrow street, falling downhill between the clammy insula walls toward the fountains. They were near the river and could hear the voice of the brown water. The stones beneath their feet were moist and stank; in a few shadows beneath the walls where the sun never quite reached, mushrooms had squirmed up through gaps in the stones, though not the kind one could eat.

In this chilled place, the women stopped.

They were not waiting for geese.

A few dropped their jars, shattering them, and turned and ran, the moment they saw what was in the street. Others stood very still, holding their breath. A corpse lay in the street on its belly, emaciated, its ribs showing through torn flesh; the arm it reached toward the women was terribly shrunken, as though prior to its death it had not eaten for weeks. Its filmy eyes stared at them without recognition, and it hissed and snarled from a mouth only half-filled with teeth. It tried to drag itself toward them with its other hand, clawing at the dusty stones, but its legs were broken. Its jaws snapped at the air. Then it moaned. The sound of its cry passed through the women like a shudder. On the next street over, there was the *clack* of a door slamming shut.

The thing's fingertips curled around a broken paving stone, and it dragged itself another inch nearer. Regina's heart was in her throat. She and the others stared at the thing, still not moving. A girl who couldn't have been more than fifteen lifted her water jar high over her head, holding it, her face white, as though she meant to bash it over the corpse's head once it came closer. Regina tightened her arm around Flora, who trembled against her, and stared at the corpse, wishing desperately that Polycarp were here, to bring his Gift to the dead and leave it unmoving, limp on the stones.

Quick, sandaled footsteps then, coming from the direction of the fountain, and Regina tore her gaze from the dead thing. From around the curve of the street, behind the crawling corpse, two men appeared. They were dressed in dark tunics, but they wore black armbands and walked with a cold, certain gait that was by itself enough to tell anyone in the Subura who they were. One carried an oak table leg that could serve as a cudgel. The other carried a long knife, its blade nearly long enough to qualify it for the Roman *gladius*, or short sword—except that it was curved, and the etching of a stylized horse into the blade declared its Numidian origin. Some horse lord of the windblown steppes above the Sahara had once carried the knife strapped to his shin. It was a lethal-looking object, and illegal.

The corpse hadn't noticed the approaching brothers; it was still trying to pull itself, bit by bit, toward the water carriers, its teeth parting in a long, hissing snarl. The men didn't hurry. Any other morning, Regina would have watched them with wariness or fear; now, her fear was focused on the dead, and she watched the men approach with only a kind of terrible fascination.

As they neared the thing in the street, the two men exchanged a look. The one with the cudgel nodded; the other stepped forward. Bending, he took hold of the corpse's hair and drove the Numidian knife hard into its skull. The thing convulsed, jerking, and the man let go of it. The corpse collapsed on its belly and lay still, its cheek against the stones. Its face concealed in its ragged hair. No blood seeped from the wound.

A sound like a sigh swept through the water carriers.

Regina's arm tightened around Flora's shoulder. She lifted her eyes from the corpse, fixed her gaze on the men in the street.

The man holding the knife was breathing hard, and he remained bent over the corpse, his blade still sheathed in its skull. His chest moved as he drew in great breaths. He had done the thing quickly and with an efficiency that spoke of an ease with killing. Still, even the months since the first dead lurched along the riverbanks in late winter hadn't been enough for a man to let go entirely of the ancient taboo against defiling one of the bodies of Rome's dead. The knife-wielder's brother stepped near and clasped his arm, squeezing briefly. To Regina's eyes, the tenderness of it seemed strange in that street where two rough men leaned over a heap of decrepit and slaughtered flesh.

The man with the knife tried to wrench the blade from the corpse's skull but the blade must have lodged deep. With a grimace, he shoved his boot against its back, then jerked the blade free. A few of the women hid their eyes; Regina didn't. The corpse rolled slightly, half exposing its face beneath a veil of filthy hair. At the sight of that face, the man's hands began to shake.

The two argued in low voices for a moment. Then the brother with the cudgel cursed and turned to the women, that crowd of both free and slave, with their wide hats and their water jars. "Follow me, see?" he called. "I'll get you to the fountain. Move. Now." He gestured furiously with his cudgel, then strode back down the street the way he'd come.

The women began to follow, whispering quietly to each other. Most gave the fallen body a wide berth—all except for one woman, plump and gray haired, who spat on the corpse as she passed. Regina helped Flora move along the street's edge, keeping an insula's wall to her back.

"We're going to be dead soon." Flora looked up at Regina with watery eyes.

Her heart raced. "No, we're not." She could barely take her gaze off that dead thing on the stones.

The old grandmother clutched Regina's arm with a grip that startled her. "When I was a girl," she rasped, "our insula had a pear tree. Great juicy pears. Juice'd run down my fingers. One time a boy kissed it off them. Gone now. Boy, pears, everything. Chopped down. No fruit, hardly no bread. And some of us as hungry as—as *that*." She stabbed a thin finger at the corpse. "Won't be long now."

"Come live at our insula," Regina urged, not for the first time. "We have bread there."

"I know. Grandson's gone before, brought it back. Kind, your father. Like an old cypress he is, branches spread over you, giving his shade. Up on the hill, the people with gardens have their praetor, and you down here have your father. But you can't fit all of us in his insula, dear."

"Someday we will," Regina whispered, her tone passionate, though the whites of her eyes showed as she stared over her shoulder at the corpse in the street and the crossroads brother with his knife standing over it. Another woman jostled her, but she said nothing. In a moment they'd be around the curve in the street, and the dead would be out of sight. Yet she didn't feel safe. Not out here. The longing in her was fierce for a wall around her, a high wall and solid and one of her choosing. It took all her will to turn forward again and focus on helping Flora on over the broken and treacherous stones.

***

The street had emptied. There was only the lone crossroads brother, now crouching on his heels by the corpse, knife in hand, an anguished look on his face. He reached for the thing's hair. Hesitated a moment. Then, sucking air in between his teeth, he gathered up the thing's filthy hair in his fingers and lifted it away from the corpse's face.

Long moments passed as he gazed at the face of the dead. He covered his mouth with his hand; his eyes were moist. Perhaps the dead had been someone of his blood, a sister or a cousin. Perhaps a past lover, a warm, living woman he'd once held in his arms and kissed, who had whispered secrets in his ear and listened to his. Perhaps it was only someone he'd known in childhood, some girl he'd played ball with in the atrium on hot afternoons and whose rotted face recalled long-neglected memories that hit him now with the violence of fire or flood, reminding him of things lost and things not quite gained, and of the sewage of time that carried everything downstream and away.

He let the hair fall, concealing the face. He clasped his hands tightly, stayed crouched there. He just sat looking at the dead woman. His eyes shone, but no tears fell. He didn't notice the honking of geese or the murmur of the Subura about him or the slow, dragging footsteps of one of the dead lurching into the street behind him out of a dark alley. The corpse approached stiffly, its head bent to one side on a broken neck, its hands half-lifted, ready to grasp. The thing moaned, low and desperate, when it had nearly reached the crossroads brother, and the man turned then with wide eyes. In the moment it took him to pull himself out of the past and lift the Numidian knife, the thing had bent over him, grasping his shoulder in one hand and his hair in the other. Even as he brought the knife up with a yell, the corpse's teeth tore into his neck.

NOON

Day came to the Subura, and with it the sweltering heat of narrow spaces packed with too many living bodies. Men napped briefly. They drank watered wine if they could. Within each walled insula, children moved about in the atrium, laughing and shrieking if they'd been fed, or sitting beneath stunted shrubs and daydreaming if they hadn't, or weeping if they'd been beaten or had witnessed their mothers being beaten. There were quite a few insulae where laughter could be heard at midday, but there were also insulae that brooded silently in the heat.

In an upper-story room at one of these apartment structures, the laughter of two girls in the atrium below could be heard through the window, but those sounds brought to the room only a bite of bitterness, like winter air seeping through a crack in the wall that has never been properly sealed, a draft that shivers its way through skin and bone. On a pallet in the room, a man lay with his eyes open and his hands clasped too tightly for him to be resting. The traces of flour on his hands and arms declared him a baker, though he was unusually lean for one. Any fat he might have had, he had burned away with worrying, which he did so deeply and so often that his body interpreted his anxiety as a particularly strenuous kind of exercise and responded accordingly.

Beside him, a plump, energetic woman was stuffing clothes into a haversack with a vigor most people reserve for shoving sandbags into a wall against a flood. She was breathing hard.

"How can you be sure the praetor will keep his word?" the baker asked his wife.

"He's a patrician, isn't he?" She crammed a rolled-up tunic into the bulging sack, then struggled to tie it shut. "Toss me that coat, husband." She nodded to the peg by the window. "We'll need to hide this 'til tomorrow."

With a small groan, he got to his feet and took the coat from its peg, then tossed it listlessly toward his wife; it hit her shoulders, and she sighed and bent to catch it as it slid to the floor.

Her husband lay back down, his eyes pale. "I'd rather not set foot anywhere on that hill," he muttered.

"Fine. I'll go. In the morning. We can leave when I get back." She was still wrestling with the ties on the sack. She hissed through her teeth, then straightened and glared at it, pressing her lips together. It wouldn't do; if she tried to carry that sack over her shoulder, its seams would split. She would have to start over; she began pulling clothing from the sack. They were all such plain garments, light wool or brown linen, all except one gown as purple as a Caesar's cloak, a hidden treasure at the bottom of the sack. It was her only relic of the past, something she'd been permitted to take to the Subura only because she was wearing it when she walked there. "I'll never understand why you get the shivers every time I talk about going uphill." Her voice was sharp. Outside the window, children were still giggling. "My *first* husband and I had a villa up there."

"A small one."

"A *villa*. That's more than you've provided for me."

She began arranging bundles more carefully within the sack.

"Maybe. But I'm here. *He* threw you out."

She stopped, her shoulders tensing. Her hands still. A few heartbeats, then she resumed filling the sack. This time more slowly.

"He threw you out, Julia." There was a softness in the baker's voice. "Your equestrian husband who wanted no empty wife. But with me you have never gone hungry."

She kept packing. Her eyes blinked back the burn of tears, then they spilled. Her husband watched her cry with his thin and sorrowful face, but he did not go to hold her. At last she forced the final bundle in, then leaned over the sack, her shoulders trembling. For once she wept not for the empty past but for the empty future, stretching before her in an endless calendar of barren days that she could not accept. She'd seen other women carrying their round bellies in their hands as they moved in their slow, waddling gait—or seen them nursing tiny infants at their breasts. Her own were dry of milk, and her womb hollow within her. Hearing the laughter of other women's children through the window, she let her tears fall over the sack, on the tightly folded undergarments and bunched tunics, the simple garments that told the world she was a baker's wife. The low-caste Christians who occupied other rooms in their insula thought her husband something wonderful—a maker of bread. As though that were something. As though that could make anything better in this sewer. It didn't matter to *her*. No amount of fresh bread had filled the hole within her or warmed the cold inside her.

NIGHT

Under tall insulae, the streets of the Subura went dark before the rest of Rome did. Quietly, a few doors opened in the shadows, and furtive shapes slipped out into the deadly streets, clad in dark cloaks and cowls. They went in pairs, or formed small groups for fear of any prowling dead. Then they stole through the narrow alleys between tall buildings as silently as though they were God's watchmen come to inspect the world while its residents slept. But they were not watchmen; they were men and women of many ages and occupations, carrying a bit of bread beneath their cloaks, ready to barter it for hope. Those sliding along the sides of insulae on the wider streets found themselves joined by other figures (and they were not few) who had stolen out of homes uphill at dusk, slipping downhill from the villas of the well-fed.

The furtive ones passed through the Subura, darting downriver through the unlit streets between tall and decaying buildings until there were a few stars above them and the buildings thinned. They crossed the pomerium, Rome's sacred boundary, and came to a street that ended in a jumbled cliff of soft volcanic rock. There was a door in the rock face, and it stood open on its hinges. A man waited there, in a dark cowl and cloak like theirs, a torch in his hand. Beside him there was a vat of oil. The man asked a question of those who approached, and they murmured the correct answer, then those who had brought torches dipped them into the oil, and the door warden lit them. With a last wary glance up the street, the dark-cloaked figures passed through the door, slipping quietly into the Catacombs beneath, down those long corridors lined with shelves on which rested hundreds of silent, shrouded cadavers. Rome's impoverished dead, interred here by families who could not afford a mausoleum on a hill.

Those without torches entered, too, and either hurried to catch up with those bearing light around some corner ahead of them, or had to walk in a darkness more complete than the void before God spoke the name of the earth. Frequently, they stumbled over some unevenness in the earthen floor, and leaning out a hand to catch themselves, encountered, with a shock, ribs or a long femur against their fingers. Since this last winter, one could not walk past the shelves of the dead—even these, the clean dead—without trembling.

In the heart of the Catacombs were several large caverns, and the nearest of these was soon occupied by maybe a hundred living men and women, of diverse castes. In the flickering light of the torches some of them held, one could even see here and there among the crowd the aquiline nose of the Roman patrician—the revered class, considered by birth and bloodline to be descendants of gods. But everyone attending wore over their daily garments that same dark robe, and a cowl that most had now tossed back onto their shoulders. The cowl and robe had served to conceal each of them as they crept through the city to the Catacombs, but now they served a second purpose as well—they concealed garments that displayed class and station. Here everyone was without adornment and without mark of wealth or poverty. Here, all of them were of one family, all of them descendants of one and the same deity.

Polycarp stood among them, garbed no differently from the rest; the others had made a little circle of empty space about the slab of rock where he stood. He carried no torch, and he clasped his hands behind him; sometimes, late at night, they trembled with approaching age. Yet his voice remained strong. As the last few of the community of the Fish entered the cavern, Polycarp began singing the *Phos Hilaron*, a hymn to the nearness of God at the day's last light, a reminder that though they worked in the dark, they waited for the sun to return.

Others joined him, and as the men and women sang softly, they brought out from under their cloaks their offerings for the night. Few had come empty-handed. A loaf of bread, if they could afford it. If they couldn't, then something, even if it were only a bite of stale barley bread, perhaps the only morsel they had left to eat. As they sang, they held the bread in their hands, lifted as though each meager piece was sacred. Perhaps for those of them that lived in the crowded, ravenous Subura, all food *was* sacred. And perhaps those who'd slipped down from the Palatine by cover of dark were relearning the holiness of bread from the passion they saw on their downhill neighbors' faces. The singing, then the hearing, then the sharing of bread that bound them each to each other: it was a rite that was becoming familiar through repeated use. Tonight, after Father Polycarp spoke and blessed their sharing of bread, they would each break the piece they held, whether it be a loaf or a smidgen, and they would pass the pieces around the gathering, until all had eaten.

"We can feed *on* each other," Polycarp had taught them, "or we can feed each other and feed *with* each other."

In the great Games of the Colosseum, the Emperor, father and *paterfamilias* of the family of Rome, would give out loaves of bread to the gathered crowds of his children, to assuage the sharpest bite of Rome's hunger so that the people might not rise in riot. But such bread was given to quiet the people, not to fill them. Polycarp, a father of this city within Rome, was interested in filling them. He meant to do so by teaching them to share bread with each other.

"I know that it has become a fearful thing to us, coming here through the dark streets," Polycarp told them now. His voice carried across the cavern, filling the silence that followed song. "But we must not fear the dead. Fear is a greater evil to us than death; our brothers and our sisters who can't yet sleep need our pity, not our terror." He lifted his hands, gesturing to the shelves on which silent corpses rested. "We mustn't fear the dead. They sleep. Those who now wake and walk can be given sleep. But we must understand—they walk not because they in their tombs are unfed but because the *living* are unfed. My brothers and sisters, let the dead feed the dead. Rome builds vast mausoleums, houses grander than the houses of the living, and holds festivals, bringing food to the dead—food no one eats—while in the Subura, Rome's living starve." His voice softened and trembled with the passion of what he had to tell. The cavern became very quiet as the gathering strained to hear him.

"I will tell you a story," Polycarp said. "Long ago, the first man to be killed by a brother was tossed into a deep pit, his legs first broken with blows of a thick staff. There was water there in the pit but neither meat nor roots, and he starved, famished until he was little more than bones on the ground. It was a hungry and a horrific death. And his spirit could not rest; he rose lurching from the earth, moaning in his hunger. And when his brother came to gloat over the body, the famished dead devoured him, after which the brother also rose, half-eaten and ravenous with need." Polycarp gazed out, seeing the horror in those many eyes. "It is the hunger of the living that creates the restless dead," he said. "The dead themselves are here, all around us, sleeping. That is why we meet here, in the dark, among our sleeping dead, to share bread among the living. It is a reminder of who we must feed, if we wish our dead to rest."

The others' faces were uplifted, eyes shining in the torchlight. He saw Regina with her eyes alight and Marcus with his face grim but his eyes fierce with a young man's fealty. Polycarp smiled. He knew that beneath their robes, they each held a loaf from Piscus's ovens; Polycarp accepted bread in lieu of rent from the insula's baker, though neither the baker nor his wife, Julia, had yet joined the gathering underground. He let his gaze roam wider; he saw faces he knew from other insulae in the Subura or from the Forum; he saw a young man with one ear who served as a merchant's stable slave and, standing beside him, a senator's daughter. His heart warmed. Once, just three or four of them alone used to meet here on the first night of each week. Now he saw at least a hundred. Such gatherings had sprung up in cities across the world, meeting in secret under the earth in old cellars or places of burial. Communication between them was rare and treasured.

"Listen to me," Polycarp said. "I will tell you about the Apostle's Gift. I will tell you about this thing that God will do through us for the city and for the world. How we will take from death its terror." His face glowed with passion. "Listen to me," he breathed. "Brothers and sisters, it is quiet here. No hunger here to distract us. All our lives, we feed on what leaves us hungry, drink from what leaves us thirsting. Because we are always left hungry and always thirsty, we begin to think that those visible objects of our hunger are what we need most. A loaf of bread, a pouch of coins, the respect of others, success, a woman's body, or a man's. Or even a person or a thing from times past, something lost and remembered that we crave. But it is not so. These are not what we need most. Our hunger thieves us from our true selves. Like a violent fever, the hunger eats away mind and spirit. In the end, everything that we truly are is gone. Only the hunger remains. Even other men and women are no longer anything but food to us, meat for our desires and obsessions. Then we are lost—unless some other brings a Gift."

He gazed out over the gathering. So many faces in the torchlight. The days to come might bring any good or any evil. Some of them might be eaten by the dead. Some of them might be found out and imprisoned by the Roman praetor. Some might face illness or doubt. But tonight, in the quiet of these underground tombs, they were gathered and ready. They had put aside the costumes of their daily lives. They had shared bread. They had opened their eyes and their ears. They'd begun to hope. They dared to hope.

"What is that Gift?" He smiled. "Seeing us, and loving us, as we truly are."

SOMEONE AT THE DOOR

THE FOLLOWING NIGHT. At some late hour in the dream country, Polycarp found himself standing in a city smoldering with crumbled buildings and overwhelmed by the innumerable starving dead. With nothing to feed their hunger, no living flesh on which to gnaw, the dead jammed every road and every alley in the Subura; they lurched against each other in their thousand thousands. Never had he faced so many.

They pressed against the walls of the villa in which Polycarp took refuge, a villa with white walls and a pleasant garden in its atrium, high on the Palatine above the ruin of the earth. The heavy cypress door rattled and shook, leaping in its hinges as the dead threw themselves against it. Polycarp took a step toward it, his heart pounding. He hesitated, fearing to face those lurching, clawing dead; his palms were sweating. Yet the moaning of so many beings torn from life and torn from death—their suffering called to him. How could he stand idle at the sound of such misery?

He groaned and looked up. Startled, he found the garden gone; instead he stood in a wheat field, the same field he'd known as a child in Thessaly, in Greece.

Then he understood. "I am asleep," he murmured. "And having a true dream."

There was some reason why he was here, some message. Something he must pay attention to.

The wheat was high above his head. The stalks tossed in the hissing of the wind, pressing against his body; behind him, distant yet too near, he heard the low wailing of the dead. He shivered, then began walking; he kept glancing at the sky, looking for something—he couldn't remember what. The sky was unhelpful, as gray as the unclean flesh of the dead.

There were faint voices far behind him, like a wind coming—and sharp, crackling sounds. He glanced over his shoulder and found that fire crackled through the wheat. Soon smoke billowed about him, thick and choking. For a while he ran from the flames, rushing through the wheat as fear-maddened as a rhinoceros in the Colosseum; his sides burned, there wasn't enough air for his lungs. He stumbled and, in that instant, saw on a head of wheat before his eyes a small red beetle, its wings out and poised, though it didn't take flight.

He stood still, his gaze fixed on that spot of color in the gray wheat.

He fought for breath.

There were noises behind him like beasts crashing through the wheat; a dark shadow rushed past him on the left. He forced himself to look away from the beetle. Behind him he saw the wheat and the sky red with flame and, dark against the flame, running men and women, some of them on fire. Their hair and their clothes burning as they ran, so that they seemed angels in the instant of their fall, messengers of the world's end. They rushed toward him and past him. The reek of scorched hair and flesh hit him with a shock. The dead were back there too, in the wheat; he could hear their moaning. Perhaps the walking corpses also were already burning, even as they hunted.

The red beetle.

He had to follow it; it had always led him before.

Its wings were out; yet it stayed perched. How could that be? This burning field where the dead and the living went up like torches in the wheat could *not* be where he was meant to be. Here he would burn, or be devoured.

He tore his gaze from the fire to look again to the beetle. Turning, he found himself staring—with shock—into the eyes of his master. Felt the master's hands on his shoulders, stopping him. "Stand, Polycarp," the Anointed One said.

✳✳✳

Polycarp bolted awake on his pallet and rolled to his side. His bedclothes stuck to him with his sweat. He gasped for air, then got his elbows and knees under him and pushed himself up, ignoring the groan and cry of his aged body. Stand. A true dream—that had felt like a true dream. And the beetle had been it, emblem of truth.

Panting, he got to his feet. The scent of burning wheat and flesh still stung his nostrils.

A clamor at the inner door. Knocking. It sounded so loud in his ears. He pushed away the last trailing horrors of his dream, drew a blanket like a shawl about his shoulders, and stumbled to his door, which led to the insula's narrow atrium. He pulled it open with a yank that nearly sprained his wrist.

"Marcus?" He squinted against the glare of light from the oil lamp the youth held. "What is it, child?"

"Julia's gone!" His eyes were wide. "She must've left before we locked the insula, and—"

"Where's Regina?" With the dream still lingering in the dark behind him, and his joints screeching their anguish inside him, Polycarp couldn't keep the sharpness from his tone.

"I'll get her, father—"

"I'm here," the small, short woman called from her open door. She was in her nightdress, but she looked alert as she stepped out among the atrium's grasses and lilacs.

Above them, on the second, third, and fourth stories, a few faces peeked from their windows. Polycarp swallowed his alarm. "Quietly, daughter. Come inside."

Marcus set the lamp on the bare floor by Polycarp's pallet, then knelt. Regina stepped inside and shut the door quietly. The it shut, Marcus began talking, swiftly, as though to make a wall against fear, a wall made of words. "There are so few of us. And now they'll know where we are, and they'll come, and—"

Polycarp lifted his hand. "Marcus, go to the larder." In the face of this peril, they would need courage and a strong reminder of who they were. "Bring me tomorrow's eucharist."

Marcus nodded jerkily, jumped to his feet with a young man's energy. In a moment he'd vanished around a corner into an alcove that served as a larder. With the widows gone, it was the only well-stocked larder in the Subura, and in a very real sense it was Polycarp's life work. Any coin that fell into Polycarp's hands, he soon translated into bread and meal to sustain the population of this midsized insula, as well as the hungry who came knocking at the door sometimes at dusk, offering their labor in return for food—or simply pleading. There was one other door in Polycarp's apartment, now closed tight, and that opened on the alley outside.

Polycarp rubbed his temples for a moment. "What has happened, daughter?" He feared he already knew.

"Julia is gone. She informed. Marcus and I are sure of it." Regina spoke tersely. She often did. Her dark hair she wore in a bun, and she paid little heed to cosmetics, which in any case she did not need: she was without doubt the most striking woman Polycarp had ever seen. To apply no kohl to her eyelids belied her Eastern heritage, but she wished little remembrance of the past, either of her own person or of her people. Her years in Rome before Polycarp found her had been years of suffering, and from them she had learned to dread wearing signs of her beauty.

Polycarp took in her words now with reluctance and fatigue. *Informed.* Such things had happened before. But not in this insula.

"Father, at first we thought the dead took her."

He glanced at her sharply.

She nodded. "There were dead in the alley on the insula's north side, earlier. Six of them. They were—*feeding*—on one of the crossroads brothers. One of the brothers!" She paled as she spoke of it. "You didn't see them, father, it was during your noon rest. They—they were tearing—things—entrails—out of his belly, and—" She paused.

Giving her time to gather herself, he folded his hands and prayed with his eyes open, his lips pressed together. Vivid before his eyes were the wasted cities and the fire in the grain. The empty houses where the dead waited behind silent windows, and no living things breathed or moved.

He would *not* let that world come to be. When the last day came and the sky rolled back at the sound of a trumpet, it must be the living, and not the dead, who lifted their arms and greeted his master's return.

This year, Polycarp had often come upon one or two dead in the streets and had done what he could. A hush always fell when he confronted one of the shambling corpses, and afterward the citizens of the Subura parted to let the father pass, their eyes warm with awe. Polycarp had been watchful since the losses of the last winter. Seven or eight dead had attacked another insula, one farther upriver, where the holy widows kept their chastity and their own larder for the feeding of Rome's abandoned—particularly the Subura's children, the many without mothers. Breaking through the doors, the dead had overwhelmed the few who'd sprung up to defend the widows: a slave wielding a broom, a few unarmed patrician youths who had begun visiting the Subura to aid the widows, and an elderly woman who took up a knife from the kitchen and barred its entrance, growling as loudly as the dead themselves. The dead had bitten many that night; Caius Lucius's guardsmen had not been far behind, burning the insula and several others near it, the dead and the living blazing within. During the assault, the guardsmen had found at least one youth from the upper castes there, which had frightened them. They hired informants now, seeking to know who in the Subura was speaking with people of the upper slopes.

Polycarp took a deep breath. The holy widows had been a community of mercy; their loss was a deep wound, one that hadn't really closed.

And now things appeared to be getting worse. By Regina's testimony, a *crossroads brother* had been overwhelmed. Had been eaten. Not by one or two dead, but by six. Perhaps the crossroads brothers had left too many streets unwatched—those streets where the landlords of the Subura, who were themselves starving men, could no longer pay the brotherhoods' fees. With a chill, Polycarp wondered how many dead were walking out there.

"It is something I never wish to witness again," Regina said quietly. "Vergilius wanted to fight the dead, and Marcus wished to wake you, but I stopped them."

"You should have wakened me," Polycarp said quietly. Faintly, he heard Marcus opening cupboards in the larder.

Regina looked down, hiding her eyes.

Polycarp sighed. "You mustn't fear as much for me, or for the insula, Regina. We have to fear for the people—out there. Now those dead will be elsewhere, feeding. We cannot let them wander on, restless and devouring and unreprieved. If we do that, why are we here?"

Regina gave a brisk nod. "I'm sorry," she said.

"Tell me the rest, daughter."

She took a breath. "When we realized there were dead in the alley, we set a watch at the door. Piscus didn't come home. So we checked the rooms. All of them. I got the key and opened up their apartment, and neither of them were there, but their larder had been emptied, and many of their clothes were gone. They left," she finished simply.

Polycarp swore under his breath. Marcus would have looked shocked if he'd been able to hear from the larder, but Regina did not. She did look shaken, and pale. Polycarp reached for her and grasped her arm, putting as much strength into his voice as he could manage. "We will move, daughter. It is not the first time."

"We've grown too big to move." Her voice was very quiet.

"Nevertheless—" He stopped.

Clear in his ears he heard the words from his dream.

Stand, Polycarp.

He clutched his shawl tighter about his shoulders. Was *this* what the Anointed One had meant? That he must *not* move? If so, he could well imagine what fire was coming through the wheat: the fire of execution pyres, lit by Roman guardsmen. His lips thinned. The red beetle had settled in the burning wheat. He had never ignored it before.

But in the dream, there had been *many* burning. Who else would suffer?

He thought of Julia's sharp voice and Piscus's silent manner and the large eyes that had earned him his nickname, Fish. *Ah, Julia, Piscus, why?*

"You are right," he said. "If they informed, then guardsmen may be here tonight, or in the morning. We cannot move everyone in that time, not without doing it visibly. And if there are still dead near the insula, it would be dangerous to try. We must stand whatever is coming." He looked to the larder, listened for a moment to the rattling of wood as Marcus fetched the communion cup. Marcus was so young. They were all so young.

"I have feared this day," Polycarp murmured.

"Father." Regina's voice was low, urgent. "We can't know what Julia and Piscus have told them, whose names were reported. Maybe the Romans know only that there are some of us here. We can hide or bury the scrolls, and the cup—"

"No," Polycarp said. "If some of us are to burn, let us do it as who we are. Without the cup and the breaking of bread, we are nothing."

Regina seemed about to say something, but whatever it was she held back, for Marcus returned from the larder with a small basket and a flask of wine. The aroma of baked bread was faint, for the bread was a day old. Still, it was *this* bread, and the scent nourished Polycarp. His senses sprung awake at last.

"We are not crossroads brothers," he said. "We desire not Roman *pax*, order and safety, but *eirene*, peace: lives woven together into a fabric beautiful and tough that cannot be torn or unraveled." He sighed. "Julia didn't understand that." He considered Regina. "You and she were close," he said.

Regina glanced up. "Not close." She appeared to be choosing her words with care. "We shared a—a few words, sometimes. Neither of us had children. I worried for her." She closed her eyes a moment, then opened them, and they were hard. "Now she is gone, and we are still here."

"Yes. We are still here," Polycarp agreed. "Come. Let's set aside our fear and our grief, for a while." He glanced at Marcus, and the youth hesitated, then handed him the basket he held. He held the youth's gaze a moment, saw his fear under tight but fragile control.

Young Marcus. Polycarp had grown fond of this fearful but desperately earnest boy. Less than a year ago, the youth had woken them all by pounding on the door of the insula. An illegitimate scion of one of the great families on the Palatine and raised among almost unspeakable wealth and privilege, in his boredom Marcus had fallen in with one of the rowdier bands of Palatine youths and gone carousing in the Subura for a lark, the night before he came to the insula; somehow he'd become separated from the others. Whatever had happened to him afterward, or whatever he'd seen, it left him shaken and changed. When Polycarp opened the door that next morning and saw the youth standing there disheveled, his face smudged with dirt and sweat, the young patrician blurted: "I am Marcus Antonius Caelius. They tell me you are trying to help Rome—make her better than she is. Even the Subura. I want to help."

Polycarp had blinked at the boy, only half awake. The name was known to him, and he was having difficulty understanding the youth's purpose in standing at his threshold. The boy was clad in a finely made toga, the regalia of a patrician, its elegant folds speaking of dignity, its white color speaking of an ancestry that the patricians chose to believe was in part divine. This whiteness could be achieved only by bleaching the cloth with urine collected by fullers from the Subura's inhabitants, an irony that occurred at least to Polycarp, though perhaps not to many patricians, whose slaves took the togas to the fullers' shops and brought them back so that no patrician ever had to smell the urine of his inferiors. Only by using the forgotten castes and keeping that use invisible could the patricians maintain the illusion that donning a toga conferred on them the dignity and half divinity they wished for, or that the performance of walking the Forum in their togas was anything more than just that—a performance.

In any case, Marcus's toga may have been an immaculate, patrician white the day before, but now the cloth was smeared with the grime of a night spent in the Subura, stained with a reality that had become, overnight, terribly visible to him.

Polycarp considered the boy. "How do you wish to help?"

Marcus just shook his head, as though bewildered at himself. "Just—help. I don't care how. However you need."

"Can you repair broken walls?"

"No."

"Can you cook?"

"No."

"Can you weave or sew?"

"No."

Polycarp looked the boy over. His skin was soft; possibly he had never even dressed himself. But he had no slaves with him now. "If I hand you some of our scarce funds," the father said quietly, "can you go to the market near the Fulvian Cistern each day and bring back bread and wine, and any fruit that doesn't look too rotten?"

The boy flushed. "That is a slave's work!"

"Yes, it is." Polycarp regarded him without letting his face show his mood. "We are all slaves here, young Marcus. Slaves of the One God who wishes to repair a broken city and bring peace to the living and the dead. He has bought us, we are his."

Marcus gazed inward for a long moment, and then something passed across his eyes. "I don't mind it." His tone went solemn. "The work. I won't mind it. All my life, I've been hungry—so hungry for my life to mean something. I think down here it might. Last night there was a—a *child*—starving. Her ribs—" Helplessness in his eyes; he wasn't able to get the words out.

"I'll send someone for her," Polycarp said softly.

"I don't think they'll find her." His hands were shaking. "She ran from me. She isn't there anymore."

Something ached in Polycarp, seeing the appeal in the boy's eyes. In their own way, the men and the women of the Palatine needed his larder and the teaching of the apostles, no less than the famished lives in the Subura did. Those who fed no one could feel as empty, as unfull, as those whom no one fed. As Polycarp swung the door wider and stepped to the side, a light of gratitude lit in Marcus's eyes.

"Come in, Marcus," Polycarp told him, "and tell us what you saw."

***

"Father." Marcus's voice was low as Polycarp took the basket. "The guardsmen might be on the way, even now."

Polycarp considered that as he lifted the cover of the basket and drew out a loaf. The bread was cool from hours of storage. "They might be, Marcus. But the Romans tend to do their violence in the open, by sunlight. And our God is the same at night as he is in the day. I think we should remember that."

He lifted the bread high in both hands, though his hands shook. He couldn't keep them still. He prayed silently a moment, then murmured for the others to hear, "We who live do not nourish the dead. Our dead nourish us. On the night of his death, Jesu, the Anointed One, took bread and broke it."

Quickly, cleanly, Polycarp tore the loaf in two. "He said, 'Take, eat, for this bread is my body.'" One half he handed to Regina, the other to Marcus. Marcus lifted the bread in both hands to his mouth and nibbled at it. Regina tore hers in half and handed one half back to Polycarp. There was a shadow in her eyes now, and Polycarp's throat tightened. Gently, he touched her cheek with his fingertips. "Take, eat, daughter," he said softly.

She looked up. After a moment, she nodded slightly and smiled. That smile, though faint, appeared to change her eyes to the color of a summer pool. Polycarp found himself reminded of a favorite pond of his youth, one alive with frogs and vibrant weeds and adorned on both its surface and its pebbled floor with sunlight. Regina lifted her bread and began eating it. Polycarp watched her eyes, and with his gnarled, bent fingers, he tore off little pieces of his own bit of bread, one after the other, and brought each to his mouth. He wet each piece in his mouth, chewed a few times, and swallowed. The taste of it filled him. He felt the softness of Regina's hand brush his—one of those small comforts a person offers another that are nevertheless mighty comforts, because they foreshadow the blessedness of the new earth that is to come.

Yet the touch troubled him. An old warmth lit in his body, one he hadn't felt in a while. He didn't know why it was kindling now—perhaps it was the sweat and dread of his dream, and his body's need to feel alive and virile. Perhaps it was because of what he'd glimpsed in Regina's eyes when she gave him that smile.

If the Romans came, he at least would be seized. Even if he were to succeed in concealing or sheltering the others, which seemed unlikely, this could be his last night as a free man. Regina appeared acutely aware of this. He saw her hands tremble. There was so much in her heart that she had never spoken aloud.

He reasoned with himself as he ate. *With this bread, I take into myself the body and the sacrifice and the love of our master. He has called me to do a task—a task that has become too large for me, it is true. But if I am to stand fast and do it, I must not allow myself distractions. I must permit this woman to remain a daughter to me and not a distraction. Else I shame our master and fail this task.*

For a few moments they ate silently. Polycarp felt Regina's gaze on him. He lifted his head, and she glanced away. He reached into the basket for the skin of wine and found that with the bread in his body he had the strength to lift it; Marcus reached in and took up the little wooden cup—wooden, for their master had been a carpenter—and held it steady as the old father poured the wine. Polycarp listened to the splash of it in the cup; the scent of it filled the little room with a hint of places far beyond this life-crammed Subura: vineyards open to the sun and wind, and quiet lakes beside which berries grew. It made him smile. He corked the wineskin and placed it reverently back in the basket, and covered it. Marcus handed him the cup.

Polycarp's voice was stronger now as he lifted it. "And he took up the wine and blessed it, and said, 'Take, drink, for this wine is my blood, spilled for you in a new Covenant with God. Do this as often as you are together, in remembrance of me.'" Gently he lowered the rim of the cup to his lips, sipped, then handed it to Regina. Again her fingers brushed his; he felt the warmth of them. She was flushed, and the soul he glimpsed through her eyes was troubled with many things. Hunger for a man to hold her but also for a father to shelter her, he could see that, had always seen it, though never had it been so near the surface of her eyes as tonight, and that concerned him. But there were other things there too. Fear—understandable. And shame, which he did not understand at all. After a moment Regina glanced down and sipped her wine.

Polycarp considered her. Regina was the gathering's only surviving deaconess; there had been two, but the other had been seized by the Romans in the month of Mars. Regina was a remarkable woman; besides her beauty and the sturdiness of her spirit, she possessed an education almost unknown in the Subura, something she had acquired in her youth in another country. She was excellent at ciphering; she held the insula (and the gathering within it) together as though she were herself the owner. During the day, Regina ministered to the poorest in their community, bringing them food and hearing their stories, and carrying some of these stories back to share with Polycarp. They worked closely together, and Polycarp trusted Regina; if she said a family on the Via Claudia XII had need, he listened and did what he could to answer the need. If she said a landowner on the Via Noctis was not withholding his promised tithe out of laziness but because one of the crossroads brotherhoods had been extorting his earnings from him until his own family was near starvation, Polycarp listened and tried to exert pressure on the brotherhoods.

Polycarp was the insula's heart, and Regina was its head; yet that seemed a strange way to put it, for Regina was a most deep-hearted woman. But her life had not always been as it was now.

***

The first time Polycarp had seen her, he'd been walking to the market by the Fulvian Cistern and had stopped, stunned. The woman who would later be the deaconess was kneeling outside the door of a cracked and graffitied insula, her head down, her wrists fastened with rough rope to a stump of an iron post. She'd been stripped to the waist, and her back was a thicket of welts. Something deep inside Polycarp growled when he saw that, even as something very like a torch's heat lit in his loins at the sight of her nakedness. He forced himself to focus not on the sight of her breasts but on the placard that had been tied about her neck and that now rested on her shoulders. *She is a slut*, the placard read, *and I put her from my house. You may cut her loose and have her, if you leave a copper in the dish. It is what she is worth.*

A small clay cup lay on its side by the woman's knees.

Polycarp stood there for a while, reading that placard and looking at the welts on the woman's back. It was not common in Rome to beat slaves so savagely, but such things happened in the Subura. Even free women were beaten so by their husbands, by men living lives miserable and without hope; it was not uncommon to be awakened in the night by screams from a nearby tenement. But then, one woke often to screams of murder or rape in the streets below one's windows, or stepped over a body at one's threshold in the morning to walk to the market. This was the Subura. Guardsmen rarely came here, and only the crossroads brotherhoods kept any real order.

This was a part of Rome where people who wished to hide hid in plain sight.

Polycarp moved across the street warily, uncertain it was wise to attract attention. He stood by the woman. She did not look up.

"What is your name, daughter?"

Her shoulders jerked when he called her that. Still, she did not look up. "Dora," she whispered. "Dora Syriacae."

His heart ached at the edge of defiance he heard under her whisper.

"Syriacae," he said. "This is a long way from Syria."

She was silent for a moment. Then she took a deep breath. "The master of this insula bought me from flesh thieves."

She was a pleasure slave then, and had no doubt been bought for the master's enjoyment or his sons'. "Why were you beaten, daughter?" he asked softly.

Her shoulders trembled briefly, and her voice rasped with pain and fear. "A tenant kissed me—touched me. Grabbed me as I walked by." She closed her eyes. "The master saw."

Her welts were many, and around them all the skin of her back was discolored. It must hurt her even to breathe. An ache and a discomfort grew in Polycarp's breast. It was clear to him what needed to be done. With the toe of his sandal he nudged the cup upright, and the ring of the coin against its clay interior brought the woman's head up, her eyes wide with hope and fear. Hope, because she clearly could not stay where she was, and who knew how long the master would leave her bound to that post, rejected, if no one bought her? Fear, because the beating you have already received is a known quantity, and a new master might be more cruel.

"You are Regina Romae," Polycarp said softly. "You have suffered too much under your old name, and it seems Rome, not Syria, is now your home. I ask you to put your old name away. Regina is a better one, I think, and you have a queen's strength, that is clear to me."

Her eyes searched him. "Am I yours?" she asked after a moment, and her voice broke.

"No." Polycarp sighed. "You are God's. It is his coin I have dropped into that cup, and he has bought you. As he bought me, a very long time ago. Though that was a different slavery, and a different coin that released me. Come." He bent and slipped a knife from beneath his tunic. Swiftly he cut the rope from her wrists. He spoke in a low voice, trying to ignore her soft breath near his face and the way it affected him. "No man owns you. You are free. I would be glad to give you a place to stay, if you need one. But you are no property of mine."

He took Regina's hands in his, chafing her wrists. She winced, and a cry escaped her lips. He wished to weep for her. He took his cloak and put it about her shoulders; it was heavy wool from the flocks of Transalpine Gaul and would have cost him much to purchase had it not been a gift. It was far too warm a garment for a summer in Rome, but other than in the middle of Augustus, Polycarp felt always a little chilled, however hot the day. Now Regina pressed her lips together tightly as the coarse wool brushed the welts on her back; tears started at her eyes. Yet she gave Polycarp a look of gratitude that was naked in its intensity, and she held it closed over her breasts, concealing herself. Polycarp nodded and lifted her to her feet. He was not a woman, but he could well understand the desire to hide from demanding eyes. He held her tightly until he was certain her legs were steady, and she made no protest.

"I will take the name Regina," she whispered, and suddenly Polycarp felt her small body shaking within the wool cloak. "Am I truly freed?"

"Yes." Polycarp took her shoulders in his hands and stepped back, looking at her face.

He did not offer to bring her to a clerk to get citizenship papers, nor did she ask. This was the Subura. No one had papers. Regina's eyes were looking elsewhere, into some other place. She was alone, he realized. Entirely alone, and realizing it. Polycarp simply held her shoulders, hoping the firmness of his hands would comfort her in her solitude.

She closed her eyes after a while. She might have been praying; her lips moved softly.

"I will come to your insula," she said.

"Good," he smiled. "There is an empty first-floor room that no one wants, because there was once a ghost there. But it is gone now, and restful, though no one will believe it. If that doesn't frighten you, you can stay there for a time. The rent I will attend to myself, until the next month. We will use the time finding you employment. I assure you, I am exceptionally good at finding things for people to do."

She stiffened. Her eyes took on a look of panic and, behind the panic, a gray shadow that Polycarp knew too well. Despair.

"No," he said quietly, and he put his arm about her and began walking her back up the street toward the insula. His trip to the market could wait. He whispered words for her ears alone, though others brushed by them in the street. His knife he still held unsheathed in his hand, and no one molested them as they walked. "No," he said, "I am not looking for a pleasure slave myself."

"Why are you doing this?" she whispered.

He glanced at her face. Considered telling her it was as his master would want. But that was not really a true answer. He might have passed her by if she had been some other slave. He sacrificed mightily for the people in his insula, both those of the gathering and those who were not—but he followed a strict policy of minding his own matters when he was out in the Subura. He pursed his lips a moment, then told her the truth, or as much of it as he knew. "I never had a daughter, or a wife. Even a sister. You might have been her. I thought of that when I saw you."

"But I am none of those." An edge of bitterness.

"No." He shook his head. "No, you aren't. Nor anything else I might want you to be. Whoever it is that you are, you may reveal it to me or not, with time, as you choose. Your body also is yours to conceal, or reveal to one who suits you. You may keep the cloak."

They walked silently for a while. When they reached the door of the insula, she glanced up at him, and he found that her eyes stirred things in him.

"Are you kind," she asked gently, "like an old grandfather—or are you only mad?"

"I have no idea. But doubtless one of those is true." He touched her cheek and smiled, and then stepped through the door, leaving it up to her whether to follow.

***

Now Polycarp settled back, folding his hands across his chest, and watched as Regina and Marcus shared the cup. What was going on with Regina tonight? It was rare to see her so unsettled or to see the desires of her heart shown so nakedly in her eyes. Marcus he understood: the boy was terrified, though now that he had eaten and sipped and shared in the Covenant, his face was calmer. But Regina—

Again he pressed his lips together tightly. Had his daughter had some part, unknowingly, in Julia's falling away? He couldn't imagine what that part that might be, but plainly something was profoundly awake in Regina's heart—and just as plainly, she was loosing the latches that she usually kept locked tight over her desire for him. He suspected that she had never fully reconciled in her own heart whether to approach Polycarp as a daughter or a lover, and she had kept her feelings under tight discipline. Now there were guardsmen coming for Polycarp, to take him from the insula, likely to suffer a painful death. They might not see each other again; indeed, the last moment might be this very breaking of bread, this drinking of wine. If there was something she must say, this could be the last moment to say it. He looked again at her eyes, and the plea he saw there pulled at his heart. Marcus didn't notice; he was looking at the door, perhaps wrestling down the last of his fears. Polycarp coughed and straightened. It was time to bring them all back to their task—himself included. Their strength must survive his death.

"My children," he rumbled, "our master calls us to repair what is broken, to heal what is ill, to bring good word to the despairing, to reclaim all that is lost." He drew in a ragged breath; the pain in his hands was sharper now. "Our master wishes us to stand fast, no matter the peril, no matter how many fall away. It is possible that when the guardsmen come, they will empty the insula. But it is also possible that they will be looking for me, and that when they find me they will not look too hard for others. We are already a city within this City. They will look for a Caesar. They likely know my name. But I am not our Caesar, who lives now in a heavenly city and not in this one. My arrest will change nothing. Marcus, there is an empty cellar beneath the larder. The entry is cunningly disguised—you must look beneath the barrel of olive oil. Look where I have scratched the fish, and it will be apparent to you. I had it made after the raid on the widows."

"We won't abandon you."

"But you will heed me." Polycarp's voice hardened. "You will protect your brothers and sisters. Crowd into the cellar with those on the first and second floors. Those on the upper stories must pray. It is possible the Romans may tire of searching empty rooms and depart swiftly." He smiled grimly. "They will, after all, have found their 'Caesar.'"

"We should have you in the cellar," Marcus protested. "If it is you they are looking for, they will spend all their effort searching for you and take little heed of the rest of us. If we—"

A scuffling in the alley interrupted him. His head jerked up; he listened. Regina paled.

"They're here!" Marcus gasped. Every line in the boy's body was tense. If Roman guardsmen burst through that door now—at this moment—they would find them all unprepared, unhidden, sitting with the wine and the bread.

The very air in the room went cold and sharp with fear.

Polycarp went very still. Part of him had been waiting to hear this sound all night, he realized, ever since waking at Marcus's knock with his mind still caught in that dream. "Listen, Marcus. God gave you better ears than that."

There was no sound of marching in the alley, no clink of metal.

"The dead," Regina whispered.

Marcus jumped to his feet. Polycarp rose more slowly, stood unsteadily and might have fallen, but Regina caught him, and he leaned on her for an instant before straightening, embarrassed. His body cried out for his bed. He was too old for the demands of this night. Yet he was the father of this gathering; he was the only one who could answer them.

He looked to the door, the outer door. The scraping of feet, many feet, half-dragged along the stones outside. A thump and then a slide along the wall. Somewhere to the right, the sound of nails scratching against rock. For a long moment they listened to the sounds, hearts beating. Somewhere up the alley outside, a low moan. Polycarp heard Regina suck in her breath.

For a moment more the shock of it held them. This was not a visitation by one or two dead, or even by the pack Regina had spoken of. Polycarp couldn't tell from the sounds how many, but surely more than ten. And these dead knew that there were living here—that moan confirmed it. Perhaps their voices had been heard through the door. Perhaps something else had drawn them to the alley. It didn't matter; they were here now.

"Father, don't!" Marcus whispered.

Polycarp had moved to the door. Now he turned. "Marcus, Regina." He stopped a moment, uncertain what to say. "What do you believe, Marcus? What do we know to be true? Nothing is broken that cannot be remade. Nothing is ill that cannot be healed, nothing captive that cannot be freed. That is what he taught us. I am going through that door, my son."

He gripped the boy's shoulder, saw both worship and fear in his eyes. They were the eyes of a young man witnessing his father at the brink of a cliff confronting harpies of Greek legend, and half the desire of his heart was to hide behind a boulder, and the other half was to grab his father by the shoulders and pull him back from the peril. Yet his eyes were dazed with the knowledge that were he to do so, he would lessen his father.

"Either I can meet them at the door, young Marcus," Polycarp told him, "or I can wait for them to break through. Except that they might not break through. They might go down to our neighbor's door. And that would be intolerable." He thought for a moment. "Go to the other rooms. Wake them, warn them, bring those you can to the cellar." That task was not too much for the boy's courage, he decided, and he would feel courageous doing it.

Marcus nodded once and, turning, almost bolted out of the room. After a moment Polycarp heard the inner door creak open and then shut. He drew in a breath, faced Regina.

She stood there with her face a mask of inexpressible pain, like one of the masks Attican actors wear in a tragedy.

"Ah, Regina," he rumbled, "please don't defy me in this. Either throw open that door, or move aside and stand behind me."

"Father, there are too many. Too many." Her voice was low and intense. "You'll be eaten!"

"Enough," he growled. "Move aside."

She sucked in her breath. "Wait." She pressed herself quickly to him, her arms going around his neck and her lips finding his. With a shock, he felt the softness of her breasts pressed to him under her tunic, the warmth of her. Her kiss was open mouthed, passionate, desperate. She smelled of love and fear. An unwelcome fire lit in his loins and spread to all his flesh.

Carefully he took her arms in his hands and detached himself from her, pushing her gently back.

"Be careful," she whispered, her eyes too full to look at.

"Regina," he whispered back. "Daughter."

Her eyes grew moist at the word. Frowning, Polycarp bent and took up the lamp of rancid oil. He held it high by his ear, just a little back so the flame would not obscure his vision. As he straightened, the taste of the sacrificial wine and the taste of Regina's kiss were still sweet in his mouth. He threw the latch on the door.

The alley was *filled* with dead. The light of the lamp Polycarp held brought them out of the dark, showing the gashes and bites in their gray skin in stark detail. For a moment his hand shook, and the light guttered. The dead slouched and slid along the wall of the insula toward him; several milling at the outlet to the Via Aquae Bruneae turned their heads with unnatural slowness, and their eyes reflected back the lamp. Their mouths opened, filling the alley with the low groaning of their hunger.

Never had he faced so many.

He sucked in his breath. That thought was so similar to his dream that it froze him. He stood in the door.

"*Father!*" Regina cried.

"Take the lamp," he muttered, and held it out to her without taking his eyes from the street. He felt the brush of her hand. Then the weight of the lamp was gone, and its light behind him cast his shadow, vast and dark, over a shuffling, broad-shouldered figure as it lurched in front of him and almost into him.

We must live lives of *unstoppable* hope, Polycarp told himself. That was the only way. Even if we cannot see above the wheat. Even here, in this place, where the walls of cramped buildings obscured people's sight of each other and of God's open sky and God's near presence no less completely than might the wind-tossed stalks of a harvest field. Even here, we must hope.

Polycarp clenched his teeth and stepped forward, lifting his hands, one gripping the corpse's throat, the other taking it by the shoulder. Others closed around him, their hands grasping at his clothes, their mouths reaching for him in a hunger too profound and unanswerable for them to voice it in any sound more articulate than the moaning that rose, breathy and loud, from deep in their bellies.

BRITTLE LIVES

SEVERAL MINUTES LATER, the dead lay about Polycarp crumpled and still, at least twenty of them, the flickering light of the oil lamp casting wild and careening shadows across their slack faces. The father swayed on his feet, like a tree chopped near the root; then he toppled and lay with his forehead to the stones. Regina let out a cry from the door to Polycarp's chamber, and the oil lamp she held tumbled from her hand and shattered in fragments of clay; the light went out, and everything in the alley was dark, the dead reduced to silhouettes. She froze, her hand whitened where she clutched the door.

She called to him softly. "Father!"

She heard him groan in the dark; the sound of it went right to her heart. As her eyes stung with tears, she ran from the door, darting up the alley to where he'd fallen, the grimed and smeared surface cold against her bare feet. She stumbled over the body of one of the dead and cried out, then caught herself on her hands. Everything in her blood screamed at her to run, before the thing she touched could twist and seize her ankle in its hard, inescapable jaws.

She had the sense, the terrible sense, that those dead might stand again, at any moment. But they lay still, they all lay still.

Crawling forward, shaking, she found Polycarp prone on the ground and knelt by him, taking him quickly in her arms. His chest was moving; he still breathed. Gently she ran her fingers over his face, his throat, his arms; he wasn't bleeding, he hadn't been bitten. But he made no response when she whispered, "Father, father." She clutched him fiercely to her, and her eyes burned. Overcome with the terror of the alley and the wonder of what she'd seen.

It had happened so fast, so fast. The corpse at the door had fallen, slipping to the side of the threshold, and Polycarp had stepped over it into the alley to confront the others, moving as unhesitantly as though he were walking to the market. Regina had stood in the door, fighting her own urge to hide, unwilling to leave him. Her lips still warm from kissing him, her heart in turmoil. She had never seen him use the Apostle's Gift before, and she hadn't seen what he'd done to the corpse at the door; it'd been hidden by Polycarp's back. She'd gazed out into the alley in the wavering light of the oil lamp, and she couldn't breathe for wonder.

Polycarp had moved among the dead with an intensity and grace, as though he were dancing. He laid his hand on each one, as gently as a parent blessing a son or a daughter. Each time he touched one's shoulder or its head, he gazed into its eyes. The first time, Regina gasped to see a living spirit flood back into those murky, dead eyes. For a moment a middle-aged woman gazed out through the eyes of the corpse, her eyes raw with regret and remembered pain. Polycarp held the woman's gaze a brief moment; then she let out a slow sigh and crumpled to the stones of the street.

Polycarp did that with each of them, his eyes deep with sorrow. He seemed to have no fear. One grasped his shoulder, pulling him back; he touched its hand and glanced back at it, and then a young man was gazing back at him. The man breathed a soft moan—not the hunger moan of the prowling dead, but the exhaustion-and-relief moan of a man letting go of a burden too long carried. With that sound he slipped to the earth and lay still, no breath stirring inside his gashed-open and half-eaten chest. One of the dead had gone for Polycarp's throat; he had caught the thing's neck in his hand and looked steadily into its eyes. Even as that one slid to the earth, two others seized upon Polycarp's arm, pulling him toward their teeth; the father simply touched them both on the head, looking in the eyes of one, then the other, as if witnessing and accepting each one's confession, in no more time than it would have taken to shout. As though each one's spirit had been bound deep within its body with chains of hunger and was now released at Polycarp's touch, escaping the body in a death sigh.

Regina had trembled as she watched from the door, her heart beating with a purely animal fear at the nearness of the dead; she could neither swing the door shut nor step through it. At the extremity of her fear, her face darkened with shame and anger. She was no Roman patrician bred on milk and water, to tumble from her chair at the first sight of something unsavory. Of Rome she may be, but of the Subura, where knives, not gossip, flashed across dinner tables. And her ancestry was Syrian, of a people whose bones were strong as the bones of the hills in which they lived. She bore old lines on her back, a savage record of what could be witnessed and what could be survived. The oil lamp shook as Regina's hand trembled, but she did *not* faint.

Now it was over. Her gorge heaved at the reek of the dead around them. In the dark of the alley where she knelt with the dead motionless about her, as restful as the bodies on their shelves in the Catacombs, Regina laid Polycarp gently to the stones and rested his head on her lap. Polycarp's head felt light, too light. The sight of his face shocked her, and she stared at him, the defiled dead abruptly forgotten.

In less time than a Roman hour, new wrinkles and crevasses had been carved into his cheeks, deeply, as though a sculptor had attacked his flesh with a chisel and a fine-edged knife. The skin about his eyes was sunken, and the shadows of the alley turned his face into an ancestral mask, an image of the ancient and honored fathers. His eyes were closed.

He looked old—*truly* old, for the first time.

"Father," she whispered, holding his head between her hands.

He hadn't been bitten.

He was alive.

He stirred slightly and began to murmur under his breath. He took no notice of her. His lips moved soundlessly and swiftly in prayer.

Something opened within her, a great well of helplessness, and she stood at the edge but refused to topple in. Squeezing her eyes shut against tears that she utterly rescinded and denied, she rocked slowly, caressing Polycarp's dry cheek with her hand. After a moment his lips stilled. His chest rose and fell. She drew in a breath, wondering if he was asleep. He looked it. Surely he had earned his sleep. She held his head, forgetful of the dead who had attacked or the Roman guardsmen who might. Caring only for this man, her father and her refuge, whom the night had nearly destroyed. She felt a little less fragile, seeing him sleep.

She had watched him sleep once before. On the first night after she'd been freed, the night when she'd discovered that she was still capable of loving. At first that had been a terrible night; she'd lain awake on her cot shaking, her gaze fixed on the ceiling with its peeling paint. Everything had felt alien to her—the air in the room, the mattress beneath her back (thin, yet far better than what she was accustomed to—and clean, it was *clean*), the even thinner light from the window looking out on the atrium. The father, she knew, slept on the other side of the wall; once, she heard him rise and move about. She stiffened then, certain that everything she'd heard and seen and felt that day had been only delusion, as she'd feared, and that in a moment the old man would come to her with dry, grasping hands and demand what all men demand. But he only paced back and forth in his little room, and after a while she heard mumbling—words too soft to make out, if words they were. Perhaps he was talking to himself, or to his God. Then the sounds stopped, and there was silence. She dared not move.

As she lay there, an agony of suspense and a horror of that silence took hold of her, until her palms were sweating. At last she couldn't bear it; she got quietly to her feet and went to the wall. Pressed her ear to the plaster. Listened. She could hear each distinct beat of her own heart. She could hear the oceanic song of her own blood. But nothing else. No footfall, no stuttering snore. She bit her lip, holding back an urge to cry out, to shriek, to hear what reaction her cry would bring. In her nightshirt she tiptoed to the door—the inner door that opened on the insula's cramped but lush garden atrium. With a gentle push she swung the door open, grateful that its hinges were well oiled. She slipped out, pressed her body to the wall between her door and the father's. Her heart pounding. Searching the higher windows with wide eyes, her shoulders tensed with memory of the beatings that followed an excursion from one's cot.

But the night was quiet. A crescent moon had just risen over the roof of the insula; its light lay soft as milk on the leaves and closed buds of the garden. All the windows were darkened and silent; unlike the home of her former master, this was not a place that encouraged carousing after dark. Unable to keep her hands from shaking, Regina slid along the wall to Polycarp's door, hesitated, then touched her fingers to its handle. There was no window to peer into; only the door permitted any sight of Polycarp's chamber. Now her heart was violent in her breast, her mouth was dry. Praying that Polycarp had the hinges on *all* his doors oiled, she nudged the door open and slipped in.

She saw his shape—surprisingly small in the dark—curled on the pallet inside. Like a small boy, his knees drawn up near his chin. A blanket tossed aside and rumpled, but still tangled about one foot as though spurned in the anguish of a sudden dream. She'd left the door open a crack, and a thin line of moonlight lay across Polycarp's legs.

He was sleeping. Just sleeping.

The whole earth seemed to slide out from beneath Regina's feet; she felt as though she were falling from a great height. Slowly she lowered herself to her knees, hardly breathing. She kept her gaze fixed on the outline of the man on his pallet, on the slow rise and fall of his breath. He hadn't stirred when she entered; he didn't stir now. Whatever dreams had visited him, he'd dealt with them in silence, without outcry, and was now at rest.

Regina sat, drew up her own knees, hugged herself tightly. Everything that had happened this day—it was too much for her. Only this morning, she had been shivering in the street, her mind lashed by the pain of the welts on her back, by the shame of her nakedness. Waiting only for the next one who would use her. Now she watched this old man breathe. Her eyes were adjusting again to the dimness, after the moonlight; she could see his face, softened by sleep. He was not so old, not truly; whatever he had witnessed in life had carved savage lines about his eyes and lips prematurely, even as what she'd witnessed had left her own back marked.

He had demanded nothing of her this day. Nor had the few others she'd met in the insula. A younger man who lived on the second story had assessed her for a few moments with his eyes, but as he might assess a woman he wished to court, not one he wished to purchase. That had been a new and exhilarating and frightening moment for her, but this moment terrified her far more. She'd never sat beside a man who demanded nothing of her. That realization hit her fully now; she trembled in the dark. Drawing a shuddering breath, she reached back, ran her fingertips over the welts between her shoulders. She could feel them even through her nightdress; the soreness of her skin lit with fresh fire at her own cautious touch, and her face twisted in pain.

What was she?

What would it mean for her, to be the kind of woman who could relate to a man who demanded nothing of her?

She thought of women of the Subura she'd seen in the streets. Some were broken and pitiable, or small and wretched, but others walked proudly, though the clothes they wore were threadbare and little better than those of the slaves that worked in their homes. They walked proudly because some at least of their time they could devote to things of their own making or their own choosing.

Some few of them had never been beaten.

This day, she'd taken a new name, a free woman's name. When she was a child, her parents had named her Theodora, a "gift from the gods"; the slavers who'd abducted her kept the name but raped it of its intended meaning, using it instead to emphasize her body's beauty when they brought her to a private sale. The master who purchased her there shortened the name to Dora, tearing away syllables even as he tore away her history and the last of her childhood. Dora was a brief name, a diminutive name, a slave's name; it simply meant "a gift." As a slave, she was property. She might be gifted to whomever her master pleased; she could not gift herself.

But Polycarp had freed her and asked that she take the name Regina. "Queen," it meant, a giver of gifts: no longer a gift but a giver, and one who might give herself where she chose. The meaning of it did a violence in her heart: what would it mean to live in fulfillment of this new name? She no longer knew what she was.

The gentle strength of this sleeping man was unfamiliar and frightening; she didn't know how to respond to him. For the first time in several years, a thousand memories of her childhood home flooded into her, moments of tenderness from her grandfather and her mother, before the flesh thieves had stolen her away. Father Polycarp had touched her cheek this day, after wrapping a cloak about her in the street; her grandfather used to do that, when she was a little girl. No one had touched her so, since. She lifted her own hand to her face now and found it wet.

***

In the alley among the crumpled dead, Polycarp's eyes slitted open at last, pale as moonlight on water. For a moment he just drew in breath and air and gazed up at her. "Beloved daughter." His voice a hoarse croak.

She bent over him and brushed her lips across his brow. She felt his breath near her ear, then the whisper of his voice.

"Our lives are—so brittle," he rasped.

"Shhh," Regina whispered, cradling his head.

The father lifted his hand, gripped her fingers suddenly. His eyes focused on her; the breath labored in his chest, as though it took great effort to speak coherently after what he'd done, what he'd witnessed. The intensity of his eyes held her; though he was clearly fighting to voice these words through a fatigue that grappled with his spirit, his halting voice held the same passion and fierce intent with which he'd so often addressed the gathering in the Catacombs. She returned his tight grip on her hand. "Some things can never—be atoned for. Can only be—absolved, or—not. Without—that grace—all rotting, we are all—" His breath hissed between his teeth, as though for a moment it hurt him even to breathe.

"It's over," Regina whispered. "They're all at rest. You gave them the Gift, father." She tried to find words for the fullness of emotion inside her, so much fullness, so much she couldn't hold it. "You saved them."

"All of them?" he whispered.

"Yes, father." She lifted his hand, pressed the back of it to her lips. After a moment she glanced up, looking out across the alley filled with unmoving dead. Above them, a few furtive stars shone in a narrow crack of sky between the buildings leaning in on them. She thought of sleeping Rome in its thousands all about them, and shivered. "I have to get you inside," she whispered. "We have to hide you."

"No—there is no more hiding." The soft hiss of his breath. "Have to—stand."

"Father—" she gasped.

He gave her a small, grim smile, his eyes opening again. They were clearer now. He placed his hand over hers. At the tenderness of it, the dry warmth of his touch, she blinked back hot moisture from her eyes. She shook her head, appalled at what he was asking of her. Panic began to rise in her, panic at the shattering of everything that had held her and kept her safe these past four years in the insula, these years serving Polycarp. The sight of him sleeping, the need to care for him, to give *him* refuge—the gentle weight of his head in her lap—all of this had held the panic back. Now her body went cold with it.

"Daughter. The guardsmen—need to find me. And not you."

"I'm not *leaving* you."

"Regina." He looked at her, his voice very soft. The pain in his eyes made her gasp. "If you love me, daughter, *go inside*. Leave me here—to talk awhile with God." His eyes were still so pale, as though every inch of his body was in pain—though he lay so still. He lifted his hand to touch her hair, and she leaned her cheek into his fingers, her lip trembling. "Our God," he breathed, holding her eyes with his, "is the same here—at night—as he is by day in our rooms. We must submit when called, daughter. We must each of us submit, each of us surrender. We are all the redeemed slaves of God. Else—else, we are—" He gasped for air a moment; his gaze became intense, holding hers. "The gathering is as vulnerable to vices—pride, self-interest—as any other group of people. Daughter, hear me. Without our submission when called, we would become only a—only a mirror—of the Palatine. Only another kind of Senate. We must remain a gathering of servants. We must choose to live in this way." He breathed open-mouthed for a moment. "I know what I must do, daughter—and I must ready myself for it. But you—I would have you safe."

"No," she whispered, "no." His God asked too much! He asked of all of them too much! "I can't—" She forced the words out, something inside her tightening. "Father!" she pleaded. "Polycarp—"

She'd never called out his name before.

She felt that everything in her, all the pieces of herself that she'd moored so carefully, were coming apart on dark waters. The insula had long since become her refuge, and Polycarp in his acceptance of her had become her refuge also. Now both refuges had been violated—by the dead, by Julia's betrayal, by the guardsmen who might even now be coming down the narrow alleys. She gave a low, moaning cry; she might lose everything tonight, everything that meant anything to her. They might all be taken or be separated forever. These moments might be the last in which she would ever see Polycarp—how could she leave him?

Polycarp's fingers curled in her hair a moment. His pale eyes searched hers, and his cracked lips parted. "You are strong," he rasped. "Strong as a queen. The others—they need you, Regina. Go now."

She took his hand, turned the palm toward her and kissed it, her eyes squeezed shut against tears. Her shoulders shook with silent weeping. "Don't," she whispered.

"Regina, Polycarp, what's happened?" A call from the door. She jolted. Marcus's voice.

Marcus. And the others. They needed her.

Strong as a queen.

She squeezed Polycarp's hand once, then let it go. She shifted the father's head from her lap and rose to her feet. She'd chosen to serve Polycarp and his God. It had been a free choice. Now they needed this of her. Her hands trembled. She wiped her eyes, took a steadying breath. Polycarp beside her was getting wearily to his knees; he turned from her, facing up the slope of the alley, then lowered his brow to the stones, an obeisance to the God he needed to speak with. All about them, the dead lay still, their spirits at rest, the bodies that'd been left behind no more now than driftwood washed into this alley by Death's river.

Regina's breast swelled with the force of her love for this man, her need for him. He meant to stand between the gathering and the Roman guardsmen, even as in the last hour he'd stood between them and the dead. How determined, how immovable he looked as he knelt among the dead, readying himself for whatever might come. Other men she had known, slave men and free: the tight-lipped and impoverished men of the insula who were so reluctantly rediscovering and reclaiming joy as they shared bread. The master who had enjoyed her body, lashing her at a whim or merely to distract himself from whatever pain or frustration he felt inadequate to face. These had been men who were not up to the task, men in whom there was no refuge, only the threat that if they wanted something of her they would bruise her in taking it, and that if she wanted something of them, they would crumple when leaned on. But Polycarp would never crumple. He could not be moved.

She could not let him down. He'd never let her down.

She walked to the insula door. Marcus waited there, and she could see Phineas and Vergilius behind him; no one had brought another lamp. She swung the door closed, with a last glance at Polycarp kneeling in the dark of the alley. Her hand trembled once, then she shut the door. She turned toward them, the wood of the door at her back. Their eyes were round with need in the dark.

"The father is at prayer." She cleared her throat. "Phineas, get a lamp." Her voice didn't waver, though she felt unsteady as a shrub with shallow roots in a high wind. "Vergilius, get everyone into the hiding place. Marcus, will you go to one of the second-story windows and keep watch tonight for the guardsmen?"

Only when they had gone from the room—Marcus giving her arm one brief squeeze before hurrying out—only then did she lean her head back against the door, closing her eyes and shuddering, biting her lip against the cries that she would not voice.

***

Regina had gone, but Polycarp knew he was *not* alone. He could hear the labored breathing of the great, dark-haired behemoth that crouched some distance behind him in the alley. He did not know if the creature approaching him had any corporeal reality, any more than the red beetle he had seen in his dream and several times in his waking life. But the *messages* brought by the beetle and the behemoth were real. Messages of truth and hope from the beetle, messages of fatigue and despair from the lumbering, misshapen beast that had now prowled into the alley. The messages they brought were desperately real, perhaps so real that they required some corporeal being to carry them, even if otherwise no such being would have existed.

As the thing approached, Polycarp did not look up but kept his brow pressed to a pavement stone smeared with offal and dried urine; he kept his eyes closed not from fear but from a weariness so poignant it wore at his bones. To give the dead rest, he'd needed to look first into each one's blind eyes and find beneath the gray scratches the remnant of the soul locked within the shambling corpse. He'd needed to witness each one's secrets, each one's sins, each one's suffering—all that each one had loved and feared and regretted in their brief lives. Only then might he absolve them and set them free and let the corpses slide lifeless to the alley floor. But he had needed to see each one's heart not through a glass darkly—the way he saw Regina's heart, say, or Marcus's, or even his *own* heart—but as clearly as *God* saw, without any veils to protect his mind from the pain of another's.

Our hearts are such small things. There is in the world both too much beauty and too much suffering for a human heart to hold.

Polycarp sobbed quietly as he rested on the mute stones, listening to the heavy paws and the wheezing breaths of the thing in the alley. Despair had come to visit him, as it had often done in the years since he came to Rome; each time, it was a little harder to send the beast away. Most often he heard the tread of its paws on nights such as this, after an encounter with the dead.

You are old, the creature whispered. *You are old, Polycarp. And there are too many hurts to heal. You are not sufficient for this task.*

"My master is sufficient," Polycarp murmured, too tired even to feel revolted at the grime he felt against his lips as they moved.

But you are here, and he isn't.

No. Polycarp braced his hands against the stones. *I am his hands, his feet. I must stand up.*

He swayed a moment, looking out at the tumbled bodies. In a moment of wild imagining he pictured them placing their hands to the street, even as he was doing, and lifting themselves up. Not as slouching, unsteady dead, but as the living called back.

Called back. Any spirit could be called back.

Go away, he told the behemoth. *I have no need of you and no time to listen to you, nor to the Adversary who sends you. You are unwanted here, as unnecessary as these bodies, these empty shells that carry no life.*

The creature Despair did not fall silent, but Polycarp kept it now at the edge of hearing. He needed to reflect on what had happened in this alley. How severely it had tired him, how vulnerable it had left him. He needed to pray, and think, without the pollution of Despair's whispered enticements.

He'd never considered having to face so many dead, more than a few at a time.

During the recent year of the pestilence, whenever Polycarp had come upon the dead in the Subura, he'd refused to conceal himself, though the approach of them made his palms sweat. Once, he'd stood in the path of a tall man lumbering down a street in the still dawn while the living peered out from their windows. The thing's entrails had spilled from a gash in its belly, and it was trailing them slickly behind it. Polycarp had stood and forced himself to breathe calmly even as the thing sensed him, raised its one unbroken arm, and let out that long, deep moan of unquenchable hunger. But as it lurched toward the father, it tripped in its own innards and lay moaning and twisting in a tangle of them, right in the street. Polycarp approached it slowly, then bent and touched the thing's side with his hand, saw the soul come back briefly into its eyes. Then the corpse went still and rested as silent as though it lay in a mausoleum and not on the grimed stones of a Suburan street. Polycarp had sat looking at the body for a few moments. Then he bent to the side and vomited up into the street.

Another time he'd been walking home and had heard screams; he'd broken into a run, pouring on speed until he feared his heart would burst within him. He was no longer made for running. Others in the street ran the opposite way, away from the screams rather than toward them; someone hit him and he fell. He might've been trampled if there'd been more people. But there were only a few, and then the street was empty. He rolled onto his side, got up onto his hands, and looked up the street. There, at the open doorway of a jeweler's shop, two dead were feasting on the small, still-twitching body of a man who may have been the proprietor; his fingers wore many rings. They had dragged him half out of the shop and were sharing his arm between them, biting deep, then tearing the flesh away in long, bleeding strips. They did not look up as Polycarp got to his feet.

The two dead were a woman, young, and a small child whose eyes were as gray as the woman's and who tore into the flesh as ravenously.

Polycarp prayed without words as he walked toward them.

Afterward, when he was done, he crawled into the dark of the jeweler's shop and leaned against a great, wooden case that doubtless held locked within it many items of beauty. He drew up his knees like a boy does and rested his arms on them. Bowed his head. The dark was quiet and comfortable; he wanted rest as he had never wanted anything before. He had never even wanted a woman so much. He hadn't even wanted *God* so much. He just closed his eyes and breathed. In a while the tears came; he felt them cooling as they slid down his cheek.

Until this night in the alley, he had never experienced a greater strain than his encounter with the two dead at the jeweler's shop. When he'd set one hand on the child's shoulder and one hand on the woman's, and they had turned growling to bite at him, he'd looked into their eyes and *seen*—

He ached with what he'd seen. His breath caught in small sobs. He rocked, hitting the jewelry case with the back of his head.

When the child's spirit had looked out of his hungering body and gazed for the briefest of instants at Polycarp, the pain the father witnessed in him had been terrible. But the woman's suffering had been worse. In *her* eyes he'd seen the anguish of a woman who'd never been told she was beautiful, had in fact been told that she was of utterly no worth, unloved and unvalued by everything that breathed, whether mortal or immortal. The whole earth could fall through the hole in her and would not fill it. She had poured wine into that hole, and the touch of men, and even her nightly rape of that small boy—the one whose body Polycarp had found feeding on the jeweler beside her. And when the dead had come to her room, she'd put up no struggle as they fed on her and the boy. She had poured them into the hole too.

***

Bad as that hour had been, this night in the alley had been far worse. Too many dead who'd never had the chance to say farewell to their own pasts, to the tears that were never shed, the joys that were never consummated, the hungers that were never satisfied. His heart had not known there was so much pain, so much loss, in the earth. His head had known, but his heart hadn't known—not the way it knew tonight, after witnessing the unveiled anguish of twenty souls.

Polycarp bit down against a groan, strove to get his knees beneath him again, then had to stop, gasping for air. His ears caught a new sound in the alley, but he ignored it. For the moment all that mattered was the air moving in and out of his body. He tried to form words for a prayer and finally cried out in silence, pleading for respite. For recovery. For strength.

The sound—the new sound—intruded again. He focused on it.

A clinking of metal.

Muted, yet unmistakable in the stillness that had fallen over the tenements since the dead appeared.

Relief settled over Polycarp's shoulders like a warm blanket. *Thank you, master. Thank you. One more test now, one more task, then I can rest.* He heard the scrabbling of unsheathed claws on the stones as the dark beast fled the alley, running not because of the clink and clatter of Roman breastplates but because, as Polycarp breathed more evenly, there was no longer opportunity for it to speak.

The clinking grew near, then fell still, and a hard voice spoke above his head.

"We seek the insula where Polycarp hides. Is this it?"

Polycarp began to laugh softly, helplessly. Lifting his begrimed face from the ground, there among the bodies of the dead, he lifted his hands too. He reached for the pair of manacles the guardsmen held ready and for the rest from care they offered, even as in an earlier year of his life he might have lifted his hands toward a lover's face.

REGINA ROMAE

IN THE HOURS SINCE the guardsmen had taken them from the insula, sleep hadn't come for Regina. She sat with her back to the rough boards of the wall in this prison shed she'd been tossed into, still in her nightdress. Her eyes on the locked, wooden door. Marcus's head she cradled in her lap; from time to time the boy moaned in the dark, stirring fitfully, and she stroked his hair. Having someone to care for helped her breathe calmly, kept her from shuddering into sobs. She had to keep it together.

There were bruises about Marcus's face, and Regina was careful not to touch them. While Regina and Vergilius had hurried the tenants from the first two stories into Polycarp's larder and into the hiding place, Marcus had been watching the alley from a high window. Seeing two of the guardsmen take Polycarp away, he'd wanted to run after them—he'd even taken up a dagger; she hadn't known he owned one. Regina had cried out to him to stop, to come to the hidden cellar; but he'd run to the door, reaching it even as the guardsmen burst through.

Regina had thrown herself before them, to give Vergilius time to shut the secret door in the larder—but it was too late. The guardsmen had come too soon; even as they rushed through the door, one of them caught sight of movement in the larder and shouted out; then Marcus was at the guardsmen with his fists, and they beat him until he lay still. Regina tried to bar their way into the larder with her body, though her heart hammered as they came at her; one seized her arm and she raked his face with her nails. With a bellow, he flung her to the floor on her back. Though she kicked at him as he bent, he shoved his knee into her belly and lashed her wrists before her with cord that bit savagely into her skin. She screamed; the man struck her. Then she lay still, dazed a moment, her head ringing with the pain of it—a terrible, gray moment where she thought she might pass out, where she didn't know whether it was a guardsman pinning her or her old master who used to crush her to the floor with his right hand balled into a fist, his left reaching for her body. Regina's breath came in short, frantic gasps.

The guardsman's voice came to her through a roaring in her ears—orders he was barking. "That larder. And every room. Search them."

The others. *The others*—they needed her. Marcus lay unmoving by the door.

"They're just tenants." She forced the words out, tasting blood on her lip.

"Maybe," one of the other guards snorted. "And maybe this is a rats' nest."

"We'll know quick enough," the guard who pinned her grunted. A blade scar sliced from his left temple across his nose to his jawbone on the right, giving his face a kind of savage beauty. His eyes were weary but without pity. The hardness in them dulled the edge of Regina's panic, enough for her to breathe. Her old master's eyes had been cruel, watery, self-indulgent. The eyes of this captor held only self-interest and determination. This man might strike a woman to quiet her—or strike a man for the same reason—but he would not do so for the pleasure of it. For a moment Regina focused on getting her breath back, regathering herself, as the guardsman turned his head toward the others. "There's no one here with more than a fist to swing. I'll take these two now—already sent Quintus and Lucullus back with the old man. You follow with whatever else you find. Praetor can sort it out. *Tenants.*" His voice was thick with derision.

The other guards stepped past her into the larder, and she screamed and tried to throw herself at them. But she couldn't get out from under the man's knee; her hands were trapped so tightly that her wrists burned as she struggled. The man who had her snarled and got to his feet. He'd left a length of cord free when he tied her; now he dragged her to her knees using it, and his hand gripping her arm pulled her to her feet. Then he was pulling her behind him, leashed like a slave new from the docks, even as she screamed for the others to stay concealed. He tossed Marcus's limp form over his shoulder, took a firm hold on the leash, and pulled her stumbling out the door and past the restful dead. The insula fell behind, and the guardsman took them through the narrow streets of the Subura, uphill toward the richer parts of Rome.

Regina knew many residents of the slum must be watching from their windows, and she hung her head, hiding her face with her hair. She burned with the shame of being dragged so, in her nightdress, through the streets in the deep dark before dawn.

She tried to tell herself that she was Regina Romae, a deaconess of the gathering in Rome. But as she stumbled over the uneven stones, bruising her toes, and as her hands went numb, she didn't feel like Regina. She felt like Dora—that slave who'd so often found herself bound, helpless, in another's power. Something welled up in her breast and her throat, a desire to beg, to do anything to be freed of this terrible, biting rope. That feeling terrified her.

As they left the Subura, her captor stopped a moment. Regina glanced over her shoulder and gasped. Dark shapes were stumbling out of an alley and lurching into the street behind them. One of them let out a deep groan. Marcus stirred faintly on the guardsman's shoulder.

"Gods," the guardsman breathed. "So many. Gods."

He cursed and dragged her forward at a run, yanking on the cord so violently that she sprawled to the stones, smacking her shoulder and crying out. At the cry, more moans erupted behind them—down the street, but too near, too near! Regina kicked out in panic, tried to get her feet under her; a hard hand gripped her arm and wrenched her back to her feet.

Then they *ran*.

The stones battered her feet; she sobbed for breath. Her side burning, she began to pray to Polycarp's God. She cried out the *Phos Hilaron* in frantic Greek syllables; in this terror it was all she could think of. *Phos hilaron hagias doxes athanatou Patros*, she cried as they ran: a prayer for light and joy on a street where the buildings leaned so close that running over the stones was like racing through a tunnel in the earth.

Something grabbed at her ankle and she shrieked, falling again; something fell on her in the dark, and she felt a cold, dry hand clutch at her face. A hiss above her. She kicked wildly, writhing, a jagged stone beneath her cutting her back. Wetness trickled hot over her thighs, the reek of urine. A face above her, its mouth open, teeth bared.

Then the weight was lifted from her, and a man stood over her. A faint gleam of metal. Again the hiss, and then the chop of iron into flesh. Regina kept kicking, and the man above her swore. "Lie still, you slut."

She froze, the sound of his voice confirming that the shape that stood over her was living, not dead. Her heart pounded. She started repeating her name to herself, silently, again and again. She was *not* Dora. She was Regina. Regina Romae. The cords bit at her hands.

Another hiss, and she cried out, her mind going blank as her whole body flinched, anticipating the cut of teeth into her flesh. The man above her danced in place, and again she heard the chunk of metal into meat. A heavy figure fell across her feet and she twisted, kicking it off. It did not grasp her or bite. Then the guardsman's hands were on her arms, pulling her to her feet again.

She swayed. It was so dark. She could hear the dead wailing, very near. The man who held her was only a silhouette against the blind night. She moaned.

His hand struck her face.

Then the ground left her feet and she was over his shoulder, his hand on her rear. She felt the hard rhythm of his strides; he was walking very quickly. There was moaning loud behind them. She didn't kick; the pain in her face had cleared her mind. She sucked in short, sharp breaths, desperate for air.

She was Regina Romae. Regina Romae.

Anger and shame lit in her, a heat that drove away fear. Not in years had she shaken apart so badly. The warmth of her own urine on her leg made her furious. She could hear her own sobbing breaths, her quiet whimpers, and she clenched her teeth, stopping them. Lifting her head, she gazed into the dizzy night behind them. She could hear the dragging footsteps of the dead; she could hear their moans. They were close.

Then the guardsman carried her out from the close streets, and he strode up a long slope, the tenements of the Subura replaced by gardens and villas; without buildings leaning close overhead, there were stars, many stars, brilliant and sharp in the sky. In their light she saw the dead shamble out of the close-packed alleys and stumble uphill after them. They didn't move fast; the guardsman was young and strong, and, if unburdened, could outrun them. But now, bearing the weight of two captives, one on either shoulder—

Regina watched the dead with wide eyes. There were thirty, maybe forty. Still more shuffled after those. Dark figures in the starlight, barely separable one from another. Just shadow shapes that had lurched out of some child's nightmare with hunger and clutching hands and a need to kill. They moaned as they followed.

The sight shook her. What could even Polycarp do against so many? And how many more still shuffled in closed rooms in half the tenements by the river, waiting for a door to open, or tumbling by accident out the window to crawl up the street seeking someone to devour?

The guardsman's breath wheezed beneath her.

"Don't stop," Regina whispered. "Run, run."

She didn't know she'd spoken aloud, but the guardsman's steps quickened; the jostling of his shoulder against her belly deprived her of her own breath. She could only watch the dead as they lurched up the hill, nearly a hundred of them now. Their moaning filled the air. As though overnight the Tiber had become the Styx, and the boatman had confused his directions and was ferrying the dead over from the farther shore.

But the guardsman's sprint was brief; he began to pant and his pace flagged as the uphill road became steeper. Regina's heart beat wildly in her ears. Behind them, four of the dead had lurched ahead of the rest. Here on the Palatine slopes, the road was sunken, a wide channel to carry away sewage, with raised steps in the middle to keep the feet of affluent citizens dry. At this time of night, there was little fluid in the road, and even little scent, for water had been poured down it after sundown to cleanse the road. But the shin-high embankments to either side of the road served to confine and channel the dead, as long as the prey they sought was directly ahead. That kept most of the dead pressed tightly together; as the group shambled forward, they impeded each other.

But those four who were ahead climbed the road steadily, having more room, one of them slouching a little to the side, another with its arms lifted and reaching for its prey. The guardsman wheezed and stumbled to one knee.

"No!" Regina cried. "Get up, get up! They're right behind us!"

Her captor planted both of his palms against the moist pavement and gazed forward at the rising slope of the hill. With a roar like a beast, he thrust himself back to his feet, both captives still on his shoulders. One hand on each, he stumbled furiously up the incline.

The dead were only a few paces behind. They did not tire or stumble.

Regina fought her bonds, twisting her wrists, panting with fear as she tried to slip one hand free. She took care not to move her hips much; she didn't want to fall to the hard pavement, to lie there bound as the walking corpses closed in on her, their hands reaching for her. She strained and gritted her teeth and pulled at her wrists; pain flared in her lower arms. She couldn't get her hands free.

The guardsman was fighting for every step; the uphill sprint had wearied him. Perhaps, if given a moment to stop and breathe, he might recover enough to finish the climb quickly.

The dead would not give him a moment.

"Please," Regina whispered, "please."

One of the dead lurched close, its eyes dull, its teeth glinting in the starlight. Stretching out its arm, its fingers clutching at her. Regina tried to twist her head away, breathing in tiny gasps. She moaned through clenched teeth, tensing.

In the next instant the corpse's cold fingertips brushed *her hair*.

A dark blur crashed into the thing's head; the creature staggered to the side, hissed, then took a step back toward them; a man in leather armor shoved the guardsman with his captives behind him, then swung a great wooden cudgel, slamming it a second time into the corpse's head. This blow knocked the creature to its knees, even as the three other dead stumbled near.

Moaning—not a moan of pain but that long, low moan of hunger—the dead corpse began rising to its feet again. Their rescuer swung the cudgel, but now two more of the dead grabbed his arms, pulling him toward their mouths. He cursed and kicked one of them hard between the thighs with his boot, but the creature did not wince or move. Regina screamed as the corpse pressed its mouth to the soldier's wrist and bit deeply. Blood welled up around its teeth, dark in the night.

The guardsman slid his captives from his shoulders; Regina felt the pavement hit her back and rump hard, and sucked in her breath. The fourth walking corpse bent and snatched at her hair. But the guardsman's knife slid from its sheath in a song of metal, and he drove his blade into the creature's chest. That did not slow it. Regina cried out as she felt her head lifted by the hair, her wrists tied helplessly beneath her. The thing's face a shadow above her, its teeth reaching for her. She tried to speak, to beg, to scream—no sound came.

A blade shone for an instant before her face. One more hard tug on her hair and then the pull was gone; she fell back hard to the stones. She saw long strands of her hair still caught in the creature's hand, the ends severed.

The guardsman's rough hand grabbed her, dragged her a few feet up the road. As other feet pounded past her, she rolled to her side and retched into the street.

Several men were wrestling with the four dead; they had cudgels, and one or two had knives. She saw one cudgel come down again and again on a hairless head that kept snapping its jaws and hissing; skin and gray matter and tissue spewed from the growing wound in its skull, until the thing just fell to the side and lay crumpled like tattered clothes tossed into the drain.

Then it was over.

Four corpses lay still in the street, and one of the soldiers bent to wipe the mess from his cudgel on a tunic one of the bodies wore.

Regina retched again, tasting her vomit on her lips and in her mouth. She groaned. Her back ached from the impact of falling several times onto hard stone. She coughed and fought to stop her belly from heaving. Her hair, cut short on the left side of her head, got into her eyes. The moaning of the larger group of dead—who must be very near now—was loud. For a moment with one side of her face pressed to the street, she could hear their approach through the rock. She could hear both the moaning and the scraping of their feet. She began praying, whispering.

There were soldiers in the street, between her and Marcus and the dead. Several armored men. One knelt, clutching his arm. To her horror, blood ran from beneath his hand and spilled to the pavement like water from a fountain, an urgent stream of life leaving him. The man groaned something that Regina didn't quite catch, and then a new man stepped into view, tall and broad-shouldered, a giant with a high mane on his helmet. An officer, a centurion. There was no *gladius* at his belt, but he held a long cudgel with a jagged scrap of bronze fixed to the end.

He stood for a moment before the wounded legionnaire.

Behind him, Regina could see the slow-moving, steady advance of the dead. They were close enough to throw stones at, with accuracy. She rolled onto her back, glanced once at the star-pierced sky, once up the road to the high, quiet villas of the wealthy, sheltered among dark, tall cypresses. Marcus lay there in the road, near enough to touch if she weren't bound; his face was turned from her and he wasn't moving or making any sound, but she could see the rise and fall of his chest.

She had to protect him. She had to do something. She forced herself to breathe. There were armed men here—disciplined, trained legionnaires; she and Marcus would *not* be eaten. She just had to pull herself together, think, survive. She had to. How the cords *bit* at her wrists!

She glanced back down the street toward the dead in time to see the centurion raise his cudgel.

"You did your duty," the officer said.

The wounded man lifted his head and closed his eyes. Regina shut hers quickly as the cudgel came down.

When she opened them a moment later, the man lay in the street, his head caved in on one side, blood running, slow and dark, down the stones toward the staggering dead.

Her belly heaved again.

The centurion turned to her captor, who stood now to one side, his chest heaving as he recovered his breath. "Run past," the officer barked. "We'll divert them, lead them back toward the river."

Regina's captor panted, tried to force out words. "There may—be others— don't get caught—between—"

"I know my work, guardsman." The centurion's face was hard, and the anger in his eyes, cold and violent, made Regina flinch—though that restrained fury was directed not at her or at Marcus but at the guardsman who had trailed a crowd of walking dead up the hill toward the parts of Rome the centurion believed worthy of defending.

Turning from them, the centurion gestured quickly with his hand; men in armor but carrying only cudgels and staves moved past in a quick but orderly line. By law no soldiers who marched in any army of the state could carry sharp iron within the ancient boundary of Rome, so in the recent disorder the magistrates had hired mercenary guardsmen to keep the streets clean of dead; Regina's captor was one of these hired men. The centurion and these twenty were not. Their training had been brutal and without reprieve or rest, and they had been tested perhaps in the swamps of Germania or along Hadrian's Wall, at those distant frontiers where most of Rome's armies held watch, far from the Eternal City. Now, striking an uneasy truce between the security of Rome and the laws of Rome, this centurion and his volunteers had ventured into the city in their armor, taking up improvised weapons that held no blades.

They were few, but they were Roman soldiers. Where they marched, the world knelt.

Regina gazed at the hard eyes of the centurion, and for just a moment he looked at her. She caught her breath at what she saw. A kind of strength she'd seen before only in Polycarp's eyes. What this man said, he would do. The moaning of the dead was loud behind them, but she believed him. He would divert the dead from the hill.

She also saw that his eyes were not those of a man who expected to survive this night.

Grunting, the hired guardsman lifted her to her feet. "You'll have to run," he growled by her ear. She nodded. He tossed Marcus back over his shoulder, gripped her arm above the elbow, then pulled her with him as he broke into a fast walk. Swiftly, they left the legionnaires behind. She heard human cries and shouts amid the moaning of the undead, but she did not look back. She kept her eyes focused on the street above her, praying that she would not stumble or trip.

The Roman villas to either side of the narrow street were silent and dark. There were no windows, for on the Palatine Hill houses kept their windows on the inside, looking into the garden. The outside was only a wall, closing out any sight of what walked in the street. Regina thought of the families in those homes, stirred from sleep by the wailing of the dead. Even at this moment perhaps a dozen mothers or nurses were clasping small children close, stroking their hair and whispering comfort into their ears. Perhaps a dozen slaves stood waiting by villa doors with staves or brooms in their hands, ordered to beat back the dead if the walking corpses should burst in. No lamps had been lit; no voices were raised in the dark. The men and women of upper Rome were simply waiting within their walls, silent and wide eyed, hoping the clamor in the street would pass them by, the way a tempest might pass by a forest of oaks.

Regina's sides burned, but she forced herself to match the guardsman's pace.

The moaning of the dead was farther behind now. She didn't dare cast a glance over her shoulder to see if the legionnaires had indeed led them away from the street. A glance back might mean tripping. She couldn't bear to lie helpless on the pavement again, not even briefly. With the dead falling behind, relieving the sharp edge of her terror, she began to worry for Marcus. She didn't know how badly he'd been hurt. He might need a poultice and a stay in bed; instead, he was being jounced about on a guardsman's shoulder.

She stubbed her toe hard on the stones, clenched her cry behind her teeth; the guardsman's hard yank on her arm kept her upright, kept her moving, though agony shot through her foot and up her leg.

"There it is," her captor breathed. "Justitia's temple."

Ahead of them, beyond the next villa, she saw a high, marble wall and, towering out of the courtyard behind it, the pillared façade of a high building, white and gleaming under the stars. Nestled against the outside of the wall was a smaller, blockier structure, an official's station. Several wooden sheds had been erected to either side of that station. A man leaned against the side of one, looking down the street at them. Another guardsman.

Regina tried to move her hands in her bonds, but she couldn't feel them; the cord had numbed them. Her captor dragged her toward one of the sheds. The other guardsman swung the door open, revealing a gaping, dark opening. It recalled to her heart the opening to the cargo hold of the slave ship that had brought her to this part of the world years ago. Her hands had been bound then too. Tears ran down her face unchecked. She'd been dragged uphill from the shattered refuge of the insula to this small shed that a Roman might toss a slave into. Of everything that had befallen her since she was pulled from the door of the insula into the street, nothing had terrified her as much as that dark opening of the shed. In her heart she cried out, though she kept her lips still. She didn't know where Polycarp was or what would be done with them—she cried his name silently as the guards pushed her through into the dark closeness of the shed. One of them—the new guard—caught her by the arms before she fell; she was pulled back against his body, and a rough hand slipped beneath her nightdress, groped her thigh with thick, seeking fingers. She flinched and made a high, keening sound that shamed her. Her body tensed like a branch bent back too far, ready to break at another touch.

"Time for that later, Decius," the guard who'd carried her said. "Reports to make, and I need you. Whole bloody Subura's full of dead—can't you hear them?"

The other guardsman grunted his assent and took his hand from her. In a moment she felt cold steel against her wrists, and then the cord parted, and her wrists were free; the guardsman shoved her to the straw. Marcus was thrown down beside her.

The door slammed to.

Regina lay panting, sobbing, on her belly in the dark. Only the freedom of her hands kept her from panic. She was not bound; she was not in the slave hold. There was warm straw beneath her, not wood chips. This was not the past.

She pushed herself up on her hands, trying to breathe through the tightness in her body. Faintly, through the chinks in the shed's walls, she could hear the moaning of the dead as they hunted in the streets of the Subura, pitting the strength of their ravenous and unmet need against the discipline and order of the Roman soldiers.

***

Dawn came, a faint and furtive light between the boards of the shed. The distant moans had been silent now for some time. Perhaps the danger out there had passed. Perhaps not. The shivers of reaction from their panicked flight had come and gone, leaving Regina exhausted, hungry, weak. She sat with her back to the wall of the shed, still holding Marcus, who groaned from time to time but did not wake. Parts of her own body ached with stiffness and bruising. Her own odor was offensive to her; her skin was coated in a grease of sweat and dirt, and she yearned for a basin of water and a clean cloth. Her emotions were fierce animals within her, prowling and roaring, making her thoughts flee about. First, her horror at the rising of the dead en masse. Would even the battle discipline of the military men avail to stop the hungry dead? She knew Polycarp, who would bring the dead absolution and rest, would have saddened at the waste of the corpses that had been destroyed during the night. But surely Polycarp had never imagined having to contend with so many. Regina found her faith shaken. Suddenly the Apostle's Gift seemed a solution meant for a gentler world; this world was one of hunger, filled with those who would devour you—both among the dead and among the living.

But she pushed from her mind the memory of those moans of hunger and those terrible, grasping hands. Better to consider that unreal, a nightmare. Focus on what was at hand; there were closer, more intimate terrors clutching at her heart. Worry for Marcus. Worry for the others in the insula—had the guardsmen found their hiding place, had they kicked or broken their way into it before giving up the search? And fear for herself as she stared at the locked door and remembered the guardsman's hand on her body. Shame, heavy and hot in her breast; the guard had touched her as though she were a whore, a slave he might own and throw to the floor when he pleased. Men had touched her that way before; they had touched Dora that way. Regina trembled. She'd been dragged from the insula into the street; she'd been bound. However much she'd screamed or kicked, it had made no difference. Her freedom and her refuge and her new name—had any of it really been true, when it could be taken from her so easily?

The thought shook her.

Yet.

There was Polycarp.

Polycarp had loved her, called her daughter.

In his eyes, she had never been a slave.

When he'd touched her hair or brushed her cheek with the backs of his fingers, there had never been in that touch any demand for her to please him. Confronted with a man who didn't demand her, for the first time she'd found herself giving. At first, she'd given to him by doing little tasks about the insula or making tea for him, or carrying messages to his tenants. Later, she had done far more, keeping the accounts and listening to the tenants' troubles. She had learned to give to all of them, all who looked to her as a deaconess who might serve and love and shelter them, and not as a slave who must please and obey.

To Polycarp, she'd given everything that he'd accept from her. Now her breath caught, remembering; she had kissed him the night before. Before the dead, before the guardsmen. She'd pressed her lips to his, knowing that he might die when he stepped through that door into the alley. She had wanted to give even that, of herself. She'd never had the choice to give a kiss before, had never wanted to before.

"*Daughter*," he'd said, as though she'd embarrassed him.

She shut her eyes against a sting of tears, feeling the ache in her heart. Here in the dark of this shed, she heard more of her heart than she ever had before. She knew now that she yearned to make a free gift of herself, but this gift wouldn't be received, for it seemed clear to her now that Polycarp didn't need or desire a lover. He was a man accustomed to thinking of others as children to care for, and he had so many of these children, so many who needed his love. "*Daughter*," he'd said to her.

And now it was too late, in any case. Everything—everything—was shattered and lost. She blinked at the shreds of light let in by chinks in the wall of the shed, her heart bleak. She was crated here like an animal.

She groaned, her grief at Polycarp's absence sharp as glass within her. She needed him to hold her or to speak to her in that firm, calming voice of his. His voice always conveyed that he knew who he was and what he was doing. Just hearing him, she felt she knew who she was too. She needed that now. She needed him. She needed him to be *alive*.

Her throat tightened. She didn't know whether he had been simply knifed in the dark or was being held somewhere for a trial. He might even be in one of the other sheds she'd seen. She thought of calling out for him—but what would that serve, except to bring some reprisal for them both from the guardsmen outside? Yet the uncertainty tormented her. Where was he now? How had they treated him? She closed her eyes against the thin light. Even if Polycarp still lived, he was going to die—she was certain of that. She drew a few shuddering breaths, refused to cry. Marcus needed her. The youth was breathing raggedly on her lap.

Bitterly, she thought of Julia, wondered where the woman and her husband were now. Not in a shed, she was sure.

With a few words to the officers of the city, the baker's wife had shattered all their lives.

***

Regina had last seen Julia the morning of her disappearance. The baker had sent some bread with Regina to the Catacombs the night before, though neither he nor his wife had come to the gathering. They never did. The morning after, Regina had climbed the narrow, foot-worn steps to Julia's small, fourth-story apartment to thank her. She climbed slowly and with some tightness in her breast; she was never comfortable or at ease talking with Julia. The woman seemed stiff, unfriendly, and not very willing to partake of either conversation or companionship.

But then, Regina had reminded herself sternly, she knew a thing or two herself about what it was like to feel alone. She straightened her shoulders as she approached the door.

No answer came to her knock, but the door was ajar. After hesitating, she nudged it open, her heart beating with a sudden fear that something bad may have happened. Perhaps Julia had fainted or was ill.

"Julia?" she called softly.

The baker's wife sat at her windowsill, gazing out at the garden. Her head turned at the call, and Regina caught a glimpse of deep sorrow in the woman's eyes before she masked it. In her lap Julia held a bit of lace. Regina found her gaze held by it.

"It's very beautiful," Regina said.

Julia's eyes stayed cold. The silence stretched into something uncomfortable; Regina had the feeling that she'd burst in during some private moment too intimate to be shared—as though she'd interrupted Julia in the midst of a prayer or a confession.

"I came to thank you." Regina bit her lip, trying to think of the words she needed. "And your husband. For the bread."

"Well." Julia glanced down at the lace, her voice detached, distant. "We have enough to spare."

Regina heard a low murmur of voices from the garden below—a few people talking outside a door. She moved slowly toward Julia, giving the woman a smile and seating herself beside her on the wide sill, her back to the other side of the window, their knees almost touching. "Do you mind if I sit with you?"

When Julia didn't answer, Regina folded her hands gracefully in her lap and looked at the lace she held. "I never had that skill," she said softly. "My hands can't make anything beautiful. Though I was taught to dance, and—other things." Her eyes darkened, and she slammed a door shut in her mind against the shrieks of furious memories. She searched instead for older, less painful memories, ones rarely recollected, in order to fill the silence with small words. "But first, when I was young, very young, my grandfather taught me numbers. My parents didn't have any sons, and I was supposed to help my father at his shop. In Damascus." She smiled.

Julia let out her breath slowly. "This would have been for my child." Her fingers tightened about the lace. Those fingers were thick, but they must have moved with particular grace to make that small bit of beauty, that gift for someone who did not exist but was only a hope.

Regina's heart softened. She gazed at the other woman, as though seeing her for the first time. The baker's wife had been hurt, many times; it was in her eyes, a deep and weary conviction that life was a sequence of losses, and amid that weariness a still-flickering flame of yearning and need.

Regina recognized the yearning, and the weariness that came of having never had a child. Regina didn't think she herself *could* have one; her body carried scars inside, not just on her back. She had faced that. And in helping Polycarp she'd learned that she had many children, many people in this insula, and in others, who relied on her—for an occasional gift of bread from the larder, or for words of comfort, or for an ear and a listening heart, to bring their cares and needs to the father. She had a community and a home; what more could she need?

"Julia," she asked softly, "are you so unhappy?"

"What have I to be unhappy about?" Bitterness in her voice, sharp and lethal—though Regina sensed beneath it a woman so brittle she might break at a touch. "I have a man, and bread to eat."

"But it's not enough," Regina murmured. The bite in Julia's tone had startled her; she searched the other woman's face, her concern growing.

Julia's eyes lifted, found hers. They were dull with an old and harbored anger. "I was domina of my own house, girl. I don't suppose you have any idea what that means."

"No," Regina said after a moment. "I don't."

She waited.

Julia's shoulders trembled. She folded the lace, carefully, precisely. Her face struggled to hold in her emotion. "I want it back. I want it all back. I'd do anything for that. Give up anything. This—this place. I don't live here, I only breathe. I can't bear a child here, it's so filthy. Someone two stories down takes a shit, and I can smell it." Her voice was low and intense. She closed her eyes, tightly, and lowered her head, holding her breath against whatever was inside her wanting to shake her apart.

"I didn't know you felt like this." Regina reached out and took the other woman's hand, but Julia pulled her hand away quickly.

"Don't," she said. "Don't you touch me."

"Julia—" Regina fought to find something she could say. "Julia." Her heart beat with alarm. How long had she felt like this? What poison was in her heart?

"No. I'm done. I thought I could bear it, but I'm done." Julia straightened, her face becoming stone. "Please go."

Regina hesitated. The pain in Julia's voice was clear as a shout. Yet her anger was sharpening now to a knife's edge; Regina didn't think sitting here with her was helping her. "I'll speak to the father," she offered.

Julia's eyes flashed. "I don't want his pity, or yours."

Regina flushed. "It's not pity I'm offering—I worry for you."

"You." Julia's eyes burned now. "You worry for *me*. What are you?"

The coldness of her voice struck Regina hard.

"A slave," Julia hissed. "That's what. A slut who thinks herself the mistress of the insula. An uppity thing Polycarp puts up with because she's good with numbers."

Regina went white.

It was a moment before she could speak. "A slave?" Regina couldn't keep the distress from her voice. "I am a freed woman."

"You, girl, are a travesty." Julia set the lace beside her on the sill, her fingers trembling, then smoothed her dress. "This entire place is a travesty," she muttered.

Regina felt a surge of panic, fought it down. Her vulnerability terrified her. Julia's voice had taken on a cant and an intonation that she recognized. The consonants were sharper, the vowels shorter—it was not the way a woman of the Subura spoke. It was the way an equestrian spoke, a daughter of Rome's merchant classes, who strolled the Forum and claimed homes on the lower slopes of Rome's seven hills. Possibly Julia wasn't even aware of the change in her voice. Regina glanced at her cold face. Wondered if years ago, Julia had spoken in such a sharp, precise voice to her slaves.

She seemed suddenly a stranger in their insula.

Regina took a breath, tried to steady herself. Equestrians came to the gathering in the Catacombs. They were no different from the rest of the people, no different from the bakers or the tanners or the fresco painters. No different even from manumitted slaves. And this insula, her insula, Polycarp's insula, was *not* the house of miserable years where Regina had been beaten, and Julia was not the domina of that house. She had nothing to fear.

"I would befriend you," Regina cried suddenly. "We all would, Julia. If you'd only come sit with us in the garden—or walk with us—or—why must you clutch your grief so tightly to your breast? Does it feel so good doing that?" Her face was flushed, her veins hot with adrenaline. "Come to dinner with us—tonight—please. Whatever you may think of us, you live here with us. Why stay locked away in this room?"

Julia's fingers trembled again, and she clutched the folds of her dress, stilling them. Watching her, Regina felt a chill of insight. Julia's grief was perhaps the one thing she owned, the one thing that told her who she was. The woman was so hurt and so alone that she'd forgotten how to love. Horror flickered in Regina's belly. She herself might have been like that. If Polycarp hadn't found her—she might have been like that.

"Please, come to dinner, Julia," she whispered. "Tonight. Phineas and Marcus and I are breaking bread together, and we'll invite the father, and I'll invite Cecilia and Portia. Just come. Don't stay up here."

"I have no intention of staying here." Julia's voice was very quiet. Something in her tone—some finality, some terrible certainty—brought Regina's head around. Her eyes widened. With a shock of clarity, she saw the window and the way Julia sat with her hips on the sill. How she would only need to lean back to topple from the sill and plummet to the garden earth four stories below. Regina thought quickly, her heart racing. Surely she was only imagining it. Julia couldn't mean to do that—she couldn't.

"You may go, girl," Julia said.

The blood rushed back into Regina's face. She was being dismissed, as one might dismiss a house slave. Her throat tightened; all the warmth left her body.

"Go," Julia hissed.

Regina wanted to say something, to protest, to plead with her, but so many feelings and fears were rushing through her body so quickly, leaving her racked and shaken. At last, she turned and fled, unable to find words, knowing only that she needed privacy now to recollect and regather herself. Leaving, she shut Julia's door with a quiet *snick*, blocking out the sight of the woman's cold, furious eyes. Old memories were rattling the doors in Regina's mind; she felt as though it took her whole being to hold those doors shut.

She walked as fast as she could down the steps and into the atrium and across the narrow garden toward her own first-story room. Glancing back over her shoulder as she moved around the lilacs, she caught sight of Julia still seated at the sill of her fourth-story window. Her cold hauteur had faded with Regina's departure; now the other woman sat with her head lowered. Framed in that window, she had the look of an animal in a cage. Not a beautiful woman but an elegant one, Julia had always seemed graceful in the way she moved and in her posture. She appeared slumped now, like one of the gazelles they keep in narrow pens beneath the Colosseum, to whet the appetite of lions who would later be loosed on the gladiators.

Perhaps this same insula that for Regina was a place of safety, with high walls to keep at bay the threat of memory, felt for Julia like a confinement. Beneath the current of her fear, Regina felt a sharp prick of fresh worry, as though she'd stepped on a thorn. Then she looked away.

***

She was the deaconess; she should've brought her worries at once to the father.

If only she'd told him.

But she'd been too shaken. Too shaken even for anger, or for anything other than hurrying to her own room, to its refuge and safety. Shutting the door, she'd leaned against it and hugged herself tightly. The words Julia had used fell on her like robbers then in the dim light of her room—*slave, slave, slut, slut*—and she whimpered through closed lips, then flushed in shame at the sound. She was *not* a slave. Not anymore. She mustn't act like one. After a few moments she stepped to the shelf along the back wall and plucked down a small flask of wine, one she kept there for mixing with water to drink. She opened the flask, nearly spilled it, her hands shaking. She allowed herself only a sip, then placed it back on the shelf.

Slave, slave.

After a while, her blood still loud in her ears, she knelt on her bedding on the floor and prayed aloud, though softly, sharing the secrets of her heart with Polycarp's God, that God he promised was always near and whose comforting presence Regina felt at rare times. The love Polycarp said his God had for the gathering, for his adopted children bought out of the slavery of their pasts, of their evils and their regrets—Regina knew about that love chiefly because of the love she saw Polycarp give to those in the gathering. But lacking the courage yet to speak her heart to Father Polycarp, she spoke instead to his God.

She prayed for most of the morning, concealed within her room. She prayed for the courage to believe in her freedom and for the courage not to flee when threatened. Blinking back tears, she prayed her gratitude that she was no longer in the master's house, no longer lashed or beaten or kicked from her bedding in the early hours, no longer answering to a name she did not want or laboring fiercely to delight and appease a man she hated. Even if she at times felt as though she were still in that insula, she wasn't. She was here. "Help me not to be scared," she whispered. "I want to help Polycarp, I want to make his work easier. It is a good work. He is such a *good* man. I hadn't known there were such men, before I met him, before he saved me. But I am frightened, so frightened. I don't even know why. Please. I just—I need—I want to be free of my past."

Her heart roared awake inside her, like a lion lashed to the earth with hard cords, roaring in both fear and desperate hope. Without words, she laid out, vulnerably, the tangle of her feelings for Polycarp. Her face was wet with tears; this part of her prayer took a long time. It brought no answers, but a little comfort, for in thinking on Polycarp, the doors in her mind that had been rattling hard since Julia's cruel words touched her ears closed tightly and stilled at last.

Finally, Regina prayed for Julia.

Then she rose, her knees screaming in protest, and moved stiffly to her door and opened it. At the outer door of the insula, several of the tenants were talking in low, urgent voices. Marcus was there, and Vergilius. She walked to them, pale but composed, determined to be again the deaconess and not a frightened slave girl. Those were both roles she might play, and if her heart did not always know which role was truest of her, she did know which she preferred. So she walked to the men at the outer door with her shoulders straight and her steps graceful and certain.

It was after midday. Outside that door, six dead were feasting on a crossroads brother in the street.

***

Piscus did not come home to the insula that day, and for a time Regina and Marcus stood by the outer door talking about that, though Regina didn't share her altercation with Julia. There was a small slat in the door that could be slid back to let one's eyes look out into the narrow Suburan street, and from time to time, Marcus or Regina slid it back and peered out—but the dead had gone hours before and had dragged the remains of the crossroads brother with them. There was still a smear of blood on the stones.

When everyone else had returned to the insula from their day's work—all but Piscus—Regina took her copy of the master key (only she and Polycarp had copies, he as father, she as deaconess), and she went from room to room, knocking gently, unlocking and peering within if there was no answer. Marcus accompanied her for the first two stories, walking beside her in his tunic and brown cloak. Those were Suburan clothes, rough and torn through much use. Polycarp had loaned them to him the day Marcus first took a room in the insula. That had happened about two months after Marcus's initial visit to the insula door; in those two months, the young patrician had walked many times across the Subura to the market and back and had seen more things that had shaken him to the heart. At last, he went with Regina and Vergilius to one of the gatherings on the Sabbath, and when they returned to the insula he did not say goodnight to trudge his way warily back up the long slope to the Palatine. Instead he stood in the doorway of the insula beside Polycarp and Regina and Vergilius and slowly stripped off his toga, folded it neatly, and set it aside. Standing in his loincloth, he gazed down on it. "Sell it," he said hoarsely, lifting his eyes to Polycarp's. "I am no longer of the patrician Caelii. I am Marcus Antonius only. I cannot go back. When I am in my father's house, I am only playing my part; nothing is real. I will share my bread here instead. I'll spend what coin I have in my pockets to lease a room here. Father, set me to any task; I cannot go back. Not after what my eyes have witnessed."

So Marcus walked beside the deaconess now in simpler clothes, and with a simpler name, one stripped of a portion of its history, a history the boy repudiated, one he chose no longer to need or desire. Watching him from the corner of her eye, Regina found herself considering him with new respect. She'd considered him a child, a boy. Yet when he'd shrugged off his toga as another youth might shrug off a child's blanket, surely he had matured. She wondered why she hadn't thought about that before. Like herself, he had found a name, one he could own with dignity as a free man.

There was a girl, Ariadne, on the fourth floor, who still wept herself to sleep some nights because a tanner's son she'd wanted had married another. Ariadne had confided in Regina a week before, and Regina had told her that there were always other men and that all pains, even the most brutal ones, dull with time, becoming only scars, only memory. Now Regina cast a glance at Marcus, considering. The two would look well together. Marcus's steady heart and unwavering devotion would heal the girl's wounds. And Ariadne's demure demeanor—almost too respectful even for a girl of Rome—would help Marcus find his backbone. He needed someone who would look up to him, even worship him, reminding him of his worth. And Regina smiled slightly; she knew something that Marcus probably wouldn't know for some time: under the daintiness of that girl there was a hot fire in her spirit, one that would emerge at first in little flickers and at last in flame, once she felt truly secure in another's love. And she was intelligent. It was likely that whatever they did in life would be done together.

Regina caught her breath. What was she thinking, imagining such a match? Marcus was a *patrician*. Of that caste with the gods of Rome in their bloodlines. Her lips thinned. A patrician might take a woman of the Subura for a slave, a slut to be cast aside after use to sleep on the floor by his bed, but never for a companion. A slow anger lit in her breast, making it difficult for her to breathe—then cooled as she glanced at Marcus again, saw the plain clothes he wore and the hardness in his eyes at odds with the soft lines of his face. No, he was not a patrician. He was Marcus. They'd eaten bread together. That hardness in his eyes meant the things he'd seen had taught him that the blood in his veins was less important to who he was than the Spirit he'd accepted into his heart. Everything else—from the clothes he chose to wear to the skin and features God had clothed him in, were only trappings that might either provide example of or disguise the man he truly was in his heart.

Regina's face heated with shame. Marcus had never looked askance at her or at any of the tenants, even the poorest. How could she think this of him, that he would spurn a Suburan woman because she lacked patrician ancestry?

She straightened and knocked at the next door. In any case, this was no time for matchmaking. As she exchanged a hurried word with the tenant who opened at her knock, ensuring all within were safe, worry bit at her insides. Who else might be missing, besides Julia and Piscus? And would there be any answer at the baker's door? There was no body in the atrium; the woman had not leapt from her window. That brought little relief; terrible and unnecessary as that death would be, it was surely better than being devoured by the dead, perhaps to rise later herself in irrevocable hunger. And the thought of it brought Regina a pang of guilt; she'd been avoiding thinking about Julia, even playing matchmaker in her head, but she needed to speak with Father Polycarp about Julia.

Regina found herself taking her time, her steps methodical and precise, not hurrying. Reluctant to reach the fourth story. Marcus began to fidget, getting antsy beside her; he clasped his hands behind him as if to control it. That brought Regina another small smile, another small distraction from her worry; whatever name he claimed, doubtless some things about Marcus would *always* be patrician, such as his concern for his own dignity. Yet she was certain his heart belonged no longer to the Palatine Hill but to Father Polycarp and his God.

"Please take the third floor, I'll take the fourth," she told him. There was no need to make him wait for her reluctance. "Just take note of any doors that don't answer; I'll come to those."

He nodded eagerly and moved toward the stairs. Regina let out a sigh and resumed her own walk. She finished the last couple stops on this second floor and then moved to the stairs herself; she could hear Marcus's rapid steps on the walkway around the third story.

As she moved along the fourth floor, each door was answered, a weary or a delighted or a troubled face peering out at her. A few words exchanged. "Peace and grace to you," Regina would murmur after a moment, then move on. As she checked the rooms, one door after another, her tension tightened in her breast. Everyone was here. No one lost, no one eaten. But no one had seen Julia and her husband come in tonight.

The Subura was not a place where men and women *chose* to be out after dark. Not, at least, if their business in the alleys was the kind that might be conducted by daylight.

Julia's door was the third from the end. As before, it was ajar. Regina felt a chill as she lifted her hand and gave a couple of hard raps on the thin pine of that door.

No answer to the knock.

Dread clenched about her heart.

"Julia?" she called.

No sound within. On the story below, Marcus's voice was lifted as though he were arguing with one of the tenants. He probably wasn't, though—he was often animated when he spoke, and especially when he was nervous.

"Julia?"

She threw open the door with a cry. "Julia!"

She wasn't there.

The room was empty.

Regina went in and stood by the table, her heart in her throat. Too empty. The room was too empty. There were empty shelves. The closet doors were open, but there were only a couple of worn tunics on the rack within.

She'd packed.

Julia had packed her things. She hadn't thrown herself from the window. She hadn't been eaten by the dead. She'd *planned* this departure.

She'd—

A low, keening cry rose in Regina's throat. She pressed her fingertips over her lips and leaned back against the table. Everything came together in her mind like so many leaves swept by the wind into one pile against a low wall, the pile growing until it might almost overwhelm the stones. *I was domina of my own house—I want it back, I want it all back—I'd do anything for that—this whole place is a travesty—I have no intention of staying here.*

"Oh Julia," she moaned, "what have you done?"

***

In the shed, Regina wondered where that woman was now, and what things she and her husband had told the praetor and what things they'd held back. Perhaps they'd held nothing back. Perhaps even now Julia was walking through a villa garden, one of those opulent gardens she'd craved, with flowery vines hanging from orchard trees, and great marble sculptures of fauns and naiads. Or perhaps she was reclining in a veiled palanquin, visiting one of the Forum markets to buy new house slaves with her thirty pieces of silver. All of those luxuries, all of those trappings—Julia would use them to tell herself who she was. In the Subura, where Regina and Marcus had found their names, Julia had been without family or identity, cast out from the life she'd valued; perhaps she had felt nameless, only a face among a thousand faces.

If only Regina had realized what Julia had been talking about—what she'd been, in her way, trying to confess to her.

Regina moaned softly and leaned her head back against the boards of the shed wall. Her breast felt tight. Difficult to take full breaths in this small shed, this holding place. She closed her eyelids and forced herself to breathe evenly. She'd been sold, like a slave—they all had.

She tried to think. She was the keeper of accounts, the observer and solver of problems, the deaconess. She had to think. What would become of them? Who had been arrested from the insula—and were they to be questioned or were they to be condemned? Where had they taken the father—what had they done with him?

Her eyes burned. Marcus stirred slightly, and she stroked his hair soothingly, holding in her tears. She knew at least one thing. Marcus lay beaten in her lap, and he needed her. She didn't know who else had been arrested, whether those in the larder had been taken, or some of those who'd hidden in their upper-story rooms while the guardsmen slammed through the door, or only herself and Marcus. But for Marcus Antonius at least, she was still the deaconess of the gathering in Rome. He was hurt, and he needed her.

At that moment there was a rattle in the lock.

Her eyes shot open.

It seemed to take a long time for the lock to turn, and as the rattling continued, her heart pounded. For a moment she was terrified that the lock wasn't turning because it was one of the dead at the door; memories of the night before fell on her. She watched the door, unable to see anything. Then the door swung open, and two men stood there. Living men. She stiffened, recognizing one—the man who had touched her. Framed in that door, he looked large as a Celt. The other she hadn't seen before; he was young, only a few years older than Marcus. They gazed in at her, perhaps taking in the sight of the smudges of dirt on her face, the bruise on her left cheekbone, and Marcus unconscious with his head in her lap.

"Look at the whore," the larger guardsman muttered to the other.

Regina's throat tightened. "I am a prisoner in this shed," her voice trembled, "but I will not take that name. I am a free woman."

"You." The guardsman stabbed his finger at her. "Are a cultist. A desecrator. You'll shut your mouth and let us have what we came for."

She stiffened, her pulse pounding in her throat. Quickly she tensed up, ready to fight. Something in the back of her mind started to scream as the large man moved toward her, his companion staying by the door.

But as he bent over her, he only seized Marcus by the arms and hauled him to his feet. The boy was still breathing raggedly, but his eyes fluttered open. The man began to muscle him to the door.

Regina leapt to her feet, her fright of the moment before forgotten in the face of a more terrible fear—that of separation. "*Where are you taking him?*"

The guardsman glanced over his shoulder, smirking at her. "He's a patrician, isn't he? Imagine that, skulking about with you rats. This little *fellator* will stand on the jury. Maybe he'll remember who he's supposed to be."

Regina spat on the guardsman's cheek; the man backhanded her. She fell to the straw, her head ringing, the left side of her face burning. She lay dazed. She heard Marcus moan her name faintly, then a scuffling sound as he was dragged from the shed. The slap of the door against the jamb. Then it was dark again, with only the thin shivers of light through the chinks in the wall.

Alone, Regina curled up and sobbed quietly.

This little shed was too much like that cargo hold she'd been chained in— so long ago—on the tossing sea journey from Syria to Italia. The clink of the chains, the leering faces of the flesh thieves who'd stolen her, crowding her into the hold with other Syrian girls they thought desirable and marketable. Their hands on her body, grasping and bruising her. That whole journey had been a fever, a nightmare; her mind hadn't been right afterward, not for several years, not until Father Polycarp had come, clothing her and granting her a room to herself, with an open window.

Now that room was gone. All those she'd cared for and who'd cared for her were gone. She was as alone here as she'd been in the galley. The soiled straw scratched at her arms.

A while later, she lifted herself on her elbows, rolled, sat up. She breathed slowly. Wiped at her eyes with her fingers. She didn't know what would become of her when night came again. But whatever would be done to her, she would not meet it weeping. Forcing her hands not to tremble, she smoothed her dress, filthied from the streets and the straw. Then ran her fingers through her hair. When the guardsmen came for her, she would be ready.

"I am no whore," she whispered.

***

Another rattle in the lock. This time Regina stood to meet it, lifted her chin. She was a woman of Rome and a woman of the gathering. She had reason to be proud.

The shorter guardsman entered, and she could hear a man laughing somewhere outside. He laughed back, then swung the door shut. Then he stood before her and drew aside his cloak; she watched his face warily but didn't move. He took something out from under his cloak, pressed it into her hand. Her eyes widened as she felt the warmth of a fresh loaf of bread against her fingers. "What is this?" she breathed, searching his eyes.

"You are not alone." Breathing quickly, the guardsman took her other hand and drew with his finger against her palm the shape of a fish.

It was all she could do not to cry out. "Thank you," she gasped. She tore a small piece of the bread away and chewed it for a moment. The bread was still soft and moist, and easily swallowed. "Where is he? The father?"

"Another shed, not far. He is well; sometimes the men at his door can hear him praying. They say there will be a trial tomorrow."

Regina felt she might faint. She swayed slightly on her feet, clenched her hands around the bread. He was alive. Father Polycarp—her Polycarp—was alive. Thank God. He was alive.

"Can you take a message to him?"

The guardsman was silent a few moments, then shook his head. "I don't believe so. I have no business at his shed, and I could pretend I'd come to gawk at the prisoner, but—they wouldn't let me in." He paused. "I should tell you there are nine others. In the other sheds. Nine from your insula. I don't know if you knew."

Regina's heart missed a beat. "Others," she whispered. "Who?"

"I'm sorry. I don't know their names. I will see if I can find out."

Regina reeled at this news that confirmed all her fears. Others. Nine of them. How would the gathering survive this? And what would become of those who depended on the gathering? What about the men who came to Polycarp's larder to get bread for their children? What about old Flora, whose water jar Regina carried?

Yet Polycarp lived. And there was a friend among the guards.

Regina tried to gather herself; so many feelings pounded through her that she felt dizzy. She tore the loaf in half, handed one half to the guardsman, and for a few moments they ate together in silence. The man brought out from beneath his garments a tiny flask and held it, waiting. This kindness was unlooked for; it was something to hold onto. It occurred to her to doubt him, to suspect some trap for her. But Roman justice needed no trap to convict her. She *had* to trust; this sudden hope was too sharp in her breast.

"Thank you," Regina breathed, between swallows of soft bread. "This is of God."

"It is," the guardsman whispered. "I'll bring you word—what news I can—before the trial begins."

She placed her small hand over his. "Don't endanger yourself."

He shook his head. "No. No danger. If I come in here a few times, the others will simply think I'm using you." His face flushed in the dim light. "You must cry out, once or twice."

Regina nodded and sucked in a breath. After a moment she expelled it in a short, shrieking cry. Then another. The guardsman jumped. "How's that?" she whispered.

"Convincing." He passed the tiny flask to her, and she took a gulp gratefully, then sputtered and choked for a moment. It held wine, not water; it stung the back of her throat.

"I am sorry for the indignity of this," the guardsman muttered. "There's little I can do to ease it without suspicion. A hired guardsman isn't usually attentive to the needs of a slave."

Her eyes burned; she risked another sip, swallowed. "I am free."

"They will choose to believe you are not."

Regina nodded, handed the flask back in hands that shook—not from fear now but from excitement. "I don't remember your face from the gathering in the Catacombs."

"I was only there once." His face lifted. "But I have never forgotten it. The words he said. About the Gift."

Regina leaned in a little, whispering more intensely. "You are right to help us. The Apostle's Gift—it is *real*. I have seen it. I've seen what he has done. And the other things he teaches—that we each have a gift, no matter who we are or what class—those things are real too. You are right about me—I was a slave. Maybe I still am, to this day, though I fight my chains each morning. But I too have a gift. I keep accounts for our insula. And you have a gift. One needs only look at your eyes to see it. I don't know what yours is. Maybe," she lifted the last of her bread, "maybe your gift is ministering to prisoners." She smiled. "I only tell you this because you need to know, whatever happens at that trial. His words are true."

"I believe it," he whispered. "Cry out again, domina—as though we are finishing our love—and then I have to go."

She did her best, though her face burned to make such sounds in the presence of a man who was not her lover. But in her heart a warmth and a strength was welling up. *Domina*, he'd called her. Lady of this house. Though this "house" was only a shed with dirty straw, he saw her within it as its keeper, not as a slave or a prisoner—despite his words earlier. She feared speaking again, for the gratitude in her was so strong it might spill from her in sobs or unintelligible sounds.

This next day might contain any peril. She might yet be beaten and raped. She and those confined in the other sheds might be burned alive or executed in any number of terrible ways. She didn't know yet what had become of those in the hiding place at the insula—save that nine were in prison sheds like this one. It was possible the Roman praetor might hunt through all the streets and insulae of Rome for those of the gathering. It was possible the hunt could spread to every city in the Empire. This had happened once before; it could happen again. Yet her hands trembled with hope. As long as a Roman guardsman could believe in the Gift and in the message, and bring bread to a prisoner who was without status or citizenship, as long as that could happen, the gathering was alive. In hiding, without refuge, yet fiercely alive. Suddenly she was certain that Polycarp was not weeping in his own shed, that he was standing and waiting for what would come, with that unbending strength of his. Her face flushed; she burned with shame at her vulnerability and her tears. She was the deaconess; Polycarp depended on *her*. The others in their sheds depended on her. This guardsman, in his way, depended on her. How could she have been so entirely without hope, so lost, weeping in the straw?

"Thank you," she managed to whisper. "What is your name?"

"I am Brutus Secundus."

"I will remember it, Brutus Secundus. You are blessed among the gathering for your kindness."

She tore a small stretch of cloth away from the hem of her ruined nightdress. After wetting it in a little wine from the flask, she began to scrub at her face and arms with it, cleaning the grime from her skin.

"I'll bring a cloth later." Brutus considered her a moment. "In fact, I'll bring a bucket of water if you wish it." Seeing her look, he added, "It won't be hard to explain. You're from the Subura. I need only tell the other guardsmen that I want my slut washed before I have her." He flushed in the dark. "Forgive the words, domina. We are rough men, and most of Rome looks down on us, even when Rome needs us. So we are used to looking down on the Subura; it can feel good knowing there *is* someone for us to look down on. It is not how *I* think, but it is how most of us think." He cast a glance at the filthy straw. "Yet no one should have to sleep in this. I'll bring water."

She understood the gift he was giving her, and why he'd used those words, though they had made the doors in her memory shift a moment on their hinges. *My* slut, he'd said. Brutus was offering her protection from the other men and asking nothing in return. Even as Polycarp had done, housing her in a room in his insula.

She nodded, her eyes moist. "Thank you," she whispered again. "Thank you."

Though she stood in peril for her life, though she'd been separated from Polycarp and Marcus and all the others, for the first time since the moaning of the dead in the alley she felt some measure of safety.

She let the dirtied cloth fall to the straw; she didn't dare tear away more of her dress. It was some relief, at least, and though she still smelled, with the sudden cleanness of her face she felt more capable, more sufficient for the needs of the day.

She drew in a breath, met Brutus's eyes. "I know Polycarp is guarded. If you have opportunity to speak to the others, please tell them that Regina and Polycarp stand firm. Tell them they must stand firm too. Tell them the gathering persists. That nothing is broken, nothing is ended. Please tell them this.

CAIUS LUCIUS JUSTUS

THAT NIGHT, the night before the trial, silence filled Caius's villa, dark and palpable. As no one had approached Livius's room for hours, the moaning within had ceased. That silence should have been a relief, a cool drink after a hot wind. Yet instead, the silence was menacing, a violence on the ears. It seemed a promise of fresh wailing, waiting only for the stumbling of one's foot to provoke a muffled curse or an unsteady tremble of one's hand to send a cup clattering to the polished marble floor. Such sounds as these might wake the horror that lay chained behind Livius's door. The slaves had performed their evening's duties in fear and now shivered on their pallets, waiting for uneasy dreams to take them.

In the praetor's study, Caius sat at his desk, his hand making anxious, jerking movements as he sketched the Latin letters of the last order he hoped to give as urban praetor and senior magistrate of the city. His hand had cramped, and now he clutched the stylus with a desperation that didn't suit the dignity of his office. He had already begun the order over again, twice. Had labored half the night on it. He stopped frequently, his expression grim. In the thunderous silence, he listened for sounds from his son's chamber, but heard nothing.

Once, he left his study and passed like a shadow through the sleeping villa until he reached his son's door. He reached for the handle. Stopped. Waited there awhile.

Caius's palms were sweating. He found it difficult to breathe. Horror of what waited on the other side of the door swept through him, shaking him like a fever. It was not grief but raw, animal *horror*. He felt that whether he turned the handle and went inside (though this he'd done a thousand times before) or turned from the door and fled, either way he would be stuck, body and spirit, into madness—if he did *anything* but stay very, very still and wait for this horror to pass.

As slowly as the creeping of a snail through the garden, rationality returned. His heartbeat slowed. For a moment he was dizzy; then he leaned against the wall by the door.

The horror would *not* pass, he realized. It would not end, not ever. Not unless he destroyed the body of his son.

But he could not do that. He couldn't.

The order he must write awaited, yet he avoided returning to the study. He left his son's door now and went to the slaves' quarters, woke one of them with a kick in the dark, sent him to bring wine to his study. Then Caius went and stood in the atrium to wait, gazing up at the stars. He had not looked at the stars for—a long time. Not since Livius had died.

The stars were lovely and cold, and he thought perhaps he had *never* seen them before, not truly. He gazed at them with his head tilted back, hands clasped behind his back in Roman fashion. Erect and dignified. His throat was tight. He could almost hear Scipia his wife laughing in the garden, as she used to. Grief welled up so full inside him that he could hardly breathe.

Scipia. How different his life was without her. Her laughter and the flash of her eyes had always distracted him from his duty, yet driven him too to excel at it. Tonight, on the eve of the trial, she would have known just what to say to quiet the troubles in his heart.

He had first seen her on the marble steps of the Senate House, wishing her aged father well as he climbed to a legislative battle over some question of public land. Caius had been one of the younger senators of his faction, possessing little rank then, only the great prestige afforded him by his family name and the dignity of a successful term as a minor official in the northern wars. He recalled standing at the doors of the House, gazing down the steps at that radiant woman, where she stood straight and slender as a statue of Rome on the steps. Caius had never been a hesitant man, and he'd presented the matter to his father in the most direct terms over dinner. A cold and unaffectionate man, with all that mattered to him concealed within an impenetrable shell of propriety and caution, Marcellus Lucius Justus had responded only with a grunt. But that had been enough. At dawn the next day, the older Lucius Justus had walked across the Palatine to the house of the Luculli and had made the marriage arrangements.

For Caius, that had been a year of Fortuna's favoring; a wedding, the softness of Scipia's lips on his, and then the miracle of her belly's gentle growth. In the Senate, Caius had spoken with passion and clarity of the need to return to traditions now fallen into disuse, to preserve the ways of their fathers. At home, he'd prayed beneath the masks of his *di parentes* and sat long in the evenings with his hand on Scipia's belly, awaiting patiently some kick or nudge from the child she would give him, the next of his family.

But Fortuna had played him false. His wife's death at Livius's birth had meant the absence of any good Roman mother to instruct Caius's son in how to live a pious life, one of proper respect for the honored fathers and fear of the Roman gods, piety that might have kept Livius safe from the Eastern superstitions that had so infected Rome. Caius himself had little to offer his son; his own father had barely spoken more than a few words to him during his childhood and his youth, and as an adult Caius had found that he was more at ease debating in the Senate or hiring advocates for the Roman courts than he was devoting time to his son at home. Buying a Greek slave girl to serve as nurse to young Livius had seemed a reasonable action to take when Scipia died, but the girl had filled Livius's mind with every kind of superstition, and Caius had sold her off in a fury before the boy was five. Buying her had been a mistake; he realized now he should have instead remarried, and at once. A quick remarriage would have meant suffering some loss of *dignitas,* but it would have been better for the boy.

And there might have been other children, if he had.

Perhaps he should *still* remarry.

He gazed up, his memories bitter within him. How beautiful those stars were, yet how violent and how cold.

A sudden wailing came to him on the night air, and he shuddered, his reflections shattered. The very sound he most dreaded: the moaning of the dead. But it did not come from behind his son's door. It was muffled by the walls of the villa. Perhaps far away. Sweat ran down Caius's face. In the night, that moaning brought a terror that could not be reckoned with or disciplined away. By day, the praetor might deal with the rising of the dead as a crisis to be met and addressed with dignity and action; by night, in this home so full of the presence and the memories of his own dead, the cries of those corpses outside were a dissolution of everything a man could be certain of. He should hear silence broken by occasional cries of birds or even a distant hum of human noise from the Subura, if he stepped out into the atrium and listened acutely. Or the sound of the wind in the cypresses on the far slope, above the Forum. There was a certain way Rome was supposed to sound, at night. No more. The wailing of the dead made what lay outside his walls in the dark uncertain. It was as though some wind had come and torn away the city he knew, leaving only moaning, chaotic darkness outside.

There was only one refuge left to him: his study, a tiny, enclosed trap of a space. Where that unfinished order awaited him. He walked back to it now, leaving the garden, and found that shutting his study door and drawing slats down over the window only muted the moans of the dead a little; he could still hear them, faint but persistent.

Before shutting the door, Caius retrieved the small silver tray left at the study's threshold by the slave he'd kicked awake, and he set it carefully on the desk; it carried a silver goblet filled with wine and a fresh bottle of ink. Caius could remember a time when such obedience and perfect discipline would have brought him pleasure, when seeing a slave leap to perform a task promptly and properly had been as cooling to his temperament as a glass of the best wine in the city. He took no pleasure in it now.

He sat at his desk. Everything was coming apart. The events of the day had speared deep into his chest. That corpse-woman crashing through his door, hands lifted and growling with a hunger to bite and tear apart everything that mattered in Rome. Polycarp's unapologetic defiance of Roman tradition, And an hour before that, Caius's interview with the slave the Christians called a "deaconess," whose words had pried inside him and found where he was vulnerable: his shame at having failed his son and having failed even his wife's memory.

He closed all of that off inside him, breathed raggedly. *Dignitas.* Duty. What was the hour? He had to finish writing that order. He reached again for his stylus and ink. Lifting the stylus in his hand, he looked at the small Latin letters his father had carved into it, before Caius was born: the family name. Caius felt the pressure of his ancestors' eyes, the open, vacant eyes of those dozens of masks, though they hung in his son's room and not in this one. They had abandoned him, those ancestors, yet still he felt the weight of their demands. Impossible, unanswerable demands.

Muttering under his breath, he hastened to make the small, angular letters of the Latin script on the parchment he'd started earlier. His mouth was dry and his eyes bloodshot; he kept lifting one hand to scrub at them with his knuckles. He did not know how late it was. He labored over the order.

***

When Caius finished at last, he felt hollow, like bark with no wood inside it, a cypress scored and burned out by lightning. Shaking from lack of sleep, his hands folded the parchment, and he set it carefully aside to take with him in the morning. He rose groaning from his seat and took up the oil lamp from his desk (its reek had filled the small study); he took up also the goblet of wine his slave had brought and which he hadn't touched yet. Gently he carried both out with him. He had one more duty to perform this night.

For a mercy, the dead, both inside and outside his villa, were quiet. Walking stiffly against his weariness, Caius went first to the atrium, to the apricot tree that stood in the northwest corner with a marble dryad embracing it. Scipia had loved that tree and that dryad, but Caius was too tired now to mourn her. He had burned himself out; he was finished. In another day, everything would be finished. Reaching up, he plucked two apricots from the branches—two golden fruit, August ripe—and, making a fold in his garment, he carried them with him, with the oil lamp in one hand, the goblet in the other.

As in most patrician families, Caius Lucius lived near his dead, and his dead slept near their living; the mausoleum was a great marble enclosure just outside the villa and nearly as large as it. A little path led from the back door of his villa up through lush shrubs and flowering beds to the great marble gate of that place of stillness. Caius murmured a prayer to Janus, god of doors, and a word of respect to the *di parentes* who had fathered his family, then slid open the gate and slipped into the courtyard of their house.

The garden within had grown wilder than the garden in his atrium; it was overrun with tangled vines and clinging flowers, and the small pond near the path was choked with nenuphars. Unpruned branches overhung the little path that wound among the shrubs and the marble chambers of the dead—all their houses, each with a door shut tightly. The many generations of his dead. Caius stopped at the doorstep of his grandfather's resting place and looked around. It was not *his* work to keep either this courtyard or his own atrium tidy—that was a slave's work. But it came to him suddenly that he had no garden slave to tend his estate. The thought made him sigh. Another failure. How mournful this garden of the dead looked. Untended. He was as complicit as any Christian in Rome in the neglect of the dead.

He poured the wine gently, spilling a little of it on the marble steps. Then he set the cup down and placed the two apricots beside it. Wearily he sat on the doorstep but kept his back straight; he was in the presence of his ancestral dead, and though their censure would be silent, here *dignitas* was more important than ever.

"I let the hearth fire go out," he said quietly. "The night my son was born. I shamed you. But still I bring you food and wine the night before every Ides and the night before every Kalends, as the men of this family have done for six hundred years." His voice trembled. "Tomorrow I will seek justice against the man who has offended all Rome's dead. And once that is achieved, I will seek justice against myself, as I ought to have done months ago. For I also have guilt toward you, honored fathers. I also must make atonement." He lowered his eyes. "I fear it, *di parentes*. And I have shamed you too with my fear." He hadn't had the courage to end it before. Death without leaving behind a son to tend the hearth fire for him could mean eternity as a wandering, wasted spirit. But he knew now that he was already living as a wandering shade. Unrestful death could not be that much worse than this faded, empty life—and it would have one crucial difference. Having cast himself upon his sword, he'd have regained his honor.

He glanced about the garden, his eyes bleak. "No son will bring food and wine for me, and no scion of our family will bring you food on the next

Kalends. I hope my actions tomorrow will bring you rest and atone for my breach of duty this next Kalends; I know there will be no rest for me. I ask for your blessing, *di parentes*. I have never needed it more."

Caius lowered his head, as a son receiving a blessing. A breeze caught at the cypresses along one wall; he heard the soughing in the high branches. There was no moaning of the dead.

Once, the silence of his own ancestors after a prayer would have chilled him, signifying as it might a removal of their protection over his house. But now he knew there were worse things to hear from his dead than silence.

***

As the sun lifted above the cypresses and the morning haze, promising the hottest day the summer had yet brought to Rome, Caius stepped down from the villa door into the street between two lines of standing, respectful lictors. He'd slept little and his body was heavy beneath the precisely draped folds of his toga, but at the sight of his lictors he straightened his shoulders. They were a visible reminder of his duty, his last duty to Rome. He must hurry to a brief bath; then he had a shrine to visit and the sacrifice of a bull to oversee, so that the gods would attend the day's trial at least partly appeased and in a good mood. Afterward, he'd repair to the temple of Justitia, where in a few hours the day's jurors would be gathering, ceremonially washing their hands and faces at the gate to enter clean into the presence of Justice.

Here, at Caius's own doorstep, the urban praetor looked out at the gentle curve of the street and at the cypresses that half hid the grounds of neighboring villas. A few other patricians were about; he saw two men in pristine togas walking slowly along the hill and, moving the other way, four bronzed slaves carrying on their shoulders the weight of a palanquin, behind whose colored veils reclined some Roman domina or some daughter of high family. Somewhere a raven called. Everything Caius saw was perfectly placed, perfectly cultivated. Every person he saw wore their clothing well; every tree wore its foliage well, trimmed and lovely. Everything here was as Rome should be, the very Rome he used to serve with love rather than weariness. For the first time in many days, he took a moment's comfort in this well-disciplined set upon which the intrigues and debates of Roman family and Roman policy were played out. Caius drew in a deep breath, tasting the warm August air; it carried the scent of lilacs from the villa gardens and, beneath that heavy perfume, the sharper, resin tang of cypresses.

Tucked neatly into the sash across his toga was the parchment he'd folded up before leaving his study this morning. That parchment would keep this Rome, his Rome, safe and clean. There must be no more violated villas, no more Roman girls stumbling down the street without a palanquin and without air in their lungs, to claw through the doors of state officials.

"This is the day on which all depends." He said the words aloud and nodded to his lictors. "Stand tall; look well. Not even a hair out of place. Today, remember that you are Romans attending Roman justice and ensuring Roman peace in a barbarous and degraded world."

"Yes, praetor," one of them said.

"The Roman dead rise furious at dishonor." His face was hard. "Today we will show them that their sons are still worthy of them."

"Yes, praetor."

Caius nodded again and stepped forth into the street. But almost immediately he stopped; his heart gave a lurch. Near enough to shout at, a figure had just come around the corner of the villa across the street and was stumbling unevenly along its wall. Its left side fell against the marble, and it stumbled along a little farther with its shoulder against the stone.

Caius's throat clenched; he held back a moan of horror. He held up his hand to halt the lictors.

Caius watched, every sense alert, as the figure dragged itself along the wall. It was a man, young, perhaps twenty. A breastplate on his chest, bloodstained. A sandal on one foot, the other bare. Thick leather. Military grade. But the man carried no weapon. His hair was cropped short, his face pale. There was a bloody wound on his arm.

Caius held his breath; he could sense the lictors holding theirs. But there was no scent of death in his nostrils. The blood on the man's arm looked fresh. He stared ahead sightlessly, but his skin didn't have the gray pallor of the dead. The military dress was an oddity.

"Soldier!" Caius's voice carried across the street.

The man's head turned, too slowly. Then he left the wall and staggered into the street toward them, one hand lifted, a moan from his lips. Caius tensed. The lictors drew back.

Then the moan became a word. "*He—eelp—*"

Caius let out his breath slowly. His legs felt suddenly weak; he forced himself not to buckle. "Get him," he snapped.

But even as a couple of his lictors stepped forward, the soldier missed his step, his body tilting to the side in a curiously graceful motion; then he fell. Cursing, Caius broke into a run, coming quickly to the man's side. Several of his lictors gathered in a helpless circle about the man; others hung back. Caius's pulse sped up. He didn't understand how this bloodied, stumbling soldier had come to the Palatine or why, but this was a Roman soldier dying in the street. He reached the man where he lay panting on the stones, then stopped sharp, everything in him going cold, as his eyes found the wound on the man's arm.

The wound was a half-moon circle of teeth marks.

As he had in that hour when a dead patrician girl had broken into his station by the temple, Caius took note of details. The man's face was flushed with fever, he was shaking. His lips kept moving as though he would speak, but his eyes were glassy. And that livid mark on his arm—Caius had seen such wounds before. On his son's body, and on the bodies of house slaves he'd sent to tend his son.

The bite. The wound that meant restless death.

The man moaned again—a sound of helplessness and anguish, not of hunger—and his eyes, horribly glazed, gazed up at Caius.

"Water," he moaned.

"Where did you come from?" Caius hissed.

"Water—please—tribune—"

"What has happened? Where did you come from? How were you bitten?" His voice sharp with urgency.

"Tribune," the man groaned. He twisted onto his side, shaking. "Tribune!"

"I am not your tribune. You are in the streets of Rome. Explain yourself."

The man's eyes fixed on some point just past Caius's ear. The praetor could feel heat radiating from the man's body as though a sun were barely concealed beneath the thin sheen of his flesh.

"Centurion—Licinius Albus sent me—find the tribune—tell him—" A spasm of coughing.

"Tell him what?" Caius demanded. The lictors shuffled their feet and stayed well back from the dying man. There were whites around their eyes. They could all see the bite.

"We fought them," the man choked, his hands convulsing in the grip of the fever. "We fought them—the risen fathers. Fought them. They pinned us—yesterday morning—in a small insula. Held out as long as we could. Not just forty, tribune. Not just forty. More came. Many. We fought them. The risen fathers. Water—please—water."

Caius's blood ran cold at both the mention of many dead at the riverside insulae and at the mention of Roman soldiers within the boundaries of the city. He thought of the medals on his wall, the rusted *gladius* in his study: military battles were to be fought along the Rhine or the Danube, never the Tiber. Battles in Rome were to be fought in the Senate House, if at all. Much good that the Senate ever did. The thought of legionnaires within the city chilled him. Yet for a single, dizzying instant, Caius's mind grasped what he might do with a legion of Rome's best at his call. Cleanse every insula in Rome of its dead in the space of a single evening. His hands shook as though he was fevered himself. No. No, he was not a Caesar. The last time a man had unloosed a thousand legionnaires within the boundary of Rome, the city had been torn in two. That must never happen again. What purging had to be done, must be done with limited civil forces, easily controlled and easily dispensed with when they were no longer useful.

The praetor took a slow breath, the momentary vision passing from him. "Where is your centurion?"

"Eaten." The man's lips curved in a terrible, fevered grin. "Tore him out through the—window. All those—hands. Couldn't stop them. Eaten—eaten."

Silence settled in the street, broken after a moment as another cough racked the man's body. Caius listened, straining to hear sounds above the low hum of human noise by the river far downhill. He could hear no moan of the dead. Yet he remembered the wailing in the night; the silence now seemed as ominous as the silence outside Livius's door—as though the dead were waiting only for some misstep or shouted word to wake them and bring them groaning up the hill.

Caius crouched beside the feverish soldier, took a better look at him. He had a scar across the bridge of his nose; it cut across his right cheek almost to the ear—a remnant of some battle fought on some far frontier against a living enemy who bled when you cut him and who tried to cut you back. The skin of this legionnaire's face was blotchy and dry, every hint of moisture baked from his flesh by the fever within him.

"Your centurion brought armed legionnaires into Rome, I take it." Caius spoke quietly, for this man's ears only. His tone low and intense. "I am not surprised that the gods dealt with him harshly for that impiety and that disrespect for our law. This is a civil problem that needs a civil solution. It is not a military problem." Caius glanced up at one of his lictors and nodded. As the togate man stepped near, Caius reached for the fallen soldier's hip, drew from its sheath the long knife he found there. The soldier was convulsing again, his arms clutched to his breast. Caius spoke through a tightened, dry throat. "May you find Elysium," he murmured, then drew the knife swiftly across the man's throat. Blood flowed out around the blade; Caius was careful not to let it touch his skin. The man gurgled and was still.

Breathing hoarsely, Caius rose to his feet. "Take this," he murmured, passing the hilt to the lictor who stood by him. "Go within and summon my slaves." The lictor stepped away; Caius did not take his eyes from the dead man, whose blood had pooled about his head. "The head must be destroyed," he said softly, to no one in particular. His hand strayed to the folded parchment at his side. Caius's certainty of what had to be done tightened and solidified into a small rock inside him. In the darkness of his study the night before, he'd been assailed with doubts and many strange thoughts. Now he was certain.

Arrests and trials and prayers to the gods weren't enough to contain this festering, hungering pestilence; the insult to Rome's fathers must be removed, must be utterly cut out of the city, as a surgeon might cut a tumor from a man's leg. Caius would burn the thread of Polycarp's life, then hand the parchment to his lictors, issuing an order against the Subura that would be executed in blood. It would happen swiftly, but it would happen one district at a time, so that all the districts would not rise together in a general riot. Wherever they found dead, the guardsmen of the city were to put everyone in that building or that street to death. Many of the living would perish—but they were only people of the Subura. Illiterate lawbreakers and blasphemers of the gods.

He could think only of his son's door and the terrible, fragile silence behind it. No more patrician families need lose their sons or their daughters to this atrocity.

He heard the creak of the villa door opening behind him and turned to see the lictor he'd sent reemerging onto his doorstep, attended by two of the villa's male slaves. Caius spared them only a glance. "Clean this body from the street. One of you run for a surgeon. The brain must be cut away cleanly, then the head sewn up. I weary of burning the bodies of good Roman men and women. This one fought in Rome's wars; let him be interred with honor—as soon as his family can be found. Make haste."

And with that, Caius stepped around the body and moved down the street, his lictors flanking him.

Anger seethed in him; he would see justice done this day.

Someone must atone for the dishonor done to the neglected fathers. For the hearth fires whose coals had gone cold. For the little shrines whose marble steps were dry and unstained by wine because those who should tend them had become cultists.

He would see Polycarp burn like a sacrifice. He would watch the old Greek's flesh curl and blacken in the heat. And then, when this duty was completed, he would hand his secret order to the lictors and would go home. He would then have done all that he could, all that he must do as a father to the Roman people in the Emperor's absence; he would be free then to focus on his duties to his own home and to atone for his own personal loss of honor. He would lock the gate of his villa and walk to his son's room and wish him well. Then to his study. There he would take down from its place on the wall the sword that had rested there since the days of his military service in Dacia, before his son's birth. He would slide the blade from its leather, look for a few moments at the reflection of his cold face in the gleaming metal, then set the hilt against the floor.

He would quietly fall on his sword. And it would be over. His honor recovered.

After he watched Polycarp burn.

POLYCARP ON THE IDES OF AUGUSTUS

THE GATES TO THE TEMPLE of Justitia swung open, revealing the carefully prepared theater of the day: a sunlit courtyard with a floor of dust and gravel, the temple itself at the far end gleaming white (the marble freshly washed). Before the temple, the white curule seat where Caius the praetor sat, the lictors in a row behind him before the temple steps, holding bundles of rods tied with ceremonial cord, representing state authority to discipline and punish. To the right, a narrow pit in the earth where a fire might be lit; to the left, rows of benches and carefully groomed, togate men seated on them. Many leapt to their feet as the guardsmen pulled Polycarp through the gate, and in an instant the low hum of conversation in the courtyard was shattered by cries of rage and fear:

"Desecrator!"

"You make our youth turn from their ancestors!"

"You starve our dead!"

"You famish our temples and shrines!"

"You sicken Rome!"

173

"I lost my *wife* to you, you filthy *fellator!*"

And one man who must surely have been the youngest there beat his chest with his hand and yelled: "Give us back our fathers' Rome!"

Polycarp let the shouts wash over him. He heard in their voices the anguish of their spiritual crisis. In the past few days, they had heard the moaning of the dead nearer their doors; the dead had attacked the very Palatine by night. Patrician Rome had wakened and looked about in horror. They didn't know what was happening or why; they knew only that they were threatened.

As the jurors on their benches clamored for his blood, Polycarp looked about him. Though considerably smaller, this courtyard was an arena not unlike the Circus Maximus where other leaders of the gathering had once been tossed to the chained dead. Before Rome had built any Circus or Colosseum or public arena, gladiators had performed their games at family feasts in the villas of the Palatine, their gory deaths a sacrifice to honor the ancestors of that family. In the same way, the deaths of the Christians in that evil time had been meant to honor and appease the disrespected, wrathful, and rising dead. Now, this day, the dead were restless again, and the guardsmen led Polycarp before the screaming jurors as a sacrifice to their dead. Before bringing him in, they'd first given him a clean white tunic to wear, then replaced the manacles on his wrists. He wore the costume of a culprit, but it occurred to him that it was also the costume of the ritual sacrifice, with perhaps one difference in the details. When a Roman bull was brought to the altar, temple attendants pulled the bull in with but a bit of white string about its horns. Polycarp felt the heaviness of the chains depending from his wrists—did they need so much metal to restrain one old man?

Polycarp looked at Caius where he sat across the long courtyard, stern and cold. Then he glanced past the praetor's curule chair, letting his gaze settle on the tall statue of Justitia where she stood at the top of the steps, one hand upraised as if to forbid entry, the other holding a great pair of scales, and a diadem on her brow—as though to suggest that in Rome, which in previous centuries had been governed by no king or queen or emperor but only a senate of men who trusted to their own hearts and minds to find consensus, that here Justice alone was regal.

How lovely, that marble face. A fold of stone cunningly contrived to resemble soft fabric covered her eyes. Justitia seemed calm, impassive, and entirely unmoved by the cries of the jury. A wry smile tugged at Polycarp's lips. "This is not what I imagined your temple would sound like, Justitia," he murmured.

At a hard shove against his back, Polycarp nearly lost his footing.

"Be silent, desecrator," the guardsman barked.

Holding his peace, Polycarp focused for a moment simply on walking over the sand toward Caius's seat. He ignored the heat of the sand beneath his feet. Heavy on his shoulders sat the fatigue of having looked into the eyes of the walking dead, and his body was sore. Yet he *must* have the strength for this day. He had a role to play, lines to speak. Not those Caius expected, perhaps. He had been playing his part on a larger stage long before this day, a stage the shape and size of a city—but this day would likely be his final act. To the Greeks and the Romans both, the world itself was a stage on which the theater of history was played out for the entertainment and delight of the gods. Men and women quarreled and fought and died on that stage, until the god descended in a machine to intervene at the end of the drama. But as a father of the gathering, Polycarp saw the stage differently. On this stage, men and women who knew God could play the active part of the device that would carry into the theater the *deus ex machina*, the god in the machine. Their role was that of God's machine, God's body. They were his hands and his feet, stepping in not just at the end but at the very moment in the drama in which they found themselves placed. Through the gathering, God might intervene early to transform the grisly sets of the Subura and the cold, remote sets of the Palatine into new places, and to change the players' costumed garb to represent miraculous transformations within their characters.

This day had been long rehearsed. Now Polycarp hoped he could call at least a few of the others in this arena—the jurors, the lictors—to play the parts they truly needed to play, to see their togas and their carefully groomed hair, and these very manacles Polycarp himself wore, for the costumes they in fact were.

Polycarp had prepared himself. All the previous night, he'd waited in a cramped shed with little sleep and no company but the occasional, distant moans of wandering dead downhill by the river. A long time he'd lain awake on the straw, listening for those groaning cries. His eyes stung with tears. In the dark, he contemplated the misery of the earth. Those moaning things by the Tiber bank had been men and women, fearing and loving and craving. Locked into little tenements that crowded narrow water browned with human waste, in life they'd hungered and found no answer to their hunger. Now that hunger had been translated into something eternal. At one point during the night, Polycarp had pressed his hands hard over his ears, unable to bear any more. He'd turned his face into the straw and wept. He was old; it came to him suddenly that he needed to find another, some other to care for the gathering. In the next day he might be dead. He didn't think about the fire pit; he thought only of the weakness of his body and the emptiness of his hands, which held no bread, could never hold enough bread to feed those who needed it. And within every set of eyes he'd seen, living and dead, there had been broken lives, so many. What had his life been worth, when the gathering was so small, the hunger so great? In those cries in the night, he heard all of Rome suffering, and he was spent.

Toward dawn as he lay half awake, he'd heard a new sound: the raucous cries of geese rising in the distance above their nests at the river. He listened, his eyes wide in the dark. The dead must be disturbing the geese, as the Celts had disturbed them in the chill at dawn, centuries ago. Perhaps those cries were cries of warning. Perhaps the cries of the geese were no less a sign than the beetle in the field of wheat—were there Romans in the city even now lying awake, listening, even as he was?

The morning light brought resolution. Polycarp's guards gave him no food and little to drink, but did bring a basin of shallow water to wash his face. He cupped his hands in it, brought the water to his face. The coolness of it had brought fresh life to him; he recalled his baptism in Thessaly. His master was sufficient to this day, even if he himself was not.

Now, as he neared the temple end of the courtyard accompanied by a guardsman, Polycarp turned his head and gave the jurors a more searching look, and caught his breath. Among them was a face he knew. On the back benches, huddled in on himself, silent, sat Marcus Antonius. The boy's bowed shoulders bore a toga in the patrician cut, and Polycarp sorrowed to see it. What was in the boy's heart, forced to wear the uniform of all that he'd rejected? It was plain to see that he did not sit there dressed so of his own accord. The boy's face was dark with bruises. His sullen eyes gazed at the temple grounds; as though ashamed of where he sat and what he wore, he didn't look at the father.

Polycarp let out his breath slowly. *Ah, Marcus, Marcus.* Something began to ache in his chest. How bad had the raid on the insula been? Had the hiding place in his larder been found? Had Regina made it out? Had anyone? A momentary guilt sat queasily in his belly. Regina had wanted him to hide all signs of their faith, conceal themselves entirely; he had refused that extremity. What pain had his choices brought now to her and the others?

The guardsman's hand clutched Polycarp's arm, and the old man stopped, straightened. He was a few steps before the curule seat. Turning his eyes from

Marcus's face, he could feel the intensity of Caius's gaze. For Marcus, at least, he must stand tall and represent the gathering well. With an inner growl, he reminded himself: his God was the same within the walls of this temple as he was outside of them. A man who served him must stand no less steadily here than elsewhere.

"Polycarp of Larissa, then of Smyrna, now of Rome." Caius's voice was coldly formal. He'd assumed the voice of the praetor urbanus, with the full weight of Roman tradition and Roman justice behind him. "You are called to give answer before the People of Rome in the presence and precinct of the goddess Justitia."

"And I have come, Caius Lucius." Polycarp made a show of looking about the temple grounds. Then he shook his head slightly, as though bewildered. "Where are the advocates?"

"You are a Greek." The praetor's voice was sharp. "And you have lived many years in the Subura, surrounded by the most disreputable persons. Your citizenship cannot be verified. Therefore none are needed; the jury requires only a questioning of the accused and the confirming testimony of two witnesses."

"I see. But you are wrong, Caius Lucius Justus. I do have an advocate, and one who will speak directly to the hearts of the jurors. Maybe they will listen. Maybe they will not." He shook his head. "Where are your witnesses, then?"

"In good time." Caius waved his hand in dismissal. "First there are questions I intend to ask. It would be best for the admissions to come from your lips. The offenses for which you stand here carry a capital penalty, but I would offer you the opportunity to die well, Polycarp."

The corner of Polycarp's lip curved. "I thank you for that respect, Caius. I hope I have lived well enough to die well." He bowed his head slightly. The chains were heavy about his wrists, and it was difficult in the heat to stay standing; he longed for a chair. But his comfort did not matter. What mattered this day was that he stand with dignity and bear witness only to things that were true, whatever the threat. His words must plant seeds in dry hearts. Those jurors would likely burn him, but he might yet with his words wake them to the futility and falsehood of the roles they played. Something might begin here that would continue in conversations and disputes and questionings around every family room in patrician Rome. It was not only those jurors on their benches who listened. His words here would matter to every member of the gathering in Rome wherever they now hid, whether in Suburan insulae or merchants' houses or high villas. His words would matter to every member of every gathering hidden in cities across the world and to every gathering in centuries yet unborn. Before so vast an audience, he must stand without giving thought to the weakness of his body or the possibilities of failure. "Ask your questions of me. I am ready."

The praetor stood very straight, Roman straight, in his seat; his white marble chair had no back. Chairs with ornately carved backs were for barbarian princes and slothful magistrates in frontier towns. A Roman wanted no prop to hold him up.

Caius watched him intently. "You do not deny that you are a leader of the followers of the rabbi from Palestine?"

"No, I do not deny it. Why should I?"

"And that you have, often and frequently, led others, both citizens and otherwise, to these strange beliefs?"

The jurors leaned forward on their benches, the low rustle of their togas and the low murmur of their voices sounding like the coming of a flood, rushing slowly nearer out of the distance.

Polycarp paused and lifted his head. For a moment his eyes shone bright. "I am an old man, Caius."

"Answer the question—"

"—I *am* answering the question." He swallowed his anger; he must not allow this praetor, who stank of fear and eagerness for blood, to prod him. "But I am old, and I talk—slowly. Also because I am old, I like to have company when I break my bread and when I go to worship. I used to have old men like myself to talk with, but now I am the only one left. Sometimes it is good to have young people who will pass you a bowl of wine and listen to your stories."

He looked at the jurors. Many of them wore frowns of discomfort. The youth who had beaten his chest with his hand and cried out *Give us back our fathers' Rome!* looked stunned, as though he'd been slapped. One middle-aged man on the back bench was chewing on his cheek—as though chewing on unexpected thoughts—much as a goat might chew its cud while resting in the pastures of Thessaly. Marcus appeared to be holding his breath.

Polycarp's words gave their anger nothing to feed on. He could see in their faces and in the way some of them turned to whisper to each other that he was not what they'd expected. After all, they had come not to perform the true duty of a jury but to see with their own eyes the desecrator, the one who starved the dead of food and then touched the dead with his hands. They had come for a quick trial and a quick killing.

It was harder to grasp the iron spear of rage in clenched fists when you had confronting you no visible monster but only an old man who talked about his life, one not unlike the grandfathers in their own families, those men who were soon to join the honored dead and to whom those families looked for wisdom and moral grounding. It was likely that when the jurors heard stories of the desecrators—those who led astray the youth of Rome and woke the resting dead—they didn't think of them in the shape of an old man. The accused who now stood before them on the sand: was he a betrayal, a perversion of everything they looked to in an aged man, or was he one of their elders calling them to account? Their faces bore the confusion of this moment.

"You will not deceive us with the smooth rhetoric of a Greek, Polycarp." Caius's voice, clear and cold, cut through the rustle of noise, his words a reminder that it was at least not a *Roman* elder to whom they listened. "You will answer questions with an *I do* or an *I do not*, with the plainness that the good citizens of our jury expect. We are not here to hear your stories but to do justice."

"I see." Polycarp met Caius's eyes, and after a moment the Roman blinked and looked quickly away. Polycarp sighed. In that brief gaze, he'd seen a grief that would howl like a wolf in the hills, if it were not tightly chained and muzzled; the praetor had blinked before he could see more. Caius was not a youth, but he was too young to carry such a weight of sorrow and remorse within him. How had he been hurt so badly? Had he no wife to soothe his cares? No children to bring him the healing of laughter? He had no gathering to confess his sins and his suffering to, and his gods were impatient with confessions.

"What else do you have to ask?" Polycarp said.

Caius looked shaken, as though he'd sensed Polycarp's searching of his heart. He drew a breath, but his voice now was hoarse. "Polycarp, do you teach to others the perverse religion of the Jews, taking from them the religion of our fathers?"

Polycarp would have liked to quibble with *teach, perverse, Jews,* and *taking*, but decided there was nothing to be gained in it. It was a simple enough question. "I do."

"Do you teach them that by eating the flesh and drinking the blood of your cult's dead founder, that they can attain immortality?"

They were speaking different languages and different scripts, the praetor and the father. Polycarp held the silence a moment—the murmur from the jury was getting ugly again— "I do. However—"

179

"Do you then consume flesh and blood?"

"I consume bread and wine." Polycarp's voice became a growl.

"An *I do* or an *I do not* will suffice, Polycarp. Do you take into your body flesh and blood?"

"I do not."

"Do your followers?"

"Certainly not."

"And is it untrue that you meet for your rites among the bodies of the Roman dead?"

A weight of dread settled over Polycarp. So Julia had revealed that. He'd feared it. The Catacombs might be watched in the future. It seemed certain now that he would not be a lone sacrifice. As in the time of Nero, there might be widespread arrests. Rome had burned once in a time of plague, and his people had burned even after the other fires were put out. Was that what his dream had foreboded? He could hear the muffled click of Despair's claws on the sandy ground. A glance across the courtyard showed the great beast settling into a crouch beside the cold fire pit. The beast was hungry.

A strange feeling of continuity came over him as he gazed across the dusty courtyard at the Roman praetor. How many had stood here—not in this walled compound, but in a hundred arenas like it, in different cities, questioned in different languages yet speaking the same lines he now must speak, held because they had devoted themselves to sharing bread and had denounced those who kept their larders locked, or because they had shared at times with their neighbors a fierce certainty that there were some things that locked doors and high walls and hired swords cannot turn back—and a fierce hope that something else *could*. He remembered Paul, who'd worn chains much like these a few generations ago. He remembered Jeremias before the king of Jerusalem and Daniel before the princes of Babylon. He glanced once at Marcus, who sat with lowered head on the jury, wondering if he too might one day have to stand in chains like his. He wondered who else would stand and give witness, after him. His lips were dry with thirst, and the heat against his scalp made his body want to sway where it stood, but he stood firm, and his heart hardened within him. This was the crucial day: he would not be standing here if his master did not have something for him to say and something for that jury to hear. He believed that. He had to. He turned his back on the beast and the pit.

"It is true," he murmured, "that we meet in whatever places seem safest."

"Your own words convict you." Caius's lip curled, though his eyes remained unsettled. "I give you this chance, Polycarp, to make amends. Do you now recant your superstition and pledge to do what you can to return the children you have corrupted to the ways of their fathers?" Recant. A hard knot of anger burned in Polycarp's chest. "Forty years and six I have served my master, and in all that time he has treated me well. Why should I turn my back and blaspheme him now?" He faced the jury, his voice rising, his patience fraying. "In our father Peter's time," Polycarp declared before Caius could interrupt him, "the Emperor of Rome threw many of the gathering into the Colosseum, where they were eaten. Your fathers wished to believe that those who died in the Colosseum were bread to satisfy the ancestors. Now we all stand here again, in this arena. Your praetor intends my death to atone for the dishonor you believe my gathering has done to your ancestors. And just as the Emperor casts bread to the crowds, your praetor intends to cast some bread to you, good jurors. Because you are hungry. You are in crisis. It is hoped that my death may relieve the bite of your hunger for certainty and safety, and that it may relieve the bite of the dead's hunger for honor. I fear you are much deceived. My death is not the bread you need. Nor are you the people in Rome who need bread most."

Polycarp grunted as though dismissing the jury and turned to the curule chair, his voice stern now. "But come, let us finish these games, Caius Lucius Justus. I do not know how long my body can stand on this hot sand."

Caius observed him a moment with narrowed eyes. The jury seemed to be holding its breath. The youth who'd called out was frowning as though a forest had sprung into being in the soil of his mind and he was now trying to find his way through it. The man of middle age was still chewing slowly on his cheek, watching the father now with a cold, concentrated look, as though to say, *Your words do not move me, old Greek.* Marcus still looked weary, resigned. Polycarp sighed softly. Though it was the others he must persuade, it was Marcus's heart that mattered to him most. It was painful to see him so. He would like to put some strength into the boy's heart, some firmness into his back. He yearned to call out to the boy: *Remember you are a child of God, Marcus. He has wakened you and adopted you from your old life. He has fed you, bread and wine. He has clothed you in his love, a finer garment than any toga. He has commissioned you, equipping you with a gift invisible yet potent: your desire to seek out truth, whatever the cost, and prune from your life all that is untrue. You are brave, my son, and you have been adopted into the family of the bravest, by one who is* paterfamilias *to all who live and breathe. Take pride in your sonship. No son of our God need lower his head at the world's scorn or its bruising. Remember who you are, my son.*

But of course he could not call those words across the sand. He could only

181

speak the words that were right for this day and this place, and hope that Marcus heard in them the words he could not say and found strength.

Caius stirred. "So be it." His eyes were dark. "Guardsmen! The first witness. Bring her."

There was a rustle; someone was being brought out from around the back of the temple. A murmur passed through the jury as a woman was led out into the courtyard—without chains.

It was Julia. Plump and red faced in the heat, she avoided looking at Polycarp, but went to stand a few strides to his left, between him and the jury. Her garments were finer than he recalled—she wore thick-soled, freshly made sandals and a gown of purple, with pearls about her throat. Though her face shone with sweat, she looked very much like an equestrian merchant's wife, and not a baker's. Polycarp glanced about, but did not see Piscus. Perhaps he was waiting behind the temple too. Two witnesses, Caius had said.

Well. Now the test truly began.

"Julia," Caius said quietly. "You carry an august name, the name of one of our most revered houses. A caprice and a prideful overreaching on your parents' part, I expect. But today you can show that you merit such a name as that of the Julii. Your words will help us decide on a just verdict and just action, and will aid us in protecting Rome."

Julia's shoulders were very tense. Polycarp watched her, a flicker of anger swiftly dampened by sorrow. The line of her shoulders spoke of pain from old wounds reopened, of regret, of bitterness directed against herself and others. He marveled that the jury could not see the way she stood; to his eyes, her pain this day was so visible, it hurt to gaze at her. What Pandora's box had she unlocked within her breast when she left the insula?

"You stand in the precinct of the goddess Justitia," Caius was intoning. "Will you speak truth and verity?"

"I will." Julia's voice was firm, calm. None of the tension in her shoulders made it into her tone.

"You lived for some time in Polycarp's insula, did you not?"

"I did. For half a year. My husband rented another place before that."

Caius watched her, his eyes hard and cold. "And what did you see there?"

She lifted her head. "There were maybe fifteen, maybe twenty in that insula who never poured libations for the honored dead, never whispered a prayer to Janus when they went out or came in, never took any fruit or wine to our insula's shrine... I..." She lifted a trembling hand to her face, rubbed her temple a moment with her fingertips. "I'm sorry," she said. "I don't like to talk about it." She closed her eyes. "Most of the time, I stayed in our room with my husband. You don't know what it was like, living there." She opened her eyes wide. "You can't imagine it."

"It is the jury's duty to imagine it," Caius said. "Tell us the rest, Julia. Leave nothing out."

Julia took a breath. "They are all mad, Caius Lucius, jurors. The old Greek is the maddest of them. In that insula, everything is—it's upside down. A pleasure slave keeps the insula's accounts and presumes to look in on everyone. Yet a young patrician man, one of a high and ancient and revered family—" For an instant she cast a glare toward Marcus, who was looking at her with horror. There was a naked fury in Julia's eyes, a *real* fury, not a play-acted one, as though Marcus's abandonment of his toga at the insula had been a personal betrayal of her, of her hopes and beliefs, of things that mattered to her. And she couldn't keep the fury entirely from her voice. "He is sent three times a week to the market to fetch bread, like the lowest, nameless slave. And then, that bread he brings, they give it out to—to *beggars* and layabouts and thieves while they themselves adjourn to secret meetings in Polycarp's room or in despoiled Roman tombs, even in the very Catacombs beneath the city, to eat their own secret meals. They themselves speak of dining there, in the dark, on flesh and blood."

Silence fell. The jurors looked breathless, as though Julia's testimony had ridden them into wild country at full gallop. Polycarp focused on Julia—how she stood in her bright gown. He watched as her chin lifted. Clearly the role she played now was that of the offended domina, stiff with horror at her night's discovery of some evil rite performed by her house slaves when they thought the family asleep. Some handling of snakes, or some chanting in a circle, some remnant of whatever magic had been native to their conquered tribe. To the offended domina, Polycarp and the tenants of his insula were doubtless lower than the house slaves; though free, the men and women of the Subura slept on thinner blankets, dressed less well, dined less well. And perhaps, the domina might think, perhaps what secret rites these half-Romans might perform after dark would be more barbarous than any a few Germanic or Dacian slaves might dream of.

"Flesh and blood? Boar's flesh, perhaps?" There was a violence beneath the cold in Caius's voice. "Or mutton?"

"No. Human flesh." She paused. "Desecrated flesh. They speak of eating the bodies of their dead."

A growl from the jurors now, deep and bestial, a growl that rose from their bellies. Marcus looked even more pale.

"The desecrated dead," Caius repeated. He leaned forward, his eyes fierce. "You had better tell us more."

She hesitated, then shrank back, as though it had occurred to her, abruptly, how very serious the allegations she made actually were. She glanced at blind Justitia, her eyes wary. "That is all I know," she murmured. "It is terrible enough. They would share the flesh in their gatherings at night. The old Greek teaches that the living mustn't feed the dead; the dead must feed the living. Is it any wonder our affronted dead arise?"

Looking at Julia now, Polycarp realized suddenly that she'd *always* borne false witness. She'd pretended to be a tenant content in the insula, a baker's wife, when her heart was elsewhere. Before that, on some villa on the Palatine, she'd perhaps pretended to be a good and devoted wife to her first husband. She was always playing a part, always wearing a purple gown. Without disguise, naked, she might be too terrified to breathe; perhaps she had not even looked at her own heart in that way, unclothed, unveiled. She wanted others to see what she chose to show them; perhaps she wanted to see only what she showed herself. He wondered suddenly what had taught her, long ago, that she needed such veils. He wondered who she really was, what she really hungered for.

His dread grew heavier. Here was one he had not helped, one he hadn't fed. He could hear the rising anger of the jury as she spoke—and faintly, beneath it, another sound: the low cry of the dead, many of them, somewhere below on the hill. But nearer than they'd sounded last night. The sound had a strange quality, as though their moaning had actually been audible for some time, though only barely, heard by the ear but unnoticed, and had suddenly become louder and more clear. That chilled him. He listened a moment, forgetting the witness and the jury.

They were climbing the hill. Dead did not often do that; they moved down streets toward the river, like water, their shuffling feet taking the easiest paths, unless they heard or smelled the living and gave chase, uphill or down. Perhaps now, one or two of the dead, or a few, had sensed some pedestrian on the high streets and stumbled toward him; perhaps, fleeing uphill, he was pulling dead after him—first a few, then a larger group that followed those.

Or perhaps they had heard the furious cries of the jury, carried toward the river on some ill wind.

Whatever had caught their notice, they were coming. Perhaps, hearing that low hunting moan, a few undead would break free of villas and gardens along the Palatine streets and join the swarm moving up the slope, until they came onward like a reeking tide, like the dead in his dream, a multitude decaying and hungry without reprieve. A few of the jurors had noticed the moaning now; several of them glanced up, and a shudder passed through them. But after a moment they turned their attention back to Julia, though with pale faces; in the past few days, they'd heard such distant moans too often for that sound to toss them into outright panic now.

Off to Polycarp's right, by the fire pit, came the slow, slouching sound of a great beast shifting its weight.

You stand condemned, Despair whispered.

"Yes." Polycarp was sweating in the sun. Convicted not by that jury but by the baker's wife and by the cries of those dead. His larder had been too small, his voice too soft. He'd done too little. This day he was called to account for those he'd failed.

Yet something in him toughened, baked hard by the sun. He *did* stand here as a sacrifice. Not the sacrifice Caius wanted, an appeasement of the furious dead. Another kind of sacrifice. Glancing at the faces of the jury, he didn't think he would be able to avoid a severe verdict or that his body would escape the flames. But his master while he lived had once said that a seed must fall to the ground, split, and die in order for a mighty tree to be born. His failures might be redeemed in this moment if the words with which he met his death could yet plant those seeds in the jurors' hearts, seeds that would later bear fruit. Maybe it was too late, with the starving dead loosed in the city. Yet he had to hope. When the evils of the world sprang out of Pandora's box in the old story, all that remained at the bottom was hope. "A fragile thing," he murmured to himself, "but it is all we have. We *have* to hope. Against the madness of the world, we have to hope. And even if I were without hope, still this is where I've been told to stand. My master is still sufficient. As long as I stand here in his stead."

"Speak loud enough for us to hear," Caius broke in sharply.

"Very well." Polycarp lifted his voice. The courtyard shimmered in the sun's heat. "This wearies me. There are no advocates present to question young Julia, no one to read in her testimony where there is truth and where falsehood. In such an absence, of what use are her words to you?" He faced Julia, whose face was contorted in the grip of her emotions. "I grieve for your pain, daughter. I regret that you found no home with us." It was the only apology he knew how to make.

"I'm not your daughter," she hissed. "My father was an equestrian, a man of worth."

"I do not doubt it." Polycarp coughed to clear his throat, which was terribly dry. "But it is not ownership of a State Horse that makes a father a man of worth, but whom he chooses to feed and how he chooses to feed them." He glanced at the jury, saw Marcus watching him now with eyes that shone with pride amid a bruised and sleep-deprived face. Polycarp took a little strength from that. "Manius Curius," he told the jurors, "lived in a cottage and devoted himself to the growing of turnips. Yet he was one of Rome's first men, whom all in Rome still revere. And I know of another just man, a writer of laws, who once left a palace to live in a desert tent, that he might teach a starving tribe to gather bread from the ground."

"Enough," Caius snapped, the sharpness of his voice cracking across the walled ground. "Jurors, your pardon, but I must hasten these proceedings. There are dead on the hill—we can hear them. Be without fear: I have guardsmen in the street to meet them. But we who are here must proceed swiftly, hasten this trial and the rites that follow, to do justice on the one who has caused Rome so much harm, bringing this dishonor, this plague, and this evil upon us. I don't plan to tarry over tales and trivialities." He turned to the accused.

"Polycarp, your violence upon Rome, upon its traditions and its health and upon the Roman peace, will be suffered no longer. I can bring another witness to confirm what Julia has told us, but I would rather avoid the delay. As the appointed magistrate of the city, I require you to recant your perverse beliefs and submit yourself to our judgment. I will ask again. Polycarp, father of the tomb despoilers, the god destroyers, the atheists, do you recant?"

But once again Polycarp had stopped listening. Or rather, he was listening again to the dead. They were nearer. There were faint shouts and cries that subsided quickly, smothered beneath the growing noise of the long, drawn-out wailing of the approaching corpses. Far too much like his dream of the dead city and the wheat.

The sun was beating hard on Polycarp's bald head, and the dust and grit beneath his feet swam for a moment under his gaze. He looked up, glancing sideways at the sun, taking its measure. The blaze of it made it difficult to think. If only that sun was a little kinder, a little more like the sun he'd known in Thessaly. He smiled faintly, remembering how he had once, as a boy of twelve summers, felt that kinder sun on the back of his neck as he sat at the edge of his parents' wheat field. He had burned that day, but hadn't noticed; his entire mind and being had been focused on a large red beetle crawling across the back of his hand. It had landed there of its own accord, and its little wings had snapped back under its shell, translating it in an instant from a flying blur of red into a small creature that crawled across the surface of the earth as men and women do. He stared at it, holding his breath. Then he got slowly, slowly to his feet, taking the utmost care not to dislodge his find. With exaggerated caution, placing one foot at a time, he moved along the edge of the field, fearful—so fearful—that the beetle would fly away. His heart was louder and more violent in his chest than he'd ever felt it before. He glanced up, could see his mother standing by the threshold of the house.

She knelt by him when he reached her, the beetle still perched on his hand. It had crawled over the webbing between two fingers (tickling him so that he nearly jumped) and then along his palm as he tilted his hand carefully to keep it from falling.

"What did you bring me?" his mother asked, her smile warming his entire world.

Without speaking, he simply held his hand a little higher, for her to look.

"A beetle?" She cupped Polycarp's hands in hers, holding his hand steady as the little creature crawled along his palm, teasing his skin with its tiny legs. "Symbol of truth and eternity," she said. "My grandmother from Kemet taught me that when I was a girl." She laughed softly as she passed her mothers' knowledge to her son, her one child (Polycarp had never had a sister), a gift as sustaining as a head of ripe wheat, as precious as a berry. And even as she laughed, the beetle's wings flickered out of its shell, tiny and fragile. Polycarp held his breath, and his mother fell silent, watching.

The wings trembled once, twice. Then the beetle flitted from the boy's hand, zipping into the air. Polycarp watched, his mouth open, as the beetle flitted to a smooth white stone, its color stark against the rock. From there, the beetle flew to an ear of wheat at the edge of the field. It clung to the ear, and the wings flickered back into its shell.

"The world is full of truth and life," his mother whispered. They were speaking in Greek, that melodic language that, as an old man, Polycarp still thought in sometimes, even after decades of using mostly Latin. *Aletheia kai zoe*, his mother had sung to him: *truth and life*. "Polycarp, my little Polycarp, you must find what is true. But you cannot hold it in your hand or keep it captive: it will fly. Truth always does. And you must follow when it does, wherever it leads you."

"Where will it fly, mother?"

"I don't know," she laughed. "But you must follow it. It might fly across the river, or over the fields, or up that cliff over there. It doesn't matter. It will take you to the one thing you need today, the one thing you need to do. Trust it. It is sacred."

He nodded and sprang from her, chasing the beetle. He slowed as he approached the field, holding his hands before him, almost cupped, ready to catch it. He stepped carefully toward the ear of wheat, higher than his head, where the beetle rested. But when he was only a few steps away, it flickered deeper into the field.

For a moment he paused, looked at the tossing sea of wheat. Then he threw himself into the grain, moving quickly but stealthily, as boys sometimes do. He could hear, so faintly, the hum of its wings. It would stop, then start again, that sound. He followed it. His body felt alive and taut; if he had to jump to catch the beetle, he felt he could jump high as the sun. Something more life-filled and vibrant than blood pulsed through him.

In the summers in Greece, with the wheat stirring in the breeze and the sky open as a woman's heart, every youth knows in his blood that he is a god, immortal, uncontainable, with a world to roam. Polycarp's heart beat in his ears as he pursued the small beetle, the tiny hum of its wings the kind of lullaby that seduces flowers into dreaming of bees. He stalked through the wheat.

Then stopped. Breathing hard.

He waited. Quick, urgent heartbeats.

He'd lost the sound.

Horror seized at him; he looked about urgently at the endless wheat—a great expanse of grain higher than his head, nothing visible but the high stalks. A breeze passed through, making the heads of wheat caress his face and arms.

Must he turn back now, return to his mother's arms?

Could he even *find* his way back?

He looked to the sky, hoping to catch a glimpse of the beetle. But there was only the sun: its heat above him something palpable he could feel, a weight on his face.

***

When he lowered his eyes from the sun, he met Caius's stern, hard look. The dead were moaning; he could smell Caius's fear. He called to mind Caius's question of a moment before. "No, I will not recant," he murmured, lifting a chained hand and passing it across his eyes to clear away the stinging sweat. "I am an old man, and perhaps I fear death more than I did when I was young. But there are other things worthier of my fear. Why should I lose myself in the wheat for you, Caius Lucius?"

Polycarp straightened and turned his back to the praetor, faced the jurors. "Now I will give *my* testimony. And you will listen, for I am the oldest one present, and I have seen more of life—and death—than any of you. It is likely I have seen things you could hardly believe."

His voice was very clear. In that moment his *dignitas*—the most important of qualities to any Roman—was so great, so intensely visible, that no one spoke or interrupted him. Even Caius remained silent now while Polycarp spoke, though the praetor's body grew tense as a bow stretched taut to the point of snapping.

Polycarp spread his manacled hands as wide as he could; an ell of chain restrained them. Among the jurors, Marcus was gazing at him out of a bruised face with that same look Polycarp had seen in his eyes the night he went to confront the dead in the alley. The look of a man who wanted to leap in front of his father and shield him, but could not see a way to do so. Polycarp smiled faintly, for him.

"You are greatly misinformed about who I am and what I have been doing," he said. "I am Polycarp. I was born in Larissa, Thessaly, a Roman citizen of Greek blood. I was born a second time in baptism in Smyrna, where for some time I served a small gathering of both citizens and noncitizens, both rich and poor, who were devoted to the sharing of bread, the teaching of our master's apostles, and to prayer and fellowship. While I was there, a message came to us from the holy widows in Rome, describing to us the severe hunger suffered in the Subura. There were many tears as it was read, for matters in Smyrna are not as bad as here in Rome, and your brothers and your sisters in smaller cities have compassion for you who live in this great one.

"Hearing the message, the elders among us appointed me to go to Rome as an apostle, and with the appointment was passed to me the Apostle's Gift. Perhaps you wonder what I mean by this; I will tell you. We of the gathering worship One God, the Giver of Life, the Giver of Gifts.

"There are many gifts, and no one who encounters the Spirit of God is without one. Some are given gifts for teaching, or for healing, or for perceiving things that are yet to come. The gift entrusted to me was that of apostleship, for I was sent out to witness and to see to and see into the souls, living and dead, who suffer in this city, to hear their griefs and to absolve them.

"I will tell you about this Gift. It is to see with God's eyes, to hear with

God's ears. It can only be given to one who is first willing to look and hear. One with the Gift sees through all veils, through all garments and costumes. If one of you were to come join me on this sand, take my arm, meet my eyes, you would find me gazing not only beneath your toga to the man beneath it, but through every cerement you've wrapped about your heart. It might be a terrifying experience for you—to have your every regret, your every fear and secret hope, naked and seen. But in that moment, if you were willing, you might also see your own self just as nakedly. You might be forgiven. You might lay all those secrets down and be as one who runs naked and free on the grass. That is a very great Gift, though a fearful one."

Polycarp let his gaze move across the jury, but each of them lowered their eyes, a few with their faces terribly pale. He gave a small nod. "It is a fearful thing, yet something each of us yearns for—to be naked before God or before another human being. To be intimate and loved for who we truly are. And if this is so with you who live, it is so, too, with the dead. Think of how burdened your hearts are. Those who die so burdened yearn and hunger even in death. Desiring intimacy, they rise and devour, for consuming another is the only way they know to take another into themselves. But I think there is one very great difference between the dead and the living. If I were to touch one of the dead and gaze into its eyes, it would be far readier than any of you to lay down its burdens and rest."

A murmur rose among the jury. The young man who'd cried out the loudest when Polycarp was brought in now hissed through his teeth, his eyes dark with horror.

"Yes," Polycarp said quietly. "It is a terrible thing to touch the dead. In the land in which the gathering was born, that touch would make you unclean; you would be cast out. And it is true that if one of the dead should feed on you, the fever will come and you will burn and die, then walk restless yourself, because the fever-death gives you no time to unveil your so carefully hidden heart to any of your brothers or your sisters, and in that way prepare for the last river crossing that is death. But what other way do we have to calm the restless dead, other than to embrace them? Do you really think that destroying these walking bodies by the sword does your dead more honor? Or that the only way to deal with that which wishes to consume you is to flee it or destroy it? Deer and fanged beasts live in such a way; men and women must not.

"My brothers on the jury, I give witness that my touching of the dead does not spread the fever, nor do I enter into your tombs with any purpose to wake or desecrate those who sleep. Why should I? The restlessness of the dead disturbs me as much as it does you. May God will that my testimony satisfies your ears better than this incoherent witness about despoiled tombs or rumors of midnight feedings. And that brings me to the other accusation I've heard today. Let us speak of that.

"I am accused of eating flesh and drinking blood. I would laugh at the absurdity of this, but you take it seriously. Very well. There is much flesh and much blood in Rome. Have someone visit my larder. See if there is less bread and grain there than one might expect. Ask the market by the Fulvian Cistern if I buy from them less often than another man."

The jurors were shifting in their seats uneasily; their faces told him too plainly that they did not believe him, or did not want to; with the wailing of the dead audible in their ears, they wanted very badly to have someone to blame. Polycarp shook his head, barely restraining the frustration that burned in him. The heat of the sun on his head, the heat of the sand beneath his feet, made patience difficult; sweat was pouring down his back beneath his tunic. "But you will not," he said. "You do not care to. Because the real accusation is that I have taken 'your fathers' Rome' from you, and that because of me, your fathers rise from their mausoleums in wrath to devour their sons, as did Uranus in the old story they tell in the country of my birth. Caius Lucius Justus, and men of the jury, if your fathers and your kin who are dead are wrathful, it is not at me. Give you back your fathers' Rome, you cry. In your fathers' Rome, men treated their own gods and their temples—and aging men, for that matter—with more respect and less noise. Why should I expect to be left in peace to serve my God with those who'll serve with me, when you are so neglectful of yours?"

The benches erupted at that, and again the temple was a clamor of angry voices. Polycarp shouted over them. "I am not done, fellow citizens—I am *not* done!—I grant you!—I grant you, it is possible that the gathering may one day stand guilty of great crimes, for though assembled by God, we are a fellowship of men and women, and we are as broken as we are beautiful. But the gathering I serve does not stand guilty today. You wish to believe that we who worship differently are therefore a different kind of people, a people capable of any sacrilege and therefore deserving of any punishment. But your wishing does not make it so! You make so much of the fact that I come to you here from the Subura. It is pointless. The distinctions you make, make fools of you. Patrician, plebian." He turned, held the youngest juror's gaze with his. "You wear the toga; I wear the simpler tunic of the people. It means nothing. Stripped of it, you and I look the same—just two men hungering and thirsting. It is only a garment. What matters is the heart." He took his sleeve between his chained hands, tried to tear it; the cloth was stubborn. "Look at it. Look at it!" he cried. "A thousand threads—different threads—woven together so they cannot break. That is what we are to be. We are to be one cloth, one body, one gathering. Patrician! Plebian!" he shouted. "You weaken Rome with your distinctions. Rome now is not one whole cloth but layers, castes, one sitting atop the other. It needs only a strong wind, and the separated layers of the city will be tossing in the air, tumbling and helpless. We cannot survive unwoven from each other. You have to understand that.

"Listen to *that* in the streets outside. Those walking *mouths* are there because you have not fed your people, and because men and women and children, Roman or otherwise, die daily, unnoticed, in the Subura. If you *had* no Subura, you would have no region for the dead to fester. What can be plainer than that? That is what you should be talking about among yourselves. The choices of your past have come home to you. They are at the gate. Maybe it is too late to recover anything. But maybe it is not."

He raised his voice, a fire burning in his heart. The words seemed to pour through him now as though from some other place, and for an instant he wondered if this was what it had been like for the prophets of old, proclaiming words God himself had given to their ears. He felt like a tunnel through which a backdraft of flame was rushing, scorching his insides, yet exhilarating in its wild energy.

"We are *all* on trial," he cried. "Our dead are here to demand answers, and we are out of time. We have to choose, now, this day. Will we have a City divided into the eaters and the eaten—a City populated in the end only by the hungry dead!—or will we build a City where we break bread together, *all of us*, Roman and Greek and Syrian, male and female, master and slave, not feeding *on* each other but feeding and sustaining each other? Give me your verdict, please, then let me rest. The past few days have been more exhausting than any in my life. I will admit that I would rather die in my bed than in a fire. But now, if you can't manage to look at the truth and decide what to do about it, I am done talking with you."

Julia was gazing at him, appalled, as though he were some kind of creature she had never seen before, whose behaviors and postures were utterly alien to anything she might expect or know how to interpret.

Polycarp merely turned aside and gazed at the statue of Justitia. His eyes glanced behind her, at the pillars of the temple and the door behind them, which must lead to the inner alcoves and the inner court, where sacrifices were made. He longed to see some small flicker of red, a beetle crawling on the marble steps, perhaps, or flitting past Justitia's blindfolded face. Some sign, some confirmation that he was this moment standing where he needed to be. He had said the words that poured into him and through him; he could think of nothing more to say. Yet he didn't think anyone had heeded him. What good was it doing, that he stood here? He kept his eyes from the cold fire pit, wondering how soon it would be lit. The dead were moaning outside, and the jury were talking among themselves in heated voices. He felt unutterably weary.

"Citizens, calm yourselves!" Caius's voice broke the air. "Guardsmen, bring the other witness."

Polycarp pressed his hand to his head; the sun was very hot on his brow. And the dead. Those moans—there might be a few corpses now literally in the very street outside. Or perhaps in a house near at hand. But he could *hear* them. So little time.

The jurors had turned in their seats to watch the second witness approach; a guardsman was escorting a woman over from where she must have been standing behind the jurors' benches. The woman was short, but she stood with incredible dignity and poise. Yet her eyes brimmed with unshed tears, and the hand she held over her heart was clutched too tightly about the torn fabric of her nightdress. She stared straight ahead, as though terrible things were to her left and to her right, as though she knew that she could only keep walking forward if she chose not to look at them.

Polycarp swayed suddenly on his feet.

He knew her.

Perhaps better than anyone in Rome, he knew this woman.

If she was here to witness against him, if she had broken, then surely all his work was broken. How would the gathering in Rome hold, if neither he nor she were left to care for it? How could the gathering anywhere hold? Her presence here was a spear through his breast, and the anguish of it a blow that all but knocked him out of the world of light and heat into some far other place, cold and dark.

The woman was Regina.

ALETHEIA KAI ZOE

The day before. An open square just outside the walled compound of Justitia's temple.

REGINA SHRIEKED AGAIN as the three-bladed whip tore into her back. The pain and heat of it flashed through her body; her legs buckled, giving out beneath her. For a moment she hung limp from the post by her chained wrists, panting, waiting for the pain to dull. Her nightdress hung in tatters from her shoulders.

The guardsman wielding that whip meant to break her.

She bit her lip hard, clenching her teeth. Over and over in her mind, above the screaming of her body's pain, she recited what she knew to be true, what she held to be true. *I am Regina Romae. I am a deaconess of the gathering in Rome. I am no slave; I give refuge and comfort for the lost. These bonds, this pain, they do not make me a slave. I am Regina Romae.*

The lash struck her again, and she jerked and screamed through her teeth. The whole world melted into the heat of the blow, and when she came to, she was sobbing, on her knees, hanging again from her wrists. A rough hand seized her hair, tugged her head back, the guardsman's breath hot on her throat. "Writhe for me, little slut," he hissed, and forcing her face toward his, he kissed her, assaulting her mouth. He tasted of bad wine, smelled of sweat. She screamed in helpless fury, but his lips smothered the sound. She fought him, thrashing, but his hand held her head still until he was done. Then he dropped her head back and stepped away, chuckling. Hot rage seared through her as she panted for breath. If she could only wipe the taste of him from her lips—but her wrists were confined high over her head, manacles biting into them. She spat into the dust.

The lash struck her across her hips, and she jerked again, then hung sobbing, panting. God, it *hurt!* Her face was wet with perspiration and tears. She found the rage within her, seized it, fed it. She was Regina Romae. She was the deaconess of the gathering in Rome.

The lash tore another scream from her throat.

She was Regina Romae. She provided refuge. She would not break.

"*God!*" she cried. The blades of the whip had struck her side, flicking around to sting her breast. She twisted away from the blow, sobbing, her face burning at the guardsman's laughter. For years, her bitterness and shame at her past had remained only a tiny seed, one she didn't allow to sprout but was unable to discard entirely. Now her captivity had made that wild seed burst into weed and flower; with a violence and a voracity that stunned her, it had grown into a raging thorn plant twining about her heart and lungs, threatening to strangle her.

She hung in a haze of pain and didn't feel or hear the guardsman step toward her—but the manacles sprang open and she slid to the dust, where she lay panting. Her back was a great blaze of heat, with lines of fire traced over it, crossing old scars. Dazed, she stared at the dust and drew in what air she could. She heard the sound of quiet whimpering and, realizing the sound was her, she pressed her lips together. She closed her eyes, started to pray silently to Polycarp's God. She felt footsteps near her body and tensed.

"Can I see her?" A woman's voice, not far away. The voice was familiar to her, but her thoughts were too scattered to give the voice a name.

"Why not, domina? I'll get her on her feet."

Large hands gripped her arms, and she was pulled up. The world swung about her for a moment, and she vomited; it splashed in the dust and grit. By some blessing she didn't get any on her body or on her torn and soiled nightdress, but her lips were slick with it, and her mouth tasted filthy to her. Cursing, the guardsman released her arms, leaving her to sway on her feet. She heard him walk away and then stop. Regina found that her dizziness had faded now that she'd retched, and she started working up enough saliva to spit.

"You're pathetic." The other woman's voice.

She opened her eyes. That woman standing before her—she knew her.

"Julia," she said flatly.

The baker's wife stood there with her arms folded beneath her breasts. She was no longer dressed as a woman of the Subura; she wore a gown of fine purple fabric, rarest of colors. In fact it was too rare—it was the kind of gown a woman of the equestrian class might wear if she wished to be seen as having patrician blood somewhere in her line.

Julia's eyes shone with a cold and bitter joy. She looked Regina over, assessing her, much as a domina might assess one of her house slaves who'd just received a beating for some infraction. Regina's face burned.

"I wonder if you have any idea," Julia said, "how sickening it was to me to see a slave girl queening it over the insula?"

"Brought—" Regina swayed, steadied, found her voice again. A cold, hard knot formed inside her. "I brought your husband broth when he was sick. I listened—tried to—when you felt alone."

"So you performed a slave's services, once or twice, and you think I should be *grateful*." Her eyes blazed. "Uppity slut. I know, you were happy there. In that—place. And you think I should've been happy too. Right? I suppose you *were* happy. After what you were, anything would be a step up. But I'm not like you, girl. My first husband—we *lived* on the lower slopes. We had a *villa*. We had two slaves. And all of that was *taken* from me. All of it." She blinked back tears furiously. "Do you think I *enjoyed* taking gifts of—of broth and—and pity—from that mad old man? Do you think I *enjoyed* living there? Do you think after what I've been, that I'd be *grateful* to you?"

"No." Her tone was cold. All the warmth had left her body. Julia's accent was equestrian again, and for an instant, at the sound of it, chains fell from the locks of closed doors in Regina's mind, and shrieking memories beat upon the doors like a thousand screaming dead. But then her blood drummed loud in her ears, louder than Julia's petty tone, and with the roar of her blood she heard Polycarp's deep voice, as though he stood before the doors in her memory, between her and the past that would devour her. His voice, telling her she was Regina of Rome, queenly and loved. And free. Brutus's softer voice, calling her *domina, domina.* And her own mind was still chanting ceaselessly against the brutal pain in her back, chanting the words, *I am Regina Romae, I am Regina Romae.*

The rattling of the doors stilled.

Rage burned hot in her body, rage so fierce she forgot even the pain that seared her. "No," she hissed. "No, you aren't like me." She lifted her head, meeting the other woman's eyes. How hateful the sight of Julia's cold smile seemed to her, and how small. "I'm bound here for your amusement, and I see you *are* amused. But I know who I am now. I *know* who I am. You—that gown you wear is nothing more than a costume. A part you'd like to play. It doesn't change who you *are*, Julia."

Julia's face contorted. "The praetor didn't order you lashed," she blurted. "*I* asked the guardsman for that."

Regina smiled thinly. "How nicely did you ask him, Julia?"

With a small shriek, Julia drew back her hand for a slap, but Regina was quicker; she caught the other woman by the wrist, tightened her fingers cruelly. For a moment she held Julia's eyes with hers. Everything in her became hard ice. "Don't—*ever*—touch me."

She squeezed her grip, and Julia's face twisted in pain. Regina held her eyes. "You should leave Rome, Julia. Tonight."

Then a hand clamped over Regina's shoulder, and she cried out as the hard fingers crushed down on a welt. Regina released her grip on Julia, hissing through her teeth. White as death, Julia backed away. Her mouth worked as though she wanted to say something. After a moment, though, she just turned and moved away at a brisk clip, retreating without a glance over her shoulder.

The guardsman turned Regina, and she glared up at him. Drew the back of her hand across her lips, wiping away flecks of vomit. At least the vomit had cleaned his kiss out of her mouth. "What now?" she asked coldly.

His eyes narrowed. Without warning, he struck her.

She found herself on her belly in the dust, her ear and the right side of her face ringing. She retched again, then sobbed with pain.

"Mouthy bitch." The guardsman's hand gripped her hair, lifted her to her knees. Her vision was a little gray, and the ringing in her ear was louder. "Be glad you're Brutus's," the man muttered.

Then the world dimmed fast as a flame dying at the end of a wick, and she blacked out.

***

"I am sorry," Brutus whispered, his back against the door in the darkened shed. "I am so sorry."

Regina lay on the straw. For the moment she lacked the strength to rise, even to her knees. She didn't look at Brutus but stared at the boards of the roof. She was not a whore. No matter how many times they whipped her, she was not a whore. She was Regina Romae, and there were people who looked to her and depended on her. Brutus was looking to her, at this very moment. "Your hand didn't wield the lash," she murmured.

"My hand didn't prevent it."

"Stop," she whispered. "Please just stop. I blame you for nothing." She shifted slightly and immediately regretted even that small movement; the pain that lit in her back forced a moan from her. She was breathing hard for a moment. The strength she'd shown when driving Julia from the courtyard had passed; tossed into the dark of this shed, shaking from pain and reaction, she was again awash with fears of what would happen—to her, to Polycarp, to all of them.

"You're the only reason I'm not raped and beaten whenever one of them is bored," she whispered. "Don't blame yourself for the things you can't do anything about."

At this moment she couldn't bear the thought of comforting another human being. She needed the guardsman to be a strong presence, someone to lean on for a moment while she recovered her breath.

Brutus came and sat by her.

"I used to watch my father beat this girl," he said quietly. "One of the house slaves. Her flesh would be cut up—so badly. I used to bring her wine afterward, hoping it would help. I will never forget her eyes." His voice was thick with remembered pain. "I was very young, domina. I would have liked to have stayed my father's hand, though it would have dishonored him, and myself. I would have liked to have said, *No more, no more. This is unjust, father.* When I heard Father Polycarp speak that one night, I understood why—why I'd wanted to stop my father so badly. But the truth is I never did."

They were silent for a while, he with his guilt, she with her pain and her struggle to retain her certainty of herself. It was as though a pit had opened beneath her and she was falling in. Polycarp would be tried and burned; the ten prisoners from the insula would likely be burned afterward without trial, herself among them. She had no refuge other than the kindness of this guardsman who knew the sign of the fish. And she lay in filthy straw in a tattered garment, beaten like a whore, and could extend refuge to no one.

She had not felt such an emptiness, such a weight of helplessness in many years, not even when she'd been carried bound up the streets of the Palatine with the hungering dead in pursuit. Her eyes were sore with crying. Every part of her body was sore, the outside and the inside. She thought of the prisoners in the other sheds. She knew each of them by name; she'd sat with them many afternoons, listening to their hopes and fears. She'd held the women close while they wept for the brutality and poverty of their lives. She'd given the men words of hope and courage when she found their shoulders slumped and their eyes defeated. She had given them advice when they had disputes or were simply angry with each other. She'd brought bread or broth up to them when they were sick. She had lifted their cares to her shoulders and carried them with her to Polycarp, all through the four years she'd lived as Regina Romae, the deaconess. She had been their refuge, as Polycarp had been hers. She was responsible for them. Her hands trembled. They were her children, yet she could do nothing to save them. The despair of it racked her, tore her more savagely than the whip had.

"Is Marcus all right?" she whispered.

"He is."

Another silence. Anger began to crackle again in her heart. "Julia came," she whispered. "To see me. After the lashing."

"The spy?" Brutus's voice dripped with loathing. "I'm surprised she's still in Rome."

That caught her attention. "Why?"

A low growl beside her, in the dark. "Caius deeded to her husband a villa in Arpinum, one that's been city property for a while."

Regina's hands curled, making claws of her fingers. A villa. All for a villa of her own. "I think she's a witness," she said after a while. "At the trial. I think that's why she's here."

"The praetor doesn't even need witnesses. With the dead on the hill, everyone's crying out for blood, someone to blame. He'll burn the father tomorrow. He won't need witnesses to get a majority vote from the jury, and a majority vote is the most he'll need, because he'll claim that without papers, the father has no citizenship." He grunted. "But he does *want* witnesses. We're supposed to talk with all the prisoners about it."

"About witnessing?" She looked on him with horror.

Brutus gazed back at her, in the dark. "Caius is offering freedom—for the witness. On condition of exile from Rome after the trial. No one's taking him up on it."

She laughed softly, then wept as the laughter made her welts burn again. "He doesn't understand. We can't be bought."

"He bought Julia."

"That's different," she murmured. "She's not of the gathering. She just lived at our insula. Polycarp gave her a place to stay when her husband shut her from his villa, and later she married a baker, who moved in with her." Her anger cooled as abruptly as it had risen, and she found only sorrow in its place. "She was never really happy. I thought it was because she missed her first husband on his hill. I didn't understand her, Brutus."

He watched her a moment. "Don't blame yourself for the things you can't do anything about," he said.

Regina began to cry softly. "I'm sorry," she sobbed after a moment. "I'm sorry." She turned on her side to try to hide her face, but moaned sharply at the pain.

She heard him shift in the dark. "Is there anything I can bring you, deaconess? There are other things in the station to eat besides bread and wine. I can bring you something more, I think. Decius and the others—they'll just think I'm—infatuated."

She smiled amid her tears. He was trying to cheer her. But she needed more right now than a pastry to eat. "Pray with me," she whispered.

He took her hand in his; his was large and calloused. Softly as though he might break them, he murmured the words:

Phos hilaron hagias doxes, athanatou Patros,
ouraniou, hagiou, makaros, Iesou Christe

"Joyous light of the deathless Father's holy glory..." The words fortified her heart; in this dark shed with its dirty straw, they seemed especially precious. So many times in the evenings, she had seen Polycarp stand in the insula's tiny atrium by the lilacs, looking at the sky, intoning those words in a Greek so musical you could cry listening to it. She gripped Brutus's hand briefly and managed the next words of the prayer with only one quick break in her voice:

elthontes epi ten heliou dysin, idontes phos hesperinon,
hymnoumen Patera, Hyion, kai Hagion Pneuma, Theon.

"Having come upon the sun's setting, having seen the evening light, we praise in song..." Brutus whispered back:

Axion se en pasi kairois hymneisthai phonais aisiais

And Regina recited the final line, her voice strengthening:

Hyie Theou, zoen ho didous, dio ho kosmos se doxazei.

"Worthy it is at all times in all seasons to praise you with glad voices, God's Son, Giver of Gifts, Giver of Life, for which the world glorifies you."

God is the Giver, she whispered in her heart. *Made in God's likeness, we are not mere gifts to be given but givers ourselves. We are givers: we must remember we are givers.*

"Thank you," she told Brutus, then added to the prayer: "I trust you can hear us, for I know Polycarp trusts you and that you hear him. Be our refuge in this hour."

A calm settled over her; freed of its despair, her mind began to plan. For a few moments she didn't even feel the pain in her body; she simply tallied accounts in her mind, as she so often had as deaconess in the insula. Then everything clicked into place with total clarity.

"Brutus," she said, "you must get me in to see Caius Lucius."

He shifted beside her. "Why?"

"You said he wants witnesses."

"He does. What are you thinking, domina?"

Deep beneath the calm that lay over her, something within her ran screaming into the smallest corner of her mind at the prospect of what she had to do. The rest of her was cold and still and clear.

"I need to be there in the temple when Polycarp is tried," she said. "I need to be a witness."

In the silence, she could hear Brutus breathing in the dark.

"Someone needs to counter Julia's testimony," she explained, "someone needs to stand with him. I need to be there—tell Caius Lucius I will stand witness. Tell him I will say whatever he pleases. I was a slave once; he will believe it of me. Tell him the lashing broke me. If you have to, tell him you had me, that you beat me afterward, until I begged to be a witness. I don't care what you say—just please get him to see me."

Brutus's eyes were pale, and for a long moment he chewed the inside of his cheek. When he spoke, his tone was hesitant. "These lies are the same as the ones I tell to the other guardsmen—that I come to the shed to make you my whore. But it troubles me to lie to the urban praetor. I heard the father speak once. He said, 'better to die than to speak untruth.'"

Regina's eyes flashed. "I will speak a small lie to one man so that I can speak the truth to many. This thing has to be done." Panic welled up within her. She *had* to be there, at that trial. "Brutus. Brother. Please. We are all God's actors on this stage of the world. There is a time when we must tear aside all the masks, let everyone see each other as they really are. That time's tomorrow, at that trial. But we have to wear our costumes, play our parts, until then—to get there. Please." Her voice quivered but did not break. "Please—you must do this. Please. The father mustn't stand alone." With a moan of pain, she lifted herself from the straw; Brutus pressed a hand to her back and helped her sit up, though his touch on the welts made her scream again.

She sat there, breathing. Then she lifted her shoulders, took a graceful sitting posture, folded her hands in her lap. "Will you do it?" she whispered against the pain.

"I will," he murmured.

Regina closed her eyes, the relief nearly unbearable. Polycarp. She would see Polycarp. When he defended the gathering, she would stand beside him.

Brutus looked at her in the dark. There was a touch of awe in his tone. "I never knew a woman could be so brave."

"Then you haven't known many women. We endure much for the ones we love." She drew a slow breath. "Please go now and tell the praetor."

He hesitated.

"Please, Brutus. I want to be alone."

When he'd left, Regina sat very still for a while in this shed that had become an unexpected refuge, guarded as it was by Brutus, a quiet place where she could rest in the dark and search her own heart. She searched her heart now. She had been a slave once. She had been a slave a long time. A man had come and freed her, given her a warm coat and a place of safety. He had reached into the empty dark and found her heart there and cupped it in his hands and pulled her near, to where there was light and warmth. She closed her eyes. The full import of what was going to happen slammed into her there, in the dark. She almost couldn't breathe with the dread of it. Fresh tears burned her eyes. They were going to kill him. Father Polycarp. Her Polycarp. They were going to burn him. And likely her as well, and the others, all those imprisoned in the other sheds. Phineas, who wrote letters every week to his three sisters in Nola and who amused and sometimes annoyed his neighbors with his obsessive fear of balding. Philemon, with his paints and his longing for a wife. Hadassah the Jewess, who had the most beautiful singing voice, though no one outside the insula had ever heard it. They were all so precious to her. Their need for her in this hour called to her. She was Regina Romae, and the men and the women of the gathering depended on her. That was the truest thing she knew, and the truth of their need, and the truth of hers—a sign of the need of every living person for shelter and succor—lit in her like a fire. Alone in the dark, she wept quietly, and prepared herself.

***

It was a surprisingly small office for the urban praetor, hardly much larger than the shed, and Regina found she had to close her eyes and force slower breathing; the walls seemed to close in on her. She stood before the praetor's desk with her arms at her sides. Each time she took a breath, the slight movement lit fires in her back. Her face was still moist from her tears, and it was all she could do to stand and keep from wincing. But she stood very straight. She would show no weakness she did not have to.

She considered him. The praetor's toga was perfectly, impeccably draped about him, as though he meant to appear as flawless and orderly as a marble statue—but his face was dark about the eyes, and his left eye was bloodshot.

This was a man who clearly didn't sleep much. Nor did he look up from his scrolls and scraps of parchment. He did that to intimidate her, she supposed. As though she were barely worth notice.

Her fingers gripped the dirtied fabric of her nightdress firmly. She would *not* be intimidated.

"Our informant had mentioned you to me as one Dora Syriacae, a manumitted slave." Now he did glance up, his eyes cold. He leaned forward slightly in his seat.

"A manumitted slave." He said the words slowly. "Yet you have no papers on your person. So I must express my doubt, Dora, that you are really free. Are you?"

"I have been free since the day I met Polycarp," Regina said softly.

Yet she was breathing too fast. Now that she was here, standing before this togate incarnation of patrician Rome, feeling his judging eyes on her as he sat beneath the rows of his medals and behind the hard weight of his official desk, she found that she was standing again over a dark pit of doubt. Did she believe the words of the hymn she'd sung with Brutus? Did she believe in the promise of a restored world to come, a world made new—justice for the impoverished and the homeless no less than for the residents of hill-slope villas, the dead at peace, loved ones long parted brought back together? In that moment, standing before the praetor's desk, with the lines of the lash on her back and fresh on her heart last night's memory of the shambling dead and the nightmarish proximity of that long-ago cargo hold on a half-floundering slave ship, she didn't know. She gripped the fabric at her hips more tightly. Perhaps the world was, after all, only what the Romans said it was: a world where the strong used the weak and the cunning used the naïve, among both gods and mortals. A world where things lost remained lost, and things eaten remained eaten. She wanted to cry out at the horror of it; she pressed her lips into a thin line.

"I am free," she said.

She *must* believe, because Polycarp did. To voice or acknowledge her doubts now would be a betrayal of him.

"Perhaps I *am* unimportant to you," she said, with forced calm. "No more than a former slave whose legality you question. But I can be useful to you, Caius Lucius. I would like to serve as a witness, in return for proper papers." His face showed no change in expression; neither did she blink. She kept her voice measured and rational. "Father Polycarp is an elderly man. His *dignitas* is very great. Is it usual to bring old men and wise to a trial? You may not be able to convict him without some ignominy, Caius Lucius."

"I'll manage," Caius said drily.

She looked at his eyes, found something there that startled her. "You haven't seen him yet," she breathed.

He frowned as though puzzled by her manner. "Seeing his followers first is instructive." A note of caution now in his tone.

Regina laughed suddenly; it welled up inside her, in a flood of relief, and she couldn't keep it silent. Caius's face darkened, and strength rushed back into Regina, a pouring like water into a cup, until she was filled with it. For a moment she kept laughing. How he sat there—so proud! Like the Nemean lion after feasting on an antelope. She fought for breath and loosened her fingers, letting the folds of her nightdress slip free from her hands. For a moment she stood straight as a queen. Well. Caius Lucius was about to meet *Polycarp* and no antelope. Let him condemn the father if he dared. Regina's face shone; her heart was so full. Polycarp was greater than this small and frightened man. He was greater than the dead that had pursued her the previous night. He and his God. He was greater than the slave ship that had carried her—for he'd taught her that she might have a new name. Even when this little praetor burned her man, Polycarp would still be greater than this moment, and she was suddenly, fiercely certain that the gathering would never forget his memory. She took full breaths. She *believed*.

Caius's face had flushed. He lifted his hand; Brutus took a step toward Regina. She lowered her eyes, her head. Her heart racing. Her laughter had endangered her. She must appear the frightened slave. "Pardon me," she whispered, taking the flame of hope within her and cupping it in her hands, trying to dampen its light to other eyes. "I meant no disrespect, praetor urbanus. I laugh because I am near fainting. I have been lashed, Caius Lucius Justus, and left without food or water. The strain is very great, too much for a woman."

His eyes were watchful. Regina thought fast. She had come playing the role Caius expected to see her in, but the praetor was a shrewd man. Now she had to look every inch the broken slave. "I know you're suspicious of me, Caius Lucius," she said softly. "But I—I don't—I don't want to be a slave again. I can't. I *can't*." Her face twisted; she summoned to the surface of her heart the very real pain that the thought of a return to slavery caused her, and trembling, she showed that pain to Caius openly, vulnerably. The risk of it—of being so vulnerable before this man—made it difficult for her to breathe. Regina let her hair cover her face, keeping her expression hidden. That afforded her some sense of shelter from his eyes and perhaps only made her appear more broken.

She felt the praetor's gaze on her for a long, silent moment.

"You'll have your papers," the praetor muttered at last. She heard him sigh. "You are right that we need witnesses. This trial must be conducted with all the proper piety. You will confess," he suggested, "that you have all eaten flesh, at his behest."

Her shoulders jerked slightly. "I will."

"You will also give witness that he abducted young Romans of good family, that he—"

"I will say whatever will please you, Caius Lucius," she whispered. "For the price I've mentioned."

Caius sat very still, measuring her with his eyes. "Very good."

Regina lifted her own eyes. The praetor's face was pale; no, this man didn't sleep much. Or laugh. Or smile. To her surprise, she felt a stab of pity for Julia, but it was a cold pity. Julia too had stood before this man's eyes. But when Julia had stood in this place, she had taken the praetor's judgment, his assessment of her, and taken it into her heart. Regina could well imagine how Caius Lucius Justus had gazed at Julia, the baker's wife and once the wife of an equestrian merchant of the lower slopes. Caius would have seen a woman who had tumbled downhill, draining into the Subura, a decayed citizen, barely a Roman, barely more than a riverside whore. How his eyes must have tormented Julia! With what rage Julia must have hurried then to find someone lower than herself, someone who could be lashed and judged in her stead. With what need she must have begged the guardsman to chain Regina to the whipping post. How desperate Julia must be now, how fierce her hope that a purple gown and a spacious villa would make her the domina she longed to be. But being a domina was not a matter of the clothes you wore or the space you inhabited. It was a matter of your relationships with others, how you treated others in the shared theater of your lives. It was about your capacity to give gifts and inspire others to give too.

Caius's cold eyes shook Regina too. But Polycarp had not looked at her so. Strengthened by her pity, Regina met the praetor's eyes for an instant, looked *in* them rather than *at* them. Saw the empty pain, like the reflection of a desert—and a vulnerability deeper than her own. As their eyes met, Caius's brow creased. He leaned hard on his desk, and something shut just behind his eyes, sealing away the emotion. Yet he kept gazing at her—not judging now, but intense, focused.

"How odd," he murmured after a moment. "You almost remind me of—" His lips thinned.

"Who was she, dominus?" Regina asked. She shivered once at using the word *dominus*—it nearly caught in her throat. But she had a tight grip on herself now; her four years of freedom would not crumble about her at a single word. And the word, like her deferent tone, had the effect she hoped for: it set Caius at ease. He looked distracted. As though he were confiding in a house slave in a moment of indiscretion. Perhaps it was the first time he'd confided in anyone in many years. It was perhaps the first time in years that he'd spoken with a woman beyond offering a polite greeting as he passed in the Forum.

"My wife," he said softly, after a few moments had passed. "She was my wife." He did not even seem to notice that Regina was still there; he was speaking to something or someone he heard in the silence of his own heart.

Regina noted again the medals on the wall, the perfectly swept floor, the crispness of the toga Caius wore, though his face showed the strain of little sleep. A moment's sadness found her. Whoever that woman had been, she surely would not have wanted to be mourned in this way—coldly and without memory of joy.

"I grieve with you," she said.

Even as Caius's eyes kindled, she knew that had been the wrong thing to say and the wrong tone to say it in. This was not a room in Polycarp's insula, and this man was not one of Polycarp's tenants. This man was proud and lethal, and he did not recognize in her a deaconess to confide in.

"Do you?" His voice was like unsheathed steel. No longer was he distracted or bemused; his entire body was tensed.

"I—" Regina groped for something to say, something she might have said, if she were truly a slave. Panic ran cold through Regina's body. What if in that lapse of caution, in presuming an intimacy with the praetor, what if she had tossed away her chance? "Forgive me."

"How *dare* you pity me," the praetor hissed. "You are nothing but a *pleasure slave*—wearing her mistress's nightdress! You grieve with me? You?" His face went livid, and Regina's heart beat frantically as Caius rose to his feet, his body taut with fury. "Get out of here," he said. "Slave. I serve *Rome*. I have *fought* in her wars. I've cleaned her streets. I've seen her most unmentionable parts and draped my cloak about her naked shoulders. I've lost family to her, lost honor, lost—" He paused, panting. For a moment he shook, visibly. His voice sank almost to a whisper as he wrestled with something within himself. "I have not served her these many years to frivol away my time conversing with whores and desecrators of tombs." He gestured for the guardsman. "She knows her task. Get her out of here."

Her task. The trial. Regina lowered her head, slave-like, but she'd gone breathless with relief. She was not just to be tossed back into the shed; she would be at the trial, she would have the chance to speak, to see Polycarp, to stand at his side. Dizzied, she felt Brutus's touch at her arm, as though to steer her, but he didn't close his grip. As Caius lowered his eyes to his papers, dismissing her, she took careful steps toward the door, not wishing to fall. She would see Polycarp. She would be able to speak for him. Her blood ran hot with elation; she lifted her head, even as Brutus guided her through the door and into the fierce August sunlight. She had done it! Whatever happened to her now, it would happen to her at Polycarp's side. She would defend him, and the gathering, speaking the truths Rome didn't want to hear. Let them *try* to silence her then! She was no slave. She might have only a moment, but she would take that moment. And speak what was in her heart, before all the world.

***

In the sunbaked arena of Justitia's courtyard, all eyes were on the drama being played out on the sand: the cold, furious eyes of the urban praetor; the eyes of the guardsmen tight with alarm and continually glancing to the temple gate and the sounds of moaning beyond it; the troubled eyes of the lictors who stood to either side of the curule seat like living props, and of the jurors, who sat on their benches as the eyes and ears of Rome's upper castes. As the woman walked slowly across that open space, the other two who stood there before the praetor's seat had their eyes fixed on her as well. Julia looked bewildered, seeing who approached. Polycarp looked stricken.

"Regina," he breathed. Caius had summoned *Regina* as a witness? How could this be? For a moment the father faltered. If Regina would not stand the test, then he had surely failed utterly, and the Romans were proven right after all: take the head, and the body of the gathering would stumble. Polycarp's legs failed him, and he found himself kneeling in the dust, his vision blurred with hot tears. Inside the heavy silence of his heart, he cried to his God. *Truth flits from our hands, and there is no faith in us.*

Despair crouched behind him; he could feel the heat of its breath, he could smell the cold-creek clearness of its body. Its paws rested heavy on his shoulders; its maw gaped for him. Hungrier and emptier than the craving dead.

"Regina," he whispered. Doubts tore through him, driven on a high wind that made his thoughts leap and spin inside him.

Regina stopped when she reached him and took her place to stand a few strides from where he knelt, between him and the other witness.

"Dora Syriacae." That was the stern, cold voice of the praetor. "You stand before a jury of Roman citizens, charged with judging a man who may stand under penalty of death. You stand also under penalty if any false word escapes your mouth, for you speak within the grounds of the temple of Justitia, most sacred among goddesses. Will you speak verity and truth, Dora Syriacae?"

"I refuse that name," she said quietly. "I will bear witness to what I have seen, praetor urbanus, but I will not answer to that name."

Polycarp heard the steel in her voice. Heat built within him, blunting the sharp edge of grief and sending wild energy coursing through his body, as though he were translated from a man to a lion. With a growl he sent the beast that crouched behind him slinking away and forced himself back to his feet. He had no time left; therefore, he had no time for despair. He blinked the moisture from his eyes and saw in a blur Regina standing straight as a pillar near him, her eyes dark and her face dry of tears. She wore the same nightdress she'd worn the night the dead came to the insula, but now it was filthied and dirtied, and torn and tattered at the back. Yet she stood very straight, and he caught his breath at the loveliness of her.

Caius stared at her from his curule chair, frowning. He looked taken aback by her manner. "Tell us what you've seen, then," he said.

For a long moment she stood silent. The jurors were silent too, gazing at the witness. The moaning in the city outside the walls of justice was the only sound. A hot gust of wind rushed into the courtyard, lifting dust and driving it across the compound in gray clouds; Polycarp felt the dust coat his legs, dry and gritty.

She lifted her head, looked across the courtyard at Polycarp. Their eyes met. The wind lifted Regina's hair and tugged at the torn strips of her nightdress. In her eyes, Polycarp saw pain and desperation; then, though he was not touching her shoulder or her face with his hand, her eyes *opened* to him, and he gazed inside the rooms of her heart, as he so often had gazed into the eyes of the walking dead. He saw rooms that were locked and chained; he could almost hear the screams behind those shut doors. He saw other rooms that were vast and wide as oceans; in one, her love and faith in him, a faith so profound and unshakable that it shook him to see it. In another room, the many moments when she'd held others in her arms and given them refuge, and the love, deep and maternal and fierce, that she bore now toward each of those she'd sheltered. He saw her loss at having borne no children, and her joy at having found children in the men and women who lived in the insula under Polycarp's care. He saw her determination to preserve them—and him—a resolve that was like a hard, cold wall of rock in her heart.

She turned back to Caius.

"I cannot say what you wish me to say," she said hoarsely. Quivering with the intensity of her emotion. "The dead are eating the city, and you want me to malign *Polycarp*—Rome's one *good* man—and the man who is trying to help you—even while the dead moan outside that wall. I cannot. Not even if you offered every other believer in Rome amnesty could I playact this farce."

She turned to face the jurors, and her voice rose, her eyes shining with rage. "I will *tell* you what I've witnessed. The ancient families close themselves within windowless walls as though stepping early into their tombs; and Roman men and Roman women scream in hunger and illness outside, while those within choose to hear nothing. I've witnessed a woman sell the lives of those nearest to her so that she can wear a finer garment. I've seen men who buy women for less price than you would buy a toga, and beat them until they can neither stand nor sit. I've seen men buy children too." Her voice rose louder and higher, carrying with sharp clarity across the courtyard. "I've seen a woman beat her slave for taking a bite of her bread without permission, while at home that slave's children are but skin stretched thin across their ribs and can't sleep for hunger. You hurl your filth and your sewage and your shit down on us, and then you look across the hills with your self-satisfied faces and don't even glance down at the people whose faces you've smeared with your stinking offal. You accuse us of the desecration of your dead, but day upon day, you *desecrate* the living!"

"Have a care, Dora," Caius growled, his eyes filled with shock.

"*You* have a care. You think I am the only witness to stand here?" Rage had translated her; her face shone, and every line of her body was tense with the violence within her. Her voice rose nearly to a shriek; she gestured at the gate and the groaning beyond it, which sounded nearer than it had before. "Your fathers witness it. They witness everything. They see what you do, and what you don't. They were never so callous as you are; they are ashamed of you. They are ashamed of how you've defiled their memory. How you leave your neighbors dying and uncared for. You deserve to have them lurching out of their tombs to devour you!"

"Be still!" Caius rose from his seat, his face white.

"I will *not* be still! Lash me, Caius Lucius Justus, if you wish! Here before all these men. Show them how a Roman praetor administers justice! But I will not say what you wish to hear. You are contemptible, a small and shrunken man presiding over a small and shrunken city that was once great."

She paused. Her eyes burned; her face was dark with fury. The groans outside were indeed nearer, and loud, as though the dead had come to witness as well, to confirm Regina's words and give their own wordless but vocal condemnation. A few of the jurors cast uneasy glances at the temple gate; the rest couldn't look away from Caius's witness.

Polycarp gazed at Regina with astonishment and pride. He hadn't known what strength she kept locked in her heart. How could he have doubted her?

Julia's eyes were round with shock. She drew in a breath to speak, but before she could say a word, Regina rounded on her fiercely. "*You* have had your say. We've heard you already. We know your quality now, Julia. You chose to serve something small. I've chosen to serve something great. I've been a slave; I will never again serve anything so small that it can fit in my heart without filling me so full that I can serve only with tears of joy."

Julia visibly withered under Regina's eyes. She swayed on her feet, as though she might faint. Her eyes looked to the jurors, then the silent lictors in their line by Caius's curule seat—so many witnesses as she was berated by a former slave. Her face went dark with shame, and she said nothing. She appeared on the verge of tears.

The jury, too, were silent, watching Regina with startled faces. It was possible that they—and most Romans—had never heard a woman speak this way, in public, in open and unconcealed anger. Certainly none of them had ever heard such a declaration from a slave. Such was the force of Regina's voice that they could not think of her as a slave, one who should be lashed for temerity; such words could only be spoken by one who was free, terribly free, more free than most women they knew, more free than most men. A few looked stricken, as though her words had stung them and called them to account; in Regina's face, streaked with dirt and sweat yet hard and intent, some saw the very face of Justitia, her blindfold removed, her eyes hot with wrath and demanding their response. Others shifted in their seats, unsettled, trying to grope for that rage they'd held clutched so tightly only a few moments ago. Their rage had been stolen from them; this woman had walked into the courtyard with an anger more just and more articulate, and in the face of it, the jurors found themselves fumbling. The moans of the dead surged suddenly loud in their ears, and a few began to sweat.

Marcus's eyes were shining. The dampened coals that all day had sat heavy in his chest had now blazed into new fire. Whatever happened this day, the jurors would remember it. They would never forget Polycarp or Regina, or the obligation of hearing and action that their testimony had placed on each of them. His shoulders firmed with that certainty and with the determination to persist in the work these two had begun.

Caius's face was pale, and his voice had lost much of its volume. "Citizens on the jury, pardon my idiocy in summoning as a witness this—this slave and whore. I think it's time we—"

Abrupt and loud, a new sound swept into the courtyard, interrupting him: the cries of geese on the wing. The jurors, Polycarp, the praetor, the witnesses, the guardsmen—for a moment all their faces tilted back and gazed at the sky. Against the glare of the sun and the cloudless heat of the heavens, a dark *V* was flapping swiftly overhead, moving south out of the city. For many heartbeats, they all watched the geese departing. The day was hot; it was too early for a winter flight. It was as though the sacred geese were fleeing a city they could no longer live in, a city no longer worthy of their warning. Or perhaps the flight itself was their last warning.

When the *V* had disappeared behind the roof of the temple, with Justitia's blind face staring sightlessly after them, all was quiet in the courtyard, though the dead still moaned in the street without. Caius's hands shook. "We are done," he said after a moment, even his voice hushed and dismayed. "Give your verdict."

THE APOSTLE'S GIFT

AS THE DEAD WAILED just outside the temple walls, the first juror stood. It was the young man, the one who'd screamed at Polycarp when he entered. Polycarp met his eyes, and the youth glanced down. "*Condemno*," he said quietly.

The second stood, his voice louder. "*Condemno!*"

"*Condemno!*"

"*Condemno!*"

One after the other, the jurors gave their sentences, some in urgent shouts, a few in quiet, almost ashamed voices. The unanimity was neither a surprise nor a disappointment to Polycarp. He let out his breath slowly; he had known, walking in through that wooden gate, that he entered a temple not to Justitia but to Timor. Fear alone was fed and worshipped here. For a few brief moments he couldn't hear the groaning in the street; the jurors' cries overwhelmed it. But then they were silent, and the moaning seemed even louder, as though it was right outside the walls.

One juror remained. A youth, a patrician—his aquiline nose proclaimed it. Slowly he rose to his feet to add his sentence. His eyes looked past the curule seat.

"*Absolvo*," Marcus said softly.

Polycarp sucked in a breath. Pride welled up fierce and hot in his chest and, following it, a wave of sorrow that made him close his eyes. *Marcus, Marcus.* That small act of enormous bravery would be unlikely to go unpunished.

The groaning of the dead seemed to rise from the very earth.

"Light the pyre." Cold resolve in Caius's voice.

Regina stiffened, and her face became very white. Polycarp simply watched as a lone guardsman strode to the pit to the right of the curule chair. For the first time, Polycarp saw that this one man held a torch; he'd held it, slow burning, all through the trial, but in the wild heat and brightness of this day, the Ides of Augustus, Polycarp had not noticed it. Now the guardsman bowed his head once to the statue of Justitia and tossed the torch in.

Flames leapt up from the pit, and the air above it shimmered; the temple wall glimpsed through that shimmer became like a painting of a temple wall left in the rain. Polycarp gave the flames a good look. To his own shock, he found in his heart no fear of the fire. He was too distracted, perhaps, by the moaning in the street. And though he felt the fire's warmth on his arms and face even from here, it was a small pit. Barely would a man fit within it; it was smaller than the baptismal pit Polycarp had once seen carved into the floor of a believer's cellar in Smyrna. "Do you light so small a fire to scorch a human life from the earth?" he asked. "Such an undertaking should require a furnace large as the sun."

"It is hot enough, desecrator," Caius said. "By the votes of the jury, you are condemned to—"

He was interrupted by the sound of something heavy thrown against wood; the noise echoed across the courtyard. The groans beyond the wall were terribly loud, making the hairs along Polycarp's arms rise.

Then a great thudding and slamming of flesh against wood, and all eyes swung to the gate to the temple grounds. The wooden door that barred it was rattling hard in its hinges. Even as the door had in Polycarp's dream. He froze, staring at it.

Caius, too, was staring. It was as though the praetor was not seeing the gate but was gazing at some personal horror private to his soul and his soul only— as if that personal horror had lurched now out of his heart and grown to a size monstrous and terrible. The guardsmen looked to him, but Caius gave no direction, only stood there with his face bled of all color. Two of the guardsmen glanced at each other. One of them nodded, and then they both sprinted for the gate. Even as they did, a wooden slat in the gate came loose, then broke; several pale hands reached through the gap, clawing. Fingers caught at the other boards, tearing and pulling, ripping pieces from the gate. The familiar, sickly stench of death came through the opening.

Outside, more groans erupted from what might have been a thousand throats. Polycarp's mouth went dry; it was all a man could do to listen to that sound without emptying his urine down his leg. The sight of the wooden gate leaping and bucking in its place as the dead tore it apart made his heart race.

Perhaps all the dead in Rome were outside that door.

There are too many hurts to heal, Despair hissed to him from where it perched now beside the curule chair.

Maybe, but a man can make a start. Polycarp took a step toward the failing gate. Even as he did, one of the guardsmen swept at the breach with his blade, and severed hands fell to the earth, but there were no cries of pain from without the door: only that low, anguished moaning. The dead tore away more of the wood, and the weakened frame buckled as their bodies slammed against it. Polycarp could see the empty eyes of the dead through the gaps.

In a voice almost more shriek than articulate words, Caius cried out: "Fire! Fire! Get him to the fire! Let his burning be an atonement to our dead!"

Polycarp's guardsman seized his arm—and the one remaining guardsman who hadn't sprinted for the gate, the one who'd held the torch, joined them also.

At that moment the gate crumpled, scraps of wood falling to the ground. The dead lurched through, arms upraised, their mouths open in the wordless wailing of their need. Their clothes were tattered; some wore nothing, their naked bodies mutilated with the terrible wounds made by gouging fingers or teeth. One of the guardsmen at the gate was dragged into the mass of the dead, his screaming cut quickly short. The other fought a retreat, sword out and flashing, but the dead seized him with many hands. As he struggled in their grasp, the corpse of a young woman missing the left side of her face tore into his throat with her teeth. Another of the dead bit away the guardsman's ear.

Julia and Regina's escorts left them and moved toward the gate, though what they might do against the tide of dead pouring through was unclear.

Polycarp's guardsmen stood very still, and Polycarp did also, unable to take his gaze from the bodies that were moving through the door and stumbling into the courtyard like a slow flood; behind those entering, the street was overwhelmed with dead: they were packed like sacks of grain in a merchant's hold. They swarmed to the door, arms lifted, beating on the ones before them, groaning in their need to get at the living.

A few of the jurors began to scream.

***

At the screams, Caius's body jolted. Every nerve in him came awake, every sinew went taut. His glanced at the jurors, Roman citizens for whom he was ultimately responsible. He had failed to protect and provide for his family, but in this moment, with the Emperor away, the Senate ineffective at best, and the dead coming through that door, he as senior justice stood in the role of *paterfamilias* for the vast family of Rome. The realization of this ran cold through his veins. For half a year he had been playing the role of the failed father to a failed son; but in this moment the screaming jurors, the lictors standing helpless, the guardsmen dying at the gate, and the guardsmen standing by Polycarp were all sons of Rome, all sons in need of their father.

Caius's snarl was feral. Shouting for the guardsmen to hold the gate, he snatched the bound rods from one of his lictors and tore loose the binding cloth. The narrow staves clattered to his feet, discarded symbols of office, but he retained two, one in either hand—thin, stout rods the length of a man's arm, with ends whittled to points. "Lictors, jurors, all of you—into the temple!" He could delay the dead while the others got inside and barred the temple door. His face livid, he strode toward the gate, even as the jurors darted past him, hurrying for the refuge of the temple. Moments before, Caius had stunk with fear; now that there was something visible and embodied to fight, his eyes burned with that cold violence that must once have kindled in the eyes of Caesar or Marius or Cato the Elder.

Caius spoke aloud to his ancestors as his steps carried him to that mass of swarming, hungering bodies. The stench of those bodies was overwhelming. "*Di parentes*," he said under his breath, "I am the last. The last *paterfamilias* of my house. Accept this sacrifice, this atonement. I will recover our honor. Fight with me. All you ancient Lucii, fight with me. I beseech you." With a cry, Caius broke into a run. He threw himself against the lurching crowd with a speed and ferocity that showed his military past; in his hands, the rods of office were both shield and thrusting weapons. With the length of a rod pressed to a corpse's throat, he held back the snapping teeth. A jerk of his hand shot the other rod's point into another corpse's skull. Even as the corpse's face slackened, Caius slid the stake free and leapt back, then stabbed again with both; two more dead slid to the ground. Hands grasped and clutched at his toga, and Caius spun, unraveling it from his body. The toga crumpled to the ground, to hinder the feet of the shambling dead; the Roman officer stood in his loincloth, brown gore dripping from the rods he held onto the trampled, sandy soil of the courtyard, his chest heaving, his face flushed, his short Roman hair damp with sweat.

The dead were closing about him, so many, their arms lifted to grab at him; in their midst he spun and stabbed, screaming hoarsely; two guardsmen, knives out, fought behind him. Caius called out the names of his ancestors, one after the other, as he spun and jabbed with the pointed rods. The names of his ancient and patrician house became battle cries as he cut into the dead. He felt their hands on him, then the sharp burn of teeth biting into his arm. Screaming, he turned and speared his rod into the creature's face. Then the others were dragging him down—such weight! He was pulled from his feet; almost he was on his back in the dust. He surged to his knees with a howl of panic and rage, one hand held immobile, the other striking, driving through one corpse's eye and into its skull, where the rod caught. He pulled at it wildly. At the weight of the corpse, the rod slid from his grip. Fingernails scraped at the back of his scalp, but his hair was too short to be gripped. Other hands caught his shoulders, his arms. Screaming, he was tugged down, their faces blocking out the sun above them—gashed and decaying faces, with ravenous, open mouths, Roman faces, old men and young men, daughters and matrons, patrician noses and the flatter noses of the Roman poor, all hissing and snarling, all ducking toward him to feed, all the Roman dead. Hands clawing at his body, fingernails digging sharply into his skin, gouging and tearing. A shriek of pain. He twisted, struggling to wrench his arms free of them, horror seizing him: the last of his house, devoured by these unclean dead; would his body rise from the earth to walk eating through the streets, unremembered and unrevered? *"Di parentes!"* he shrieked. Agony in the right side of his face, one of the dead biting into his cheek. *"Livius!"*

***

The guardsman's grip on Polycarp's arm tightened, and the father was pulled a step nearer the fire; it was very near now. The other guardsman was gazing at the disaster at the gate, and he was pale as a Celt, his eyes showing their whites. Caius's shouts could be heard above the groans of the dead.

In a quiet, cold voice, Polycarp said, "Do you really mean to burn me while your temple is overrun?"

The guardsman who held his arm didn't look at him. His voice, too, was carefully controlled. "I am a Roman. I do my duty."

"So do I," Polycarp said grimly.

The heat of the fire on his face was like a second noon sun. Fear and anger and shame rushed through him like some dark alcohol, muddying his mind. He would burn then, as the dream had warned. And he had achieved nothing. The dead had come and would devour everyone here. What did it matter then, that his words and Regina's had shaken the jurors, or that seeds had been planted in unready hearts? Those seeds would not last the day.

Cursing, the guardsman gripped both of the old man's arms and began to move him across the dust—only to draw up short. A long knife was pressed sharply to his throat, the blade glinting in the sunlight.

"No more." The other guardsman's words were hardly louder than a whisper. "Keys. Now."

The guardsman who held Polycarp didn't move, didn't release his prisoner's arms. His eyes just flicked from one side to the other. His adam's apple twitched slightly, just above the knife. "Cassius had them."

The other man's gaze shot back to the gate, and he cursed. "All right, let him go."

Polycarp felt the grip on his arms release, and he stepped to the side, unsteady on his feet. The cracking voice of the fire and the heat of its hunger on his face made him feel faint. He stepped back, saw the two guardsmen, the younger one now removing his knife from the other's throat. Beyond them, the dead were milling about the other end of the courtyard; they had dragged Caius beneath them and were feeding. But already a couple of them, unable to get at the meat that was twisting and shrieking on the dry ground, were turning and stumbling toward Polycarp and the guards. And others appeared to have some of the jurors trapped in a corner. Polycarp couldn't see Regina or Marcus or Julia. He began to pray softly under his breath.

The younger guardsman stepped to him, took the prisoner's right wrist, began picking the lock on the manacle. Polycarp could feel the rattle of it all the way up his arm. He stood with the fire at his back, begrudging every second that kept him from moving to face that crowd of dead, from moving to help his people.

"Brutus—" The other guardsman stood by, his face aghast.

"Shut up." Brutus wrenched the manacle free of Polycarp's wrist and dropped it; it dangled at the end of the chain from his other wrist. His eyes met Polycarp's; they were wide with fear and there was a plea in them. "We need you, father," he said softly.

In the next instant two of the dead were upon them, hissing; Brutus leaped back, and the other guardsman plunged his own knife into one's chest; the thing seized his arm, and the guardsman let out a screech of fear that would have shamed him in any place or any moment other than this one.

"Not yet time to rest," Polycarp murmured. Taking up the chain in his left hand, he lifted his right and stepped between the hired guardsman and the dead.

***

Even as Caius threw himself into the dead, Julia froze, her face white, staring at the approaching corpses. "Come on!" Regina cried to her. The deaconess glanced wildly about the courtyard, taking in the temple door, the jurors rushing past the blind statue and through it, and Polycarp standing between the guardsmen near the fire. Some of the dead were very close, lurching and stumbling, and they came between Polycarp and the witnesses. Several turned toward Julia and Regina, closing on them, hands reaching, clutching—it was like that night fleeing the Subura, except here in the bold sun the dead looked more terrible, because they looked more human. Not silhouetted shapes looming in the dark, but bodies horribly torn and broken, jaws slack in their moaning hunger.

Julia voiced a long whine of fear, still unmoving, and Regina grabbed her arm, her heart pounding. "Wake *up*!"

"They're inside," Julia whispered.

"It's what the man you betrayed wanted to *prevent*," Regina cried, wanting to scream in exasperation and fear, every nerve in her body sharp with the need for flight. She had to get Julia moving inside where she'd be safe, and she had to get to Polycarp.

The dead closed in, and Regina yanked Julia with her, scrambling back across the dust and grit. Julia came with her, shaking, and for a moment Regina felt pity pierce through her. Everything Julia had taken refuge in had shattered with that splintering of the temple gate.

"Come *on*, run!" Regina pulled Julia with her, stumbling toward the temple steps. One of the dead lurched to their side, and Regina sprang away, her heart pounding, not loosing her grip on Julia's arm, but the corpse reached in and seized Julia's hair. Regina heard Julia's shriek and kept pulling her, but the corpse held her, and then there were other corpses on them, hands grasping. Desperate, Regina drove her foot into one's shin, a panicked kick, but it didn't buckle or even wince, just hissed at her, its blind eyes fixed on her. Then the dead were fastened on Julia, strong hands pulling her back, tearing her from Regina's grasp; with a cry Regina fell back, other hands reaching for her.

"*Regina!*" Julia's shriek. "Caius—Regina—help me!" She had fallen, was on her belly; Regina caught a glimpse of the dead covering her, one dragging her back by her ankle, several crouching over her, one on top of her—she disappeared beneath them. Regina stumbled back, one of the dead pursuing her, then turning at Julia's shriek. One raw shriek, then nothing but the cracking and sucking sounds of the dead feeding. The corpse that had taken a step toward Regina hissed, then stumbled back to join the pack crouching over the other woman. Regina shook with horror, her hands trembling as though she were naked on the ice on a winter night.

She was gone. Julia was gone.

Just like that.

Gone—all of her regrets and her fears and her rage and her self-loathing and her bitterness, and any moment that had ever made her laugh or ever made her smile. Her husband, wherever he sheltered, was severed from her. She was gone. The suddenness of it was a spear of ice. There had been no moment to hold her as she died, or remonstrate with her, or curse her, or forgive her, or absolve her. She was simply gone, without farewell. Everything broken and unfinished. With a clarity as violent as lightning on a hill, Regina grasped the import of Polycarp's Gift as she never had before. To finish what had festered unfinished, to say goodnight, with grace, to those who had lain terribly awake. She stood stunned, gazing at the feasting dead where they hunched over that unseen body on the earth.

A hard hand grasped her arm, and she jumped. A voice at her ear. Marcus. "Come on! We have to hide!"

"No," she whispered. "We have to stand." Something in her hardened. "Where is he?" She ignored Marcus's pulling at her arm, his pale face; she scanned the courtyard. There. Her breath caught.

Father Polycarp was walking *toward* them. He was maybe twenty feet away, across the courtyard. He was walking in the midst of the dead, like Moses parting the sea. A haze of gold about his hair. His hands touched their shoulders or their faces, and with his gaze into their eyes, emptied bodies slid to the earth.

Yet there were so many. Even as Polycarp came near, several of the dead grasped the loop of chain that hung from one of his hands, pulling him toward their jaws; others grasped his shoulders. One bit deep where Polycarp's neck met the shoulder. A scream tore its way up Regina's throat, and she tried to leap toward him, but Marcus held her. "No!" the youth yelled in her ear.

"Let me go! He'll *die*!"

"It's too late!" he cried.

In panic, Regina slammed her elbow into his gut, then tore free. But even as she ran, she felt herself shoved to the side; then the guardsman, Brutus, was before her, swinging a great torch in his hand; she felt the warmth of it on her face. Grim, he lunged in, stabbing with the torch at the faces of the dead, who hissed and snarled and gave way before the heat. One's hair went alight, a woman whose eyes had been torn from her but whose mouth still gaped open, the gums drawn back from the teeth. The creature fell backward, its face wreathed in flames.

"Grab him!" Brutus yelled, reaching out himself, seizing Polycarp's shoulder and pulling him free of the dead, fending off their groping hands with the flames. They still tried to press forward, so many corpses with their mouths open and hungering, their hands grasping for a garment or anything to clutch. Regina took Polycarp's other arm and then they were dragging the father with them, falling back, the dead closing in from either side. Brutus danced from the left to the right and back, flailing the torch, stabbing with it when one of those things came too close. The smoke from the torch brought no tears to the corpses' eyes.

Marcus got beneath Polycarp's chest and heaved the old father up onto his shoulder, his face red with strain. Turning, he ran for the temple door, the dead grasping at his sleeve but not catching it as he passed. Regina hurried after, a glance over her shoulder to see Brutus with the dead half-closed about him. Waving that torch he must've plucked from the execution pit. "Go on!" he roared. "I'll follow! Go!"

Regina ran.

Her breath sobbed; a stitch burned in her side. There were snarling faces, grasping arms everywhere, to either side, a few dead now between her and Marcus and the door; but Marcus ducked and wove through them, staying free of their hands, shouting wordlessly in his fear and desperation. Then he was through and heaving his way up the marble steps, past the blind and unwatching Justitia.

The doors were ahead in their shadowed recess behind great pillars, and they were closing.

"Stop!" Regina screamed, but her voice was hoarse and small. Something grasped at a strip of her nightdress, but the strip tore free and then she was dashing up the steps, barefoot and disheveled, something inside her screaming at the sight of the blood running down Marcus's back from Polycarp's body.

Marcus reached the door and thrust his hand into the crack as it closed; a howl of pain, and then he got his other hand in the crack, Polycarp precariously balanced on his shoulder, and he was pulling the door open with a roar. Regina reached him and dug her own small hands into the space, gripping the cool cypress wood and pulling. There were frantic shouts within—jurors and lictors, some hysterical with fear. "No! You can't bring him in here! You can't bring him in here!" one of them was shrieking. "He brings the dead! You can't! You can't!"

Regina didn't dare glance over her shoulder; her heart might give out if she saw the moaning dead lurching up the steps behind them, hands outstretched. She put all of her small weight into wrenching open the door. Then a man's voice at her side snapped, *"Get back!"* and a hand thrust her head down. There was a great shove of the torch past her head and through the half-open door, and screams inside. The resistance against the door fell away and it swung open, and then a great hand on her back shoved her through. Regina tumbled inside into the dimness, crumpling to her knees, her breath rasping. Then Marcus was beside her, laying Polycarp on his back on the cool marble. She heard footsteps as the others inside fled farther back into the temple, away from the door. Brutus was shouting at the door, and there were snarls of the dead, the hiss and crackle of flame through the air, the snap of the door closing. Then a drumming of hands, a beating of dead hands on wood.

Regina was tearing a great strip from her dress, leaving what was left of it in tatters. Polycarp's life was pulsing out through the great gash at his shoulder— so much blood and life, spilling over the cold marble and then over her hand as she fought to press the cloth into the wound. His eyes, which had been open and gray and barely seeing, now squeezed shut, and the father groaned at the touch on his wound, a sound that terrified Regina with its weakness. She sobbed and pressed the cloth harder. "Help him," she cried to the others. "God, help him!"

***

Pain wild and hot at his throat and shoulder—Polycarp spun dizzily in the dark, panting softly. Eyes tightly closed, teeth clenched against the sharpness of the wound. A bit of cloth pressed there by someone's hand. Nearby there was pounding, relentless pounding, a drumming Polycarp not only heard but felt as a tremor in his body. Thick scents of incense and blood.

Others were crying out, voices moving about.

"Those doors won't hold!" Marcus's voice. That was Marcus.

"Quick!" A deeper voice. The guardsman who had grabbed him out there as he stood among the dead. "See if there are torches in the alcoves—we need more fire!"

"Wait! Barricade the doors first! Brutus! They're coming through!" Marcus's voice shrill with fear.

A cracking of wood, the guardsman cursing, then frantic slamming of objects against each other.

He was needed. He had to stand up. His master had told him to stand, and now the others needed him on his feet. But the pain beat in his throat and side, and he spun again into the dark.

A touch of gentle fingertips on Polycarp's cheek; for a moment he thought of his mother, now buried in a hillside plot far away in Thessaly above the fragrant sea. *It will take you to the one thing you need today, the one thing you need to do. Trust it.*

He coughed, his breath wheezing. Over his mother's voice he heard another woman's. He opened his eyes, saw through a haze of pain Regina's face near his, and above her a low, marble roof. An alcove along the side of the temple's interior, perhaps. It was dim in here.

He drew in breath raggedly.

"No. Don't you leave us! Please. Father. Polycarp." Her voice thick with tears. Regina's hand pressed cloth firmly into the wound at his throat; swallowing back the pain, he looked at her, saw her disheveled hair, her face shining with sweat, and her left shoulder naked and lovely. She had torn away a great strip of her already ruined nightdress, a wad of linen she now held pressed to Polycarp's throat; a flap of ragged fabric hung back over her breast, baring the top of it. Her skin shone softly in the faint sunlight coming in from somewhere above and to the right. He gazed at her in wonder, as though at a messenger in a dream. Her beauty and the vulnerability in her eyes had always called to him, had always been a temptation, but he had never known she was this lovely.

Polycarp drew in another breath, hissed at a flare of pain.

"Don't leave me," Regina whispered.

"I have done my work in the world," he rasped. Lifting his hand to her face, he felt the softness of her skin, held her eyes with his. A moment's regret and yearning swept through him, stronger than the pain, swift and fierce as a fire through wheat, and he almost cried out with the force of it. If he had walked other paths, met her in other circumstances, been other than who he was, she might have been his, and he hers.

But he had no time for regret.

He could feel the last strength leaking from him. He turned his eyes, glimpsed her hand red with his blood. He wet his lips enough to speak again. He could not stand any longer. He was too weak now to carry the Gift. He had to pass it on.

He struggled to speak clearly and to find the lines he must say; the world was still blurred, and that pounding he heard threatened to shake him right out of the world and into the empty dark. "The Apostle's Gift to me, I pass to you." He forced the words out, raised his voice loud enough to hear. "It is yours now to face the living and the dead, and bring them peace. I bless you and anoint you, Regina Romae, mother of the gathering in Rome, in the name of the Father, the Anointed One, and the Comforter of Our Souls."

Her eyes were round and moist. Her lips parted, her face translated in wonder: for the briefest instant Polycarp glimpsed a nimbus of soft light about her and saw a few strands of her hair rise from her head about his hand. His body felt suddenly lighter.

The Gift had been passed.

Regina drew a shuddering breath; the enormity of it filled her eyes.

"Tell Marcus—the others—to hope," Polycarp rasped. "Hope."

"I can't," she cried, taking his hand in hers, taking it from her cheek and pressing her lips to his fingers. Tears pooled in her eyes. "We *need* you," she whispered.

"What do you believe—Regina? What do you know to be true?"

The tears rolled down her face, leaving streaks in the sweat and dirt. "Nothing is broken that cannot be remade," she whispered after a moment, her clasp on his hand tight.

"Yes," he breathed. He was dizzy; Regina above him blurred. He closed his eyes a moment, opened them. Everything was faint. That pounding. And splintering—and hoarse shouts.

"Nothing is ill that cannot be healed." Regina's voice trembled. "Nothing captive that cannot be freed. Polycarp—" Her eyes pleaded with him, with God, with death. "Don't go—don't go—don't go."

"It's all right," he whispered. "If my body wakes, you will give me rest. I do not fear. Now you are needed—at the door. Do not need you here. Regina." His breathing came in short gasps. The temple had become very cold, both the stone beneath him and the inside of his body, everything cold.

He tasted blood in his mouth. Regina and Marcus grew dim, but he could see, beyond their heads, flitting in the shadows about the edge of the chamber, that red beetle, bright, a beacon. Everything else grew dark. He smiled and got slowly to his feet, cold and light as though he were no more than a head of wheat. That beetle darted along the wall, red as fresh blood, inviting him.

Once, in Thessaly, he'd followed a red beetle through a field of wheat and across a mighty stream. He had done so with no sound of wings in his ears and no sight of any beetle red against the sky. He'd had only the faith that he would find it. Across the stream, in a stand of poplars as old as the world, he'd found the little creature again. He'd been shaking from the cold of his swim, and his skin was scratched and torn from his climb up the bank through that hostile brush whose roots cling to the edges of rivers with the same tenacity one sees in barnacles latched to a galley's hull. Yet as he stood panting, there was the beetle, quivering on a bit of twig in the thatched roof of a small cottage above the bank. A cottage with a little garden for turnips and beans behind it, and the poplars to break the wind. The tiny beetle was violently red against the gray of the roof, like a shout.

He stood there looking at the beetle for some time. Then his eyes dropped and he noticed the door was open. A short, stout man with a gray beard—an Easterner—stood there, leaning against the jamb, his ears very large, his thumbs hooked into the sash he wore about his drab, foreign clothes. A few kindly wrinkles had taken residence around his eyes to keep them company.

The boy cleared his throat. "I am Polycarp."

The man nodded. "I am Peter." The boy heard rolling gravel in the man's voice, like the rough song of a fishing boat's keel against the shingle. Peter jerked his head as though to indicate the dark interior of the cottage. "This is the house of Cornelius, and I am a guest in it. But I don't think he will mind if I invite you in."

The boy didn't cast one glance back at the stream he'd forded at peril or at the wheat field behind it; he just glanced up at the beautiful red beetle, whose wings were flicking in and out, in and out, as though it wanted to take flight again but was only waiting on the boy. His heart beat fast, but his body was tired, and his steps were slow as he moved up to the door. The fisherman turned without speaking, and Polycarp the boy followed him into the cottage.

Thinking of that boy, Polycarp the old man laughed once, a dry sound like the clack of two sticks of kindling struck together. Then, having followed his master forty years and six, he stepped off this broken stage of the world into the dark.

FINIS

STRANGERS IN THE LAND

BASED LOOSELY ON
THE EVENTS OF JUDGES 4-5

CIRCA 1160 BC

---

for my daughters River and Inara
may their lives be full and free

HISTORIAN'S NOTE

IN THE THIRTEENTH CENTURY BC, several wandering tribes of Hebrews were crossing the desert. They were a young and vigorous people, flushed with life. Few of them had ever seen a walking corpse.

They were freshly displaced from the fertile fields of the Nile, where the dead were carefully contained; indeed, many Hebrew workers had broken their backs in hard labor, making or hauling brick to build the high tombs in which the cities of Kemet (that land the Greeks called Egypt) housed their dead. Those of Kemet cherished the memory of their dead and did all they could to send the deceased to the judgment hall well prepared.

There, the recently deceased handed its heart to the gods, to be weighed in scales against the feather of virtue. Often, the heart, burdened by the evils of this life, proved heavier than the feather. Then, the people of Kemet believed, the soul was cast back into the body. Deprived of the fruitful fields beyond death, it rose from its sarcophagus in a mind-devouring hunger.

The bodies of the dead must be securely entombed against this possibility. Hoping that any wakeful dead might yet find peace, the people of Kemet inscribed the insides of the tombs with hieroglyphics and magnificent art—spells and prayers and histories, everything that a risen corpse might need to remember who it had been. Perhaps, if a corpse could be made to remember the life it had lived and its hope of new life beyond death's river, the spirit might return to its gray eyes and it might offer an acceptable sacrifice and atonement using the incense, fruits, and ornate vessels of fine drink that its relatives had left with it in the tomb. Then lie down in the sarcophagus and return to the hall of judgment with a lightened heart. So those of Kemet hoped as they slid closed the massive doors of the tombs.

In our own era, several unwary archaeologists have slid open those same doors to find themselves food for the cursed and hungry dead—a testament to the utter forgetfulness of death and the smallness of the human voice, which even with its strongest stories and most beautiful pictographs cannot yet reach across death's river to bring messages or remembrance to the lost.

In time, Kemet adopted other practices for securing a successful journey across death's river. The brains of the dead they scooped free of the skull, and the other organs too, placing them in canopic jars. Mummification effectively prevented resurrection; the bodies were now but hollow shells closely enshrouded in linens. In time, the plague became virtually unknown in Kemet. Yet that cultural legacy of a pronounced concern for the well-being of the newly dead persisted. Over the centuries, the brick tombs grew greater and more magnificent, and many laborers—both Hebrews and men of other ethnicities—died in the toil of making them.

In caring so meticulously for their own dead, the people of Kemet oppressed bitterly the living members of other tribes, and the tale of the revolt of the tribes is among the most dramatic of the stories that come down to us from our spiritual ancestors. The Hebrews have left us many folktales and songs that tell of the coming of their Lawgiver and his confrontation with the Pharaoh, their liberation from oppression, and their march into the wilderness to find their own land and their own deity.

The story is well known and frequently retold. Yet most modern storytellers end their tales and let their voices fall still after the celebratory departure, the exodus from Kemet; it is hard for us to gaze steadily at the dark years in the desert and the trials that turned a frightened people of former slave workers into the hardened, efficient, and even brutal tribes that a generation later invaded fertile Canaan, slaughtering many of its people and setting up their tents in the valleys near the burned and smoking towns.

What happened to these people in the desert?

***

Their exodus from a land lush with food yet dark with oppression into barren hills with few oases strikes us as both magnificent and naïve, perhaps in equal measure. The Hebrews starved in the desert, and thirsted, and even lamented the loss of a life of enslavement that at least had not required any of them to be responsible for their own provision. Better to be oxen pulling brick than be men, some of them cried. It is too hard to be men. The women offered their own complaints: along the Nile, their more lovely daughters may have been prey for lusty overseers, but at least they had been fed and clothed.

This season of innocent misery came to an unanticipated and terrible end one night when the dead stumbled, groaning, out of the rocks and canyons and fell upon the tents. We do not know where these dead came from, or why they were so many. Dead have been known to travel together en masse, shambling slowly like animal herds across an empty landscape until they encounter food. It is possible some other tribe had succumbed to the illness and had slouched into the dry hills without direction or destination, there to wait for years or even centuries until drawn by the noise of the Hebrew camp.

We do know that the death toll was severe. Even if we accept the Hebrews' written memories as the most extravagant of exaggerations, the loss of life must have been catastrophic. When dawn came, the Hebrews faced the hard reality that many of their people had been eaten and many others bitten. Some of the latter were already lurching unsteadily to their feet, their hands reaching to clutch at the survivors.

**

How the Lawgiver ended the pestilence is a narrative that I will refer to elsewhere, not here; it is at any rate no story to tell after dark. More important is the way of life the survivors adopted in their fierce intent never to suffer such a crisis a second time.

That time of terror in the wilderness redefined how the Hebrews understood their world and their duties within it. They saw themselves now as alone—desperately alone in a complex and threatening world they had been taught to believe was simple; in the empty desert they had few things to rely on. In their need for certainty, they established a Covenant with the God they had encountered in the desolate wastes, and they chiseled the first words of their Pact into tablets of hard stone, which they then kept with them always in a sacred Ark. In Kemet, they had seen contracts written on scrolls of papyrus, a vegetable material that perished if exposed to moisture; the desert demanded that a covenant as important as this one be recorded on some substance less fragile. Only a contract written into stone that would last as long as the earth could assure them of its reliability.

Among other exacting rules, the Covenant demanded a sharp separation between the living and the dead. The living were to clean their hands and arms up to the elbows before and after touching any dead meat, and the meat of some animals could not be touched at all; they were not to touch with their naked hands the body of any dead man or woman; they were not to leave any dead body unburied, for any reason. The punishments for breaking the

Covenant were severe, even as the promised reward for keeping it was great: an eternal inheritance in a clean and fertile land and divine protection from the hungry dead.

One consequence of that Covenant was a profound and lasting distrust of tribes not their own. The Hebrews both envied and feared the less restricted lives of their neighbors, who lived by no exacting Covenant. To cite one example of the many customs that worried and at times disgusted the Hebrews, some of their neighbors left their enemy dead unburied after a raid or buried the dead too shallow. How terrible it must have been to walk among the fallen, unclothing the slain and checking for bites that they may have concealed in their fear even from their own people. The Hebrews believed it was better to simply bury all the bodies—bury them deep if the soil was soft or pile high a cairn of stones over each corpse to crush it securely to the ground so that none might ever rise, moaning, to catch and devour the living.

The commandments by which the Hebrews lived left no room for unwary haste or compromise, whether with one's own dead or with another's: pile high the cairn, and if necessity required that in doing so you touch the bodies of the dead with ungloved hands, then wait afterward outside the camp for the required seven days until your uncleanness had passed.

To minds hardened by the crisis in the desert, compromise meant the deaths of others in your tribe. Those might be deaths you couldn't predict or prevent, but as they rose, wailing, those dead would cry out your guilt to God.

***

Studying the fragmentary but eloquent records these tribes left behind, I find myself struck with both admiration and horror. Admiration for their ability to both survive and establish a code of law that would permit them to remain human while surviving. And horror at their readiness to exterminate or enslave other peoples who were less aware and therefore less cautious of the ravenous dead.

In our own time, this globe has suffered one mass genocide at least once every decade for more than a century. Despite this, we are today a sheltered people, and we are losing our memory. Yet it is vitally important that we remember. Like the Hebrews, we are at a moment of terrible choice, where we too must decide what we will do with those who live as "strangers" among us, those who labor in our towns or starve in our streets. Those who speak a strange language and who some of us choose to believe are not of our People.

Some of us have already made the choice. Some of us appoint watchmen with authority to hold and harass and contain the strangers we fear. Some of us erect fences along the border of the land or gaze at the sky and shiver in fear of falling planes.

The ancient records hold lessons for us, hard lessons we too often ignore. Our ancestors, like the Hebrews, yearned for the durability of their covenant passionately enough to write it in stone—not in tablets within an Ark, but on the pedestal of the Statue of Liberty. We will at times regret and wish to deny the covenants and the commitments our fathers have made, regardless of whether they were right or wrong, foolish or wise. And at times we will fear their consequences, real or imagined. Yet if we cannot honor the covenants we make with those who live among us, then we may prove equally unable to honor the covenants we make with God, or with our own kin, or with ourselves. Like the Hebrews, we are newly come to a land we now consider our own, and though we think of ourselves as one constituted people, a people set apart, we remain in fact many tribes intermingled, giving worship to many gods both sacred and secular.

In the lean years to come, when the dead moan outside our walls and our homesteads, nothing will matter more to our ability to survive—and to remain true and human—than our readiness to honor the covenants that our fathers and that we ourselves, the living, have made with each other. To do otherwise is to forget that we are strongest together, and that God, who does not make promises lightly, has issued us no guarantee that the ideas that save us will come from a banker in Chicago rather than an assistant electrician in Los Angeles. And to do otherwise is to be less than who we've said we will be.

***

Our narrative opens a few brief generations after the desert. A people without a standing military or any significant arsenal, the Hebrew tribes had raided when they saw land worth taking; now, having taken it, they were weary, and most of them desired only rest and the chance of a new life in a lush and fertile land. The aggressive deforestation of later centuries would let in the desert, but in

1160 BC, the land of promise was not as it is today. Israel was more humid then, and in some places richly forested, a land of milk and honey.

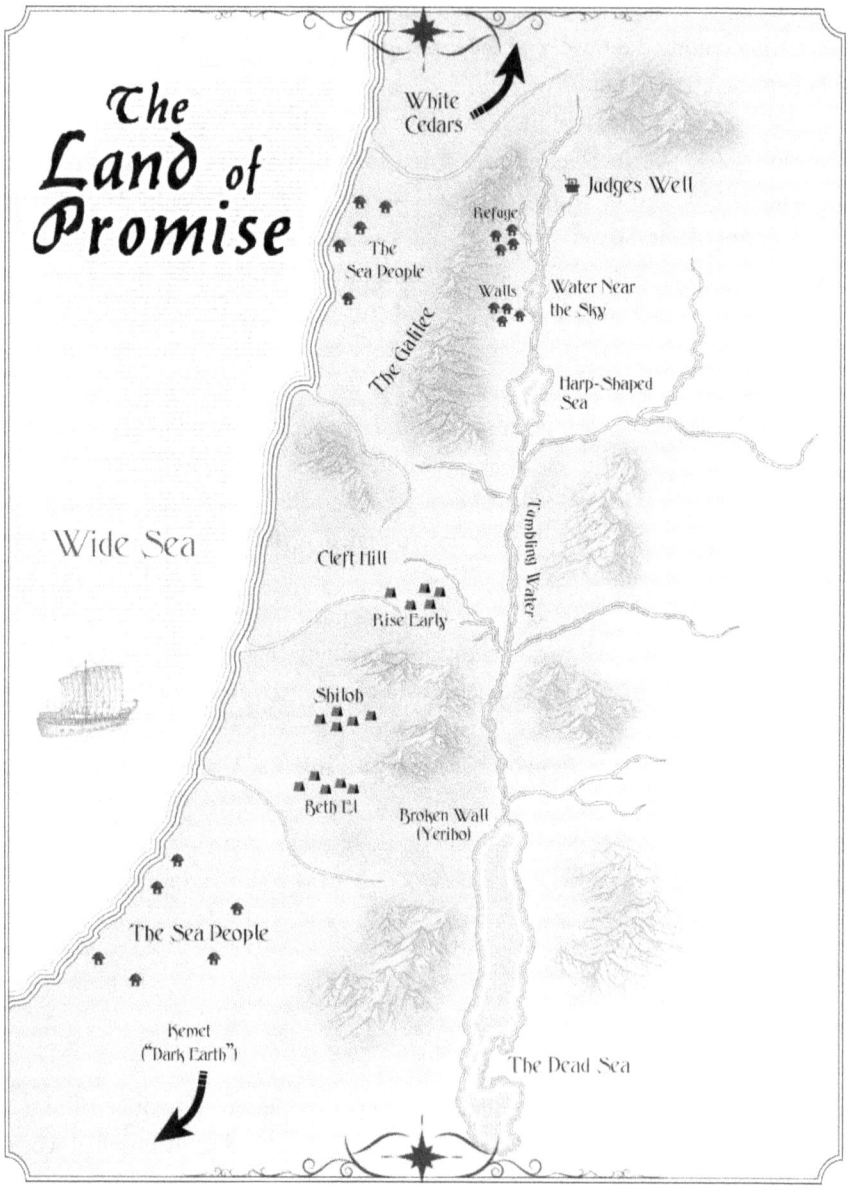

Many of the Hebrews were eager to keep to their own kin on their own lands, trusting in the judges of the Law to arbitrate disputes and keep the region clean of the dead. The Canaanites who had lived in the land before them now had few leaders and fewer armed men; with those few who remained, the Hebrews had made a covenant in the valley that the priests later named Weeping because of their regret for the truce established there. Now most of the Canaanites kept to themselves in small settlements of wooden houses or hovels, or lived and worked among the Hebrews as slaves or second-class laborers. Yet their presence had already begun to change the Hebrews they lived among. Though many of the Hebrew encampments still consisted of tents amid pastures filled with herds, in places a few houses of cedar could already be seen, a few vineyards, a few olive presses.

PART 1. SHILOH

NAVI

THE PEOPLE OF THE COVENANT had many judges, but only one *navi* who told them the future and the past and found truth. She heard their pleas four times a week from a wooden seat her husband had carved for her beneath the great olive tree on its hill near Shiloh. The tree had branches that spread wider than the roof of a cedar house, and it had been standing there, tall and green, when Yeshua the war leader first led their ancestors to the land. Still rich with life, it served now as a visible reminder to all who came before the *navi's* seat that the fertility and possession of this land of promise, this land of milk and honey and olive groves, came with a high cost: the keeping of the Law and the Covenant, that commitment to ways of living that alone kept the People clean and secure in a world where heathen tribes or the living dead might rise up in the night and devour them.

To keep the Covenant meant olive oil and abundant fields of wheat and barley, many births among the flocks, and many children.

To break it—that meant a curse: blight and barrenness and unclean death.

Let the People look to the *navi's* seat and remember this.

Devora the *navi* sat there now with the full authority of the Law at her back, her eyes hard among early wrinkles, her graying hair glowing in that softened light that comes before sunset. A massive, broad-shouldered man stood behind her with a stout ashen spear ending in a bronze head and the long, uncut hair that was the visible sign of his vow. As a nazarite, Zadok lived a life that had no meaning but the wielding of the spear and the defense of the tribe of Levi. He had trained his body for this. Zadok was not a farmer, a tanner, a vintner, or a priest. He was one who preserved life and dealt death when needed. In all the land, only four others shared his vow.

Two supplicants had just turned from Devora's seat to make their way down the slope, one with a relieved look, the other with a scowl. Their argument over the possession of a bull had nearly drawn blood, and the details of the case were such that the seventy judges in Shiloh could not decide it and had sent the two men to the olive tree. But no vision had come to Devora to reveal where there was guilt and where there was not, and in her frustration the *navi* had resolved the matter by deciding that both men together would take the bull and give the animal to the priests, who would offer it up as an *olah*, a burnt offering before God. In this one act they would sacrifice their dispute and atone for the discord they'd brought to the camps of the People. This case, like others that day, had reminded Devora how divided the People were, how provisional their commitment to the covenants they'd made with God and with each other. In light of the evil news this morning had brought to the valley below, this division alarmed Devora. She sat very still, anxious to end the day's judgments and return to the camp. She was intensely grateful for Zadok's steadying presence behind her.

The people gathered on the slope below parted to let the two supplicants by. There were maybe thirty men and women, some standing, others seated on great slabs of rock that past supplicants had pulled free of the scree on the west side of the hill near the cairns of the dead. Beyond the supplicants lay the valley, filled with the white tents of Shiloh. That land was lush with tall grasses and stands of oak and terebinth near the water; faint from the far slopes across the river came the lowing of herds, many of them her husband's. The slow river wound eastward on its way to meet the Tumbling Water, which ran through all the land from the Galilee hills in the north to the dead sea in the south where no fish were—and where the salt in the water was so thick a man could lie on the surface without sinking. Where the salt on the shore stood in tall white pillars, shaped like tents or women or creatures the Hebrews had not met before even in nightmares. Like so many reminders that the land was strange to them and they still strangers in it, and their possession of its fields and waters a blessing that could yet be revoked, a promise that could yet be rescinded.

As Devora looked out over the supplicants, she decided she had time before sundown to sit in decision over one more case. It was her responsibility to see as many as she could, yet she was weary. She yearned for a restful Sabbath meal with her husband. The cases of the day had not succeeded in distracting her from her real worry—the armed camp that had set up a few miles downriver around the tent of a chieftain called Barak ben Abinoam, bringing with it news of walking dead in the north.

Devora searched the supplicants' eyes—herdsmen, levites, craftsmen—for some sign of an easy case, though only the most difficult were sent to her. A stir among those lowest on the slope drew her attention. People were drawing together as though to form a wall as a woman approached them, climbing unsteadily up the hill with a bundle clutched in her arms. Her lank hair hung forward over her face, and she was wrapped in a blanket that looked to be coarse wool. A salmah, the poorest of garments. One shoulder was free of the wool, bare and dirtied with the stain of a long and sweaty walk. Devora did not recognize her from the nearby camp at Shiloh nor from any of the herders' camps in the surrounding valleys. She might have come a long way, wearing nothing but that salmah and her long, ragged hair, and carrying nothing but that bundle she held.

One of the supplicants, a white-robed levite, stepped directly into her way and must have said something that Devora couldn't hear from her seat; she saw the young woman—a girl, really—lift her head and spit in the levite's face. The man lifted his hand but did not strike, as though reluctant to touch with his bare skin this woman who came strange and dirtied to the *navi*'s hill.

The other supplicants formed a circle around the girl. A few who did not share the levite's hesitation began shoving her, as though to push her back down the slope. Seeing the girl stumble to her knees, Devora hissed through her teeth. She didn't want complications; the day had been tiring enough. The seat of decision was hers and there would be no stoning or reviling or barring of any supplicant from her hill unless it was at her word. She wanted to know what was going on, and quickly. She lifted her hand.

"Let the girl come!" she called, her voice sharp and clear in the late afternoon heat.

Silence fell over the hill.

The supplicants stepped away from the girl, a few of them with visible reluctance, and left an open path to the bare, trampled space before the *navi*'s seat. Now all their eyes were on Devora; she felt them, even as she kept her own on the girl who was stumbling the last fifty paces up to the olive tree. The *navi* put up her hand once the girl had come near enough, and the girl stood there with her eyes lowered, her shoulders shaking, her hands clutching the bundle as tightly as though it were her very life.

Devora knew at once something was wrong, badly wrong, and Zadok stirred almost imperceptibly behind her; he felt it too. The bundle the girl held drew the *navi*'s gaze.

"What brings you here, girl?" she said softly, without lifting her eyes from the bundle. "Who has wronged you?" Those four words were her ritual, her invitation to any who came to speak with her beneath the olive. Her promise that she would hear them before making a judgment.

The girl shook without speaking, and Devora saw the terror and wild hope in the girl's eyes. She also saw that this was not a girl of their People; her sharp cheekbones and the kohl beneath her eyes, smeared from the girl's tears, betrayed her. She was a Canaanite girl, though it was possible she was captive or wife to one of the People. Her features were those of the north, of the Galilee hills, and the state of her sandals and the half-healed scrapes on her shins beneath the ragged hem of her garment told the story of a long journey on foot, carrying her bundle down out of the hills to this olive tree.

The anguish in the girl's eyes was a loud demand, though silent; it made Devora wary. The girl was heathen, keeper of no Covenant, a threat to the sons of the People. Devora wanted suddenly to turn the girl away. She could do this easily. The girl was not of the People. And she had not been sent here by the seventy judges—she had walked right to this hill and tried to shove through the supplicants who were already waiting. Devora could just send the girl to Shiloh to wait.

Yet.

This girl had come willingly to the olive tree, in a land her strange, soft people had once possessed. She had come even as any daughter of the People might, to seek the *navi*'s knowledge and the *navi*'s justice. And the words of the Law spoke of how the People were to treat such as her:

Shelter the stranger you find in your land, for you also were strangers in the land of Kemet where none gave you shelter. Forget not your suffering in the land of Kemet.

Even had there been no such words in the Law, this girl had come to her. To the *navi*. With that anguish, that demand in her eyes.

She could not be turned away.

Devora felt a chill, a premonition that was instinct and not prophecy. She made her voice stern. "Who has wronged you, girl?" But suddenly that seemed the wrong question. She could see it in the girl's eyes. Whatever this girl might tell her, it would not be a situation where justice could be meted out between her and another. Whatever judgment she would ask would not be one Devora was prepared to make.

"*Navi*—" The girl's voice broke. Her hands whitened around the bundle she held.

"You stand before the Law and the Covenant," Devora said sharply. "Why have you come, Canaanite?"

"Help me." The girl's voice was raw from crying. The plea in her tear-reddened eyes was one of panic, one woman's cry to another. "They say you approach the Hebrew God without any veil between you. Please. Beg him to help me."

Her hand shaking, the girl peeled away one corner of the bundle, and Devora wrinkled her nose at a stench of ripe decay. The bundle was a swaddled infant, less than a week old; the girl's back was to the other supplicants below, and only she and Devora and Zadok behind the *navi*'s seat could see the infant. See what was wrong. Devora's breath hissed between her teeth.

Unclean! A wild cry in her mind, a cry as ancient and forlorn as broken tombs in a desert place. A cry her people had made around fires in the wilderness long before she or anyone she knew was born. *Unclean!*

The infant opened its reddened eyes and reached its hands feebly toward the *navi*, tiny fingers clutching at the air. Its mouth opened and let out a high-pitched moan. Devora felt terribly cold. The child's skin was gray. Much of the infant's left leg was gone, where some creature had bitten into it and torn away flesh and soft cartilage, perhaps only a moment before the child's mother had been able to rescue it.

Its eyes gazed on the *navi*, but those eyes were dull and dry like small stones.

The infant was not alive.

It would never again draw milk from the young Canaanite's breasts. It would never crawl or learn to walk. Its hair would never grow even a fingernail's width, nor would it ever void its bowels.

But it *would* hunger.

Devora listened to that high, unwavering moan for one long moment, feeling not only chilled but old: the ache in her wrists and fingers, the sharp needles that lived in her back. Swallowing against the dryness in her throat, she motioned to the man who stood behind her. After an instant's hesitation, Zadok set aside his spear and plucked from the girdle about his waist two gloves of dried goatskin. He drew them on, then moved forward quickly to seize the child.

The girl shrieked, tried to leap away with her infant, but the man caught her arm, pulled her savagely back, even as she kicked at him and screamed, her eyes dark with horror. He took up the baby by its remaining leg, wrenching it from her. He held the girl away from his body, and she clawed wildly at his arm, thrashing. Her salmah fell open, revealing a body thin and wasted, with great folds of skin slack from a childbirth that could not have happened more than a couple of weeks before.

"*Navi!*" the girl screamed. "*Navi!*"

The man hesitated, looked to Devora, even as the girl fought his grip. The infant wriggled in the air, hissing like an asp, its small arms moving. The people below on the slope could see it now, and several of them cried out.

Devora tensed. That corpse writhing in the nazarite's grip was her most terrible fear made flesh. "Zadok," she said—

Then, between one beat of Devora's heart and the next, it happened.

The air around her *heated*, as though the *navi* were standing in a desert. A dry and violent heat that overcame her and swept into her. Devora knew what it meant; it was the *shekinah*, the holy presence of God, the same heat that dwelled over the Ark in the Tent of Meeting at Shiloh. Devora braced herself, and then the vision came. The seeing of what might happen.

She saw shambling figures lurching through the valley below. Some of them were on the slope below her, others were by the river. Still more were among the tents, small at this distance. Herds of them, all swaying as they walked. Arms lifted as though yearning for an embrace. The scent of decay stank sweetly in Devora's nostrils. She coughed painfully and passed her hand over her eyes, which burned now with strain.

Her vision cleared, mercifully. There was only the girl screaming and Zadok the nazarite with the child clutched in his hand. And the supplicants below with ashen faces, the hill on which they stood, and around them the wide fields of heather and barley under a pale sky. No other dead, only that small, moaning infant.

Her lips tasted of salt; in the heat of God's presence all the moisture had been baked from them, leaving only that taste behind.

She forced herself to breathe. Deeply, fully. It was the future she had seen, but it was not the truth. Not yet. It couldn't be. It mustn't be. In her mind, she heard the screams outside her mother's tent, screams that went on and on until they died in a gasp of breath. That was a memory, that was the past. She tried to shove it back as she turned cold eyes on the Canaanite girl. Thirty years ago, her people had brought the unclean death into the land. Now it was happening again.

"Please, *navi*," the girl cried, her face twisted in pain and fear. "Please, pray to the Hebrew God. There must be something the gods can do. He didn't die of illness or hunger or any wild animal. It's *unjust*. The gods have to give him back! Please, *navi*, please, *navi*!"

The girl's cries pulled at her, but Devora could not afford to pity her. The miracle the girl hoped for was not Devora's to provide. It was brutally clear what she had to do, to avert what she had just foreseen. Her life had been a series of acts of extreme and necessary justice. Keeping the Law, protecting the People—this mattered more than one girl's pain. She met the Canaanite's eyes and made her voice hard as the edge of a blade. "Don't be foolish, girl. Only one thing can be done. Go home; your husband will give you more children." Devora turned to Zadok. "Do what must be done," she said.

The nazarite gave her a grim nod. Unlike the others who'd taken the nazarite vow, Zadok ben Zefanyah had not made his covenant with the high priest, but with the *navi*. Devora had been there the night his father died defending the priests, had been the one person in the camp to stop and speak with the boy as he stood by his father's corpse.

His vow and the events of his life had shaped him, she knew, into a man who grieved deeply but did not flinch; when the corpses he'd seen and the acts that had been required of him returned to his heart in the dark hours of the night, he would drown the memory of them in the heaviness of barley beer (the only violation of his vow that he permitted himself) or in the sweet softness of a woman's body. The dawn would find him slumped over his cup or over his lover's breasts, weeping. But his cries would pass. He would stand, unsteadily a moment, then leave the beer-house or the woman's tent and return to his covenant and his duty. And whatever that next day required, he would not flinch.

He did not flinch now. He held the Canaanite girl at arm's length and set the bundled infant upon the ground. Then he took up his long-hafted spear from where he had set it aside.

"*No!*" The girl began to shriek. "You Hebrew bitch!" she cried. "*You Hebrew bitch!*" The scream tore its way out of her throat, raw and frantic, as she tried to struggle past Zadok.

Devora closed her eyes, said a short prayer under her breath. She could hear the murmur of the supplicants—none of whom had moved. She heard the tiny moan from the corpse that had been an infant; it ended in a hard *thock* of bronze driven into flesh. A choked, sobbing noise from the mother, as though a scream had caught in her throat and would be lodged there for every night of her remaining years. The *navi* kept her eyes closed a moment more.

When she looked on the world again, the girl was on her knees, her face ashen, still making that choked sound. Zadok stood beside her; he'd cast his spear to the grass. Down the hill, some of the other supplicants were on their knees as well, overcome by horror. The bundle at Zadok's feet didn't move or make any sound.

Grimly, Devora rose to her feet. Too old, she felt too old today. Much too old for seeing…this. She stepped forward until she stood by Zadok and the Canaanite, with the small corpse at her feet. Glanced down at it. The head had been crushed entirely; one of the little hands was still curled as if to grasp at some flesh warmer than its own. There was no blood beneath the body, nor any on the bronze head of Zadok's spear that lay beside it, for only living things bleed.

It was a small, mangled thing, without face or any color to its skin. It did not seem ever to have been human. There was a burn of moisture in Devora's eyes; she forbade it. If no one had been watching she would have sat down beside that body and remained there until the world was old.

She glanced up, noted the position of the sun. Perhaps two hours before dark. Dusk would come swiftly, and with it the Sabbath bride. They must be in the tents before then or sleep on the heather; from sunset this day to sunset the next, she must rest. Yet she could not simply hurry to the tents and leave this body unburied through the Sabbath.

She whispered the words of one of the six hundred and thirteen *mitzvot*, commandments given to their fathers in the desert for keeping the camp clean of disease and the dead:

You shall bury the flesh of the dead, and raise above it a cairn of stones, that God will see it, and remember, and make the land clean.

The People sheltered and hid from the dead within the mighty tent of the Law, and the poles of that tent were the living pillars of the Covenant, strong and binding promises between the tribes and God and between the tribes and each other; yet the roots of those pillars were intricate and fragile, for those roots were the acts of the People that upheld and sustained the Covenant. Devora sat in her seat of decision to pass judgment wherever the roots had been broken or eaten away by unclean choices, in order to keep the whole tent of the Law from collapsing and crushing the People beneath it. Now she could sense that mighty canvas of the Law tearing in the wind and heat of her vision. What this day had brought to her. News of herds of dead moving through the high Galilee, a migration of corpses into the land such as she had never before heard or imagined. And one of them brought even here, to her feet, at the olive tree.

Her hands were trembling; she could not still them.

"We must bury it," she whispered. "And we must hurry."

CAIRNS FOR THE DEAD

SOME HORRORS DEMAND that we have words to explain them, but Devora had none. She stepped past Zadok and the girl to gaze down the slope at the ashen-faced supplicants. Behind her, the girl's sobs became high-pitched and sharp, like the sounds of some small animal dying in pain. Devora took a steadying breath, carefully sewing her heart shut. She did what had to be done.

A wind sprang up, pulling at her hair and her dress. She raised her voice over it. "This hill is cleansed," she called to them, "and a cairn will be raised."

"*Selah*," the supplicants murmured back. *Always.* And the wind took away their voices. Their eyes were wide; they stared into a darkness that was their own fear and their own expectation and their own waking at night. They had come here to stand before the olive tree to receive justice, rather than visiting justice upon each other in blood and heat and the glinting of knives. Now they were pale. They had heard rumors of the moaning of the dead in the high Galilee and the coming of armed men to seek aid from all the tribes, but the Canaanite woman today had brought that distant terror that they could ignore here to this very hill above the tents of Shiloh and the holy Ark itself. Surely the hunger cry of the dead infant meant some savage and irremediable justice had been visited upon them, upon the land and the People. That God who sat in decision over the Hebrews and over the whole earth had taken away his hand of protection. That they were no longer supplicants but rather men marked for death and burial.

The cleansing and the silencing of this one small, restless corpse brought no comfort. They gazed at the *navi*, awaiting some judgment or vision from God. She felt the weight of their need, their demands on her.

But what could Devora tell them? That she had foreseen the dead moving across the holy valley in great herds and didn't yet know what God wished her to do to prevent it? They didn't need to hear that.

"Go back to your tents," she cried at last. "The *navi* has left her seat."

They gazed up at her listlessly.

"Go home! Observe the Sabbath. Live by the Law, and the land will be clean."

Some of those standing or sitting on the slope below her had been there before the sun rose to offer the earth its warm kiss. Some had been months in Shiloh while their cases were debated among those levites appointed to sit in decision over the People, before they'd been referred at last to the *navi* who received special insight from God. Yet now they didn't complain; they began leaving the hill, one after the other. Some of them walking slowly back to the tents, some quickly as though fleeing. As though they understood that their demands on the Law and on God were rescinded or postponed. Perhaps, in the days ahead, they would wait in silence to hear whether the valley would fill with the voices of the dead preparing to feed or with the clack of stone against stone as cairns were raised over the corpses to hold them unrising to the earth.

Devora watched for a few moments as they moved away through the heather. Delaying her next task. She lifted her eyes, gazing across this land of promise from her high place, and listened to the wind move in the olive leaves. Softly as the wind, she heard the Canaanite weeping.

She didn't turn yet to face that mother and the infant in need of burial. She couldn't. There was little time, but she needed one moment to breathe. She glanced down at the valley, at the mighty flock of white tents perched like cranes by the river. That was Shiloh. A yearning lit in her for a quiet meal and rest in her husband's tent. But she knew there would be no rest for her tonight, no real rest.

The men from the Galilee had pitched their tents a few miles downriver to the east. She could see them from here. Not a permanent camp like Shiloh, but a hasty one, mostly small tents that could be rolled up and carried on a man's back. In the high land where those men lived, the dead were feeding, groping through fields of wild barley or along creek-banks, hunting animals or men or women. Or reaching through windows for infants asleep in the cedar houses built by the Canaanites.

Years since she'd seen one of the unclean dead.

Except in her dreams.

Except whenever she lay her head down and closed her eyes and pursued sleep through the weeds and fens of her nightmares.

Turning, Devora found Zadok standing over the infant with his back to her, and the girl still on her knees. She had drawn her salmah back around her, but Devora recalled how thin and exhausted her body had looked, as though the journey to her olive tree and the ordeal she suffered in her heart had bled the girl's body of all her strength and health. The Canaanite glanced up at the *navi* with swollen eyes.

"A cairn," the girl said. "You said a cairn. Please. My child. He needs to go into the water. He's not a Hebrew. Please. He must pass into the fish, and the fish into the people, so that he can come back."

Devora went cold with horror at the thought. What if it took only one unclean corpse to defile an entire lake, all the fish in it, all those who ate of the fish? Who could say what would happen? Thirty years ago, the heathen dead had wandered, moaning, into Shiloh camp and devoured much of what mattered to young Devora. She had known since that day what a peril the Canaanites and their customs could be.

"Enough," she cried. "I'll have none of your heathen ways, girl. They've brought this on us. Your gloves, Zadok."

When the nazarite didn't answer, Devora stepped toward him, glanced at his face, and received a shock. That face showed no expression: Zadok simply stood with his dark eyes fixed on the small body.

"Zadok?"

No answer.

Alarmed, Devora approached him, trying to catch his eyes with hers. He didn't move or show that he'd heard her. His massive body just breathed in and out, his chest moving like a great bear's, his entire attention on the corpse. Devora's heart beat faster. It had been a long time since one of these moods had overtaken Zadok. It used to happen every time he stilled one of the unclean corpses—but the last had been nearly ten years ago, and the one before that had been four years earlier.

The worst time, when he was still but a youth, Zadok had stood completely still for almost two days. When he'd come out of it at last, he'd been violent, enraged, lashing about with his spear. For a few minutes, then he'd collapsed from exhaustion. He'd slept for a day and a half and woken with no memory of his fit, nor any clear memory of the death that had prompted it. Zadok and two other nazarites had been clearing an oak grove of dead, several hours upriver from Shiloh. Some caravan merchant had died there, then risen; he'd eaten his wife and one of his slaves, and the rest had fled, leaving three bodies restless and unburied. The dead had surprised Zadok in the trees, but he'd dealt with them. Afterward, one of the other nazarites had stayed beside him while Zadok stood still as a tree, his memories gripping at his heart. The other had run to Shiloh with word, and had told Devora. After a quick word to her husband, the *navi* had hurried out to the grove, and she had been there sitting by Zadok when he woke at last.

But that had been over twenty years ago.

She had no idea how long this one would last.

The *navi* glanced at the declining sun. Felt the small, sharp teeth of panic. The Sabbath was coming; they had to get back to the tents. But they could *not* leave a corpse on the open ground, with no stones over it. Her breath hissed through her teeth.

She struck Zadok hard across the face.

He didn't even blink.

Devora's right hand stung, and she rubbed it with her left. Her heart was pounding now. She glanced about, cursing under her breath. Wishing she'd kept the supplicants at the hill rather than dispersing them. The area was quiet now but for the wind. There were only the three of them—Zadok, the Canaanite girl, and the *navi*. Alone with the tiny corpse.

"What's wrong with him?" the Canaanite whispered.

"The dead are a shock to anyone," Devora muttered. She must do without Zadok. She caught the hems of the goatskin gloves at his wrists and peeled them free of his hands, one, then the other, careful not to touch the fingers or the palm, anywhere the leather might have touched the corpse. Under her breath, she recited the words of the Law. That was a ritual of hers when she needed calm.

You shall not touch the flesh of the dead, for the dead body is unclean. If a man touches the flesh of the dead, you shall put him from your camp and watch him. Seven days you shall put him from your camp, until his uncleanness has passed.

The gloves were much too large for her; her hands felt silly inside them, and she worried they would slip off her fingers, which were damp with sweat. She kept her hands curled to prevent this. She reached for the infant.

"Leave him alone!" the girl whispered, without looking up.

"You brought this child to me," Devora said. "Now it is my task to do what I must." The *navi* took the tiny body in her hands, lifting it carefully, not letting the gloves slip. The infant was very light, as though she held a bundle of leaves. She hooked the swaddling cloth with one gloved finger, lifting it from the ground too. She could wrap the body in it later.

For an instant she glanced at Zadok's spear where it lay in the grass. That bronze spearhead would probably make digging a grave easier. But she shook her head. The spear was Zadok's. She would leave it with him.

"Come, girl." She began walking briskly down the slope.

***

In the lee of the west slope there were cairns in great number, several hundred of them, orderly stacks of flat stones like stunted pillars set in the earth, a forest of monuments. Some of the dead beneath them had died of age or illness, a few from bloodshed, some from a judgment of death by stoning. Set a little apart from the others—because the bodies beneath them were defiled—a stretch of eight and sixty cairns marked the resting places of those who had died the unclean death on that terrible night thirty years ago, when the walking dead had come to Shiloh.

Carrying the infant's body at arm's length, Devora moved slowly among the cairns, weighted down by the crushing burden of the past, which even the Covenant could only partially lighten. Behind her the Canaanite followed numbly.

Devora lay the infant by the cairns of the defiled, and the Canaanite knelt by the body, her head lowered, her hands clutching her knees. Devora left her there and hurried to a bit of scree nearby where a rockslide some years before had exposed the guts of the earth. Beyond the scree and the curve of the hill she could see the white tents of Shiloh again, as alluring to her as a flock of white doves alighting in a dry wilderness. But the tents must wait.

The stones she gathered had to be large ones—large enough to crush the dead to the earth. The corpse's head had been shattered; it would not hunger again. Yet it was unclean and might spread the blight to anything it touched. You couldn't know what might sicken from it—living people or living crops. So you pile stone above a dead body, any dead body, no matter how dead or how still the body may look. The time in the desert, when Devora's ancestors had seen corpses rise moaning to their feet, had taught them to take no chances, none.

***

Devora felt the strain in her arms as she carried the last of six slabs of rock from the scree to the place she'd chosen beside the other cairns. Sweat began to trickle down her back, making her itch. Devora tried to move quickly, but her fatigue was catching up with her. After more than forty years of life, her body was aging; there were days when she felt no pain, and days like this one when the weariness was as present as the breath in her lungs. Devora glanced back once to see Zadok standing still as a cairn himself by the olive tree on the slope above. She chewed on bitter words for Zadok in the privacy of her heart, but those words were quickly swallowed in remorse. She'd left him up there, trapped in who knew what darkness of the heart. Spearing the dead had brought back memories for him, too. She should have expected that. She should have taken up spear or stone herself and borne the burden of that act on her own shoulders, even as she was now bearing the burden of this stone. Her face heated with shame; the nazarite's vow was to defend her life, not to suffer in her place.

The Canaanite girl still knelt by the small body. At first, Devora had feared the girl might grab the infant and flee, but she seemed to be in shock. The salmah had slipped from her shoulder, nearly baring one breast, which was so swollen with milk that her skin was red and each vein could be clearly seen. It must have hurt terribly, yet the girl did not appear to notice. Nor did she cover herself. She just stared listlessly at an empty spot of ground beside the infant and did not twitch or do anything but breathe as Devora approached.

With a groan, the *navi* let the rock fall to the earth beside that scrap of flesh and bone that had once been a child. Then rested a moment, breathing hard. She didn't spare the Canaanite another glance. Just listened to the beating of her heart and the breath coming in and out of her body. Calm. She needed calm. She glanced again at the sun, held up her hand—four fingers' width between that blaze of heat and the tops of the hills. Little time, little time. She didn't intend to spend the Sabbath on this hill among the cairns, with a weeping Canaanite girl and a nazarite lost in his own private nightmare. She needed to get back. She needed to tell the priests of her vision. Needed the solace of her husband's arms—she knew well that her own nightmares would visit her tonight, after dark.

Taking up a jagged rock to use for a shovel, Devora began digging in the soil beside the body, parting the roots of weeds and hollowing out an infant-sized resting place in the warm ground, as though shaping a small womb in the earth for the child's body to return to. She panted as she worked. A quick glance at Zadok—he had not moved.

"Don't put him in the ground," the Canaanite said, her eyes sore and red.

Devora didn't look up. "You can't take it from the hill," she said quietly. "Or to any water the People might drink."

"You've taken everything from us," the girl said. "Everything. Our men toil like slaves in your fields. Your priests burn our gods." A quiver of despair in her voice. "Can I not even care for the body of *my child?*"

Devora cast the jagged rock aside and reached for one of her stones. Each was roughly rectangular, about the length of her arm and the height of her hand. Grasping the edge of a stone with both her hands and digging in with her fingers, she lifted and tipped, rolling the stone into position. Her back itched furiously, and her arms and shoulders and neck burned with pain.

"I hate you," the girl whispered. "I hate you."

Devora glanced at the Canaanite girl, a rebuke ready. But she was caught by the girl's visible anguish and cold defiance. The Canaanite wasn't the kind of heathen Devora might have expected to meet. She carried in her hand no trivial god of wood or stone. She had no war paint. This stranger in her land was only a girl, one who had suffered and labored in the birth tent to bring one small life into the land to set against all the unclean death. The midwives had pulled that infant wet and helpless from this woman's own body and handed it to her as it cried in its horror at the strangeness of the world beyond the womb. Devora thought of those moments she'd never known but had witnessed, when the mother and the infant weep together and the midwives press warm, moist cloths to the mother's exhausted and torn body to stop the blood.

The grief in the Canaanite's eyes was so intense it was nearly feral. It took Devora aback; the rebuke died on her lips. She had felt grief before—grief that tore at her in the night. But whatever this stranger was feeling, *that* Devora had never felt. For a moment Devora pressed her own hand to her belly, and something clenched tight about her heart. She had never brought any child crying into the land. What would it have been like to bear one, from one harvest season nearly to the next, feel it growing inside her, and birth one, and then lose one?

The Canaanite's travails had not ended with the lifting of her child to her breast. It could not have been many days later when she'd risen and stumbled all the way here out of the settlements in the high Galilee, carrying that bitten infant, her own body still bleeding from its birth. She must have needed to rest often, near fainting, only to push herself unsteadily to her feet again. Perhaps the infant had been alive and feverish when she began her long, desperate walk. Perhaps it had died along the way, then risen to the mother's horror with that low cry of hunger. Yet the girl had kept carrying it, kept on her feet, all the way here, to the *navi*'s olive tree. It might have taken her days. Perhaps Devora's words of comfort had been colder than she'd realized; perhaps there was no husband. Perhaps it was the husband who had bitten the infant and eaten its leg. She didn't know. She only knew that the Canaanite girl had come here alone, carrying her infant across a land that had once been hers and her people's.

"The cairn is a necessity," Devora said softly. "It is also a promise. A promise to the dead that the People will not forget. A promise that even God will look down and see the cairn and remember. And a promise to the living *and* the dead that the unclean death will end here, at these stones, and spread no further. We must bury the child the Hebrew way. Or more children may die."

She wished she might wipe sweat from her face, but dared not lift the gloves to touch her skin. She kept her eyes on the Canaanite, saw that her words meant little to her.

"Girl," the *navi* called softly, "what is your name?"

"Hurriya." The girl's eyes were hopeless. "I am Hurriya. The father was Malachi ben Aharon."

"That is a Hebrew name," Devora said sharply.

"He *was* Hebrew," the girl said. "A laborer at an olive press near Judges' Well. My father sold me to him when I was twelve."

Devora cast an uneasy glance at the cairn she'd raised. The father had been Hebrew. If he were here, he might beg the *navi* to sing the Words of Going for his son.

"Did the child have a name?"

"No," Hurriya whispered. "He was only seven days old. I knew in my heart you couldn't help him. But the hope. The hope was all I had."

The horror of it made Devora's throat tighten. On the eighth day, every male Hebrew child was circumcised and given a name. This infant had perished without name and without any mark of the Covenant upon its flesh. It was not of the People. It was not of *any* People—it had no name. Yet if no Words of Going were sung over the cairn, this infant and its father would be forgotten. God might see the cairn, but how would God know who was beneath it? The thought of one of the People being unremembered—that was the grasp of a cold hand about her heart.

She let out her breath and returned her focus to the physical work of raising the cairn. She arranged three great stones in a triangle around the little pit she'd dug—that made a wall, or a frame, for the cairn. Like the foundation of a small house, a house for the dead. She reached for the infant and lowered what was left of it into the small depression she'd made in the earth.

Muscles that she probably hadn't used since she was a young girl were screaming at her. She clenched her teeth and lifted one of the other stones. With a groan that felt like her bones were coming loose from each other, she slammed the stone down across the top of the cairn's foundation, covering half of the small grave, forming half a roof. Her gloved fingers still clenched tight about the edge of the stone, she lay over it, wheezing. For a moment she just lay there.

Finish. She had to finish this.

She pushed herself up.

Only two more stones. One to complete the roof and one to sit atop the cairn, sealing it. Two more, only two. The infant was already half concealed. She could do this.

But she could still hear that moan, that unliving moan, in her mind. Worse, she could hear the moans outside her mother's tent, thirty years ago, and the screams. Her hands began shaking again. If she were to close her eyes, she'd be *there*, in that tent, as a child. She used to visit that tent in her dreams, night after night. But it had been a long time now since she had. She knew she would be there tonight. When that happened, she couldn't be alone. After so long—she feared the dreams would shatter her, that her body would convulse and clench up and she would sob in her blankets until morning. She couldn't afford that kind of weakness, that kind of terror. Israel couldn't afford it. She needed her husband tonight.

She lifted the next stone, straining. A cry ripped from her throat as she let the great rock fall into place, roofing the cairn. As she gulped in air, her palms flat against the cold stone, she felt the slightest tremor in the ground, through her knees.

She lifted her eyes.

Three horses were riding up the valley below toward her hill at a swift canter, one well ahead of the other two. They were sleek animals, good ones, probably trades from across the Water. They were riding from the northeast, from the northern camp, and with the sun behind her Devora could see them clearly. The riders were tall men, one broad-shouldered with a thick, dark beard. The other two lean and wiry.

Taking a breath, she returned her attention to the cairn. It must be finished. The earth was cool against her knees, but strands of her hair had strayed across her face, sweaty from the exertion. Not how she would have chosen to meet men of her People: on her knees, sweaty, and dirtied. She hissed through her teeth. Burying this corpse was more important than her dignity. She reached for the last of the stones. She would finish this, and then she would hear what these men wanted, these men who'd taken up the spear when the dead rose, and ridden out of the north.

Men from the Galilee

THE FIRST OF THE RIDERS pulled well ahead of the other two; he rode at a gallop right up the slope, only slowing when he reached the cairns, so as not to break his horse's legs against some mound of stone. Horses were rare in the land, a gift of God to any who possessed one. Sacred in their own way and not to be risked heedlessly. The man riding this one checked his steed, slid from its back, and strode toward Devora among the cairns without any sign of deference or respect for the *navi*.

Ignoring his approach, Devora was fighting to lift the last stone into place, and she nearly passed out from the exertion and from the pain in her back.

Suddenly the weight was gone, and she nearly fell. Blinking sweat from her eyes, she found that Zadok had taken the stone from her and was raising it to the top of the cairn as effortlessly as though he were lifting no more weight than a full waterskin. The stone settled into place with a reassuring *clack* of rock against rock.

Zadok!

Her whole body lightened with relief.

The nazarite turned to her, his eyes grim but present. "*Navi*," he said quietly.

"About time," she gasped, then swayed on her feet. Zadok's hand caught her arm, and for a moment she leaned against him, just breathing, heedless of the impropriety. But she had no time to rest or breathe; the war-leader was approaching between the cairns. The Canaanite looked numbly on without rising from where she knelt. Devora's own limbs were shaky, but she forced herself to step away from Zadok and stand without support. Her dress was smeared with soil and sweat; there was dirt beneath her nails and scrapes on her hands. She felt filthy, and vaguely defiled, though her naked skin had not touched the corpse. She longed desperately for a cold river to dip into and dry clothes, but there wasn't time.

The stranger stopped when he was near enough to speak without shouting. A lean man, tall with the height of the northern tribes, his hair braided in the war knot. One of his eyelids drooped a little. That would have made another man look sleepy; it made this man look sinister, secretive. His lip had a bit of curl in it. As his gaze took in Devora and Zadok, then lingered on the Canaanite, that curl twisted into a sneer.

Devora braced herself, not liking the look of this man.

"A heathen," the man called out, without bothering to introduce himself. "Even in Shiloh I find the stink of them."

The Canaanite looked up from the cairn, and her eyes burned hot.

"She's a supplicant," Devora said quietly. "Let her be."

The man spat to the side, and Devora tensed. This was where the dead were buried—how *dare* he— "Who are you, stranger?" she demanded.

He showed his teeth. His hard, cold eyes glanced past her, at Zadok. "I am Nimri ben Nabaoth, of Naphtali tribe. I lead herdsmen in the hills above Judges' Well. Why does the woman speak for you?"

"She is the *navi*," Zadok said. "She speaks for God."

"Ha. Ask God to choose a man for the next *navi*."

"Perhaps he will," Devora said smoothly. "You've come from Barak's camp?"

"I've come from *my* camp. Barak happens to be camping near me."

The other two riders were approaching now. They dismounted some distance from the cairns to approach on foot, showing respect for the holy ground where the dead were buried, and for the *navi*. Nimri glanced over his shoulder at them, tensing slightly. Then he shook his head and shot Zadok a look. "Let *them* talk to this woman if they want." Then he mounted his horse. "The high priest—I can find him down there?" He jerked his head toward the white tents.

"It is nearly the Sabbath," Zadok said.

Devora didn't say anything. Her hands were clenched with rage.

"After the Sabbath, then," Nimri said, his tone dismissive. His gaze flicked across them all once, contempt for the woman who spoke for God and a violent hate in his eyes when he glanced at the Canaanite. Then he turned his horse and kicked it into a canter, nearly riding down the other two men. The men leapt to the side, and then Nimri ben Nabaoth was past, and he and his horse tore down the slope as quickly as they'd come.

"If that is the kind of man mothers raise in the northern tribes," Devora muttered under her breath, but didn't finish the thought. The other two were near now. One of them stepped forward, his eyes glancing at the nazarite and the two women. Devora took a careful look at the war-leader approaching her. His hands were rough from working an olive press; his legs were long and lean. There were few wrinkles in his suntanned face. Some of that was youth. Devora suspected the rest was that this was not a man who worried much or deliberated much. A great, slanting scar crossed his nose and cheeks, probably a witness to the efficacy of Sea Coast iron and to the youth's ability to face it head-on, without fleeing. Or, Devora supposed, a witness to this man's inability to duck.

She nodded at the man, and he halted a few strides from her. Then the man looked the two women over, appraising them for a moment as he might appraise slaves he wished to purchase for his bedding. The Canaanite didn't appear to notice; she still knelt by that cairn, her head down, silent in her suffering. But Devora flushed, and her eyes went cold. "Do you also come to insult God's *navi*?"

The newcomer cast a glance back at Nimri, his face amused. "That is a proud man. Nimri insults everybody. Someone will gut him with a spear one day. But we are all proud men in the north." He looked back at her, grinned. "I like you. They did not tell me the *navi* was a lovely woman."

"The *navi* has been a woman for three generations."

"God's ways are strange," the northerner remarked. "They *did* say you were a woman. They didn't say you were beautiful. I am told the last *navi* was a wrinkled old thing. Not every doe ages well." He glanced at Zadok. "Is she yours?"

Devora seethed, but Zadok spoke before she could. "I serve her. I have taken the nazarite vow." Zadok's voice was calm, but every line of the man's body was tense, watchful.

"The hair. I saw." For the first time, the northerner's voice deepened with awe. "We haven't seen you in the north, but we've *heard*. They say a nazarite knows no trade but the spear. They say he fights like ten men."

"They are wrong," Zadok said grimly. "I fight like twenty."

"Ha!" The northerner slapped his thigh in appreciation and pointed at the nazarite. "I like you too."

Devora lifted her voice. "What is your name and your tribe, stranger?"

"I am Omri." He drew himself up. "Of Zebulun tribe."

"And what are the chieftains of the north doing in Shiloh valley, Omri of Zebulun tribe? There are no dead here. Does Barak ben Abinoam lie in his tent enjoying his wines while the dead feast?"

The amusement faded from Omri's face. "We've come to find what visions God has sent the *navi*," he said, the flirtation gone from his voice. "And to ask the *kohannim* for the Ark."

"God sent a vision this very day," Devora replied. "I have seen the dead lurching through fields of barley and wheat. In numbers greater than the cranes in the marshes. I have seen the whole land defiled and blighted. It is God's warning. This is what might happen. You and the men in that camp must see that it doesn't."

Omri looked stricken by her words; he fell silent. The other man's face grew grimmer, colder. Devora considered him curiously. Dark, curling hair about a sun-roughened face. He held in his right hand a tall staff with its top swaddled in wool and its end planted firmly in the earth. That made Devora think of a herdsman, but the man's hands were stained with red and purple— the juices of grapes. A vintner, then. Perhaps he needed the staff because he was infirm. Yet he did not lean on it. He wore a heavy wool cloak, which was strange in this heat. He did not bear scars across his face as Omri did, but his dark eyes and the set of his shoulders spoke of a wrath and a strength barely restrained. There was something lethal about this man. She would not care to be alone with him. She felt sure she could remind Omri of his place, and hers, but this other man…

"When we left," Omri muttered, "there were just a few wandering herds of corpses up by White Cedars. The northernmost encampments were at risk. Nimri's, mostly. We sent word to other tribes. Set our camp down there—" He waved at the valley. "Where else would we all gather but Shiloh? Though it means leaving our barley and our vineyards undefended for a few days, we need help." His face flushed with anger. "We need *much* help, if God has shown you—that. If I am not hearing only a woman's fears."

Devora ignored the comment, focusing instead on what Omri was implying. "How many men have come, Omri?"

"Five hundred and fifty," he said.

Devora started. "So few?"

"Maybe less now. A few slipped away as we came down out of the hills. They did not want to leave their farms unwatched." He showed his teeth.

Fear gripped her heart. "How many tribes?" Her voice breathless with horror.

"Zebulun and Naphtali have come. A few from Issachar, very few—but Laban is their chieftain, and when he lifts his axe, he's an entire raid by himself." Omri's eyes glinted. "The northern tribes have gathered. But the others...the chieftains of Reuben sent this message to us in the hour before dawn today: *Let Barak defend his vineyard, and we will defend ours.*"

Three tribes. Only three. Three could not take the Ark of the Covenant with them, nor the blessing of the *kohannim* who stood before God for the People. Three tribes out of twelve could not take God with them into the north.

"Omri, not in all our years in possession of this land have the People risen with so few as five hundred and fifty men." Devora felt her control slipping. The infant, the weeping of the Canaanite girl, the vision of the dead devouring the land, the shock of Omri's news—it was too much.

"The other tribes feel no threat," he muttered.

"What threatens one tribe threatens all. Have our People forgotten the desert?" Her fear rose like a river in flood. "Where is Barak? Why hasn't he come himself? I would speak with *him*, Omri."

"He is here."

The man who'd spoken was Omri's companion, the grim, lethal one. He cast his wool cloak back over his shoulder, revealing a bronze breast-piece, polished though dented from past raids. Bronze greaves strapped to his calves. He took a step forward; as he did, he unwound the cloth about the head of his staff to reveal a lethal slice of bronze that flashed in the lowering sun. A spear, not a staff.

Zadok took his place by Devora's side, tall and menacing, and the man did not approach nearer.

"Barak is here," the man said. His voice was strange, rasping a little as though he rarely used it, as though he rarely indulged in conversation with other men or with women. Yet his voice rose from deep in his chest and was powerful. "And *I* would ask things of God's *navi*."

BARAK

BARAK WAS A MAN WHO liked to have warm earth under his hands, or the cool, healthy skin of green vines. His vineyards were not the best in Eretz Israel, but they were close. His presses gave wine that sold not only to the sons of the People but even to merchants traveling through on their way to the great cities on the coast. Over the door of his house hung a bronze spear and a shield, from the days when he'd led the men of the north in repelling a raid of young warriors from those coastal cities. Though he'd had four hundred men at his back, he'd fought in those days only to defend his own house, which to his mind was his whole tribe.

His wife, a Canaanite, had died half a year ago in pregnancy, both she and the child, and at times the pain of it hit him so hard he stood still in the middle of his vines under the hot sun, vision gone wet with tears, just waiting to be able to breathe again. He hadn't taken another wife yet, though he must do so soon or his seed would be lost. Yet his grief was bitter, and he did not forgive Hadassah for leaving him nor God for taking her.

He would never forget the fire he'd felt in her flesh as she died; she'd been burning up from the inside, and his child had burned inside her. And then, between one breath and the next, she was gone, and what was left of her retained its warmth for a time and then cooled slowly, like a charred coal. He had remained with her body until the sun rose, defiling his hand each time he touched her face to feel her warmth dying away. In the morning, he'd carried her to the slopes above his vineyard. Set her in the earth, raised a cairn above her. Pitched a tent beside the stones that marked her memory and remained there seven days until his uncleanness passed.

When the seven days ended, he had returned to his cedar house and found his slaves and his wife's mother with ashes in their hair, mourning by the hearth. Without a word to his mother-in-law, he'd gone to her alcove and dug out her gods from beneath her bedding. He had tolerated them for the sake of his Canaanite wife. Now she was gone. God had taken her. He feared what else God might take from him. He'd made it halfway to the hearth before Hadassah's mother had flown at him, screaming and snatching at the gods with her aged hands.

She had screamed and kicked at him, and in the end he'd had to tie her, binding her at the wrists, ankles, and knees. He'd left her rolling on the floor behind him as he'd burned her gods, one after the other. She had shrieked and called him vile things and spat at him, but he had not turned his head or responded, until the flames were licking at the carved face of the last of her gods. By then she was out of breath and sobbing.

"Burn," he'd murmured without turning to face her. He had kept his eyes on the flames. "When God is near, everything unclean catches fire. Nothing unclean must remain in my house. I will invite no more fire in my house."

He watched the coals long into the night, ignoring the weeping of his wife's mother. Seven days. His wife Hadassah had been dead only seven days.

***

Now, months later, Barak stood before the *navi*, taking her measure. The *navi* was aging but lovely; she was not tall, but the way she stood and the hardness in her eyes conveyed presence and command—something he had never seen before or expected to see in a woman. The man standing behind her was a giant, and his legend as giant as he, but unlike his chieftains, Barak ignored the nazarite. After an initial glance, he ignored the Canaanite girl too, though her face pulled at his heart, troubling him; she looked so much like Hadassah.

But Barak did not like to be distracted from a thing that he needed. He focused on the *navi*.

"What would you ask?" Devora's voice sounded a little hoarse. Good. She was off her guard, then.

Barak lifted his voice, intending to speak in a way that demanded her submission, but to his own surprise he found that his tone grew hard with anger.

"Each year, we in the hills send a tenth of our harvest to Shiloh. To *feed* Shiloh. So you can speak to God, protect us from the dead." Barak thought grimly of the caravans moving south through the hills—and of the screams of Hadassah's mother as the fire devoured her gods. He had done his part to keep Law and Covenant. "Now the dead have come," he said. "What happened?"

"What happened." Devora's face tightened. "Each year fewer tithes come. Each year fewer children are dedicated to the priesthood. Each year as I sit in decision here, I hear more offenses against the Law and the Covenant, more lawlessness in the land. And now, this day, I hear that the People have need of spears to protect them, and only three tribes have come. It is not Shiloh that has failed."

Barak's eyes glinted with anger. But he held his tongue. That this *woman* should take him to task…but the *navi* was set apart from all women. She was *kadosh*, she was holy. She was God's. A man could not strike her. Nor could a man ignore her words.

"I demand assurances of God." Barak planted the end of his spear haft into the earth, but he did not lean on it. "I have heard things in the hills that touch my mind with fear. Who is to say El will stride before us against the unburied dead?"

"Have the men of this land become weak, brittle? Moseh the Lawgiver but lifted his hand, and raiders from another tribe tumbled into the dust—for he knew God was near. Do you and your men know nothing but your own fright, roaring louder in your hearts than anything else you might hear?"

"I hear *you*," Barak said grimly. "And I believe you hear God. If God is with us, *navi*, I will not fear." Barak held her gaze. He did not know what he would find when he returned to the north, what he would have to face. But this woman did. This woman could see what would happen, see what God might give and what God might take away. He would not allow himself to lose his temper with her; he needed her. His men needed her. "I'll not lead men on a raid they won't survive or to a battle I can't win. If we have no sign that God is with us, if you will not go with us into the north, then I will go home to my vineyard, and likely each of the men will seek out his own door, to stand in defense of his own home, until the dead come. Let all other men fend for themselves."

DEVORA'S DECISION

"…IF YOU WILL NOT GO…"

Dread sat in Devora's breast, a clammy mass wrapped in damp, clinging cloth. If Barak did not lead the tribes into the north, surely the vision she had seen would become real. And the infant she had buried would be only the first of many. The cold presence of all the cairns on the slope seemed suddenly intense; the outlines of those farther up the hill stood sharp against the sky, a demand. Like so many silent watchers waiting to see if the judge and *navi* of Israel would keep her promise. That the unclean death would stop with the raising of these stones and devour no more of the land's children, whether Hebrew or heathen.

But there were *dead* in the north, many dead. To go with the men—it would be like returning to the night of the attack on Shiloh, or to that other, earlier night in her mother's tent. She could hear, faint and distant, the death-shrieks outside that tent. She held the memory at bay with an effort of will.

Behind her, Zadok growled low in his throat, like a wolf coming awake at a threat to his own.

Devora fought to stay calm. "Do I look like a man to you, Barak ben Abinoam? Like one who takes up the spear?"

Omri actually *leered* at her—as if thinking that, no, she didn't look like a man to him—but Devora ignored him.

"We both go, or neither, *navi*," Barak said.

"He is right," Omri said. "The men are frightened."

"When God calls a man to take up the spear," Devora cried, "he does not ask him to count the enemy."

Barak's eyes narrowed.

"*I* do not count them," Omri said. His smile didn't touch his eyes. "I am here. I am ready for a fight. That jackal Nimri is too. But other men shake in their tents or their houses. Maybe they have grown old and weak in their hearts. Or maybe they are just sleepy—who knows? Those with a bit of loot, a few fine garments, a girl or two, are ready to rest. I have brought home no slaves and have little to put in my house. So I'm not done with the spear. But there has been a lot of fighting: the raids of the Sea People, strife with the Horse People east of the river, threats from the chieftains of White Cedars to our north. But now no spearmen come out of White Cedars to raid us, only the unclean dead."

"Will you come?" Barak asked, his voice cold and quiet.

Devora swallowed. "You would force the hand of God's *navi*."

"I would."

For a moment Devora glimpsed grief in the man's eyes, a grief deep as a scream but silent.

"I have heard the dead near my vineyard," Barak said, "and I have done what I could to gather men to silence them. But I am not Moseh. I am not

Yeshua, or Othniel, or Ehud. And God has taken much from me." His eyes were dark and intense. "Like a woman, God promises out of one corner of the mouth and curses out of the other. Let God send a sign that she favors us. Let God send the Ark—or send you."

The wind had picked up again, and strands of Devora's hair flicked across her vision. Her throat felt very dry.

The men's eyes were on her. They were so strange, these men of the north. Hardly better than heathen. Perhaps they *were* half-heathen. More than any other tribes in Israel, they'd mingled with other peoples who burned *olah* before gods of the sea or gods of the rain or gods of the forested hills. With people who did not cleanse their bodies or wash to the elbows before they ate. People who ate foods that defiled them. People who touched the dead bodies of their kin, who raised no cairns over their dead or who fed them to fish. People who defiled the land.

Devora exhaled slowly. She thought of the chieftains losing their courage and returning each to his own territory, and each man to his own crop. The thought horrified her. Those dead she'd seen in her vision—they would devour each homestead, each tent, as easily as a child might pluck berries.

Yet to go *with* these men, to seek out the dead herself—it would be like riding right into her memories.

Her mother's screams were louder, nearer. The green leaves above her tossed in a sudden gust. There was sharp pain in her palms. Slowly she forced her hands to open, saw where her nails had cut her skin.

She sat in decision over the People, with the Law at her back like an old woman with a hand on her shoulder to guide her. But what would guide her in *this* decision?

As if in answer, a wave of heat and a wave of vision. Again she saw the slouching dead moving through barley fields, and recoiled from the sight. For an instant she glimpsed a young woman wielding a bronze peg, a tent peg. A young woman with eyes that hurt to look at.

Then the vision passed, and there were only Barak and Omri before her, and Zadok behind her, and the Canaanite girl weeping silently by her child's cairn.

But it was enough. For the vision had shown her what she needed to know—that the dead could be dealt with, and that Barak ben Abinoam could not deal with them alone. Once, long years ago, Devora had hid shaking in her mother's tent, helpless in her terror, while everyone she knew died. She would not let that kind of fear determine her choices now.

She motioned Barak closer.

When the northern chieftain stood before her, Devora spoke softly, for his ears alone. "There will be screaming in the Galilee. But the God who gives me these—visions—he is the same God who parted the sea for Moseh. He gave our fathers bread in the desert. He has shattered walls and broken the spears of chieftains whom men feared. He makes the barley grow and gives heat and light to the earth. And with this God, with *this* God you have made your covenant, Barak." Her voice had dropped, and he leaned in to hear. "Learn not to demand assurances," she whispered.

"Nevertheless," he murmured, "you will go?"

"I will go," she said.

Seeing the relief in his face, she realized that for all his bravado, Barak hadn't been sure she would come—or what he would do if she refused.

"I would like to meet the woman who mothered you," Devora said. "She must have torn out her hair in exasperation."

"She is ten years beneath a cairn," Barak said.

Devora made a small noise in her throat. Barak did indeed have all the traits of a man who had little to do with women and had neither wife nor mother to counsel him or soften his edges. But enough. She had made her decision, it was done. Though she felt so cold. She must turn now to practical matters.

"Provide a white tent," she said. "One befitting God's *navi* to whom the priests at Shiloh listen. My husband has a horse that I will ask for, so you need provide no more than the tent."

"It will be done." Barak nodded. "I will send one of the chieftains for you after the Sabbath, *navi*." The man began walking back to his horse. Omri gave the *navi* another look and grinned at her, then followed Barak.

"Barak!" Devora called out suddenly.

He turned.

"Something else God has shown to me. You have approached God with doubt and demands and not as your fathers' fathers did. The renown for this victory will not go to you or to your kin or to your tribe. God has shown me that he will deliver the dead into the hands of women."

For a moment there was silence on the hillside.

"Then let us hope those women know what to do with them," Barak said, and turned from her.

THE ANGEL OF DEATH

As Barak and Omri mounted and rode away from the cairns, Devora looked after them, troubled. It occurred to her suddenly that she might be vulnerable among these men of the north, who only granted a grudging acknowledgment of her holy position. Clearly, Nimri and Omri looked at her and saw only a woman, rather than a levite anointed by God. Yet Shiloh's women were set apart from all the women of their People. Many of them had been dedicated as children to the service of the Most Holy God. They wove the clothing that the high priest wore when he entered the *shekinah*, the holy presence within the Tent of Meeting. Their hands carried incense to the door of that Tent, preparing a sweet scent for God. They were not as other women.

Now the behavior of these three men of the Galilee reminded her that women elsewhere in the land had *not* been dedicated to such holy service. Women elsewhere might anoint their bodies or their bedding with sweet scents for men, but none of those other women carried sweet scents before God. And their lives were more slave-like. They might be beaten, for instance, if they failed to please their father or their brother or their husband, whatever man was their keeper. They might be deprived of food or bartered away if their man tired of them. That bartering was against the Covenant, but she knew such things occurred. Devora sensed that the women of the north lived different lives than those she had known.

She felt Zadok beside her, a tall, firm presence. "Ride north with me after the Sabbath, Zadok," she said. "God's *navi* needs a nazarite beside her."

"Your will, *navi*," he murmured.

She lowered her head. "I am glad you—woke—so quickly," she said.

He didn't answer. Devora could feel his shame. Like a drumbeat in the air.

"I should have remembered," she said. "I shouldn't have placed that burden on you."

"I have taken the nazarite vow—"

"Yes," Devora said. "You have taken the vow. And I was wrong to abuse it."

Before Zadok could answer, the *navi* turned and approached the Canaanite where she knelt by the cairn, holding her salmah closed with one hand. If there had been scant time before, the arrival of the riders had only made her urgency greater. The sun was nearly touching the far ridge; the Sabbath bride was already walking across the eastern hills toward them. And she must yet decide what to do with the heathen girl.

Devora stopped when she stood near the Canaanite.

"You are unclean," the *navi* said to her, for the girl had carried a corpse for several days. "I cannot bring you to the tents at Shiloh. But I can find you some place to sleep at the edge of the camp."

The girl didn't look at her. Her face was pale and exhausted, as though she herself were one of the dead, whose cairn had been inadequate to hold her to the earth. "Leave me here," she whispered. "Let me die near my child." She lowered her head, leaned it against the cairn. Began singing softly, Canaanite words that Devora didn't know. It sounded like a go-to-sleep song, one of the simple, slow melodies mothers sing to infants. Despite her need for haste, Devora watched her a moment, caught. Her own mother had sung to her once like that, other melodies, but just as soft.

Then Devora sighed. "Zadok, carry her."

The Canaanite's voice fell still. The nazarite's mouth twisted in distaste, but he didn't hesitate. As he stepped toward her, Hurriya looked up at last, her eyes hot. "Don't you touch me!"

"He won't hurt you, girl. Nor will he touch your skin. Come, now." Devora gripped the girl's left arm near the shoulder through the thin wool she wore, careful not to touch her bare skin, for she was unclean. She lifted Hurriya to her feet. Hurriya looked wildly from her to the nazarite.

"We are not going to hurt you," Devora said again.

The girl acquiesced as Zadok lifted her into his arms, her body rigid with tension. Devora shook her head. She could not leave the girl on the hill; she was a supplicant. The *navi* had an obligation to her. But neither did she know what to do with her.

Devora led the way, and she and Zadok circled the hill. The nazarite was watchful. They could see, below in the valley, the two horsemen racing the dusk, hurrying back to their own camp. As Devora and her nazarite reached the slope beneath the olive tree, the *navi* glanced up toward her seat.

And gasped.

No. No, this couldn't be. Her body went rigid with attention; she stopped breathing. Was it only a trick of the light, of the setting sun? It *must* be. Yet even as she gazed, she saw—she was *certain* she saw—

She broke into a run, ignoring Zadok's shout behind her. Climbing the hill was an exertion, and her sides burned, but she forced herself on and came quickly to the olive tree. Even as she approached, she knew that it had been no trick of the light. The tree was changing. The edges of its long leaves crinkling, drying. As though the tree were dying one of the long deaths of trees, accelerated into the brevity of a handful of days, quickened so that she could *see* the death, even as one might see a fever taking a child's body, relentlessly, from one brief hour to the next. She reached up, touched her fingers to one of the yellowing leaves. The edge of the leaf crumbled even as she touched it; it was dry, brittle. She let out a low cry and leapt back from the tree, taking in all of it. The leaves along one entire half of the tree were drying away, dying—the half of the tree that faced the north.

"Are you hurt, *navi*?" Zadok called, hurrying to her side, leaving the Canaanite standing below.

"The tree," she gasped.

Zadok approached quickly, his gaze darting to the branches. She heard him suck in his breath. For a long moment they stood quite still. The tree appeared to wither even as they watched; whatever part this olive tree, like all others in the land, had shared in the Covenant of God, it was now dissolving away, like papyrus exposed to water. The sight of it drew all the warmth out of Devora's body, left her shivering. She thought of the unclean flesh she had laid in the earth on this very hill, so near the tree's roots, and a low moan rose in her throat. She closed her lips tightly to hold it in.

"What does it mean, *navi*?" Zadok breathed.

Devora let her hand fall from the branch. "It means—the promise is revoked. That the unclean dead will overwhelm the land because we have broken Covenant with God. That blight and plague will no longer pass over us without touching our soil." She stared helplessly at the tree. "It's the *malakh ha-mavet*, Zadok. The *malakh ha-mavet*. The angel of death."

CRIES IN THE OLIVES

"IT IS ONLY ONE TREE," Zadok said as they hurried down the long slope toward the tents. He carried the Canaanite girl in his arms as if she weighed no more than a linen cloth. Their voices were hushed, breathless as they rushed through the heather at nearly a run, the slope already cast into shadow. Less than an hour now before dark, when the Sabbath would come like a bride to the People, her face veiled by the night sky, to free the People from work, give them rest, remind them they were free and possessors of a land of their own, with no overseer's whip and no foreign gods to take from them their labor and their harvests.

But though it was customary to greet the bride with song or with a slapping of hands against thighs and exuberant shouts, tonight the delight of Sabbath barely touched Devora's heart as she struggled to keep pace with Zadok's mighty strides. Her heart was clutched in the withering roots of that olive tree. Her face very pale.

"It is *not* only one tree," Devora protested. "What sickens one plant can kill an entire crop. What sickens within one woman's heart can poison an entire People. You know this, Zadok. Why else did you take the nazarite vow?"

"It is *one* tree," Zadok said, "and all about me I see a land fertile and lush, a land of olives and great herds."

"This day I have seen the land filled with herds of the ravenous dead." Devora's voice shook. "Zadok ben Zefanyah, the Law will defend the People from the dead," Devora breathed, "but only if the People live by it. How many times have I sat in judgment over acts that tear at the very roots of the Covenant? Brothers killing brothers or robbing them. Bodies left unburied. And always, I hear of—of *her* people, mingling with ours. Of Hebrew men who permit deities of wood and clay to reside in their homes, or who dance at Canaanite festivals in the hill country. Zadok! What *if*—"

Zadok made no answer, and Devora did not voice her fears. Her side burned; though she was aging, she was the *navi* and she climbed and descended this hill often. And her need and her anxiety drove her. Yet their haste was taking its toll on her, and her growing dread seemed to choke away her breath.

Glancing at the silent girl Zadok carried, Devora wanted badly to hate her, to loathe her for the withering that was coming on the land, a blight in which her strange people and their small, useless gods had surely played some part. And hate would be easier on her than this cold, clinging dread. But the little flame of hate flickered out; she could not sustain it. The girl was too weak to hate.

Hurriya was a ruin, barely alive; she'd likely been held together only by her need to seek out the *navi*, to bring her that tiny corpse and beg for the impossible. Now the Canaanite stared out at the valley and at the white tents they were approaching. Unblinking, apparently unaware of the day or the hour or of anything but what lay within her own heart, in her own grief.

The *malakh ha-mavet*!

Every Hebrew child knew the story. How the night before their fathers' exodus from a foreign land, the *malakh ha-mavet* had visited the homes of the men and women of Kemet, from the lowest farm worker to the home of Pharaoh himself. And in each home, the firstborn had been struck with the uncleanness, the fever, the drying out and convulsing of the body, then the quick tossing of the spirit into the empty dark and the stillness of a corpse cooling slowly on its bed. And then, in the hours before dawn, when the Nile was calm and quiet as a lake, the firstborn rose hungering, and the grieving of their parents turned to shrieks of terror as son devoured father and daughter devoured mother, as parents turned on the bodies of their children with spades or shovels or sharpened styluses. That night of the risen dead had left every house in Kemet spattered with blood.

Every dwelling place but the Hebrews'.

For God's hand had covered them.

The Hebrews commemorated that night each spring at the festival of Pesach, the Passing Over, even as they commemorated the time of wandering in the desert each harvest at Sukkot, the Feast of Tents. Each year, the *kohannim* reminded the gathered celebrants in the fields about Shiloh that so long as they kept the Covenant and lived by the Law, God's hand would cover Israel. Their sons and their daughters would be as many as the stars in the night sky; their tribes would grow as fruitful as the branches of the olive tree.

But now the olive tree above Shiloh had withered.

The three in the heather were approaching the camp swiftly; Devora could see men and women among the white tents ahead. She found that she was reciting one of the *mitzvot* softly, though she barely had breath for it; for once, the words of the Law brought her little calm. The burn in her side was fierce.

***

When they had approached within shouting distance of the camp, they halted where a dip in the land would conceal the girl's uncleanness from the sight of the tents. While Devora leaned forward with her hands on her legs above the knees, gasping for breath, Zadok took his cloak and, with only a moment's hesitation, laid it out across the weeds and blossoms. Then he placed the girl gently on it. He would need to find a new cloak; he would not get this one back.

The girl lifted her hand and caught at Devora's sleeve. The *navi* tensed.

"I heard you talking with the men," she whispered. "There are more dead. Many more dead."

"Yes," Devora said.

"We're all going to die. Like my child."

"We most certainly are not," Devora snapped.

"They came out of the olive grove. There were eight of them, and their bodies had been torn open and eaten on, as though a lion or a wolf had been at them. But they were walking, they were *walking*." The girl's eyes showed their whites.

"I know," Devora said.

"Malachi was at the olive press, and they *ate* him. They snarled like animals. They dragged him down and tore at him and *ate* him."

Devora shivered.

"I was in the shack, and I tried to hold the door. I tried to keep them out— I tried—I tried—" She began weeping, without tears. "They were too strong. They wanted the baby—they wanted my baby—"

In her mind Devora could hear the shrieks of her mother again, dying outside the tent. "I know," she said again, her voice hoarse. The girl's misery seemed terribly familiar, a dark mirror of Devora's own. The girl had come to her seat for judgment, but there was never any forgiveness for the deaths of your kin. Whether you could have prevented their deaths or not, they were gone. Devora knew this too well.

Some days a woman can only save one life, the old *navi* Naomi had tried to tell her when she was a girl. Yet surely if that one life were always your own, that was an abomination in the eyes of the God who sits in decision over the living and the dead. Unable to look away from Hurriya's quiet misery, Devora realized that the Canaanite, like she herself, stood alone and still breathing among the corpses of her kin. And even if Hurriya survived her heart's grief and her body's anguish, she would still stand there, every night of her life, every morning. Though she had sacrificed everything she had and everything she was as she struggled out of the hills, wasting her body away as she bore her dying infant in her arms, still her child and its father were dead. She, she only, was alive. There would never be forgiveness for that. Devora knew this; she had fled alone out of the death of her parents' camp when she was twelve, had listened and waited for mercy, and had received only barrenness in her womb and night terrors when her memories came back to her in the dark, and hard burdens to carry.

Devora felt that she must say something. She could not just leave this girl grieving here in that woolen cloth that could only be called a garment by an act of the imagination, with her body thin and exhausted and torn from childbirth, her breasts swollen with milk that had become futile, a curse to her.

"You did what you could," Devora told her after a moment. "Try to sleep, and forget."

"Forget," Hurriya whispered. She began to laugh softly, helplessly. Letting go of Devora's sleeve, she curled up, bringing her knees to her chest as though to protect an unborn child, though she had only her own ravaged heart to protect, only her own body to shield.

Devora exchanged a look with Zadok, then stood.

"I can get bedding for her," Zadok said. "But if we leave her here weeping, a wolf will come for her."

"Guard her tonight, for me."

"Your will, *navi.*"

Devora's shoulders sagged beneath the weight of her unseen burdens. What if the girl *did* die out here? She glanced at Zadok, saw the weariness in his eyes.

Shelter the stranger you find in your land.

Yet like Hurriya fleeing her hills, Devora had done what she could. It was not enough, but only a small crescent of the sun was visible now above the hills. She'd lingered too long already.

"When your uncleanness has passed," she said without looking at the girl, "you can wash linens in the camp, be given meals, a place to sleep. Until we know if any kin live who can claim you. Forget, girl. That is all you can do. There will be other children."

The girl just sobbed. The sound wrenched at the *navi*'s heart.

Devora turned and hurried toward the white tents, walking fast.

SHILOH

SHILOH CAMP was both a monument and a defense against the past. It lay on the land like a great map beneath the gaze of God that charted the People's history and their orientation toward their deity. The *kohannim* boasted that no matter where a Hebrew found himself in the land, he always knew which direction he was facing. For a People whose fathers had lost a generation wandering in the desert and hiding from the restless dead, knowing where things were was vitally important. Where there was water, where there was sand, where there were quail to eat or deer to hunt. Where there were enemies and where there were kin. Where you were and where God was in relation to you.

The camp was a great square, tilted so that its points faced north, west, east, and south. The eastern quadrant held the tents of the *kohannim*, the priests who'd gone through seven-day rites of purification and cleansing and could now approach God's presence without fear, bringing burnt offerings to atone for the uncleanness of the tribes. The doors of their tents faced east, toward the Tumbling Water, the great river the People had crossed when they took the land. Their tents faced the past.

The western tents held those levites who were not of the priesthood. Scribes and craftsmen and the young dedicates who were brought to Shiloh as children, to be raised as levites if they were boys or to be raised as wives for them if they were girls.

The southern quadrant held the tents of the seventy judges appointed to resolve disputes. These faced the vast settlements of Benyamin and Yudah tribes, the most populous in the land.

And across the camp, facing north and away from the People, as though keeping watch toward those hills where there were still many heathen, stood the tents of the nazarites, those who'd taken the harshest of vows to defend the Ark, the holy tribe of Levi, the priests, and the *navi*. In the midst of their tents lay a great cleared space of dirt and sand where the nazarites danced the spears each morning, training for battles with either the living or the dead. The nazarites were few. There were in fact only five in Shiloh this year. Though in the north there were raids from the fortified towns on the coast or from the heathen settlements in White Cedars where the hilltops were high enough for snow, those were the concern of the northern tribes. The rest of the land had lain quiet for a generation. Few now took the nazarite vow or kept it. Many of the older nazarites had even gone through the rites to be released of their vows. Of the generation who remembered the night the dead had come to Shiloh, only Zadok was left.

And finally, broad and mighty at the utmost east of the camp, standing between the People and their terrible past, stood the Tent of Meeting, many-colored and stretched over a frame of wooden poles. It was the reason for Shiloh's existence. Within it, behind a heavy veil, was the *kodesh kodashim*, the

Holy of Holies, which held the Ark of the Covenant. Inside that great chest of wood and gold were tablets of stone on which were inscribed the Ten, the words spoken by God to the People at Har Sinai, the words that had initiated the Covenant, the first words of the Law. And above that Ark, in an empty space between the outspread wings of carved golden angels, dwelled the *shekinah*, the heat and presence of their ancient desert God.

Even in their ancestors' time when Shiloh had moved often, this Tent had never been raised *within* the camp. It always stood just outside, in hope that the uncleanness of the People would not offend God to wrath. In the outer part of the Tent, in a tiny censer prepared by levite women and placed before the veil, incense was burned at all hours, to sweeten the scent of the camp, so it would be easier for God to live near them. The *kohannim* taught that this God they'd found in the desert was not like the handcrafted gods of wood and stone that the heathen revered, gods who might be housed within your own tent without fear, small gods who were powerless to protect those who honored them from either the spears of the living or the teeth of the dead.

No, the Hebrews' God was *el kadosh*. He was a mighty and holy God, and the unclean dead and the unclean living alike would wither if they approached him. At all times he was set apart from the camp, so that if his anger burst into flame, perhaps only a small part of the camp would burn, those tents nearest him. He must be approached with care. His heat could kindle not only against the enemies of the People, living or dead, but against the People themselves. For though the *kohannim* believed this strange God had consented and chosen to dwell among the Hebrews alone out of all the peoples in all the lands beneath the sun, the *kohannim* also remembered that before this God, all peoples, even theirs, were small. If God's slightest fingertip touched the land, that touch might dry a river or scorch crops. What then would happen if, looking about and seeing the evil the People too often did to each other, how the People too often failed to care for the living or confine the dead, what if God in wrath should strike the land with his fist? Would not the very hills smoke?

***

Devora passed the Tent of Meeting as she hurried into Shiloh, and she passed the charred earth beside it, that silent memorial to the night of wrath thirty years past. Her heart hardened at the sight of it. That night it had been

Canaanites who had brought the unclean death to the camp. The heathen who could not be trusted to place their dead beneath cairns or to keep their camps clean of dead meat or even to wash their own arms up to the elbows before lifting their fingers to their mouths. The heathen who all but *invited* the coming of the unclean dead.

At the doors of the white tents, the *kohannim* and their wives stood singing, in robes and gowns of white with embroidered hems. The men sang first, deep voices lifted in ululation to greet the Sabbath bride, who came over the hills clothed in the *shekinah*. Even before the men's voices fell silent, their wives lifted their own, lovely voices calling out their worship of the God who gives and takes away, the God who stirs new life in the womb and closes us each in the womb of the earth when our brief lives have ended.

The men and women of Shiloh camp inclined their heads respectfully as the *navi* passed, and despite her haste Devora slowed her walk enough that she could pass them with dignity—though her white gown was stained and torn in places from her work in raising the cairn, and her feet were sore within her sandals. The song she heard all about her was a comfort; it eased the anxiety that had choked her after the withering of her olive tree. With so many men and women singing a greeting to God, it was unthinkable that God was not here among them. Perhaps the withering had only been a warning, nothing more.

As she approached the high priest's tent—her husband's was still many tents beyond it, in the western part of the camp—Devora halted and looked at the high priest and his wife as they sang outside the door of their tent. She had to tell him, she realized. She had to tell the *kohannim* of her vision.

Eleazar ben Phinehas ben Eleazar ben Aharon was the head of Levi tribe and the one man who might pass within the last veil to speak face-to-face with the *shekinah*, the hot presence that dwelled over the Ark. He alone could give offerings there, sending up a sweet smoke to renew the Covenant between God and People. Among all the People, only he was permitted by Law to speak without the veil between him and the divine ears.

Only he.

Except that God, too, could draw aside the veil. Without consulting priest or levites, the *shekinah* might sometimes fall upon a *navi*, showing the prophet things that otherwise only God's eyes would see. It was an uneasy relationship, that of the high priest and the *navi*.

Eleazar's robe was white like the other priests', but over it he wore the *ephod*, a loose garment gold like the sun. And over that he wore an ornamented bronze breast-piece. It was the sign of his office, the *hoshen mishpat*, the breast-piece of decision. Embedded in the *hoshen* were twelve smooth river stones from the Tumbling Water, on which had been inscribed the names of the Hebrew tribes, and also two stones with no letters on them, one dark as a cow's eye, the other pale as dead flesh. The *urim* and *thummim*, a last resort, a device for divining God's will in uncertain matters.

Beside Eleazar stood Hannah, his wife, in a white levite's gown with the blue sash of the midwives about her hips. Her head tilted back in song. She was a tall woman, nearly as tall as the priest; she had always towered over Devora.

"Eleazar!" Devora called out.

The priest stopped his song, and his wife beside him fell silent. They looked at Devora curiously. Disheveled as she was, the *navi* likely was a strange sight to them.

Devora found herself out of breath, trying to gasp out what was in her heart. "*Kohen*, there are dead—the olive tree—it withered—and there are dead. So many." She swallowed, gathered herself. "God sent a vision."

"What did he show you?" Eleazar murmured. There was respect in his tone, but wariness too.

Briefly, Devora told of her vision, of the lurching herds.

"This is horrible!" Hannah gasped. And Devora saw in the other woman's eyes that she too remembered the night of wrath thirty years before. No one who had been there would ever forget it.

Eleazar's eyes had become windows into a desolate place. "What you have seen is like cold water on my heart," he said after a moment. "The men of the Galilee sent a messenger here today."

Devora stiffened. "What did he say?"

"He said the other tribes were refusing to come at Barak's call. He asked for the Ark." Eleazar looked grim.

It was said that in the days of Yeshua when the People took possession of lands east of the Tumbling Water, the levites had carried the Ark on stout poles in advance of the host. The few dead walking in those valleys had stumbled out of the fields with their lifted arms and their moaning voices, only to wither before the Ark like dry wheat before a desert wind. So it was said.

"But they have come with only three tribes, *navi*. They cannot take the Ark. They think God does not care if his People are divided or together."

"Maybe we should talk, all of us, after the Sabbath," Devora said quickly. "What I've seen—if there are so many dead—"

"We are one People, *navi*."

"I *know* that. But perhaps it's time to cast the *urim and thummim*, to find out if God *wishes* to go north with the men. Why else would he have sent me such visions?"

"Perhaps. But right now it is time to greet the bride," Eleazar said, cutting her off. And he turned toward the door of his tent.

"Eleazar, please—"

"We will talk after the Sabbath, *navi.*" He spoke without turning and disappeared into his tent.

Devora stood a moment, afflicted again by a terrible sense of not having done enough. Hannah gave her an understanding look but said nothing. Devora turned to leave, then stopped. Fresh to her mind had come the sight of the Canaanite curled up like a wounded animal in her travel-stained salmah, nothing but a woolen blanket to shelter her body and her grief.

"Hannah," Devora called.

The priest's wife had her hand at the door of the tent. She glanced back at the *navi.*

"Hannah, please. After the Sabbath. There is a girl at the edge of the camp. Zadok is tending her. She is weak from childbirth and likely ill. She'll need ointment, and herbs, and warm water and cloths. You'll know what else she needs better than I. Will you go to her, Hannah?"

Hannah gave her a curious look. "Who is she?"

The *navi* paused. She could hear the sides of the tent flapping slightly as a wind moved through the camp. It seemed to her that the wind carried to her the sound of a faint moan, as if from the hill. Then a quiet, gasping sob, the grief of a bereaved woman. Perhaps visions came to her ears this day and not only to her eyes. Or perhaps she only imagined it. "A supplicant," she said. She could not say *a heathen,* nor explain why it suddenly seemed so important to her that someone see to the girl. She had no time to argue with Hannah.

Hannah gave a small nod. "I will see to her. Good Sabbath, *navi.*" She paused. "The other wives are dining with us. Will you join us?"

"Not tonight," Devora said.

Then she walked swiftly, almost at a run, toward her husband Lappidoth's tent. All through the camp, the priests' songs were falling silent; the Sabbath had arrived.

And then Devora *did* run, forgetful of dignity.

THE MAN WHO DEFENDED HIS CATTLE

DEVORA HAD BEEN twelve the first time she had seen him; he had been twenty. She was traveling alone on her way to Shiloh after the dead had devoured her mother's camp and all her kin. By night she lay in the weeds, shivering. By day she moved with caution, listening for any moaning dead and keeping away from any cart paths or any living men she saw, who might be tempted by a girl alone and without the protection of her tribe. It was easy to tell at a distance whether a figure striding through barley or tall grass was living or dead, for the dead staggered and lurched, but either the living or the dead could be dangerous to her. She was the only one left of all the men and women and children she knew; the fourteen others in her camp were dead. She was weak from hunger, and she hurried from one small pond or mud hole to the next, anxious for water.

The day she first saw Lappidoth was the second day of her flight.

She heard the moaning first, faint but unmistakable over the music of nearby water, and for a long time she stood still, terribly still, in grass higher than her chin. When she moved a little, as silently as she could, she came to a stream and saw the dead—and *him*—on the other bank. He was defending his herd from them. One of the cows had been torn apart; the others huddled in the middle of the stream. There were four corpses attacking. One was naked with a great gash in its side, its ribs white in the sun. Another of the dead had only one arm, yet it clawed at the air with the other as it came at the herdsman.

The young man had cast aside his cloak so that they could not grasp at it to pull him toward their biting teeth; he wore only his loincloth and a cattleherder's gloves, his body covered in a sheen of sweat. He held a flint hatchet, and he ducked and darted among the dead like a desert fox among serpents. Devora watched, breathless. The herdsman was so careful not to touch them with his hands, not to defile himself. He brought his hatchet down at one of the corpses' heads, shearing away the ear, then neatly flipped the hatchet about in his hand and swung his right arm back, driving the flint blade into the corpse's head. Then he leapt back out of the others' reach; they staggered after him. Devora held her breath, her heart in her throat. The dead hissed, and she could hear again her mother's shrieks and the shambling feet of the dead in her camp. Devora shrank back, though it meant the tall grass obscured her sight a little.

Even as she watched, eyes wide, one of the dead closed with the herder while his hatchet clove another's head; leaving the hatchet stuck in the first corpse's skull, the man ducked beneath the second's grasp and got his gloved hands on its hips. In a moment he lifted the rotting corpse high above his head and hurled it bodily into the stream.

The corpse in the stream splashed on its back like a turtle trying to right itself in the water. There was no time for the herder to try retrieving his hatchet; the corpse that was still on its feet was reaching for him. He leapt to the side, grasped a fistful of its hair in his gloved hand, and tried to pull it from its feet, but the corpse's scalp peeled free with the hair and the thing was still grasping for him, moaning, a bared patch of its skull shining in the sun. Devora bit her hand to smother a scream. She wanted to flee, to get far, far away from the dead, but something in her held her there, hiding in the tall grass, watching. Her own camp had been helpless against the dead, but this man wasn't. Her eyes shone with admiration.

The man stumbled; he fell to the dirt and then rolled fast to his left as the corpse turned and staggered after him. He got up into a crouch and then sprinted across the sand, putting distance between himself and the corpse. The other unclean corpse had risen from the water and was coming at him too. The man ran to the water's edge and bent and took up two large stones in his hands, one a blunt river stone the size of a clay bowl, the other a jagged rock that had been broken in two sometime before and would serve for a hatchet. With his eyes hard, one rock in either hand, he turned to face the oncoming dead.

***

In the end, they lay at his feet, unmoving. The herdsman stood panting, the rocks still clutched in his hands, dripping brown, viscous fluid, his head lowered. He might have been praying, or mourning, or simply spending all his energy just breathing, just staying on his feet.

She had watched him for so long. A warmth lit in her heart.

But he was a man, a strange man, and she was still a girl. She slipped away through the grass; glancing once over her shoulder, she saw through the tall blades his face lifted, peering after her. He must have heard her rustling retreat.

He must have looked up. Her heart pounded, and she fled. She didn't stop running until her sides burned and her legs gave out under her.

The man gave her something to think about on the long walk to Shiloh. Something other than her mother's face. By day as she walked—drinking from small streams and chewing on grass to dull the bite of hunger, her ears attentive for any sound of the dead—she thought about the man and the way he had stood between the moaning dead and the riverbank. The way the sun had blazed on his bare shoulders and arms. She had not known what a man was, not really. There had been men in the encampment where she and her mother lived, and there had been her father, though they were gone now. They had been merely adults, taller and mysterious beings. Now she had seen a man. It seemed to her she had never truly seen one before. Her heart thrilled at it. The memory and wonder of it gave her the strength to keep placing one foot before the other.

But at night there was no escape from her terrors.

At night she lay awake, shivering, as the breeze tossed the blades of grass overhead. She could only lie still, listening, imagining terrible noises in the dark. Remembering how she'd wakened to see her mother's torso disappearing through the flap of the tent; something had her feet, was dragging her out. Her mother clutching frantically at the rug. The whites of her eyes.

Then she was gone; the rug slid out behind her. Devora had trembled, staring at the tent flap as her mother's screams broke the night, terrible screams. The sound of teeth tearing flesh. Screams that went on and on. Devora had covered her ears and just rocked back and forth, too scared even to cry.

Sometime in the hours that followed, Devora had taken up a clay pestle her mother had used to grind meal, the pestle cool in her hand, and had waited, shaking. At sunrise, a gray hand with strips of its flesh hanging loose had peeled aside the door of the tent, and her mother's face had peered in. What was *left* of her mother's face. Much of the flesh about her jaw had been chewed away, the bone showing under one gashed cheek. The corpse's dull eyes had looked directly at Devora, its mouth opening in a hiss.

Afterward, she had fled her mother's tent and the remains within it. The encampment had been full of the dead, shuffling back and forth. One of them was her father—who had been eaten as he slept in another tent. He had been weak. He had not saved her mother, or her—had done *nothing* to help them. Seeing her come out of the tent, he moaned, and then they were all moaning at her, all of her dead kin, and she ran. Ran fast and far across the low slopes, until she couldn't hear them anymore.

When the world was dark, there was no escape from the memories of her mother's camp. But by day, as Devora stumbled and half ran at times through the long grass, uphill and down, she forced the night shivers from her mind and dreamed instead of the man she'd seen fighting for his cattle, the man who, unlike her father, slew the dead and defended his own. His strong hands and the way the sunlight glistened on his back. She thought of him holding her, taking her in his arms, pressing his mouth to her throat as she had sometimes seen her father do with her mother. The warmth of that dream sustained her on the long walk. Whispering to God as she moved through the weeds, she vowed that she would find that man again one day.

***

Yet it was four and a half years before she saw the herdsman again, and in that time the entire shape of her life had changed. She had become the *navi*, had faced the dead again, had seen the fire in the tents. She'd even been kissed, but the man who'd kissed her was now beneath a cairn.

The year she turned sixteen, there was a rich harvest in the land, and more people than usual came to the Feast of Tents, that gathering where the men and women of the land leave their permanent camps or their towns and come to pitch tents in the fields near Shiloh for seven nights, in memory of their time of wandering in the desert. Many of the young women danced hill dances they'd learned from the Canaanites or the wilder desert dances of their own People. For the first time, Devora danced too—for she found her herdsman by accident as she spoke with a few chieftains among the tents pitched by Ephraim tribe. Their eyes met, and she excused herself from that moment of council, because some things are more important than talk or planning or Shiloh itself.

She danced that night for Lappidoth, whose eyes shone as he watched her. She knew he did not remember her; probably he had not seen her face that other time. Probably he had seen only a movement of the tall grass as she ran. But now he gazed upon her, and she burned as he looked at her, burned as though he'd touched her. How she danced! She let her hips sing of her desire as she moved in the moonlight; she had thought of him so many times as she lay waiting for sleep.

After the fires at the Feast of Tents were coals and the people had gone to sleep, she rose from her place and sought out his tent. There was no woman there; he was alone. She slipped onto the wool carpet he lay on and woke him with a whisper in his ear, a whisper she herself could not hear, for her heart and the blood in her ears were louder. It was the boldest moment in her life. She had no family, no tent of her own, only the visions that came to her sometimes from the God of the Covenant and the memory of her first sight of this man, a memory she'd held close for years. Those two were the only things she had, the only things that meant anything to her then. She whispered to him about her longing, how strong and like a man he'd looked to her when she had first seen him. Then his hands grasped her arms and he pulled her beneath him; she gasped as she felt his weight on her. His face above hers was struck with wonder, like a man who has been told that though he had never known it, he is the son of a chieftain. Or like a desert man on a long journey who crests a hill to find an unexpected, clear lake at his feet. "Who are you, girl?" he asked hoarsely.

"Devora," she whispered. "Your wife."

***

Before the Feast of Tents was finished, Devora and Lappidoth stood beneath a canopy together, and it seemed to the young *navi* that all Israel celebrated with them. They had reason to. The nazarites, though now few in number, had fulfilled their vows well, cleansing the low valleys of the restless dead. It was becoming rare to hear of a corpse walking. And though the Feast of Tents was a reminder of deprivation and hunger in the desert, it was also a reminder that beneath the sheltering roof of the Law, the People had *survived* the desert.

When Devora and Eleazar and the *kohannim* met and talked in the afternoons, they spoke of the need to push all the tribes to make sure that none of the Canaanites sent their dead to the water or left bodies unburied. And that none of their own people did either.

During the short, warm summer nights, Devora's mind was on other matters.

***

For thirty years, Devora had hidden away the memory of her mother's camp, and Lappidoth had found less reason to fear for his herd. Now the dead were back.

As the reverent hush of Sabbath fell over Shiloh camp, Devora drew aside the heavy canvas door of her husband's tent and found Lappidoth already within, seated cross-legged on his red cushions, and she found with warmth in her heart that he was the same man she had seen fighting for his cattle, the same man she'd danced for. He was still strong, and sturdy as an oak. Life in this lush land had been good to him. The fine threads and fringes on the rugs and cushions within the tent he shared with her were a sign of his wealth. He had many cattle in the fields and ten hired herdsmen and was an astute trader. In his lap he held a great clay bowl of grains, and before him was a round wafer of unleavened bread, about the size of his two hands.

"You're not eating the Sabbath meal with Hannah and the priests' wives?" His voice was a low rumble in the dimness.

Her throat felt tight. "I'd rather eat here with you, my husband."

He nodded and held out his hand to the cushions at his side. She went to him and knelt gracefully there by him. He pressed a clay bowl into her hands; it was filled with water. Devora set it before her and washed her hands and arms up to the elbows as the *mitzvot* required, then her face. The water felt cool against her skin, and she sighed softly as some of the sweat and dirt of the day flowed away into the bowl. Lappidoth took up a piece of the unleavened bread, breaking it in two.

After a moment Devora set the bowl behind her and leaned against his side, her head on his shoulder, as she had often done long ago, as a young woman. She pressed her face to his garment, which smelled of cattle, and cried without tears, her body shaking as though coming apart. Lappidoth's calloused hands were warm and comforting on her back.

She just let him hold her. He waited, neither eating the bread nor pressing her to eat, and not asking her any question. He just held her.

After a while she whispered, "There is a windstorm in my heart."

Lappidoth put his arm about her, held her tightly to him. With his other hand, he took a small stone and set it beside the bread. "This is my wife's heart," he rumbled. Then covered the stone with his cupped hand. "This is my love for my wife, covering her heart. That the winds may pass over without tearing through her."

She smiled despite the tightness in her breast. "I love you," she whispered.

Yet as she gazed at his hand cupped protectively about that small stone, she shivered. His words reminded her of what she'd seen at the olive tree, and her worry howled louder inside her. What if God had removed *his* hand?

SCREAMS IN THE NIGHT

THE *NAVI* BOLTED AWAKE with a cry, clutching at her breast. She sat up, heaving for air. The pain and terror of her dream so violent, she felt she'd black out. A roaring in her ears.

Then her husband's strong arms were about her, his voice low in her ear, murmuring to her, calming her. He caressed her hair as he spoke, almost as he might caress the neck of one of his horses, calming it after a rearing and a cry of panic. Horses, nightmares, the ravaging dead—nothing ever really fazed Lappidoth. Devora clutched him, her heart pounding, grateful that in the spinning dark there was one thing to cling to.

She gulped in great breaths of cold night air, her wool covers tangled about her legs, her body nude but for a sheen of sweat. She hated this. *Hated* waking like this. It was always a few moments before she even really knew who she was. She reached for the wool, drew it up about her. Lappidoth laid her gently back and helped her cover herself; his body was pressed to hers, warm and firm. He kissed her cheek and neck. "Shhh," he murmured. "Shhh, Devora."

Devora realized he was kissing away tears. Her face was moist. "Don't let me go back to sleep," she whispered.

Lappidoth's arm squeezed her, a promise. He shifted so that his hip rested on hers, so that his body partly covered her beneath the wool. It comforted her. He was large and warm, and his weight held her to the present, to this specific moment in his tent, in his bedding.

After a moment she put her arms around him, though her hands still trembled behind his back. He didn't try to make love to her, just held her, occasionally kissing her face, the line of her jaw, her lips. Devora listened to her husband's breathing, like that of some huge animal in the dark. She could feel his heart beating where his chest pressed to her. She began to breathe more slowly. Full, deep breaths, filling her body with air and life. Her heart stopped racing.

She pressed her face into the soft place between her husband's neck and his shoulder and breathed in his scent. He had always been a distraction to her, a distraction from everything.

She felt something stir against her hip, and her senses came alert. She moved her fingers slowly over his back, thinking. She held her breath a moment, then decided that if he wanted her again, she would voice no protest, though she also wouldn't invite it—she wanted only to be held. But lovemaking too would distract her from the past and the future. And she knew with an ache between her ribs that each time he touched her might be the last.

His large, thick hands began to caress her arms slowly, though he made no other movement. His breathing was a little faster. After a moment he murmured her name in that soft growl of his, and she caught her breath, remembering the night he first said her name that way—repeating it a moment after she made a gift of it.

***

Some time later, she found herself warmed and content and safe as she lay under him and felt his strong body on her and inside her. She loved the way his breathing felt after he finished. She drank in the smell of him.

"I'll ride with you," he murmured.

She gasped, her content fading. "No, you won't," she whispered, worry sharp within her.

He lifted himself up on his elbows, and she looked into his eyes in the dark. "I'd be ashamed to stay," he said. He had faced the dead before.

She lifted her hand to cup his face, felt the roughness of his beard against her palm. He covered her hand with his own. A large hand, a herdsman's hand. Once strong, so strong. Now so wrinkled, the veins thick like cords, but—so beautiful. Her husband was a man who sat with others in the evening and discussed the Law. He was a quiet man, though furious when roused. For an instant, heat rushed into her, scorching her, not a passion-heat but a God-heat, and she saw her strong, gentle husband in the grip of the dead, many of them, *so many*, the unclean dead tearing him off his horse and bearing him to the ground, their nails and teeth digging into his flesh. She gasped, and the vision left her, leaving dizziness in its wake. The tent spun around her a moment, and to keep herself from spinning with it she clutched Lappidoth's arms as tightly as she had during their love. She forced herself to breathe, and the world stilled.

Kisses soft and moist on her brow, on her eyelids. His rumbling voice. "Are you all right?"

She kept her eyes closed, fearing the tent would spin again. "Please, husband," she whispered. "I beg you. Stay, defend your cattle. You have no herds in the north." She felt the tension in him, but he didn't speak. "I will be with armed men, I will be safe. I will serve our God better knowing you are here." She opened her eyes at last, saw the pain in his. It made her ache. Making him promise to stay, when she left and put herself at risk, was cruel. But he was not a young man now. And what she had *seen*!

She spoke softly, hoping to save his pride. Her wonderful, strong, aging husband. The sharpness of worry in her heart. "Please. Stay, and take your best yearling bull to Eleazar. A sacrifice to the Most High, so he'll give us victory and bring me safe home."

He looked at her for a long moment, then nodded. She let out the breath she'd been holding, and Lappidoth kissed her slowly, warmly. Then he moved within her, making her cry out, startled. It had been long since they'd made love more than once.

This time, it was more effort than passion, but she did not care. She clung to him, felt the warmth of him, kissed his shoulders and neck, and thought, This is my husband, my husband. He was the one thing in the world that was truly hers and that she need sacrifice to no other and to no duty. She drove the visions from her mind, wishing she did not have to leave this tent. For a while—for a little while—she let herself forget everything, everything, and clung fiercely to him, willing this night and the Sabbath day that would follow and the night after to be without ending.

WIND IN THE CAMP

A FEW MILES AWAY, Barak also endured a restless night. The wind had picked up, and he lay in his pavilion with his eyes open, grateful for the roar of the wind against the canvas. The noise prevented him from imagining that he could hear the moans of the dead.

Hadassah's mother had known the dead were in the hills before he did, and his vines had realized it even before her. They had even tried to tell him; how many mornings had he stood, his brow furrowed, holding a blighted leaf or a withered stalk in his hand? The grapes had begun to dry up like raisins, right there on the vines that should have fed and fattened them. Even the ground began to look gray rather than that deep, rich earth color he'd always seen before.

Then the moaning began. At first very distant—on the extreme edge of hearing, in the faint hours before dawn when sleep changes how everything in the world feels, even the air on your skin. He had bolted up in bed and strained to hear, only to have the sound fade like the cry of a heathen god on the high air. He shivered once, but lay back down to sleep. He had imagined it. He must have.

But Hadassah's mother was certain. He found her each night standing at the door of their cedar house, gazing toward the hills. He had to put his hands firmly on her shoulders and, speaking softly, half-coax, half-force her to her bed.

The blight on the vines grew worse. Such a sickening of the plants was a terrifying thing. If a man's wife sickened, he could drape a shawl over her shoulders and order her to bed. When a crop sickened…that was an unnatural thing, and he could only stand helplessly by, seeing neither cause nor cure. Praying to God with a dry mouth and a heart clamorous with horror. On crops they all depended, and on God who, fickle as a woman, brought rain or withheld it as she pleased.

One night he heard the moans and was no longer able to ignore them. The dead were nearer now, wandering aimlessly about, perhaps on the slopes of the nearer hills. Shaking, he stumbled out the door to stand at the edge of the vineyard, gazing straight up at the sharp and brittle stars so that he wouldn't need to look at the dark, brooding silhouettes of the hills to the east.

"God!" he cried in a hoarse, loud whisper. "Is it not enough you took Hadassah? And the child she would have given me?"

There was no answer. He almost felt he could hear the vines withering as he stood there, a dry rustling sound, like brush on a desert wind, very loud in the silence between distant moans. A rage burned low in his belly, though he didn't know if it was directed at the land that was betraying him or at the dead whose distant moans were now too loud to ignore, or at God, who, like a woman, could not be trusted to keep her promises. Both women and God might abandon a man one day. Leave him crying amid his vines.

He turned and went inside and slammed shut the cedar bar across the door for the first time in years, the first since the last, worst raids from the Sea People. But he could not shut out the moans of the dead.

***

Rolling onto his side in the tent, Barak gazed at where his bronze shield and spear and breast-piece were propped against one of the poles that framed his tent—gear he had taken from a Sea Coast raider he'd killed. With a sigh, he got to his feet and began arming himself, strapping bronze greaves to his shins, settling a leather jerkin over his shoulders and then the breast-piece over that, lifting his spear and testing its heft. He didn't know how near dawn it was, but it was surely near enough.

By the time he stepped outside, the wind had settled again and the camp was quiet, most of the men asleep except for sentries and a few of the chieftains arguing in low voices around a nearby fire. Laban was there, as broad-shouldered as a nazarite, and Omri too. Barak walked toward them, his bronze clinking slightly.

"Get the men ready," he said. "It's time to leave."

Laban gave him an uneasy glance, and Omri looked startled, but they both stood without comment and began moving through the camp, calling out for their men. After a moment, those men began to emerge from their tents, their weary faces drawn with fear.

Barak stood amid the shouts of men gathering their gear without taking much notice of it. He looked to the north, at the silhouettes of hills against the sky. Up there, north of the settlements at Walls and Refuge, was a narrow valley of vineyards and barley fields and his own homestead, his own house of cedar and thatch. A few days, and he could be standing again at his own door, stepping inside to a warm welcome, Hadassah's soft body pressed to his, her kisses moist on his throat.

No.

Hadassah was gone.

A fresh pang of grief in his breast, surprisingly sharp. He drew in a shuddering breath and banished both grief and memory. Began moving through the camp. There was much to see to.

A shout made him turn; Nimri was walking toward him in haste, his eyes bright with that fanatical fury Barak knew too well. Barak kept walking, forcing Nimri to fall in alongside him.

"What is it, Nimri?"

"It's the Sabbath, that's what." A snarl in the man's voice.

Barak's eyes hardened. "The Law says: if your cattle fall in a ditch, it is no violation of the Covenant to haul them out. I have no cows in a ditch, but I may have dead in my vineyard. No other tribes are coming, Nimri. We've wasted enough time here."

Nimri's face twisted. "What I'd expect," he muttered, "from a man who took a heathen girl to wife."

Barak stopped short, and his voice went cold. "My father was a Hebrew, Nimri. My mother too."

"I do not deny it." Nimri smirked, then cast a glance down toward Barak's groin, and sneered when he lifted his eyes. "Yet you stink of them."

Barak fought his anger. He had no time for this. His fingers twitched, but he did not reach for the knife at his hip. "Before you insult me again, think carefully about whether you want a battle with *me*." If his voice had been cold a moment before, it was ice now. "Stay here and wait if you will. I will leave horses, such as I have; you can catch up when you've done as we agreed."

Nimri tried to speak, but Barak held up his hand. "Enough," he growled, and turned away, walking on through the camp. His back was tense, but he did not expect a knife in it; Nimri was trouble, but he was no coward. Barak did not look over his shoulder to see if Nimri still stood there or whether he had gone back to his tents. He just proceeded through his own camp, stopping a man every once in a while to give a command or ask a question. Already men were folding the tents. The wind was back, and all about Barak loose canvas flapped in the wind, with a sound like a hundred giant birds all taking flight at once. Strangely, the sound calmed him a little. Surely a camp that could make that much noise would prove large enough to cleanse their land of the dead.

If Nimri had spoken as he had in the hearing of other men, Barak could not have ignored it. But he ignored what he could afford to, for he was used to it. Since the day he had seen Hadassah by the well in Walls and looked into her dark eyes, the day he'd met with her father and taken her to his house, he had heard the jeering of other Hebrews. That he, who had been known as a man raiders from the sea might fear—that he should take a heathen girl as a wife rather than a slave.

Still struggling with his anger, Barak reflected that at least Nimri would be out of his camp for a while. And perhaps Nimri was the kind of man he should leave behind to push at the priests of Shiloh, in any case. A man with a passionate faith in the power of God and his Ark and his Law, but who would not be awed by any other man, even a levite, even a priest. Nimri would not be likely to back down at a refusal.

MISHPAT

DAWN'S COLD LIGHT. The Sabbath bride had visited the People for a night and a day. This was now the morning that followed. Lappidoth had already left to see about a horse for his wife. In his tent, Devora dressed swiftly but with purpose; she was acutely aware that what she wore this day, and what she carried with her, might be as important as any words she spoke. Even as she cinched tight the girdle about her white dress—white, the color of the Levi tribe—her fingers faltered an instant. She glanced at the bundles and parcels at the back of the tent, her eyes drawn to one long, slender bundle in a corner, half-concealed beneath the rest, a bundle bound with a red cord. Two things there must go with her as well, two things she had not taken in her hands in a long time. If she was to ride into the north and see fields that were occupied by the hungry dead, she could not leave it to others to carry out her judgments. To do so would be to invite a kind of blindness. The kind that kept her from seeing the weight that the burden of executing her judgments placed on Zadok's shoulders.

It should have been her hand that silenced the infant, not only her hand that buried it. It must be her hand that attended to the dead.

God had given her visions of things to come. That meant the burden was hers. It was right that it should be. She had never borne a child, but she was a woman of the People and she understood how to bear burdens, she understood how to shoulder those hard necessities required to preserve life. She had once carried a corpse in her arms like a beloved child a mile through dank reeds because it was unthinkable that another should have to.

Devora moved to the goatskin bundle and unwrapped it. Took up the scarlet cord first and held it in her hand a moment. Then she gently drew aside the goatskin, revealing the item it had concealed: a blade longer than her arm, polished to a sheen, slender and feminine in its delicacy. A hilt of white bone. She gazed at it grimly. Both the blade and the cord she held were heathen in origin, yet they were items that had proven useful to the People and had been consecrated for their uses, even as the fields and hills that had once been possessed only by the Canaanites were now places set apart and chosen out of all lands for the Hebrews, places holy in their own way.

"We must have a truce, you and I." Devora spoke to the sword and to the memories it recalled for her. "I will lift you and carry you with me, because the dead are in the land again and there will be butchery to do before the land is clean. But you mustn't expect me to use you. Only when I must. You were once unclean with the blood of a woman who was the best woman in Israel, the wisest. I will not like you or the necessity of carrying you. I unbind you and will need you ready to my hand, but don't think that I carry you as a man would, with any joy in your beauty."

The blade lay there mute yet eloquent in the shimmer of dawn light on its cold metal. Iron, the only iron blade she'd ever seen. Sea People had smithied it, in their walled towns on the coast to the west. The blade had come to Devora as a gift in the darkest of circumstances. After she'd done what she must, she'd wrapped it tightly in that goat hide and bound it and bound with it the pain of that day. Released now, that pain leapt at her and clawed at her heart as she gazed on the sharp metal.

"I will name you Mishpat," she whispered to the blade, "the Judgment. That will help us both remember what you are and what you are not."

A judgment on the dead. A judgment on her. The swift cut of decision, severing what limbs must be severed from the body of the People so that the rest of the body might thrive and not decay.

She considered the blade a few moments, as if watching for some sign of its consent to the name. Idly she wrapped the scarlet cord about her hand, feeling its coarse, aged fiber against her skin. Then bound it about her waist like a girdle. A dark mood fell over her, and she pressed her hand to her belly with a gentleness that would have surprised any who saw her.

She listened for a long moment, but heard nothing there. An ache opened within her, deep as the ravines of the Tumbling Water. There was no life stirring within her after the lovemaking of the past two nights. As *navi*, she would have known if there were; she felt certain of it. Tears stung her eyes; she blinked them away.

She knew her barrenness to be a judgment on her for the choices she'd had to make as a younger woman. As with any shattering of Covenant, barrenness had been visited on her, even as barrenness and blight now threatened the People and the land itself.

"Devora?"

She turned, saw Lappidoth at the door of the tent, peering in. She drew in her breath. She could be vulnerable, here in his tent. Once she stepped outside, she could not be. Out there, where she was going, weakness would be lethal— for her, and for her People.

Lappidoth came to her, sat beside her, and put his arms about her. "I'd nearly forgotten you had that," he murmured into her hair, and she knew he meant Mishpat. "You are taking it?"

"I am. It has only ever been used for one thing. Where God is sending me, I may need it." Devora closed her eyes, just feeling his warmth. "Why have you never been angry?" she whispered. "I deceived you when I came to you."

She had not told him she was barren, or why. Yet he had sheltered her in his tent all these years, not because she was the *navi* but because she was a woman, a woman he loved. Nor had he ever taken a second wife—though this meant his seed would not be passed on. He had once told her there was only one woman he wished to see bearing his child within her.

This morning might be the last she would ever see him.

"You didn't know." His voice a rumble at her ear, his presence heavy and strong in the dim light.

"I feared it," she murmured. Then she shook her head, breathed out slowly, straightening her back, refusing to lean any longer into his arms. She wanted to, so badly, but she could ill afford to begin this morning weak. Tears were a luxury reserved for women who did not have a People in their care. Her eyes hardened again, with purpose and with denial of all weariness.

"Sarah was barren," she said suddenly. "Our father Abraham's wife. Her body aged and she bore no child, and bitterness ate at her heart. Then two men came to her husband's tents beneath the oak trees. Only they weren't men, they were *malakhim*, angels of *El adonai* our God."

Lappidoth pressed his face to her neck with a soft sound in his throat, to comfort her.

"They said to Abraham, we bring you *niv sefatayim*, fruitful words from the God in high places. A year from now your wife will give birth to a boy." Devora lifted a hand as she spoke, moving her fingers gently through her husband's hair. "Sarah was within the tent, concealed from the sight of men who were strange to her. When she heard the words, she laughed. A cold laugh, for she did not think God could bring anything green and alive out of the desert she felt her body had become." Devora's voice fell, became soft. "But a year later, she had the boy. Then she laughed a second time, with tears. Isaak I name you, she said to the boy as he suckled at her breast, Isaak, my laughter.

"I have tried to live a life as holy and set apart, as *kadosh*, as Sarah's," she whispered, "but when I was a girl I broke the Covenant twice, and God remembers it."

Lappidoth's arms were around her.

"There will be no laughter for me in my old age." She gave him a small, bitter smile. "And perhaps I will not come back from the hills."

"You *will* come back," her husband growled. She could hear in his voice that her words had upset him. He gripped her chin suddenly, turned her face toward his. His eyes were fierce in the dim light. "You have a covenant with me, not only with God. And how can you keep it from beneath a cairn? You will come back." And rather than wait for an answer, he kissed her.

At that moment there were shouts outside, sharp cries of fear. Devora stiffened, and Lappidoth's eyes went dark with alarm. Swiftly he rose from beside her. He strode toward the tent door, cast it to the side. Devora got to her feet, had time to cry, "Wait!" but then Lappidoth was already through the door, and gone.

Devora's heart pounded. She started toward the door, stopped. Glanced back at the blade that lay unsheathed on the rug. It looked lethal. A moment ago she had been mourning her inability to bear new life. That blade was meant to sever life.

Another cry outside, a scream. This time one of pain.

With a moan of dread, Devora bent and took up the blade, then hurried out the door.

THE SOUNDING OF THE SHOFAR

DEVORA BURST from her husband's tent and was nearly trampled down by a man on horseback; she let out a cry and sprang back, tripping. Then the man was past with a glance at her over his shoulder as he rode, and Devora had a shock. For his eyes and his cheekbones were those of the northern tribes. And in one hand he carried a long knife, nearly the length of a man's arm between elbow and wrist. The knife was red with blood.

Then man and horse were gone amid the tents. Lappidoth was nowhere to be seen. Devora broke into a run, moving as quickly as her long woolen skirt would permit, Mishpat's hilt cold in her hand. She didn't understand, couldn't understand! But she sensed the camp, *God's* camp, was under some kind of raid. As she dashed through the tents, others began to bolt past her running the other way. There were screams and, somewhere ahead, the clang of bronze striking against bronze. Panic choked her.

The commotion was coming from near the Tent of Meeting. Holding Mishpat out to her side, she darted past the tents, dodging to the side as another horse galloped past her. Caught a glimpse of the rider's face. Hebrew. Another northern face. Her heart burned hot within her. That Barak—that Barak!—*what had he done?*

There were levites on the ground among the tents now—their white robes gashed open and reddened with blood. She ran faster, leaping over the bodies, breathing hard, a stitch in her side. Then she was around the last of the priests' tents, and she could see the Tent of Meeting and the scorched earth around it and high on its pole near the Tent, the ram's horn, the *shofar*, untouched, no alarm blown. Had there been no time?

Several northern men were dismounted by the pole, and one was bent over the body of a fallen priest. Zadok and another nazarite were fighting to get into the Tent, the door barred by a lean man whose face was turned away from her; the man held a bronze blade and a round shield. Zadok lunged in with his spear, but the man caught the spear on the edge of his shield and spun the shield in one quick, smooth motion, ripping the spear out of Zadok's grasp and sending it clattering away. The other nazarite had only a knife in his hand, and he danced in place, awaiting an opening.

Devora had only a moment to take in the scene—the battle at the door, great gashes in the side of the tent, the body in the dirt, and the men moving away from the pole now to flank Zadok—when there was a bellow like a bull's voice to her left, and her husband leapt around one of the tents with a tent pole uplifted in his hands. Lappidoth ran at the men and drove the end of the pole into one's face, sending the man sprawling limp some distance away. He spun the pole at another man's head, but the man ducked. Then Devora was at her husband's side, screaming loud enough to drown out her fear, and they were facing three from the northern tribes, tall, lean men wielding staves of cedar. They carried no shields; those staves served them for both attack and defense.

The blade wavered in her grip; these were living men, men of the People, and she had only once before in her life raised Mishpat against another's life. But these men meant to kill *her husband*. They meant to defile the Tent of Meeting, *had* defiled it. And they meant to kill Lappidoth.

Everything in her went cold.

She swung the blade.

The eyes of the men facing her widened in horror at the sight of this white-robed levite woman bearing down on them with a blade of iron that seemed not of this land or any other, slender metal, a white slice of death such as they had only seen perhaps in the hands of men of the Sea Coast during raids from the walled towns in the west. The strangeness of the sight and the hesitation it provoked was lethal; Devora's blade slashed across the face of the man in the middle. A spray of blood, some of it spattered warm across Devora's neck and her cheek. The *navi*'s heart was pounding. She screamed again and swept the blade down at the legs of the man to the right, even as Lappidoth blocked the man's club from striking her; the iron blade slid through sinew and bone as though they were milk, and the man crumpled with a shrill cry.

As her husband faced the last of the three, Devora caught a glimpse of the Tent of the Meeting past the enemy's shoulder. The second nazarite lay still on the ground, a pool of blood beneath his head. Zadok had taken up the fallen man's knife and was dancing to the left, then the right, with the kind of grace one sees in desert asps or in the lethal mamba of Kemet, the serpent that strikes unseen from the trees. But Zadok could not get within the northern man's reach; the man's war braid and the colored stones he'd woven into his belt declared him a chieftain of men, one who had survived many harsh raids in the north. In less time than the beat of a heart, Devora's eyes took in the nazarite's peril and the great cuts in the side of the holy Tent.

The Tent had been violated; there was at least one man within who had not been consecrated or prepared to enter the *shekinah* and who dared to bear sharp bronze before Holy God. Yet no fire blazed from the Tent to wither the northern man where he stood, which Devora couldn't understand. But then, these were not strangers in the land who raided the Tent but men who partook of the Covenant and the promise. Perhaps God, whose ways were not the ways of men and women who walk on the earth, was waiting for his Hebrews to clean up the evil of their own. She didn't have time to think of it—it was only a silent cry of astonished horror in her mind.

Other northern men had emerged from among the tents to the right, one with a bloodied spear. Devora sprang away from her husband and his opponent, bolted the few steps to the pole by the Tent. She reached up for the peg from which hung the shofar, the curved ram's horn, the voice of the People's need or the People's might. Snatched it from its peg and lifted it to her lips. Blew on it the *t'qiah*, the notes of challenge and alarm.

The call was deep and clear; after a moment the call seemed to return, doubled, from the slopes of the hills.

There were shouts in the camp. And footsteps, white-robed men rallying to the Tent at the call of the horn. Somewhere, a woman's scream. Hannah, the midwife. That was Hannah's voice.

There was no time for thought or judgment, only action. Devora ran toward the other northern men who were closing on Zadok and her husband, looping the shofar about her neck by its leather cord as she ran. She brought Mishpat up, and the blade was slender and violent like a scream out of God's mind in the desert. She knew no art of its use, but she was furious and desperate, and one of the men fell back before the rage in her eyes, and the other took the blade across his right shoulder and spun to his left and dropped to his knees, where Devora's sandalled foot took him in the face.

Then a third man was before her with a club in either hand, and the *navi* was slashing the blade in great strokes through the air that made her arms ache and left her open and vulnerable had she known it. But the other man simply avoided her strokes and did not strike, his eyes round with astonishment. Perhaps he guessed she was the *navi*; perhaps it was only that he found himself met in the dance of spears by a woman and didn't know what to do. But then other men of the camp were behind Devora and at her side, and the northern man fell back. Powerful arms wrapped around Devora from behind, pinning her own upper arms so that she could hardly swing the blade. She screamed and kicked back at her assailant. Heard a rough, low voice in her ear. "Easy, Devora, easy. It's over, it's over."

Lappidoth.

She collapsed back in his arms, panting for air, and Mishpat hung limp at her side. She was shaking. She just let his arms hold her for a moment, then the reality of what had happened seized her. "The Ark!" she cried.

Lappidoth released her, and she turned to the Tent. Zadok stood there with a shallow cut along his cheek, his hand gripped fierce about the invader's throat. Somehow he had gotten past the enemy's blade and taken the man's throat in his hand and wrenched him from his feet. Now the man had been forced to his knees, and the nazarite loomed over him, squeezing his throat, his other hand holding the man's right wrist at a cruel angle, though the northerner stubbornly clung to his sword's hilt and would not drop it.

With a start, Devora realized she knew the man.

Nimri. This was Nimri, that chieftain of Naphtali who had spoken so scornfully by the cairns, before the Sabbath. Her heart went hard and cold.

Zadok's eyes were those of a killer, but in a moment, two of the camp's other three surviving nazarites were beside him, and they pulled Zadok loose, muttering low words in his ears. One of them then kicked the invader onto his back, then held him down with a foot over his throat while his companion disarmed him. Zadok stood silently by, his eyes still hot with rage, his hands flexing as though it were taking all his will to keep from leaping upon Nimri and choking away his life.

But Devora spared the men little attention, for now she could see through the wide door of the Tent of Meeting.

And what she saw winded her.

Within, the altar had been toppled to the side, and two northern men lay slain beside it. A white-robed priest knelt by them, clutching his belly from which a darkness flowed that could only be his life leaving him. A spear lay discarded to the side, its bronze head wet with the priest's blood. In his hand, the dying priest still held the flint knife that was used in preparing sacrifices for the altar; this morning, it had sacrificed only the two northern men who lay dead within. Beyond the priest was the veil that concealed the *kodesh kodashim*, the Holy of Holies, from the eyes of those who hadn't been consecrated to meet God face-to-face like a lover. But the veil had been ripped aside, like a rape. Through the tear, Devora could see the Ark of the Covenant tipped on its side and its lid fallen away, revealing the scrolls of the Law and the two stone tablets on which were chiseled, durable as the land itself, the words of the Ten.

The bleeding man turned toward the door, but even before she could see his face, Devora could tell who he was from the *hoshen mishpat* he wore.

"Eleazar!"

The priest's eyes showed recognition; then he swayed and fell.

In another moment Devora was within the Tent, despite the sacrilege of it; she knelt and lifted Eleazar's head to her lap and cupped his face in her hands, her heart stricken with ice. This was the high priest of her People, struck down by a spear within the very walls of the Tent of God. Those walls stirred loudly in the wind, and the veil fluttered, a fragile thing.

"No," Devora said, her voice thick. "Oh no."

Eleazar's gaze lifted, focused on her though dull with pain. "Ark," he gasped. "They wanted the Ark. Told them. Law forbade. Ark can only go— where *all* the tribes go. Not just two or three."

"Shh," Devora whispered, and brushed strands of lank, sweaty hair away from his face. "Don't talk. Just rest, *kohen*. Just rest. Until Hannah is here."

His mouth worked a moment without words. Then: "No time. Your vision. The dead. You must go. Where God needs you to be."

"Please don't talk," Devora said, desperate. She took cloth and pressed it to his wound, but the dark blood kept pulsing out. He was dying. Devora felt a firm hand on her shoulder and didn't need to glance up to know Lappidoth was there with her, silent and strong behind her. As he had always been.

"My sons," Eleazar rasped. "In Beth El camp. Send for them."

"We will," Devora said, gripping his hand tightly.

Gazing past Devora's shoulder as if at the sky, Eleazar gasped, "Don't let the People be—eaten—or—or burned—"

Devora didn't understand, but she nodded. Everything in her felt wrung tight.

"*Sh'ma*," Eleazar forced the words out. "*Sh'ma Yisrael adonai eloheinu, adonai echad.*" Hear O Israel, Adonai our God, Adonai is One. A Hebrew's death prayer, since the time in the desert. Speaking it, Eleazar was saying, *I may die, but I die in service to Holy God, as my fathers did before me. You who live, see that you do likewise.*

The breath left his body in a long sigh that stopped abruptly. A sound more terrible in its way than the moans of the dead. Devora stared down at him. He was gone. The high priest of Israel. Gone. She'd been too late. Once again, as on that other night three decades before, when there'd been fire in the tents and many who'd mattered to her had perished, she'd come too late.

Gently Devora laid the priest back on the bloodstained rugs that floored the Tent. She took his left hand and placed it on his chest, then brought his right up to join it. Even as she did, another woman entered on silent feet and knelt across the body from her, then took the priest's face in her hands. This other woman was weeping breathlessly. It was Hannah. She too had arrived too late.

"He is dead, Hannah," Devora said gently. "You mustn't touch the body. When it cools, he'll be unclean."

Hannah shook her head, her eyes wet with her tears.

Devora lowered her head, her own grief rising within her like a wind. She and Eleazar had never been close, though they had shared a bond, as had all the survivors of that terrible night so many years ago. The bond that all the old shared, that none of the young could truly understand. Devora had seen the others who had lived through that night die in recent years, of old age or disease or weariness. Maybe a day would come when only she would be left. She alone.

As she looked down, her gaze caught on Eleazar's breast-piece and the stones placed within it. The stones on which were carved the names of the tribes, and the *other* two stones. The *urim*, dark as a horse's eyes, and the *thummim*, pale like dead flesh. Gently, reverently, Devora lifted those two from the breast-piece; Hannah, lost in her weeping, didn't appear to notice. For a moment she held them in her hand. The stones were very small. They were rarely used.

"Does your hand still cover Israel?" the *navi* whispered.

She cast the stones. Letting them roll across the rugs within the Tent. Held her breath as she waited to see which would stop rolling first.

The two stones rolled.

The *urim* settled, dark on the earth-colored threads. The *thummim*, the "no" stone, rolled a little farther.

Devora let her breath out slowly.

The *urim* had stopped first.

The "yes" stone.

The answer was yes.

She rose and picked up the stones. One, then the next. Held them in her hand, pressed them to her lips. She needed a moment, just a moment. She was shaking.

The answer had been yes.

Her fist tightened until her nails dug into her palm and she felt she could feel the *urim* and *thummim* pressing right against her bones, through her skin. She drew in a fresh breath with a hiss. God still covered his People. Provisionally, perhaps, but God was still here. *Still* here.

Hannah's weeping behind her was quiet.

Devora could act again with the authority of God's *navi*. And action and judgment would be needed. For a great violation of the Covenant had been committed.

Devora rose stiffly to her feet and left the tent, emerging into the morning sun. The shofar still hung about her throat, Mishpat in her right hand. She gazed numbly at the blood on the iron. She'd meant to wield Mishpat against the unclean dead, not the living. Wind tugged at the slashed sides of the Tent before her, though within the recesses of the Tent the veil hung limp, gashed and still, as though that veil were God's hymen, torn and then held to be of little value. A flicker of heat lit somewhere on the cold plain of her grief and grew until the flames consumed her heart. Lappidoth spoke to her, but she did not hear him. She saw Zadok standing near and she said quietly, "Take me to him."

The nazarite nodded, his face still hard with violence. He turned and led the way, and heeding neither Hannah's weeping nor the cries of the wounded, Devora moved through the camp. Rage burning in her heart. She did not even feel her husband's gaze on her.

She found Nimri held out in the heather beyond the Tent, between two nazarites who had pulled him away from the camp as though he were unclean. Now he stood among the purple blossoms, and the wind tugged at his hair. He hardly seemed to notice Devora approaching, but when he saw Zadok, he spat like a cat. The other two nazarites gazed at the *navi* with something in their eyes that she had never seen there before. Awe, perhaps. Devora's long, silvered hair bannered in the wind; her white gown, though dirtied and splashed with blood, billowed about her legs in a way that suggested a mighty bird swooping through the heather. The shofar about her neck, Mishpat held out bloodied at her side.

Devora stopped when she stood before Nimri, her eyes hot with fury.

"Whose command?" she demanded. "Who sent you here?"

Nimri lifted his chin. He'd been bruised about the face, and the marks of Zadok's fingers were dark on his throat. "Go home to your tent, woman."

"I am the *navi* of Israel, Nimri! *Why are you here?*" Her voice cracked sharp as a lash in the air.

He watched her a moment, a brooding look in his eyes. "Asking for the Ark."

For an instant there was only the wind in the heather.

"You might try leaving your spears behind when you ask," Devora said. "Where is Barak?"

"He's left for the north, woman." Nimri sneered at her. "I'm to meet him there at Walls, with you and the Ark."

"Left? This morning?" It made no sense. His camp was only a few miles away. Surely he would have waited an hour or two for Nimri to return.

"Yesterday."

Devora cried out, enraged. "On the *Sabbath*! Has he forgotten the *whole* Covenant?"

"What does a woman know of the Covenant?" Nimri's voice went quiet with menace. "Judgment, of either Barak or the dead, is for men to decide. You have no place here. Get back to your husband's tent."

Devora struck him.

His head whipped back, and then he looked at her with rage-darkened eyes and blood on his lip. His face reddening. Devora held his gaze, her eyes hard. "I speak a *navi*'s judgment and a *navi*'s curse," she said, and at the words, a little color left the man's face.

Devora's words welled from some hot pool of fury within her, and heat washed through her body, the heat that had always presaged for her the nearness of God and the nearness of the future. Her voice hard as the tablets in the Ark on which were chiseled the Covenant of their People. "You will come once at each planting and once at each harvest to Shiloh. You will come on foot, without sandals or waterskin, relying on the mercy of the levites to give you water to drink and oils for your feet. You will bring to them a white bull, without blemish, and beg the priest to sacrifice it for you, to atone for this day's evil. You will do this year after year, until the priests release you."

She drew in a hissing breath. "That is my judgment." Her voice rose, shrill and cold. "*This* is my curse. Nimri ben Nabaoth, until the priests release you, you will take up no spear nor blade nor any implement of metal, nor any bludgeon, nor so much as lift your hand to strike another man. The instant you do, your hand will wither and your whole body will be struck with the white sickness—for with your own hand you struck down a priest of our God. And my friend." For he had been. She knew in this moment that he had been. However uneasy they had at times been with each other.

Devora was almost shrieking the words now, the heat of the future, of prophecy and curse, crackling along her skin, making her hairs rise. Nimri's face had gone white. "You will be a leper, unclean, begging at the roadside with stumps where your hands were. Your manhood will decay and fall off. You will be spat upon by all who are true to their Covenant. I, Devora, the *navi*, who sees what God sees, I speak this curse. Whatever covenants you made with Barak ben Abinoam, you must abide the consequences of their breaking, for you will never again march with other armed men."

WORDS OF GOING

DEVORA HAD SEEN too many burials; this one was harder than most, for it seemed to promise other burials to come. An hour after banishing Nimri from the camp, Devora led a procession through the heather and up the slope of her hill to the forest of stone cairns. As she climbed, she glanced to the east and saw that Barak's camp had indeed slipped away. The tents there were gone, leaving only spaces of trampled dirt amid the weeds. Like guilty men leaving a corpse. Her face tightened. Nimri had spoken mockingly of Barak ben Abinoam, yet Barak had left him behind to bring the Ark and the *navi* north. What commands had Barak given him? Had Barak meant to seize the Ark by force? In either case, for loosing this wolf on the tents of Levi, Barak had much to answer for.

Behind the *navi*, twenty priests climbed the hill, and Shiloh's last few nazarites climbed with them, each bearing a body safely wrapped in a linen shroud. Behind the bearers walked women from the camp, veiled in their grief like northern girls, climbing in silence. The morning's terror had left them too exhausted even to weep. Hannah was with them. Zadok walked just behind the *navi*, carrying Eleazar in his shroud.

Devora led them among the cairns without word or cry, but her mind was loud within her, and she could not calm it. She struggled to understand how this thing could have happened, that *Hebrew* men—Hebrew, not heathen—should try to seize the Ark from the priests by force. She knew the People had been spreading out through the land, further and further from the Ark and from God and from the Law at Shiloh. What if they were ceasing to be a People—becoming mere scattered encampments, no longer tribes but homesteads, isolated among the homes of heathen? She repressed a shudder. Was that why the dead had come, surging out of the cedar forests in the far north? To drive the People together again, like scattered deer fleeing a storm, rushing together down long slopes to gather in one valley, before one Law?

Or were the People altogether forsaken, and the dead here merely because God's hand had been removed from covering Shiloh and the land? The *urim* and *thummim* had suggested otherwise. Yet. She remembered the *malakh ha-mavet* and the way the Tent of Meeting had been cut open and no fire from God had withered those who toppled altar and Ark. Devora did not know, *could* not know, if the herds of dead moving in the north were a chastisement meant to drive the People together, or a revocation entire of the Covenant and the promise.

Here among the cairns, the men from Shiloh set out the bodies in a great line, as they had once before, thirty years ago, after another attack on the camp. Devora stood by the bodies, her head bowed, feeling the memory settle heavy on her shoulders. All about her, the men gathered up stones, mighty stones to bury the dead. Zadok stopped a moment beside the *navi* without speaking, just giving her the comfort and solidity of his presence. She glanced up at his face, saw it drawn with pain. The memories were heavy on *his* shoulders too.

Devora looked out over the cairns. Many of the corpses beneath them, especially the oldest ones, had become anonymous now, hidden in a field of dead whose names she didn't know. One of the cairns was even crumbled in upon itself, as much a ruin as the body it buried. For the human memory is short, and even when we write it in stone we quickly forget and the stones crumble and even those stones then forget.

The men laid Eleazar in a shallow grave and then piled the stones above him, a house humbler than the pyramids of Kemet but alike in purpose and no less effective. Devora wished for a moment that she could see his face, but he was shrouded, and then there were stones over him and she couldn't see even his shape, and his laughter and his love for his wife and his exuberance for the Law were buried forever.

When the cairns were finished, Devora stood facing Eleazar's with her arms folded, preternaturally straight and still, her gaze fixed on the pile of rock. She lifted her voice, clear on the crisp air, chanting the Words of Going. There were words in that lament that were Hebrew, and there were words of Kemet, for many generations of their mothers and grandmothers had sung those words over the bodies of their sons, beaten to death in the labor of raising the great tombs and cities of the dead in that land of river and dark earth. In those words could be heard the tears of all the women of the People and all the tears the men had feared to shed. The song was older than the *Shirat ha'Yam*, older than the praisesongs of the *kohannim*, older than any *navi* or any vision given to man or woman by the God of their Covenant. The People had known death and loss and despair, and the screaming in the desert, before they had known God.

Devora sang for Eleazar and for the other dead priests, and for the nazarite Nimri had slain. And, after the briefest hesitation in her heart, she sang even for a small child, a nameless child with a Hebrew father and a heathen mother, who had died somewhere in the north and then been buried here. She sang for the child because the infant's mother had no way to say farewell herself, here, so far from the water. She sang for the child because of her dreams and her terrors of the night before. Because when the unclean death separates child and mother, some atonement must be made, some words of parting. There were no words in the Law that demanded she sing over a child who was not of the People. But there was a Law written on her heart that did demand it.

***

The young Canaanite didn't stand as Devora approached her on the outskirts of the camp, her blade still held in one hand, her throat a little hoarse from singing over the cairns. Hurriya was lying in thick pelts that Zadok must have thrown there on the earth, and nearby there was another hide rumpled, where Zadok had probably slept. The *navi* considered her a moment. This wouldn't be easy. Bracing herself, she stepped toward the girl.

"I need a guide in the Galilee," Devora said.

Hurriya lifted herself up on her elbows with an effort, and the pelt that covered her fell away from her. Devora recoiled half a step, appalled at her condition. The girl smelled of sweat and blood and dirt; her face was very pale, and her salmah looked stiffened. Devora wondered how long it had been since either that woolen cloth or the girl within it had been washed. There were hollows under Hurriya's eyes as she looked up at the *navi*.

Perhaps the Canaanite girl had kin in the north. Someone who could care for her there.

"I thought I was *unclean*," the girl said, and the bitterness in her voice was like a slap.

Devora glanced about quickly, noting a discarded waterskin and a cloth that had probably been brought here in the morning with bread in it. She let out her breath slowly. The girl had been fed at least and given water to drink. But she had given birth to a child not long ago, and her body had not healed well from it. The walk down from the Galilee, in exhaustion and terror, must have been brutal. It was a wonder the girl was even conscious.

"You've lived all your life in those hills," Devora said. "Neither I nor Zadok have ever been in the Galilee. And you know more about what's happening there than anyone in this camp." She didn't add that she would trust a heathen before she'd trust that dog Barak and his chieftains. "If Zadok rigs a sidesaddle for you, can you ride a horse?" she asked aloud.

Hurriya just sank back and closed her eyes. "I've never ridden a horse."

"You'll ride before me on my husband's horse, then."

She shook her head, pale with misery. "Let me die, *navi*," she whispered.

"I am *not* going to do that," Devora said sharply. "You came to me. I have an obligation to you, girl; I mean to keep it. I am taking you north. You can show me when to turn to the left, when to the right, until we get there." She thought for a moment. "We will have to get you your own waterskin, and keep your skin covered at all times, to prevent contact. You *are* unclean." Her heart sank; she couldn't bear to lose the hours it would take to gather up a spare waterskin and food and supplies for the girl and to beg clothing for her from one of Shiloh's women, clothing that could not be returned. She had to leave, now. She meant to catch Barak.

"I am unclean," Hurriya repeated. "This whole *land* is unclean." Hurriya began laughing, a cold, bitter laughter that shook her until she coughed and clenched up in pain. Devora gazed down at her in dismay.

"I don't care what you do," Hurriya whispered after a few moments. "Tie me to your horse if you like. I don't care."

Before she could reply, Devora heard hooves behind her and turned toward the tents. There were two horses approaching, one dark as beer from Kemet, and massive, the other smaller and white, with a dark patch near its nose. On the dark horse rode Zadok, who seemed even more massive in the saddle. He wore a breast-piece of bronze, and his spear was strapped to the side of his saddle, counterbalanced on the other side by several waterskins—bless him, that solved one problem—and a small pack. The man's face was grim. He sat that dark horse like danger and threat incarnate.

Lappidoth rode the white horse, his face drawn and pale. Devora cried out when she saw him, fearing for a moment that he meant to ride with her, whether she willed or no. But he saw her face and shook his head.

"The horse is only for you, Devora," he said. "I am staying."

Devora blushed. Of course. When Lappidoth her husband made a promise, he kept it.

"His name was Arvad, the wanderer," Lappidoth told her gravely as he halted near her, "for he was wild on the steppes before a caravan from Midian brought him to Shiloh. Now he is Shomar, because he guards his rider." He slid from the horse's back. Zadok drew his horse up beside but stayed in the saddle.

"I need speed more than safety," Devora said. She noted the bedroll and other supplies attached to Shomar's saddle. Her heart was warm with love for the man. Here was one man in Israel who kept his covenants, all of them, every one.

"Oh, he is fast, wife." Lappidoth shook his head and patted Shomar's neck. Devora stroked the other side of the horse's neck, marveling at the animal's beauty. She felt powerful muscles move beneath her hand when the horse turned its head to nuzzle her ear. Devora's eyes shone. Horses were rare in the land.

"He is fast enough," Lappidoth said, "but then, Barak's men have few horses. They will be on foot. So safety *will* matter more than speed. I will not have my wife falling from a fast, nervous horse who startles at an asp on some hillside far from my tent." The horse whickered, and Lappidoth caressed the animal's chin. "He is a good horse," he said slowly.

"There are three other nazarites still alive in Shiloh," Lappidoth added in a lower voice. "Will you take them with you, wife?"

Devora shook her head. "They'll be needed here. And Zadok rides with me. I am *kadosh*. Why should I fear to journey in the land of our People?"

Lappidoth looked troubled. "You are *kadosh*. Yet men lifted arms against you this morning. The Ark is *kadosh*. Yet men turned it on its side, trying to drag it from the Tent where we meet God. Eleazar was *kadosh*. Yet he lies dead."

Devora swallowed against a tightness in her throat at these grim reminders of the day's evil.

The men of the north had much to answer for.

"I do not trust the northern tribes," Lappidoth said.

"Nor do I. But they will have what they want. They will have the *navi*, to remind them God is with them as they cleanse the land."

"Wife," Lappidoth said, and the hard, urgent way he said the word made her focus on him.

"Take the men," he said. "Please. You are *kadosh*, and it has not been my way to command you or to govern you too firmly. But please take the men."

She hesitated a long moment, then shook her head. "Shiloh is my home," she said softly. "Husband. Shiloh is my home. I can't leave it without its spears. Thank you—for worrying for me. No one will harm me while Zadok is with me. Even if they should wish to."

But Zadok's own brow was furrowed, as though he himself was uncertain of the merit of either accepting or refusing Lappidoth's plea. His eyes were pools of grief and guilt—a guilt Devora knew too well. The burden that settled, hot and tight, in your breast when you could not save those lives that were your responsibility.

Quietly Zadok dismounted and helped Devora bind Mishpat to her saddle.

After a long, searching stare at Zadok, Lappidoth gave his wife a brisk nod. Seeing this, Devora's heart went warm with gratitude—for a husband who could remain behind without it breaking his pride and his strength, and who could watch a younger man guard his wife without jealousy, and who could trust her when she said she would be all right.

"I know Zadok will keep you safe," Lappidoth said gruffly. "He is an able man."

"And you are a good man, my husband," she whispered. "You have my heart."

"Just bring Shomar back." He forced a smile. "I traded ten head of my cattle for him. I have never seen a finer horse."

He stepped back, and Devora tried to think of some further word of farewell, but words failed her. She just held his gaze, her eyes full of her heart. Zadok bent and lifted the Canaanite from the ground, careful not to touch her bare flesh, his face grim at the small cry of pain she made. He settled her into the saddle before Devora, then gave Shomar a pat on the gelding's rump and muttered, "Keep these women safe, horse."

Devora put her arm about the Canaanite's waist and held her tight, fearful the girl would panic and spook the horse. Hurriya's eyes were wide. "Shomar is my husband's," Devora whispered near her ear. "He will not let you fall."

The Canaanite gave a terse nod. "Don't leave me alone with him," she whispered.

"What? The horse?"

"That man." The girl was gazing at Zadok, wide-eyed.

"Peace, girl. Zadok won't harm you."

Though affronted for Zadok's sake, Devora was grateful to see the girl's fear. Fear was better than numbness, better than despair. It meant her heart was still beating, her blood still loud in her ears. That was perhaps the best Devora could hope for; she didn't want the girl to die on her along the way. And making sure she didn't would give the *navi* something to distract her from the vast lake of grief that lay dark beneath her feet, ready to swallow her.

"*Navi*," Zadok murmured. "Hannah sends a message."

She glanced down at his hard face. She was certain she could guess what the wife of Eleazar had in her heart.

"She says, *I call for judgment on Barak ben Abinoam, who killed my husband and the high priest of Israel.* She asks you to do this for her in memory of the day in the reeds. She says you have always protected her and those bound to her."

"That is true." She gazed to the north, thought of the shambling dead, and wondered if God had already prepared a bitter judgment over the men of the north, Barak and others. "Barak will atone for what his men have done," she said.

As Zadok remounted his own steed, Devora glanced back at Lappidoth, and the man looked wearier than she had ever seen him. "God be with you, Devora," he called to her.

"And with you, Lappidoth," she said.

She dug in her heels. "*Hai!*"

Shomar carried her over the uneven ground at something near a gallop, and the tents sprang away behind; then they were in the heather, Devora and her horse, riding around the edge of the camp. She glanced back once, her hair streaming across her face in the wind. Saw Lappidoth still standing by Hurriya's discarded bedding, one hand lifted. Gazing after her.

STRANGERS IN THE LAND

DEVORA, THE *NAVI* and judge of Israel, rode from Shiloh with Hurriya before her and Zadok beside her. They rode as though their horses had caught the scent of God and were rushing to find him. Yet God was behind them, not before, and the blasphemy of that torn veil had perhaps ensured that God would not follow them into the north. Devora spurred Shomar on, almost cruelly, her insides so hot with rage that she saw nothing to the left or to the right. She rode blind. Her only thought was to find Barak ben Abinoam and demand of him a dire atonement for the evil of this day. That he could have treated their God—*el kadosh*, the weighty, the mighty, who could rise over the land in fire and storm and scorch it to a desert that would not bear seed for a thousand years, or who could fall gentle as rain and urge wheat from the soil that would grow at his touch taller than the height of a man—that Barak could have approached this God, *this* God, and treated him as a mere object to be acquired and moved about. Did he think he was dealing with one of the wooden not-gods of the Canaanites, a mute thing that you might carry in the palm of your hand? She hissed Barak's name as she rode, and the midmorning sun lifting over the land found her horse streaking through the fields, and Zadok on his own steed a spear's cast behind her, laboring to catch up.

***

Yet she could not keep that pace; it left Hurriya shaking and faint. Devora didn't know how much of that was her anguish and how much of it fear of being on horseback, but the sight of her pain cooled the *navi*'s fury, and she slowed, consoling herself with the thought that Barak and his men were on foot.

So they trotted their horses northward through fields white for harvest. From time to time, Devora leaned to the side and let her fingers trail through the high wheat or plucked up some to chew as they went. This was the *land*, beloved of their mothers and fathers, and its beauty pulled at Devora's heart and abated her anger, almost brought her tears. The day was long and her wrath burned out, though no doubt it would flicker into fresh fire when she caught up with Barak at last. With the land of promise rich and fruitful about her, a kind of quiet awe settled over her. Each field and each hill about her was shaped delicately by the hands of God, each one with a name and a story. Here, the dead seemed only a tale told to frighten. An impossibility. Yet there in the north, where the hills were taller—they were there, somewhere. Hurriya's pale face was testimony to it.

Riding with Hurriya before her in the saddle and her arm about the girl's waist was a strange experience. With the exception of Lappidoth, Devora had never spent so many hours so near another person. This Canaanite girl in her arms neither spoke nor cried as Shomar carried them through the wheat; she simply rested limp against Devora's shoulder, taking shallow breaths. Sometimes she slept. Devora began to feel a strange protectiveness, riding with her like this. She could feel the warmth of Hurriya's body through her salmah.

***

They passed Cleft Hill on their left in the early afternoon and saw the tiny wooden houses of Rise Early clustered beneath the slope, with olive presses just outside the town and barley fields behind it. That had once been a walled town, one of the strongest of the Canaanite towns, but it had never really been rebuilt after the Hebrews had taken violent possession of it. Devora spared the cookfires one uneasy glance as they passed. Strangers in their land, so many in their land.

An hour or two later, Devora lifted her hand for a halt and brought Shomar to a stop by a wide pond north of Rise Early and let him drink. Zadok lifted the Canaanite from Shomar's back and laid her gently by the edge of the water beneath one of the leafy terebinth trees growing there. In their branches cicadas sang loud as thunder, recalling moments from Devora's girlhood in Shiloh, where a hundred such insects had roared in a line of terebinths outside the girls' tent.

Zadok walked a little way from where Hurriya rested. Then stopped and gazed, brooding, at the pool. Devora tended to her horse, patting down his flanks with her own shawl. Then she stroked Shomar's neck for a few moments and whispered soft words.

Devora glanced at Hurriya, who had her eyes closed. The *navi* smiled slightly, still warm from holding her. She supposed the girl was asleep. After a moment, Devora joined Zadok at the water's edge, and they walked along the bank for a while in silence. A kingfisher darted in and out of the water. She glanced to the north. From here the land rose steadily, climbing toward the Galilee and toward the snow-capped mountains of White Cedars in the north beyond. In the near distance, Devora could see the Hills of Teaching and of Cleansing towering over the land. There was smoke rising from the slope of Cleansing, but not enough for it to be a camp of armed men. Probably herdsmen. If they were nearer, they'd probably hear the bleating of goats.

The earth at the bank was soft here, nearly mud. "But no hoofprints," the *navi* murmured. "Nor feet. Barak and his men didn't stop here."

"I will finish looking," Zadok said quietly. "Go back and rest, *navi*."

She glanced at him—his face was tight with grief.

"You fought well," Devora said softly. "It is not your fault the high priest is dead."

Pain flashed across his eyes.

"My father died that night," he said.

Devora had no need to ask what *that night* meant. For her too it would always be *that night*.

"He died defending the Ark, and the levites, and the *navi*. I was seven. He threw me within his tent, commanded my mother to hold me there. I have never forgotten his face. I will not give to the fulfilling of my covenant less than my father gave to it."

Another silence. She did not break it; she knew the importance of silence when the heart is sore.

"I fought well," he said at last. "But the high priest is still dead."

He just looked out over the water. Devora felt stiff, as though she'd slept badly. She could not yet cry for Eleazar or the other dead in Shiloh.

She thought of pressing him, but it would do little good until he was ready to speak. After a moment she left him standing there in the reeds.

Returning to where the Canaanite lay in the damp grass beside the water, Devora saw with a sinking of her heart that Hurriya was weeping. The young woman was gazing up at the branches above her, her tears leaving pale streaks through the dirt and sweat on her face. Devora approached and knelt by her, very near but not touching, folding her hands in her lap. The girl looked only half-alive, lying there pale in her anguish amid the lush vegetation.

"Do you have any kin in the Galilee?" the *navi* asked softly.

"Leave me alone," Hurriya whispered. She was looking at the pond. "I want to die here. Here, where it is so beautiful. Where there's water. Please just leave me here."

The vulnerability in her voice tugged at Devora, and angered her. "I lost all my kin, girl," she said sharply. "Everyone I knew of as my tribe. All of them. Mother, father, the elders, the other children I'd known. In a single night, they were gone. You can't let yourself speak of dying. There are always other people who need you. Right now I do; you're my guide. There must be others in the north, kin who need you. Someone we can take you to."

Hurriya shook her head. Then whispered something Devora couldn't hear. The *navi* leaned closer, and Hurriya repeated: "Sister."

"A sister, yes. At Judges' Well?" Devora asked.

Hurriya was silent for a few heartbeats. "There was this olive tree," she said, her voice hoarse. She sounded not as though she were speaking to Devora but as though she were speaking to herself, aloud, because she needed to. "The tallest one. Anath would climb to the very top. I'd call up to her. Could never get her to come down. She said up there she could see the whole sky and the goddess's face." Hurriya stared at the water. "I want to tell her—I saw the whole sky too, and the goddess's face. In my little—" Her voice broke. "For only a few days. A few days." She sobbed.

Devora felt a flicker of unease at the mention of a deity not her own, a deity she couldn't trust, but the girl's sobs quashed her unease and took her whole attention, for though nearly silent, Hurriya's sobs seemed to shake her whole body and risk breaking her. It was clear the girl would never make it into the north like this, and Devora *did* have an obligation to her. The girl had come to her, and she was suffering.

With a sigh Devora took the Canaanite into her arms, wrapping the salmah tighter about her and then holding her. Hurriya was shaking; Devora held her pressed close with one arm, and with her other she tore off a bit of her dress and dipped the linen in the water beside them. The water was very cool.

Gently, and taking care not to brush Hurriya's face with her fingertips, Devora washed her face with the cloth, clearing away the grime of travel and grief. "There," she said softly when the left side of Hurriya's face was clean, "a woman can at least mourn in dignity."

Hurriya made no answer, and Devora finished, then rolled up the cloth and laid it gently in Hurriya's palm, in case she wanted it.

"Are you bleeding?" she asked, keeping her voice low so that the nazarite wouldn't hear. She could see Zadok out of the corner of her eye; he'd finished his circuit of the pool and was tending the horses.

"What do you care, Hebrew?"

"By the Covenant, girl, be civil. I am trying to help you."

"I don't want your help."

"Another ride and you may." Devora tried to dampen her frustration. "Let me tend you." There was no other woman here to do so, Hebrew or Canaanite, so Devora would have to care for the girl herself. Stranger or no.

Hurriya made no sign of assent or denial. Devora cast a quick glance about her, then called out, "Zadok, look away and do not approach, please."

The nazarite didn't turn toward them. "Your will, *navi*," he said. His voice cold with his own grief.

With great care, Devora unwrapped Hurriya's salmah. Keeping the cloth over her arms, Devora gripped her above the elbows and lowered her gently onto her salmah like a blanket. Seeing her body unclothed, Devora gasped. Her breasts were still swollen in a way that must have been torture. Dried blood on the girl's left thigh and leg, though not enough to endanger her. Gently Devora took the scrap of linen from the girl's hand where she'd clutched it loosely, wet it again in the pool, and slowly washed her thighs and her womanhood. Then she rose and walked grimly to Shomar, to her saddlebag, retrieving the spare waterskin.

Zadok was currying his own horse. "Is she well?"

"No woman's well who's just had a child," Devora said curtly, and walked back.

She knelt again beside the young woman, who was no longer crying but only gazing up at the branches. Devora recalled what she'd said about the olive tree and her sister. The protectiveness she'd felt for the girl earlier was fiercer now, and she wondered at it but had no time to think too much about it, for the girl's need was so great. She had forgotten for the moment that she was Hebrew and Hurriya was heathen. Or rather, it wasn't that she'd forgotten it—it was that the fact that Hurriya was a young woman grieving and in pain seemed so visible and immediate that the other fact paled before it like a torch in bright sunlight. Devora submersed the waterskin in the pool until it was full. Lifted the skin to the girl's lips. "Drink," she said. "Small swallows."

She watched as Hurriya drank slowly, and tilted the waterskin up for her until the young woman lifted her hands and grasped it. Devora let her have it.

"I forgot how far you'd walked," she murmured. "My mind was on—other things. I'm sorry."

Hurriya took a few last swallows, then lowered the skin to her side. Her eyes were a little more alert. "Why are you doing this? When you despise me."

A twinge of guilt. "I don't despise you, girl."

"You despise my people."

Devora paused. "You came before my olive tree. You are my responsibility, my care." Her tone was fierce and it surprised her.

Hurriya lay back. "I'm grateful for the water."

Devora nodded.

"My people—there are only remnants of us in the land." Hurriya closed her eyes. "And most Hebrews see us as labor, either in the fields or in their beds. You're different. You see us as a threat."

Devora hesitated a moment, a turmoil within her. She was trying to sort through her feelings for this strange girl.

"You Canaanites invite the rising of the dead," she said at last. "When the People came to the land and there were raids between our tribes and yours, you tossed your own dead into the water and left ours unburied." Her voice went low and intense. "The unburied dead cry out to God. They moan. Ceaselessly. They even rise from the earth and walk, seeking burial, feeding to sustain their walking until that burial is given to them."

"I have seen that," Hurriya whispered.

***

When they left the pond, the slow pace of their riding made Devora hiss in exasperation, but her own body was grateful for it. Already her thighs burned from chafing against the saddle, and the rolling gait of her husband's gelding promised her livid bruises later. The girl actually moaned for the first few minutes of their ride, then mercifully fell asleep, though the look of misery did not leave her face even in slumber. Devora yearned to pronounce some curse against Barak as dire as the one she'd given Nimri. She should not have had to chase after his army on horseback. She should not have had to take this girl with her as a guide—she could have left the girl dying at the edge of Shiloh camp and been done with her. Yet she knew she could never have done that.

As they rode, Devora began watching the rising hillsides, alert for moving figures. Already, she feared to catch some glimpse of an unsteady, lurching corpse. But there were none. Which only made her more anxious. They'd left the barley fields of Manasseh tribe behind and were climbing toward the high lakes of the north.

Hurriya snored softly as she slept against Devora's shoulder. She was still so pale, and her body so thin within her salmah, as though God had formed her not out of a man's rib but out of leaves and dry twigs.

She was so small, so vulnerable. At one point, the *navi*'s hand twitched with a powerful urge to stroke Hurriya's hair in comfort, and Devora reminded herself angrily that the girl was unclean.

Devora had never caressed another woman's hair, and it was some time before the memory came to her of her own mother caressing hers, and singing softly to her, when she was eleven. Before she'd bled and before the walking corpses had come to her mother's camp. Though it surprised her to realize it, this memory of her mother brought Devora no pain or fear, only warmth and well-being. It felt good, riding in the late summer heat with Hurriya in her arms and with the warm strength of Shomar beneath them, bearing them both. It felt good. Though her thighs and rear were sore, Devora found herself nearly dozing, lulled by the warmth of the girl she held and the smooth, rolling rhythm of the horse, and would startle awake after a few minutes of drowsy stupor. For a time, she forgot what they were riding to and what they were riding from.

Until she glanced back at Zadok and felt the darkness touch her heart again. The nazarite hadn't forgotten. His face was grim as a man's who'd just stood by while his brother died.

***

After a while, Hurriya woke. She seemed more alert. With each mile she looked about her more, her face drawn with pain but the worst of her anguish fading from her eyes as though each step Shomar took was erasing an earlier step. Erasing the long nightmare of her walk to the *navi*'s seat. As though her child and her pain had never been. As though all of that had happened in the dark dream country, not in her waking life. Yet she remained terribly pale. Devora made her drink often.

They came to the high country, and Zadok emerged from his brooding and began watching the tall grasses and the scree on the slopes. There were a few hours of light yet, as the days this time of year were long. Devora began asking

Hurriya softly for advice on the way they should take, and to her pleased surprise the weary girl offered an occasional gesture or word of direction. They picked their way among well-traveled paths into the broken hills that hid from their eyes the Kinnor, the Harp-Shaped Sea. They passed the two peaks of the Hittim, skirting them on the east. Devora considered Hurriya's wan face and then glanced at the smoke that hung over the tiny settlement on one of the hills. They could stop, perhaps, and ask for herbs for the girl. Yet she was in haste, and there would be women with herbs following Barak's camp, she was certain. Uneasy, Devora pressed on.

Hurriya cast a glance at the settlement too, but without any expression of longing. Perhaps she simply didn't care.

The Kinnor Sea called to Devora's heart as they moved carefully along the cliffs that confined it on the west. Near the shore, the water was that shade of blue that water only gets when it is viciously cold, for the shadow of the hills lay over it. Innumerable white birds dipped and glided over the water, far below the women and the nazarite. Their voices came up to them in faint, shrill cries, like the voices of God's own host diving out of the sky to give battle. Even from this height, Devora could make out little houses clustered near the water and small boats on the surface.

"*Kinnor*, the harp," Devora whispered. "I have never seen this sea. It is beautiful."

"*Kenar*," Hurriya said.

Devora glanced at her. "What?"

"*Kenar*. The sea is *Kenar*. Not *Kinnor*."

She frowned. "Is that a Canaanite word?"

"It's Canaanite. Look." She gestured at the water. "My mother told me there are more fish in that water than there are men and women on the earth, and a god sleeps at the bottom of the sea, and his name is Kenar. The fish swim out of his dreams into the water, and because his dreams are deep and don't end, the fish will go on swimming up to the nets for all time, as long as the god stays asleep. The men who go out in the boats are careful to speak very quietly when they're on the water. They don't want to wake the god."

"A heathen story," Devora murmured. "There is no god actually under that water."

"Do you know that? Have you swum down there to look?" Hurriya's voice turned bitter. "You asked me to guide you. Yet you believe this is your water and your land, and me a stranger in it. And you don't believe what I tell you about it. How should I guide you, *navi*? You should have left me to die near my son."

Devora fell silent. Hurriya's words depressed her. They reminded her of how dependent she was on the Canaanite here, and how dependent the Canaanite was on her. She did *not* know this part of the land. Yet she needed to find in it five hundred living men and a great many dead ones. She looked down at the sea—*Kinnor*—and for a while she watched the water and the great white cranes swooping over it. Whatever the sea was called, it was breathtaking when seen from here, so near the sky. As pure and beautiful indeed as a harp's music.

When she did turn her head at last, she found Zadok riding beside her, and gave a start. The man's face was stricken with awe, his eyes moist though he shed no tears; he was staring at the sea. Devora looked away; it seemed indecent to witness such naked emotion on Zadok's face. She hadn't known the nazarite was capable of being moved at such beauty.

***

They climbed farther into the hills and left the cliffs of the sea behind. Following not the Tumbling Water in its deep ravine but a caravan road that wound up toward the heights. They found dusk falling over a land of dark and wooded ridges, cut sharp and beautiful against the sky. After pointing out the wagon track she thought would lead them toward Walls, Hurriya fell into a sleep that was deep and desperate, her head cradled against Devora's shoulder, her mouth open. As the last light faded, Devora tensed and became more alert, listening now for sounds she feared to hear—for they had reached the high Galilee.

They stopped to refill a few of their flasks with water at a small well where a few boys were tending sheep, Zadok asking questions of them. Hurriya opened her eyes long enough to take a look at the boys, then fell back into her sleep. Devora sat her horse near enough to the boys to see the terror etched into their faces, carved there like letters in stone. Their eyes wide. They had seen things, in these hills, recently. They shook their heads when Zadok asked about the dead, as though too afraid to remember. But they did let the nazarite know that many armed Hebrews had passed the well earlier that day.

Devora motioned Zadok to her side and whispered so as not to wake the girl. "We must try to ride at a trot."

"The horses need rest."

"*I* need rest," she said, her voice sharp with fatigue. "The horses can take us until moonrise, at least. At a faster walk, as long as this wagon track doesn't vanish."

Zadok watched her a moment with dark eyes, then nodded. He cast a glance at the boys, who were already beating their sheep away from the water and up toward the slopes. "They saw something, but ran before taking much of a look, I think." He frowned. "These Canaanites are like mice, always ducking behind a wall or into some hole."

"They are boys," Devora snapped. "And they were brave enough not to leave their flock behind."

Zadok gave her a puzzled look, and Devora turned away quickly, nudged her horse back onto the caravan road, one arm around Hurriya to keep from jostling her.

The *navi* had startled herself. Zadok was right: these *were* Canaanites. How strange that she found herself defending them.

HARDLY DARING TO CLOSE HER EYES

THEY HAD RIDDEN only a little way beyond the well when the day's last faint light was eaten by the sharp ridges rising about them. When Devora tried to press on anyway, Zadok reached out and wound his fingers through Shomar's mane, his eyes dark against the darker night. "This has not been an easy Sabbath day in your husband's tent, *navi*. You cannot ride to confront Barak ben Abinoam or to face the dead, in the dark, so weary that you could lift no hand against them. And you might kill the girl trying."

She knew he was right. Yet the thought of delaying even an hour—

"The dead are out there, Zadok," she whispered. "In these hills. Maybe over that next ridge or behind that stand of trees." She rubbed her eyes with the back of her hand, but carefully, not wanting to stir Hurriya from her sleep. "We have to find Barak's camp. They're on foot, they can't be far. We can't stop."

The nazarite did not relinquish his hold on Shomar's mane, and the horse began to slow his walk. Devora gave Zadok a baleful look, but the nazarite's face was impassive.

"My covenant is to defend you," he said. "We will rest for the night."

"I should have left you in Shiloh," she muttered, yet she breathed easier. Somehow, with all this quiet, dark land about them and somewhere in it herds of moaning dead, knowing that Zadok was with her was a fierce comfort. Glancing around at those dark ridges against the sky, hearing the snap of branches in the wind, her pulse quickened and she admitted to herself the real reason she didn't want to stop.

She didn't want to close her eyes.

She didn't want to face the nightmares. Not out here, without a tent, without Lappidoth's arms to hold her and bind her to the present.

"That looks like a stand of terebinths," she whispered, nodding to the left. "We could take shelter there."

***

In a few moments they were setting up camp for the night in the lee of the terebinths, each tree ancient and creaking in the wind. Zadok chose a spot for a fire pit, then lifted Hurriya and laid her near it. Devora took Mishpat, a waterskin, a small bag of grains to eat, and the wool roll of her blanket and then turned Shomar loose to graze, trusting he'd come at her call. After watching the Canaanite wrap her salmah tightly about her body, Devora sighed, took up her own blanket, and covered the girl with it. Hurriya's eyes watched hers a moment, but her face could not be read. Devora stepped away, resigning herself to a cold night. Her thighs and rear were sore from riding; she supposed Hurriya must be far more sore. She got the bag of grain; the girl would need to eat something, exhausted or not. Taking one of the waterskins, Devora poured a little over her arms and washed them, though she spared no water for her face. She could feel the dust of travel, a coating of it on her skin, and she yearned fiercely to wash it away, but water on a journey in the hot weeks before harvest was not to be wasted. She took the waterskin to Hurriya and let a little run out into her cupped hands. "Scrub up to the elbows, girl," she said, and Hurriya gave her a look but obeyed.

They ate in silence while Zadok cracked dry branches into kindling, dug a fire pit, and laid the wood within. His rough, powerful hands scooped up dry, fallen leaves, and he covered the wood with them. Hurriya hummed a little of her go-to-sleep tune, the one she'd sung on that Sabbath evening by her child's cairn. Then she fell silent, eating with her head lowered. Devora felt she should say something to the girl but didn't know what. So she chewed the grain slowly—too fatigued to put much energy even into eating—and waited for the fire.

She felt the dark close tight about her, pressing in on her heart. She glanced over her shoulder more than once. The wind-talk of the trees sounded ominous now, a portent of death. For a few moments the old primeval prey-fear of a fierce wind at night overtook her—the fear of being caught, helpless, and swept off the earth, or the fear that the wind would bring something predatory and godlike swooping down upon her as she shivered in the grass. Neither moon nor stars were visible, and the dark beneath the trees was like blindness. Like *hoshekh*, the dark that fills the mouth and nostrils and gets inside the heart until the spirit itself is cold.

She wanted light badly, but considered telling Zadok to stop making the fire. The cracking of branches had been so loud—though perhaps hidden in the cracking the wind was causing in the trees behind them. But the fire—the fire would be bright and visible for a long way. Raiders she didn't fear; they would not trouble Israel's *navi*, and she pitied the raiders who would choose Zadok for a foe. But the dead—what if there were dead near enough to see the fire?

Drawing in her breath, Devora beseeched God silently for a vision of the night to come. She heard wood rubbing quickly against wood and knew Zadok was making fire. Near her, Hurriya had lifted her eyes toward the trees too. For the briefest moment, Devora felt scorching heat on her right side, the side nearest Hurriya, but the heat did not pass into and through her as it usually did. No vision came. Devora sighed. At least that momentary heat was *something*. God had not forsaken her and her People entirely; he was still here, somewhere. She could still feel the touch of that *shekinah*, that desert-heat presence. It just wasn't *showing* her anything.

"There's something in the trees," Hurriya said.

Devora looked up quickly, peered beneath the trees. Glanced at Zadok, saw him setting his spear by his hip, ready to take it up at any sign of movement. For a while they all watched the dark.

But beneath the trees nothing moved, only the branches overhead. Zadok began rubbing the sticks together again.

"What did you see?" Devora asked the girl.

Hurriya just shook her head. "I'm sorry. I must've imagined it."

The fire roared up, and the nearer trees leapt into being. The shadows were dark and strange beyond the circle of light.

"The wind has you uneasy," Zadok said in that low rumble his voice made when he was tired. "Will you sing, *navi*?"

"What?" Devora didn't look at him, her eyes on the wood.

"Sing. There is no *kohen* here to sing to God and to remind the land and the trees and the night that they belong to God. Will you sing?"

Slowly, forcing herself to deepen her breathing, she turned to face him and the fire. On impulse, she decided to do as he asked. Anyone near—or anything near—would hear the song, but perhaps God would hear her better too.

> *Ashirah lahashem ki-ga'oh ga'ah*
> *Sus veroch'vo ramah vayam!*

Devora sang softly at first, then loudly, defiantly, the Hebrew words rolling one into the other and then galloping from her like horses riding across an open place, not to be halted or challenged, free and strong and fierce.

> *And you, God, you breathed on the face of the waters,*
> *Made a dry passage and we passed through,*
> *Water on our left,*
> *Water on our right.*

> *The stranger said, I will pursue the People,*
> *I will overtake them and devour them,*
> *I will divide up their herds among my men,*
> *I will enjoy their women,*
> *I will end them with a bloody hand.*

> *And you, God, you breathed on the water,*
> *The waves covered the stranger, the deep swallowed him up.*

Devora let the words rise from her belly and her throat and her lips, out into the night, in a wailing, exuberant cry, the high, screaming song of a woman of a desert people.

> *Ashirah lahashem ki-ga'oh ga'ah*
> *Sus veroch'vo ramah vayam!*

When she fell silent at last, she lowered her eyes, not wanting to share the pain in them with the others. She had sung that song with Eleazar once, thirty years past when she was barely more than a girl and much of the repairing of Shiloh had fallen to her. She and Eleazar had sung that after the cairns were raised, tossing the words back and forth between them, even as their forebears had done on the lethal shore of the Red Sea. Devora pressed her fingers to her lips. The problem with aging was not that death was near, for death was always near. The problem with aging was that a woman began to carry too many memories within her.

"That's what you sing when you're afraid?" Hurriya's voice sounded small and bitter. "You sing about your God killing my people?"

"No," Devora said wearily. "Not *your* people. It is the *Shirat ha'Yam*—the Song at the Sea. The first *navi* sang it. She and her brother the Lawgiver and their brother the first high priest sang those words on the day of Israel's deliverance from a foe who killed more of our People than the unclean dead ever did." She glanced at the Canaanite. "In Kemet, where we were made slaves."

"Now you are here," Hurriya said, "and you make my people *your* slaves."

"That is not how it's supposed to be." Weariness overwhelmed her. She realized her hands were shaking as if with extreme cold, and she held them between her thighs to keep them still. What was wrong with her? She felt as though she'd fallen off Shomar's back and was tumbling down a long slope. Too much had happened in the last few days. The infant. The raid on Shiloh. Eleazar's death. Too much.

"Zadok, keep watch, please," she said quietly.

"Your will, *navi*."

"Get some sleep, girl," Devora called across the fire. Then she lay down in her own bedding. She no longer cared what dreams might come. Sleep was suddenly its own necessity and its own end that justified any terrors it might hold. Devora tilted her head back and gazed at the sky. There were still no stars—she wished desperately that she could see stars. They would be a reminder of the promise that came with the keeping of the Covenant, the promise God had given their fathers in the desert.

Can you count the stars in the night sky?
Even so will your children and your children's children be beyond counting.

Those sharp points of cold light were a better defense against fear than the bronze points of a thousand spears. The unclean dead never looked to the sky. The dead had no promises, no Covenant. The People, though—they had the eternal promise that their seed would never die in the earth's dark soil, that they would grow and fill the land, planting after planting, harvest after harvest.

The stars would have been a comfort.

Reluctantly she lay down on her back, folded her hands over her breast, and closed her eyes. Reciting to herself the ten conditions of the Pact written into stone within the Ark, she shut out the crack and sway of terebinth boughs, the sound of the wind, the uneven earth and roots beneath her back, even the soreness of her thighs and rear from the day's riding. But she found she could not shut out the fear, so she caught it instead and put it in a little wooden box inside her mind and snapped that box shut and held it there in the dark. That is where you belong, she told the fear. If there was anything in the trees, Zadok could watch it. It was for her to sleep, to be rested when God or her People would need her. She slowed her breathing. Listened to her heartbeats. Recited the Ten again. *You shall have no other gods before me...You shall remember the Sabbath and keep it sacred...You shall not steal...You shall not bear false witness against another...*

***

Her eyes flew open. She could still hear the silence after her mother's shrieks and then the wet sounds of the dead feeding. Could still feel the cool clay pestle in her hand, clenched tightly because her palm was slick with sweat and she had to keep hold of it. Breathing hard, Devora struggled to reorient herself. She was lying on her side with a fire before her. Hurriya sat across the fire, her eyes reflecting back the flames. She was singing softly. That same go-to-sleep song Devora had heard her sing before. The melody tugged at Devora; there was something so wistful about it. Like a woman alone in a boat on a lake singing to another woman walking alone along the shore.

Somewhere to the left, Shomar whickered softly. Zadok was not at the fire; he was gone.

Devora wrapped her arms about herself and bit her lip to hold in a whimper. Anger flashed through her, a heat that didn't warm her. She could not suffer these dreams now. She could *not*. The People needed her.

"Did I cry out in my sleep?" Her tone was sharp, bitter.

Hurriya stopped singing and shook her head. Kept watching the fire. She had a strained look now that she wasn't singing, as though it was all she could do to hold back her pain from overwhelming her.

"Where is Zadok?" Devora asked.

"He heard something."

"What did he hear?"

"A deer. He said."

Devora looked to the trees. The wind had died down and the trees were no longer full of menace but only mournful. Because they trapped the dark and held it beneath their branches even as some men and women trap it in their hearts.

"A deer," Devora murmured.

She thought it unlikely that a deer would have drawn the nazarite from the fire. She shivered, glanced away from the trees, saw the girl watching her.

"He was alone with me," Hurriya said after a moment, her voice holding a faint hint of relief. "He didn't touch me."

"You are unclean," Devora said, irritated. "And Zadok does not take women unwilling. He's a nazarite; he'd hardly need to."

"That's what Hebrew men do," Hurriya said.

Devora felt a rush of anger at her and beneath it a touch of pity that she let the anger smother. This girl had endured things she had never heard of a woman enduring before. But she couldn't afford to think about that. Devora looked away from the girl and watched the fire, wondering where the nazarite was and whether indeed he had heard or sensed the dead moving in the thicket. She shivered, and when she glanced at last at the Canaanite, she saw that the girl was shivering too.

No, she was *shaking*.

Devora watched her with growing alarm; the girl's eyes stared just over the fire into the dark beyond it, and her eyes were those of someone staring at things God had hidden before the making of the world and had never intended to be seen by living eyes. Devora rose and went to her side. The *navi* could feel heat rising from the girl as though she were sitting next to a fire blazing as high as the roof of a house. But after a moment the heat was gone, simply gone. Hurriya blinked, then her shaking subsided.

And suddenly Devora understood. She caught her breath.

"You *saw* something," Devora whispered. "Something that isn't here, not yet. And you did earlier too. When you saw something in the trees."

Hurriya glanced at the *navi* but seemed disoriented.

"Answer me, girl," Devora snapped. "Has this happened before?"

"Twice," she whispered. "Twice before this night. While I was with child."

Devora tried to take this in. It shouldn't be possible. Could the girl be imagining it? Yet Devora had felt the heat. She *knew* that heat. God had shown this girl things that usually only his eyes saw. Yet how could this be? She wasn't Hebrew.

"What did you see?"

"A man, Hebrew, I think. He was beating my sister." She began shaking. "I would rather die than see this. I wasn't dreaming."

"I know," Devora said quietly.

"Then I saw you. You were sitting beside a dead man. I don't know who he was. You got up to gather stones." Her eyes were vulnerable. "What does it mean?"

Devora took a breath. "It means you are chosen to be the next *navi* of Israel." Hardly believing her own words. "It means you see what God sees."

Hurriya laughed that cold, bitter laugh she had. "I've been touched by your God, you mean."

"Yes." Devora's voice sounded very small to her.

"I don't *know* your God."

For a moment only the fire was speaking.

There was strife in Devora's heart. This woman was *not* of the People.

"It seems *he* knows *you*," Devora said. "This is a very great burden, and a great gift. No veil between you and God. I have to think about this."

Devora got up quickly, paced out to the shadows beyond the firelight. She set her back to the nearest tree and just breathed evenly.

That Hurriya should be chosen, that was a sign.

But a sign of what?

That, revoking his promise, God had chosen another People? Or that the survival of the Covenant and the People depended on strangers? Or something else?

She glanced around the bole of the tree, saw Hurriya at the fire in her salmah. Thought again how inadequate a garment that was. A new and strange thought occurred to the *navi*—what if God had left the People unsheltered because they themselves had given no shelter?

Shelter the stranger in your land…

If Hurriya was the next *navi*, it was because God had something for her to say to the People, something only Hurriya could see, something only she could tell them. Something they must hear. Something about the strangers in their land.

The sickly sweet scent of death assailed her, making her belly heave. With a gasp, Devora turned her gaze away from the fire and gave a start, her heart pounding. A tall figure stood there in the dark, massive and looming over her.

Its eyes glinting in the light of the fire.

It was not Zadok.

THE CORPSE

FOR SEVERAL HEARTBEATS Devora stood paralyzed, caught by the thing's eyes, which were empty and cold and only gave back firelight the way metal gives back a dull sheen. The corpse's sides moved in and out as it took quick breaths. Then it snarled, a sound that had nothing human in it, and lunged into her, knocking the breath from her, pinning her to the tree with its weight. Devora lifted her arm to shield her face and throat, felt the thing's neck pressed against the heavy wool of her sleeve. Its breath on her cheek, cold as the air over a frozen lake. The corpse leaned hard on her arm, its teeth snapping a mere breath from her throat; it had lurched right out of her night dreams and into her waking life, it had come for her, she'd always known it would. She found her breath and screamed shrilly. Turned her face to the side, fighting to hold it off with her arm, but the thing was *strong*. Another moment and it would be *feeding* on her—

A flash in the dark, and the corpse's head was severed half from its neck and fell limp against its left shoulder. The thing's hissing went silent, but still its cold hands grasped at her. Wide-eyed, Devora saw Hurriya standing behind the corpse, naked, Mishpat lifted in her hands.

With a cry, Devora dropped to her knees and threw herself to the side in the dark, heard the corpse scrambling after her as she rolled. A cry from Hurriya, and as Devora rolled onto her back she caught a glimpse of the sword flashing again through the air, and then she was on her belly again and then had her hands and knees beneath her and was pushing herself up to her feet.

The corpse was impaled on Mishpat, the blade driven into its chest; its head hung limply behind its shoulder, and its hands were groping in the air. Hurriya was ducking them.

"The head," Devora gasped. "The head!"

Hurriya wrenched the sword free of the corpse's belly and began swinging it like a wood-axe, chopping the blade into their assailant's head, shoulders, and arms. Again and again. The body went down and she stood over it, lifting

Mishpat high and sending the blade shrieking down through the air. Sobbing as she chopped into the body.

For a moment Devora looked on with horror. Then staggered toward her, panting. "It's done," she rasped. "It's done, girl!"

Hurriya didn't seem to hear her; she just kept lifting the blade and chopping. Her face wild with anguish. Bits of necrotic flesh flew through the air. Some of it spattered across her legs.

"God's Covenant, girl! Stop!" Devora cried, her eyes wide.

A sound of crashing through the trees to her left, and she spun to face it. Hurriya did as well, lifting Mishpat, but then there was a man's cry from that direction: "*Devora!*"

For an instant Devora was startled—Zadok had never used her name before, nor had she permitted it—but relief overwhelmed the brief shock. "Zadok!" she cried.

The nazarite burst into sight, his spear in his hand and three waterskins looped over his shoulder. Taking in the scene at a glance, he cast spear and skins aside and swept Devora up in his powerful arms, startling her. In a moment he'd borne her to the fire and set her beside it. His eyes were hot with fury, but he said nothing. He ducked into the shadows of the trees, and in a moment he returned with spear and waterskins and Hurriya walking beside him, naked and shaking, her legs bespattered with bits of flesh and tissue. She carried Mishpat out to her side.

Devora got hurriedly to her feet. "Zadok, my waterskin—"

He tossed it to her. "*Why* did you leave the fire?"

"Why did *you*?" Devora cried.

Zadok looked at her a moment. "Stay here," he said firmly.

She nodded jerkily. His bronze spear clutched in one hand, the nazarite rose and hurried back into the shadows beneath the trees. Devora looked into the dark for a moment, shivering. Were there more out there, more dead?

But she had a problem here, near at hand, something she had to tend to. Something she *could* tend to.

"Sit," Devora said to Hurriya. "Quickly."

Hurriya lowered herself unsteadily, the firelight showing goose bumps along her arms and on the skin of her breasts, from the cold. She held Mishpat out to the *navi*, and Devora saw now that the girl had wrapped a small cloth about the hilt, so that her skin did not touch it. Devora would have been relieved, but she was too shaken with fear. Hurriya set the blade before Devora and removed the cloth. She did so slowly, as though reluctant to let the blade go.

Devora set the blade aside—it would have to be cleansed—and then poured out the entire waterskin over the girl's thighs and legs. Swept up some dry brush and began scrubbing her legs.

Hurriya gasped at the pain of it.

"Be still," Devora snapped. "You have bits of—of *it*—on you. Be still, girl."

Devora bent low over the girl and looked at her legs carefully in the firelight. Hissed through her teeth and brushed at a spot just above her knee. She glanced at the hair between the girl's thighs, then gave a closer look though her face burned. But nothing had spattered that high on her body.

When Devora was satisfied that none of the unclean flesh was left on the girl's body, she began brushing fiercely at the ground, pushing dirt and offal into a small pile that one might cover with two hands, if one dared to touch it. Devora straightened and turned toward Hurriya, still breathing fast.

"Never do that again," she snapped.

"It stopped moving," Hurriya breathed. "It stopped."

"Yes, it did."

"And it didn't bite you. Or me."

"It didn't." Devora's voice was sharp. She wanted no comfort or help from this heathen girl; now that she was sure the girl had no bits of the corpse still clinging to her, Devora wanted to be left alone, to hold herself in her own arms and shiver. She realized she was still on the edge of panic. A whimper of fear rose in her throat, and she held it back. She bit her lip, hard, tasted her own living blood. Began to breathe more calmly. The girl was right. The corpse hadn't bitten the *navi*, hadn't even touched her bare skin. She was all right.

"You don't know what I saw." The Canaanite stared into the fire. "Coming down from the hills. With my child. The things I saw. I couldn't watch another woman be eaten."

Devora knelt by her and sat back on her heels. She watched the firelight play across the younger woman's face. Then glanced over her shoulder at the dark under the trees. With a shudder, she wondered if she would ever again be able to sleep near trees.

"Thank you," she whispered, and glanced back at the girl. But Hurriya had lost consciousness.

Devora watched her a moment, saw again the leanness of Hurriya's body as she lay naked by the fire. Her breasts rising and falling with her breath. That ghastly pallor to her skin, almost as though she might be one of the dead herself. And now, great bruises forming on her thighs and the beginnings of sores where the saddle had rubbed her raw even through her salmah.

A terrible unease was growing in Devora, as though some beast had given birth in her heart, and its clawed pup was growing, scratching at the walls within her, feeding on all that Devora now saw. Many times Devora had suffered her nightmares and night terrors, seeing again her mother's face and the lurching dead in the camp. Often she had cursed the heathen in her heart, those who would cast the dead into open water, uncovered and unrestrained and utterly without burial, if the Hebrews who possessed the land permitted it. Devora hadn't forgotten the Canaanite cheekbones and eyes of the dead who'd fallen upon Shiloh camp thirty years before. When Canaanites were brought before her seat beneath the olive—which was rare, for cases involving them were easily dealt with, without the *navi*'s intervention—but when they *were* brought to her, Devora had dealt her judgment harshly, knowing that only the strictest observance of the Law could keep the People safe. One Law for the Hebrew and for the stranger in the land, and a stoning and then burial beneath the stones if the violation of Law was so severe that no lesser cleansing would suffice.

Often, she had remembered the Canaanite features of the dead.

But never had she imagined having her life *preserved* by one of the heathen.

Hurriya shivered in her restless sleep. Devora crouched beside her, held her hand an inch above the girl's brow. Warmth. The beginning of a fever, perhaps. For a moment the panic rose again in Devora. What if it was the fever of the dead? But no, the girl did not have that look. This was a fever of the living body, some uncleanness that came of having a child and losing it and suffering after. At least so Devora hoped.

She rose shakily and walked about the fire. Took up Hurriya's salmah and brought it back to where she was lying. Draped it over her. Hurriya didn't move beneath it.

***

Devora set to the task of cleaning her sword, with as much care as she had cleaned Hurriya's body. She shuddered as she wiped the flesh and stains from the blade with a handful of grass. She did so meticulously, slowly, careful not to get any of it on herself. "I was right to bring you," she whispered to the blade. Her eyes round in the dark.

Glancing up, she caught a glimpse of movement beneath the trees and gasped. Her heart wild in her breast. She gripped Mishpat's hilt and was about to cry out, but then Zadok's enormous shape emerged from the darkness, and he stepped out into the firelight. He had on his goatskin gloves and was dragging the corpse behind him by its ankle, carrying his spear in his other hand. He gave Devora a grim look and cast the body down at the edge of the firelight. "I think it is the only one," he said.

"You think?" Devora whispered.

He set his spear aside. "I may be wrong. You and the girl must stay by the fire, *navi.*"

Devora nodded. She was full of questions, but she glanced down at the corpse, and for the moment her questions choked in her throat.

Now that it wasn't moving, the corpse seemed indeed a pitiful thing. Its left shoulder and the left side of its face had been terribly hacked open by the sword. The rest of it—a husk and only a husk. As though God had sucked out the breath of life that he'd blown into the human body at the beginning of time and left behind something fragile as papyrus but upon which no letters Hebrew or other could ever be written again. In this leathery flesh that remained, no hopes or fears could be inscribed, and even if a man were to pull the unclean bones free from this withered corpse and chisel words into them as if into stone, even those bones would merely crumble away. Gazing at that corpse, Devora felt a horror of the brevity of life and the transience of all lives human and animal, which in the end are eaten or devoured whether by their dead or by some rogue lion or only by wind and soil. Whether God will remember them or not.

"Where were you?" she breathed.

"By the water," Zadok said. "There's a stream downhill, beyond the trees, barely close enough to hear a shout. I heard something in the trees while you slept, and I went that far looking for it." He paused, his regret showing in his eyes. "That was a mistake."

"It *was* a mistake," Devora said hoarsely.

Zadok was silent a moment. "I am used to doing this alone," he said. "When the levites send me out. When there is some corpse in a man's barley or feasting on his flock. Forgive me, *navi.*"

"We are not hunting, Zadok." Devora couldn't keep the edge from her voice, and no longer wished to. So the man was grieving. So he felt he'd failed Eleazar. He still had responsibilities to *her.* "Not until we find Barak and his men. We need to *find* Barak. And you need to stay here and defend us until we do."

Zadok gazed into the fire, the lines of his face tense. "There were three sets of footprints by the stream."

Devora was silent a moment. Zadok's words doused her anger like ice water. "The dead?"

"They did not walk like living men." His gaze flicked down to the corpse. "We must hope the other two have walked on."

"Surely my scream would have brought them if they hadn't," Devora said uneasily.

Zadok shook his head. Then he crouched by the corpse. His gloved hands turned its head to one side, then the other. Devora gasped. The body was missing both of its ears. Indeed, now that it lay in the firelight she could see that the right side of its head had been torn open from where the ear should be to the middle of its hair, baring tissue and torn muscle and a white glint of bone.

"Ears are easy to tear away," Zadok muttered. "If one of these is feeding, it is likely to go for the throat or the cheek or the ears. Soft places where the teeth can dig in and tear. This one may have been in the trees all evening, *navi*. Yet it did not moan or approach our camp. It did not hear us." He gave her a grim look.

"So the others could still be in there." Devora peered into the dark beneath the trees.

Zadok didn't answer. His hands were shaking slightly.

"*Don't* freeze on me," Devora breathed.

"Your will, *navi*." The nazarite's voice was hoarse. Without lifting his gaze from the corpse, he pulled out his bronze knife and set the blade against his left palm. Drew it swiftly across his skin. For a moment he closed his hand around the blade. Devora looked on, disconcerted, as blood leaked between his fingers.

She rose to get a cloth, but Zadok shook his head. "Let it bleed a while," he muttered.

She watched him a moment. "This will keep you alert?"

He lifted his eyes to hers. Dark with pain.

She nodded, glanced at the corpse, then at the fire and the girl lying beneath her salmah near it. Trying to gather her thoughts. After a moment she realized Hurriya was awake and watching them. Her face still terribly pale, her eyes cold.

"Is the girl well?" Zadok asked hoarsely. He was gripping his sliced hand tightly with the other.

"Yes," Devora said.

"She must not panic. It's best if we stay quiet tonight."

Devora nodded.

"She took up your blade." Zadok's eyes shone in the firelight. "Brave girl. For a Canaanite."

Hurriya could probably hear their words, though they kept their voices low; she was only a spear's length away. But she did not appear to react to them. She was staring at the corpse.

"She hates them," Devora whispered. "She doesn't *fear* them anymore, not as I do. She just hates them."

"Hers are a strange people."

"Yes they are." Devora glanced back at the trees, peering into the *hoshekh* beneath the branches. Nothing there. Nothing that could be seen. She glanced down at the corpse's ravaged face. It was male, but she could tell little more about it. Neither what color its eyes had been nor its age. "I can't tell if he was Hebrew or heathen," Devora muttered. The uncertainty of it weighed on her. It seemed now vitally important to her to know who had unraveled the roots of the Covenant: the heathen in the north or the uncareful Hebrews. She gave the corpse's face another hard look, then her gaze strayed down its body, settled on its hips. She drew in a quick breath as a solution to her uncertainty occurred to her.

Devora averted her eyes quickly, her face warming. Found herself facing Hurriya, whose eyes seemed to read hers. The Canaanite woman got unsteadily to her knees, one hand clutching the salmah tightly about her. Hollows about her eyes—the day and the night were exacting a fierce toll on her body.

Hurriya crawled near, then bent over the corpse, swiftly tugging its clothing aside. Devora couldn't look. She fought a surge of nausea at what Hurriya was doing, at her closeness to the dead. But the girl was already unclean; it would make no difference.

"He was Hebrew," Hurriya rasped.

Devora said nothing. Zadok watched the Canaanite with that quiet wariness of his.

"You Hebrews mark your bodies," Hurriya said coldly. "A Canaanite woman always knows what kind of man has assaulted her."

Without another word, Hurriya rose and returned to her place across the fire, keeping her salmah wrapped tight about her.

Devora looked after her a moment, thoughts leaping through her, quick as a flight of deer through a wood. She exchanged a look with Zadok, then went to Hurriya. The girl lay shivering. Devora knelt by her, trying to think through what the girl had said. There had been signs enough for her to interpret, but she had to step carefully. She watched the girl's face.

"The child's father. Malachi ben Aharon. You were his slave?"

Hurriya didn't answer.

"He bought you and was cruel to you?"

The Canaanite just stared at the fire.

Devora waited for a while. She heard Zadok digging, for there was a body to bury. The *navi* was just about to give up and try sleeping again when the girl spoke.

"My father couldn't feed the three of us—my mother, my sister, and me. So he sold me to one of the other workers in the olive grove. A Hebrew, who could afford me. He sold me because I was old enough to be—desirable. When that man—" Her voice broke, but she recovered quickly, and Devora felt chilled at the anguish she heard. "When he touched me, I thought I'd die. The way he hurt me—he *liked* to hurt me."

Not knowing what other comfort to give, Devora reached out and gripped Hurriya's shoulder through the salmah. Her breast felt tight. Nothing of which Hurriya spoke was against the Law. None of it was a breaking of the Covenant. But the fear and hate she saw in the girl's eyes—no woman should have to endure that. It was women who gave the Covenant to their children, who bore in their wombs the living sign of the promise. With God, together they made the future of the People. What had happened to Hurriya was not against any words of the Law, but surely it could destroy the Law and the Covenant all the same.

"I tried to hide from him once," Hurriya whispered. "He beat me until I couldn't rise from his bedding for three days. And little Anath had to hear it. Every one of my screams. Malachi only lived a stone's throw from my father's shed. They worked the same presses. When I took water out to him at midday, I would look up and see Anath in the treetops." She fell silent.

"I have erred," Devora whispered. "You have no kin to return to. None who will keep you. I should've found another guide. Yet the things you see—" She thought for a moment, her heart aching. "You must return to Shiloh with me—after this. You must be near, where I can teach you."

Hurriya shook her head. "I'm not going back there." She paused. "I don't care about these visions," she added after a moment. "Or your God. But help me find Anath." She swallowed. "And the dead. If you want to help me, tell me everything you know about the dead. You have so many rules about the dead. So teach me."

"Girl—"

"I am no *girl*. I am Hurriya of Judges' Well. I have lost my child. Those corpses—they *took* my child. My *child*. I have one sister, and that is all I have. I will find her, I will help her stay safe." She was speaking rapidly now, trembling with urgency. "We are going to a camp of armed men. When—when I am *clean*—" She mouthed the word with distaste, "help me find clothes. And a knife. And my sister. That is what I ask of Israel's *navi*."

"I will see that you have clothes. And we will have to find herbs for your fever. If I teach you about the dead," Devora added after a moment, "I must teach you the whole Law. And you must abide by it."

"Your Law." Hurriya laughed coldly, bitterly. "Always your Law, your strange and terrible Law. You would cast a woman from the tents because a corpse touched her, or stone a woman for placing a bowl of fruit before the goddess."

"If necessary, yes," Devora said hoarsely. "The People must be kept clean."

Hurriya turned her face away, shivering in her salmah. "Teach me, then. I don't care."

Devora's temper flared. "You *do* care, you impossible heathen!" she hissed through her teeth. "*Damn* you. Filthy, unwashed—you think your gods and the corpses of your dead are both things to keep in your houses! You bring the dead down on us, bring the blight and the curse and barrenness to the land— and then you lie down ready to die and you don't care! You *do* care, damn you!"

"It was a *Hebrew* corpse in the terebinths," the girl whispered without turning her head. "And a 'heathen' who saved you. Now I am so cold—please. Let me be. Please."

The bitterness had left her voice, only weariness now. Her tone doused Devora's temper. The girl was feverish and suffering. Of course she didn't care at times; she hurt too much to care.

Devora sighed. She had a double obligation to this strange girl—as a supplicant and as the next *navi*, who must learn from her. She reached for the girl's waterskin where it lay discarded by the fire pit and held it to Hurriya's lips. "Drink. As much as you can, before you sleep. We have to cool that fever."

Hurriya didn't open her eyes, but her throat moved as she swallowed. Devora tilted the waterskin, and to her relief the Canaanite drank deeply. "We'll talk after we've slept," Devora said, then lowered the waterskin and left it by Hurriya's hand.

A clack of stone behind her, and Devora turned to see Zadok piling rock upon the pit he'd dug in the earth. The body was out of sight, already in the ground. She breathed a sigh of relief. The corpse had unnerved her. More than that, it had ripped loose the already fragile latches on her memory. A glance at Hurriya showed that the girl had already fled back into sleep.

Devora too lay down in her bedding; she was shaking again. She could feel the cold of that corpse's flesh through her sleeves, where it had seized her. She kept her eyes open. All too clearly, she could imagine other dead stumbling out of those trees while she slept, waking her with their low moans only moments before they grasped her and—

She held herself tightly, turned her back to the trees with an effort, and faced Zadok, who was crouching across the fire from her, making a triangle between the three of them. The back of her neck twitched; she couldn't stop thinking about what might creep out of the dark behind her. With that vast, menacing *hoshekh* behind her, the fire was little comfort. She glanced at Zadok's eyes, saw them reflecting back the fire, tried to summon up her anger at him for leaving their fire. But her anger was like damp kindling that wouldn't light; the fear was too great.

After a moment, Zadok lifted his gaze toward the sky, and she followed with hers. Drew in a deep breath, let it out slowly. The wind had died and the clouds were drifting apart; there was a great fissure in the sky, like a ravine cut into the darkness, and in it shone bright stars. Devora found herself calming.

"Bless you, Zadok," she murmured. He must have seen her glancing often at the sky earlier. Must have known what she was hoping to see.

She willed her body to relax.

Closed her eyes.

Immediately she saw her mother's face. Vivid as though her mother were crouching beside her, teeth bared.

Devora's eyes flew open. She clenched her hands tightly around her arms, breathed deep for another moment. If she couldn't banish that memory from her mind, sleep would be out of the question. She would end up weeping through the night.

She watched the stars a few moments.

At last she sat up. Put her back to the fire and reached for Mishpat. She laid the blade naked across her thighs and looked into the dark beneath the trees.

"How many dead do you think are out there, Zadok?"

"Too many."

A stick cracked in the fire.

"Yes," Devora said. "Too many." She shivered, gazing out at the dark. She didn't turn to look at the nazarite. Instead, she watched how firelight and shadow played across the rough stones of the cairn.

It had been long since she'd slept without Lappidoth's arms about her, yet now she was here, alone, without him. Desperately she thought of him, wondered where he was. Was he sleeping that deep sleep of his, or was he standing, perhaps outside his tent, gazing up at the same stars in the same sky, praying for his wife? Devora yearned suddenly for the warmth of his body against her back and for the smell of him. Lappidoth smelled of cattle and wind and heather and wild barley, for he would run his hands through the barley that grew wild in the pasture as he walked toward his herds.

The cold panic was rising in her again. During the day she was in control, she could cut through her fear like her own iron blade. But now, after dark, after seeing that corpse—she needed some way to survive until dawn. With that cairn so near, and the darkness beneath the trees, and no tent over her, no arms about her—she couldn't do this. She breathed faster. Then an idea occurred to her that was comforting, but it gave her a pang of guilt, too. She didn't know how to ask for it without it seeming like—

She wrestled with it.

"Will you lie beside me, Zadok?" she whispered finally.

She heard him stir slightly.

"To hold me, while I sleep?" Her shoulders alone betrayed her tension. "I know we will both have evil dreams tonight. Yet I would like very much to sleep, if I can." She swallowed. "And not wake screaming."

She felt terribly vulnerable, even naked, asking for this. It meant setting aside her dignity as the *navi*, it meant—too many things. It should be Lappidoth here. She should be asking him.

Yet Zadok had always had her entire trust.

She felt the nazarite settle beside her, sitting by her. A powerful, large presence. She didn't look at him.

"You miss him," his voice rumbled in the dark.

She didn't have to ask who he meant. "Yes." Her throat tightened. "I wish he were here." If he *were*, if Lappidoth *were* here to hold her, he only and no one else, she could let herself cry. She could let herself shake apart in terror, until the fear had passed over her like the angel of death, knowing that he would still be there holding her, without judgment, while she put herself back together again.

"It is a strange thing I ask," Devora whispered, burning with anger at herself for showing the nazarite how vulnerable she felt. "You can refuse."

"I don't." His voice softened.

Devora nodded wearily and lay down, and after a moment Zadok lay behind her, his beard scratchy against her neck. His arms closed about her, warm and strong. She shivered.

"Thank you," she whispered.

He squeezed her gently.

"Don't fall asleep."

"I won't, *navi*."

She lay still in his arms a while, willing sleep to come. The Canaanite had begun to snore softly. Devora could hear from Zadok's breathing that he was still awake, and a calm settled over her. He would watch. It was all right. And if she woke, his arms would hold her to the present, as her husband's did. His arms were strange, more muscled than her husband's. She felt another twinge of guilt, yet it was strangely pleasant being held in them. There was so much of his father in Zadok, so much of Zefanyah. She felt his breath on her shoulder and found her heart beating a little faster.

"Zadok," she whispered.

"Navi."

She paused. "In the trees, you called out my name. My name. Not *navi*."

He tensed a little.

"You called *Devora*. As though my name belonged on your lips." Lying in his arms, she was suddenly alarmed at the intimacies the two of them had taken that night.

"I was frightened for you, *navi*," he said. "I intended no insult to you."

"Don't do it again," she said quietly.

"Your will, *navi*." He sounded weary.

She didn't say anything more. She watched the darkness under the trees warily. She wondered if Zadok *cared* for her. In that way. She'd felt for a moment that she could sense it in his breathing as he held her. And he'd called her name, her own name, freely, even as a husband might call out his wife's name. He'd never done that before. She wondered how she felt about it if he *did* feel that. It had been a long time since she was a girl, and pursued. She was not one now.

And she needed Zadok to be *Zadok*, the Zadok she knew, the man who stood with his spear behind her seat beneath the olive tree. A man she could trust to perform any task without flinching, whether the task was to spear an infant corpse or hold her while she slept. He had always been reliable, as few men were. What if there were passions, longings, in his heart that she did not know? What if, in the uncertain north, he was to become strange to her as well? If she could not trust Zadok—if she could not trust even herself, even her own heart—what was there left in the land that she *could* trust? What stood between her and the moaning in the dark?

She clung to his arm with her own small hands and closed her eyes, forced herself to breathe evenly. Whispered a few words of the *mitzvot* to calm herself—

If a living man touch any unclean thing, a corpse, or the carcass of an unclean beast, or the body of any creeping thing, then he too is unclean.

She thought of the Law stretched like a great tent over the People to keep them safe. She felt Zadok's chest against her back, strong and sure. Felt his breathing. He was still awake, still watching. One by one, Devora doused the fires of the busy camp her thoughts had made in her mind. She could not allow her thoughts to dance madly in the firelight, like the shadows dancing on the cairn. Right now she needed sleep and someone to watch over her during the hours she was defenseless. That was all that mattered. The rest must wait. She breathed slower.

Though she barely remembered it, there had been a time when she had not recited the Law before sleeping. A time when she'd had no nightmares to ward off. A time when she had been young, had not been the *navi*.

PART 2. SHILOH, YEARS PAST

THE GIRL WEEPING

THE FIRST TIME Devora ever glimpsed a thing that did not yet exist, she was twelve years old and only recently a woman. The vision came to her the day before her mother's death. It was just after dawn and there was frost on the heather, one of the last frosts of the year. Devora was carrying a ewer down to the stream outside her parents' camp to fill with water, humming to herself. The frost made little noise beneath her feet, for she'd wound heavy cloth around her sandals to keep her feet warm, and this muffled the sound. Her mind was on the changes and the soreness in her body and the prospect of being permitted to go to the Feast of Tents for the first time later that year. She broke into a run for the sheer joy of it, just to feel the wind in her hair. This was a pure kind of joy, a kind she would rarely experience again.

Without warning, heat blazed within her as though she'd leapt from the frost right into the smoke above a fire pit. She gasped for air and stopped, almost falling to her knees. Even as she did, she glimpsed across the stream, startling her, a young woman who looked identical to her. A woman who had her face. She was running through the grasses, weeping. Devora held her breath and would have called out, but in a moment the other woman was gone. Just gone.

WHAT GOD'S EYES SEE

THE SECOND TIME, Devora was fifteen, and the vision came to her only moments after her first kiss.

At that time, Devora lived in the girls' tent in Shiloh, a vast, four-sided pavilion shielded on one side by a wall of tall terebinth trees, like a green veil between the girls and the tents of the priests. At first Devora resided there as a ward of Naomi's, a waif who had wandered to Shiloh out of the hills, crying incoherently about the dead. The old *navi* Naomi had listened to her and sent the nazarites out to find the camp from which Devora had fled. Several of them returned to Shiloh days later, their faces grim, the wooden staves they carried darkened with fresh stains. Devora had watched them enter the camp, wide-eyed, and then had hidden beneath her blankets in the girls' tent until her trembling stopped.

The other girls had resented her. She was not one of them. No father had brought her to Shiloh to give her to God along with bushels of wheat or a young, unblemished bull. She had no father at all, and no priest had spoken for her, asking for a betrothal, as had already happened with many of the other dedicates. Devora was a stranger in the girls' tent. And she often woke them, screaming, from her dreams. The other girls tormented her, and Devora in her misery struck upon an unusual solution. In the middle of one night she got up and knelt in the middle of the great pavilion and pressed her face to the earth and cried out, waking the others:

Ata adonai, whose hands made earth and sky,
Who breathed life,
I bring you a gift,
a small gift,
the only gift I have.
I give to your service and your use,
this girl Devora of Ephraim tribe,
this girl is yours,
consecrated to you,
kadosh, kadosh,
she serves you.

Hannah, the oldest of the girls, gave an indignant cry when Devora finished and lifted her face. "You can't dedicate *yourself!*"

"I just did," Devora said quietly, and she faced the other girl with a new boldness in her eyes. "No less than you or the nazarites or the *navi*. I am God's."

***

Devora had begun running through the grasses that morning of her mother's death, and though she now lived in a permanent camp, she hadn't stopped running. In those first summers in Shiloh, Devora fought to banish from her memory the death of her mother and the growling of the dead in that camp. Her memory seemed to her a badly woven basket; things obviously were capable of leaking through gaps left in the weave, for she'd forgotten things before. So she packed her mind with the six hundred *mitzvot* the way a farmer packs a basket with grain, leaving no unused space, hoping that the more she filled her mind with the Law and the traditions that kept the People safe, the less space there would be for the terrors of the past.

In the ferocity of her study and her flight from memory, Devora knew she seemed grim for a young woman. The one joy of girlhood that remained to her was to watch the young nazarites on the fighting ground each morning, admiring the way the sun had bronzed their powerful arms, noting the sheen of sweat on their bodies as they danced the spears. Young Devora had a favorite among the nazarites, a man who bested most who came against him. In his strength and certainty, he reminded Devora of the nameless herdsman who had defended his cattle from the dead, that man who appeared often in her dreams.

The nazarite had a birthmark on his shoulder in the shape of a spearhead, and the other young men teased him over it. Devora was drawn to him for that. He was not godlike and unreachable; he was like her. He too was nettled by his peers. Devora admired him with a fierceness in her heart for the way he responded. For the nazarite would clap his brother on the shoulder and laugh. "We will be fighting on some high slope and God will look down out of his wide sky and see us all sweating in the heat, and he will be looking for some man to bless that day. His eyes will notice my shoulder. And God will say, *There is my servant Zefanyah, I will bless him.* The rest of you will all have to find other ways to attract God's attention."

***

To Devora's delight and embarrassment, her nazarite took to watching her in the evenings. He would stand within earshot of the tables where Eleazar the high priest taught the six hundred *mitzvot* of the Law, one table for the sons of priests and one for the dedicates who might become their wives and thus must know more of the Law than the wives of herders or tanners or caravan merchants. Devora would flush when she felt the nazarite's gaze, and one evening, for the first time, she failed to answer one of Eleazar's inquiries correctly. The high priest gave her a prolonged stare, then grunted and moved on to ask a question of the other table, without any reprimand beyond that small, noncommittal noise. But Devora's face burned as though God had placed a sun in front of her. And the other girls whispered quietly about it, which made her burn even more.

That night, Devora stayed behind, feeling an embarrassed need to apologize to Eleazar. The apology only made him cross.

"Get some rest, Devora. You're only, after all, a woman," he muttered, waving a hand dismissively.

Devora's eyes darkened at the comment. It was viciously unfair—she had a better memory than any of those who sat at the boys' table—but she didn't have a response that wouldn't earn her a beating or a week of chores about the camp, so she turned on her heel and stalked away through the tents, thinking dark thoughts about God's appointed high priest.

She had just reached the shadows of the terebinths in their line behind the girls' tent when she felt a strong arm about her waist. The soft laugh behind her, a laugh she recognized, stilled a momentary panic. In a moment she was pulled up against a firm, male body, her heart wild within her. She had just time to glimpse his face and gasp before the nazarite covered her lips with his, and the shock of the kiss rushed through her like fire and flood. A weakness came over her that was almost like drowsiness, but beneath it there was a thrill and a heat tightening up deep within her. She yielded willingly to the kiss, so many feelings rushing into her and through her, like cattle stampeding through a grove, the force of their passage tugging the leaves from the lower branches and sending them whirling about. After a few moments she found herself gazing up at his face, her lips still parted. Hardly enough air.

He smiled.

"You *are* pretty," he murmured. "Sleep well tonight." He cupped her cheek in his warm hand, and she just stared up at his face, blushing, because it was unlike her to have nothing to say. Then he kissed her again and she made a small, soft sound as he did, overwhelmed by the taste and scent of him and the strong, uncompromising way he held her. Then he released her, brushed the tip of her nose with his lips, and moved away through the dusk beneath the terebinths, leaving her standing alone, shaking a little. The cicadas were louder than anything she'd ever heard, and she could see every shadow and every patch of dim light beneath the trees cut as sharp as though the world had been made only moments before. She lifted her fingertips to her lips. Her body still felt warm and weak. This wasn't *anything* like how Hannah had described kissing in her stories in the moon tent.

It occurred to Devora as she stood beneath the terebinths that if this nazarite asked for her, she would be his second wife. She knew he had a wife whom he went to visit each Sabbath, an afternoon's walk from here at the encampment of Beth El. A woman of Manasseh tribe that Zefanyah's father had bought for him after his mitzvah. He might even have children; Devora wasn't sure. She would have to find out; surely the woman would come to Shiloh soon for the Feast of Tents. She felt a little unease, but she had never expected to have a husband. No man in the camp had spoken for her before, and she had no father to provide a dowry. This kiss was new—and unexpected.

She wondered if she *was* pretty.

Even as all of these new joys and anxieties rushed through her like wine and water, Devora lifted her eyes and saw the *navi* walking between the tents with two other women of the camp. A heat rushed through her that was nothing at all like the warmth she'd felt deep in her belly when Zefanyah had held her and pressed his lips to hers. This heat scorched her and dried her out and left her pale and faint. Then the vision came, and the shock of it was too great. After a moment she slid to the ground, fainting.

***

A touch on Devora's shoulder woke her, and she came to with a cry of panic. Old Naomi was seated beside her, her brown face wrinkled and furrowed like a freshly plowed field.

"Calm yourself, girl," Naomi said. Her voice was firm and had a hard edge to it, though it wasn't unkind.

The *navi* touched Devora's brow, and her hand was dry.

Above her, the cicadas seemed loud as thunder.

Devora drew in great swallows of air.

"Why did you faint?"

"I grew dizzy," Devora said. "And afterward I fell."

"Your flesh was hot as coals when I reached your side. But now you are cool. There's no fever."

Devora moistened her lips with her tongue, for they felt so dry they must crack.

"You saw something, girl."

She hesitated, then nodded.

Naomi watched her a moment, her eyes hard and unrevealing. At last she made a small noise of assent. "Do you know what it is like to be the *navi*?" she asked.

Devora shook her head.

"God terrifies us all. The *kohannim* do not dare to take off their sandals and step onto the holy ground within the Tent unless they've first washed for seven days." Naomi gave a wry smile. "I wish men in the land might do that before entering into their own tents to lie with their wives. They would smell better. But there, God scares them more than women do." Naomi looked toward the Tent of Meeting, and her eyes hardened. "Yet they do fear *me*. Did you know that, child?"

Devora nodded.

"God sends visions to my own eyes and does not care whether I wash first. In fact, I do not kneel or ask for him to show himself, he simply does. His *shekinah*, his presence, falls on me like wind and fire and nearly scorches me to the ground. A heat almost too fierce to bear. You know what I'm talking about, girl?"

"Yes," Devora whispered, frightened.

Naomi's gaze pierced her.

"What did you see, child? Before you fell?"

Devora shook her head vigorously, and Naomi's eyes narrowed. "You have pluck, girl. Not many people try to hide something from God's *navi*." She lifted a few strands of Devora's hair between her fingers, looking at them as though she might find in them the answer to her questions. That wry smile again. "Very well. You and God may keep your secret, for now. But listen to me, child. I want to know whenever you have one of these dizzy spells. I need to hear about it. And I think you will come visit me in the mornings. We are going to have a lot to talk about, you and I."

The thought of approaching the old *navi*'s tent, alone, to be questioned by her—that would have filled Devora with dread, if the old woman's words had not already given her more dread than she could carry. Naomi helped the younger woman to her feet, and for a moment Devora clung to her, feeling unsteady. The fear of what all this might portend, what it *must* portend, gripped her.

"Please," she cried. "What does it mean? Why am I seeing these things?"

"It means you are the next *navi*," Naomi said quietly. "It means you are seeing what God's eyes see."

CARRYING THE DEAD

THE NEXT AFTERNOON changed everything.

It was Devora's turn at the washing. As she left the white tents to make her way upstream, she hauled a washing board under one arm and carried a basket of heavy, soiled cloth on her shoulder. The sun was late-summer hot, baking away what strength she had, and she moved beneath it in a daze. In the sky behind her, cloud was piling upon cloud, promising thunder.

Doing the washing meant a long walk. The women of Shiloh kept the Covenant and were careful not to soil the stream that ran through Shiloh before rushing east past many camps of the People on its way to the Tumbling Water. Instead, the women took the clothes to small, isolated pools that formed in the mud near the stream. In the early dawn the water in these wash holes was cool and clear, but a little splashing of clothing in them and they became brown and more soiled than the tunics and robes a woman hoped to wash. So as the day aged, the women had to move farther up the stream to find new wash holes, often walking far from the camp. Once the clothes were laid out to dry, there was a brief respite. A woman could lie out on the grass and watch the thunderclouds build on the horizon or stare for an hour at a small beetle clinging to a reed. Or, if she was far enough from the sight of the tents—and if she dared—she might strip away her own tunic and leap into the cold river with a shock like being born. There, swimming between sand and sky, a woman could feel, if just for a little while, completely free and clean.

Today Devora had to walk far; as her feet squelched in the river mud and the tents of the encampment fell far behind, she could see through a haze of green reeds Hannah and Mikal, the women of the shift before her. They were bathing. Devora hoped to find a clean wash hole after passing them. She tried to hasten, but the weight of the basket on her shoulder made her grunt, and twice she slid in the mud, catching herself on a splayed hand but splattering her face and breasts with mud. By the time she reached the bathers, she was livid and in an ill mood. She cast them a glowering look that neither of them noticed. They were enjoying the river and had no room in their minds for anything but the fresh, cool water. Hannah was leaping and diving as though she were part fish.

It was the upcoming Feast of Tents, not only the cool water, that had them in such a good mood. Some of the girls were already considering who they hoped to dance for; a few had even begun quietly sewing decorative patterns into their dresses: flowers, or shapes of people crossing a desert (for the Feast commemorated the time in the desert), or trees.

Now even Hannah called out to Devora cheerfully.

"Come swim with us, Devora! The clothes can wait!"

For a moment she hesitated. The thought of joining them and letting the water wash the dirt and mud from her skin and the terrors from her mind—it was an attractive thought.

But she turned away from them, shouting back, "I will keep to my work, thank you. You can play like fish if you like."

She heard the groans and boos of the girls in the river, but ignored them and moved on through the river mud. She couldn't bear the thought of being among other women just now. Naomi's words resounded in her mind like drumbeats: *The next navi...you are the next navi...you are seeing what God's eyes see.*

Devora had spent the early morning in the old *navi*'s tent, in what Naomi promised would be the first of many talks between them. The old woman had questioned her keenly about the visitations she'd had from the *shekinah*, and Devora had found herself telling the *navi* of her first vision—the one that had come to her when she was twelve. The words had flowed from her like water and blood, until she was nearly sobbing with them. She told of her mother's death and of how she had seen herself grieving—how she had been *warned*—and had said nothing to the elders in the camp.

"They would've thought I was dreaming. That I'd fallen asleep when I should have been bringing water to the camp." Devora's eyes burned with tears. "I didn't want to be beaten. And they're all dead. Because of me. *Because of me.*"

Naomi had listened in silence, her sharp eyes peering deep into the girl, then sighed. "Don't be foolish, girl," she said. "You didn't know better. You do what you must, you trust the rest to God. Some days, a woman can only save one life. That day, it was your own life. Some day yet to come, it may be another's." And Naomi clapped her hands, and a slave came in with hot tea.

But when Naomi sent the younger woman from her tent at last, Devora felt little comfort. She believed old Naomi—she was the *navi*. God was sending her visions. The enormity of it was unbearable. Because she'd said nothing. She'd seen and said nothing. She searched her memory. The fear she'd felt then, of being beaten by the elders for telling lies—that seemed another girl's fear and not her own. She could remember the fact of it, but not what it had felt like. Now as she stumbled on through the mud with her washing board and her basket, Devora burned with anger at herself. The girl she'd been—that girl had been too afraid to do what was necessary to keep her people safe. Devora could never forgive her for that.

She came to a waterhole, one where the water was clean and the laughing of the girls was distant, and she let the basket down with a groan. She cast a glance back at the girls bathing. It must be nice to be Hannah or Mikal. To have never seen the dead. To have never truly suffered or feared. To worry only about whether they would be a man's first or second wife and whether that man would be young or old, handsome or foul. Devora's own hopes of the night before, and the way she'd been flustered at that kiss, all seemed so foolish to her now. Bitterness gnawed at her heart.

You are the next navi.

If that were true, there would be more warnings. What she had seen the day before must have been another warning, and she swallowed uneasily, realizing what the warning must mean. She made up her mind to tell the *navi* of it when she returned from the washing. Naomi the Old was right. She must never again hide anything she had seen. Not if it was from God.

She bent over the basket, reaching for a tunic. She made a face; the water before her was clean, but she had not picked her spot well, for the reeds here *stank*. There was a scent of decay, of something rotting under the weeds—

Something cold grasped her ankle.

A savage pull, and the ground rushed toward her. She slammed onto her belly; her fall shoved the air out of her before she could shriek. She kicked wildly, glanced over her shoulder and saw—*it*. A face half-torn away, its mouth open now in a hiss; eyes gray and sightless, a thin hand clutching her ankle with terrible strength while the other hand clawed forward to grasp a clump of reeds near the roots; with a groan, the creature pulled itself forward, toward her.

Its rotting torso slid free of the brush, and for a moment Devora was certain that she was back in her mother's tent, and the thing that had been her mother was crawling back into the tent after her, grasping at her. The body below the waist was gone, and it trailed entrails and scraps of tissue behind it. The reek of it did violence against Devora's insides. She tried to scream but managed only a breathless whimper. Its cold, dry hands gripped so tightly. Making her unclean.

She kicked at it, but it only snapped at the kicking foot with its teeth, and Devora twisted and writhed in panic. She looked desperately about her, hands scrabbling among the soiled clothes that had fallen around her. She wanted a stick, a rock, anything—she gave a low, keening cry as the thing's other hand seized her calf, and she heard the slither of its body through the reeds. In a moment it would have its head above her leg and would dig into her skin with its teeth. It would eat her—it wanted to *eat* her!

Her hand struck something.

Wildly, she grasped it with her fingers—a hard surface—

The *washing board*!

With a cry she lifted it in both hands and rolled to her side, brought it crashing down on the creature's head as it hissed just above her captured foot. She heard the smack of the wood against soft, rotting flesh. A growl from the creature. Screaming now, the air back in her lungs, she smashed the board down on the creature again and again, putting all her strength and terror into each blow.

When she stopped, the corpse was still, the top of its head mashed. One eye had been crushed by the washing board; the other stared dully at the sky.

Panting, Devora reached down, pried the dead fingers from her leg, then pulled her leg quickly away from its hands. With trembling fingers, she examined her shin and ankle. There were no scratches there, just a developing bruise where the corpse had clutched her. Her lip began to tremble, and she stilled it. She would *not* cry, not here.

Devora got to her knees, shaking. She could hear cries nearby, splashing. Then running feet. The girls from the stream. Hugging herself tightly, Devora looked at the thing that lay still now in the grass, smelling like a cow found dead in a field days late. Though the thing's strength had been terrible, it was small. She looked at the cut of its hair, at the tatters that remained of its garments. A boy. It had been a boy. A small boy.

Then the other girls reached her, their hair wet about their shoulders, dry cloth wrapped quickly around their bodies.

Hannah swayed on her feet, her eyes wide. Her hand went to her mouth. "Oh God, oh God, God, God," she moaned through her fingers.

"It's Nathan," Mikal whispered. "It's Nathan."

Nathan was Hannah's younger brother—gone a few days before to carry a message to the camp at Beth El for the priests.

Hannah moaned and fell to her knees.

"It *was* Nathan," Devora said hoarsely, remembering too vividly her mother's face in the door of the tent. "Now it is unclean. It's not him." She shivered; a breeze touched her cheek, and then without warning it became a wind, driving ripples across the water hole and making the reeds whisper, and the heat was gone from the day. Devora was sweaty and shivering in the wind. "We have to make a cairn," she whispered.

"There aren't any stones here," Mikal said, her face tight as though she were holding back tears.

Devora looked out over the reeds toward Shiloh. The camp was a long walk. They could go to find men, but that would mean leaving the body in the weeds. That would be unthinkable. And in any case Hannah would not leave the body like this. One of them could go. But the others would have a long time to wait, and—she glanced at the corpse. It had been half-eaten; there were other dead near, somewhere. None of them should wait here, where other mangled dead could already be crawling through the weeds. A fire lit in her, and her terror flickered out. She was not shivering, crying, useless in the reeds. She was not standing by while others confronted the dead for her. She was not helpless, as she had been in her mother's tent.

"My skin is already unclean from its touch." Devora stooped over the body. "I will carry him to the camp. The men can make a cairn for us." She kept her hands from shaking as she slid her arms beneath the reeking, broken thing that had been a boy; she lifted it. The corpse was very light—lighter than the basket of clothes she'd carried. Its intestines trailed to the ground beside her as she held it. Devora averted her eyes. "Gather up the clothes, Mikal," she murmured, and then took an uneasy step forward, then another. She tried not to think of what she was carrying; when it shifted slightly against her, she bit back a scream, swayed for a moment, eyes closed.

"Let me help." Hannah's voice was hoarse with crying.

"Touching it means being put from the camp." Devora's own voice was harsh. "That should only happen to one of us."

Hannah stifled a sob. Devora ignored the sound, kept walking. The mud by the river sucked at her feet. The wind, which made waves of purple blossoms in the heather and made the reeds hiss like serpents, kept tugging her hair across her face. She gritted her teeth, pressed on. There had been no opportunity for Hannah to say goodbye to the child. Devora understood her pain, but she had no time for it and could not permit herself to think about it, or she would begin crying as well.

"Maybe we should leave the body," Mikal whispered, her eyes wide.

"We do not leave one of our dead unburied." Devora's voice was cold.

Hannah cast her a grateful, tearful look.

"Run ahead to the camp, Mikal," Devora said. "Tell them."

Mikal bit her lip, then nodded and sprinted through the reeds. In a few moments she was far ahead, running fleet as a gazelle.

Devora gazed ahead, fixedly ahead. The camp seemed an eternity away, as though it were in far Kemet and she had a wilderness to walk across before she could get there. Her arms ached beneath the small weight of the boy. Yet she did not let herself stumble or stop.

***

By the time Devora and Hannah stumbled out of the heather and reached the first of the tents, Devora's rough washing dress was pasted to her back with cold sweat, and despite the wind her hair clung to her cheeks and neck. She feared falling ill, but the grim resolution within her was stronger. She still carried the dead child.

The *kohannim* and some of the other levites had gathered at the edge of the camp, and Mikal was there speaking urgently, tearfully, with them. The high priest stood with them, his sleeves bloodstained from a recent sacrifice, an *olah* in the Tent of Meeting. He'd been listening to Mikal with a grim look. But then one of them saw Devora and Hannah and cried out, pointing. They all fell silent.

The levites parted, making a path for the two girls. Eleazar's eyes were wide with shock, his gaze fixed on the burden Devora carried. She saw Zefanyah, and the look *he* gave her lent her strength, strength she badly needed. Devora held her head high and carried the boy's corpse into the midst of the camp.

As she reached the *navi*'s tent, two nazarites ran up with a woolen cloth and laid it a few feet before the door of the tent, so that Devora could set the body down without defiling the earth within the camp. Then the cloth could be lifted to carry the corpse to the slope where cairns were raised, and the body could be wrapped in the cloth, lowered into the earth, and covered with heavy stone.

But Devora did not lay down her burden. She stopped with her toes nearly touching the edge of the cloth and waited, holding that small, dry weight in her arms, her eyes on the woman who stood in the door of the tent.

Naomi wore the white dress of the levites, and though she had never been tall, in the moonlight at the door of her tent she looked as regal as a queen of Kemet. Her gaze took in Hannah's tears, the corpse Devora carried, the brown stains and gore on Devora's sleeves.

Her eyes grew cold.

"Were any of you bitten?"

"No, *navi*." Devora held her head high, though she wanted to slip away and hide; the hardness of Naomi's face shook her. Devora stood very still. "I was the only one it touched."

She heard a half sob behind her. Hannah.

Naomi searched Devora's eyes for truth. Her face remained hard, her emotions masked. This was not the Naomi who had smiled wryly at God's secrets or Devora's "pluck." This was Naomi the Old, judge of Israel, who had been alive when the People had taken possession of the land. Naomi, who had learned from the first *navi* and whose responsibility was keeping the land clean from the dead.

"I believe you, girl." For a brief moment, Naomi's eyes showed her pain. Devora took in a quick breath, but did not otherwise react. She had to be strong if she was to face the consequences of her choice without tears and without terror.

"Set down the body; a cairn will be built for it."

Devora obeyed, though she felt that any movement might make her collapse in fatigue. She yearned for Naomi to say anything to her, anything personal. Bending at the knees, she laid the corpse gently on the cloth before her feet. Straightening, she looked at it. Lifeless and still, it seemed more pitiful than perilous; a wisp of torn flesh and sinew, a torn-up face without any breath in it. Sunken and small. A thing once made in the image of God and then withered and savaged until nothing left of God could be seen in it.

Devora stood and lifted her eyes. "You wanted to know what I saw," she said softly. "When I fainted."

"Yes." Naomi's eyes were keen.

"I saw you." Devora met her gaze without flinching. "Standing in front of a burning tent. There were corpses in the tent. Then you fell, all at once to one side without bending your legs, and when you hit the ground you were gone. And I saw myself standing near. I saw myself grieving but I had no tears."

Silence.

The men were gazing on with horror. It was the first time anyone but Naomi had heard Devora speak of having a vision. Even Hannah's sobs fell silent, and the girl looked at Devora with wide eyes.

"Were you older when you saw yourself stand there?" Naomi asked.

Devora shook her head, something inside her beginning to quail. "No, I don't think so."

Naomi gave a small, slight nod. Her face giving nothing away, her voice clipped and sharp. "Did you see anything else?"

Devora shook her head.

Naomi made a quiet, dismissive noise in her throat, as though setting what she'd heard aside until its importance was clearer. She looked out over the gathered men of the camp. "This girl is a *navi*. She brings us the *niv sefatayim*, the fruit of God's wisdom. God who sees what has been and what may be. You had best listen to her." She turned her gaze back to Devora, and her voice grew colder. "But she is also unclean. For seven days she is unclean."

Devora lowered her head, blinking moisture out of her eyes.

"Devora of Israel," the *navi* intoned solemnly, "I put you from the camp. You will take neither food nor water nor clothes. You will touch no item in this camp. You will touch no crop nor any well filled with water. You will keep yourself separate from the People, sharing neither nearness nor speech. For seven days."

Devora swallowed. "*Navi*—"

Anger flickered in the old woman's eyes. "*Go.*"

The word was as sharp as a slap.

Devora's face burned. She had tried to plead, to ask for one kind word—whether from the *navi* or the levites or from Hannah or from anyone, she didn't know. She'd been rebuked. She'd deserved to be. For a moment she searched Naomi's face for some compassion or love, but found only that mask, as though her weathered face had been chiseled from stone, immutable law written into it in crevasses and hard lines, even as the Law had been written into stone tablets long ago on Har Sinai. There was in that face no pity or reprieve or farewell, only the cold justice that Shiloh hoped would keep a People from perishing from this earth.

Devora glanced behind her, saw Hannah watching her with reddened eyes and tear streaks on her face. Mikal white as though she were ill. The levites had their eyes on the corpse, and they too looked pale.

Suddenly she needed to be *out* of this camp, away from Naomi's hard eyes. Devora turned and ran. The levites stepped back out of her way, careful not to touch her with so much as a fold of their garments. That brought a fresh sting to Devora's eyes, and her feet pounded the soil as she sprinted, her hair flying behind her.

But as she reached the last of the tents, she heard a man's voice call out her name, not loudly. She stumbled, then straightened and turned. Through her tears she saw Zefanyah approaching at a jog, a waterskin slung over his shoulder. Her face burned with shame and she looked away, furious with herself that the nazarite should see her like this, not only unclean but her eyes tear-swollen and surely hideous.

"Devora, take this with you," he called. She glanced up, and he tossed her his waterskin. Without thinking, she caught it out of the air with both hands. She could feel the weight of it; it was full. Enough water for a few days. He was giving the waterskin to her, a true gift, for she could not bring it back with her, neither to him nor to the camp. She would have to bury it out in the wilderness; her touch had defiled it the moment she had caught it out of the air.

She hugged the waterskin to her breast and looked at him through the strands of hair that her run had left disheveled across her face.

"Thank you," she whispered.

He smiled, and there was such warmth in his eyes that she couldn't bear it. She turned from him and ran again, ran harder, not looking back to see if he was watching her. The city of tents fell behind her, the low voices of the camp fading to a hum like that of bees.

Once she was halfway up the slope, Devora slowed, then bent over, gasping for air, the waterskin still clutched to her breast. The day was getting dim; with the hills looming so high around Shiloh, especially to the east, dusk came early and dawn came late. The cold reality of what had happened fell on her, as sharply as though she'd ducked under a fall of ice water. She sank and sat in the heather, the lovely blossoms swaying about her in the breeze that had replaced the earlier wind. She was cold, and her body itched with dried sweat. She lifted her hands and she could feel the cold of the dead boy's flesh. She was defiled. Unclean. *She had touched the dead.*

Devora clutched at the stems of the heather and tore at them. She let out a long, raw scream, tossing her head back and screaming until she had to gasp for breath again. Yet still her breast ached as though there was a great bruise across her body. She sat for a while in the weeds, just catching her breath. Then she chafed her arms against the cold, trying to think as the night gathered about her. She heard the cries of jackals, but they were far from here. Later, even as the first stars appeared, she heard the low moan of one of the lurching dead. Even though it was far away, she shivered at the sound of it. She had no weapon in her hands, neither knife nor washing board. She had only the waterskin Zefanyah—bless him—had tossed her. And even had she had something lethal in her hands with which to defend herself, she had no desire to see another of the loathsome dead.

Yet.

She had carried that child. She had done what she must, what she feared to do.

The thought gave her strength. She bent and searched among the stems of heather. It took her some time to find what she needed, but at last she pulled a jagged rock free of the dirt, and she held it up before her eyes, looking at it in the starlight. It was longer than her hand, and thinner. And this stone knife had not been handled by any of the People, had been touched by no one but God who had shaped it and placed it here in the earth for Devora to find. And at the end of her seven days, Devora could simply toss it aside.

She forced herself to her feet, her eyes wide in the dark. She had heard the moan; she knew there were other dead in the hills. But she refused to lie crying in fear.

As she moved across the slope to find shelter, the wind picked up again, as if to hurry her. It rushed through the heather, even as it had when she was carrying the body toward the camp; the heather flattened before it as before the rush of God toward his Tent. It was very beautiful—the blossoms moving like a single living creature beneath the stars—but it was ominous too. As though something powerful and unexpected was coming to the valley.

KINDLED LIKE STRAW

FOR THE WEEK of her uncleanness, Devora lived by filling her waterskin from small creeks in the hills about Shiloh and by foraging for berries and roots, which were plentiful this close to the harvest. She kept her waterskin and her stone knife with her at all times, even once when climbing a tall tree to take eggs from a bulbul's nest. Yet she was nearly always hungry. She washed her dress and bathed sometimes in the mornings in streams she found, but by nightfall she felt sweat and dirt caked on her skin, which was a misery to her, and her dress became ragged and stiff, as though it were a part of her uncleanness.

Dutifully she avoided the herds of cattle that ranged farther up the valley, and once when she saw the smoke of campfires on a ridge and caught the scent of roasting meat, she turned and ran through the heather, putting distance between herself and those tents, until her mouth stopped watering.

Several times she heard a corpse moaning, and once she heard two dead moaning, as if to each other, from opposite slopes across the valley. She found it difficult to sleep, and when she did, her dreams were violent and evil. Sometimes she sat in the weeds fingering the edges of her stone knife and looked at the sky or gazed down at Shiloh's tents, and thought of Zefanyah or of the cattle herder who she'd seen fighting the dead years ago. That was far more pleasant than thinking of the dead. She imagined her return to the camp, her reintegration into the People. She imagined the nazarite sweeping her up in his arms and kissing her, having missed her and yearned for her for seven days.

She tried his name on her lips.

Zefanyah.

She decided it was a beautiful name, a mysterious name. Even an erotic one. Zefanyah: "God has hidden him." The word meant hidden like a secret or like a treasure, something you store up to give to someone at the proper time. Devora began to pray softly and silently in the dark. New hopes, strange hopes, were blossoming inside her, and she dared to wonder if perhaps God did not hate her, if perhaps God had forgiven her for her helplessness the morning of her mother's death. Forgiven her enough to have stored up this treasure, this secret for her.

***

On the final night of her exile from the camp, Devora sat near the summit of the hill of cairns where Shiloh buried its dead, with her back to a great olive tree. She had spent the past two nights in this same place; the olive was a comfort to her, something warm and alive and straight at her back, something that reached toward God's stars. Though she was still unclean and outside the Law, she at least felt as though the Law was *there*, a great tent over the valley sheltering the People, and one of its poles firm against her back. It gave her comfort. She gazed up at the stars and thought of the invisible roof of that tent. She thought of telling Zefanyah about it.

Even as she thought of him, the moon lifted above the opposite ridge.

Looking up at it, she stopped breathing.

Most nights, the moon glided gracefully into the sky over Shiloh valley like a great white crane. But tonight the moon shone dark red, a great sore in the sky. Devora shrank against the olive tree; she suddenly felt terribly exposed on this hillside; her instincts screamed at her to hide, even if it meant digging at the earth with her fingers to make a burrow, like some beast of the hills. All thoughts of Zefanyah had fled.

The moon crept higher.

One by one, the little fires of the camp far below went out.

She breathed shallowly; she kept watching that moon. It was unnatural, that color, and the size of it—as though the moon had swallowed up much of the sky around it. She waited for some vision that would warn her or help her interpret what she saw in the sky, but no vision came, no touch of dizziness. The air was cool and clear.

She couldn't sleep; she just watched the moon creep, bloodied, across the sky, until it set.

Then for a long time the night was dark again, and chill. Sometimes the jackals cried in the hills, and Devora shivered, both relieved and frightened that the moon had gone, leaving no hint as to what it portended.

A shriek shattered the night like glass. Devora froze. The cry was distant—it came from the direction of the camp. The cry went on and on.

Then there were other screams, thin and distant. Her eyes grew round in the moonlight.

A deep, deep call—a single rolling note—filled the air, and the hills deepened the sound and rolled it on and gave it back to the air amplified. Devora felt it in her feet and legs, in the slamming of her heartbeat. Someone had blown the shofar, the ram's horn, down in the camp. One long note, now fading to silence except for echoes from the more distant ridges—the *t'qiah*, the note that means *God is mighty, beware, this land is his!*

As if in answer, another sound erupted, quiet at this distance but distinct enough to make Devora shudder in the night.

The moaning of the dead.

The wailing of many, many throats.

She got to her feet, gazing down at the tents, her heart in her throat. There were sharp, terrified screams on the air and, under it all, that moaning. The ram's horn did not call again.

"*El adonai*," she whispered, "*adonai*, help them."

A flame went up in the night, a tower of fire rising over one of the tents, as though some power had spewed fire toward the sky. She watched with wide eyes. She felt a rush of heat across her face, crackling along the skin of her arms. It was the same as the feeling that came when she had a vision of things to come, the rush of the *shekinah* through her mind and body—yet *this* heat was immeasurably stronger, as though someone down in the camp had opened the door to a furnace the size of a mountain. The heat rushed *into* her and through her, and she cried out, every part of her burning; in a moment it might wither her like a dry leaf tossed into a fire pit.

Yet even as the scream left her lips, the heat was gone.

It had passed through her.

The cool air again touched her skin. Thirst parched her; she tasted salt on her lips.

Then she was running.

Below, the fire was spreading through the camp, and still there were moans and screams, a few male voices raised in a psalm of battle and defense. Panting, Devora rushed down the long slope, rushing through the thigh-high heather, feeling it slap against her ragged dress. Rushing as though if she could only get there in time, the camp might live. She knew that she needed to be there, with those she had begun to love. She began calling their names, calling their names in the dark as she ran, the glow of the fire on her face. Her sides burning.

***

Devora reached Shiloh and the tents of the *kohannim* just as dawn reclaimed the sky from the dark, her legs streaked with dirt and sweat from her run. The early light showed her smoke rising from many tents that had been set afire; men were moving about. With heavy gloves on their hands, they pulled charred bodies from the ashes and dragged them out, setting them in long lines. A small girl huddled with her arms about her knees by the lines, rocking back and forth. No one knelt to speak with her or shoo her away.

There were so many bodies. Forty, maybe fifty. Some were missing limbs or had great gashes in their sides. Many had been blackened in the night's fire, skin and flesh baked away to leave only stretched, sinewy things behind, like heathen doll-people made out of sticks.

A small boy of perhaps seven winters stood by the line of bodies. Behind him stood a lone woman, standing straight and silent as though unwilling to let pain bow her shoulders. She was veiled like a heathen girl, her eyes lowered to conceal her private grief from the view of others.

There was something familiar about the boy's face, and Devora watched him, troubled, as she approached the line of bodies. She saw that his eyes were hard; they were not the eyes of a child. In the moans of the dead and the roar of fire, that small boy had learned, in one wrenching of the heart, that the same God gives and takes away.

She also saw something more. Something in the shape of his face.

Feeling as though she had stepped off a cliff of stone and was falling through a great expanse of air, Devora made her way to the boy, until she stood before him and his mother.

"You are Zefanyah's son," she said softly.

The boy didn't answer her. His eyes remained hard, and he kept his gaze on the bodies.

"Your father—he is here among the dead?" She could not keep the pain and shock from her voice.

The boy nodded and looked down at one of the bodies.

Devora shivered and followed his gaze. The corpse the boy was staring at was charred almost to soot, the face unrecognizable, white teeth and eyeless sockets facing the sky.

"Zefanyah," she whispered.

The boy nodded again. The woman standing behind him made no sign that she'd heard, or indeed that she was capable of seeing or hearing.

Devora gazed down at that scorched body. How many nights she had dreamed of being held in his arms, being kissed, being his. How in her dreams he and the man she'd seen defending his cattle by the river—how they had become one, youthful, strong, vital. A rock a young woman might lean on. Now all that strength, all that life, all that fierce will and heat, how it had all been doused in the brief dark between the moon's setting and the sun's rising. She could not understand. She could not. It had been one thing to carry the body of a tiny boy through the reeds, to feel that boy reduced to mere bones and sinew, but that a man she had seen sweating on the training ground, whose muscles rippled in the sun's heat, a man who might wrestle a lion to the earth and whose grin lit such fires in her body—that *he* might now be nothing more than brittle bones within a shroud of ravaged and burned tissue. How could it be possible? She drew a breath, and she turned to the boy. The boy and the silent woman Zefanyah had left behind, with none to pitch a tent for them. "What is your name?" she asked the boy.

"Zadok." His tone was flat. He didn't look at her.

Zadok, the righteous one.

She took his face in her hands, made the boy look at her. Found his eyes. "Zadok." She spoke intently, desperately, and after a moment she could see through her tears that the boy saw her, was returning her gaze. "You must find stones. Heavy stones. Ones that hurt to lift. Help the men bury your father. Whenever one of the People dies, you bury them so they cannot rise. You raise a cairn high, high enough that God will see and remember them." Her voice broke. "Do you understand me?"

The boy nodded. He looked as though he might cry too.

Devora straightened, glanced at the woman grieving. "God will remember your husband." Her voice broke. "God will remember all of them!"

Then Devora turned and walked along the line of bodies, shaking. Forcing herself to look at the faces. Those whose faces were still recognizable—she knew them all. All of the freshly dead.

At the end of the line of bodies, a girl sat on the ground with brown fluid and bits of flesh spattered across her nightdress and a knife held loosely in her hand. Devora knew her.

"Sarai?" she called softly, kneeling by the girl.

Sarai looked up. Her face was smudged with dirt. "They're all dead," she said, without emotion. Her eyes were dazed, in shock.

THE ZOMBIE BIBLE

"What happened?" Devora whispered.

Sarai just looked past her, at the lines of bodies. Devora followed her gaze. A young man was moving down the lines with a heavy stave in his hands, and as he passed each corpse, he struck its skull hard.

Devora flinched and looked back to Sarai's face. Her friend's eyes were distant. Devora took Sarai's face in her hands and pressed her forehead to hers. "Don't look," she whispered.

Sarai brought her hands up, placed them on Devora's, but made no effort to draw back from her touch.

"Sarai, it's all right. It's all right." She spoke as softly as she could, though fighting her own horror. "Shh, it's all right," she whispered.

Sarai moaned.

A hand gripped Devora's shoulder from behind, startling her, and then a voice she knew, a man's voice: "Devora, the *navi* is calling for you."

She glanced up. "Eleazar!"

He looked at her numbly. "Will you come?"

Devora nodded numbly, rose, and walked beside him, letting him lead the way through the white tents. Zefanyah, *Zefanyah* dead. So many dead. Where was the *navi*?

"Where did they come from?" she whispered.

Eleazar answered her but didn't seem to have heard her question. His voice sounded dull, hollow, as though he were speaking from the bottom of a well. "I was sleeping. We were all sleeping. Those things were *feeding* in the tents by the river—who knows how long before someone blew the shofar."

"How many?" Devora felt a sense of unreality closing on her, like a fog descending over the camp and shrouding the carnage. Her head felt curiously light.

"Fifteen, maybe twenty." Eleazar's eyes were bloodshot. "Herdsmen, still wrapped in their wool. Heathen. Canaanites. They stumbled in from the slopes."

"Canaanites," Devora repeated. Anger bit at her.

"Yes. They bit—so many." He stumbled, caught himself. Devora looked at him, appalled at his fatigue. He seemed to be on his feet only by sheer effort of will. "The nazarites—they saved me. Some of the others. And I got several priests to the Tent of Meeting and we brought out the Ark. We brought out— and the camp—the camp burst into flame. The dead lit as though they'd been doused in oil, yet they walked about still moaning even as they burned—" His voice dropped and he whispered words of the Law under his breath:

The people must not be burned with fire
not consumed with flame
but buried beneath clean stone.

"God's judgment on them was so entire, so complete," he said. "Some burned away until not even bones were left behind."

Devora shivered. She recalled the leaping of flames into the dark as she had seen it from the hill, and the sense she'd had of heat passing across her skin, though the fire was so far away. And how it had felt like the heat that came when she saw things that hadn't yet happened. Behind the leaping of visions into her waking day there rested a Power and a Presence that might burn the world at a touch. The appearance of the visions was the gentlest of its visitations, as though a great mother bear with teeth the length and lethality of knives had chosen to nudge her hip gently with its nose.

"Not even bones," Eleazar whispered. He looked around them at the camp. Men and women were moving past them now, some with bandaged arms or with bloodstains on their robes.

"We will have to watch for signs of fever," Eleazar said, in that hushed voice that was so unlike the exuberance of the priest who taught in the evenings. "Some in the camp may be hiding their wounds. Many people touched the dead last night. We have to find out who is clean and who is not."

"Why are you telling me this?"

Surely Naomi the Old had given orders for everything that needed doing?

But before the levite could answer, they reached the *navi*'s tent. Eleazar drew aside the flap and inclined his head respectfully. With a tremor of unease, Devora stepped through.

***

Inside, the *navi* was propped up on cushions, her face pale and damp with sweat. No one else was there with her. Her eyes shone, and her hands trembled where they clutched at the cushions. Her garment had been cut away from her right shoulder, where a livid bite could be seen in the skin above her breast, a fierce half circle of red marks, the marks of human teeth. Devora sucked in her breath as she saw it.

Naomi looked up, gestured her close. Devora hurried to her side and knelt there. She reached for Naomi's hand, but the old woman cried out, "*Stop!*"

Devora stood still. She could feel the heat from her flesh through the air between them, as though the woman lying on those cushions carried hot coals inside her body.

"I am unclean, girl," the *navi* rasped. "Do not touch me."

"No," Devora whispered.

The *navi* had to swallow twice before she could speak further. "They brought you to me, the priests. I hoped they would," she managed.

"I'm here," Devora said.

"The Canaanites brought this on us," Naomi said quietly. "There will always be strangers in the land, and they will be neglectful of the Law. Until it is too late. You must help the People remember the Law." She tapped a small clay jar at her side. "Open this," she whispered.

Devora did so, careful not to touch Naomi's hand with hers. Careful to touch only the top part of the jar. In a moment it was open, and the *navi* lifted it in one shaking hand. "Bow your head, girl," Naomi said, and then upended the jar over Devora's head. A little olive oil trickled out over her hair and her forehead. Devora closed her eyes as it ran down her face, slick and sweet-scented.

"You have been like a daughter to me," Naomi murmured. "As they all have. But you are the one who sees. I always thought it might be you. The way you remember the *mitzvot* as easily as other women remember the names of their kin. I wish I'd had the time to prepare you. To tell you things first...I anoint you, Devora. I anoint you the *navi* and judge of Israel."

Naomi lowered the jar, lost her grip on it. It rolled aside until it stopped against the side of a cushion.

"Don't die," Devora whispered. She opened her eyes, and took in the sight of the old woman burning up on her cushions. The reddened bite wound. The fever sheen in the *navi*'s eyes.

"Girl," Naomi murmured. "You'll have time to mourn me later. Only be strong, for they will look to you. The *kohannim* know already what you are. I made sure of that. Now we must act, girl. Before this fever takes what's left of me." She lifted a hand weakly, pointing at a pile of furs in the corner. "Bring what you find. Be quick."

Choking back her anguish, Devora hurried to the furs, knelt there, and tossed them aside, revealing a long, narrow box of plain cedar, no jewelry or adornment, just God's own wood.

"Do what needs to be done. With that," Naomi croaked.

Slowly Devora slid the lid from the box. Inside she found a long blade with a hilt of bone. The blade was much longer than her arm. She touched the metal gently, heard her fingernails ring quietly against it. "This isn't bronze," she breathed.

"Iron." Naomi was breathing hard between the words she forced out. "A gift. Sea Coast man—I saved his life. He left me that. Take it, Devora."

In anguish, Devora turned and gazed at the *navi*, whose eyes seemed glassy now. Naomi kept moistening her lips with her tongue, as though to fight the desert heat in her skin the only way she could.

"I can't," Devora gasped.

"At dusk, the *kohannim* will." Naomi's hand twitched on the cushions. "I would rather it were you. Because you are the *navi*. And you have seen the threat. As none of them have, not truly. You took that small boy in your arms—" Her breathing was labored. "It is you, Devora. They will look to you for judgment. Because you see what God sees."

"I *can't*," Devora cried. She had slept little in the past seven nights; now her hold on the waking world seemed tenuous. Her memories crowded upon her, ready to do her violence: the thing that had been her mother looking in at her through the tent flap. Its mouth open in a hiss. The firm, cool surface of a stone pestle in her palm.

She made a little noise, like a whimper.

"*Devora.*" Naomi held her gaze, though now her entire body had begun to shiver violently. "Listen to me. It is kinder for me to die this way than in the lingering fever. I want to know that my body will not stand from these cushions when I am gone. It is kind, Devora. Listen to me. You have seen how God is a father who burns away what threatens his children, and you and I have felt his heat. But God is also our mother. As a woman, I know this. That her heart is a deep, deep lake dousing all wrath and flame. That she kisses us when we are born. Quickens new life within us when we have become women. God made both Adam and Eve, both in God's likeness. And if this is true, Devora, what I tell you, what Miriam who was *navi* when I was a girl told me, then God who is like our mother and has compassion will forgive us the evils we cannot avoid and the lives we cannot save."

Naomi moved her shaking hands, folding them weakly over her breast. "Do this for me, Devora." She closed her eyes, panting softly, her face slick with perspiration. "Do it quickly."

Devora's vision blurred. She had seen this. She had seen a vision of Naomi dying. She had foreseen her own grief at her mother's death. And in neither case had she been able to save either her mother or the mother of Israel. The tears hot on her face. Try as she might, Devora could not think of God as a mother. Distant, delivering visions and then demanding action, and *not* maternal, not one who might embrace or hold a grieving, shattered girl.

Naomi whispered the words of the *sh'ma* and closed her eyes. For a few moments more, Devora stood shaking, the hilt of the iron sword clutched tightly in both her hands. Naomi did not open her eyes or speak.

A great cold settled in Devora's heart.

This could not be avoided. It could not be delayed. She saw so clearly in her mind the face of her mother, distorted and hissing. If she were to see Naomi like *that*, it would break her; she would collapse and never again stand.

"I love you, mother," Devora cried, and lifted the blade.

JUDGE OF ISRAEL

DEVORA STEPPED from the tent, drawing the bloodied sword behind her, the blade's tip trailing in the dust. The levites and the young women parted for her, standing silently to either side, watching her. Devora's face was terribly cold. All the heat had been sucked out of her and out of the world. As she walked by, one of the levites began to weep quietly. She didn't look at him.

"We need another cairn," she said softly.

She walked slowly through the camp, feeling embers crunch beneath her sandals. An occasional metal ringing from the blade as the edge struck some rock along the way. Doubtless there would be some nicks, some damage in the sword; she did not care. She looked about her at the bodies and at the young men already gathering great stones to make the cairns. So many cairns. She looked at them and walked on. Until she stood at the very edge of the camp, gazing out across the reeds by the bank. There were more bodies in the water, she saw, facedown and caught against some rock jutting into the river or dragged half onto the bank. Perhaps some had not caught at the bank but had drifted free, like leaves blown into the water by a high wind. In the confusion of the night, some of these bodies might have escaped, slipping downstream to pollute the Tumbling Water and the fields of their People.

She did not care.

She stared out at the reeds and the heather on the high slopes behind and the dark, rising ridges of the Galilee hills to the north. She smelled smoke and burned flesh and decay. She heard weeping and low talk among the men at their work. For a while she recited in her mind the names of those she'd known who were now gone from the land: Mikal with her laughter and her love of mischief; Tabitha, who had dreamed of love and rich herds in the lower valleys; practical Leah, whose hands were so clumsy, though she worked harder than any of them. Even Zefanyah, who she had so admired on the fighting ground. Zefanyah, who had kissed her. Who had given her his waterskin. He too had been among the night's dead.

They were gone. All gone, for all time. The land on which they'd stood had been defiled and filthied; it might be a generation before the stink of the dead was gone from Shiloh.

She recited some of the Law quietly to herself, seeking calm. Most of the *mitzvot* were stored up in her heart, and reaching for one was like reaching for a memory of a beautiful summer day. She had replaced most of her memories with *mitzvot*; how would she ever be able to replace the memories of this night?

"Devora?" A man's voice. She didn't turn her head. Eleazar. He was breathing hard; he came to stand beside her. "Devora?"

She didn't answer. She kept looking at the heather, which was moving now, softly, in a breeze.

"Devora? *Navi?* Has God shown you what must be done?"

"You must wait," she said.

She said nothing more, and at last the high priest turned back to the camp.

Devora stood there, weak and faint because she hadn't eaten. Still, she stood looking across the heather. As the sun slid to the edge of the hills, she whispered, "You are cruel, *adonai*, but I understand why you must be."

The wind picked up in the heather, but there were no words in it. Just the rustle of weeds bending so they would not break.

She turned her eyes to the hills, saw the way their ridges cut at the sky in the gathering dark. "I will judge the People for you, as she did." Her voice gathered strength. "I will keep the land clean."

It was the only thing she could give Naomi—or any of them. She covered her mouth with her hand and held her feelings tightly within her. Let loose, they would tear at her and devour her as ravenously as the dead.

She must build a cairn over her feelings, a high cairn, so that she could stand before the People.

***

When dawn arrived, Devora turned and walked back into the camp. As she reached the Tent of Meeting she stumbled; two levites caught her by the arms before she could hit the soil. She moaned softly; they brought her unleavened bread and mutton, and after washing quickly to her elbows, she held the bread in both hands and tore at it until she felt like vomiting. They brought her water, but refused to let her drink more than a few quick sips at a time. Her stomach lurched within her. She clutched at her belly with a groan, and they stood patiently by.

When she was able to stand again, she motioned to them and they helped her to her feet. She stood there in the tattered shift she'd worn throughout her exile from the camp, the shift still stained with brown streaks from her fight with the dead boy in the reeds. She drew in a breath; she reeked of death and sweat and unwashed girl. She wrinkled her nose once, then composed her face and lifted her arms, like Moseh in the desert. She called out the words—the words of the Lawgiver that would summon the People to her.

The women came stumbling from their tents and the men from their work; they had piled the cairns high, and all but a few were now finished. They gathered about her in a half circle, their faces stained with blood and dirt, their eyes weary. A few gazed at her with cautious hope.

"I am Devora of Israel," she said, "and I see what God sees." She took a breath, her eyes glancing only once to the tent where Naomi had died.

Then she faced her People and began making judgments, separating the clean from the unclean.

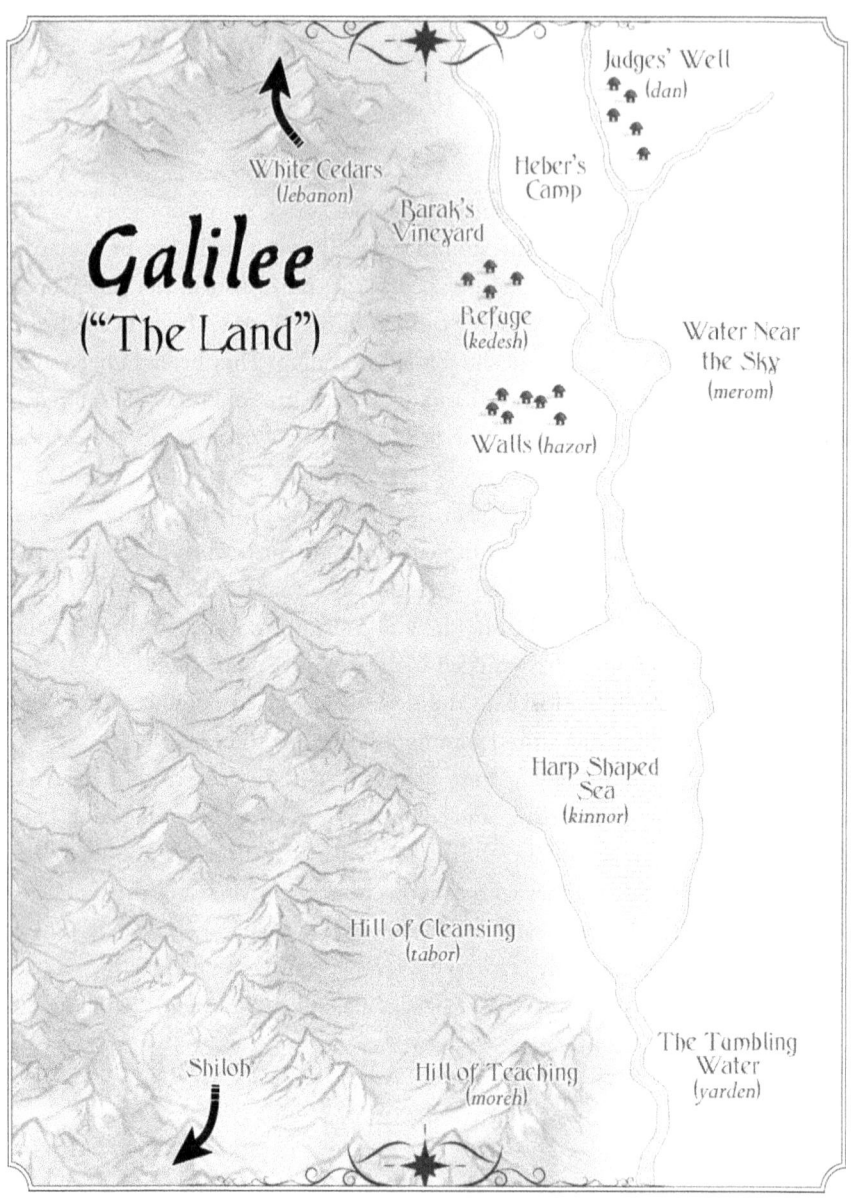

PART 3. THE HIGH GALILEE

WATER NEAR THE SKY

HIGH IN THE GALILEE, where the Tumbling Water is just a stream one can wade through by brute force, there is a high plateau the Hebrews call *Merom*, Water Near the Sky. There a small lake reflects back the stars; lilies and other delicate water flowers cover its surface near the shore. Shielded on all sides by a bowl of earth and rock, the lake is far more placid than the Harp-Shaped Sea, and the fish there, though few, are fat and slow, and they sleep as they swim. If the fish in Kinnor are like dancing, leaping deer, the fish in Merom are more like lumbering oxen. They are not as pleasing to taste, but the Canaanites in those hills have many ways of preparing them that give delight to the tongue and gladden the heart.

The boats that plied this small lake in that time were flat-bottomed and small, nearly coracles; in each, a single man would stand with a spear and a small net for catching the fish he impaled. In the warmer months, the boats would slip out on the quiet water in the dark before dawn and return as the sun rose, each with its cargo of bloodied fish. Salted and dried, the fish would fill great bins; the people who lived in that earthen bowl were well fed. Once, a mighty town had stood there, with a steep slope at its back and a circle of high walls of baked clay. Walls, the Canaanites had named their town, a boast to others who might wish to seize the lake from them. Now the walls were only a ring of tumbled and cracked bricks; not even a wooden palisade of cedar from the hills had been raised in their place. Hebrews had come there, with spears and cries in a language the Canaanites did not know, and they had brought with them a new God who apparently did not care for walls in his People's path.

Tearing their way through the walls, the Hebrews—the last of the Hebrews, for other tribes of their People had already found fertile valleys in which to

363

pitch their tents far to the south—these weary and hungry and furious Hebrews set fire to half the town and killed many of the men whether they were armed or not, in their fury to possess this place near the sky. Women were dragged from their dying houses and thrown to the dirt streets, where sweating, ragged men forced them even as the slaughter continued on every side.

The Law that had been given to the People of the Covenant in the desert forbade this treatment of captives:

> *When you see among the captives a beautiful woman and you desire her and bring her to your tent, she will shave her head and weep for her father and her mother who are dead, for one full month, and in that time you will not touch her.*

> *And if you find she doesn't please you, then you will let her go where she will. You will not sell her or make her an item of trade, for you have known her.*

Those *mitzvot* the judges had declared in the desert, part of the great Law to bind the tribes to each other and to the God who'd found them thirsting and perishing in the dead-haunted ravines. And often these *mitzvot* had been followed in the south, where the levites had demanded that the men remember the cost of breaking the Covenant. "Our fathers' Covenant, not ours!" some of the men would cry. And the levites in wrath would shout: "Is this then your fathers' land and not yours?

Hear, men of Israel! Our God in the desert made this Covenant not with our fathers, but with us, with each of us who stand here alive this day.

And the men, hearing these words, had held back their hungers and heeded the levites. It would not do to break the Covenant and to spurn the God who gives and who takes away even in the moment of taking possession of the land he'd promised them.

But these last tribes that raged northward after all their brothers and sisters had found land in which to lift their tents—these last tribes were not eager to let any Law restrain them. Few of the women of Walls were given time to mourn their dead. Some were held to the ground, their garments torn from them, even as their husbands or fathers bled to death in the dirt beside them. The screams of the dying and the screams of the survivors tore the air.

The newcomers, however, did keep the *mitzvot* that demanded cairns for the fallen. They dared not break *those*. In the days after the death of the town, many women gazed out of tent flaps, their faces bruised and tear-stained, the numbness in their eyes replaced for a few moments by wonder as they watched the Hebrew men gather massive stones from the slopes behind the town and pile great cairns above each of the dead, both Hebrew and Canaanite, until a forest of stone monuments stretched along the bank of the Tumbling Water where it emptied into their lake from the north. Never had they seen the dead treated so; their own way had been to weight the bodies and give them to the lake, that in time, through the digestion of fish, they might be taken back into the people. In shock, these women watched as the cairns went up, not knowing what it meant, only that it was strange, wondering that the Hebrews took time to tend to their enemy dead as well as their own, and bewildered that they feared the bodies so much that they would pile heavy rock upon them, nor give them to any fish that might be eaten by a man.

Later, some of the women would weep bitterly for the loss of the spirits of their people, but first there was only shock. The town was gone, the men they had known were gone, their own bodies had been torn and used for the pleasure of others who did not even know their language or their names. Everything was different, everything.

The winter that followed was the hardest Walls had ever known, for the Hebrews were yet strangers in the land and the land did not know them nor did it consent to feed them. The survivors, conquerors and conquered, squatted in the charred ruins of ancient houses or shivered in their tents; the fish stored in the bins had been squandered by the raiding spearmen, and coracles had to set out on the water even in the bitter cold to look for food. Parties of men began to leave the town, pressing north, farther into the hills, to raid the smaller villages of the Canaanites. Some perished, and some settled where they found food; few came back.

In Walls, some of the Canaanite women were killed because they could not be fed, but most were not. And when the first caravans came through on their way from the steppes of the Horse People to the cities of the Sea People on the coast, more women were bound and bartered to them for the goods needed to make life possible again along the shores of Water Near the Sky.

Yet it was just as likely that the desperate men might barter away a Hebrew woman rather than one of the captives, for the Canaanites who had lived uneasily beside the Hebrew women through the winter knew many useful things—including when the caravans could be expected to come through and which goods each carried. So many, indeed most, of the captives remained in the tents of those who'd claimed them. And before a year had passed, the ruins of the town were filled with the cries of infants. These children would grow up with Hebrew fathers and Canaanite mothers, and in them would survive a love of wooden houses rather than tents, and a desire for gods you could hold in your hand, and the wisdom to make the fish taste like a divine gift.

The grandchildren of those children lived in Walls now, and Walls persisted as a town of scattered houses of wood and thatch. In some, little gods carved from wood or clay were concealed; in some, they weren't. In the quiet hours while the lake lay dark, the little coracles set out again upon the water, moving silent as dreams over the lake, and in them stood patient and grim men whose blood was Hebrew or Canaanite or both, wielding the spears the conquerors had brought against fish now rather than men. They were the wealthiest and best-fed settlement in the Galilee, for they had the knowledge of two peoples and the strengths of each.

Yet they had also the griefs of two peoples, the griefs of desert grandfathers and lakeshore grandmothers. They lived fiercely and drank deeply of barley beer brought up from the valleys of Manasseh and stored in great barrels in the town's beer-house. They danced Canaanite dances at the full moon and they kept within their houses on the Hebrew Sabbath. They loved fiercely and faced death grimly, the people of Walls. Rarely did any of them send children to serve God in Shiloh, and rarely did any go to the Feast of Tents, to remember the time in the desert.

Exasperated, Naomi the Old had sent a levite to live among them, to remind them of the Law, and they had tolerated him—it was important, after all, to have someone who could sing the Words of Going after cairns were raised—and in time they even loved him, but they did not listen to him much. Their homes by Water Near the Sky were all the land, and the men and women of their town all the People.

***

As Shomar picked his way down from the ridge toward the camp Barak's men had pitched on the shore of Water Near the Sky, Devora thought the lake very lovely, even lovelier than that larger lake now a day behind them, the one they called a sea and over which cranes flew and beneath which fish apparently swam out of the mouths of gods. Before her on the saddle, in her arms, the *navi* held Hurriya, whose breathing was a little shallow. Devora could feel the heat of the girl's fever even through her salmah. The previous night had not broken the fever, though it had not worsened either; Hurriya had wakened with it, exhausted by a long and restless night. Devora herself had wakened earlier, sore from the previous day's riding, yet strangely relieved of her fatigue; she'd wakened with Zadok's arms about her, strong and sure. His breathing light, for he was awake. He had not let her go during the night. Neither had he ceased watching. And he had let her sleep until daybreak.

She had flushed, finding herself held so. She had slipped from his arms gently, not daring to look at his face. She felt his gaze on her as she washed to her elbows, nearly emptying her waterskin, then chewed on a little bread from the store Zadok carried in his saddlebag. Her tension grew. The trees seemed dim and hostile in the morning light. Hurriya still slept, though fitfully; a look at her face and a hand held a feather's width over her brow confirmed for Devora that the Canaanite's fever hadn't broken. The cairn was an ominous presence, reminding her that the dead were near. And Zadok's gaze made her acutely uncomfortable. What had she been *thinking*, lying in his arms like that, like a wife, no matter how frightened she had been of her dreams? What if he misunderstood, thought she were seducing him? What if—?

But she couldn't spend the morning in turmoil. She needed her strength of mind. She rounded on him, the words on her lips stilled by the amusement in his eyes.

"Intolerable," she muttered, and turned her attention to the girl. "Saddle the horses, please," she called over her shoulder.

"Your will, *navi*." The nazarite's voice was rough with sleep. He made very little sound as he rose and got to work breaking their camp.

Devora focused on the Canaanite, seating herself by her and calling her name until she opened her eyes.

"You're very ill, girl," Devora said softly. "You might as well know it."

"I know it," Hurriya said wearily. "Being heathen does not make me a fool."

Devora paused, then gave her a quick nod, though she didn't know whether she meant it as acknowledgment or apology. "I am just tense, girl. There will be more dead today. And more the next day. May God send one of us a vision with some comfort in it."

"Does he?" Hurriya rasped. "Those he's sent me have been like—like nightmares."

"No, he doesn't. He sends visions when they're needed, and then they are unlikely to be pleasant." Devora cast another uneasy glance at the terebinths. "And they are needed now."

She gave the girl a little water, and as soon as Hurriya had swallowed it she slipped back into sleep, and Devora gazed down at her in dismay. She hoped they did not have far to travel this day to catch up with Barak and his men. Who knew how the girl would survive another day on horseback.

She went cold inside at the thought of Barak ben Abinoam and what he had either commanded or permitted. But as she gazed down at the sleeping girl—the sleeping *navi*, she reminded herself—she knew that she had a more pressing matter to attend to than her fury at Barak.

She rose and went quickly to where Zadok was readying the horses. The nazarite had just lifted Shomar's saddle to his back; the horse whickered softly. Devora stepped near enough to speak for his ears only. Yet standing so near him—she was more aware of him today than she had ever been before. His strength, his solidity, the way the muscles in his arms moved, the masculine scent of him. She suppressed the shiver this sent through her, felt her face burning again. She forced her thoughts to the matter at hand.

"Zadok, I want you to watch over the girl's safety."

Zadok stopped, his hand still on the girth strap. "You care for her," he said in a low voice. Devora could hear the disapproval in it. "I know. I have eyes. But she is *heathen*."

"She is the next *navi*," Devora whispered.

Silence.

Zadok's eyes showed his bewilderment, as though she'd told him the sky was made of tree leaves and she expected him to gather them up for her.

"She is the *navi*, Zadok. God sends visions to her."

"How can that be?"

"I don't know." Devora pressed a hand to her temple. "I really don't know. God's ways are strange."

Zadok's face darkened. "She is heathen. I will make no covenant with her. You, I will defend."

"You'll defend who I ask you to defend," Devora said sharply.

Zadok just growled and turned back to the horse, which flicked its tail.

"Damn it, Zadok, it's strange to me too. But the life of the next *navi* must be preserved. Even if—" Devora swallowed. "Even if I should die. The younger *navi* has to make it back to Shiloh after this."

Zadok moved around the horse, checking the saddle and the bags.

"Do you trust me, Zadok?"

"I trust you, *navi*." He gave her a pained look, and Devora was reminded sharply that he'd spent the night holding her.

"Then *trust* me. This girl is the *navi*. I don't understand it either, or like it. But God has chosen her."

A pause. "Your will, *navi*." His tone heavy with reluctance.

"Thank you," she said. "I need you, Zadok." *I need you to stand at my back,* she thought but didn't say aloud. *I need you to enforce my will when I make decisions. I need you to trust me. I need you to not mention last night, not act as though I am any other woman, not try to speak to me of it or—or kiss me. I need you to be as reliable and unbendable as that spear you carry, as reliable as you've always been.*

"You had better wake your Canaanite again," Zadok muttered after a moment.

Devora nodded and watched his face a moment before moving wearily to stir Hurriya from her restless sleep.

***

They spent much of the rest of the day in silence, and Devora sorrowed over it. It was as though someone had planted a thicket of willows between them, and they could hardly see each other through the veil of hanging leaves.

It was also a day of delay, for they stopped often to give Hurriya rest or to grant Devora a few moments to look through the grasses for some herbs that might calm her fever. She found only a few leaves of mint, had hoped for ginger root. She made do with what she had, but it did little good, and she wished bitterly that she had some of Hannah's knowledge of herbs. Even as girls, Hannah had never been good at remembering *mitzvot*, but she had always known where to find a particular blossom or a particular root and what to do with it once you found it. For Devora, there had been only the Law.

In the end, she and Zadok walked their horses, easing their way through the last miles. Perhaps there would be herbs at the camp or at that settlement on the lakeshore—surely at Walls Devora could find a midwife with knowledge of herbs and fevers.

They had spent the day tense, their eyes on the slopes about them, watching for the dead. Once, only once, Devora saw three human shapes moving along a distant ridge, walking in file like living men yet swaying from side to side like trees in a wind. She rode on without mentioning the corpses to the others, though she suspected Zadok had probably seen them too. It was more important to find Barak's camp than to pursue a few straggling dead across the hills—but it was long before Devora could tear her gaze away from those distant, ominous figures.

The fact that they didn't see more was unnerving; after the attack in the night, Devora had been ready to see herds shambling toward them, moaning and hungering for her flesh. The emptiness of this country, the constant vigilance, Zadok's tense silence, the shallow, feverish breathing of the Canaanite girl in the saddle before her—all this made Devora so jumpy that she was nearly nauseous. And the saddle rubbed her thighs terribly raw, adding an acute physical discomfort.

***

Now dusk was falling and Barak's tents lay below them by the water. The *navi* saw the open sky reflected in the lake, and when she glanced to the side she saw the lake reflected in Zadok's eyes.

"Few tents," the nazarite said quietly.

"Fewer even than I thought," Devora agreed.

The tents were pitched tightly together, like a flock of birds eyeing with dread the sharp hills surrounding them. Ready to spread their wings in a moment and leap back into the sky, leaving the land to its own horrors. Quiet in the dusk ran the Tumbling Water, which the lake fed but which didn't start tumbling until after it flowed out of this narrow valley and began descending out of the hills. The smoke of cookfires wafted across the water toward the cedar-and-thatch houses of Walls, a half mile around the edge of the lake.

But only silence wafted back.

Some of the men of the camp were standing at the shore, tiny at this distance. Perhaps they were gazing across at the eerie town. Towns were loud. So were encampments of tents and flocks—but towns were louder, and the men knew this. The beer-house at least, even at this hour of dusk, should have been boisterous and awake with firelight.

This town, however, was utterly still, utterly silent.

Devora didn't like it.

"Zadok, ride ahead, please. Tell them the *navi* is here. That she wishes to speak with Barak at once. And ask for herbs for the girl."

"Your will, *navi*." Yet Zadok cast her a glance that showed his reluctance to leave her side; Devora wondered at it. She did not think she would be in danger riding into the camp. She was *kadosh*. And she and the Canaanite girl were unlikely to be attacked by any dead on this open slope as they neared the tents.

Devora cast an uneasy glance over her shoulder at the ridge behind them, half expecting to see corpses silhouetted against the sky. But there was nothing there. Not even a bird. As though the entire land had gone silent, waiting.

Like that settlement across the water.

Perhaps it was only that Zadok was uneasy leaving before speaking whatever words he'd hidden in his heart since the morning. For a moment Devora both dreaded and hoped that he would say something. But the nazarite only turned and gazed down at the camp grimly, then nudged his horse into a canter.

As he rode ahead, Hurriya whispered, "I don't have to fear him, do I?"

"No. Other people do."

"What is he?"

"You must have heard stories. Everyone in the land knows about the nazarites."

"I know they fight."

Devora watched Zadok approach the tents below and felt sorrow and a strange kind of possessiveness for the man. Zadok was hers. Had been, ever since he took the nazarite's vow, swearing it to her and God. Even before then—ever since she gave him words of comfort that day he stood by his dead father. It was right that she should speak for him. "Fighting is *all* they do," she said. "They do not tend the land, they say no prayers and perform no priestly duties. They do not trade or barter. They defend those who keep the tablets and the Tent of the Law. They give up everything for that. No, girl, you don't need to fear him."

Hurriya started shuddering. Devora felt the tremors against her body and tightened her arm about the young woman. "What is it, girl?" she whispered.

"The faces," Hurriya whispered back. "The faces."

Devora was suddenly aware of an intense, familiar heat emanating from the woman she held. Her eyes widened.

After a moment the heat flickered out as abruptly as a candle's flame. Yet Hurriya kept shaking. "The town is full of lost things," she whispered. "We have to go there."

"You saw something," Devora murmured.

"Only for a moment. A glimpse. Faces. There was a fire and all the faces were burning."

"I don't see any smoke over the town." Devora thought for a moment. Had God sent a vision of what had happened there, of what would happen, what might happen?

"The gods are cruel," Hurriya said, her voice thick. "Do they think I'll hate them less for taking my child because they bless me with knowledge they keep secret from others?"

"It is no blessing," Devora said dryly. "The *navi* brings words men need to hear, visions they need to see, not visions they *wish* to see. You see what God sees, but men don't want to see what God sees. It's not a blessing."

They were nearing the outskirts of the camp now, and Devora heard a horse coming toward them. It was not Zadok's horse. After a moment the rider cantered away from the tents and approached them, and Devora saw a scarred face and braided hair. She knew this man, and her lips twisted in distaste. Omri, the Zebulunite.

"You are here," he called as he approached. "Where is Nimri?"

"Ask him when he arrives," Devora quipped. "Where is Barak?"

Omri's eyes narrowed. "Have a little respect, woman." He drew his dun-colored horse up alongside Shomar. "You were supposed to come with an Ark," he muttered.

"Barak will have to settle for me," Devora said icily.

Omri grunted and rode beside them a moment. Then he leaned near, attempted to glance down Hurriya's salmah. Devora felt the girl tense.

"A Canaanite," he said. "And a curvaceous one. Is she for sale?"

"No, Omri." Devora's voice was winter. "She is not."

"Still." He leered at the girl. Hurriya stared fixedly ahead.

"She's unclean, Omri." Stressing each word, Devora added, "For seven days." Actually, only six days of her uncleanness were left, but this northern savage didn't need to know that.

The man recoiled and rode just behind them, his face unreadable. Devora turned her shoulder to him, speaking in a low voice to Hurriya. "Because you are unclean, your feet must not touch the ground within the camp."

Hurriya glanced over the *navi*'s shoulder, and her eyes flickered with hate.

"Ignore him. Don't even look at him. Think of him not as a Hebrew man like the one who owned you but as a small boy watching a dragonfly to see what it will do. Now imagine the dragonfly not moving, not even a flicker of its wings. The boy pokes at it. The dragonfly still does not move. So he loses interest and goes to trouble some other."

"There are no other dragonflies," Hurriya murmured.

"What?"

"No camp followers. Didn't you see? You and I are the only women here."

Devora gave a start. She halted and heard Omri halt a little way behind her. She gave the camp ahead a hard look, and considered what she *hadn't* seen, riding into the valley. Hurriya was right. There was the camp, but there were no camp *followers*. None of any kind. Devora knew enough about the raids that plagued the land to realize that any camp of armed men always had followers. Thieves ready to pick the unclean bodies of the dead. Carpenters and weavers who might be called upon to mend a broken cart or a torn tent or coat. Old Canaanite women with packets of herbs, ready to tend to fever or foot rot. And young women, Hebrew and Canaanite and mixed, women without husbands or fields to glean, who in the final extremity of their hunger would barter their bodies for food. Usually there were far more camp followers than there were men in the raid. But not this time. There were none. Not when the men were going to seek out the dead.

That made her uneasy—it meant she and Hurriya were alone in a camp of men. Already others in the camp were gathering outside their tents, not near enough yet to shout to, but near enough to watch Devora and Hurriya ride in. Omri wasn't the only one who was famished enough for sex to cast an eye on the *navi* and the woman who was with her.

"It doesn't matter," Devora murmured. "I am the *navi* and can't be touched. And you are unclean and can't be touched. These men are bound to the Covenant and the Law."

"I have seen how they keep it here," Hurriya said coldly.

Devora straightened. She didn't want to think about that just now. About how the keeping of the Law may have decayed in these hills. She cast the men an uneasy glance. Remembered Lappidoth urging her to take the other nazarites with her. "*We* will keep it," she said. "And so your feet will not touch the ground within the camp. Stay in this saddle until I can arrange for bedding and a tent outside the camp."

"Where I'll be defenseless," she said quietly. "Your rules are ridiculous."

"And necessary." Devora's voice was sharp. She was keenly aware of Omri's eyes on her back. "We don't know what kind of touch allows the uncleanness to pass from one body to another. So we must assume any touch may defile."

"But this fever isn't—it isn't *that* fever." A sharp intake of breath. "It isn't, is it?"

"No." Devora softened, and started Shomar toward the tents again at a walk. "No, I don't believe so. It is all right, girl. But the words of the Law remain. The Lawgiver in the desert demanded seven days. He wrote that into the Covenant. To make sure the People would never become too hasty, never endanger the camp by bringing someone unclean back into it too quickly. Our

Covenant holds the living together and gives them hope, and keeps the dead buried and still. Look around at the terror in these hills, and see the consequence of neglecting it."

Omri interrupted then by nudging his horse alongside Shomar. His grin showed all his teeth.

"Where are the dead, Omri?" Devora asked, cutting off whatever the man had intended to say.

"God knows. We've been waiting here for Nimri since early morning."

"I see. Have you sent men to scout the hills around? Why is the town so quiet?"

"Why doesn't God send us visions to tell us?" Omri muttered. "Why else have you come?"

"God may send warnings," Devora said, "but I doubt our God intends to do the work that the men of this camp can do."

"He didn't send us warnings that the dead would be eating tribesmen up by Judges' Well. So what good is he?"

Devora stared at the Zebulunite in disbelief. "You northerners marry heathen, allow heathen gods to be worshipped in your tents and your houses. Someone up here leaves dead unburied, untended. And the dead rise and begin eating, and you want to blame *God* for not forewarning you? Your actions, your—callousness toward God and Law—these are warning enough!"

"You're the one with a heathen slut on your horse," Omri grinned. For some reason he didn't seem rattled by Devora's outburst, and with a shock she realized that she had diminished herself in his eyes. Just a woman getting upset and railing at a man, like any other who didn't know her place. That's what Omri must be thinking.

"There's too much God in you," he told the *navi*, then looked her over as he had on the hill. Devora's jaw tightened.

"A lot of woman too, though," he grinned. "I am glad you are with us."

Devora said nothing in reply; her unease grew. Hurriya was tense in her arms. Perhaps the girl had a point about the men of this camp.

"I saw the nazarite," Omri said as he nudged his horse closer, "but not your husband. Why didn't he join us?"

Devora's throat was tight. She couldn't say that she had begged Lappidoth to remain behind, for this would diminish him in the eyes of the northern men, making him seem a slave to his woman. Yet anything else she blamed his absence on—his age, or fear, or a devotion to other duties—would make him seem no less small to them. She kept her lips closed and held down a flash fire of fury at Omri for the question. And truly, she wanted—needed—Lappidoth here. He had always been the tent over her, the shelter for her when her fears were fiercest.

"Huh," Omri grunted. "At least I have something to look at that's prettier than Barak's old face."

Devora felt her face burning. The Zebulunite was *flirting* with her. Yet she was the *navi* and had a husband, and if she'd had a son when most Hebrew women had their sons, that son would now be Omri's own age, or older. What was he thinking?

Devora nudged Shomar to a slightly quicker pace, but Omri stayed beside them, complimenting her eyes, the line of her jaw, the cradle of her hips. Devora's face burned hotter.

Hurriya shifted as though about to act or speak; Devora clenched her hand tightly around the girl's arm through the wool of her salmah, forbidding it.

"I like the way you ride that horse," Omri crooned. "Would you like to ride something else?" As Devora refused to look at him, Omri sidled close enough to place his hand on her thigh, his fingers gripping her in the most nauseating manner. She turned on him as quickly as a serpent. "What are you doing?" she whispered fiercely. "Do you think I won't cry out and have you stoned for trying to possess another man's woman?"

"I don't see another man here," Omri grinned. "He seems to have lost you."

As if she were a sort of misplaced trinket that had rolled out from under her husband's watchful eye and might now be picked up! Lappidoth had taught her that men were capable of valuing all of a woman, not only her thighs or her womb. This oaf apparently wanted only to rut with her. She was the *navi*; who did he think he was?

"Get your hand *off* me," Devora hissed.

Omri's fingers dug into her thigh as his face flushed with anger. Perhaps he had not heard that commanding tone from a woman since he was a small boy in his mother's tent.

Devora's eyes went dark. She reached for Mishpat.

Just then there was a clatter of hooves, and glancing over her shoulder Devora saw Zadok riding toward them from the tents at a clip that was just a little too quick to be casual. Relief swept through her like a summer wind.

Omri followed her gaze and scowled. "Does that dog always heel you?" he muttered. His hand left her thigh.

"Only when the *navi* needs him to," Devora said quietly. "I am *kadosh*, Omri. Holy. Not to be touched."

He sneered. "You are still a woman."

"Not your woman."

"Huh. The Galilee is a long way from Shiloh."

Devora's insides went cold. How dare he. Did he think distance lessened her husband's claims on her, or hers on him? Or did Omri mean to threaten her, to indicate *he* could claim her as he pleased, here in the north, among his own people?

Zadok was nearly up to them. Omri whispered, "If you find your need is hot on you, woman, and you need a man between your legs, my tent is easy to find."

"Shouldn't you be making plans for dealing with the dead?" Her hand clenched about Mishpat's hilt, a fact that Zadok's eyes didn't miss as he reined up beside her. Massive and brooding and watching Omri with his cold, dark face.

"Omri," Zadok grinned—though the grin did not touch his eyes. "Is there any beer in the camp?"

Omri bristled, as though expecting a challenge. But Zadok offered none.

"Ride with me," the nazarite said. "There's a lot we need to talk about." He said that with a bit of an edge to it, and in a moment he'd grasped the pommel of Omri's saddle and was steering the man's horse away from the women. Devora let out the breath she'd been holding, but her hand did not lift from Mishpat's hilt.

"You still think I should sleep alone at the camp's edge?" Hurriya asked quietly.

"*I* will be sleeping at the camp's edge," Devora said firmly. "I am *kadosh*. My tent will stand apart. Zadok will be at hand. You will have bedding outside my tent. Be alert and cry out if you need to. But you won't need to. No one but a fool would cross Zadok."

Hurriya looked ahead, at the men standing outside their tents. "I see nothing but fools," she said.

Choosing not to answer that, Devora watched Zadok and Omri cantering ahead, then lifted her eyes, looked again at the placid lake and the too-silent town on the farther shore. Cold clenched about her heart. She didn't know what Hurriya's vision meant, and the younger *navi* was untrained, unable to interpret the things God showed to her. But Devora did know this. Whatever was to happen here in the north would begin there, at that lake.

At the town of Walls, which no longer had any. Among houses silent as cairns for the dead.

***

As Shomar followed Zadok's horse among the tents, Devora began to notice how *odd* this camp was. Not at all what she might have expected—but then, her experience of fighting men was largely limited to the nazarites, who were well-armed, disciplined, and who acted as though ferocity were an essential, if unspoken, part of their vow. This camp was *not* a camp of nazarites. It was something else entirely.

For one thing, the men were barely armed at all. Only a few with shields, some without even spears, just farming implements or sharpened poles. These were northern men; their fathers hadn't taken any lions' shares of the loot from the cities whose walls had tumbled in the south where the Tumbling Water stopped tumbling at last and moved lazy and wide through green fields. And the glances of desire they cast at the two women riding past could not disguise their underlying fear. Devora saw the way their hands trembled, the pallor of their faces. Was it *these* men she had come north for? These were only children, fearing the dark.

The men gathered near as she walked Shomar through the tents, and the horse shied, having never been among such a press of people. Devora patted the horse's flank to calm him. Feeling the shiver that passed through Hurriya, Devora said softly by the girl's ear, "My husband's horse will not drop you."

Hurriya gave a terse nod.

"Anath loves horses," the Canaanite said after a moment, keeping her eyes on Zadok's horse ahead of them, refusing to glance at the men who crowded close to either side. "She even found one, a wild horse by the river. She tamed it and used to ride it in the early morning. She thought none of us knew, but *I* knew." Again the shiver. "I need to tell her horses hurt. They hurt. Why does she always look happy after riding?"

"A horse doesn't always hurt," Devora smiled. "We just haven't ridden much, you and I. We will heal." Privately she wondered if that was true of the girl. It was perhaps a miracle that she was still this lucid. Would herbs help, or was this journey in the north consuming the girl's last strength? She cursed Barak in her heart for making such a journey necessary.

She tried to ignore the fear in the many faces around her. But what good would a camp filled with terrified men be to her or to God?

"*Damn it,*" she whispered.

She kicked Shomar to a gallop, startling a cry from Hurriya. Then a shout from Zadok, who had turned in his saddle at Hurriya's cry. Devora made for the center of the camp, pulling up her horse where the tents were thickest. Men gathered in a half circle about her, and she lifted one hand high, her other arm about the Canaanite.

"Tribes of the north!" she cried. "Put away your fear! Bury it. Raise a cairn over it. Shun it as you would the dead. It will do you as much harm, or more. Remember that you are men. And men of Israel, whose fathers wrestled with God in the desert and wrung blessings from him!" Her voice rose nearly to a scream. "God gave you this land of promise, took it from others who were here before you and gave it into your hands. Now defend it!"

The men looked at her, but none raised their voices to affirm her words. Their faces were still pale with fear. Devora faltered. She was used to men listening attentively when the *navi* spoke, before springing to action. But these men had never stood before the *navi*'s seat. In their faces, Devora saw that her words neither shamed them nor inspired them. In their eyes, she saw that they were merely listening to a woman because a few moments ago there had been no woman in the camp, and she was strange to them.

"Listen," she told them, trying to keep her voice steady. Their gaze unnerved her. "Everyone fears the dead," she said. "I do too. But the dead are weak, and the God of your land is strong. Do you fear to face the dead without spears, shields, with just a fence pole in your hands? The dead don't even have that. They are just stumbling, clumsy bodies. Taking them down," she chopped her arm through the air, "is like cutting trees. Our fathers broke a strong wall at Yeriho. The dead are not stronger than a stone wall."

The men stared at her in silence.

"Be strong and courageous," she urged them. "Show our God that you do not doubt, that you are not less than your fathers were." She faltered. "Do you not know who I am?" she asked at last.

"You are from Shiloh," one man called out.

"I am the *navi* of Israel," she said. "I see what God sees."

"God has turned his eyes away," another man called. "We passed an orchard—it was blighted."

A murmur rose from the men, an angry, despairing sound. Hurriya shuddered, and Devora's arm tightened about her. She understood; the men had seen the *malakh ha-mavet*, even as she had. And the only vision of victory she had to share was an image of a woman driving a peg through a corpse's skull. She'd told Barak that women would protect Israel. But if she told these men that, these cruel northern men, they would surely only laugh at her with that cold, bitter laughter that she knew all too well. What could she tell them? These were not supplicants waiting on her judgment beneath the olive tree— yet they *were* waiting on her judgment. They were waiting to hear what God might say to them, what accusation God might make to explain the presence of the walking dead, or what defense God might make for the removal of his protection. All their eyes on her. So many eyes filled with dread.

"God will defend us," she said hoarsely. "He fights with us." The inadequacy of her words shook her.

"Let's go," Hurriya whispered, turning her head so that her lips were not far from the *navi*'s ear. "Please, let's just go."

"Be still," Devora whispered back. She gazed out over those despairing faces and understood the Canaanite's panic. She had miscalculated. All it would take was the wrong word spoken, and these men might take their despair and terror out on *her*. She could feel Zadok's tension behind her, as though all the air around the nazarite was stretched tight, ready to snap. Omri at least had slipped away, no doubt uncomfortable around the nazarite.

Lappidoth had wanted her to take all the nazarites with her. Swallowing, she conceded that he might perhaps have been right.

But her anger was stronger than her fear. These men would *not* wilt like a dying crop and leave her and this Canaanite girl and the other women of the land to face the dead for them. "Where is Barak ben Abinoam?" she cried.

Mutely, several of the men gestured toward the shore, and Devora glanced there and saw by the water one tent larger than the others, a great pavilion dyed in earth colors, rich browns and reds. Devora lifted her eyes, caught Zadok's gaze, nodded toward the pavilion. Then she turned her back on the scared men, coldly, deliberately. Keeping her arm tight around the Canaanite, whose breathing was quick and shallow, perhaps from fever, perhaps from fear.

Devora gave the tent a grim look.

She would make sure this was a meeting Barak ben Abinoam would never forget.

KADOSH

BARAK WAITED, cross-legged, on the rug-covered floor of his pavilion. He could hear the *navi*'s voice outside, speaking to his frightened men. He cursed

Nimri in the silence of his heart for failing to bring him the Ark, that he might burn the unclean dead from the land. As a child sitting between his grandfather's knees, he'd heard of how the Ark had burned dry the Tumbling Water itself, which south of Kinnor Sea was not the stream it was here but rather a roaring, crashing river falling out of the high hills. He'd heard how the tribes had crossed over on dry ground. Of how the Ark had brought drought to their enemies or kindled their tents like straw. He glanced at his spear where it rested against one of the four poles of his tent. A spear was enough for a man to carry against raiders from the sea—but against the dead?

Barak heard the sounds of horse and saddle outside of the door of his tent and straightened. She was here, the *navi*, just outside.

He dreaded this meeting but had determined that Devora would come to *him*, here. He would not argue with a *woman* where his men could see and hear. Especially *this* woman.

She was *kadosh*, set apart. Which meant she couldn't be understood, no more than God. She was a woman; when he'd faced her on her hill above Shiloh, he'd seen the fineness of her features, her smallness, the shape of her body within her dress. She should be in her husband's tent, pleasing him or mending his garments, or preparing stew and warm milk for him. But she was not in her husband's tent. She was here. And it was to her, out of all the men and women of the land, that God chose to speak and reveal what was to come. She and the Ark were both vessels to carry words spoken by God. One vessel of wood, one of flesh, both were reminders that God was at hand.

He took a small breath; he didn't know how to handle her.

***

Zadok entered Barak's pavilion first and moved aside to stand by the door of the tent, tall and glowering, the light from Barak's small fire playing off the hard, unforgiving edges of his face. A moment later Devora swept in with a swish of her long, travel-stained white dress and fury in her eyes.

The *navi* did not do anything Barak might have expected of a woman entering his tent. Devora did not kneel before him on the rug nor did she sit. She strode across the tent, giving him hardly time to lean back from the intrusion before her hand whipped across his face, striking him hard enough to black his vision for an instant.

He caught her wrist even as she drew it back, held it tightly. Her eyes were dark as the midnight at the bottom of a lake.

"Release the *navi*'s hand." A growl from Zadok at the door of the tent.

Breathing hard, his pulse pounding in his temples, Barak gazed into those midnight eyes a moment before glancing past Devora to see the nazarite standing like a tower, filling even the war-leader's voluminous pavilion. Barak's own growl was deep in his throat. But this was the *navi*. She was *kadosh*. Forbidden to touch her. He let go of Devora's hand, his teeth bared from the effort of holding in his rage. His cheek stung.

"How *dare* you," the *navi* hissed, standing before him. "Israel *needs* you. How *dare* you betray the Covenant so."

He rose slowly to his feet, breathing deep. "Where is Nimri?" he growled.

"Dealt with." Devora nearly spat the words, and the threat in them took Barak aback. His anger flickered down like a fire growing cold; he was bewildered. What had the *navi* done to that belligerent herdsman of Naphtali tribe? What *could* the *navi* do?

"Give one reason, one, why I shouldn't deal with you likewise." Though Devora's head barely came to Barak's chin, her presence filled the tent. "God is not an idol of wood you can cart about, wine-drinker. You think God is a—a weapon for your hand!" Her face was flushed with fury, those eyes darker by the moment. "But you are a weapon in *God*'s hand, Barak!"

He bristled. He would *not* be upbraided by this woman, like some boy come late to dinner with unwashed hands. "I am no god's weapon and no man's," he growled. "I am a vintner who has been eleven days from my vineyard while dead prowl about it, and I fear for the harvest." He lifted his hand when she started to speak, and to his surprise she stopped and listened, though her eyes flashed. "I do want the Ark. I see it isn't coming." For some reason he found himself needing to persuade her. His voice had an edge to it. "Some of the men in this camp want to thieve our few horses and ride after the dead now, this night, and be done with it. Men of Omri's sort. Others wish to slip away when I'm not looking. It is only by a *hair* that I hold this raid together, *navi*!" He was shouting now but could not stop. "These men *need* an Ark. Something holy, something *kadosh*, something they can keep their eyes on, that will tell them where they are supposed to stand and where they are supposed to walk, in what direction, whether to fight or flee. Something they will trust more than they trust me. They need an Ark. I sent Nimri for it—" He took a breath. "I had little time, and I hoped he would deal with the high priest in my stead—"

"Nimri *slew* the high priest."

A silence brittle enough for a single word to shatter. For several moments, no word did. Barak's face went completely white. The tent seemed to tilt toward him, and he could hear every beat of his heart.

Unthinkable.

He fought to breathe.

"I—did not mean that it should come to that," he whispered.

The silence stretched until it was taut and tense. Devora's face grew colder. Zadok loomed by the door of the pavilion with his arms folded across his chest, like some monument in fertile lands on the other side of the desert. Their eyes were on Barak with an intensity that shook him. His palms were sweaty, his throat too tight for words.

The *high priest*. Slain.

Nimri—what had he done? A scream was rising somewhere in the back of his mind.

"You're more heathen than Hebrew," Devora said at last. Her voice was like the winter wind through a door. She turned with a dismissiveness to her movements, as though she had no more time to waste with him. Zadok drew aside the tent flap and preceded her, and in a moment she was gone and the tent was too full of thunderous silence. Barak swayed on his feet.

The high priest was *dead*. The blight in Barak's vineyard appeared vividly before his heart. He had taken up the spear, pleading with God to shelter his vineyard while he defended the vineyards of other men. What wrath had that ass Nimri brought down on them all? Barak's covenant with God was already a fragile, provisional thing.

He burst into motion, sprang from his tent. Outside, dark was falling.

"Navi!"

She was already on horseback, with a young Canaanite in the saddle before her. Zadok was mounting his black gelding. Men stood at the egresses of nearby tents, watching with wide eyes.

"You can't leave!" Barak shouted, his voice pitched in a way that shamed him. "The men—"

"I am not leaving." She nodded toward the lake. "I am riding to that settlement."

Barak shook his head. "Not alone—"

"God has something to show me there. There was a vision as we came down from the hills." She nudged Shomar forward, turning her head enough that Barak could hear her speak over her shoulder, though she did not look at him. "There's something in the cedar houses I need to see."

Barak glanced at the lake and the silent houses. "I'll get men."

"I'll hear God better without them." She and Zadok spurred their horses to a trot.

Aghast, Barak called to the men outside their tents. "Stop them!"

Several men sprang before the horses. Even as they did, Devora unsheathed Mishpat and held the blade ready at her side, where it shone in the starlight like an invitation to death. Clean and white and unanswerable as an act of God. Barak gasped, for the blade was clearly iron, not bronze. Once only in his life had Barak ben Abinoam seen with his own eyes an implement of iron; the heathen champion who'd led the coastal raid Barak had repelled years ago had carried such a blade, and it had cut through the bronze shields of Barak's men as easily as if Barak were defending his vineyard and theirs with only sticks of wood—as though a heathen not-god lived within the metal, thirsting with the need to sever and kill.

Whether at the sword or the oncoming of the horses or the fury naked in the *navi*'s eyes, the men fell back. The *navi* and the nazarite sent their horses into a brisk canter. In a moment they were gone from the camp, riding out toward the shore.

"*Damn it!*" Barak yelled. "Omri, Laban!" The war leaders were already near, drawn by the shouts and the hoofbeats, and they ran toward him. "You each gather up ten men, your best. Follow me!" Barak shouted the words as he ran for his own horse. As he saddled Ager and then leapt astride, his heart pounded fiercely. Women and God always brought trouble to a man's house. This woman and her God more than most. "*Ya!*" he roared, wresting Ager's head up and digging in his knees.

THE SILENT TOWN

DEVORA AND ZADOK had a good start, and Barak didn't catch up to them until their steeds had carried them into the town, past the settlement's cistern and up a long street between two-story houses of cedar and fir. No voices called out from the houses, either to greet or challenge these strangers in their town. Nor did Barak call out to the houses. The gaping holes of the upper-story windows opened on lightless rooms as dark as though God had never created light. *That* kind of dark.

Fears rose in Barak's mind that he hadn't shivered under since he was a small boy—when he'd cry out for his mother, and her soft words would drive away the unclean, lurching things with which his imagination had peopled the night. His mother was not here now. And the irremediable dark within these deserted houses might conceal anything. Bodies, whether still or in motion. Bodies rising from the floor, mouths open and hungering, silently approaching, arms outreached to grab at him. His blood was loud in his ears, loud and demanding as God's voice at Har Sinai. It took everything in him not to turn his horse and bolt from this strange town.

But there was no scent of death. Just stillness.

There was no sound of hooves behind him; the other men he'd called for were no doubt riding to catch up but hadn't yet reached the settlement. He glanced down at his saddlebag. There was a curved bulge where he'd packed the shofar he carried. If he needed it. He made the sign against evil quickly with his left hand. He had lost the Ark; he intended to keep at least the *navi*.

Barak caught up with her, his horse wheezing, even as Devora slid from her own steed's back where she and Zadok had halted outside a tumbled ruin of rafters and soot. One of those houses of cedar—a very great one—had burned to the ground; heaps of charred wood rose from the ashes the way lost kin rise from the mists in our dreams, fragments of our past demanding attention. There was no smoke rising from the cinders and no glow of embers—the fire must have been out a few days—but the scent of burned wood remained thick in the air.

Barak pulled Ager up before the ruin, a few steps from Devora. "What are you doing?" he whispered fiercely, glaring down at the *navi*, ignoring the tall nazarite who stood by her. "There could be dead here."

"There most likely are."

"Then what are you doing here, *navi*, without more men?"

Devora glanced at him, her eyes still dark with anger.

Zadok's voice was a cold challenge in the dark. "If the *navi* says there is something we must see here, then there is something we must see."

Devora glanced at the nazarite. "Even if there wasn't," she said quietly, "we must find an herbalist, or her supplies. For the girl."

Barak gave the Canaanite an uneasy glance. The girl was gazing about, frowning as though looking for something she might recognize. Her eyes were a little glazed, and she was very pale. With a start, Barak realized she was ill with fever.

"That girl," he said hoarsely. "Is she—"

"It's not that kind of fever," Devora said. "But she has touched the dead." With her gaze fixed on the charred ruin before them, the *navi* unstrapped a waterskin from the side of the saddle and handed it up to the girl. The Canaanite took the skin and held it, but didn't drink.

"Wait for my men," Barak said.

"Are you afraid, Barak?" An edge to the *navi*'s voice.

He didn't know how to answer that. Admit his fear to a woman? He turned his head and spat on the hard-packed dirt of the street.

"So am I," the *navi* said. "Let's take a look." For a moment the *navi* turned her attention to her horse. The gelding's eyes were showing their whites, and Devora scratched under his chin a moment. The gelding whickered softly, but his eyes stayed round with fear. Leaning in, Devora whispered in the horse's ear. Then she stepped away from her horse, with Mishpat unsheathed at her side.

"Zadok, watch over the girl, please."

"Your will, *navi*."

Devora left her horse, and the nazarite sat his with an uneasy look that Barak could well understand. As the *navi* walked slowly to the ruin, Barak looked at the charred timbers, then his gaze darted to the houses at either side, which were solid and intact. Only one house had burned. There must have been no wind. Still, a fire in an encampment or a town was a furious thing; there must have been men here to put the fire out before it devoured the other homes. But how had they salvaged nothing of this one house yet kept it from the others? It was as though this one house had been struck by a firebolt of divine judgment from the sky, or as though the people had stood about it with water and blankets, keeping the fire contained. Watching it burn. It made no sense. *Nothing* about this town made any sense. He had been here before, twice, years ago. Once when he met Hadassah as she drew water from the town's cistern, once when he came to speak with the town's elders at the gate, during the worst raids from the Sea People. It had been a grim settlement but a thriving one. Now these silent houses—it was as though the settlement he knew had never existed. Or as though he were no longer even walking in the waking world—as though somehow he had ridden Ager right into the dream country. He shivered.

"That fire was not accidental." Devora kept her voice low. "Look. There's wood piled against the wall that fell, and fragments of a broken oil jar."

Barak gave a start and took a closer look at the ruined structure. Yes, he could see the woodpile now—a great heap of embers and charred ends of boards, hidden half from sight under the collapsed wall. And a few pottery shards in the ash. He glanced at Devora, noting the confidence and rigid certainty of her posture, the cold in her face. *She sees what others do not*—that's what was whispered of her in the land. *She finds justice; the defiler and the defiled cannot hide from her.*

"Why would someone burn an empty house?" he murmured.

"It wasn't empty," Devora said quietly.

Barak's pulse quickened. He took another look, a careful one. There. His throat tightened. Crushed beneath the fallen timbers, a body charred and blackened, only its legs visible. One shred of cloth wound about the left leg had somehow escaped the fire as if by an act of God, who loathes above all deeds a murder committed in silence without eyes to witness. The betraying cloth was white, though smudged now with ash and soot.

Devora stepped with an old woman's care through the ruins. Barak watched her without dismounting. The white cloth gave him an uneasy feeling in his belly, like nausea, but weaker than that; he felt that he knew what kind of cloth the man had worn and what it must signify, but he would not look at it in his mind. It was like the dead in his vineyard—he knew the horror was there, he could hear it rustling among the vines, but he could not see it without stepping closer to peer between the green leaves—and that he would not do. If some man had been murdered here in his own house, his shelter burned down about his head by his neighbors' malice or fear, let God whisper the secret, if he would, into the ears of his *navi*; Barak would not go digging among the cinders to find it. He had trouble enough.

In the saddle, the Canaanite began humming softly to herself. The sound of it was very lovely, and the tune was simple and familiar, though it was a moment before he knew what it was. Barak felt his eyes burn and scrubbed the back of his hand across them quickly, and only then realized it was the same go-to-sleep song Hadassah had used to sing while holding her belly, when she was with child.

"Be still, woman." His voice was hoarse.

The song stopped. Hurriya looked at him.

"We're all going to die here," the young woman whispered.

Barak jerked. "I said be still," he snapped.

"Something's wrong here. All wrong. Some of the people didn't leave. And the ones that did left parts of themselves behind. And now we won't be able to leave."

Barak lifted a hand to slap her, to bring her out of whatever fit she was in or merely to silence her. But at that moment Devora turned back toward them. Barak lowered his hand.

"Something very wrong *did* happen here," Devora murmured when she reached them, and her face was cold.

Hoofbeats interrupted her, and Barak snapped his head about to gaze down the street, the way they'd come. Several horses turned the corner—eight, maybe nine horses. All that the camp had left, since Nimri had not returned. He recognized Omri at the front and Laban right behind him, a man nearly as large as Zadok, with his great axe strapped across his back. Both of these chieftains bore torches, the firelight revealing their faces in the dark. As they rode nearer, it was clear the others were men of Laban's, hardy men of Issachar. Barak breathed a sigh of relief. He could bear the silence of this town better if he had men at his back.

"Chieftain!" Omri called as the men pulled up beside the ruin. "More men are coming. On foot."

Laban gave the ruin a dark look. "What is this?"

"They burned the house," Devora said, nearly trembling with fury. "These half-heathen. They *burned* this house and him in it. He needs a cairn." Her voice rose, something near panic. "They *needed* to give him a *cairn*."

"Why kill him at all?" Barak asked. "He was a levite. I saw the robe."

"He was already dead," Devora said. "They locked him in his own house. His body likely stopped breathing long before the fire was lit. His neighbors boarded up his house, shutting him in. They could hear him thumping against the walls inside. They could hear him moaning." Her eyes had a distant look, and Barak wondered suddenly if she was *seeing* what she described, not as a woman imagining it or deducing it, but as a *navi* witnessing it, witnessing events that were already past as clearly as he himself might witness some event in the present. He felt a chill.

Then the look passed from her eyes and she drew in a slow breath. "It took them a long time to gather up the courage," she murmured. "They stood there praying and weeping in the street. And finally they burned the house."

"God," Barak whispered. "Holy God."

"They *spat* in the face of Holy God when they set fire to a body made in his likeness," Devora said coldly, turning from the ashes and striding back to her horse. "Only God has any right to burn lives from the earth. Bodies belong beneath clean stone, with raised cairns so they can be remembered. Who will remember this man?"

Hurriya, still in the saddle and shivering a little from her fever, was gazing on the ruin with a fascinated, focused look.

"Men are different in the towns," Laban said, his voice deeper even than Zadok's. "We believe we are twelve tribes, *navi*, but we are really two. Men of the tents, men of the cedar houses. Issachar still lives in tents. Here, in the hills of Naphtali tribe, men have raised houses or live in houses the Canaanites raised. Men of the tents hold to the Law. We know how fragile our tents are. Men of the houses—" He shrugged. "The houses are large. They like to have many people in them to share bread. They learn strange ways, are quicker to do strange things."

"This is no Canaanite custom," Hurriya called faintly, "to burn our dead. We take our dead to the water."

Even as Devora climbed into the saddle behind the girl, Barak glanced down the empty street, pondering what commands to give Laban and Omri.

They were here. They might as well do this right.

"My men and I will look around." He looked to the nazarite. "The women stay here."

"Zadok," the *navi* said, her voice cold and authoritative. Without another word, Devora got her horse moving and walked him down the street, with the Canaanite breathing shallowly, her head resting on the *navi*'s clothed shoulder. The nazarite gave Barak a warning look and followed.

Barak cursed. "Laban, search the west end of the settlement. See if you can find any of the people who lived here. Take the men. Omri, with me."

He turned Ager and rode after the *navi*, overtaking her. He heard the clatter of hooves from Omri's steed close behind him and, more distantly, the hoofbeats and the voices of the men moving off in the other direction. Seeing that woman riding ahead with that wild blade unsheathed, fury and confusion burned in his breast.

Barak moved his horse alongside Shomar and pressed the gelding's side aggressively, his leg brushing Devora's a moment. "Do you think you can ride where you will," he whispered fiercely, "like a man?"

"I think I can ride where God sends me," she said.

Omri drew up alongside Barak on the left, holding his torch away from his horse, and he gave Barak a look that made it clear the young chieftain would enjoy beating this woman and teaching her her place. Barak held up his hand to forestall any fool's speech from the younger man. He pitched his voice low. "*Navi*, you are not in Shiloh. You are in my camp, among my men. You will go where I tell you and stay where I put you."

The *navi*'s eyes flashed. "This is Walls, this is not your camp," she said.

"If you leave the *navi*'s side, you will die tonight." The Canaanite kept her eyes lowered in the way of a northern woman, with respect, but there was a bite to her tone.

Barak's eyes widened.

"What have you seen, Hurriya?" Devora asked quietly.

"The dead." The Canaanite gazed ahead with that same, glazed look. "They filled the street."

"And you saw Barak fighting them," Devora murmured. "So it was not a vision of what has already happened. Hurriya has visions, as I do, Barak. She sees what God sees. You can trust what she says."

Two women who were *kadosh*. Two of them. But Barak didn't have time to dwell on it, for the girl's words seeped in past his anger and unease. His palms began to sweat. "There are dead in the houses or somewhere near," he said.

"I saw them in the street," the heathen girl said faintly.

They walked their horses slowly, watching and listening. They had kept their voices low. Their horses' hooves seemed too loud against the hard dirt. The street grew a little wider around them, and instead of houses there were now low shops, structures with three walls and thatched roofs, open to the street. Walls had been the largest settlement in the north, and there were many shops on this narrow market street that ran the length of the town. In most of them, the wares still hung, exposed to any thieving hands, as though their owners had fled without tarrying to pack away their livelihoods. Barak saw pottery, lovely in its beauty but with a thin sheen of dust settling over it. He saw dyed cloth brought in by camel and caravan from the coast, he saw beads and jewelry from the Horse People east of the Tumbling Water. One shop sold small gods and goddesses. Devora hissed through her teeth as they passed that one.

At last the *navi* stopped beside an open shop where dozens of small leather pouches hung on cords from the roof, and bound sheaves of leaves and herbs hung beside them. She rode Shomar right into the shop without dismounting and talked with Hurriya in a voice too quiet for Barak to hear her words. The *navi* brushed her fingers across the leaves, sometimes bringing her hand to her nose to catch the leaves' scent. She opened some of the pouches.

It seemed to take a long time, and Barak's palms kept sweating. He peered down the street at the dead market and the empty shops. Omri fidgeted beside him, drumming his own saddle with his fingertips. "Why do women take so long at everything?" the younger man muttered. "Take half a day to a market, come late to a meal, come late to bed. When I own a girl, I'll—"

"Shh." Barak held up his hand again. Omri subsided with one last mutter, then kicked his horse and rode ahead a little. Barak waited by the shop. He wondered suddenly if he should muffle the horses' hooves by winding cloth about them. He felt wary of making any unnecessary sound. Even the crackling of Omri's torch sounded too loud to him. He glanced at the grim nazarite and saw in Zadok's eyes that he too was anxious, though he sat very still in his saddle. Barak lifted his head and took the air's scent, but could detect no decay in it. He looked about at the emptiness of Walls with wide eyes, his heart beating fast. The girl's words kept echoing in his mind. The dead were here. Or somewhere close.

After a moment he thought he heard humming, and caught his breath again. The Canaanite; she hummed only a few notes, then stopped. The loss of it wrenched at him; for a moment she'd sounded very like Hadassah.

"What is that song?" he whispered as loudly as he dared. He'd never asked Hadassah what the words meant, but hearing the melody now, with Hadassah dead beneath her cairn and forever lost to him, the strangeness of the tune and the heathen words of it haunted him.

When Hurriya spoke after a moment, her voice was cold and distant. Devora kept looking through the herbalist's wares, appearing to ignore the girl.

"He grows tall as a cedar tree," the girl whispered, and Barak had to strain to hear her. "He will have fine things to delight him. Olive oil and perfumes for his body. And a woman who is scented and lovely for him. And when his mother has died, he will hear her voice whenever he walks by the water where her body is. I—I sang it to my little one, walking out of the hills. Until he died. Afterward, when I tried, he—it—the moaning—"

She fell silent.

Barak gazed at the girl in horror.

Devora held a few leaves in her hand, and now she plucked a few more from their sheaf by the roof above her head. Barak recognized the first as mint but had no idea what the other leaves were. The *navi* handed them to the girl and said softly, "Chew these, girl. We'll brew some into tea later. Chew, it'll help."

The girl took one leaf and nibbled on it, her breathing shallow.

Devora backed her horse out of the little shop. "That song. Why do you Canaanites promise soft lives to your children?" she asked, her voice quiet and bitter. "You make it too easy to forget the desert. You give them lies to hope in. Life is—brutal. It might be given to us or taken from us. Painting your eyes with kohl or wearing dyed cloth from the sea does not change this." Her face darkened as she gazed about at the abandoned shops. "You heathen will never be as vigilant as we are. You have not suffered as we have."

For a moment, only the sound of hooves on the hard, packed dirt.

"*I* have suffered," Hurriya said, biting off a little of the leaf.

Devora flushed and said nothing.

"And you are wrong. Maybe my mothers and fathers never had to fear being eaten in the *desert*. But, knowing the danger, we might be as careful as you! And we *know* things, useful things. Walls—our fathers *built* walls, but yours tore them down. Walls could have saved my—" She choked and fell silent.

"Walls couldn't have saved this town," Devora said. "Whatever happened here happened inside the houses."

Down the street, Omri began to thump the butt of his spear against the packed earth, and Barak bristled. Did he have to make such noise?

"Look," Zadok said sharply.

Barak and the *navi* both followed his gaze and saw, far down the street, beyond the shops, where another street lined with houses crossed this one, there stood a mighty house, much larger than any other they'd seen, an elder's house. This house also had gone up like a torch. The walls still stood, but they were charred and blackened from fire and there were great holes in their sides. The roof appeared to be entirely gone. More than anything, the house reminded Barak of the way blackened cedars sometimes stand on the hills for years, their insides hollowed out by lightning and the wrath of God.

His throat tightened. This town, like his own small homestead, had been prosperous. It sat by a lake filled with fish, a day's walk from plentiful fields, a land of rich vineyards and soft rains. The land they'd been promised, milk and honey. Grape bunches large as a man's chest. Hadassah, her body warm in the soft night. Where were those promises now? Burned out, blighted, ash and cinders.

Cold sweat. His tunic stuck to his back.

They cantered slowly past the shops toward the house, and Omri joined them, lifting his spear. He looked a little pale. As they rode closer, Barak thought he saw movement in the shadows before the door of the house. With a shock, he realized there was a figure on its knees, bent over another figure that lay still on the earth. Barak gasped. That figure supine on the ground was a corpse, an unburied and defiled corpse. All the flesh and muscle had been stripped from the legs, which were only bones. Only the torso still resembled a living person. The body was small—a child or a dwarf; its face had been torn and gnawed, making it impossible to tell. The belly had been gouged open, and the thing leaning over it had its fists full of entrails, lifted slickly from the torn belly to its hungering mouth. As Barak halted his horse, the thing glanced over its shoulder at him, its mouth and chin dark with blood, its eyes—*terrible* eyes—dull and sightless in the starlight. It snarled, teeth bared, like an animal warning scavengers back from its prey.

The eater was a woman.

A sound of hooves behind him, then Devora was beside him on her gelding with the Canaanite riding before her. The *navi*'s face was hard and cold, the Canaanite's twisted in a hatred that blazed like a flame no amount of water could put out. Together they gazed at the hissing thing, which gazed as fixedly back.

Lightheaded, Barak gripped Ager's mane, fearful that he might slide and fall from his horse, like a boy only just learning to ride.

Slowly the thing that had been a woman rose to its feet, the entrails on which it fed still clutched in one hand, like a tether attaching it to the other corpse's belly. One of its slack breasts visible through a rent in its garment, swaying as it moved. It bared its teeth at Barak and Devora, took a lurching step toward them, dragging one foot behind it. A sudden breeze brought its reek to their noses.

Barak saw Devora lift her blade and held up his hand to stop her. Though his hand shook. Yet it was he who defended the tribes and their women. He would not send one of those women against the dead—not even a woman carrying an iron blade.

Grimly Barak hefted his spear.

"Be careful," Devora said. "It's stronger than it looks. Cut into the head. And remember it is unclean—both the one feeding and the body it feeds on. Don't let it touch you."

Barak nodded and raised his arm, readying the spear, then rode hard at the shambling corpse, a scream rising in his throat that he held back and would not loose. His palm was slick with sweat where he gripped the haft of his spear. As he hurtled toward it, the corpse opened its mouth as though to offer a kiss, lifted its arms as though to embrace him.

THE MOANING DEAD

BARAK'S SPEAR took the corpse in the shoulder, spinning it about and nearly unseating the chieftain from his horse. Then his spearhead ripped free of the necrotic flesh. The haft remained in Barak's hand. Suppressing an urge to keep on galloping until he'd left the corpse far, far behind, Barak wheeled Ager about, and horse and rider threw themselves at the corpse again, though Ager let out a panicked squeal that no man should ever hear his horse make. The thrust of the spear into its shoulder had turned the corpse about, and now it was facing Barak again as he came at it from the opposite direction. It hissed and lifted its arms again. Barak roared in defiance of his fear. The warm wetness down his leg and the sharp scent of urine warned him that he had unmanned himself, but he didn't care. All that mattered was getting that horrible, lurching corpse to *be still.*

His spear took it in the jaw this time, and caught; his own velocity tore him from the saddle, and as he fell Ager reared and squealed again and then tore off down the street. Omri wheeled his own steed about and hurried to catch the fleeing horse.

Barak landed hard in the grit of the street, which had been packed firm by generations of sandalled feet. The wind was driven out of him. He rolled to his side, gasped for air. Saw the corpse staggering closer, splayed hands reaching down at him, the gaze of those murky eyes fixed on him. His spear had caught in the thing's jaw, and the haft was dragging behind it along the ground. The corpse stank, a negation of all life and breath and every touch of God's fingers on the land.

His heart wild in his chest, Barak ripped his knife free of its sheath on his hip, but even as the walking corpse closed on him, its face burst apart, bits of its head and scalp splashing aside like something half-liquid. The corpse slumped to its knees. The bronze head of a spear protruded through what had once been a face. Barak's knife dropped from his hand and he clutched his chest, gasped for air.

Zadok rode up, his face grim, and his gloved hand took the haft of his spear and wrenched it free of the corpse with a sound like a foot coming free from clinging mud. The dead woman fell backward to the ground.

Then Zadok stepped his horse over to the lifeless body the woman had been feeding on and stabbed its head with his spear too.

The nazarite swung the spear up so the point jabbed toward the sky, and his dark gaze held Barak's. "You have never faced the dead," he said. "Only the living. I see it in your eyes, Barak ben Abinoam. I have faced the dead, and the *navi* has faced the dead. Now you have also. Render the *navi* of Israel more respect." Then he turned and trotted his horse back to where the others waited, leaving Barak heaving for breath on the ground.

Barak found his hands were shaking. He had never known fear like this.

He'd been afraid during the great raid from the west, facing the warriors of the Sea People with their iron blades and bejeweled ears, but usually he'd been afraid only *after* the battle, when they lay dead around him and he'd turned and retched into the grass, trembling with reaction.

But this—this corpse. It had been a *woman*. And it—it had come after him like a lion or a wolf, something hungering and mindless, its hands grasping. The way it had *moaned*—

Still needing more air, he got shakily to his feet, looked for his horse, then remembered that Ager had bolted and Omri had ridden after him. Such was his own terror that he did not think even to be angry at the other chieftain for his flight. Nor did he even flush dark with shame when he saw Devora and the Canaanite girl looking on. Panic still rushed in his blood like winter water.

Suddenly every house in the street to either side held a menace in the dark. Barak stilled his hands, slowed his breathing. He was a chieftain of Israel. He could not afford panic. He swallowed, several times, moistening his throat enough to speak again. "Let's get out of here. Now."

"We came here to find the dead, Barak," Devora said. "Not hide from them."

"They *devoured* Walls," Hurriya breathed. The girl's hands were trembling where they clutched Shomar's mane.

"And maybe other settlements too." The moon had risen over the thatched rooftops, and Devora's eyes shone in the light. "But take heart, girl. Your sister has *not* been eaten. You had a vision of her."

"Not a good vision." The girl looked faint.

"She was alive in it."

"Yes, she was alive," Hurriya whispered.

Devora looked at the corpse a moment, then her gaze moved to the door of the burned house behind the corpse. A great bar of wood had been locked across it, holding it firmly shut. The door was charred, but it stood. "Everything has gone wrong," she said softly. "Something has torn the Covenant."

"Who?" Barak said. "Who has broken the Covenant? Who is God furious with?"

Devora shook her head wearily and slid from her horse, leaving Hurriya in the saddle. The Canaanite's eyes widened; she looked as though she didn't trust the horse not to bolt away with her alone in the saddle.

"You don't simply *break* the Covenant, Barak ben Abinoam," Devora said sharply, gazing at that door. "You loosen it. Think of the roots of a crop field, intertwined beneath the soil, strong. A hundred tiny acts each day loosen the weaving of those roots. Untruths, betrayals, infidelities, cruelties, blood spilled without cause, bodies left unburied—all of these eat at the roots like the gnawing things you find when you dig up the earth. The roots are the People, the soil is the land of promise, the weaving of the roots is the Covenant." Devora glanced at him in the dark. "Then a wind comes. A storm. If the roots are loosened, if they aren't bound tightly together, the wind tears away everything, soil and crop." She approached the door, touched it a moment with her fingers, drew them back as though she'd been burned. Her voice became distracted. "You won't find just one guilty man somewhere in these hills, some man we can stone and be done. It is a thousand small evils that bring this emptiness upon us."

She placed her aged hands beneath the bar and tried to lift it. Barak heard her breath wheeze.

"What are you doing?" he called, alarmed. He didn't want to know what was in that house—or any of the others. He didn't want to see anything more. He wanted to get back to the camp, regroup, gather his men.

"Taking a look," Devora said. "Help me please, Zadok."

The powerful nazarite dismounted and moved toward her. His face was calm, which staggered Barak, and shamed him. Yet he understood it. The nazarite had work to do, had a task, something definite that could be done in this town whose silence mocked all possibility of action. Zadok gripped the cedar bar and lifted it for the *navi*, then opened the latch on the door and swung it open; part of the door, soot-blackened, crumbled away as he did.

They gazed into the interior. Moonlight came through a high window and through a great gap that had been burned in the roof. It was a great house, two stories; the window was on the second, and there were no windows on the lower story, though the fire had burned away the far wall. All across the floor were dark shapes, and a lingering scent of charred meat. Barak sucked in his breath.

Devora peered in, one delicate, bony hand clutching the jamb. Her eyes glinted faintly, and her hand tightened around the doorframe as though she were dizzy. Zadok gave her his arm to steady her. Barak held his spear in both hands across his chest, reassured by the solidity of its wood.

"Burned," Hurriya whispered, gazing over their heads at the interior. "Like the levite's house. They burned this house, with the dead in it." A touch of awe in her voice.

"Twenty-three." Devora was tight-lipped. "We do not burn the bodies of the People, we bury them."

Barak could not count the shapes in the faint light; his eyes could not pick out one from another. But he did not question Devora's sight. "God of our fathers," he breathed.

"It *is* terrible," Hurriya said suddenly. "But the people of this town found a way to protect their kin from the dead. What right have we to judge them?"

Devora spun to face her, her eyes livid. "And where are those people now? Are they here? Do they live? Do you know?"

Hurriya didn't answer.

"Did—did *this*—help any of them?" She waved her hand at the house. "Shut the door, Zadok."

He did, and replaced the great wooden bar over it, locking the bodies within. For just a moment the nazarite leaned against the door, as though overcome by what he'd seen. Barak just sat his saddle, overwhelmed.

"Look," Hurriya called softly.

The others glanced up. After a moment Devora saw what Hurriya meant and pointed. Barak saw that a narrow strip of linen hung from the charred window on the house's second story. By some miracle a little of that linen had escaped the flames, and he could see that it was dyed scarlet; against the charred timbers it seemed garish and utterly out of place. As though someone had decided to hang up fine clothes to dry in the heat of a burning house.

Devora exchanged a look with Hurriya, then gazed at the cloth steadily. "A brave act," she whispered.

"I don't understand," Barak muttered. "It's a scrap of cloth. What does it mean?"

Devora's voice was soft in the dark. She sounded awed. "Someone— someone living—led twenty dead inside, so that her kin could slam shut the door and bar it behind them. She must have escaped to the upper room and pulled up the rope ladder behind her so that no dead could follow." For a moment Devora only gazed up at that window, her face pensive as though struck with thoughts that had never occurred to her before.

"Think of it," Hurriya breathed. "Just think of it. She stood up there alone. With twenty dead hissing beneath her. Their hands reaching for her."

"It is not only men with spears who have courage," Devora said.

"She?" Barak's eyes had widened in horror. "How do you know it was a woman?"

"Not a woman, a girl," the *navi* said. "Don't you recognize the linen?"

"It's just a scrap of cloth."

"Nothing is ever just a scrap of anything, Barak ben Abinoam. Everything made bears the shape of its maker's hands and can betray who its maker was, even as every hill and thicket in the land bears the imprint of God's shaping fingers. Everything is clay, everything is marked."

"It's a maiden sash," Hurriya said. "A girl wears it beneath her breasts when she wishes to beg Astarte for her breasts to grow full. For her blood to come. A girl wears it when she tires of being just a girl."

"Yes." Devora gazed at the window and its limp linen, and her voice hardened. "This town, also, is more heathen than Hebrew."

"But brave," Hurriya whispered.

Barak gazed up at that linen, struck with horror. He tried to imagine standing alone while twenty of those—those *corpses*—waited below you for your foot to trip. And the flames licking up the sides of the house. "She didn't burn," he said, looking at the window. "She jumped out. Led them in, then leapt from the window."

"She did," Devora said quietly. "It *was* very brave. Though she died for it."

"Died?" Hurriya gasped.

"That rock in the earth there, by the wall—it is smeared with old blood. She cracked her leg there, or her head."

"Maybe she rose to her feet, and lived," Barak said grimly.

"There is a wide swath of soil, like a furrow, leading away from the rock. She was dragged away, eaten. Not all the dead were in the house. And the dead caught her right after she leapt—otherwise the neighbors would have come for her first."

The desire for this to be wrong gripped Barak's heart so fiercely it startled him. "No, a neighbor saw her wounded—one of the men who barred the door. And came to pull her away. That's what the marks in the soil mean."

"Would he have dragged her body along the earth between the houses? He would have lifted her and carried her in his arms. What she did was holy, Barak. God gave her a great task, and she leapt for him. You do not carry an injured holy one to safety by dragging her body through the dirt."

He winced at the thought. The scene Devora suggested was too terrible. That a girl—a child—might risk so much, and achieve such a victory, only to fall to her death: it was an injustice that blasphemed God and mocked the Covenant. He could not bear it, or accept it. A *navi* Devora might be, but she did not have that look in her eyes now, the look that meant God was showing her visions. And these were only marks in the dirt. They might mean something else. They might mean anything. It was only dirt.

A cough in the street behind them interrupted, and Barak turned to see Omri walking his own horse toward them, with a tether about the neck of

Barak's steed. In the light of the torch he still held, Omri looked pale. As he drew near, his gaze flicked to the corpse in the street and the body it had been eating. He stopped and sat his horse, staring down.

"Rare for there to be just one," he murmured.

"Yes," Devora said. "It is rare."

Omri stepped the two horses in a wide circle about the body. Their eyes rolled, and Barak's horse shied, nearly tearing the tether from his hand; at last he was near enough and he tossed the tether to Barak, who caught it deftly out of the air. "Horse nearly galloped back to Shiloh," Omri said, tearing his gaze from the horror in the street. "I should ask you to barter that breast-piece for him."

"He's worth more than a breast-piece, Omri."

"Then trade me her." Omri attempted a smile and gestured at the *navi*, who swung about with her eyes dark and fierce. "She'd be pleasant. Worth the loss of a horse."

"She's *kadosh*," Barak said, taken aback.

Omri seemed to notice how they were all looking at him: Zadok, Devora, Barak. The Canaanite's eyes were lowered, but her shoulders were tensed.

"She'd do," he muttered.

"Touch her and die," Zadok said quietly.

Devora just gazed at the Zebulunite coldly, which seemed to bother him more than Zadok's threat.

"You needn't act like I tried to lift your skirt," Omri said in a subdued tone. "If a man doesn't break this silence with a jest, it'll madden him."

Barak gestured at a cache he'd spotted to the side of the burned house, a great pit dug into the ground, likely walled with stone, concealed now beneath a great wooden cover. "Break open that cache, Omri. May be supplies we can use. Supplies this town won't need." He cast a grim look at the burned house.

The Zebulunite walked his horse toward the cache, grumbling beneath his breath. Omri had challenged Barak for the leadership of the camp while the men were still gathering, days ago. Barak had bested him; now it seemed Omri wanted to show Barak he was still a man. But Barak had no time for this. He stepped beside Devora quickly and growled, "Don't entice him, woman. I'll not have the two of you bring shame on my camp."

Devora flushed dark with anger. "*You think*—"

"You must have glanced at him," Barak muttered irritably.

Devora hissed through her teeth, but Barak was already moving, mounting Ager. Stroking the horse's neck to calm him, he nudged Ager into a trot around the corner of the broken house toward that cache. Even as he did, Omri pried beneath the lid with his spear and levered it up, then tipped it over. That great cedar lid fell back and slammed down against the earth, a sound that echoed up the street between the empty houses, revealing a great hole in the ground. A sickly-sweet stench rolled out, and Barak gagged a moment, cursing silently in his heart. Fool townsmen had stored *meat* in there. But it had gone bad; surely they'd *salted* it, at least. He'd hoped desperately to find vats of grain, unfouled grain.

"Whoa," Barak murmured to his horse, which was shying nervously at the reek. The animal whickered and stood breathing hard. Barak leaned down over its neck. "Good, good," he whispered in his horse's ear.

"*Navi.*" Zadok's voice was urgent.

Barak glanced over his shoulder at the nazarite and the *navi*, saw Devora's eyes widen. A small figure was climbing up narrow steps out of the cache, a silhouette against the shadows. A dull sheen of eyes in the moonlight. Several other shapes were coming up the steps after it. Lifting its foot from the last step, the first moved out of the cache and staggered across the trampled earth toward them. It was small—stood no taller than Devora's belly. Some of the others climbing out behind it were even smaller.

Children.

These were children.

He took a breath. Something unsettled him, but he felt a flood of relief that drowned any uneasiness. Children. The promise of the Covenant, that the People would live and thrive and fill the land, no matter what came. A rush of faith into his heart such as he had not felt since he was a small child, sitting at his grandfather's knee hearing stories of their People's escape from the brick pits of Kemet and their taking of the land. This was surely a mighty sign. During the raids a few years ago from the fortified settlements on the coast, it had been common enough for encampments to hide their children in pits or caches concealed beneath thick brush, to be retrieved later once the threat was past. This town had been eaten by the dead, and perhaps its last men and women had fled into the hills with the dead close behind, after first ensuring their children's safety in that cache.

"Children!" he called to them, the joy in him nearly choking his voice.

At the sound of his voice, the children—so *many*, climbing out of the cache—lifted their arms in the dark. And with a shock, Barak knew that something was wrong. Badly wrong.

Those dull, glinting eyes.

High, wavering moans as the children lurched out into the street.

Devora let out a wordless, anguished cry, and Hurriya made a small, choked noise. The *navi*'s cry fell upon Barak's heart like the stone that triggers a landslide. He lurched into motion, wheeling his horse about. "Back!" he called hoarsely. "Fall back!"

Zadok swore and lifted his spear, moving his horse between the *navi* and the advancing children. Devora just sat her horse, gazing at the children with a horror as though she were watching the entire land burn. The children were lurching toward her horse; in a moment, they would close about Zadok's horse and hers like a tide about a rock.

"*Navi!*" Barak's voice was too high, like a child's. "Ride! Ride!"

She didn't move.

Omri too sat his horse as though frozen.

Zadok let out a battle shout and sent his horse into the dead, laying about with his spear, using it more as a staff then an impaling weapon, knocking the small corpses from their feet with the force of it. It took them a moment to get back up, and Zadok wheeled his horse, spinning his mighty staff as easily as he might a child's toy. But there were too many. Their moans filled the air, drowning out all thought and hope.

Barak saw two small girls lurch past the nazarite, toward the *navi*'s horse—he could almost hear words in their moans. He was certain—he could almost hear words. The moans tore at his mind. Barak screamed and drove his own gelding between the *navi* and the children. His heart beat, cold sweat stung his eyes; he lifted his spear but froze, those tiny, glinting eyes gazing up at him; he didn't know what to do. Children. Children of the People. He couldn't spear children of the People.

A hand grasped his calf, closing about the bronze greave, the fingertips digging into the exposed skin at the back and pulling. Panting, Barak of Israel gazed down into a hissing, livid face, a face gashed and darkened with dried blood, the eyes scratched and unseeing though fixed in the direction of his thigh. The thing that had been a small girl hissed like an asp, its teeth stark in the night, gums drawn back.

"El," he gasped. "El, El, El—" The name of God, over and over and over, like a child's syllable chanted against some groping terror in the dark. He couldn't move; he felt the tug on his leg, so strong. The face bending toward his calf, even as the other girl reached and took his foot. Other children—such small, small beings—staggered against his horse, their little hands reaching up at him. The animal trembled violently, its back rippling beneath Barak, but it was well trained. This horse had carried him in a charge against raiders from the coast. The horse shook as with fever but did not bolt.

Devora's high voice startled him from his paralysis.

"Run, girl! Move! Now!"

Hurriya slid from the saddle and fled, stumbling, for the far side of the ruined house.

Then Devora cried out in a screaming ululation that rose in pitch like a shriek of steel, then fell into words, a battle song, old Hebrew, the dialect of their grandfathers in the desert, when every hand, living and dead, had been raised against their tribes. Devora rode at the children. Her white horse slammed bodily into the crowd of dead, beating aside the small bodies with his great flanks; in a moment the *navi* was at Barak's side, her face stern, her eyes cold fire, her hand white about the hilt of that iron blade; her arm swept down, and the weapon scythed through small bodies, cutting away arms, shearing flesh and bone. The girls fell away from Barak's horse, cut open, hands and arms severed from them—but even as they fell beneath Shomar's hooves, there was no blood. There were no screams. Only those keening moans of hunger all about them.

Then Devora had ridden past, taking her wide-eyed gelding in a wide circle through the street, her blade slashing and cutting. Zadok fought his way to her side, and the two rode together, spear and blade. Even as Barak shook away his panic and hefted his own bronze spear again in his hand, he saw the two girls lurch back to their feet near his steed. Their arms were gone; one's chest had been crushed by the hooves. Yet their dull eyes were fixed on him; their mouths gaped in wordless hissing. The stench of them was vile, worse by far now that their bodies had been carved open. They were unclean. They were reaching for him.

With a shout, Barak lunged to the side, driving the spear into one child's brow. The small, decaying body went limp, but the spearhead had caught in its skull and could not be pulled free; the child's corpse hung as a dead weight on the end of the spear, nearly pulling Barak from his horse as the girl's knees buckled. The other came at him, and Barak drove his sandal hard into its face, driving it back a few lurching steps as he fought to pull his spear free. He was drenched in cold sweat; his heart hammered within him.

Devora's song rose into those high, desert wails, then fell again and again into words, as she rode among the dead. Numbly Barak lifted his eyes to her, saw her bound hair shining in the moonlight, her sword an arc of white in the air, never still. Behind her galloping horse, a trail of bodies, shattered and reeking. A few staggered to their feet or crawled along the ground after her; the rest were still, their heads carved open in terrible wounds. Zadok had ridden now to the edge of the cache, was spearing the corpses as they stepped out. Omri had joined him there and lent his spear to the fight, though he looked ready to be violently ill.

The body by Barak's horse hissed, and with a curse the chieftain plucked out his knife and drove it hard into the thing's forehead. He shuddered as it twitched and went still, sliding off the blade and dropping to the earth, on its back. Panting, he gazed down at it in cold horror. It was a girl. Just a small girl. It still wore the dirtied remains of a woolen dress; the cloth had been torn away from its right shoulder, baring a breast as flat as a tablet of stone. Barak ducked his head to the side and vomited, his midday meal rushing up his throat in a steaming flood. He choked and coughed, drew the back of his hand across his lips. His other hand gripped the haft of his spear, rigidly, a child's body still impaled on the bronze head.

Barak the vintner, war-leader of the northern tribes, sat his horse shaking. He drew from his saddlebag the shofar Laban had brought to him when he first formed the camp. The ram's horn Othniel himself had blown when he fought the first raiders from the sea, when Barak had been just a boy. Now Barak lifted the shofar to his lips and blew a long blast. He needed his men. He needed God. He needed someone, anyone, to share with him the terrible responsibility of fighting these walking corpses that had once been breathing, laughing children. The call of the horn echoed through the town.

THE OLAH

THE CHILDREN tried helplessly to reach up and grasp at Devora's feet as she rode through them. They strove to catch her, to pull her from her horse, but their small bodies were no match for either the strength or speed of the gelding Lappidoth had given her—or the savage reach of the *navi*'s blade. Behind her by the cache, Zadok and Omri jabbed their spears downward again and again, like Canaanites on the lake spearing fish. The light from Omri's torch shone on the hissing faces.

A few moments more and it was done. Devora turned and cantered back, taking out the few that were still staggering or crawling along the ground. The blade cut through scalp, skull, and brain. In the end, there was only a street filled with bodies, strewn across the packed dirt from where Barak's steed stood shying to the open cache.

She rode to the cache and glanced down the steps into it. Small bones lay scattered at the bottom. Bones of children. Bones picked clean and cracked open for the marrow. In the deaths of so many children of her People, whether mixed with heathen or no, Devora could see the death of the Covenant. She could see the touch of the *malakh ha-mavet*, as though its mighty wing had swept over the town and all those touched by its shadow had died, regardless of promises made or promises kept or promises broken.

She made a high-pitched, furious sound like a beast discovering a trap about its paw, then rode back. None of the children lifted themselves from the begrimed earth to challenge her. Beside her, Zadok dismounted and left the cache and walked slowly among the bodies, making sure each of them had been speared or cut through the head, making sure all were still.

Hurriya made a choked sound from where she watched from the corner of the charred house. Her eyes were round and dark in the dim light. Omri walked his horse away from the cache. For once he did not even look at the women. He had eyes only for the bodies in the street.

Barak still sat his horse in the middle of the street, in shock, the shofar now held in one limp hand. Devora cantered toward him until she was near enough to address him without lifting her voice.

"Do not hesitate again, chieftain of Israel." Devora's voice was a shard of winter. "These were not children. These are the dead. Look at their eyes, not their bodies. Whether they wear a levite's white or a young girl's sash, whether their face is that of a spearman or an infant, the eyes of the dead hold nothing. They are only bodies to bury." She kept Mishpat carefully extended, though it tired her arm—for the blade was spattered with unclean gore. "Did any of them touch your naked skin?"

The look Barak gave her was distant, distracted, and her heart skipped a beat. "Barak?" she asked harshly.

"No," he said after a brief hesitation. "None."

"Are you sure?"

"They touched only my greave," he said hoarsely.

She held his eyes a moment, then accepted this as the truth and looked back at the stillness in the street, the unholy stillness. She could not think about what she had seen and done; there were judgments to make. "Before you enter the camp, you must cut a strip from your cloak, Barak ben Abinoam, and wrap that wool about your fingers. Then pluck away the greave and cast both bronze and wool to the earth. Do not touch the bronze with your hand. In this way, you can enter the camp clean and under no judgment."

"It will be as you say, *navi*." He seemed hardly to hear her; his voice was a croak.

She turned from him, holding back her own dread. What had happened this night would rattle any man. Barak seemed frozen with horror now, almost like Zadok had often been, though his eyes flicked from the left to the right; he did not seem unaware of the bodies at his feet or the charred house before him. Dismissing him from her mind, Devora began walking Shomar away.

Omri rode up alongside her, still clutching his guttering torch, his eyes round with fear and wonder. "That blade," he said.

"Yes, I can wield it," Devora said sharply. She had no patience right now for the man.

"It—it really *is* iron," Omri breathed. His gaze was fixed on the *navi*, as though wondering if she too were made of some strange, foreign substance of which other women were not. Devora ignored him and walked her horse back down the street. Shomar stepped nervously over the corpses, and the *navi* caressed his neck softly, whispering in his ear. She met Zadok's eyes as she passed him; the nazarite straightened and gave a weary nod. It was done, then. The nazarite drew his knife and cut his hand grimly, then sheathed the knife.

She led Shomar to the corner of the burned house and glanced down at Hurriya, who was shaking. After a moment Devora dismounted to stand before the shuddering girl. The girl's horror pulled at her heart.

"Close your eyes," Devora said softly.

Hurriya gave a small shake of her head. She stared at the children in the street.

Devora took a saddlecloth and pressed the cloth to the young woman's eyes. "No, girl," she said. "There is no ruined house, no town. You are in the olive grove, and there are no dead. You are watching your sister play in the branches."

"The town," Hurriya whispered, without trying to remove the cloth. "The whole settlement. Like my child."

"No." Devora glanced at the dark hole of the cache. Her body felt cold, everything inside her was cold. "Not the *whole* town. They probably locked the children in to keep them safe, then lured the dead away, all that they could. They must have meant to circle back."

"Only they haven't," Hurriya whispered. "They haven't circled back."

Devora was distracted from answering by the sound of hoofbeats. She glanced over her shoulder. The other men were riding down the street toward them, summoned by the sound of the shofar. Laban rode at their head with that massive axe of his ready in his hand, held as lightly as though it were only a hatchet. They stopped near Barak, looking down at the shattered corpses, their faces stricken.

"It is all right," the *navi* called, raising her voice in a shout. "There were dead in the cache, but—"

The door of the nearest house across the street jolted hard in its hinges, then shuddered again, a sound as of bodies thrusting against it from within. Devora swung to face the door, her face white with shock.

The dead. Roused perhaps by Devora's battle song or by the shofar to stumble about within the house, looking for the living. Perhaps they had been on the second floor and had finally tumbled below. Now, alerted by Devora's shout to the direction in which they could find her, they had thrown themselves against the door.

"Spears!" Barak rasped. He dismounted and tugged his own spear free, and several of his men left their horses and ran up, one with a spear like Barak's, the others with poles or rakes or whatever they'd improvised along the journey.

"Break the door," Barak gasped, unable to find enough breath to make the order any louder. "Let it out where we can slay it."

The men were as pale as he. Devora heard the breaking of cedar, the sharp crack of the door coming apart; the door splintered and wrenched aside, and dead lurched out into the street, their teeth bared. Their arms reaching for warm flesh. Barak's men were between her and the corpses, and they shoved their spears hard into the corpses' bellies and thighs, pushing them back by brute force. But the dead still groped for them and moaned, not heeding the wounds.

"Their heads!" she cried. "Strike them between the eyes! Between the eyes, men of Israel!"

As if wakened by her cry, Barak surged into action, leaping forward and driving the bronze point of his spear into one skull, driving it in by the ear, the flesh parting at the metal's touch like a rotting apricot.

Devora moved toward the house, but Zadok stepped near and took her arm in a firm grip, peering into her face. "*Navi?*"

"There are dead in the houses," she said numbly.

Her hand tightened about Mishpat's hilt, and she tried again to step toward the door, but Zadok thrust her behind him with one powerful arm. One of the dead had pushed a pole aside and now grasped one of Barak's men by the shoulder, pulling him toward its jaws. Zadok's spear drove into its open mouth, and he lifted the corpse free of the door; it jerked helplessly in the air, impaled and writhing with the cold metal driven into its throat.

Devora gasped as Zadok spun, his spear sweeping through the air. The incredible strength of the man! The corpse came loose and was flung through the air, slamming into the ground. A snap of bone. The corpse got to its feet, one arm limp at its side, and lurched toward them again. Others were still pushing out at the door, being barred only by the long-shafted weapons and the desperate strength of the men. Those men were ashen-faced, panicked, screaming as they held the dead back, the long fingers of the dead catching at their hair, their cheeks, their arms. One man was pulled in close, and a hissing corpse bit down on his ear and tore it away with a long strip of tissue and flesh.

She saw Barak leap away from the door, screaming orders. While Zadok and Laban and a few men held the dead back at the door, four others ran with Barak to the cache and wrenched its massive lid up from the ground. They brought it swiftly to the house and pressed the wooden lid against the door, pushing the dead back into the house by sheer might and barricading the door with it, holding it in place with their own living bodies. The massive lid shook as the dead pounded against it from within.

The house had two stories, one window for each; the lower window was barred with wood, but now Devora could see gray, half-eaten hands reaching through cracks in the wood, some of them missing fingers, tearing chunks of wood free, ripping away the covering over the window. Devora lifted Mishpat and stepped near even as the wood slats came away and a corpse's face appeared at the window, pale against the darkness behind it. The left side of its face that of a young woman, the right side eaten away almost to the bone. It hissed at her, and Devora thrust Mishpat at it, cutting across its cheek. The corpse fell back from the window into the darkness of the house; she could hear it hissing and spitting.

The men at the door were screaming, Barak roaring louder than any. The door was rattling.

There was a cracking of wood above her; she glanced up, caught the glimpse of another torn and half-chewed face gazing down at her out of the dark frame of the second-story window; then the thing was coming through, climbing out. It toppled and fell toward her with a slow and terrible grace, as though falling through dark milk instead of air. Devora screamed, then something else slammed into her side, knocking the breath from her. She sprawled in the dirt, glanced up, wheezing. Saw Zadok ben Zefanyah standing over her, his eyes cold as though there had never been warmth in the world. The corpse had fallen almost at his feet and was staggering upright when the nazarite drove his spear into its face. The point passed through the thing's skull and out above the base of its neck. Zadok pressed his boot to the body's shoulder and shoved it free of his spear; it fell back and crumpled to the earth as lightly as though it were only a heap of clothes.

"Get back, *navi*," Zadok growled. "Away from the houses. Into the market. These are for me to fight."

But now, as Devora looked about her, she saw the doors of the nearest houses bucking and shaking as well; there must be dead in most of the houses on this street, corpses locked inside. She could hear moans muffled behind the wood, and she shivered. She heard the clear, deep voice of the shofar lifted, louder than the wailing of the dead, louder than the slamming of their bodies against the doors. Barak had his shoulder pressed to the great lid, his other hand held the ram's horn to his lips. Living men came running through the market shops toward them, perhaps twenty, thirty men. As though the shofar had called them. But they were on foot and must have left the encampment moments after Omri and Laban did, and then taken this long to reach their chieftains who'd ridden in on horseback.

Devora backed up and stood in the midst of the street with Mishpat gleaming in her hand. She saw the cracks appearing in wooden doors up and down the street. Whatever dead had waited concealed within, the battle and the voices outside their doors had stirred them. The lid that Barak and the men held to the first door leapt like a living thing, and one of the dead within forced its arm out. Then the corpses were pushing the men back, with a strength born of unstoppable hunger, a strength that would not give out, for the dead felt no fatigue, no hopelessness.

With a roar, Zadok threw himself hard against the door, lending his weight to that of the shorter men, and the lid slammed back into place so sharply that its edge severed the decayed arm. It fell to the ground and lay there like a piece God had discarded when shaping men at the beginning of time.

Another corpse began climbing out through the lower window, and Devora impaled its head on Mishpat. Breathing raggedly, she realized that the men could not contain the dead in these houses. More corpses would spill into the street at any moment. And though other men were now running to join them with staves and knives and makeshift spears, they would not be enough.

Omri had let his torch fall in the midst of the street when he had taken up the lid with Barak and the other men; the torch still lay there, blazing in the dirt. Now Hurriya ran from the corner of the burned house and took up the torch, panting as she staggered toward the house, toward where Devora stood at the window the dead had torn open. Realizing her intent with a shock, Devora leapt in her way, seized her arm, wrested the torch from her. "No!" the *navi* cried. "Not with fire! These were the *People!* Not with fire!"

The Canaanite tugged wildly to get her arm free, her eyes intense. "Let me go!" she cried. "We *have* to! This was my vision. What the gods meant me to see!"

Devora looked at her in horror, holding the torch away from her, out of her reach. The Canaanite woman's face was translated in revelation, in sudden, awestruck belief that the gods hadn't abandoned her, that the blessing or the burden they'd given her was more than just a caprice.

"We have to burn the houses," Hurriya shouted. "We have to burn them! As the people here did."

"No," Devora breathed. She glanced suddenly at the torch she held in her hand, at the flames. Words of the Covenant rang in her ears in the deep, calm voice of Eleazar ben Phinehas ben Eleazar ben Aharon:

> *The people must not be burned with fire*
> *not consumed with flame*
> *but buried beneath clean stone.*

And, faintly, the rasp of Eleazar's dying words: *Don't let the People be—eaten— or—or burned...*

"We have to!"

"We are *not* heathen," Devora cried.

Hurriya took her arm wildly, clutching her through the thick wool of her dress. Her eyes alight. "So you Hebrews have ways to keep the dead from rising. Your cairns, your graves, your Covenant. But the dead *have* risen, *navi.* And the people here have found ways to deal with them *then!*"

"It is a heathen way!"

"Yes!" Hurriya screamed. "Or we die!"

Suddenly Devora's own words from earlier that night were recalled to her mind as clearly as though spoken to her this very moment by God:

> *The navi brings men words they need to hear, visions they need to see, not visions they wish to see.*

Hurriya too was a *navi*, and she'd been given a vision of faces burning.

A man near her screamed, a shrill cry like a doe when a lion tears into its shoulder with his teeth. Devora looked up in time to see a corpse-gray arm wrapped around the man's breast and a ghastly head tearing flesh raw from the man's throat. For the briefest of breaths she met the walking corpse's eyes and saw nothing there; then the thing had pulled Barak's man through the window, and his legs were disappearing into the house. Devora leapt for him; her fingers brushed the bronze greave on his leg, then he was gone. Not even another scream. Just gone. She made her decision and with a shriek she thrust the torch through the window and dropped it there before springing back. Other gray faces filled the window, hands reaching out; men sprang past her on the right and on the left, their spears thrusting at the window, shoving the dead back, the way boatmen shove long poles against a riverbank. Then the dead faces were backlit by bright flame; something had caught within.

"Torches!" the *navi* cried. "More torches! Burn them! Burn the house!"

***

Men improvised torches using bits of wood from shattered doors or from whatever they could find, and Laban swung his torch from one to the next, lighting them. Hurriya retreated to lean against the wall of another house; she took a crumpled leaf—all this time she'd clutched the herbs in her hand—and began chewing on it. She was very pale.

Devora didn't watch either the men or the Canaanite; she had eyes only for the burning house, her face twisted in grief. In this place where she could not tell if the living or the dead were Hebrew or heathen, where the *mitzvot* were hardly kept, where no tithes were sent to Shiloh nor any young men or young women sent to the Feast of Tents, the Covenant had been hacked through and shredded, as though a mad harvester had attacked the crop of the People with a sickle before the crop was ripe. And now she had hacked through the Covenant herself, burning bodies rather than burying them. Yet what else could she decide? The Covenant demanded that she keep the People safe from the dead, keep the land clean—yet the land was now so defiled that sword and clean stone were not enough to mend it. Only fire could cleanse the unclean death from this town.

Dark smoke poured from the upper window and then flame, licking its way up toward the roof, hungrier even than the dead. The sight of it seared her mind. A burning, an atrocity, this smoke they were sending into God's sky, the sharp scent of meat burning. Like a perverse, horrible *olah*, a burnt offering, an atonement for the breaking of Covenant, an atonement for their failure to keep the land clean and undefiled. But this *olah* must surely reek in God's nostrils, must surely make their God vomit and heave in revulsion at what was happening in the land he dwelled in.

Then the men were lighting the house to the left, and Devora could hear the moans of the dead within. The dry cedar cracked and sang its fierce death song as the fire spread faster than tears or prayer. The roof of the first house cracked open with a clap of thunder, then crumpled inward, and the moans within fell silent, buried beneath the broken timbers that crushed them down and covered them like a cairn of wood and charcoal rather than stone.

Devora spun in a slow circle, taking in the gray, filthy ash drifting down from the blazing rooftops, dark against the firelit air. Some of it fell on her arm and burned her, and she cried out, not knowing whether the ash had come from a burning bed or from one of the bodies of the People. She gazed in horror at the sky, dark with smoke.

"*El!*" she shrieked. "*Elohim! Adonai!*" Anguish tore at her, stripping pieces away from her mind. She screamed for her God. Begged for his mighty hand to return and cover this town and the land.

The ash fell from the sky. More of it now. Everywhere the cracking of roofs and walls giving away. The shouts of desperate men, the low moaning of the dead who did not feel any pain of fire or spear but only the pain of being unable to feed, unable to fill their hunger.

The smoke spread out above them, unfurling across the sky like dark wings, like the *malakh ha-mavet*.

Devora stopped screaming, her throat hoarse and on fire. Barak was gripping her arm and shouting something, but she could not hear him. Then, after a long moment, sound returned to her world, and she heard the fire and the rattling of doors up and down the street, other dead trying to get out, trying to get at them. The sound clasped her heart in a cold grip.

"Burn everything!" she hissed. "Burn it all!"

Then she shook Barak away and ran, her feet pounding over the ground, the ash still drifting down. She reached up and beat it from her hair. She glimpsed Shomar turning in circles in the street, terrified but unsure where to bolt. She cried his name, ran to him, seized his mane and sprang to his back.

Even as she mounted, she heard a scream that came to her ears piercing above all the rest. Hurriya!

Devora saw where the dead had broken free of one of the houses and were stepping over the body of a fallen man. Hurriya had taken up the man's spear in both her hands and was stabbing at the dead. She speared one in the brow and the corpse dropped to its knees, but before the young woman could pull the spear free, another of the corpses grabbed the haft and used it to pull Hurriya close. With a cry, Devora sent Shomar galloping toward her, the smoke stinging her eyes. Leaning from her saddle, one hand wrapped in Shomar's mane, Devora caught up Hurriya in her arm and with a desperate strength that would have shocked her on any other night than this, in any other place, she pulled Hurriya up into the saddle before her. The spear was ripped from the Canaanite's hands and left in the grip of the dead. "I'm getting you out of here!" she cried in the girl's ear, and Hurriya clung wildly to the horse's neck.

"Run, Shomar! Run!" Devora cried, digging her knees in hard. The horse leapt beneath her with a ferocity like something being born. Dead moaned behind her, and dead spilled from a shattered door into the street before her, and Shomar rode them down, permitting the Hebrew and the Canaanite only the briefest glimpse of their sightless, ravenous faces, the white of cheekbones through torn and missing flesh. Then they were riding out of the town, Hurriya bent low over Shomar's neck, her hair in Devora's face. Hurriya kept sobbing, "They took my baby, they took my baby—" The *navi*'s heart pounded as she urged Shomar quickly out along the shore of the lake, everything in her tight and desperate and ready to unravel in grief. Her nostrils seared with the scent of flame and smoke and decay.

IN THE SILENCE OF GOD

DEVORA DID NOT let Shomar slacken his pace until they had ridden some distance across the shingle. Then she halted and gazed out over the water, her heart still racing. The town burned behind them, and Devora could hear the distant crack of wood beams breaking in the flames and the shouts of living men. There were no longer any moans from the dead.

Suddenly she couldn't hold it in any longer—the doubt, the anguish, the fury at what she had done and at God for letting it be necessary.

"*God!*" she screamed.

Hurriya tensed in her arms.

"*Ata adonai!*" Devora's rage and despair echoed across the water. The reflected firelight on the lake was strangely beautiful.

"Where are you?" she screamed. "This—this burning—is not an answer to our need! *It's not an answer!*"

Hurriya whispered, "The dead will hear!"

"*Let* them hear," the *navi* snapped.

She urged Shomar back to a canter, heard the splash of water under his hooves as he bore them along the shore. She was riding away from the town and away from the camp, out into the dark and the silence. She could not bear to see the *malakh* spreading across the sky, hiding God's stars with its dark wings. She could smell the smoke in her hair.

"None of the gods are listening," Hurriya said.

"God *is* here," Devora cried. "He is *still* here. He is still covering us. He sends you visions." Lifting her voice, she shouted across the water, "Send *me* a vision! Send *me!*"

"What if he doesn't?" Hurriya said, her voice brittle with pain. "What then? Will you crawl back to Shiloh?"

Devora brought Shomar to a halt again, sat breathing hard on his back, felt the horse's sides moving as he breathed between her legs. Something soft and powdery touched her face, and she looked up in the dark and realized flakes of ash were falling, even here. She shuddered.

The town behind them was not only silent, it was dead. And she could do nothing, had done nothing. She had barely ridden from the burning houses with the one other life her horse had carried into the town. She had saved no one but Hurriya.

Vividly she heard Naomi's words in her heart—*Some days a woman can only save one life*—but those words seemed empty to her, a riddle without an answer or without any answer she could bear.

"There were children," Devora whispered.

No visions came to her over the water. No answer.

Hurriya was gazing back at the fire far behind them. She was shaking more violently now, and Devora could feel the heat from her body, a heat that was not one of vision.

"Chew your leaves, girl," the *navi* muttered.

"I lost them."

Devora's heart sank. Perhaps the leaf the girl had been chewing before the dead attacked would be enough to calm her fever for a while. But she didn't know; she was no midwife or herbalist. They would have to get more. At that, Devora's momentary fury flickered out, and exhaustion fell over her like a collapsed tent. She slumped a little. She felt old.

"Those houses," the girl murmured. "Those houses full of dead. The people—they couldn't bear to kill the sick. They couldn't do it. So they locked the sick into the houses on that street. Trusting the doors to hold. That's what happened. I can see it. No vision, but I can see it."

"A corpse is stronger than a living person," Devora said wearily. "They don't hold back. They don't hesitate. They don't doubt. They don't care if they destroy their bodies to break a door. They just kill and eat. The People, who are living, are capable of restraint. Of weighing choices and consequences. Of judgment. The dead are not." She glanced at Hurriya. "To be without restraint, to be without *Law*, is to be like one of the dead. Without the Law to hold you back, you may break a door, you may shatter some obstacle, but you will break yourself too."

"They couldn't let their dead go," Hurriya rasped, as though she hadn't heard. "You can't either. You aren't grieving for the dead, you're screaming out your guilt to them. That's what was in your voice, when it echoed over the water. You want your God to give you a vision of the next day, or the next, but you're gazing at the past. Ever since you took me from Shiloh. You're gazing at the past, and so no visions come to you."

The words shook her. Only Lappidoth had ever touched that bruised part of her heart, and he had never done so with words. No one else had ever seen this in her—her guilt, the sense of crushing responsibility, the conviction of all those she'd failed. Zadok's pain. Her mother's death and, later, Naomi's. The many deaths in that burning town. All of them her burdens to bear—and only holding herself and her People strictly to the Law had kept their weight bearable.

Until now. Glancing up at the smoke that had taken the stars from her—taken even that visible sign of God's presence and God's promises—she felt as though even the Law, even the Covenant, had been stripped away, like the roof of a tent torn aside in the wind of a violent storm. She had torn some of it away herself, turning the bodies of the People into ash and dust.

"You can't carry the dead with you," Hurriya whispered out of the dark, and her voice was that of a feverish, suffering woman with a heathen accent. But her voice was also that of the *navi*, speaking of things she and God had seen that for others remained unseen. "You can't. If you can't take some part of them back into your heart as sustenance, take joy in having known them—if you can't hum a sleep-song to them or talk to them quietly in the evening—if they cannot sustain and nourish you in the water you drink and the fish you eat, then you have to at least do it the Hebrew way. You cannot bear them; you have to bury them."

Devora knew Hurriya was right. The dead from her past were like corpses she'd hefted onto her shoulders and now struggled beneath, carrying them in search of a cairn rather than laying them down and going to gather stones. But she did not know how to gather stones for the dead whose presence she felt within her. She didn't know how. She gazed out over the water and wondered if God too was watching the reflection of the flames on the lake.

"If God is silent," she said, "I will act as though he is not. When God sends no visions, when we don't know if he is with us or if we are left to die in the ash among the corpses, we must still act as though his hand *does* cover us. Our responsibilities are unchanged. Nothing else will suffice." Under her breath she added, "*I* will not demand assurances."

She guided Shomar back toward the fire and the distant settlement and, farther along the shore, the tents of the northern men. In the firelight, she glanced at Hurriya's face and gave a start.

Hurriya's cheeks glistened with silent tears.

Devora felt a pang of remorse. The girl was exhausted. Shomar, huffing softly in the dark, was exhausted too. This was no time to be riding along the shore in the dark, fleeing her night terrors. She put her arm about the girl's waist and pulled her back against her breast, holding her tightly. "Shh," the *navi* whispered.

"Further north," Hurriya whispered back. "I have to get further north. I have to find Anath. I have to find her."

No Survivors

THE RISING SUN found Barak walking with the other war-leaders through a strange land of falling ash and ash underfoot and ash in the air they breathed. Omri and Laban spoke in low tones about what to do next, where to lead the men, where to seek the dead, but Barak walked in grim silence. He could not stop thinking about the hours of flame and heat and sweat. His men had worked right there amid the flames, shoving the flaming dead back into the houses, fighting to contain them as they burned and withered.

Those *faces*, melting in the flames. Hissing and snapping their jaws even as they burned.

"How many men died last night?" he whispered.

The others fell silent.

"Five of mine," Omri muttered after a moment. "And eight others."

"Mordecai ben Enoch was dragged into the fire." Laban turned and looked back up the street. "He was a strong man, and he killed twelve of the Sea Coast raiders when they came through the Galilee. Four wives will be watching at the window of his house, but he won't come home to them."

Thirteen. Thirteen men.

"And how many unclean?" he said.

"Eight men bitten and lived," Omri said.

"Show me," Barak said.

Omri and Laban exchanged a look.

"I know," Barak growled. "Show me."

***

The eight knelt in a line in the street where the children had died, with two armed men standing guard behind them. As Barak approached with the other chieftains, he saw the *navi* moving along the line with slow but unfaltering steps, with that wild blade unsheathed and held out to the side. The nazarite, for once, was not at her side. Devora's face was grimmer than Barak had ever seen a woman's face before, and she stood straighter and fiercer than any woman he'd known, her posture one of uncompromising duty; she might almost have been a man.

"Is it right that a woman should do this?" Omri muttered.

Barak held up his hand, and the Zebulunite fell silent, though his body was rigid with tension.

Some of the eight knelt in the ash between the tall houses of their own free will. Three were feverish and trembled where they knelt, one of them barely conscious. Four had been bound, their wrists lashed together and then secured with short cords to their tied ankles. One had struggled until he'd toppled to his side, and one of the men assigned to guard them had moved to him quickly and, gripping his arm with a gloved hand, pulled him back to his knees. "You shame your kin," the guard hissed in his ear before stepping back.

As the *navi* stopped before each of the kneeling men, she asked the man's name, repeated it after him, and then met his eyes with hers. "You fought to defend the People," she said. "The Words of Going will be sung for you."

A few of them thanked her. One did not look at her, and she placed the tip of her blade beneath his chin, gently lifting his face until he did. Barak saw that she was careful not to touch any of the men, though she stood near them. She did not shrink away or scream. She did not do anything he might expect a woman to. Her face remained hard as stone.

With each man, once she had heard his name, the *navi* lifted Mishpat and the blade swept down through the air with a sound like a bird's wing. When the ash at her feet was soaked dark, she stepped away and stood before the next of the men.

One of the Hebrews down the line wept, but none of them screamed as the sword fell. Not one. There had been screaming enough during the night. Perhaps they had screamed so much that they had lost the ability to, like singing until you're hoarse. Or perhaps the horror of what could await them was greater than the horror of the swift, delicate blade.

Looking on, Barak shivered and felt again the touch of the dead on his leg. In the hour before dawn, Barak's pavilion had been moved near the edge of the town, and he had gone to it once he could hear no more moans of the dead. He'd cast aside his spear and fallen to his knees inside his tent the moment the flap fell back, plunging him into a warm, comfortable darkness that was utterly different from the cold night within the town. The floor of his tent was spread with rugs of Canaanite design, many of them woven even here in Walls, others to the north in Judges' Well; he felt the weave of them against his knees. He'd fallen to his face, pressing his brow to the rugs, moaning, praying, begging, though he didn't know for what. He could not rid himself of the sight—in his mind—of that little girl impaled on his spear.

With a groan he'd rolled to his side and lifted his knee to his chest, his hands feeling quickly along the skin of his leg. There was no bite there, no scratch or wound. But his skin felt to him like ice. Like dead skin. He breathed raggedly through his teeth, exploring his calf with his fingers. He kept moving his fingers up and down along his skin, gasping for air. He was alive. He was alive, but they had *touched* him. Those things—those corpses—unclean corpses—they'd touched him. He squeezed his eyes shut against the sudden rush of tears. "Make me clean," he moaned, "make me clean."

He wanted then the wine of his vineyard, not to drink but to wash his leg, even as he might wash out a wound. He had clutched at his leg, breathing hard, trying to grapple with what had happened this night. The silent town. The children. The dead girl's touch. He felt almost as though he were in the grip of a fever; he shook and twisted on the rugs. Called out once for his wife. Hadassah, whom God had taken. As God had now taken an entire town. An entire *town* of the People.

***

Now, as Barak ben Abinoam stood watching the holy woman take the lives of eight of his men, his leg remained ice cold and the ashes on the ground warm against his sandalled feet. He lifted his eyes and gazed bleakly at the burned-out husks of what had once been great houses of cedar. He had known this town; he'd met Hadassah here. Now everything here was unfamiliar to him. He did not know how to act, what to decide, what traditions either of his People's or his wife's might apply. He had burned her mother's gods that the God of his own fathers might keep his crop and his land safe and unstrange to him. But everywhere he turned, he saw all that should have been safe now contorted and burned.

At last the *navi* finished her dread work. As Barak watched her she glanced up, and for a moment their eyes met. Hers were cold as the lake. Barak looked away. When he lifted his gaze again, the *navi* was already a long way up the street, leaving the dead. The two men who'd guarded the bitten now stood by their bodies, which lay like bundles of clothes on the ash-covered ground. Looking more like some child's joke than the bodies of dead men.

Omri and Laban stood silent beside him. He could sense their horror. There were no words for this, there had never been and never would be. The bodies lay very still. A little way beyond them, Barak could see the crumpled corpses of last night's children, all of them covered with a fine layer of white ash so that they no longer looked like the bodies of the dead but like the monuments of Kemet where their fathers' fathers had toiled to make brick. But the statues in Kemet were said to be forms of beauty, while these statues of ash were the forms of children that appeared as though they'd died in terrible torture. Chewed and bitten, some with their bellies eaten. Their scalps cloven by an iron blade. Their faces distorted, frozen for all time in expressions of abominable and unanswerable hunger. Suddenly and for the first time, Barak was grateful that his seed had borne no lasting fruit in his wife Hadassah's body. Had it done so, he might have had to see his own flesh become one of— one of *these*. He was a man of the north; he had survived blight and bad harvests and raids from the coast. He had survived many things. He did not know if he could survive that.

"How did this happen?" Omri whispered. He had his face averted, as though he could not look directly on the bodies.

"The *navi* may know," Laban rumbled.

Barak shook his head. He did not need a *navi*'s vision or any words whispered out of the dark by God to guess. "The men of Walls concealed them in the cache," he said quietly, "then most of them left. They must have hoped to draw away the dead, lead them away from their children."

"But we found the dead here," Omri said.

"Only some—those that died in their houses, perhaps even after the others left, the living who had no fever and could still walk. They locked all the houses, and they closed up this cache. All we've found are the men and women they left behind. The unclean ones."

Omri looked pale.

"We only found one of the dead that wasn't in a house. That one must have burst out somehow—something drew its attention before we even came here. It was—feeding." Barak swallowed uneasily. "Maybe someone came to the town before we did. One of the men coming home perhaps. Or someone from another village visiting kin."

"*Elohi*," Laban breathed.

Barak lifted his eyes toward the stark, surrounding hills. The groaning dead who were in the streets of Walls must have groped their way over the stones and up the slopes after the settlement's men and women, pursuing them with a hunger that would never rest, never halt. It had been a good plan, whoever among the men and women of this town had devised it, when they realized there were too many dead to burn. But for the children, it had been too late. Maybe one of the children, or several, had been bitten, had become unclean. Had fallen and lain still and then risen and sought to devour the others. Secured in the cache with their small flasks of water, waiting for their parents to return bringing safety and food, the children had no way to flee or hide from an enemy that was locked inside with them. Those who were not entirely eaten had succumbed and risen also, until the entire cache was just filled with those small bodies with sightless, waiting eyes, silent in their decay.

Had the parents returned, they might in their despair have been devoured by their own children when they lifted the cover at last from the cache and reached down to pull them out.

But the parents hadn't returned.

"How long has the town been silent?" Laban said quietly.

Barak shook his head. Long enough, certainly, for the ashes of the houses the townspeople had burned to grow cold, the smoldering of embers to cease. Long enough for all the bodies of the children in the cache to stir. A day? Several? He wondered if any of their parents still breathed. The men of Walls might have had spears to fight with, but Walls had not suffered a raid since the coming of the Hebrews to the land, and those spears had likely only been wielded against the fish in the lake since the time of their grandfathers. And they would have had women with them, and old men. What chance could they have had, fleeing the dead on those slopes?

A cold, choking guilt settled in his throat to match the cold touch on his calf and the cold fear in his belly. He had arrived too late for this town.

Barak turned and began striding back toward the tents. Omri and Laban followed. "We will build cairns over each body," he growled as he walked. "Even the burned ones. Dig them out of the ashes if you have to."

"Are you serious?" Omri exclaimed.

"I am, and you do not want to argue with me, Omri of Zebulun. I am not in an arguing mood."

"But *every* body—there must be dozens—"

"At least. See that it's done. Laban, will you make sure none are missed?"

"If you ask it," the somber giant said carefully.

Barak gave him a brief, grateful look. "I do ask it."

"Do you have *any* idea how long that will take?" Omri snarled.

"It is what the *navi* would wish."

"Since when does the *navi* command the spears?"

Barak turned on him, and his face was lit with such wrath that Omri fell back a step. "The Covenant says to build cairns, we will build cairns!" He was shouting. "Look around you, you fool. Do you want to question God's ways in this field of ash?" He glanced at Laban. "We will not leave one body unburied! I want none of them left! Am I clear?"

"You are," Laban murmured. Omri merely gazed at him in shock.

"Gather stones!" Barak shouted. Spun and strode back up the street. Enough of this ash and smoke.

***

Zadok stood still as a cairn himself amid the ashes and fallen timbers, his spear fallen at his feet. Devora approached wearily until she stood at his side. After a moment she set Mishpat aside near her feet. Straightening, she scrubbed at her face with her hands, trying to smudge away the dirt and ash. Then she just stood there. She watched his chest rise and fall. His eyes were dark pools that gave nothing back when she looked in them. All around them, men with gloves and rolls of tentcloth gathered bodies and shrouded them, bearing them to where Barak was having cairns raised on the shore of the lake. Sometimes the men cast looks at Zadok, and their faces held awe or bewilderment. Those who had seen him the night before had seen how he fought.

"Zadok ben Zefanyah," Devora said after a while. "I need you."

Devora reached for the small bronze knife Zadok wore sheathed at his hip. She tugged it free and reached for the nazarite's hand. Gently she opened his fingers and drew the blade across his palm, making a slit deep enough to bleed for a while. His breathing changed a moment later; it must have taken his body a moment to feel the pain. Then his head turned, and those dark eyes focused on her.

Devora placed the hilt of the knife in Zadok's hand, pressing it against the cut, then closed his enormous fingers around it. "If there was ever a man of our People who needed a wife to look after him," she said, "that man is you, Zadok. Why don't you have one?"

"I could not defend both Shiloh and a woman." His voice was deep and hoarse. Hearing it was a relief to her. "A day would come, *navi*, when I would have to break one covenant or the other."

She nodded and looked out over the ashen street. Saw the men bearing away the last bodies of children. It was too much; she felt as though she were drawing in death through her eyes, aging and crumbling away like ash as she watched. But she couldn't close her eyes; what waited in the dark behind her eyelids would be far worse.

"What do you see, Zadok? When you close your eyes."

He watched her for a moment. "They were in the tents." His eyes shone a moment, surprising her with their moisture. "I ran out to look for my father. They were everywhere. The stench—" He shook his head. "They were crouching over my father, four of them. Outside the Tent of Meeting. They were eating him. Behind them, Eleazar took up the shofar, blew the call. My father had saved his life. I tried to get his body away from the dead, tried to *fight* them—"

He fell silent.

"I'm sorry," Devora said.

"I failed him. Every time I face the dead, I fail him."

"No," Devora whispered. "Zefanyah would have been proud of you. You are the kind of man he would have liked. The kind he would've wanted at his side. I know this, Zadok."

He just looked bleakly out over the ash.

"I need you, Zadok," Devora said. The pleading in her voice did not shame her; she had to lean on someone, if only for a moment, or fall over. "I am barely holding it together. Those—children—" She swallowed. "I understand your suffering now. Why you stand still, the way you do. I encountered the dead as a girl, you as a boy. But since, you have gone out time and again to hunt them and raise cairns over them, whenever one has been seen in the land. Wherever Shiloh has sent you. How do you stay on your feet, Zadok? Tell me."

"I remember who I have to protect," Zadok said.

Devora laughed coldly, bitterly. Something in her heart cried: *But I am a woman! I am the one who is supposed to be protected.* But she knew better. She was the *navi.* Judge and mother of Israel. It was her burden to bring God's visions to the People and keep them safe. Her eyes hardened, and she stifled her laugh.

"Did you see it, last night, Zadok?" Devora asked, forcing the words out. "The *malakh ha-mavet?* Did you see it over the settlement?"

"I saw smoke," Zadok said grimly.

For a moment they both listened to the sounds of the men laboring by the lake.

Zadok wiped the blade of his knife on his cloak and sheathed it. Then bent and took up his spear. "I have taken the nazarite's vow. It does not matter if God is here or not." His voice was rough. "Or if the angel of death is here or not. *I* am here. I have taken the vow."

Devora let out the breath she'd been holding. His words sounded so much like her own words to Hurriya during the previous night. "All right. If anyone made it out of here alive, where did they go?"

"Kedesh. The town of Refuge," Zadok said. He was quiet a moment, and when he spoke again his voice was softer. "...I did want a wife once."

Devora glanced at him, jarred out of her thoughts.

Zadok nodded, his tone strangely subdued. "A woman who lived in Shiloh, who would always live there. I thought—" He glanced at her eyes, then looked away. "I thought that any act of mine would defend both her and the tribe of Levi. Nimri's raid taught me differently."

Devora's eyes widened.

"Me," she gasped. "You wanted *me*."

He just looked at the lake.

Devora recalled Zadok crying out her name as he rushed toward her through the terebinths. She recalled the way his breathing had changed as he'd held her. Yet—she had known him so long. And she had never known this. With a sudden blush, she wondered if other women in Shiloh camp had known. She who saw what God's eyes saw—might she have been blind to what other women might see? Had her husband known of Zadok's heart? Had *she*? Her head spun and she felt a great urge to sit down, but there was nowhere to seat herself that was not covered in the ashes of the dead.

"You chose Lappidoth when I was a boy of eight," Zadok muttered. "When I was a young man, Lappidoth seemed to me to be very old. I thought he might die, and I might ask you then, after your time of grief. I had a fool's heart. Forgive me, *navi*, so that I will be released of this burden I endure."

She watched his eyes a moment, saw the suffering there. How like his father he looked in this moment. The hard lines of his face, the depth and uncompromising purpose in his eyes. The only thing different was the anguish. Zefanyah had died before he could know pain like that.

She shook her head. "You've broken no covenant, Zadok, none with me. There's nothing to forgive."

"If you wish me to relinquish my vow—"

"Stop," she cried softly. "By the tribes, stop, Zadok. Just—be quiet a moment. Let me think."

She lowered her head. She could feel his gaze on her, and it was warm, undemanding. Yet she wanted to flee. The feelings in her heart and the feelings in his—whatever they were—it was too much. Everything she had encountered in this dead settlement was too much. She needed to go up into the hills where the wind was loud and the People were quiet. She needed to find some place to kneel and weep and pray.

But what did she fear? Zadok was younger than she, but he was not a boy. She lifted her gaze and saw him looking on her with concern. The anguish beneath it was deep but faint, like old coals after a fire had burned down all night. She sighed and stepped nearer to him, took his face between her hands, the scratch of his beard warm against her palms. He didn't move either to hold her or draw away. A tenderness welled up in her like a spring. She was conscious that the men dragging the bodies from the street could see them, but she didn't care. This moment was between the *navi* and her nazarite, and she would not let watchful eyes or any rumor they might start disturb it.

She looked up at him. "Who do you protect, Zadok, now that the high priest is gone?"

Zadok met her gaze without flinching. "Israel's *navi*."

"Then keep protecting her," Devora whispered. "And Devora, the woman, loves you for it. I am my husband's, I cannot be yours. But you do not *offend* me, Zadok. You are so important to me. You have to know that."

Zadok caught her hand in his, held it in that firm, unyielding grip. His eyes searched hers. Then he nodded. "I know it," he breathed.

"Thank you for sharing your heart."

"Thank you for sharing yours," Zadok rumbled.

A smile touched her lips. "We've grown old, Zadok."

"Maybe the *navi* has." He returned her smile. "But I can still outrun or outfight any man in Israel."

"Beast," she murmured. She was grinning now. His boasting cheered her. Zadok bore deep pain, but nothing—neither the rising dead nor the hard burden of slaying dead children nor his yearning for her—nothing could still the fire he carried within him. That cheered her. Even the *malakh ha-mavet* seemed no more than a shadow cast over sunlit ground, in the face of Zadok's enduring fortitude.

"It's good that you never took a wife, Zadok ben Zefanyah," Devora told him, lowering her hands from his face, regretting the loss of that warm beard against her palms. "You would be too much for her. You and Lappidoth are the only men I have ever met of whom that is true. Other men, women can work with." She smiled again and turned to glance up the ashen street. Men toiled there, but if they had been watching her, they were not now, and whatever judgment each of them had made on her was locked for the moment within the silent Ark of his own heart. There would be cairns by the water, new ones. She must go and sing over them. She must resume her burdens. She took Mishpat up from where she'd set the blade aside.

Zadok set a powerful hand on her shoulder. "*Navi*," he said. His voice had grown stern again, but it had lost some of its grimness, and the sound of it was a comfort to her.

"Refuge is where we'll find any from the town who still live and breathe," he said. "But we will not find any survivors, *navi*."

BREAKING CAMP

THE MEN HAD moved some of their tents to the edge of the burned settlement, raising a forest of canvas around Barak's pavilion; this had allowed the men to take the work of cleansing the town and raising cairns in shifts. After singing the Words of Going over the cairns, Devora's mind and heart were so full, so turbulent, that she stumbled toward these tents without a word to anyone. She wanted only to throw herself to the rugs and sleep until the men broke camp and she had to get to her feet again. Devora hardly even noticed the looks men gave her as she stumbled by with Mishpat still clutched in her hand. Their eyes held awe or fear—she had become strange to them. They were not looking at her as they had the evening before when she rode into the camp with a feverish heathen girl before her. Gazing at her now, their eyes still said *woman*, but those same eyes held alarm rather than desire. They did not know what to think about her or what to do with her. She was *kadosh*, set apart—as alien to them as God.

Even the glance Omri cast her as she passed held this strangeness, yet his gaze roved over her body. He stood, stroking his jaw with his hand, his eyes thoughtful and dark.

Laban was standing at the edge of the tents, sending men this way and that, and he saw the *navi* and directed her to a massive white tent. It had been his, but it was the levites' color, and he gave it to her. She didn't know where Laban meant to rest and did not have the energy to care. Nor did she know where Hurriya or Zadok were; neither was by her tent.

Inside, Devora stumbled to her knees and held Mishpat upright before her, the point resting on the earth, the hilt before her eyes. Before singing over the cairns—while waiting for the last ones to be raised—she had cleaned the blade and then polished the metal to a sheen; no trace of the unclean dead or of those bitten remained on the immaculate, though dented, metal. Now she stared hard at the blade. And felt things hardening within her.

She could still feel the slight resistance of each man's neck against Mishpat's blade, she could feel the tension of it in her hand. A night of terrible judgments. Not all of them hers. She spoke quietly to God in the dimness of her tent.

"Where are you?" she asked. "Have you truly lifted your hand from us?" Anger tightened her throat. "How have we offended you so greatly? Is it that our People mixed with the heathen? Yet—in that town—many of them fought to live with such strong hearts. Did all they could to preserve their *children*. As Hurriya did. They were not strangers to the Law—they could not have been strangers to it in their hearts. Why didn't you bless their acts? Why were those for nothing?"

Her tent flap drew aside and she glanced up with a sigh, expecting Hurriya or Zadok. But the man who stepped into her tent was shorter than the nazarite, his face hidden beneath a hood, one hand holding a heavy wool cloak closed, the other at his side carrying a bloodied knife.

She gasped, but the man murmured, "Do not scream, *navi*," and she recognized Barak's voice.

"What is this?" she hissed, her eyes wide.

Devora pressed a hand to her breast, waiting for her heart to stop pounding from her moment of fright.

He could not mean violence against her. That didn't make any sense. She watched in puzzlement as the war-leader tossed back his hood, revealing a wan face and haunted eyes. She drew in a breath; the man's hair had grayed. His hair—it had streaks of gray in it, gray as Lappidoth's hair—but there had been no gray in it before. She gazed at him in horror. "Barak?"

"I have come to your tent and the men will gossip," he said quietly. "But in here it must be. I will have no prying eyes for this. Do not cry out; I don't mean you ill."

The man opened his cloak and with his left hand drew out a dove, clutching it by the legs, the severed neck dripping blood onto the ground. "I will make a covenant with you, *navi*," he said. Breathing raggedly, he crouched across the tent from her and began carving into the bird with his knife, cutting the feathered body into two halves with a brutal, quick efficiency. Devora rose unsteadily, watching him, her heartbeat back to normal, her mind catching up. A covenant? A covenant to do what?

Barak separated the two halves as far apart as his arms could reach, then set them gently on the ground. He glanced up at her then, his eyes fierce. "I will promise you something you desire," he said. "You see further than men's eyes. And you are unshaken by the dead and know much about them, that is clear. I will hear you before the decisions I make. I will let you strike down my word if you know the decision to be wrong, and I will trust you as God's *navi*, holding back only those decisions that safeguard the lives of the men."

Devora looked at him, assessing him. The man was sincere. However reluctant he had been to acknowledge her or afford her respect, he was sincere now.

"And what promise do you ask of me, Barak?"

He glanced down at the two halves of the dove, then back at her. "Can you look, *navi*, and see whether I will survive the cleansing of the land?"

"It doesn't work like that. I can't answer your questions. God sends what he knows I need to see, to preserve what he wishes preserved."

He was silent for a moment. "But it's going to get worse."

"Yes," she whispered.

"Then I ask a simple thing, *navi*," he said quietly. "If I should be taken by the dead, my body defiled and half-eaten and rising unclean from the ground—" His hands began to shake as he spoke, and he set the stone knife carefully aside and got to his feet, facing her, his eyes filled with fear such as Devora had rarely seen in a human face. Her throat tightened.

"If my body should rise," he repeated, low and intense, "ride after me, *navi*. Ride and find my body. Pile clean stone above me, with your own hands, even if I have been dragged far away." He took a slow breath. "I have no seed, no inheritance in the land. If I live, I will take another wife and ensure my seed persists. But I may not live. And I will not wander the land unclean."

She gazed at him, and it seemed to her that the tent filled with the scent of ash and smoke.

"Do this," Barak said, without any quiver in his voice, though he passed his hand over his brow. "Make covenant with me. And any strife between us is at an end." His eyes were so terribly earnest, so desperate, it was all she could do not to look away. "You are the first judge of Israel, and you are the *navi*. Where you tell me I must ride, I will ride. Where you tell me to cast my spear, I will strike. Make this covenant with me."

She glanced down at the two halves of the dove. This was no small thing, to make a covenant. What they did here, God would watch, and remember, even if they should forget. Yet she had always been quick to make her decisions. Delay threatened life.

"I will," she said.

The relief on Barak's face was so naked that she looked aside.

They passed between the parts of the bird seven times. Each time they recited—first Barak, then Devora—the ancient, simple words of the rite:

426

Let it be done to me
as it was done to this bird, and more
if I break this covenant
or fail to keep it.

When her voice fell still the seventh time, Devora felt the responsibility of this covenant settle over her shoulders like a heavy wool cloak; it was an almost physical feeling. The bond of responsibility between her and the war-leader could not be severed, not by death nor by anything that might happen in life. It was as sacred and as real a covenant as that which she had made with Lappidoth her husband many years ago. It was as real as the covenant the tribes had made with each other, and the covenant they had made with the remnants of the heathen peoples at the vale of Weeping, and the covenant they had made with God on the mountain in the desert. Upon its breaking would follow a curse.

One did not make a covenant lightly, and Devora wondered what consequences this covenant would have that she could not yet see. Yet she did not regret her act. Barak was bound to her now, and surely what he had asked of her was no different than the responsibilities the Covenant between God and the People had already placed upon her. She was accustomed to being bound to a duty; this one did not frighten her.

Barak stood, and to her relief, he took the remains of the bird with him. He gave her a nod, then left her tent as abruptly as he'd come. Devora breathed softly in relief and sank to her knees in the silence of her tent. Alone once more. She couldn't bear having to speak with another person right now. She could not bear the thought of having to carry one more burden.

Her need for rest fell upon her as savagely as a growling bear, but she shrugged it off and got to her feet. No. She would pace and think. She would *not* close her eyes, not until she was very far from this place. Not until the moans of the dead were less near in her memory, less loud in her ears.

***

When Devora left her tent a while later, the air still smelled *burnt*, and a film of ash had settled on the surface of the lake, turning the lilies on the water to pale corpses of themselves. All around her, men were breaking camp and preparing for the half-day march toward Refuge. Devora went to Shomar and curried him, then saddled him for the day's ride, though she winced at the thought of that saddle between her sore thighs again. Barak and the other chieftains appeared to sit their horses without discomfort; riding must be something a woman could get used to. She talked to Shomar softly and listened to him whicker softly back. She began reciting the words of the Law under her breath, to calm the edge of her anxiety:

And these words, which I command to you this day, will be in your heart: and you shall teach them to your children. You shall talk of them when you sit in your house, and when you walk by the way, and when you lie down, and when you rise up.

"We have raised the cairns," Devora murmured to God as she patted Shomar's neck. "We will *not* forget our promise. And I trust your promises hold true also."

She didn't know if God was listening.

A sharp crack of wood disturbed her thoughts, and she glanced toward the last wooden houses that stood, their roofs bearing blankets of ash. Devora caught sight of Laban at the door to one of the houses, swinging back his great axe and slamming it into the wood. Three other men stood behind him. Large, lithe men of Issachar with makeshift cudgels ready in their hands. Devora nodded, approving from a distance what they were doing: breaking into the last houses to check for any lurking dead before abandoning the camp and the town. She turned back to her horse, checking his hooves, then giving him water to drink and grains to eat from her small store of them, for this was no time to turn him loose to graze. His eyes were soft and liquid in the midmorning light.

She listened without watching as Laban and his men went from one house to the next. Once, she heard a man's scream, followed by the wavering moan of a walking corpse. Devora shivered.

Then the moan was cut short. Perhaps Laban's axe had done its work.

She strapped her waterskin and Mishpat to the side of the saddle.

She glanced about for Hurriya and at first didn't see her. Then she glanced toward the burned settlement and was startled to see the Canaanite approaching out of the town, coming from the houses the men had already checked. Zadok walked beside her, and as he looked toward Devora, for the briefest moment she surprised a look in his eyes of yearning and regret that battered at her heart. She looked away, embarrassed to have caught that look.

He *did* want her, then, as a man wants a wife. She sighed. It was clear that he would continue to treat her with great respect. But how was she to treat *him*, knowing what she now knew?

The sight of Hurriya distracted her. The girl was carrying a fistful of green leaves that must have come from the herbalist's shop in the market, and she was no longer wearing her stained salmah. Instead, she wore a thick woolen gown, dyed green. It must have belonged to one of the wealthier wives of the town, and it reflected a Canaanite's sympathies: a love of bright colors and things that draw the eye in the sun. Devora found her own gaze held; though Hurriya walked with discomfort and though there were dark bruises about her eyes from nights without rest, she looked suddenly beautiful. And little trace remained of the unease she had once shown around the nazarite. Then the girl stumbled and leaned heavily on Zadok's arm, and a flame of jealousy lit within Devora's heart so sudden and so fierce that it shocked her; she damped it swiftly, furious with herself.

"Those clothes are unclean," she said as Hurriya approached her with a wary glance at Shomar. Zadok gave the *navi* a nod without looking directly at her and departed to help the men with the tents. And Devora breathed easier.

"So am I," Hurriya said wryly. Her left cheek was full of herbs, and she chewed them slowly. Her eyes had lost their glassy look, but she was still deathly pale. "Why does it matter?"

Devora sighed. "I'm glad you found clothes," she said after a moment. "And you look lovely in them, Hurriya."

The young woman glanced at her, perhaps surprised to find Devora calling her by her name.

Everything was strange now. The problems over which she sat in decision this day were very different from those she had judged when men of the People came to her olive tree with broken pacts or broken in spirit. Her own decisions were strange to her—hard necessities that were driven not by the Law but by the panic she saw in men's eyes and the bursting of the dead through wooden doors. The very sky above her was strange, darkened by ash and by the burning of lives and the burning of the work of men's hands. Zadok's heart was strange to her, concealing within it things she hadn't suspected. Even Hurriya was strange to her, in this green gown. She looked—whole—in it. As though not only the edge of her fever but also some of her weariness and her grief had fallen away, even though her body showed where it had been ravaged by fatigue.

"I don't know how to restore the Law," Devora whispered. "In this place."

"By giving me a waterskin," Hurriya said. "By helping me find my sister. By helping these men protect their houses and their kin from the dead."

Devora looked at her. She took Hurriya's waterskin from its strap on the side of the saddle and passed it across. Hurriya took a small drink.

"I think I understand your Law better than you do," Hurriya said, passing the waterskin back with both hands. She held it almost reverently, and Devora wondered how often she had gone without water on her long walk from Judges' Well to Shiloh.

Devora gave her a sharp look but said nothing.

"You say your God gave you this Law in the desert when he looked at you, when your Lawgiver looked at him. When they faced each other on Har Sinai."

"Yes," Devora said.

Hurriya leaned forward, her eyes intent and far more lucid than they had been the night before. "When you see another's face—the face of a child, or another woman, or the face of the goddess, or the face of someone hungry or hurt—their eyes, they look back. They look at you. They ask your love, they ask you to hear their crying and know that you and they are both alive, and some day you may be hurt, you may be hungry. It may be your child carried dying in your arms." Hurriya choked a moment, then went on. "When I look at you, you look back. Only the dead don't look back."

Devora thought about that as she bent to tighten Shomar's girth straps.

"You think the Law is a pact with your God, a pact with others of your People. But it's not just a pact."

Devora just listened, thinking hard.

"It's an answer," Hurriya said intensely. "You have rules for everything. But it's not the rules that matter. It's that you *want* to make them. You want to answer the suffering you see in another woman's face. You want to give her safety, or justice, or comfort. That's what matters. That's why you have your Law, why you love it. But when you sit in decision at your olive tree, or on this horse looking at the burning town, you have to find the right answer to the suffering you see. Your fathers in the desert found the Law, found that answer. So it guides you, like I guided you into these hills. But you still have to find the right answer to each face you see."

Devora rose, looked at her over Shomar's back, swallowed. Suffering could give a woman insight, she knew, and surely few women had suffered as this Canaanite had. "I misjudged you, Hurriya. I treated you as only a child. A bruised, grieving child."

Hurriya's smile was only a little bitter. "I am the *navi*, remember."

"I remember," Devora said softly.

Hurriya gazed at the ruin of Walls. "Both our Peoples suffered there," she said quietly. "Do you still blame mine? For the dead?"

"God sits in decision over us all," Devora conceded. She swung into the saddle, wincing briefly at her soreness. "Come," she said.

"You are a stubborn old woman," Hurriya said. Devora helped her up with a grip on her clothed arms.

"As an aging olive," Devora agreed as Hurriya settled before her with a groan at her body's pain. "Come, girl. Let's talk about your visions, since only you are having them."

Canaanite the girl might be, but there was no denying what *else* Hurriya was. Or what duties Devora had to her, to teach her and prepare her.

Shomar whickered as Devora nudged him forward.

"Let's talk about being the *navi*," she said.

ZADOK'S RUN

A FEW HOURS later beneath the hot sun, Devora received a fresh shock when she and Hurriya and all of Barak's men reached a ridge overlooking the town of Refuge. Gazing down into the valley, Barak cursed. Hurriya shivered once. Devora merely stared; even the nightmare at Walls had not prepared her for this.

The town was no longer a refuge but a trap.

With the valley of the Tumbling Water before it, a high cliff at its back, and strong walls on its east, south, and western sides, Refuge conveyed strength. It was one of three such settlements in the land, walled towns that Yeshua the war-leader had wrested from the Canaanites and established as safe places the People could go to in time of need, or that a fugitive could flee to in search of justice if pursued by one who wished to kill him. Perhaps that fierce chieftain, Yeshua ben Nun, who had torn down so many walls in the river valleys of the land, had one day gazed up at some sheer stone fortification and realized his People might eventually need such a defense themselves. Or perhaps he had foreseen how divided the People would become and realized that there would be a need for neutral cities, places where it would not be permissible to kill for any reason, even the execution of justice.

Let there be three towns of refuge, where a fugitive may flee his enemies who would devour him. And one of these shall be in the north.

Whatever Yeshua had been thinking when he declared those words, he surely had not anticipated this.

For there were indeed enemies now in the north who sought to devour the People.

And they were here.

Hundreds of corpses pressed against the south and east walls, and others behind them pressed forward, crushing the first line of the dead against the stones in their mindless, urgent hunger. The wind carried up the reek of them and their eerie moaning, a sound that crept inside Devora like shivers from extreme cold, until her hands were shaking and she had to clasp them behind her to still them. Beneath the moans, another sound: like the rattle of a landslide but softer, like a hundred drums that were not keeping rhythm together. Or like hands, many many hands, beating upon stone.

The men stopped on the ridge and let their packs slide to the ground. The chieftains on their horses gazed down with mute horror. Vivid in Devora's memory was her vision beneath the branches of the olive tree, her foresight of great herds of the dead lurching through the land.

For a long while, no one spoke. They just watched the hundreds of dead slamming their decaying flesh against the stone walls below.

"They need bows," Hurriya whispered at last.

"What?" Devora whispered back.

"Bows. Like the Sea People have. Look. A few of the dead lie still. They've been throwing things from the walls at them. But they need bows."

Devora had heard of bows, of course, but had never seen one. Yet she saw how they might be useful. If one had the ability to kill at a great distance, greater than a spear's cast, and more accurately—if one had that, one could simply slay the dead from the walls, then issue out to build cairns once all the dead were still.

To his credit, something had hardened in Barak during the afternoon's march. He sat his horse a few moments watching the horror below, then turned and called out, "We are men of Israel, and that is a settlement of Israel. Let's relieve that town by nightfall, men."

Some of the men shouted, lifting their spears or whatever implements they held. Others just gazed down at the walled town, learning new fears.

"Omri, Laban." Barak strode up toward a promontory of rock that jutted out from the ridge, and the other two men strode to join him. Devora did not. She had no interest at this moment in the plans of men. She listened to the thudding of those hands and bodies against the walls of the settlement below and realized with a dull inevitability that this ordeal of facing the dead in this strange hill country would go on, and on. That God alone knew how many dead they would have to bury, how many valleys they would have to search, before it was done.

Even as she struggled with this, Hurriya's body grew fiercely hot against her breast, and Devora gasped, for the flash of heat nearly scorched her. Then it was gone, as quickly as it had come, and it was again a mere heathen girl who leaned against her in the saddle and not a living torch.

"They're going up the river," Hurriya breathed as she came out of the vision. "All of them, right now. They're fleeing, but the dead follow. Men and women from Walls, many of them."

Devora caught her breath. Suddenly it was clear to her what had occurred. Those fleeing Walls had come here, to Refuge, only to find the dead waiting outside. So they had kept running, going up the river. Taking some of the dead with them.

"Stay here," Devora whispered, and she slid from Shomar's back, wincing at the stiffness of her body. She took a breath and broke into a run toward the outcropping of rock where Barak and the other war-leaders stood, debating how to attack the dead below. "Barak!" she called out. "Barak!"

The man turned.

"We have to go!"

"What?"

"We have to go! The refugees from Walls. They're fleeing up the river. Hurriya has *seen* them. A vision—a vision from God!"

Barak swung down from his horse and strode to her, his breast-piece clinking. Omri looked on bewildered, Laban looked pensive.

"What are you talking about, *navi*?" Barak growled as he neared.

"We have to hurry north. There are men and women in the open field, in the vineyards, with the dead close behind."

Barak's eyes widened, he shot a glance to the north. Nothing could be seen there because of the curve of the river valley between the steep hills.

"My vineyard is up there," he breathed. Then shook his head. "We have to relieve those in the city. Then their strength can join ours."

How could she convince him? "No. We must first preserve the lives of those of the People who have no walls."

Omri nudged his horse closer. "What is this woman's talk?" he muttered. "The dead are here. Sound the shofar, Barak, before these men feel their manhood wilt. Before they slip away into the hills."

Barak looked from Devora to Omri, his face pale.

Devora rounded on the Zebulunite. "Hurriya had a vision!"

"She's a Canaanite," Omri sneered.

"She's a *navi*! She sees what God sees! What God needs *us* to see!"

Barak gripped Devora's arm, his eyes intense. But she did not flinch. "If your girl has seen a true thing, we will have dead before us and dead behind," he whispered fiercely in her ear. "And if the dead have overwhelmed the vineyards and homesteads along the Tumbling Water, then going up that river we will have dead to either side." His eyes glanced toward Refuge below. "And I have *kin* in that town."

"All the People are your kin, and the safety of their houses and their tents is your responsibility. These at least are safe behind a *wall*."

"For how long?"

"We have a covenant." Devora leaned close. "This is *not* where you will cast your spear, Barak. *God* shows the way to victory, Barak. *God* shows us how to clean the land. Not our own wisdom, which is small. If you break covenant with me, Barak ben Abinoam, if you ignore the visions he sends, I swear to you, every last one of your men *will die*. Do not do this."

He cursed and gazed at Refuge, a muscle twitching in his cheek. For a moment Devora had doubts. This was a war-leader who'd sent men after the *Ark*. Why did she believe he would respect a covenant with her any more than he had one with their God? Would he hold true?

"We *cannot* leave them to die," Barak growled, releasing her arm and pacing furiously.

"They have a wall," Devora cried. "We'll come back for them."

"*They* don't know that!"

"Barak, don't listen to her," Omri hissed. "Look at her. She's just a woman. And she wants us to listen to the fever-rambling of that heathen slut? Don't be a fool, Barak! Look at the men. We have to fight *here*."

Barak glanced at Devora, his face pale as a fish's belly. "We'll have to get them some message. The people in Refuge. Those men and women, those children. They have to know we'll come back for them."

Devora let out her breath. He was listening to her. She looked down at the town and something clenched inside her. The dead slamming their hands and their bodies against those walls—who could make it through *that* to bear any message to the town?

"Who do I send?" Barak breathed. "Who do I send?" Wide-eyed, he glanced at the other war-leaders. "Omri, you or I might do this thing, but none of the men could. They're farmers—they couldn't get through that—they'd have to go around to the far wall, they'd have to get to it without being seen. Fight if they are seen. They'd have to—" He stopped, helpless.

"I'm not doing it," Omri grunted.

"Nor you, Barak," Devora whispered. "The men need you."

"I will make the run," a deep voice said behind her.

Devora turned slowly. Her face went very pale. "You can't," she breathed.

Zadok stood there, his face set, a fire in his eyes. The men looked on Zadok with fresh awe, and Devora could see reflected in their eyes the fierce legend of the nazarites. "No," she whispered.

"This could mean your death," Barak said. "An unclean death."

"I have known since my seventh winter that I will die," Zadok said firmly. "And I chose *how* I will die: in service to the Ark, or to the *navi*, or to the sons of Levi. The day of it is God's to choose."

Devora met Zadok's gaze, saw the fire in it, saw deeper, saw the certainty and the devotion and the fierce glorying in the task, the knowledge that if he ran to that town, in that act his failings would be forgotten both by himself and by God. The knowledge that he would at last have fulfilled his vow.

"Zadok," Devora said, "you don't have to do this." She couldn't lose him.

"None of Barak's men have my stride or my skill. I am the only one who can." He smiled grimly. "And I *can* do this. God's hand is on me; I will reach the walls." He met the *navi*'s eyes. "I can finally do a thing worthy of my father."

Devora's throat tightened. She stepped near him, so near their bodies nearly touched. What she had to say other men mustn't hear. She whispered fiercely in his ear, pleading. "I've seen the *malakh ha-mavet*. Twice. God's hand is *not* on us."

He looked at her, his dark eyes above hers. "If we leave these people with no message, you will suffer. I know. You know too how bad it will be. I *can* do this."

She sucked in breath between her teeth, her panic rising. Before she could speak again, Zadok nodded to the plain below and said, "*Navi*. That outcropping of rock. To the west. It'll hide me most of the way. It can be done."

Her gaze followed his nod. She could see the outcropping, almost a low wall of stone rising at a slant from the land, as though God had driven a massive stone into the soil like a spearhead. Beyond it, a stretch of open grasses, then the west wall of the city, the only wall with no corpses beating against it.

But she saw something else, too.

"Zadok," she said, "there's no *gate* in that wall."

It was true. The walled settlement had two gates, one in the east wall and one in the south—both had dead beating against the timbers, which must surely have been reinforced heavily from the inside. In fact, the reason there were no dead pressing against the west wall was likely because no one had fled into the city through it when the corpses had first descended on the valley.

"The men of Refuge will lower a basket for me," Zadok said.

"You don't know that. They're terrified. Who knows what they'll do."

Zadok smiled grimly. "When I make it past those dead, *navi*, Refuge will want to speak with me." His smile widened, showing his teeth. "I promise it."

"Zadok—" But her throat tightened, choking off her words. So much she didn't know how to say.

He gripped her shoulders in those powerful hands, held her gaze a moment. Then he glanced over her shoulder at Barak. "Keep and preserve her life, in my stead. The Canaanite too."

Barak gave him a brisk nod, his face drawn.

Zadok nodded back, then stepped away from the *navi*, releasing her. Quickly he unbuckled his breast-piece and cast it aside; it would be too heavy, a hindrance rather than a defense. His greaves, too, he slid from his legs. His tunic he pulled off over his head. He stood a moment in his loincloth and his sandals, his body muscled and bronzed by the sun, his dark hair long and uncut. He took it up in firm hands and bound it in several knots near to his scalp, where it would be less easy for the dead to grasp. Then knelt on one knee at the *navi*'s feet, lowering his eyes. His fingers moved quickly, tightening the laces on his sandal. "Bless me, *navi*," he asked.

She didn't want to bless him. She wanted to keep pleading with him not to go. She wanted to ask him to stay with her. Slowly Devora set her hand on his head, felt the thick curls of his hair. For a moment she didn't speak. When she did, her voice sounded frail to her.

Adonai bless you and keep you,
Adonai make his face shine on you and be gracious to you,
Adonai look on you with favor and give you peace.

She didn't lift her hand from his hair. Another, she was going to lose another of her tribe, her family. She'd lost Naomi. She'd lost Eleazar. She was going to lose this man too. "Zadok, you—" She tried again, managed to keep her voice calm. "Tell them where we're going and why. That there are people with no walls and no refuge, and we go to shield them. Tell them we will be back and that as long as they remain within their walls, God will be their shield and their tower. Tell them the *navi* is with Barak's men and that she promises them this. Zadok—" She paused, gathered herself. Her voice low and intense. "You make it to those walls, Zadok ben Zefanyah. You *make* it there."

She lifted her hand, and Zadok got to his feet. His eyes met hers, and they were unveiled. The passion in them she had only seen before in Lappidoth's eyes.

"*Navi*," he said with another duck of his head, and then he turned and bolted into a run, flashing past Barak and the gathered men, darting down the slope. Devora found she couldn't breathe, watching him move. He was fast, fleet as a deer, leaping and ducking through the brush.

Almost absently Barak gave the chieftains commands, calling to ready the men for the march upriver. But his gaze never left the valley below, and the other tribal leaders walked away slowly, looking over their shoulders.

At last, only Devora, Barak, and Omri stood on the high rock. Omri's face was pale with horror, Barak's awed. Devora, however, felt that she had been struck through the breast with a spear and was now in shock and waiting to feel the pain of it. She glanced once back the way she'd come. Shomar's head was down; he was grazing among the rocks. Hurriya sat huddled on his back, watching Devora with eyes glazed with pain and vision.

"Holy God, the man can run," Barak breathed.

Devora swallowed and turned her eyes back to the valley. Had she been a young woman, she might have offered to run herself, hoping that God would bless her and shield her as his *navi* and bring his words through her to the settlement.

Once again, Zadok carried her burdens for her.

The nazarite was sprinting along the outcropping now, keeping the low stone bulwark between him and the dead; there were perhaps only a few spear casts between him and the southern wall where the dead moaned and beat on the stone. He would have to run northwest along the stone, then round the far end of the outcropping and make for the west wall, hoping either that the dead would be too preoccupied to see him or that his legs would carry him so swiftly to the wall that he could be hoisted up before they reached him.

It was desperate.

And wondrous.

She watched Zadok's powerful body race along the rock. In him she saw his father, Zefanyah, who had danced the spear so furiously on the training ground that none of the other nazarites could best him. Zefanyah, who afterward would stand laughing among the other men on the packed dirt, sweating, his chest heaving, until he would glance over to where Devora watched with the other girls and smile at her.

And she saw her husband, Lappidoth, as a young man, slaying the corpses that had come for his cattle, his bronzed skin shining in the sun, his blows powerful and sure. His eyes full of purpose and will and the determination to hold firmly to what was his.

"I have never seen a man move like that," Omri muttered.

"Until this last night and day, you had never seen a nazarite," Devora said, her heart swelling with pride even amid her fear.

"He is one man," Barak said. "There must be four hundred beating on that wall. At least."

"He is Zadok ben Zefanyah," Devora said.

"He's rounding the end of that rock," Barak said quietly.

Below them, Zadok came clear of the rock, but even as he did, several figures lurched out of a fissure. Eight, nine of them, barring his way. Devora found she couldn't breathe. There had been dead hiding *in* the rocks. Possibly someone working the fields had taken refuge in some den within the rocks and been followed and eaten, and the dead had stayed there until stirred by the sound of Zadok's footsteps and his breathing.

Now they were upon him.

A hush fell over the hill. Devora's blood was loud in her ears. She could have forbidden him to go. She was the only one whose forbidding he would have heeded. Yet she knew that this would have broken him.

The moaning of the dead was faint but terrible in her ears.

She watched helplessly as Zadok leapt among the dead, his spear flashing in the sun. Two figures lay still on the ground. He spun and danced—he *danced*—darting forward and back, leaping over one corpse that had tumbled to its knees, landing on his feet and bringing the spear up, stabbing with the bronze head, wielding the butt end like a weapon itself, knocking corpses back. Then he wielded the spear one-handed—though its weight was not light—and his other hand plucked out his knife, and that too flashed in the sun as he leapt and fought.

"He's going to make it," Omri breathed. "He's actually going to make it."

Zadok fought in utter silence. No raiding cry, no prayer, no voice that came faint to Devora's ears. Just focused, silent discipline.

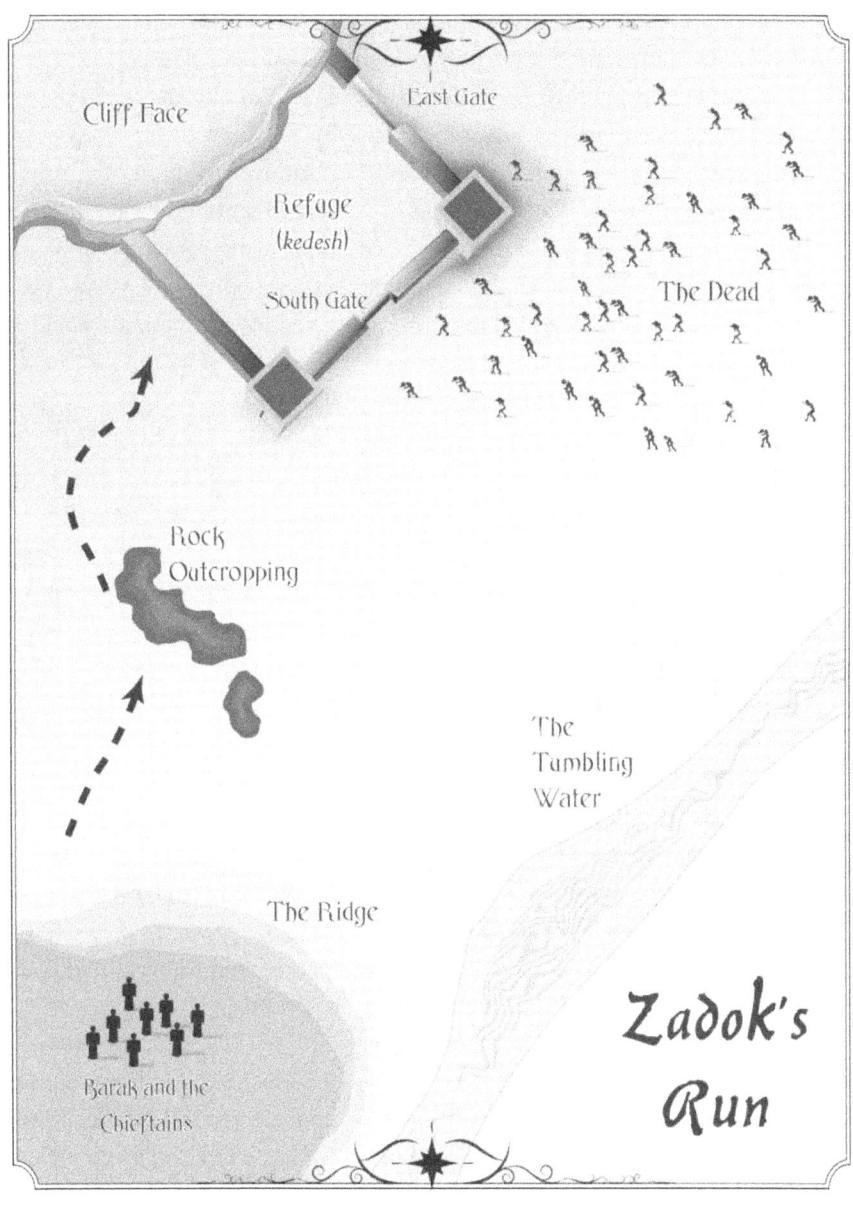

"*Navi!*" Barak gasped.

"That does it," Omri muttered.

Some of the dead were breaking away from the south wall, lurching out over the open grass, their attention drawn by the moans and snarls of the corpses that had closed on Zadok. Devora bit her lip and prayed silently, her palms damp with sweat. Below the ridge came the sounds of men shouldering their burdens, unaware of the grim battle the nazarite was fighting.

But now Zadok thrust his knife into the face of one of his assailants, and it appeared to stick in the corpse's skull, for he shoved the corpse aside, abandoning the blade, and broke free, bolting out over the grass. The way he'd run before had stirred the admiration of his watchers, but now he *truly* ran. It couldn't be less than two hundred strides between the rock outcropping and the west wall, but he tore across the ground like a stallion in full gallop. Veering north to buy time as the lurching corpses moved toward him, a reeking herd flowing along the wall and over the grass.

"He won't make it," Barak said softly.

Omri just shook his head.

"He will," Devora said forcefully. "He *will*."

Run, Zadok. She mouthed the words, without sound. *Run, Zadok. Run, damn you.*

He had perhaps eighty strides to go—but there were dead all around him now, and dead between him and the wall. He dodged and darted between them, sometimes knocking one aside with his spear, then spinning past. Devora saw the dead thicken about him, and she felt almost dizzy.

"*Run!*" she cried aloud.

She saw the sunlight on his shoulders and back where he shone with sweat. He dodged and the point of his spear cut the air. Then the dead were thick between him and the wall, and he didn't hesitate, didn't turn back or flee. The nazarite ran directly *into* the corpses, wielding his spear and using the sheer force of his run to shove the walking corpses aside.

Omri cursed. *They say a nazarite fights like ten men,* Omri had told Zadok when the two of them met, both taunting him and questioning.

No, Zadok had answered. *I fight like twenty.*

Now Zadok proved it. He spun on his heels faster than Devora had ever seen any man move, ducking and thrusting among the dead, his lethal bronze slicing and piercing scalp and face, throwing corpses to the earth. Still they closed on him, hands grasping for his shoulders, his arms, uncaring that he was armed. Their fingers brushed him, defiling his skin, yet he struck with both blade and shaft of the spear, as though it were only heads of summer wheat touching him and the spear he held a scythe. More corpses fell. But now he could not move forward farther, so he stood and fought. The moaning dead pressed in on him, the ones behind shoving those before them, and after a moment Zadok went down beneath the sheer weight of their bodies, and Devora let out a low cry; she couldn't help it, it tore its way up her throat. She saw the corpses bending over that piece of earth where he'd fallen, only thirty strides from the wall. She wanted to look away, but she couldn't. Something was tight and hard in her breast. She remembered the scorched, unrecognizable face of Zefanyah as he lay stretched out on the ground in a line of dead.

"He *rises!*" Barak yelled. "He rises! *Navi! I can see the sun on his spear!*"

Devora gasped. It was true; she could see it too. The flashes of light as the spear thrust up from the ground, twice, then again. And then with a roar she could hear even from here, even over the wailing of the dead, Zadok ben Zefanyah, nazarite since he was seven, burst to his feet, the dead still clutching him, one of them even with its jaws about his left arm, blood running down to his left hand. Yet Zadok stood, screaming hoarsely, thrusting against the dead with the shaft of his weapon. His hair had come loose and it swept about him as he fought and turned, hair longer and more flowing than any woman's, hair that had never been cut. Bloodied now about his shoulders. Dead grasped at it, pulling his head back; a corpse tore into his left shoulder with its teeth. Still he remained on his feet as they ate at him, still he roared and battered at them with his spear, using it more now as a pole and shield than as a thrusting weapon. Bodies lay still about his legs, dead he'd silenced, yet others clambered on top of the fallen to clutch at him. He drove the butt of the spear back, crushing the face of the corpse that had his shoulder, destroying its head; he shook his arm and shoulder like a man shrugging off a cloak, and the body fell away. Blood ran down over his chest from the deep bite in his shoulder. The dead still held his hair and his left arm, yet he turned, and gripping his spear near its head, he drove the point like a dagger into the eye of a corpse behind him. He was bleeding, he was unclean, still he fought. Still he fought to get the *navi's* message to that settlement.

People had come to the west wall now and were hurling shards of pottery and ewers and even beams of wood down on the dead who moaned between the wall and Zadok, though with little effect.

"He is still fighting," Barak breathed. "He is still fighting."

"He is a nazarite," Devora said again. Everything in her numb.

Then the dead tugged Zadok beneath them a second time, and on the ridge Devora and Barak and Omri waited, but there was no flash of sun on Zadok's spear nor any surge of the man to his feet. Only the dead, bending over that spot and feeding, covering Zadok so that his body could not be seen through them. A pain sharp near Devora's heart. His body. Zadok's body. It would be left down there, to be fed on, to *rise*—if the dead left any of him intact.

With a cry, Devora turned and moved as quickly as the her soreness would allow, running for her horse.

"*Navi*, no!" Barak tore after her.

In a moment Devora felt the man's weight slam into her, bearing her to the ground on her belly, driving the breath from her. Wheezing, she kicked wildly, but he crushed her to the earth.

"We have to get his body!" she screamed. "We have to get his body!"

"It's no good! Be *still*, you fool woman!" His growl in her ear.

"No! We have to!" She shrieked and thrashed under the chieftain's weight and heard him cursing wildly as he fought to hold her. All she could think of, the one terror in her heart, was that Zadok was down there being torn and eaten, that she had sent him to die and could not leave him there, not like that. Zadok, who had loved her and sworn to her, who had been her defender and her right arm and her strong cedar to lean on, these last days of their nightmare journey into the north. She could not leave his body there among the dead. She could not betray him so.

Sobbing breathlessly, she kept fighting, and Barak wrenched her wrists over her head, pinning them in a grip that she could not escape. With his other hand he wound leather tightly about her wrists and knotted it; a strap perhaps from the leather beneath his breast-piece or from his greaves. She spat and bucked but could not dislodge the man. Felt him lifting her, carrying her over his shoulder as she kicked and pummeled his back with her bound hands.

"Stop fighting me," Barak whispered fiercely. "There's nothing we can do. Nothing."

She kept struggling, barely hearing him. The ground moved dizzily beneath her as he strode, carrying her toward her horse. And still she screamed with the moaning of the dead in her ears. Screamed her throat raw in protest, screamed to Zadok and to Barak and to God who was watching somewhere in his terrible silence.

PART 4 - ALONG THE TUMBLING WATER

THE WITHERING LAND

THE MEN MOVED north, with Devora tied to her saddle, her wrists thonged to the pommel. Hurriya clung to her waist from behind her. North of Refuge there was no road and no town—just the broad valley of the Tumbling Water, a strip of well-watered earth a quarter mile wide, nestled between steep hillsides. The land leveled out for a while as they followed the water north, and the river here flowed slowly. On the west bank there was a cart track that led them past small vineyards that drank in the hot sun, between water and hill. Behind each vineyard could be seen a low house of cedar or pine, like a tired bear with its back to the steep rising of the land.

In any other year, this might have been a cheerful place. At this season the vines would have been green and lush for harvest, with fat clusters of grapes almost too heavy for a man to lift.

But Devora felt no cheer. She sat her horse rigidly. She was uncomfortable and sore. But that was nothing compared to the humiliation hot in her breast. She rode beside the men, tied to her horse, like any slave. With her wrists bound, she could not lift her hands to cover her face, though she felt their eyes on her. She felt naked. Any grief she might show would be terribly public.

And as she'd told Barak, in all things made or done by God or by men there was a message that could be discerned. The message in the strap about her wrists was clear to her. Surely she would not be respected as the *navi*, not here, not among these men. Not now that Zadok was gone. Zadok's presence too had been a message, a sign of her authority, a sign that she was set apart. That sign was gone. The men might look at her now and see only a woman in a dirtied, stained white dress. Once Omri even rode to her and sneered, "Just a woman." She didn't move or look at him, and she dreaded for a moment that he would grip her thigh as he had done once, but at that moment Barak's voice came sharp from where he rode a little ahead. "Omri!" And cursing under his breath, the man let her be.

As she watched him go, Devora felt the bite of anger. Only another woman. Prone to tears or hysterical screaming, of value because her body created life, but not to be trusted outside a man's tent. What if, seeing her so, the men stopped listening to her? Certainly Omri had; his brief moment of awe that night in Walls had not survived seeing her screaming like a slave girl as Barak tied her and tossed her onto her horse. How could she help her People if her words to them were no longer the words of one who sees what God sees, but only the words of a woman who rides without a man beside her?

Her gaze flicked down to Mishpat, which was still strapped to the side of her saddle. The blade had not been taken from her—for she was *not* a slave. And though she could not reach it, the sight of that sword hardened her. She was still Devora of Israel, whether free with a nazarite and the mighty presence of the Law behind her, or trussed to her saddle like a raid captive.

And even her humiliation, even her grief, were small things compared to her dread at what she now saw before her and behind her and on every side. For this was *not* a lush valley ready for harvest. The dead had been here first. And with them, its sere wings scything through the vines, the *malakh ha-mavet*. Where its shadow had fallen, the vines were withered and dry as brambles; there were no lights in the houses.

Barak grew visibly tense as the slow tread of the men brought them farther upriver, and Devora recalled his words at the lakeside: *I am a vintner who has been eleven days from my vineyard while dead prowl about it, and I fear for the harvest.* This was Barak's country: the vineyards of the north Yarden, famed in Israel. The people of Walls, Hebrew and heathen, had led the great herd of the dead straight up this valley, where the vineyards awaited them like a long row of riverbank blossoms to be trampled. There would be no harvest.

As they passed up the cart track beside the dying fields, silent as mourners, they came upon strange sights. A walking corpse that crouched amid the vines and dug at the ground with its fingers, with relentless, slow movements that seemed utterly without purpose. The corpse did not even glance up as Omri approached it from behind and drove a spear into its skull.

After that, they found a corpse pinned, half-crushed, beneath a wagon with a broken axle; perhaps the man had died there. Now he lay on his back, the wagon holding him at the waist. The corpse writhed and growled at the men who passed, twisting to the left and to the right, struggling helplessly to get on its belly and crawl toward the living. The men at the head of the line stopped and stared at it a few moments. For once Devora felt nothing seeing the corpse twist and strain to get at them. It was only one more corpse in a land that was itself becoming a corpse.

It didn't really matter.

After a few moments, Laban strode forward with his axe and took off the thing's head. The head rolled away from the wagon and stopped with its face toward the sky. The jaws didn't move, but the milky, dead eyes did. Laban growled and brought the axe down on its brow, swinging like a man splitting wood. Hurriya glanced away with a shudder; Devora just looked numbly on.

As the line of men began to shuffle uneasily past the wagon and the still corpse, Barak detailed five men to make a cairn. Then he rode to Devora's side and drew a small knife from a sheath he'd strapped to his shin. With calm, measured movements, he set the knife to her bonds and cut them; Devora felt the cold of the bronze against her skin, but Barak was careful and he did not cut her. When her hands were free, she lifted them slowly, rubbing her wrists, wincing as life came back to her numb hands, hurting them.

"I am sorry," Barak said quietly. He had the grace at least to look ashamed. "He died bravely."

"He died." Devora's voice sounded small to her, and hopeless.

Barak said nothing.

"His body will rise."

"I know." The war-leader coughed. "When we return, we will end that and raise a cairn for him."

"I should never have let him go." Devora closed her eyes.

Barak rode beside her a moment, as though he were trying to think of words to say. Then he sighed and kicked his horse into a canter and left them. Hurriya squeezed Devora slightly, her arm about Devora's waist, and whispered, "He died serving those he loved. The gods will remember him. Your God will too."

***

They stopped briefly about two hours before dusk, and the men shared some of their diminished rations without fires or means of heating them. Sore and exhausted, Devora passed Hurriya's waterskin to her, then lay down in the weeds by the riverbank and looked at the sky. She didn't want to eat. She couldn't cry, couldn't sleep.

After a while, someone settled in the grass beside her, and she felt a hand stroking her arm gently through her sleeve. Soft humming. That go-to-sleep song of Hurriya's. Devora didn't turn her head to look at the girl, she just listened. The grief and terror and fatigue of the morning and of the previous night hit her all at once. Withered fields. An entire settlement, gone. That girl who longed to be a woman, leaping to her death. Zadok, her Zadok, dead. Beneath all those feeding corpses. Tears stung against her eyelids; she rebuked them. She yearned suddenly for Lappidoth, for his strong arms about her, holding her so that she could sleep without fear. Letting her hide her face against his chest so that she could weep without shame.

But here she had only Hurriya and her melody and the soft touch of the girl's hand through her sleeve.

"Thank you," she said.

Hurriya stopped humming. "We Canaanites don't let a woman grieve alone," she whispered.

"Neither do we Hebrews." Devora reached and gripped the girl's own arm through her dress, returning the touch. "Did you really see them, girl? Survivors from Walls?"

"Yes. With the dead behind them."

Hurriya and Devora were silent for a while. Then the Canaanite said, "Tell me about this God of yours, who sends these visions."

Devora opened her eyes and gazed at Hurriya's deathly pale face and the empty sky above her. In her dress the girl looked nearly skeletal. Her eyes were weary and glazed with the slow return of her fever, but they held no hatred, only concern. A tenderness for her touched Devora's heart. The girl was ill and fading a little, yet she had come to where Devora lay and had hummed that song for her. This was a woman who had already walked the length of the land once, bleeding and carrying a child. Her fever and illness were unlikely to keep her from doing what she felt she needed to do for those who needed her.

And Devora *did* need her.

They were two women alone. And they had been through fire and death and terror together. Only Lappidoth had ever seen Devora's heart as naked as this girl had seen it.

She should be caring for and comforting and guiding this new *navi*. Instead, she was being comforted *by* her. Devora sighed and sat up, drawing her responsibilities back about her even as she had often seen Hurriya draw that salmah about her thin frame. "We know little of God, even we who see things that only God sees," she told the girl. "We only know that he's made promises and that when he's made promises in the past he's kept them."

Hurriya was quiet a moment. "What promises *has* he made?" she asked.

"That we will possess the land always," Devora said wearily. "That we will have children, as many as stars in the winter sky. That he will dwell here among us."

Those promises seemed so empty to her now. The land they possessed was reduced to withering fields and ash. An entire settlement had lost its children. And her own womb was barren. Sarah had borne a child out of the aging desert of her body—but that was only a story of the past.

Maybe Sarah had been right to laugh bitterly.

"That your people will always possess this land," Hurriya repeated, an edge to her voice. "Your God doesn't love my people. Why then does he curse me with visions? Does he think I haven't suffered enough?"

Devora could hear the tremor in Hurriya's voice. She shook her head. "I don't know."

Before they could say more, a short call on the shofar interrupted, summoning the men and the two women to their feet. It was time to move on. The sun above was hot and lethal in the sky, and it was all Devora could do just to get to her feet. Yet she turned and took Hurriya's arms in her hands, feeling the fever warmth of her through her sleeves, and lifted her to her feet as well. The woman almost fainted from the effort of rising. Devora didn't think she could have stood on her own. For just a moment Hurriya leaned against her, and Devora allowed it, a protective fire in her heart.

THE VINEYARD

BARAK KEPT the pace quick, leading the men in their long file along the rising riverbank past fields of barley and vineyards that were dying away like weeds in a fire. His shadow stretched out before him to his right now, long like the shadow of a tree. It was late, yet somewhere ahead there might be refugees fleeing the dead—if that heathen girl really *was* seeing things God saw. They had covered a lot of ground this day, and unlike any men and women fleeing Walls, they'd had no need to hide from the dead; they'd slain those they'd passed. No doubt the survivors of that burned settlement had traveled slower, hiding when they had to and always watching for some chance to shed pursuit and double back toward Walls. They might even be within reach this very night.

And Barak had another reason for haste. They were very near now to his own vineyard. And still all the land about them showed evidence of blight and death. His anxiety clawed at him. He had to know. He had to know for sure. As he took note of whose fields they passed, he ceased to think any more of the heathen girl or her refugees or of the *navi*, or of how Zadok had fought as though he had no fear of any corpse. His whole mind was bent on his vineyard, nearer with each step.

When they reached his vines at last, the sun was already kissing the hills with fire. Though Barak had always loved the sunsets of the Galilee—had often stood outside his door with his wife to watch them before taking her inside to his bed—he did not love this one. The burn of it along the ridges made him think of the fire at Walls. Made him think of the fire that had devoured the gods Hadassah's mother had cherished. Made him think of the nights afterward when he sat silent by his hearth, watching the coals, grieving for his woman. Made him think of things lost and never recovered.

And what Barak saw now in his field, he did not know how to bear.

He rode Ager out into the vineyard a way, then slid from his horse and staggered toward the first row of his vines like a drunken man, swaying on his feet. Behind him he heard Laban riding up and down the line of men, urging them to keep moving. Omri just sat his horse, watching his war-leader and shaking his head grimly. Devora nudged Shomar past him, and Barak heard Omri growl at her, "Your Shiloh God has abandoned us, woman."

But none of this made much impression on Barak ben Abinoam. He stumbled on toward the heart of his field.

Nothing lived in that field, nothing at all; the ground was dry, the earth itself drained of color and richness. The shriveled remains of vines limp upon the dead earth like weeds upon a shore, or hanging brown from their straightening poles like the skins serpents shed and leave behind. Barak lurched through this wasteland of his crop like one of the dead himself, then stopped and just gazed at the dead rows. Only when he felt the dry, brittle soil against his knees did he realize he'd stumbled. For a time he just knelt there in the midst of his desiccated field.

"Barak? *Barak?*"

A woman's voice, coming through the roaring in his ears as though from a great distance. Barak ben Abinoam turned his head, saw Devora standing near, and behind her Omri and others of his men. Her lips moved, but this time he did not hear her words. He should get up, he should go to find his house, his beautiful home of cedar and thatch. But he didn't yet have the strength. The dryness of his vineyard had crept inside him the way a desert wind can creep through the flap of a tent that's been poorly fastened.

He reached down, took a handful of gray soil. It felt more like sand against his palm than dirt. A moan rose in his throat.

"You," he groaned. "You are more like a heathen whore than the God of the Ark, the God this fool woman prates of. I left this field, I went to lead your People, I took down the spear." His voice rose, he was nearly shouting, venting his fury and despair without rising from his knees. "I stood in that burning settlement, I stood at Walls, I fought. How can you let my harvest wither? Are you not God of planting and of harvest? You took my Hadassah, you took the harvest I expected of her womb. And this—you take this." He lifted his eyes to the silhouettes the hills made against the darkening sky, that dark, unknowable expanse from which came rain and day's heat and which the evening's first stars did so little to light. "What covenants do *you* keep, you whore?" he cried.

He saw the *navi* step before him. Saw her lift her hand. Then the left side of his face rang from the slap.

"Be silent, you fool," the *navi* snapped.

Barak just looked at her a moment. Then he began to laugh, loudly, the laughter building from deep in his belly. He just knelt there and laughed until tears poured down his face.

Devora watched him, aghast, and when he fell silent at last, gasping for breath, she hissed, "Get *up*. Barak, we can't stay here. Grieve tonight in your tent, not now."

He shook his head. His hands clenched in the soil.

"*Barak!*"

"You cannot ask that of me," he breathed. "You cannot. This is my land, these are my vines. This is my house, my land." He would not look up at her. "Omri can lead the men."

"Omri can lead the men of Zebulun. But who will lead the men of Naphtali? Issachar? If not you?"

A long silence.

"Find another," he whispered.

"Barak ben Abinoam!" Strain in her voice. "Whether God and you keep covenant or not, you have made a covenant with *me*, and I call you to fulfill it."

He met her gaze. "Why? Why ride when I have neither field nor wife to defend?"

"Defend the *People*," the *navi* cried. "Defend the Covenant!"

"I have no Covenant," he said. "God keeps no Covenant."

"Then defend *me*. Help me, Barak. Help me take these men against the dead."

Barak gave her that same empty look. Then a shrill cry tore the air—a woman's scream of panic. Barak felt his breath catch in his throat. His body stilled, listening. The air erupted with moaning, the distant wailing of the hungry dead.

Barak stirred at last, rising to his feet. He stared hard across the vineyard. "That came from the house," he whispered, going cold with horror. "*Hadassah.*"

It seemed impossible to him in that moment that only half a year ago he had stood in this vineyard toiling beneath the sun, near where he stood now, and one of the field slaves had run to him, calling his name. The man had been out of breath, and it was a few moments before Barak could grasp the man's message—that something was terribly wrong with his pregnant wife. Barak had tossed his pruning tools and his gloves to the dark soil and bolted for the house, charging down the long row between the vines, panting for breath. That had been the day God had taken his wife from him, the day he had arrived almost too late. The fever had burned through her all too quickly; when he stood in the door gasping for breath, she had turned her glassy eyes to him and whispered, "I'm glad you're here."

The last words he'd heard her say.

Now Barak leapt to Ager's back and swung the horse about so hard the gelding nearly foundered. He sent Ager galloping hard between the rows of shriveled vines, his blood cold. He *had* to know who had screamed, what woman had cried out from his house.

He heard Devora's horse galloping behind him, heard her cry, "Quickly, Shomar!" but paid her no heed. In moments he could see a long house of cedar above the dead vines, and then he was out of the withered stalks and riding toward the door of the house, but others were there before him. The stench of them ripe in the air. He caught a glimpse of a living figure slipping through the door of the house and slamming it shut. Corpses staggered after it, throwing themselves at the door. Others beat at the walls of the house with their hands or hurled their bodies into the wood. Thirty or more. Some of them naked, their bodies torn and chewed, terrible wounds. Others disheveled, their clothing rotting on their backs, their bodies rotting within their clothes. Another shriek from within the house. Roaring, his whole mind filled with Hadassah's memory and Hadassah's death, Barak ben Abinoam lifted his spear and rode down the dead.

HEBER THE KENITE'S STORY

THE NEXT FEW moments were the most terrifying Devora had known since childhood. There were shouts behind her, but her whole mind was fixed on the man riding hard before her, out of reach. And on the dead slamming their bodies into that house. She heard the shriek from within, and Devora herself screamed silently as Shomar bore her toward the ravenous dead at a gallop.

Ahead of her, Barak leapt from his horse, landing on his feet with his spear clutched in both hands, and then he was at the door, wielding that bronze weapon with a ferocity Devora had never seen him display before. The butt of his spear slammed hard into one corpse's belly, sending it flying from the door; then the sharp bronze point drove into another corpse's skull. Devora slowed her horse, and Shomar reared with a shrill animal scream as several corpses turned from the wall and lurched toward her, their hands reaching for her, for the horse, for them both. The stench of them ripe in the air.

"Hold on!" she gasped to Hurriya. Unsheathed, Mishpat whined through the air.

Another shriek from within the house, then an abrupt end to the cry.

Heart pounding, Devora took off one corpse's scalp, and the little circle of hair and flesh spun through the air. Still the unclean thing came at her, growling like an animal. Its brain exposed and pulsing. Then there were dead all about the horse, grasping at her legs and Hurriya's. All those murky eyes staring up at them from faces that had been bitten or chewed half away. The Canaanite took up a waterskin, nearly full, in both hands, and brought it smashing down on one corpse's head, using its weight to knock the corpse away. It staggered back, then caught its balance and came at them again. Devora lifted her voice in song, shakily, but felt no desert ferocity, only raw, pounding terror as the corpses' fingers caught at her dress, tearing it, trying to pull her from the saddle. Mishpat slashed across faces and hands.

A glance showed Barak standing in his door, having forced it open, and spearing the dead as they came at him. He kicked one hard in the belly, driving it back as he wrenched his spear free of another corpse.

There were shouts behind them in the field, men running on foot. And a horse's hooves, galloping hard. Then Laban was with them, his axe swinging in the air, splitting one of the faces that had been snarling up at Devora and Hurriya. Hurriya bent low, slamming the waterskin against the hands that grasped at her; then one of the corpses got its fingers in her long hair, and with a scream she was wrenched from Shomar's back. Devora reached for her and caught only a fistful of green dress that tore away in her hand. "*Hurriya!*" she shrieked.

After a panicked heartbeat, the *navi* slid from Shomar's back into the dead, their hands on her flesh, her gown, making her unclean. Screaming, she carved with her sword, cutting away the terrible dead faces. Hurriya. *Hurriya!*

Cold breath on her throat and the cold of a hand clutching one side of her neck, pulling her toward the corpse's teeth.

Devora spun into the corpse, saw its eyes inches from her own, her sword trapped between her body and its cold flesh; panicked, she brought the hilt up and smashed the hard bone into its face. She shoved the corpse back with a strength that only terror could give her. Another cold hand on her shoulder, pulling her back, wrenching her from her feet; she fell. For a moment she lay on her back and saw their two faces above her, and screaming she brought Mishpat up and cut into them. Quickly she rolled to the side and got back to her knees, barely keeping herself from vomiting. One of the dead she'd cut stumbled after her, and she drove her sword into its head like a spear. Its toppling weight tore Mishpat from her grasp and she scrambled to the corpse's side and retrieved her sword with a desperate pull at its hilt. Heaving for breath, she looked up and saw Laban with his arm about the Canaanite, pulling her up onto his horse, her dress torn open at her left side. The girl was shaking and weeping; four dead lay still, their heads cloven by Laban's axe. Drawing in a ragged breath, Devora realized it was over.

Laban rode to her and leaned half out of his saddle, extending his hand to her.

Devora shook her head. "No, unclean—" She glanced at the weeping girl. "Did any of them bite her?"

"No." Laban's voice was a deep rumble. "Take my hand, *navi*. Uncleanness doesn't matter now, not up here where the dead have touched everything. Another week and we will all be unclean, whether we live or die."

Devora gazed up at him. The deep brown of his eyes, his weathered face. Once before a man had offered her help when she was unclean. She remembered Zefanyah tossing her the waterskin when she'd left Shiloh, that time the old *navi* had banned her from the camp. She remembered the warm leather of the waterskin in her hands, how she had cherished it those days and nights when she was alone in the heather.

Laban's face too was kind.

"I can't," she whispered. Pleading. "The Law is all we have. Our only tent. Without it, we are only leaves in a high wind." She pressed one hand to the earth, splaying her fingers, and forced herself to her feet. Hurriya's tearful eyes gazed at her as she rose.

"Are you all right?" Devora asked her.

The Canaanite nodded shakily.

"Thank God." Devora yearned suddenly to hold her, to pull her close. Instead, she turned toward the house, saw Barak still standing in the door, leaning on his spear, his chest heaving as he caught his breath. The dead lay about his feet in a heap of reeking flesh and tattered cloth. His gaze met hers and there was a look about him that she had never seen in anyone but Zadok.

He cast his spear aside with a bitter expression and turned to go into the house, and Devora stumbled toward the door, stepping with a shudder over the bodies strewn about it. She heard Laban's deep voice and Hurriya's faint, exhausted voice behind her, and then footsteps, and she waited at the door for the Canaanite. Hurriya was as white as if she had no blood left in her body. Her legs shook within the remains of her dress. Devora caught her arm, pulled her near, put her arm about her to steady her, and they went in. Behind them Laban turned and rode back toward the men approaching on foot over the field.

The interior of the house was dim, with the day's fading light coming in only through a few untended gaps in the thatch between the stout cedar boards that made up the walls and roof. There was a large window in the far wall but it had been closed and barred with wooden slats. To the left, a wall with a few bundles leaning against it and a ewer for water. A few clay bowls. To the right, some bedding left in a corner and a doorway covered with a heavy, hanging rug, likely leading to the room where Barak used to sleep. In the center of this main room they found a short man with a sun-weathered face, aging but still lean with muscle, crouched over a woman whose face had gone still with death. The man was clad in leather armor. For a cloak he wore a once magnificent gazelle pelt, now dirtied and stained. He held a bloodied knife in his hand; there was a great gash in the woman's left breast.

To Devora's horror, the woman's womb was round with child; she was pregnant, and the man had killed her. The *navi* drew back with a gasp, then saw the livid bites on the woman's arm.

The man held out his hand as if to ward them away. "I had to kill her," he said quickly. "She was bit. I only killed her because she was bit!"

Barak stared at the corpse for a long moment. "She's not Hadassah," he said softly. The rage went out of his eyes like a doused fire, leaving them cold and dim.

"Of course she's not," Hurriya said softly. "Our dead don't come back to us, Hebrew. Not unless they come back in hunger."

Barak didn't answer; he just gazed at the corpse. Hurriya stepped past him, gave the man with the knife a wide berth, went to lean against the open doorway at the other end of the room. She lowered her head as though to seek what privacy she could as the fright of her near escape took hold of her. Devora watched her, worried, but did not go to her. Her heart had not stopped pounding.

"Who are you people?" The man with the knife looked from one of them to the other. A flicker of recognition in his eyes when he glanced at Hurriya's face, though the Canaanite didn't appear to notice.

Devora turned her gaze away from the Canaanite. "I am Devora, the *navi*. I see what God sees."

The man sneered. "God doesn't see anything anymore. She's left us. Left the land. She's gone."

Another day, Devora would have rebuked him, would have had sharp words. She had none today. Not with that corpse on the floor and so many of them outside, lying in the blighted field about the house. "That might be," she said. "But if God does have anything to show us, I will see it. Or she will." She nodded toward Hurriya.

The other man followed her look, but Barak cut in. "Where are the dead?"

"Everywhere. Hills stink with them. You can't do anything but run."

"We didn't come here to run," Devora said quietly. "Are you bitten?"

"No," he muttered. "I'm likely to end up the only man in this forsaken land who isn't." He considered her with that look the northern men gave her that meant she was strange to them, a woman but something else as well. That look that meant they didn't know how to speak to her.

"I'm Heber," he said.

"You're a Kenite." Devora recognized his accent.

One side of his mouth curved, half a smile. "I am."

The Kenites were desert men. Rare to see one west of the river. They were not of the twelve tribes, but had bound themselves to the Hebrews with many covenants in the wilderness years, and had sheltered vulnerable Israel out where the wind screamed in the rocks. The Lawgiver himself had taken a Kenite wife, and the Kenites had sworn to live by the same Law, worship the same God. The Kenites were known in the land as a wild tribe, hot-tempered and skilled with bronze.

"You have a camp nearby?" Barak asked.

"Up there." Heber waved his hand vaguely upriver. "Had four men with me. Dead ate them. Ate my horse. Ate theirs. I crawled through the river a while and lost them. Fell a few times, then got up and went on. No use dying in the water, unburied, for anything to eat. Two nights back. So dark, those clouds, no moon even. Couldn't see anything. Even God must have been blind in that. Finally find a little place to get out of the water, up onto the high bank. Can't get back to my camp—too many between here and there." He shook his head. "We'd had a good raid," Heber said. "Against the heathen," he added quickly, seeing the look Devora gave him. Hurriya must have heard him, but she didn't look up from her grief. Impossible to know if she was even listening.

"I don't care to get the blood of the People on my knife," Heber went on. "A good raid, though. Loaded most of our goods on horseback. We meant to trade at Refuge and hear who had seen the dead and where. Set out that way, didn't make it. Our horses. They ate *our horses*."

"Your camp. How large is it?" Barak asked. "Is anyone left there?"

"No, just my goods. Some woven rugs, a slave girl. And my other horse, Ira." He scowled. "I did not come easily by that horse, and now I'm on foot, with the dead on every side."

Devora gave him a sharp, appalled look. His *other* horse. When she and Zadok had left Shiloh, they had taken with them two of the only three horses in the camp. Barak's camp had only eleven. And this *raider*, who lived by taking the possessions of other men, spoke casually of his *other* horse. She glanced at Hurriya, but she was still leaning against the doorway, silent in her grief.

"At dawn, there were dead along the bank, just wandering there," Heber muttered. "So I lowered myself over the edge before I was seen, and there was a wolf's den under the weeds, in the wall of the bank. I slipped in. No wolves now. They don't like the dead either, they don't. Nothing living does." He glanced up at Barak and Devora, and his look was haggard with memory. "Had to stay there in the dirt all of the last day and this last night and most of this day too. No food. Didn't dare crawl down to the river for water. Didn't dare sleep. One of the dead fell from the bank once, right into the water, made my heart nearly stop. Waited for it to get up—where it was standing it would have seen me—but its body broke in the fall, its back maybe. It just moved its head from the left to the right, facedown in the water. Couldn't even moan with its face in the water like that. Probably still there. Hope it rots there." He lowered his voice fiercely.

"Sometime this morning, the dead wandered on, all but that one in the water. So I got up, climbed quietly as I could onto the bank. Walked downriver a bit, climbed back down for water, then up. Kept moving. Have to keep moving now. Found refugees coming up the river to meet me. From Walls."

"They're alive!" Devora cried.

Hurriya looked up quickly. It had been her vision of survivors that had sent them here.

Devora felt a surge of sudden hope. If this were true—if there were truly refugees from Walls, men and women who still lived and breathed and had survived the death of their settlement—if Barak's men could find them and protect them—perhaps everything would be all right. If they could save some of the People, surely they could cleanse all the land. Surely it would mean God had not forsaken them. Whatever reason God had for sending no visions to his servant Devora since their coming to the north, for sending visions of what might come only to a Canaanite girl who did not worship him—whatever it all meant, if they could save these people, they would know, they would *know* God was with them. And all these deaths—the children in that town, and this pregnant woman who lay dead on the floor of Barak's house, and *Zadok*—these deaths would not be without meaning.

Heber nodded. "Fifty, sixty of them. Fleeing the dead. Said Refuge was besieged. Said I could join them, they'd be grateful, they would, for another knife and a man who knows what to do with it. But I wasn't going to try going north again." He shuddered. "Thought I'd be able to slip by the dead, if I was quiet. I'm used to being quiet. Then I met her." He nodded toward the corpse. "She wanted to try getting back to Walls. Made a pact with her—"

He stopped. His face went ashen. He was staring past them at the corpse.

HURRIYA

DEVORA GLANCED over her shoulder and froze. The corpse was *moving*, its fingers twitching against the cedar floor. Though it had a knife wound in its breast.

"*El kadosh*," Heber breathed. Holy God.

"*El adonai*," Devora whispered. She lifted Mishpat and turned toward the body. By the door, Hurriya's face twisted into an expression of loathing and hate.

Even as Devora stepped toward the corpse, its eyes opened. Devora gasped. There was nothing in those eyes, no emotion, no awareness, no life. The woman's eyes did not reflect back either Devora's face or the blade lifted over her. Devora recalled Hurriya's words to her amid the ashes of Walls—that in the eyes of anyone living, be she Hebrew or heathen, you could see her life and her need and the reflection of God in whose likeness she was made.

But not in these eyes. These eyes might drink in what the corpse saw, but they gave nothing back.

The corpse's lips parted and it drew in its first breath, lifting its heavy womb. Then it let out the breath not in a wail like a new life being born, but in a long, slow moan, a sound that swept into your ears and inside your mind and under your ribs and into your heart, the voicing of a need so great it could never be met, not even if the one voicing it should devour all the world.

The corpse rose up on its elbows and rolled to its side, those dull eyes turning toward Devora's legs, the moan dropping to a hiss.

"God!" Barak choked. "Slay it!"

Heber stepped near, his bloodied knife ready. "Step aside, woman," he said.

Devora could not look away from the corpse's eyes. She felt cold throughout her entire body. Then the thing's arm lifted, fingers curling to grasp. It reached for her leg.

"Damn you," Devora breathed.

She brought Mishpat down. The iron sank into the corpse's head as easily as a keel sinks into water. One shudder and the corpse went still. Devora's blade held it up on its elbow for a moment, then the body slid from the sword and fell back. Its hands hung limp. A great gash in its head, cleaving it nearly to the eyes. Those eyes were open and unchanged.

It did not bleed.

After a moment they heard the sounds of anxious voices outside, the men talking. And a scratching against the wooden floor in the other room, probably the flight of a mouse.

"God," Barak breathed again. "God."

"It's what happens," Heber muttered. "Seen it before. Never get used to it, though."

Devora just stared at the corpse's womb, so large and full. This woman had carried life for the People, had carried within her own body the survival of the Covenant and of her tribe. Now she lay dead and unclean. Devora could see no movement against the skin of the corpse's belly, but still the sight of that distended belly struck her with horror. What if some small, waiting life yet moved in there? She had an almost overwhelming urge to bend and press her hand to that unclean flesh, to feel for some movement or some beating of a tiny heart.

"Get it out of here, please." Devora swallowed.

Barak nodded, his face stunned, and he stepped toward the outer door, then through it. They could hear his voice lifted outside.

"You did it right, girl," Heber said. "Went for the head." He lifted his gaze from the body, gave Devora a bewildered look. "What are you doing with a man's blade?"

Devora ignored him, stepped away, and looked to Hurriya. The girl still leaned against the edge of the inner door. Her eyes still glassy from the lingering fever, yet intent on the body.

"How many have to die?" the Canaanite whispered.

"Some days a woman can only save one life," Devora muttered. Glanced at Heber. "It looks like today we saved yours."

"The men with you did," Heber said. He nudged the body contemptuously with his foot. "Not that I'm not thankful for it, Hebrew." He looked around at the dim room, glanced up at the rafters. "May be enough room for the men in here. Could wall up the door, be safe until dawn if we're quiet."

"There are five hundred men by the river," Devora said. She gave the walls of cedar a look of distaste. "We'll sleep in the tents."

Barak stepped back in, and two men with him. They had gloves. Grimly the two took up the corpse by its feet. Devora stepped aside as they dragged it out through the door. Hurriya stared at the corpse until it was gone.

"Cairns," Devora whispered.

"They gather stones already," Barak said.

"Thank you."

Heber glanced from one of them to the other, the bewilderment in his face growing. He sucked in his lower lip, chewed on it.

Barak's face was drawn with pain, and Devora remembered that his fields and his very house had been defiled. Devora stepped beside him. "We will cleanse the land," she said for his ears only. "And there will be another vineyard."

"I will keep my covenant," the man said wearily, and Devora realized that though she'd meant to comfort, Barak thought she was doubting him.

Before she could say anything more, she heard that scratching sound from the inner room again, louder now. Frowning, Devora glanced at the rug hung over the door to the inner room, then gasped. The rug had been pulled aside a little, and a corpse was looking through it. A mangled body on its elbows, most of its face chewed away, only one eye intact, both ears gone, a thing deaf and nearly blind and no longer bleeding or feeling, yet still moving, crawling and scratching its way across the floor in terrible purpose. Even as Devora glimpsed it, the death-stench filled the room, pinned back previously by the heavy rug and now freed to warn them all, though too late.

It happened fast. Too fast. The thing's rotted hand reached out, grasped Hurriya's ankle, and tugged sharply. The Canaanite fell to her knees hard, then slammed down on her face with a startled cry. The corpse tugged Hurriya half under the rug as it pulled itself forward, climbing onto her. Ripping her dress open and gouging into the woman's side with its fingers and teeth. Even as Devora leapt at the corpse with Mishpat in her hand, she saw the rush of blood, red and thick, and torn meat.

With a scream Devora swung the blade, slicing through the corpse's face and carving the top of its head away. The body fell to the side and did not bleed or stir. Devora cast her blade aside and threw herself to her knee beside Hurriya. The wound in the girl's belly was lethal; the blood coming out was black and sluggish, and her face was pale, so pale. The girl was breathing in shallow little gasps, but she was aware, and her eyes looked helplessly up at the older *navi*.

"You didn't tell us there was a corpse in that room!" Devora cried over her shoulder.

"I didn't *know*!" Heber sounded shaken. Perhaps realizing that it might as easily have been him leaning against that door.

"Get out. Both of you."

The men hesitated.

"*Get out!*" Devora screamed.

Footsteps. She heard Barak take up her blade and wrap a cloth about it—as though to signal her that he would make sure her sword, her waterskin, and her horse were seen to. But Devora didn't turn or acknowledge him. Another moment, and she and the Canaanite were alone. Heber's knife lay on the floor near them, forgotten. Devora took up a fold of Hurriya's torn dress and pressed the fabric to the wound, but the blood welled up, soaking it. There was nothing she could do. Even if Hurriya could survive such a fatal wound—even then—Hurriya looked up at her, kept her gaze on the older *navi*'s face.

"I—I'm dying," Hurriya choked. Her eyes wild with the sudden, terrible knowledge of it.

Devora reached for her hand, gripped it, brought it to her breast. The girl's hand was unclean, but Devora was unclean also. Even if she weren't, in this one moment she could not care. What did it matter?

"Can't die," the girl gasped, her eyes wide. "I didn't find Anath. I didn't find her."

"Hurriya—" Helplessly, Devora gave the cloth over the wound more pressure. Without effect. She didn't have long.

"Please," Hurriya whispered, "find her."

"I'll try." Devora could hardly speak through the tightness of her throat. Her promise to try was all she could give.

"Oh gods." Hurriya's face was white, and the pain in her eyes was terrible, like a reflection of the pain in the eyes of God. She gasped for air a moment. "I'm sorry. I'm sorry I—hated you. Blamed you."

Devora's eyes moistened. "I'm sorry too," she whispered.

Something passed between them, something for which there were no words and would never be. Hurriya squeezed the older woman's hand once, and Devora returned it.

Then Hurriya's gaze flicked to the side of the room where the dead woman still lay. "Don't want to be—like her."

"You won't."

"My body—should go to the fish—"

"I can't," Devora whispered. "I can't do that. I'm Hebrew."

"I know. Hebrew." A plea in her eyes. "Devora, we are both women."

"Yes," Devora whispered.

"Your Law," Hurriya said faintly. Blood pooling beneath her. "Made to shelter, preserve your People. Your People weren't—weren't made to preserve it."

"Don't talk. Just breathe. Just breathe." Devora moaned. She was losing one more woman she loved. She couldn't bear it.

"You'll lift stones above me?" Hurriya rasped.

"Yes."

"And sing over my body?"

"Yes."

Hurriya's eyes glistened. "I wish I could—could hold him again. My baby." Her hands were shaking.

"I know." Devora lifted the girl's hand, pressed it to her cheek, holding back her tears. "I know."

"He was so small," she whispered. "So small."

Hurriya's eyes closed, and Devora could hear her body fighting to breathe now, in little gasps.

"Hurriya," the *navi* whispered, but the girl didn't open her eyes. With a shock she realized Hurriya's eyes would only open again if she rose from the dead.

Her chest tight, Devora hummed the first few notes of Hurriya's song, in a desperate hope that hearing it, she might come back. But she didn't. Instead, her breaths grew shallower and shallower. Lifting her hand from the bit of dress she'd pressed uselessly over the wound, Devora took the girl's hands gently in hers, feeling their warmth. She held them a while. They were so small, like a child's.

"Sleep, then," Devora whispered, sniffing back tears. "You sleep now, daughter. Sleep."

One last, small breath. Then Hurriya's chest no longer moved. She was still. Devora held the girl's hands fiercely, but there was no longer any pulse in them. A quiet, keening noise rose in her throat. Hurriya was gone. Her daughter was gone.

Shaking, Devora folded the young woman's hands over her breast, then reached and caressed her hair softly, tucking it behind her ears and laying it smoothly about her shoulders. Her tears cooled on her cheeks. "No," she kept whispering. "No, no."

She bent low over Hurriya's body and kissed her lips, gently. Hurriya's lips were soft but dry. Devora kissed the girl again, and a third time, and felt that if she were to try and stand and leave the girl's side, she would break apart, frail as clay.

Yet she had to. She glanced at the knife Heber had left on the floor. There wasn't much time. Still she gazed down at Hurriya's still body. On an impulse she unwound from about her own waist the scarlet cord that she had used there as a sash, the same cord that had once held the furs wrapped about Mishpat and that had come with her all this way into the north.

Gently Devora wound that faded scarlet cord about Hurriya's wrist. The cord looked lovely on her, even in its lack of color—as though Hurriya had been wearing it like a bracelet for years, while she gleaned in the fields or picked olives from the branches of the orchard by which she'd lived. As though she'd carried it with her all the way from the north, then all the way back again. It was weathered; it had endured, even as she had. And like a cairn, the cord was a covenant, a promise. The cord bound them both to each other. Like her iron blade, that cord had a history. It had belonged to the *navi* before her, who had been given it by Rahab herself, the Canaanite girl who had preserved the lives of two Hebrew spies during the taking of the land and who had then hung the scarlet cord from her window, a sign that her house was inviolate and sheltered when the Hebrew raiders burst at last through the walls of that settlement.

It was not only that the cord had bound Rahab to the People and brought her into the tribe; it also bound the People to her. So that their men would know that Rahab was one of theirs, not to be harmed, and to be treated as a woman of their own People might be treated. A sign that the People had a responsibility now to those women who had survived the falling of their towns' walls. Devora had a responsibility. Hurriya had tried to tell her that, tried to show her.

"Unseeing," Devora whispered, "I permitted injustices." She had sat in decision so many years with the Law at her back and the People before her, both Hebrew and heathen; perhaps she had not looked often enough over her shoulder at the Law, and so had forgotten what to look for when she gazed out on the People. She had forgotten to look for justice for the strangers in the land. Though it was the Hebrews who possessed the land, a land of promise, a land they held to be theirs and held as theirs, yet the Lawgiver had declared that there must be one Law alike for the stranger and for those born in the tents of the People. *Shelter the stranger, for you also were strangers in the land of Kemet.*

Yet her People had not done so. How many women had been left unsheltered, with only a salmah to clothe them? How many?

But Devora had no more room for thought or for anything but the deep, wrenching grief that assailed her. The house had darkened until she sat beside Hurriya's body in deep shadow.

She caressed Hurriya's hair once more, whispering her name. Then reached for Heber's knife.

***

The evening light outside the house seemed bright and harsh to her after the dimness inside, though in fact the sun had now slid behind the ridge to the west and dusk was upon them. Barak stood there talking with Omri in a low voice, and he turned at her footsteps.

"*Navi*," Barak said.

"I will camp here tonight," Devora said numbly.

After a moment Barak nodded. "I'll set a watch and tell the men to keep silence." He looked as though he wanted to say something more but could not find the words he needed.

Devora simply stepped past him, ignoring his gaze on her and the lustful gaze of Omri the Zebulunite. She had no time or space in her heart for either.

Walking as though asleep, she moved to the place at the edge of the field where the men were raising the cairns. Laban was there; he took one glance at the *navi* and then turned grimly toward the house. As he left, Devora sank to her knees by the cairns, her face drained of life. The other men glanced at her but did not disturb her.

Devora gazed out over the blighted field.

"She was the *navi*," Devora whispered to God. "Your *navi*. How could you."

No answer came to her out of the withered vines or the wide sky, and Devora knew in that moment that none ever would. Even if God were to show her a hundred visions more, there would never be any vision that would give a reason for Hurriya's death. Devora's eyes glistened, but her grief was too sharp for any moisture to wash it out. Her breast felt tight and it hurt almost to breathe. She watched dully as Laban came out of Barak's cedar house carrying Hurriya's body in his arms, tightly wrapped and shrouded in a blanket, neither face nor feet visible. Devora saw a red area in the cloth where her head must be and knew it for blood from the knife wound she had inflicted. The *navi* moaned softly and covered her face with her hands.

***

Devora worked the men hard, raising Hurriya's cairn. She made it the highest one in that line of silent promises to the dead. When Laban lifted the last stone, it clacked into place nearly level with his head. The other cairns were already done, and only a few men remained there to see if the *navi* needed help. The other men had left quickly, not wanting to spend longer than they must in the presence of the dead.

"Go," Devora whispered. "All of you."

Laban hesitated, one hand resting on the top of the cairn. "She was not of the People," he said.

"She is of my tribe," Devora said softly. "I accept her as one of my tribe. Please go."

Laban looked at her another moment, then turned without a word and began walking away through the dead field.

Devora leaned on the cairn, her eyes cold as a winter sea. Then she lifted her voice. Though hoarse, she sang with such beauty that men raising tents in the field stopped and stood still, turning to face the cairn and the *navi* beside it.

As the darkness fell, Devora sang her farewell to a woman of her People.

***

Barak offered a room in his house to her, but Devora could not bear the thought of sleeping there. She staggered out into the withered vines in the dark, moving toward where the other war-leaders had set up their tents with hers nearby. The tent Laban had offered her. She wondered a moment if Mishpat and her saddle and her waterskin were there in the tent and whether Shomar had been well cared for, but her mind was too weary to hold the thought. It was dark now, but she did not walk with any alertness. She felt like a vessel with its oil poured out and left to dry in the dust.

Walking so, she nearly collided with a man, and he called out sharply in the dark. Looking up wearily, she saw Heber's hard face in the starlight.

"Covenant and Law, woman," he growled, "watch yourself."

"I am sorry," Devora said. Her gaze took in the man—he had a bundle on his shoulders and a waterskin slung at his hip. "You're leaving," she murmured.

"I'll not stay to wait for the dead," he said.

"There are five hundred men here, Heber," Devora said. "The land will be clean in a few days, and there will be rebuilding and replanting. Raider or no, a man with a strong back will be honored here."

"Clean?" he said. He looked at her intently, then laughed, hard, a laughter eerily like Barak's when the chieftain had knelt in the ruin of his vineyard. A laughter devoid of any joy, just mirth at the savage futility he saw. The Kenite wiped tears from his face, wheezing with laughter. "You don't. You don't understand." His sides shook. "I've been hurrying south for weeks. Weeks, woman. After raiding in White Cedars. There are thousands. Thousands in White Cedars."

All sound left the world, everything but the beat of Devora's heart. She just stared at Heber, the night terribly dark around them.

His mouth was still moving, but it was several moments before she could focus on his words. Then: "All of them moaning and staggering toward us, every last one of those heathen corpses. These you're seeing are just the first. The first few."

"Thousands?" It came out in a whisper.

"Or tens of thousands. Even God has never seen so many dead." Heber laughed again, shaking his head. The sound chilled her. "I'm going to keep moving, *navi*. I don't plan to stay with your camp. You're dead already. All of you. You just haven't stopped breathing yet." He glanced away to the south, his mirth dying out, the haunted look returning to his eyes. "Make for Kemet, most likely. Get a vast river between me and those walking dead."

"Kemet!" Devora was struggling to collect her thoughts, still the racing of panic inside her. "But this is the land of promise. Kemet—our fathers were slaves there!"

"*Your* fathers. What should I care? They feed laborers well in the dark land. Here, we'll be free and eaten. God keep you, *navi*." And he walked away into the shadows. After a few steps he called back without stopping: "If you reach my camp upriver and my slaves haven't been eaten, you're welcome to them."

Then he was gone.

Devora stared after him into the night.

Thousands.

"Merciful God," she whispered. "Cover us. Let the *malakh ha-mavet* pass over us."

***

Pale as a corpse, Devora made her way back to her tent, which Laban had pitched for her a little apart from the others, for she was *kadosh*, and apparently to him at least that still meant something. The tent was just barely within earshot of the others, and now Devora looked over the night wasteland of the withered field and drew in her breath sharply. Maybe it wasn't a good idea for her tent to stand apart. No nazarite stood watch outside the tent's door. If the dead came lurching across the field, only a thin wall of canvas and the possible protection of God's hand would stand between her and their grasping hunger.

Thousands.

She shivered in the dark.

Shomar was tethered just outside her tent, sleeping on his feet. Devora saw that someone had placed a basin of water within the gelding's reach and that he'd drunk half of it. A little relief touched her; her alarm at Heber's words had cracked the numbness about her heart like the shell of an egg, and for just a moment she stood leaning against her horse, putting her arms about his powerful neck, breathing in his scent. This had been a hard journey for him too. And he was a little part of her husband, here with her. The two of them strangers together in a strange camp. She rested against her horse, not letting herself think of Hurriya or Zadok. There was moisture on her cheek, and she rubbed it away against his sleek hair. She permitted herself no more tears than that, and after a bit she straightened, knowing that if she did not go into her tent now, she would fall asleep right there, standing on her feet like a horse herself.

She didn't know what nightmares she would endure tonight with neither Lappidoth nor Zadok beside her, nor what the next morning might bring. The refugees they'd been pursuing might have been eaten already, or not. Barak might stand and lead the men, or he might crumble in his own grief. God might protect them, or not. She didn't know. She couldn't even find the strength to care. She wanted only sleep.

Drawing aside the door flap of her tent, she stepped in where it was dark and warm.

She had the briefest sensation of not being alone—then someone grabbed her, a powerful arm pulled her back, crushing her against a firm body. Her eyes flew wide as she felt naked skin against her, breathed in a man's sweat scent. Even as she sucked in a breath to scream, a hand, rough and calloused, covered her mouth. Smothering her cry.

A fierce whisper in her ear. "I don't see any nazarite dog heeling you here."

ALL FALLING APART

DEVORA BREATHED in desperate little gasps, through her nose. Omri's breath was hot on her throat. His lips brushed her neck and she jerked in his arms.

"Shhh, hush, woman," he growled in her ear, his hand pressing down more cruelly over her mouth, bruising her lips. "Hush now."

Fury and fear pounded through her, like fire and ice. Every inch of her body wildly alert. She could feel his rough palm against her lips, his belly pressed into her back, and something swollen pressed to her hip. He couldn't be doing this—she was *kadosh*, not to be touched! She was married. She was *unclean*, though she had yet to tell the camp that. This couldn't be happening.

She tried to bite his palm, and he jerked her head back hard against his shoulder, his mouth moist on her throat. Kissing her. He was kissing her. He did it roughly, bruising her neck. She screamed again into his palm and twisted in his arms, but his arm crushed hers to her sides. She dug her nails into the skin of his hips, but he only breathed louder by her ear.

"That's it, woman, that's it," he groaned softly. "I knew you were baiting me that day. Riding here alone with that nazarite and no husband. Did he enjoy you, that dog? You're going to enjoy this a lot more."

He dragged her back, pulling her with him toward the bedding at one side of the tent. She fought him, but he was *strong*. She kept crying out into his hand, hoping men in the other tents would hear, but the sounds were small and muffled. And she couldn't get *loose*. Panic rushed through her like cold water. He was doing as he pleased, and she couldn't stop him.

She was forced down onto her back, his weight on her. He pinned her upper arms with his elbows, leaning into the hand he held pressed over her mouth, hurting her. His eyes fierce and dark, just above hers. She struggled but was hardly able to move, unable to get him off her. She cried out as his knee forced her thighs apart.

"I can smell your cunt," he breathed, and bit her ear.

She thrashed under him, shoving at his sides with her hands. She had to get him *off* of her. Her eyes shot to the door of her tent, but Zadok was not outside. Zadok wasn't anywhere. Her eyes flicked to the small bundle of her garments and her waterskin, to her left, the length of a man's body from where she lay. She could see the glint of her blade beneath the clothes.

She couldn't get enough air.

"You hush," Omri whispered in her ear.

Devora squirmed, nauseated, as he began thrusting his hips against her, through her dress.

"You don't get to talk tonight. You had us all so convinced you were the *navi*. That you heard *God*. Well, fuck you. Anyone with eyes can see that the Covenant is falling *apart*." The man licked her throat—the animal *licked* her. She shook with rage and fear. "You saw what happened to Zadok," Omri whispered to her. "And so many others. You saw the *dead*. God isn't in the land anymore. God isn't here. If he was, he'd have sent the Ark. Do you hear me? He would have sent the fucking *Ark*. It's all falling apart. So what should I care?"

His hand left her lips, then his mouth was on hers and she screamed into his mouth. Felt the grasp of his hand at her hip, gripping her, then tugging her dress up. She kicked, her knees hitting against his hips. She threw herself to the side; his weight held her in place, but she twisted her left arm free and went for his face. Dug her fingers into his right eye.

Omri reeled back with an anguished yowl, his hands lifted to his face. A hard shove with her hip and he was off her. She rolled away across her bedding, reaching. And as quickly as she might draw a breath, she'd swept Mishpat up in her hand and rolled onto her knees. Brought the sword up in one smooth movement even as Omri came at her, and the blade severed his neck as cleanly as though he were made of thin cloth rather than flesh and bone. His head hit the rugs flooring the tent and rolled toward the door; his body fell to one side of her.

On her knees, holding her bloodied sword to the side, the hilt cold in her hand, Devora screamed in anguish and rage. Panting, gazing down at the headless body. It lay completely still. Devora took in great gulps of air, sobbing for breath. Her heart loud in her breast. She worked her tongue in her mouth a moment, then spat on him. Spat out the taste of his mouth.

He'd meant to defile her. Use her. As though she were some girl he'd taken in a raid and not the *navi* and the mother of Israel.

"The Covenant *is* falling apart," she whispered.

Men were shouting outside, in the other tents. Men who'd heard her cry out. Shaking, Devora forced herself to her feet. Stumbled to the door of her tent, Mishpat bloody in her hand. She glanced to the right, where the head lay faceup, still contorted in that last expression of shocked fury. The eyes already glassy, emptied of life.

Breathing hard, Devora hurried from her tent. Shomar was still tethered just outside. She leapt astride him, not bothering with saddle or any bags, just laying the blade across her thighs. Men were running toward her. Barak was there. "*Navi*, what has happened?" he cried.

For the briefest moment she hesitated. The night around her was strange and dark and there was no moon yet. Behind her in the tent, a slain man, his blood dripping from her sword. Somewhere out there in the blackness over the fields, lurching dead. Thousands.

And no moon yet.

Her right hand tightened around Mishpat's hilt. Her left gripped Shomar's mane.

Everything was falling apart. They could not delay for a night, nor even for a moment.

"We end this tonight!" she called to Barak. "We are not staying here! We *end* this! Bring the men and follow, Barak!"

Then, trusting him to follow and knowing she must ride whether he did or not, she dug in her heels and drove Shomar galloping into the empty vines.

FEAST OF THE DEAD

NOW SHE WAS alone. Entirely and utterly alone. There was only the moaning of the dead in the hills on every side, the warm reassurance of Shomar's mighty body between her knees, and the dead bone of Mishpat's hilt in her hand, slick with her sweat. She was panting. She didn't even know if *God* was here. Perhaps the words Omri had hissed in her ear had been true. Perhaps even God was gone. There was only her.

She could still feel Omri's touch loathsome on her thighs, and she wanted to find a quiet place to sit and grieve, but she held herself together. She had to. She had no idea where the dead were; she had to be alert. When she glanced behind her, the camp was just a glow of fires in the distance. For a moment she thought she could see movement on the bank, perhaps Barak following. She didn't know. Out in this dark, she might as well be riding through a land already dead, the Covenant nothing more than torn and discarded scraps of roots, the People a once-green olive tree wrenched from the earth and cast aside. Heber's words dug into her mind: *Thousands, thousands in White Cedars.*

And Hurriya's words. *We are both women.*

"Yes," Devora whispered again, "yes we are."

She made it to the riverbank, discerning it by the faintest shimmer on the water, the only thing that passed for light in this darkness. Shomar galloped hard along the edge of the water. Abruptly she heard faint screams ahead, somewhere in the night. Many of them cries of pain and terror. Then the moaning of the dead, as though the dark itself had taken voice. Devora's fingers tightened in Shomar's mane.

A sliver of moon appeared over the hills, and glancing up, Devora cried out. The moon held her eyes. She stared at it, her heart pounding in her breast. She had seen such a moon before, over Shiloh, that terrible night. The light felt *wrong*. She felt it like a scream beneath her skin. The shine of the moonlight on the dark river to her right was like blood on the water. In horror, she saw its light on her hands and felt it beating on the nape of her neck, the way the sun beats on you on a desert day, that kind of insistence, that kind of draining of energy and strength. But this was cold, so cold.

Then Shomar took her past a stand of dark oaks, and spread before her was a field of trampled barley. In her first wild glimpse of that field, Devora saw things that afterward she would pray and beg to forget, and never would.

There were dead in the barley, hundreds, the stench of them overwhelming. Some shambled through the tall crop by the water, pursuing a small group of living men and women who ran and stumbled before them, likely the last survivors of Walls. Other dead crouched over their victims in small groups throughout the field, and their eyes shone red, luminous in the moonlight.

One corpse was dragging a flailing woman through the barley by the hair, while four other dead lurched after her, bending, their hands grasping, trying to clutch at the living woman, who was young, too young. Nearby, a man had been torn apart, drenching a patch of the field in his blood; one of the crouching dead was chewing on a hand, another on a foot, a third had an ear. One corpse was seated with a pile of entrails in its lap like a nest of dead serpents. It lifted the glistening intestines to its mouth with a slow grace, like a dignified grandmother at a banquet.

The living by the river did not scream as they ran; many of them fled half bent over, as though winded. One, a woman Devora's own age, had cast aside her robe or her salmah and now ran naked in the barley, forsaking dignity for speed. Even as Devora looked, the woman stumbled, and three of the dead fell on her. One grasped the woman's leg in its hands and tore strips of flesh from her thigh with its teeth. The woman kicked with her other leg and screamed, shrill peals of pain and terror. The other two corpses tore into her breast with their fingers, ripping her open and reaching in for those parts of her that God had hidden within her body before birth. The corpses' arms were bloodied to the elbows; one reached low and pulled out the entrails, and the other corpse snatched at them; the first turned on the second and hissed like a cat. The woman's shrieks went on and on, terribly similar to the screams of Devora's mother. But gazing at that woman dying in the barley, this time Devora did not see her mother's face in her mind, her mother dragged screaming out the door of her tent. She saw only Hurriya's face. Hurriya, her life bleeding out, dying helplessly where Devora could not reach her or console her. Fury rushed through Devora like flame roaring from one tree to the next. She held Mishpat out to the side, ready, though her arm felt the strain.

No more of the People must perish.

"*Ride*, Shomar," she whispered fiercely, and sent the horse surging beneath her in a gallop that tore up the dirt.

Faces of the dead turned toward her. A song of metal in the air, slicing down as her horse carried her into this rot in the tall barley in the Galilee night. She rode down upon the woman being eaten amid the trampled plants, and her sword took away first the top of the woman's head, silencing her screams. Then she wheeled about, and Shomar's hoof took one of the dead in the face, sending it sprawling. One corpse still gnawed at the woman's leg, the other rose snarling and lunged at Devora, its gray hands grasping for her sandal, her leg. Mishpat cut away the hands, then carved through the thing's head, and the body fell like chopped wood.

Then Devora was riding about the field, slashing. With her knees she kept a tight hold on her horse, her heart hammering, her mouth hot and dry, her mind gone in one long scream of horror.

The terrible, half-unfleshed faces of the dead—

The moonlight dyeing the grasses the color of blood—

Her own screams reaching her ears—

Her frantic glances about the field showed just moaning, lurching figures and a few dying men and women twisting on the ground, the others in the distance fleeing. Her horse had carried her through to the other side, where the hills rose again and there were fewer dead. She grasped Shomar's mane and dug in and wheeled him about once more, riding back at a canter into the dead. Her body was covered in a sheen of cold sweat, she was shivering. She fought for focus, rode at the first standing corpse she saw and took away its head with her sword.

Another corpse was devouring a boy who struggled weakly under it, and she stopped her horse, and as it reared she carved down into the creature's head. After the corpse fell to the side, she leaned over and drove her blade through the boy. Then she was trotting her horse through the moon-red field, and tears were hot on her cheeks, and she was fighting and killing in a blurred world. She heard sharp cries and deep, hungry moans; she rode through the midst of them, brushing tears and sweat and dirt from her eyes and gazing into faces as she passed, but none of them were her mother, none of them were Naomi, none of them Zadok or Hurriya. And she could save none of them. None of the bitten. Just a chop of the blade she held, butcher's work.

***

Barak rode hard, and Ager wheezed under him. He could hear the *navi*'s hoofbeats ahead of him, though distant, otherwise there would have been no way he could have followed her in this terrible dark. Yet he rode blind; trees rushed by on one side or the other like grim presences, brief touches of some dark heathen god on his mind, looming large and horribly close, then gone as he rode deeper into the night. He was panting, his eyes wide, straining for some glimpse of light; he rode in terror of losing the *navi*, in terror of his horse stumbling. He had not paused to look in her tent but had run for his horse; as it was, he had barely saddled in time to pursue her. Behind him he could hear the faint hoofbeats of a few horses following. Laban perhaps. A glance over his shoulder showed him torches and their reflections on the water, and the dark silhouettes of armed men hurrying after their chieftains on foot. When he heard the screams ahead and the low moaning, it shook him. This was not how he'd wanted to come upon the dead. No plan of attack, no hiding of men in high places where they could rain spears down. Just a headlong gallop into a valley of corpses with his men far behind and leaderless. He cursed under his breath and drove Ager to greater speed.

Then the moon rose, and it rose the color of blood, and he heard the screams in the moonlit field ahead. Everything turned cold within him, and he saw the corpses bathed in the red light, their eyes blind and unblinking. He saw their feeding, saw the People being violated and devoured, heard their shrieks in the barley. Saw the *navi* ride into them as though into a field of wheat, her sword flashing in the moon. Ager carried him into the field after her, in a rush; the reek of decay slammed into his nostrils, stronger than he'd ever encountered it, powerful enough that he nearly slid from his horse.

One moment the dead were far out in the field; the next he was among them, attacking two-handed with his spear, a thrust to the left, a thrust to the right, their faces crowding near, hands reaching for him. He struck at them desperately as his horse surged past them. He was too panicked, sweating, to look and see if his blows had any effect. He tried to keep his eyes on the *navi* ahead; he called out to her, but the moans of the dead overwhelmed his voice.

He was wrenched backward and off his horse, and he landed with a cry in the tall barley, his spear flying from his hands. His stallion sped on, but he could not hear Ager's hooves above the noise of the dead. A hand grasped his ankle, others clutched at his throat, hands cold like water in a pool at the bottom of a cave, but dry as soil baked by the sun. A face swung over his, a face with no eyes but with a gaping mouth filled with teeth. Howling, he shoved his hands against the creature's chest, toppling it over. He reached down, plucked from his hip the small bronze knife he kept there, but others were on him. He kicked and fought, slashing with the knife, his heart pounding wildly in his chest, too much terror to think of where to strike the creatures. He laid open one's belly—it made no effort to defend itself, a thing that had once been a plump woman; its organs spilled from it now, and it still reached for his throat with fleshy fingers. He hacked away another's hand—his knife was sharp—and still it bent and dug its teeth into the leather strap covering his shoulder. The world, the unclean faces, the bright harvest stars and the waving ears of barley between them and him—it all vanished in a white fury of pain and terror. A shriek went on and on—his.

Then he could see again, he was shoving the ravenous corpse off him, pulling his knife free of its skull. He rolled, gritting his teeth, his shoulder on fire. Hands were grasping at his armor; he hacked them off and stumbled, crawled through the barley. Somewhere nearby now he heard the cries of living men. And above it all those long, wailing moans, a sound that was a rape of the mind, a sound that took away all his senses and battered him with unreasoning, animal fear.

He found himself on his hands and knees and he crawled swiftly through the barley. A shape loomed over him. He rolled to the side, somehow got on his feet. His knife found its home in the creature's throat, and he felt hands wrap about his own throat as he sawed, cutting away its head. The body fell lifeless, the hands slipping from Barak's throat. The head fell to the side, and as

Barak glanced down at it, he saw the eyes—those murky eyes—*still moving*, tracking him. The jaw still working silently. With a cry he sent it away with a kick of his foot.

He gazed around the barley field, wild with terror, his shoulder burning. Other figures were stumbling toward him, arms outstretched, eyes bright in the moonlight. He cast a frantic look ahead—he could not see Devora anywhere. Only the stumbling dead, so many. A glance over his shoulder showed him the glow of the torches of his men on the edge of the field. Gasping, he staggered toward them, then caught his breath and burst into a run.

No man could face this field of dead alone.

Tall ears of barley whacked across his skirt of leather and his bronze breast-piece as he ran. Sweat poured from his brow. There were dead all about him, but always he looked for where they were thinnest and darted through before they could seize him. His sides, his shoulder, his very lungs burned with fire.

He stumbled over a body and nearly cried out, but then he saw the eyes and saw that she was a woman, one of the living, her mouth open in silent pleading, and he reached down to take her hand and pull her to her feet, panting as the dead closed in. Yet when he pulled at her arm, she was strangely light and her eyes rolled back in her head. He glanced down and screamed, for her belly was torn open and nearly hollowed out, her entrails fleshy and half chewed away, and as he pulled, only the top part of the woman came with him. He dropped her and fell in his horror and shock. Then he scrambled away through the barley, lurching figures all about him, reaching down for him.

His mind, his breath, his whole being was taken up in the effort of flight. Ducking low through the barley, hoping to avoid being seen by the dead. There were too many between him and his men now, but at last he reached the riverside edge of the field and collapsed behind a stand of terebinths. He threw himself into the shadows behind one of the trees, dropping his knife to the ground. There he shook and sweated, certain they were following him, their dark shapes staggering through that field. But he was unable to get up. He clutched his shoulder and cried out. With a need fiercer than he'd ever felt, he longed for his own house and for the cool taste of the grapes from his vines. He clenched his eyelids shut and breathed in through his teeth, losing himself in the throbs of pain, agony that beat like a drum in his shoulder with every pulse of his blood.

He had seen what had happened to the woman in his house. Had seen her eyes open, heard her low wail. He remembered clearly the bite in her arm. He was unclean, unclean, and the wounds the dead left were lethal.

Not daring yet to look out into the field, he set his hand against the bole of the terebinth, forcing himself up onto his knees, baring his teeth against the pain and fear. His throat felt terribly dry, his body seized with thirst. He unstrapped his bronze breast-piece and cast it aside. Tore the leather jerkin beneath it up over his head with frantic, fumbling hands. Ran his fingers across the tender skin of his shoulder, wincing. His shoulder was one great bruise; the leather had been mashed into his body by the force of that corpse's jaws—but when he lifted his fingertips to his eyes, there was no blood on them. Panting, he clutched the jerkin, explored the leather with trembling fingers. He found impressions there, but the leather was tough; the teeth had not cut completely through it. Clutching the jerkin to his chest, he closed his eyes and moaned.

He had *not* been bitten.

Not bitten.

He was whole.

Tilting his head back, he sucked in great breaths of the night air, filling his chest. Alive. He was alive.

On his knees beneath the terebinths, his chest bared, he clutched the leather and just breathed. He could hear water; glancing up, he saw that the ground disappeared into a ravine perhaps a spear's cast from where he stood. Below must be the Tumbling Water, or whatever trickle would later become Tumbling Water farther south; up here on the high, cliff-like bank, the roots of the terebinths likely dug deep toward that enticing water.

Breathing fast, Barak began to shrug the leather back over his head and shoulders. Then strapped the bronze piece back on above it. It had saved him once this night; he might need it again. He cast about him; the knife he'd dropped by his feet seemed a pitiful blade to carry against the dead. After a moment he found a long branch, nearly straight, that had fallen from the tree overhead. He bent and took it up, skinning twigs from it with the knife and then hacking desperately at the narrower end, improvising a spear point. The branch was dry and he feared it might break, but at any moment a corpse might stumble in under the trees and see him. He wanted something with more reach than that knife in his hands.

"Get out," a voice hissed softly.

Startled, Barak nearly leapt up from his hiding place. Glancing sharply over his shoulder, his heart pounding, he found two eyes peering up at him amid a face smudged with dirt. A young man—hardly more than a boy—was hiding in a hollow beneath the terebinth. He'd blackened his face with dirt and was lying with his belly to the ground; he'd drawn the year's first fallen leaves over his body to conceal himself.

"Go!" the youth whispered fiercely. "This is my place. You'll bring them!"

Recovering from his shock, Barak muttered, "Who are you, boy?"

The boy lifted his head just a little, trying to peer out into the field. "Yehoyakim. From Walls."

"What are you doing down there?" Barak said sternly. He felt revulsion clenching up within him. "Your kin are dying out in the barley."

Yehoyakim met his gaze. The whites of his eyes showed. "What are *you* doing here?"

The words struck Barak like a slap. Shame burned through him. He caught his breath, swore bitterly. Cast a glance out at the field. Several lurching dead were very near now, moving toward the stand of trees. He could still hear distant screams and the low moans and nearer, the trickle of water over stones in the ravine below. Stiffening, Barak tested the heft of his makeshift spear.

Something went cold and hard inside him. His breathing calmed. He was Barak ben Abinoam, and no boy to hide behind a tree.

"Fear would devour us all, even as the dead," he muttered. He looked at the youth. The boy had lowered his chin to the ground again. "Stand and have courage, Yehoyakim. Hope that God is no woman to weep or gloat while we die, but a strong man, mighty and furious, as some of the levites say."

"So let *him* fight the dead," the boy whispered.

"Why should he? If God is a man, he will scorn you for shivering so. If God is a woman, she will not admire you or desire you. Either way, your submission to your fear makes you alone." Barak's anger was fuel and fire in his breast, and he straightened, his back to the tree, the spear ready in his hands. The dead were near now. He could hear one of them dragging one foot behind it. He took a steadying breath. In a softer voice, he added, "A day ago I saw a man take on four hundred dead by himself."

"Did he live?" the boy whispered.

"No. But we will never forget him. Neither will God." Barak's hands tightened about the haft of the spear; its weight was reassuring. He could do this. Out of the corner of his eye he caught a glimpse of flame. Looking carefully around the bole of the tree, he saw torches moving through the barley. "Look," he breathed. "The men of the north fight the dead, Yehoyakim. Come with me."

The youth shook his head, but Barak could not see him. After a moment's silence, the chieftain said, "Fine," and then he leapt around the tree and *ran* at the approaching dead. Lifted his voice in a great roar, even as his father's father must have roared at the walls of Yeriho and the burning of Ai, when the

People were still newcome to the land and were strong. His blood burned; he lifted the terebinth spear high and drove it hard into the face of the nearest corpse, then swung hard to his right, wrenching the corpse to the side and down. It slid free from the sharpened wood and fell, and the wood did not break. Barak slammed the butt end of his spear backward to his left into the chest of the next corpse even as it closed with him. The corpse sprawled into the grass hissing, and two more were upon him, their milky eyes gleaming in the moonlight. He leapt back and brought up the spear, thrusting toward one's head, even as the corpse that had sprawled to the side a moment before scrambled back to its feet.

The air smelled of smoke. In the field near at hand Barak saw fire rising and the figures of his men and of the lurching dead dark against the flame. Barak fought with a ferocity he had never before felt. He did not know anymore if God was male or female, weak or strong, reliable or fickle. But he had seen how Zadok fought before the walls of Refuge. He had seen the nazarite fight as though possessed by a god, as though he were no mere man but whirlwind and fire in a man's body. Whatever God Zadok had known, whatever that strange God was like, Barak hoped to catch that deity's attention now. And he knew that whatever God might be watching, that God would respond only to courage.

TO SAVE ONE LIFE

DEVORA HAD NOT seen Barak ride into the field and hadn't seen him unhorsed. She rode now along the rising cliffbank of the river, dealing grimly with those dead who were pursuing the refugees. She grunted and panted with the exertion, the burn in her arm as she swung Shomar about again, and again. Whenever she had breath, she screamed at the living. "Downriver!" she screamed. "Circle around! Downriver! There are tents. Downriver! Go downriver!"

Some listened and bolted to their left, darting into the field to try cutting through and heading back the way they'd come, trusting her. Others kept moving north, up the rising slope of the land. In their panic they were no longer men or women but only frantic, darting animals, deer being chased by wolves.

Then there were dead all about Devora's horse, and she was sweating in the cold and her arm nearly giving out each time she brought the blade down. Shomar reared in terror, his belly and flanks covered with splatters of decayed flesh. His hooves struck out, but the dead, who did not fear horses, only grabbed at his legs. Without success, for the horse was quick, its body massive and powerful. Yet as Shomar came back down on all four hooves, gray hands reached up, clutching at Devora's skirts and at the horse's mane. Devora screamed and carved away the hands, but there were many, and now they were all about her, more of them pressing in, so many eyes red in the moonlight. In a moment, a breath, a beat of her heart, she and her horse together would be tugged beneath them, even as the refugees had been.

A man's shout rose above the moaning, a deep-chested roar. A horse with spotted flanks was driven into the dead at her left, and Devora glimpsed Laban's face. The chieftain of Issachar had his great axe lifted high, and he brought it smashing down, the head of a corpse splitting beneath the bronze. The man held to his pommel with his hand and lifted his right foot, kicking the faces of the dead with a giant's strength, knocking corpses from their feet.

"*Navi!*" he bellowed. "To me!"

Laban forced his way through the moaning dead, and Devora cut her way to his side. Then they were riding among the dead together, chopping with axe and sword; Devora's skirts were stained with bits of gray flesh and tissue. In a moment they were free of the clinging press of corpses, free of the intense reek and the clutching of hands at her garment. Their horses took them far out into the barley; then Devora wheeled about. "No!" she cried, and sent Shomar galloping back toward the bank, where there was still a great throng of dead and a few refugees trying to elude them northward.

"*Navi!*" Laban roared.

She glanced over her shoulder, saw him gesturing downriver with his axe. She turned, then she saw it too. Some of the panic eased from her heart.

The men of Barak's camp had come.

They were on foot, and they had lit torches and were now charging into the field, shouting. Devora realized they could see her over the barley—in her white robe on her white horse, with her sword uplifted like a slice of the moon. They were charging into the field for her, because seeing her there, they believed at last that God was here in the field, ready to fight the dead with them.

The men of Israel drove against the dead, waving their torches before them, and the corpses fell back hissing before the flames. Perhaps eighty, ninety men had come. Devora didn't know where the rest were—perhaps shaking in their tents. Parts of the field went up in flame as the barley caught, for the men were desperate and they swept the torches before them wildly, their eyes showing their whites and reflecting back the fire as they confronted the snarling faces of the dead. Sometimes one of the corpses went up in flames too, its ragged clothes catching from the barley or from a torch slamming into its head and setting its hair afire. The dark above the faces of the living and the dead was alive with sparks and strangely beautiful.

Without a word to Laban, Devora sent Shomar into the fray, cutting fiercely with her blade. She kept Shomar moving, rushing among the corpses, some of which turned toward her but too slowly to grasp the fast horse, others of which went down beneath her blade without ever knowing she was there, their faces fixed on the men who were advancing with flame. She heard a scream as one of the men was pulled down, and she turned Shomar toward the cry. One of the dead had fallen, its leg crumpling beneath it. Though the corpse's back and buttocks blazed with fire, it had dragged a living Hebrew down, its arms wrapped about the man's legs. The man's scream rose in pitch as the corpse crawled over him and bit into his face. That scream!

Riding in, Devora clove the corpse's face in half, then turned again, and even as several corpses lurched into her horse's flanks, she grasped Shomar's mane tightly and leaned out to the side and took away the top half of the Hebrew's head, cutting off his scream.

One of the dead got hold of her skirt in both hands, and she clung to Shomar frantically. The cloth tore, but now the dead were pressing into the horse like a wall of cold flesh. Devora heard a shout and knew Laban was beside her, and in another moment he was among those dead with his axe. To her horror, the corpses grasped his axe and pulled the great man from his horse. There was fire in the field all about them now, and the smoke stung her eyes and throat, and she tried to force Shomar through the press of dead to where Laban had gone down, but he was covered with corpses. She heard him roaring, still struggling and fighting beneath the weight of the bodies, even as Zadok had.

But when Devora finally fought her way to him and struck down at the dead, screaming as she slew, when she cleared enough of a space to look down at the corpses that lay cut and spattered over the ground, there was little of Laban left. His face was gone, his chest torn open and emptied, the dead having pulled everything out of it. One more person she had seen die and been unable to help.

Devora stared down at his remains, but no scream would come. Wild-eyed, she lifted Mishpat high and wheeled Shomar about, though the horse's flanks and sides were flecked with sweat and bits of decayed flesh, and the gelding was half-mad with horror. Yet he obeyed when Devora sent him rushing back against the herd of shambling corpses. The *navi* no longer saw anything about her, not clearly; it was all a fever of screams and moans and hissing, inhuman faces, the faces of the true strangers in the land. She cut and thrust and slashed, and backed her horse free with the dead following her, and cut down and slashed again. And in her mind she saw crowding about her not the actual faces in this field but the faces of *her* dead: Eleazar the high priest with his eyes turned sorrowful in the moment of his death; Laban roaring as he went under; leering Omri, as she swung her blade toward his neck; Naomi the *navi*, her eyes glazed, pleading for a swift end and a high cairn; Zadok, her own Zadok, his eyes caring and intense, binding his long hair back before starting his run; her mother, shrieking and clawing at the rugs with her fingernails as something pulled her from the tent; a small infant with only one arm voicing a long moan; Hurriya, lovely Hurriya, frail and thin yet so beautiful in her green dress, dying with her face inches from Devora's own. The *navi* screamed and hacked wildly at the dead.

***

At last there came a moment when Devora lifted her blade and looked about and there were no more dead on their feet. Just men, living men and women, moaning and crying in the trampled and withering barley. And fires blazing all about them, lighting up the night. The smoke stung her eyes and she shivered, recalling the destruction of Walls. Panting, she walked Shomar across the field, listening to the groans and screams of the wounded and the bitten. Shomar's breath heaved beneath her; even her husband's magnificent horse was tired and near collapse. It took all Devora had just to stay upright on his back and withstand the reek of the field.

She halted and gazed down at a patch of crushed barley. There lay the body of a girl, one who could not have seen ten winters before she began hungering for flesh. Half the girl's scalp was missing, chopped away. It might have been

Mishpat that cut her; the blade, slimy with gore, hung limp from Devora's hand. The *navi* gazed at the girl and had no tears. She sat her horse. Breathing. Just breathing. She brushed sweat from her eyes with the back of her hand. That girl who lay dead had never been to the red tent, never heard the laughter of the older women, never learned the secrets they would tell her. She had never grown breasts, never known love or the kicking of a child inside her. Yet she was gone, like wheat cut from its stalk before it had an ear, like the infant whose body Devora had buried on the hill above Shiloh, like Hurriya closing her eyes in that cedar house.

Another girl, a little older than this one, had once shivered in her tent while the dead fed on her mother just outside. She had not even dared to cry, for her body hadn't yet learned that tears could be silent. She just hugged her knees and rocked, back and forth. After a very long time, a bloody hand drew the tent flap aside, and a face looked in, a face that was like her mother's yet torn, one ear chewed away and the eyes gray and empty. Her mouth gaped and she *hissed* at the girl.

Devora glanced down at her aging hands, remembered the heft of the pestle she'd lifted, her mother's own pestle she'd used to prepare meal. She remembered bringing it down, her arm rising and falling, bits of flesh and droplets of dark fluid staining her arms and her nightclothes; she had washed all of that ruin from her body and her clothes much later, in a shallow pool far from the camp. Then she'd huddled in the tall grass by the water while her clothes dried. Her knees drawn up to her chin, her arms about her legs. Her sobs beside that pool had been the last time she had ever let herself weep fully, without any restraint.

A girl had died in that tent as the pestle struck again and again. Devora had never carried that girl's body to any wide field within her mind, had never piled any cairn of heavy stones above her.

With her sword tip, the *navi* lifted a little of the dead girl's soiled hair and dropped the strands across her eyes, hiding them. In a hoarse voice, she whispered the Words of Going for them both—the girl who lay here in the barley and the girl who had died long ago in that tent. Sitting her horse in this gore-drenched field, Devora missed that young girl with a yearning that *ached*.

She glanced about the field, saw the men dragging bodies through the barley. There was grieving and ugly work to be done yet tonight, for none of the wounded could be permitted to live. And she could not bear it. Where was Barak? She longed to hand this night to him and rest. She wanted to lie down. She wanted Lappidoth's arms, or Zadok's. She wanted somewhere warm to sleep where there was no moon and no reek of the dead—she could smell it now even in her hair—and no memories but ones she chose to recall.

Men began to gather about her, weary but their faces flushed, because this night they had faced the moaning dead and silenced them. Farmers and carpenters and tanners and herdsmen, they stood with their hands clenched tight around the handles and hilts of implements spattered with flesh and decay—hastily fashioned spears, shovels, hammers, fence posts, a few bronze blades. She looked out over their faces and knew that these men looked to her for judgment or affirmation, or for some vision from God to confirm what their hearts hoped—that their work was now done, and after these fires burned down and the sun rose over the smoke, they could return to their homes and rebuild and replant, and lie with their wives and give the People new children to replace the ones that had been lost. Devora saw in their eyes no contempt for her as a woman, only awe. She was the *navi* to them now, truly, the messenger of God, strange and terrible and holy and set apart. A sword in her hand. She wanted to laugh bitterly, for she had never felt less like the *navi*. She was covered in grime and sweat, her body was unclean from the touch of the dead, and her dress hung off one shoulder, torn and disheveled after her struggle with Omri and after the grasping hands of the corpses. Yet the men needed her now, and she didn't know what to do. The tent of the Law was in tatters; the younger *navi* was dead. What was still holy? What still mattered?

A few of the men around her began to chant, their loud, deep voices opposed to the darkness and filth of the night and the work ahead of them:

Urai! Urai! Devora!
Arise! Arise! Devora!
You have shielded your people,
You have cut apart the foe,
You have taken earth and sky from him,
Urai! Urai! Devora! Arise, arise!

They chanted Devora's name, and she listened but could not speak. She lifted her blade high, though her arm ached from the weight of it. They needed her. Yet she knew she had to tell them that their work had not ended, that there were more dead to come. And how was she to do *that*? If Naomi the Old stood here in her place, she would have had something sharp and strong to say that would put hearts of hard stone into the men's chests and stiffen them against what must come. But she was not Naomi the Old. She was only Devora the Old. And she was unclean.

The men who were chanting fell silent. For others were emerging now from the barley and the smoke, and these others were sunken-eyed and wasted thin and carried no weapons. Exiles in their own land, these last refugees from Walls had lost their homes, their kin, their ability to sleep or sing. Their haggard faces were haunted by an anguish greater than any Devora had ever seen. Yet their ordeal had only begun. It would not end. Even if the thousands of dead coming down out of White Cedars were stilled and buried, for these men and women it would never be over.

We will find those who still breathe, Zadok had told her, *but we will find no survivors*.

One of them—a woman Devora's own age, but so *thin*—reached and clutched at her skirt, and she found she could not look away from the demand in the woman's eyes, a demand made without hope but with only the utter necessity of hearing its answer.

"Yes," Devora said hoarsely. "I have been to Walls." In those few words, in her tone, in her eyes was everything she had to say and couldn't. The deaths of the children. The ash in the air. The line of silent cairns by the lakeshore.

The old woman let out her breath, and something seemed to flicker out in her eyes. She understood.

"I—I'm sorry," Devora whispered.

"Night has fallen," the old woman rasped.

"Night's already here."

"A blood moon," the woman said, looking past Devora toward the sky. "When God turns his back."

Devora shivered, then reached down for the woman's hand and clutched it tightly. The *navi* was unclean. Perhaps the woman was too. It no longer mattered. "You listen to me," Devora whispered fiercely, leaning close enough for the other woman to hear her. "You listen. God has not turned his back. I promise you. He will lift this blight from the land. *He will*. Tonight is a sign of it. If we do not lie down and die, he will lift the blight."

"A few seedlings may grow out of these ashes," the old woman murmured. "But I am old, so old. I have no seeds. Why should I stand like an old tree in an empty field?"

"Who else will give the seedlings shade?" Devora asked.

The woman laughed. It was not a bitter laugh, only a very tired one. "I am going home," she said, and she turned from Shomar and began walking across the dying field with small, painful steps. Devora watched her go, in anguish.

One by one, the other refugees followed her. The men of Barak's camp fell silent, then set down their burdens and parted to let the exiles pass. The starving men and women walked south along the riverbank, back toward the camp, back toward Walls. They stumbled away under the red moonlight, exhausted, spent, the ghost of a people. Perhaps they would make it to the camp and collapse, and those of Barak's men who had lacked the courage to march tonight against the unclean dead would creep from their tents and bring food and water to these, the barely living. Or perhaps they would not stop. Perhaps they would go on walking, with those same slow, anguished steps. They would walk through the night and on into the next day and on until they came at last to the cinders and ash and the few standing houses and shops that had been Walls. Perhaps they would not stop even then, but would go on, down out of the hills and down the whole length of the promised land, following the steps of Hurriya before them, a silent witness to the violence and the misery in the north. They might pass through the entire land, past Hebrews and heathen who had never seen the dead and who would watch them with wide eyes, uncomprehending yet unable to look away. They might pass out of the green fields into the wide desert and come at last even to the dark earth and the high monuments of Kemet itself, the land of their fathers' slavery, as though to say with their shambling gait and their sunken eyes and their slack, thirsting mouths, *The People who went out from here have perished; only we have come back.* Perhaps even then they would keep walking, until they died on their feet and their emptied corpses still moved slowly over the wide earth, moaning their anguish, their grief, their hunger for all that was lost.

***

When the exiles had gone, the Hebrew men stood silent in the barley. Devora caught the eye of a young man, one of Barak's. Motioned him close. He ran to her side. He was a youth, really. Perhaps he had not even lain with a girl before, but tonight he'd fought the dead, taking up a torch and a sharp-bladed shovel to fight with, while other, older men shivered in their tents.

"Where is Barak?" Devora demanded once he stood by her horse. "We need him."

Pale, the youth pointed toward the ravine and the water in it. "I saw," he said. "The dead had him backed against the water. I saw him, *navi*, he fought like a nazarite! But he fell from the bank, and the dead went over the edge, following him."

Devora's heart sank. These men needed their war-leader. Omri was dead, Laban was dead. If Barak was gone, who was to lead these men? Wasting no time in replying to the youth, she drove her knees into Shomar's powerful sides and sent her horse galloping toward the ravine. She pulled him up almost at the last moment, then peered down at the water and the damp earth and sand. There were several broken, moaning corpses in the water or at the water's edge, and wherever sand rose above the low water it was covered in footprints. She glanced upstream, but the creek curved too much in its deep bed for her to see far. She thought she could hear distant moaning coming down the ravine, but that might be no more than the sound of her terror.

Devora sucked in a breath through her teeth. Clearly in her mind she could hear Barak ben Abinoam's voice:

If I should be taken by the dead…ride after me, navi. Ride and find my body. Pile clean stone above me, with your own hands, even if I have been dragged far away.

Those footprints. The dead had not remained here; something had drawn them away. There was a chance that Barak was alive, that he'd fled upstream, pursued by the dead. Perhaps injured from his fall.

The *navi* glanced over her shoulder at the men in the barley. None to lead them. She could perhaps hold them together. She was *kadosh*, and tonight had proven that being *kadosh* might still mean something—even to men who were kin to Omri of Zebulun tribe. She could urge them toward Judges' Well, where there might be a wall they could get behind. Or south to Shiloh, to plead again for help from the other tribes. Surely if Devora the *navi* spoke of her visions and shared the warning of Heber the Kenite, surely men of Manasseh and Ephraim and Gad would hear her. Surely they would gather with strength to face what was coming. If she had to go to every encampment herself, with nazarites beside her, to speak with the chieftains—! Surely they would come!

These men needed her.

Yet.

She gazed up the ravine. She was certain she heard moaning now. How many dead? And Barak alone, limping and splashing up that stream, with corpses in pursuit. *Ride after me, navi. Ride and find my body.*

She'd made a covenant with the man.

In the tents of the north, the Covenant with God was uprooted and torn apart—but she still had her own covenants to keep. If she were to turn now from this riverbank, if she were to leave Barak to the teeth of the dead, how would she be any different from Omri or Nimri?

Still she hesitated. This was a terrible choice.

She thought of Hurriya gazing up at her, her eyes glassy with fever. *We are both women.*

The decision of one man or woman to stand between another and harm or injustice: that was the foundation of the Covenant. It was the one essential act on which *shalom*, peace, depended. Without it, there was no Covenant, no Pact between people or between people and God. Hurriya's eyes had told her that. She had learned it, not in her mind but in her heart, deeply, as she'd sat watching Hurriya die. She could not unlearn it now. She could not betray Hurriya's memory that way. And she was done with leaving her own dead behind her, unburied, moaning in her memory, driving her to panic and tears at night.

She made her decision.

***

"What is your name?" Devora asked the youth, who had followed her to the riverbank. Other men were approaching a short distance behind.

He drew himself up. "I am Gideon," he said.

That made Devora smile slightly, even in her haste, for the youth was arrogant to name himself without mentioning his father's name or even his tribe—as though his name might be known in and of itself—but it was an arrogance she liked. If a youth could still be arrogant after tonight, he was strong enough for the task before him. "It's a good name," she said. "Gideon, tonight you must lead the men from here, though I have no oil to anoint you." She saw his eyes widen. "Be strong and courageous, Gideon. Gather the men and raise cairns. Then go to Shiloh; I will follow when I can. Make sure you don't camp too near—they will not be pleased there with the men of the north. The high priest is a boy; you want to talk to his mother, Hannah. Ask for messages to be sent to every encampment in Israel, both Hebrew and Canaanite. Have messages sent to the Kenites and to any friendly chieftains across the Tumbling Water. Tell them what has happened. Tell them there are more dead, thousands, coming down out of White Cedars. This is the word of the *navi*."

"Your will, *navi*," the young man breathed.

She hesitated, taking the measure of this young man. "There is one more thing. The men must be checked for bites, all who fought in this field tonight. You remember Walls? The clean and the unclean must be separated. Check them all."

486

The young man went white. Seeing this, Devora leaned close, lowering her voice. "Gideon, we won tonight. Don't forget it. Check the wounded. Keep the men clean. Shelter the stranger and the fatherless. Any covenants you make, keep them. Live by the Law, and God's hand will be on you."

He nodded.

Devora turned her attention to the river below, while Gideon watched her. Her face became grim. If Barak had indeed fled upriver, she might find that she needed to get down there to help him or to retrieve his body. The thought of standing between the high, closed walls of the riverbanks, perhaps dragging a dead man with her through the water while the dead lumbered after her like a trapped herd of water oxen—the thought made her dizzy with dread. Clambering down that bank would be like descending into some other place, some dream country that was without Covenant and knew only teeth and blood.

In any case, she didn't see how she could get Shomar down that bank. With a sigh, she slid from the gelding's back. She turned to Gideon. "This is my husband's horse," she said quietly, "and the finest in Israel. Take care of him and receive a *navi*'s blessing. Lose him or endanger him, and receive a *navi*'s curse."

"Your will, *navi*!" He looked with awe on the horse, as though the animal had been touched by God.

Leaning her sword against her hip, Devora took the gelding's head in her hands gently and kissed Shomar's nose. Shomar, who had borne her so far and through so many perils. "I will see you back safe to Lappidoth," she whispered, looking in the damp pools of the gelding's eyes. "I promise."

Devora gave the youth a stern look, then patted Shomar once more on the neck, took up her blade, and stepped away. She began to walk, as quickly as she could, ignoring stiff muscles. She did not look back. Mishpat she carried unsheathed at her side as she moved along the edge of the bank, watchful of both the water below and the barley grasses about her. Not all the barley had blighted, and some patches of it here by the bank were still full of life; the brushing of it across her arms was strangely comforting as she walked.

For a moment she felt that she was again that small girl fleeing her mother's camp, leaving behind her a field of bodies and hoping against every fear in her heart that somewhere ahead of her was a refuge and a tent to rest in. After a few moments Devora halted and bent with a moan at the ache in her body. She took up a handful of dirt and rubbed the soil into her palms, grimacing. She didn't need to be any filthier, but her hands were sweating, and if later she had to climb down that bank, she did *not* want to lose her grip halfway down. And, with a little satisfaction, she noticed that the dirt on her right palm gave her a better grip on Mishpat's hilt. Straightening, she resumed her walk and set her mind firmly on her task, on the fulfilling of her covenant.

She could hear old Naomi's voice as truly as though the woman were walking beside her. *You do what you must, you trust the rest to God. Some days, a woman can only save one life.*

God Rising Over the Water

EVEN BEFORE Barak opened his eyes, he knew he was in trouble. It wasn't just the pain in his right leg or the ice-cold of water under his back.

It was the moans.

They were many. He forced his eyes open, saw his feet first, one bare and without a sandal. The water, cool and dark. The embankment he'd slid down, perhaps only moments before. He looked up farther, saw the starlit sky and dark silhouettes against it, at the edge of the bank, gazing down at him. Moaning in such persistent hunger that he began to shiver violently where he lay in the water.

Even as he watched, one of the dead leaned out, its hand clutching as though to grasp him, and the corpse toppled down the embankment. There was a crack of bone, and with his heart pounding, Barak saw the thing lurch to its feet perhaps a stone's throw from him, one arm limp at its side. Two others were already standing in the middle of the creek, lurching toward him.

Panic shot, violent and cold, through him, as though he'd been speared to the riverbed. For a moment he lay there in the water, watching them approach. Then with a cry he leapt to his feet, glancing about wildly for the spear he'd fashioned from a terebinth branch, but it was gone—either left up on the high bank above him or borne downstream on the water, though that seemed unlikely, as the Tumbling Water here looked to be only knee-deep in the middle. Nor did he have his knife.

The dead closed on him; others now were falling from the bank or being shoved by those behind them. Barak stumbled out of the water, half-dragging the leg he'd injured in his fall; his right leg was torn and bleeding, but it was not broken. Vaguely he remembered a desperate fight at the bank and then being shoved over the edge by the press of the corpses. He could hear distant screams and more moans of the dead and a crackling like flame. He couldn't have been out for more than a minute or two.

He stumbled along the edge of the water, staggering upriver, stubbing his good foot hard against a rock. Pain shot up his injured leg at each step. He could hear the dead splashing behind him, *close* behind him. Cast a glance over his shoulder, saw them reaching for him. Hissing in pain, he fought to push himself to a run, but his leg felt like giving out. With his hands he tore at his bronze breast-piece and tossed it aside as he lurched on. It landed in the water and shone there, would shine there perhaps for years until a patina of green caked to it. It would not have protected him against the dead, and he needed to shed any extra weight. He had to get out ahead of these corpses and climb back up the bank and fight his way to his men. He knew that was what he had to do, but panic coursed through him, urging him to just run, *run*, until he could find some place to hide. He was unarmed, he was injured. And his next glance over his shoulder showed him twelve dead lunging after him in the water, and more falling over the edge, and still more following him along the line of bank above, shambling along in a grim mockery of his flight and of human movement.

Barak left his leather jerkin on—it had saved him once before—and he forced himself to greater speed, still nearly dragging his right leg behind him, as though he were himself one of the dead. The water was cold about his feet and shins. The muscles of his neck and shoulders tensed, expecting the touch of cold fingertips behind him. He had felt the cold, dry touch of the dead before; if he were to feel it again, he was certain he would start screaming and wouldn't be able to stop. He tried to remember his words to Yehoyakim, remember the momentary strength he'd felt in his blood as he'd fought the dead in the barley near the bank. As though he'd been a nazarite himself, blessed by his people's strange God and knowing no life but sweat and the spear and the fall of emptied bodies about his feet. But now, with the river icy about his ankles, he was only Barak the vintner again, a man without woman or child or even any growing field ready for harvest, a man with nothing left but the body he wore. He held back whimpers of fear as he staggered up the river.

He fell once, his face and chest plunging into the water. Sucked in the river through his nose and then heaved himself up on his hands and knees, coughing and spewing out water, shaking with cold. He felt the brush of fingertips across his sandal and the lightest touch on his heel, the first of the corpses behind bending to grasp at him, and he sprang to his feet with a sobbing cry. On he ran, forcing his body on against the pain in his leg.

Once he glanced at the sky. The red moon was not visible between the two cliffs of the bank. There were only the cold stars, the sign of the promise, the sign of the Covenant. Breathing raggedly, he gazed at them a moment, head tilted back as he ran. They had never seemed so beautiful. This might be the last time he would see them; there was a violent stitch in his side, and his breath and strength were giving out. He clung to the sight, needing it, needing that hope. He'd been stripped not only of kin and land, but also of all his certainties; they'd been cast aside as abruptly and completely as that breast-piece. He had tried to command and own the women of his house and the women he needed to use, but with Devora this had proven impossible. He had learned that at Walls. He had hoped to command God also, to control what God might do, or not do, using his keeping of the Covenant, even to the burning of the small gods in his house, to hold God to terms. But God too was ungovernable. Now he had no assurances from God, he had no spear in his hand. He had nothing to lean on nor any weapon. All he had was that sight of cold stars, stars that no blight or unclean death could touch. Those bright points of light gave him the hope he needed to keep his legs moving, to keep running despite the low moans of the dead behind him. Because those stars were one thing at least that could never be removed, and though Barak himself had no seed in the land, perhaps the promise—that the seed of the People would be preserved—would never be removed either. Even if all else he might trust or hope in was gone.

Stooping, he took up a jagged branch from the water, wrenching it free of the silt and river stones. The sand on the bark gave his hand a good grip on it. The wood wasn't strong or green; it would break. But it was something in his hand. He felt calmer. He looked over his shoulder again; there were no longer dead on the high bank, but there were perhaps thirty corpses in the stream behind him, strung out, those along the edge of the water moving faster, those knee-deep in the river moving slowly and falling behind. Barak fought for breath. He was a little ahead of the corpses, but was no longer any faster than they. He didn't know how far he had run—far past the barley field, he was certain of that. He could no longer hear screams or the roar of fire. He clutched the branch tightly, certain that his running scramble was at an end. He could press on until his limbs gave out and he lay gasping and helpless at the water's edge, like a wounded gazelle. Or he could stop and turn to face them.

Whatever God had pierced the sky with those stars and hung promises on them admired courage. He was certain of that at least.

He turned toward the dead and bent, leaning over and panting for air. He drew in heaving gulps of it, sweat pouring down his face even though the water about his feet was cold. Keeping a tight hold on the branch, he watched the dead stumbling toward him, their eyes like small, luminous stones in the starlight. He bared his teeth and straightened, lifting the branch in both hands like a club.

Then it happened.

A warmth on his skin, gentle like the touch of a linen that had been heated by a woman's body. Then the warmth was inside him, a sense of comfort, the way a man feels when the sun has risen on the Sabbath and he is half-awake but restful in his bedding with his woman still asleep and naked, her head on his chest. Barak thought he heard a whisper, and he turned his head, gazing again upriver. There was a little mist farther up the ravine, concealing the walls of the riverbanks only as much as a thin veil might. Even as he looked, it lifted, and Barak let out his breath in a low sigh, for from one bank to the other the ravine had filled with that pleasant warmth, and he could feel someone whispering to him, though he could not make out the words. But with a certainty as potent as Moseh's when the Lawgiver looked upon the bush that burned and yet did not blacken or crumple to ash, Barak knew that God was there in the stream.

Slowly, as in a dream, the vintner lifted his weaker foot and tugged his remaining sandal free, then dropped it into the water.

"*Kadosh*," he whispered. Holy ground.

In that moment, he was no longer aware of the splashes of dead feet in the stream behind him, or of the sharp and brutal cold of the water on his skin, or of the sweat running like oil down his face and back. There was only the lifting of the mist, and the nearness, the impossible nearness of God. He let his breath out slowly, standing still, arms limp at his sides, watching the mist rise. The God who filled the space between one slippery embankment and the other one was other than he'd imagined, other than he'd believed. Not a cold, aloof woman planting or scything crops, but a warm *shekinah*, a presence. Like hands cupping his face, like a scent of blossoms from a distant grove, like a strain of pipe music almost too faint to hear, like a whisper carried to him on the wind, like love and light and a woman's kiss, thrilling everything in him. He cried out suddenly, a raw shout from his throat, a wordless sound of awe and praise.

Then, as gently as it had come, the sense of that nearness, that *shekinah*, that warm feminine embrace, was gone. And even as his eyes lifted, he saw several tents with a stand of oaks behind them, above the high bank, perhaps twenty feet above him. He stared at them for a long, focused moment. Tents. People.

The living. The tents could mean help—a waterskin to drink and other men to stand with him against the shambling corpses.

He heard the moans of the dead close behind him. A glance over his shoulder showed them less than a spear's cast away, their arms lifted to take him. Casting aside the branch, he bolted, splashing through the water and throwing himself against the far bank, which had a little slant to it; he grasped for roots, rocks, any handhold he could, began pulling himself wildly up the bank. Damp soil crumbled and slid beneath his feet; with a gasp, he pulled himself furiously up the cliff, digging in with his toes and his fingers. The burn of pain in his torn leg became a shriek of fire, and he was screaming in the agony of it. The dead were beneath him now, he could feel the thud of their bodies against the bank below him, felt a fingertip graze the underside of his foot. With a howl, he reached his right arm up and found a tuft of weeds to grasp, began pulling himself higher. He gasped and sobbed with the effort. Glanced up, saw the bank and the overhanging oak boughs and above them now that wild, red moon. Only a few feet more, and he could grasp the edge of the bank, if it didn't crumble beneath him. He clung helplessly to the cliff; only a few feet more, but his legs and arms were shaking. If he moved, he'd fall. He knew this. He'd *fall*. The snarls and moans beneath him made him feel as though he were made of water.

Reaching, he grasped a root and gripped it, pulled himself up just within reach of the bank. But the root tore free of the soil and began to swing his upper body away from the wall of the bank. With a desperate cry, he took the root in both hands and pulled himself along it back toward the comfort of earth. But more of the root was pulling out; his heart beat with panic. He reached for some other handhold, grasping desperately, his fingers brushing the wall of the bank.

Suddenly a hand grasped his own, and he gasped, a shiver running through him. But the small, delicate hand was warm with life, and lovely and dark in his own. He gazed up and found a girl leaning over the edge, young, perhaps just old enough to bear a child. A dusky Canaanite girl with the high cheekbones of her people, her dark eyes only a few feet above his own. She was so unexpected, the warmth of her hand and the depth of her eyes so different from the cold, moaning death beneath him, that for a moment he just held completely still, awestruck, as he had been when he'd felt the living presence of God rise over the water.

The girl's grip on his hand tightened.

"Come on," she whispered.

WHO GIVES AND TAKES AWAY

A HEAVE, THEN Barak fell onto the weedy bank, coughing and gasping. He grasped a root and rolled onto his back, straining. Took deeper breaths. The pain had become acute; white fire shot up his leg to his hip, and his breath hissed through his teeth.

The young woman who leaned over him was lovely in the starlight and naked as though she were his lover or his purchase. Her face had the Canaanite cheekbones and that cast to the eyes. He found he couldn't take his gaze from her; she was so like Hadassah, though younger and smaller. Her own gaze flicked over his body and she muttered, "Not bitten." She got to her feet.

The moans of the dead at the water below were loud.

Barak scrambled up onto his knees. The girl was walking toward the cluster of tents. A horse was waiting there by a cold fire pit outside the largest pavilion, a small, sleek desert horse so black its hair shone. The girl held in one hand by her leg a wooden *teraph*, a goddess charred by fire yet recognizable as an Astarte, the goddess of planting and birth and harvest and love. Her other arm held a wolf pelt. There was no breeze, and the girl's hair hung lank about her face and shoulders, caked with dirt. There were bruises on the girl's cheek, her breasts, her thighs, her legs. To see her so bewildered Barak, who could not understand why a man would beat a girl so severely, especially this girl. To Barak she was beautiful, lush as the wooden Astarte she held, and the bruises on her body as wrong as the red moon in the sky.

"Wait!" Barak cried.

The woman turned, her fingers already curled around a clump of the gelding's mane. She stood and stared at him. Her eyes caught at him; they shone in the terrible red moonlight. After a moment she swept the wolf pelt about herself, concealing her body.

"Whose tents are these?" he called.

"Heber's." He heard the hate in her voice and suddenly understood. She had been a raid captive. "The men are gone," she said. "A boy was left to watch me, but he is gone too."

"Who is your mother?" he called softly. It was the traditional call of a man to a village girl he wished to court. "What is your tribe?"

He could hear the branches of the oaks tossing.

"I have none," she said.

He gazed at her, and in his wonder he realized that she was not the only young woman he had seen these past days who had reminded him of Hadassah. He realized where he had seen this girl's eyes and cheekbones before. "You're that girl's sister," he gasped. How strange that he should find her here. It seemed miraculous that it should be so, as though this moment had been touched by God. These past days he had seen so few signs of God's touch, only signs of her absence. Until that mist in the ravine below. Until this bruised girl had reached down her hand to help him up. "You're Hurriya's sister."

Her reaction to the name was immediate. She turned with her eyes bright and her face alight with hope. "You know her?" she cried. "My sister—you've seen her! Where is she?"

"She took refuge with my camp," Barak said, and stopped. The light in the girl's eyes was beautiful; to see it go out would break his heart. That light—that *hope*—how long had it been since he'd seen that in a woman's face? In anyone's face?

He saw the light start to fade as she guessed the worst from his silence. Everything else had been torn from her; even her goddess had been charred and burned, perhaps tossed carelessly by some raider to the edge of the fire. He could not take this from her too. "No," he said quickly. "She is well. A few of my men—they led her, and others, west toward the Wide Sea. There are walled settlements there, where she'll be safe." Where this girl might be safe too.

The light blazed again. He saw the girl shaking. "Tyre?" Her voice was breathless. "Or Sidon?"

"Sidon," he said.

"I'm going to find her," the girl said. Clutching the gelding's mane, she leapt onto the horse's back. She winced, for her body was badly bruised, but still she clung tightly to the horse, and her eyes had in them a fierce determination Barak had only ever seen in the eyes of one woman before: the *navi* of Israel.

"Wait!" Barak stepped closer. "Tell me your name!"

"My name," she whispered. She looked distracted, as though searching for the answer to his question. She hummed a few notes of a melody, very quietly, recalling something to herself, something from before her bruises and her pain.

Barak knew the melody well. It was Hurriya's song, and it was Hadassah's song that she used to sing to their unborn child, holding her belly. His throat tightened.

"There were standing dead beneath the olives," the girl said softly. "I found my sister's hovel empty, blood on the walls. But no bodies. Just—my sister and her baby were gone. So I went to find her. And these men found me. And hurt me." Her eyes burned with hate. "In their tents I was Ya El. A joke of theirs. I carried the name of a goddess of my people, so they made me carry the name of their God instead. I hope they are all dead, all of them. I hope they were *eaten*."

"Then I'll not call you Ya El," Barak told her. "What should I call you?"

She bent low over her gelding's neck and kissed the horse's ear. "Anath," she said after a moment. "When the sun comes up, I will be Anath."

Then, before Barak could say anything more, the girl Anath was riding away, past the tents. He watched her, thinking of that hardness in her eyes, thinking of Inanna riding down the gates of Sheol to rescue her lover in the story the Canaanites told. Half expecting the woman and her horse to crumble away on the still air, a thing of ashes and dreams, not flesh and blood. But still he could see her, galloping away from the riverbank and out over the tumbled, unplowed landscape in the red of the moon, riding up the rising land and into the hills.

***

When she had gone, Barak listened a few moments to the moaning of the dead in the river below. He hoped the girl found her way safely to the gates of Sidon. She might barter the horse for food and a room. He hoped so. The thought of it made him strangely calm—that there might be escape, for someone, from this long night of the dead.

The low wailing in the ravine seemed suddenly sorrowful to him. So many people had died up here. He could still hear Anath's song in his ears, and he yearned again for Hadassah, remembering the warmth of her in his arms, how she had taken his hand in hers and pressed his palm to her belly the night before her death. She had told him she could feel the baby kicking, and though he couldn't feel it himself, he had laughed and kissed her ear and told her he could, told her that he was glad she was bearing him such a strong son.

Forcing himself to take deep breaths, he glanced about at the tents and the oaks behind them. He was far now from his ruined vineyard and the camp of his men, and he didn't know how his men and the *navi* had fared against the dead. He hoped the corpses in the ravine below would move on if they could not see him or hear him. He could follow the bank back and look across at that barley field, and if he could do it unseen by the dead, climb down this bank and back up the other. Find and regather his men.

He considered the tents.

He needed meat, something to give him the strength he would need to get back. He could hardly stand, he was so weary. And water. He needed water. Yet he was hardly prepared to climb back down to that corpse-filled stream to get it.

He moved toward the largest of the pavilions grimly. When he drew the flap aside, he could smell the reek of death—that same smell that had surrounded him in the field. But nothing moved within. Nothing shuffled toward him. Nothing moaned at him out of the dark. After a moment, he let the flap fall closed.

A few unsteady paces took him to the little fire, which was just dead coals now, but there was kindling there and dry straw and flints. In a few moments he had a small blaze and was able to make a torch by shoving a short branch into the fire and letting the dry leaves kindle and burn until the fire reached the wood and began to sing and crackle in its joy at sating its hunger to devour all things. Lifting the branch, he returned to the tent. He paused for a while with his hand at the flap, unable to bring himself to open it; he shook and sweated as with a fever. He had seen too much tonight. He did not think he could bear to see one more of those—those *faces*, lifted toward the torch, gray eyes and a bloody mouth opening in a hiss or a low moan.

Bracing himself, he laid the branch at his feet—he could not bring it too near the fabric of the tent. The whole thing would go up in flames. He drew the tent flap aside, peered within.

One of the dead was there, but it was not moving. A bronze peg, a tent peg, had been driven through its skull. Its mouth was open in a hunger that was both silent and eternal.

Slowly Barak let out his breath.

There was nothing else in the tent but bedding, which smelled of urine and semen—but the scent of decay overpowered the other smells.

It took great control not to retch, but covering his nose and mouth with his hand, he stepped into the tent and crouched by the body and waited for his senses to adjust to the offensive smell of the tent.

The tent flap settled behind him. Outside, the branch flickered and burned; its glow passed through the gap between the flap and the tent wall, and the faint red light fell across the dead face. The face was intact; the brow and the skull above it had burst open like an overripe fruit at the passage of that metal peg.

He crouched there a long time, breathing shallowly through his fingers. Once he reached out and touched the blunt end of the peg with his fingertips. He withdrew his hand quickly.

He thought of Hurriya's sister, who looked so much like his wife yet was so fierce-hearted. She was the only living person he had encountered in this camp. And her horse had awaited her by the door of this tent. It must have been her hand that had slain the corpse. Barak thought of that girl lying naked and beaten on these very rugs until that hungering corpse drew aside the flap and peered in at her. He shuddered. He thought of her wrenching that peg from the earth.

Devora's words came back to him. *You must understand this, Barak. The God of our mothers and fathers will deliver the dead into the hands of women.*

Barak laughed quietly. A woman with a blade no man of the People had ever held. A naked slave girl with a bronze peg. Women had always been strange to him, strange as God herself, unreliable and unknowable. To be wooed, perhaps to be possessed and placed in a man's tent where they would hopefully stay a while where he put them, where they could be enjoyed and used. But the women he had seen these past few days and nights were stranger than any he'd known. Or perhaps all women were stranger than he'd known. The levites who kept the Law taught that God had made woman to be an *ezer kenegdo* to man, a help, even as God herself was an *ezer*, a help to the People, her arms surrounding, embracing, comforting, lifting up whom they held. Barak felt suddenly a yearning to know what an *ezer* truly was—to know what the levites actually meant. For if a woman could ride at the dead with an iron blade flashing in the red moonlight or drive a bronze peg through a dead man's skull—and yet weep and lie as weakly as the *navi* had lain in the weeds during their halt that afternoon, then he did not know what a woman was or what a woman was meant to be.

And he did not know anymore what a man was.

He watched the silent face, and a sorrow grew in his heart. He found he could not stand; those lifeless eyes held him. They looked like little river stones with a film of some gray slime stretched thin across their surfaces. His grief for his vineyard and his anger at God suddenly seemed small. *He* seemed small, his complaint and his fear the cry of a small mouse in a wide field. That face—that face, and the faces he'd seen in the barley and in the riverbed—what was happening to the land, to the People? This creature with the peg driven through its brow—he looked at its lips, saw the blood there. It had been feeding shortly before that girl slew it. He shuddered. This broken thing had moaned with a hunger for flesh that could never fill it, never sustain it, never nourish it. It consumed everything it encountered with a hunger like a god's hunger but made no covenant with anyone it fed on. It would use the flesh it consumed to make nothing, grow nothing, produce nothing. It would not have any young. It would not grow any vineyards. It would only feed and devour, and give nothing back. It didn't live: it merely craved.

Yet this had been a man once.

A man who'd tended his vines or his herds, then died. A little circle of tooth marks on his arm told the tale of that death. He was not elsewhere chewed; perhaps he had beaten off the corpse or stilled it, then run into the hills to hide from the People. He had been unclean, defiled; he would have known what his fate would be if the others learned of it. Perhaps he had even hidden his arm beneath a heavy robe for a few hours or a day, even in the heat of the Galilee summer; perhaps he had shuddered each time someone brushed against him as he moved about the tents. In the end, the fever would have grown fierce, burning him from within. He would've had to flee. And here, in these hills, perhaps in this very valley, he had lowered himself among the stones or in the wild grasses, and shivered and vomited until he was done. Then he'd lain still, completely still, under the wide sky. His eyes empty, his chest sunken in on itself. Time had passed, a wind moving over him through the weeds. Perhaps a small antelope had grazed near him for a while.

But at some point his chest had moved, filling slowly with air. Beginning to rise and fall. The body had begun to breathe. Then the mouth had begun to move or the fingers to twitch. Only the eyes remained entirely the same, dull and dead. No spirit returning to look out through them at these hills that had known the footprints of God.

How long had the creature lain there, just breathing? How long before it had climbed to its feet and lurched slowly away through the tall weeds?

That could have been him. Fleeing the dead tonight, only a few strides ahead of their grasping hands, their teeth—that could have been him.

Barak was shaking. "The land has become strange to me," he whispered, gazing at that lifeless face frozen in its moment of famished need. "I wanted only evenings in my house and Hadassah in my bed, her breasts in my hands. I wanted only my vineyard, only the ripe grapes, the coolness of them beneath my feet, the taste of wine. The long battle with soil and worm is enough for any man of Naphtali. God, you give and you take away, and we are only ashes. We are only ashes."

SH'MA YISRAEL

THE MOON must have set and the fire must have died down again to coals, for no light fell now on the dead face, and the dark within the tent became oppressive. Barak didn't know how long he'd sat there. He was numb inside, hollowed out. He tried to recall the comfort he'd felt when the mists rose over the water, the nearness of a God who did not loathe him, a God who might nourish him. He got to his feet and stumbled toward the door of the tent. He had to get back to his camp, his men. It did not matter how bruised and overcome he felt or what kind of God might heal him. There was work to be done and no one else to do it.

He pulled the flap aside, then caught his breath. A figure was standing there in the dark, a little shorter than he was. It must have been listening right at the door of the tent. Even as Barak realized it was there, the corpse grabbed his wrist in its hands, lifting Barak's hand toward its lips and ducking its head, biting quickly. The pain was deep and sharp. Barak roared and tried to pull his hand back, but he only pulled the corpse with him.

With a shout, he turned and pulled the corpse toward the fire pit and slammed it down on the ground, crushing its chest down with his knee. The unclean thing held his wrist tightly, kept tearing at his hand with its teeth. Screaming from the pain, Barak took up one of the fist-sized stones from their ring around the fire pit, and he brought the stone down on the corpse's skull. And again. And again. Its snarling fell silent, and the thing grew still, one side of its head flattened. Its dead eyes did not change; it simply stopped moving.

Panting, his back bathed in cold sweat, Barak dropped the stone and grasped its fingers, breaking two of them as he pulled its hand free of his wrist. Then he tore his hand from its jaws, leaving some of his flesh between its teeth. His face gone the color of maggots, Barak fell back on his rear and sat there by the corpse, gasping. He caught a glimpse of its face; the left side of its face had been chewed almost entirely away. The right side had been the face of a youth, no more than a boy—doubtless the boy Anath had mentioned, the one left to watch Heber's camp, the one she thought was gone. Barak groaned and leaned back, lightheaded; he glimpsed the stars high above his head. His hand and his arm were pulsing, and he lifted his hand before his eyes, stared at the red gash where a chunk of flesh had been torn free; he supposed that piece of him was still held in the dead boy's mouth. For a long moment he stared at his hand. Then he began laughing, shaking his head and laughing, as the blood poured down his hand from the bite and ran warm along the length of his arm. It was all too strange, and life too fragile a thing to understand. He kept laughing quietly until he felt too weak to. Then his vision went gray.

***

Barak heard the sound of sticks cracking and opened his eyes. It was a moment before he could focus. His face felt dry and hot, and his insides were baking. There was coarse cloth wound about his hand. His heart lurched; he could see a human form sitting in the dark by the cold fire pit. Barak was on his back near the pit. The figure glanced at him, and in the dim starlight he recognized her graying hair and the flash of her eyes.

"*Navi*," he murmured. Not one of the dead.

"You've been bitten," Devora said. Her tone one of cold resolution. She was taking up sticks from a little pile she must have gathered while he lay senseless. She cracked the sticks and arranged a little tent of them over the coals.

Barak lifted his hand, saw that it was swollen and dark. He laughed quietly, then coughed from the pain the laugh brought him.

"Some days a woman can only save one life," Devora said. "The old *navi* tried to teach me that, Barak, but I didn't understand. I do now. When you save one life—when you keep Covenant and save even one life—you save the People." She paused. "I am sorry I was too late to save yours."

Barak just breathed for a few moments. He didn't know why he'd thought he was baking; now he shivered with the greatest cold he had ever known. "Stay with me," he rasped.

Her eyes gazed down on him, unreadable as ever. "I will," she said.

All about him were the raiders' tents and the leaves of the oaks dark against the sky. He yearned for his own vineyard—to die beneath his own vines, amid the scent of grapes and growing things. But his vineyard was already gone; it had died without him, and he was left here lingering in fever like a last cutting from it tossed aside to wither on its own. He kept watching the oak leaves and listening to the quiet fire. He had imagined dying at a spear's thrust or of old age, not of the bite of the dead on strange soil. But the *navi* was here, waiting while he died. She would raise a cairn over him. He would be remembered. He took comfort in that.

"I felt the *shekinah*," he whispered. "It rose over the water. And God was neither judge nor wife to me. I do not know what God is."

"You were feverish," Devora murmured.

"No." He shook his head, panting. "This was—before. We think we know what God is, but she is entirely strange to us. Stranger than the land, stranger than the heathen. We lie to ourselves when we say we know God, when we judge God or fear God or speak of God. Maybe God can be loved, as the priests do. I don't know what God is anymore." He shook from the cold, and his teeth chattered, but he forced the words out. "God gives and takes away. Blessed be the name of God."

"*Selah*," the *navi* whispered. *Always.*

He felt the touch of a waterskin to his lips, drank a little, choked and spluttered most of it up.

"The dead," he rasped after a few moments, his throat sore and violent. "Must put them all—beneath cairns. God has not forsaken the land."

"He has forsaken only his *navi*," Devora said. "No visions come. No seed I've planted has borne fruit." She gave a small, bitter laugh. "Nor any seed planted in me." She was quiet a moment. "I violated the Covenant. I killed my mother, twice. Now my daughter too. There is no longer any way to keep the Law. God has forsaken me, Barak. If he has appeared in some way to you, I am glad for you. But all my joy is gone, and all my hope."

"Not all," Barak rasped. "Your girl—the Canaanite. Found her sister. Alive." He was finding it difficult now to speak, his throat was so dry.

Devora glanced at him sharply, then her eyes softened. "Oh, Hurriya," she whispered, then said nothing more.

Barak coughed a little, then gazed past the oak branches, at the sky. At those same distant stars he'd seen from the bottom of the Tumbling Water's ravine. He barely heard Devora's words. He was just focused on those bright stars. His body kept shivering, but he felt again the warm touch of that holy presence in his heart. He was glad there were no sandals on his feet. He wished Hadassah were here, and even her mother, whom he'd sent away to Refuge when the dead came. But especially Hadassah. The things he would tell her. He would hold her, kiss her, and have her, if there was no other way for him to tell her, if he could find no words. All the deeds of his life seemed suddenly trivial to him, but this brought him no despair, only a yearning to hold Hadassah in his arms again, to feel her warm belly swollen with life. And a skin of clear water in his hand to share with her.

"Didn't tell her. I didn't tell the girl about Hurriya," he said.

There was silence for a while.

"I'm glad," the *navi* replied at last. "Where is she now?"

"She rode away. Toward the sea, where it's still safe. She was so *hopeful*. So beautiful."

"Thank you for telling me that." The *navi*'s voice was softer. Even a little vulnerable.

Barak could feel himself slipping beneath the fever. Everything blurring, even himself. He closed his eyes. "*Navi*, tell me the stories of our People. I want to hear them."

He felt a damp cloth against his brow. Then Devora's voice, cool and calm in the heated dark. He caught the stories in bits and pieces, moving between waking and sleep, between the world that is real and the world that isn't. But it didn't matter. He knew all the stories. His grandfather had given them to him when he sat between the old man's knees as a child. It was a comfort, though, to hear them again. To call them to mind. All these stories that made him more than just a vintner and more than just a man who carried a spear whom other men were willing to follow. More than just a man who lay dying. The stories made him one of the People, who would never die.

Devora's low voice told of his fathers Tubal Qayin, who first discovered the shaping of metal, and Yubal, who made the first music so that the *malakhim* themselves came out of the sky to listen. And Yabal, who began the keeping of sheep and goats, the herding of cattle, the pitching of tents. He heard of the brothers Qayin and Hebel—how Hebel was beaten across the head with a great stick, then thrown into a narrow ravine, there to starve until he died. How he rose to his feet some days later, hungering and rotting, until he found and devoured his brother.

Devora told of how the dead filled the land, every land, until God looked down on the hunger and the violence in the earth and was grieved. How a vintner like himself—a man with a wife and three sons, who enjoyed wine as much as any Canaanite—had built a great box of wood, an Ark. Not to carry stone tablets but to carry human lives, which to God's eyes were no less sacred.

Rains fell while Barak ben Abinoam tossed in his fever. Rains fell, and the parched and hungry earth drank them until it could hold no more water and vomited the water back up, and there was mud, then flooding, then a great sea that drowned everything beneath it, and the dead floated in the sea moaning. Waves drove the corpses against the sides of the Ark, and their decomposing hands beat upon the wood. How terrible for the few living hiding within—to hear the thunder and the fury of rain on their roof and the slamming of many hands against their walls. And always the moaning, louder than rain or wind, the ceaseless voices of the dead.

"God overwhelms us," Barak rasped, interrupting the tale. "Whatever we do, God is too vast, too deep. I wanted to command God, as I might command a woman." Barak moistened his lips with his tongue; it was so difficult to speak.

"You should lie quiet, chieftain of Israel." Devora's voice, unexpectedly, held concern. "The fever is burning you up."

"God is like—like the *land*," Barak whispered. "You can cultivate the land. You can grow fine things on it. You cannot command it or control it or say, Bring me a fine harvest. You have to work it. God is like that. I didn't understand."

He lay shaking for a few moments, unsure if he was speaking to the *navi* or to Hadassah or to Hadassah's mother. There was a woman here, he knew that much. "I am sorry I burned your gods." His whisper almost too quiet to hear. "I thought I could hold God to her promises. But the land makes us no promises. There are no promises."

"There *are* promises," Devora said sharply.

"I am sorry," he breathed, not heeding her. "Sorry I tried to take the Ark. That I sent Nimri."

She looked at him dispassionately.

"Laban," Devora said after a moment, "would have been the better choice. You should've sent Laban. He might have talked Shiloh into it."

No time left. He lifted his eyes, hoping to see that mist between him and the stars. There was nothing. Yet he knew—knew the God of his fathers was near. He was not afraid. Not anymore.

"*Sh'ma*—" He had to stop. His voice was but a dry croak. He tried to wet his lips, tried to swallow. There was nothing. Then the rush of cool water over his lips and into his mouth, like water from the rock in the desert. Someone was leaning over him, between him and the stars. Someone was pouring water into his mouth. He swallowed, and again, until the water stopped.

"*Sh'ma!*" he gasped. "*Sh'ma Yisrael adonai eloheinu, adonai echad…*"

Then the heat in him was too fierce for words and he moaned as he slid into the grip of it, burning, burning, nothing left but the fire. Breathing was too great an effort when his throat and his insides were so scorched, so after a while he stopped doing it.

DEVORA'S VIGIL

IT TOOK DEVORA a long time to gather the stones. The windstorm had returned to her heart. When she closed her eyes, meaning to rest for only a moment, she would see her mother's face or the contorted face of Hurriya's infant. She'd hear Heber's words. *Thousands, thousands in White Cedars.* Then she would jerk awake with a gasp and move on to gather more stones. There was no rest for her in sleep, no safety. There would probably never be.

Gritting her teeth, she lifted the last great rock to the top of the second cairn (for she'd buried the slave boy first, then Barak), letting the stone fall with a hoarse cry. Then she leaned on the pile of stones, panting. Her eyes stung with salt; in that moment, remembering how Zadok had once placed the stone at the top for her, Devora felt Zadok's loss keenly.

All the strength left her limbs, and she wept for a while. It wasn't that here, alone, she could afford to, but that here, at the utter limit of her strength, she could no longer hold any of it back. The winds within shook and battered her like an old tree in some violence of the air out of the desert. She had raised so many cairns. In a few generations, the stones of these two new cairns would topple or crumble or be overgrown with weeds, and those lying beneath them would be forgotten by all but God. With terrible clarity Devora grasped that the tribes were a transient People, whatever promises they clung to. Transient not only because they lived in tents or remembered living in tents, but because all peoples are transient, and once they move on, the land does not long remember them, even if God does. Even the Canaanites' walls and cedar houses were a transient thing, a vanity. Canaanite, Hebrew, living and dead, they were all strangers in a strange land.

A hasty search of the tents and belongings of the raiders revealed little of use to her—a little bread, a few empty waterskins, many items of luxury that a

Canaanite might enjoy but that she refused to, and a corpse, another corpse for her to bury. But she did find one thing she took—a small bag sewn from a goat's bladder, full of small things that clacked together as she lifted the bag and set it by the fire pit. Not coins, but smooth, polished river stones, not yet engraved with any names. She went to sit with her back against Barak's cairn and emptied the bag of stones between her feet. They were beautiful, not as gems are but as stones are when the river has kissed them, and they were many colors. After a moment she picked out one that was a pallid white like the moon grown old, and another that was dark like Shomar's eyes. She held them both in her right palm. Her hand was unclean; perhaps the stones would bring her no true sign. Yet perhaps soon no one's hands would be clean.

"You showed Barak Hurriya's sister," Devora whispered to God. "She lost everything, even her child. But her sister lives. That has to mean something.

"You gave me an answer in Shiloh. I ask for another. Does your hand still cover the People?"

She cast the stones.

***

In the quiet that followed, she sat with the cairn at her back and looked at a sky so full of stars that it made her eyes ache. She still held the dark *urim*, the "yes" stone, in her hand. She recalled her words to Hurriya by the shore of the lake. *In the silence of God, I must act as though he is not silent.*

Yet perhaps God had not truly been silent at all. He had sent visions to her through the Canaanite, had spoken to her through Hurriya. Devora had been bewildered—what message was it that only Hurriya, only a Canaanite, could bring to the People? Now she realized that Hurriya *herself* had been the sign, the message. Some part of her had known this since Walls, since tossing that flaming torch into the house of the dead.

No. Some deep part of her had known it earlier than that. She'd known it from the moment she had seen Hurriya struggling her way up the hill toward the olive tree, naked within her salmah, bruised, carrying the half-eaten remains of her child. Even then, Hurriya's presence at the olive tree had been a message, a demand for justice, for the strangers in the land no less than for those born in the tents of the People. And the suggestion that even tribes who were strange to each other could teach one another something about preserving life and withstanding the unclean dead, something about God. That even a woman who did not know the Law, a woman who feared the Law, might teach an older *navi* more about the nature and the demand of the Law than she had ever before known.

Hurriya had delivered her message. She had done so merely by suffering in Shomar's saddle and by speaking of her grief and anger. And by dying with her hand clasped in Devora's own.

Devora glanced at the stars. She had to believe that God was still watching. That the tent of the Law still covered the land. Otherwise why had Hurriya had visions, and why had her longing for her sister's safety been answered? Why had the *urim* stopped rolling before the *thummim*? Why was Devora herself still breathing?

Devora leaned her head back and breathed deeply for a few moments. She could not stay here, but she could not stand yet; the grief was too violent within her. After a while she took up a small rock with a jagged edge from beside the fire pit and began to carve hard, deep Hebrew letters into the river stones, one after the other, while she sang the Words of Going hoarsely. She did not sing for Barak only, and his name was not the last that she carved into the stones. She carved *Zadok*, on a stone the color of fertile earth, and *Naomi*, on a stone the color of the sky. Then *Hurriya*, on a stone whose purple hue, though faint, suggested blossoms of heather. Her grief choked her voice when she carved the letters of that strange, Canaanite name that had become so dear to her. The thought of Hurriya's sister riding somewhere in these hills comforted her a little, enough that she could carve the letters without her hand trembling; something of Hurriya still lived.

Devora took her time, making sure the letters were well-carved and deep.

The last stone was simply *Am*, mother.

She wished for needle and thread, some means to sew the stones into the shoulders or the sleeves of her garment—for that was how levites carried name-stones, even as the high priest carried the names of the tribes in his breast-piece—but having neither, she settled for taking up the empty goat-bladder bag. But she did not put the five stones away immediately. Instead, she sat looking at them, reading the names again and again; she put them away, one after the other, until only *Am* remained. She could hear Naomi's words: *God will forgive us the lives we cannot save.*

She scrubbed the back of her hand across her eyes and looked to the sky; it was no longer so dark. In fact, the sky was nearly the blue of morning, and the stars were going out. And the scab-redness of the moon was long, long passed, as though it had never been.

"Forgive me for my mother and for Naomi," she whispered, not lowering her eyes from the heavens. "This time I do not ask you for a child. Only do not forsake me now. Forgive me. For her. And for my daughter, whose life I couldn't save." She bit her lip until she tasted blood.

Holding the *Am* stone in her hand, she closed her eyes but did not sleep. The memory sprang upon her and this time she did not flee it. She faced it and mourned.

***

The pale light before sunrise found Devora still sitting with her back to Barak's cairn, still awake, with Mishpat lying unsheathed across her thighs. Some of the death-reek had faded from the camp, and a gazelle now walked gracefully among the tents, nibbling here and there at a patch of heather. She was a doe, her striped sides moving gently with her breathing. Devora watched her with the kind of hushed fascination a girl might feel, a child who has never seen a doe before. Amid the horrors of the north, Devora's heart had nearly forgotten such grace and beauty could exist. She had nearly forgotten there were such things as gazelles in the world. Once, the gazelle lifted its head and looked at the *navi*, its gaze focused and unblinking. Devora hardly dared breathe. At last the gazelle looked away and walked past the fire pit, almost within reach, looking for more heather blossoms to eat.

Devora rolled her shoulders back, breathed deeper.

The land was not dead yet.

She watched the gazelle for a while, but then the doe straightened sharply and turned to stare at the stand of oaks. Her ear twitched. Then with a few quick bounds the doe sprang away between the tents and was gone.

That alerted Devora to the danger. Without taking her gaze from the oaks, she took up some soil from the trampled ground by the fire pit and rubbed the dirt on her palms. What she wouldn't give for a bath and a safe refuge in which to sleep…

With a grim look, she rose to her feet and stretched her arms and legs thoroughly, ignoring the protest of her stiff muscles and her soreness from the saddle. She lifted Mishpat and swept the cold iron once through the air, letting her arms feel its weight, letting her body get used to it again. She let her weight rest on the balls of her feet and loosened her hips as though she were preparing to dance before her husband.

She recalled how Lappidoth had fought the dead that day, when they came for his cattle at that stream that was now so many desperate miles to the south. How he had ducked and darted among the corpses, swinging his hatchet about as though it were part of him. Devora gazed at Mishpat, recognized the cold necessity of her blade, a thing lethal and cruel, yet a thing as balanced, as beautifully designed in its own way as the Covenant itself. "I intend to see Lappidoth again," she whispered to the sword. "So you and I must dance together, whether we like each other or no."

***

When the dead lurched out of the oaks, arms raised, their skin ashen gray and their eyes wide and unblinking, the *navi* was ready. She watched the dead stumble toward her. Four of them. Great strips of flesh hung loosely from one's chest; another still carried a man's hand in its grasp, chewed off beneath the wrist. One had been male and in life had been a large man and one of some wealth; the tatters of a woolen cloak of many colors still clung to its body. The others had been women. Two were naked, and the third wore a faded green dress and about her waist the blue sash of a midwife. Her gray face was wrinkled; she had lived a long life and had likely brought many lives screaming into the world. Now she took them screaming back out again.

Devora spread her feet a little, crouching slightly, ready to spring to the side or leap forward or back. She held Mishpat before her, both of her small hands on the hilt. "You are unclean," she called to the dead. "An abomination. We do not want you walking in the land. Lie down and be still."

The dead midwife made a spitting noise like a furious cat and lurched toward her, with the others close behind.

"Come, then!" Devora cried, her throat dry. Without hesitating, she leapt forward, spinning on her toes and bringing Mishpat gliding through the air with a hum of wind and death; the cold, dispassionate blade sheared through the midwife's head just above the ears, and the body toppled lifeless to the earth. Devora brought her blade back before her just as the other dead closed on her. They did not fear her blade as the living might; they did not hesitate or slow their lunge toward her. Devora sliced away an arm that reached for her, and as it fell cleanly from its shoulder, no blood spurted, though the stench of rot and uncleanness worsened. She sprang back even as one of the other corpses grasped for her, its fingertips sliding for an instant along her wrist.

One of them opened its mouth in that terrible moan, that wordless, mindless cry that spoke of a hunger that would devour all life and all creation and yet still be famished. The other two took up the moan, and the sound filled the space between the oaks and the tents.

"Shut up," Devora said coldly.

She ducked low and brought her blade cutting through their legs, first one, then the next. Two of the dead fell and lay moaning and twisting their torsos on the ground, and the other loomed over Devora, its hands fastening on her shoulders. The corpse pulled her up toward its mouth, and even as it ducked its head to bite at her throat, Mishpat slid between its breasts and carved upward, releasing stench, cutting right up through its throat and then through its face, carving the top part of the body in two equal halves. It jerked a moment, then its grip on the *navi*'s shoulders went limp, and with a cry of revulsion and fury Devora lifted her knee and drove it into the corpse's chest, knocking it away.

The thing that had been a woman seemed to fall as slowly as a body in a dream. When it hit the earth at last, faceup, its back splattered open and it lay lifeless and tragic in a pool of its own insides.

Devora walked back to the other two, stood over them, sweat running thick as oil over her face, her hair lank and hanging before her eyes. She stayed just out of reach of their flailing arms. They twisted, trying to writhe nearer to her. She felt empty, looking down at them. They were not people, whether Hebrew or heathen. They were not even alive. Their hands and faces were stained with fresh blood, and she thought of Hurriya's tale of how her child and its father had died. These dead spat and hissed and reached for her, their gray eyes dull but their faces twisted in hunger and hostility and loathing and a longing to end life.

"There is no place in the Covenant for you," Devora told them quietly, and brought Mishpat, the Judgment, scything down.

***

The burn of noon found Devora exhausted from raising the new cairns. Yet she did not lie down, she did not sleep. She took up her sword and a bit of cloth from the raiders' abandoned bags and began cleaning the blade.

She knew what she must do.

She was alive and she had covenants to keep. She would follow the remnant of Barak's men south. She would make her way as Hurriya had before her through the strange hills where the dead were. Listening for God in the silent places, she would make her way, night after night, toward the heart of the land. Wherever she was forced to halt by an onset of the walking corpses, she would raise cairns over the Hebrew and the heathen dead. She must be hard and silent as the blade, yet not blind to the suffering of those whose homes and kin the dead had taken. They were all strangers in the land, bereft of shelter and beset on all sides by the stench of death. Knowing that she was herself a stranger in the land, unhomed and unclean, no other woman or man could any longer be strange to her. Hurriya had been right—their dwellings, and those of the Canaanites, were threatened alike. And they'd be strongest facing the dead together.

For seven days she would remain unclean, but it might well take those seven to get to Shiloh on foot. She might find the dead all about her. If God meant her to meet them as she now was, alone, she would do so. Such things had been required before of those God called. Moseh had been sent against the Pharaoh of Kemet and all his chariots and his cities with just a stick in his hand and the promise whispered from a burning bush: *ki ehyeh immakh*, I will be with you.

Devora did not have even that promise, or any stick that would perform wonders. But she understood now the story of the burning bush as she never had before. It was not enough simply to sit beneath her olive tree and decide what to do about the suffering that was brought before her. The *navi* must go out into the land and do what she could for the suffering she found there, whether she witnessed it in the eyes of her own people or in the eyes of a bereaved stranger wrapped in a salmah. She could not sit with the Law at her back, for the Law must look into the eyes of the People. The Law must listen to the heart. Otherwise the Law, which was alive like an olive tree, would blight and decay, until it became unable to yield any life-sustaining fruit.

She would deliver Hurriya's message to the People. And she would blow the shofar, call together the chieftains of the tribes. Tell them what Heber had said. Tell them they were all marching north, and the Ark of God with them. Maybe they would find tens of thousands of hungering dead when they returned to these hills. It didn't matter. She had to trust that they would see the fire of the *shekinah* burn like wildfire on the slopes, hotter than any *navi* had ever been touched by it, hotter than anything made of flesh and bone could endure. That they would see the dead razed from the land, even as they had been razed from Shiloh thirty years ago. But even if the Ark lit no fire, still they must stand together against the dead.

510

For a moment she looked to the north over the tops of the oaks, where hills mounted higher and higher until she could glimpse the sharp line of the mountains of White Cedars beyond them, where snow fell like white feathers out of the sky. Somewhere north of her was an olive grove where a girl used to watch over her sister from the branches of a high tree.

"I'm sorry, Hurriya," she whispered. "I don't know where Anath is or how to find her. But I know she will be all right. You trusted me to help you, you hoped you could trust me when you came to my seat. I let you down then. Maybe I'm letting you down now. My daughter." Her voice choked. "Please trust me again. She will be all right. Your Anath. I know she will; she survived this camp and she survived the dead and she has a horse that will carry her far. I have to trust her to that horse and to God. I have to. The People need me, Hurriya, both our peoples."

She turned her back on the oaks and the higher ridges and the distant suggestion of peaks that knew the softness of snow and the seductive death of the extreme cold. She could do nothing more here.

Waterskin and goatskin pouch slung over her shoulder, Devora carried Mishpat at her side and began walking south along the high bank. She listened and watched intently, for it was not a question of whether she would encounter more walking corpses today, but when. She thought of Lappidoth waiting for her in the white tents, but this did not lighten her heart.

Whether God stayed silent or roared loud as thunder in the hills, her longing for rest was a seduction and a luring away from her responsibilities. She was the *navi* and the judge, but she understood that she too was judged. As she watched the pain of the People, God watched her. She knew she would not rest nor set Mishpat aside until there were no dead walking anywhere in the land. The burden of facing the dead was finally and entirely hers to bear. She *would* bear it. She had to.

FINIS

NO LASTING BURIAL

BASED LOOSELY ON
THE GOSPEL OF MARK
AND ON THE LEGEND OF
THE HARROWING OF HELL

FIRST CENTURY A.D.

---

for Inara, my fierce Inara

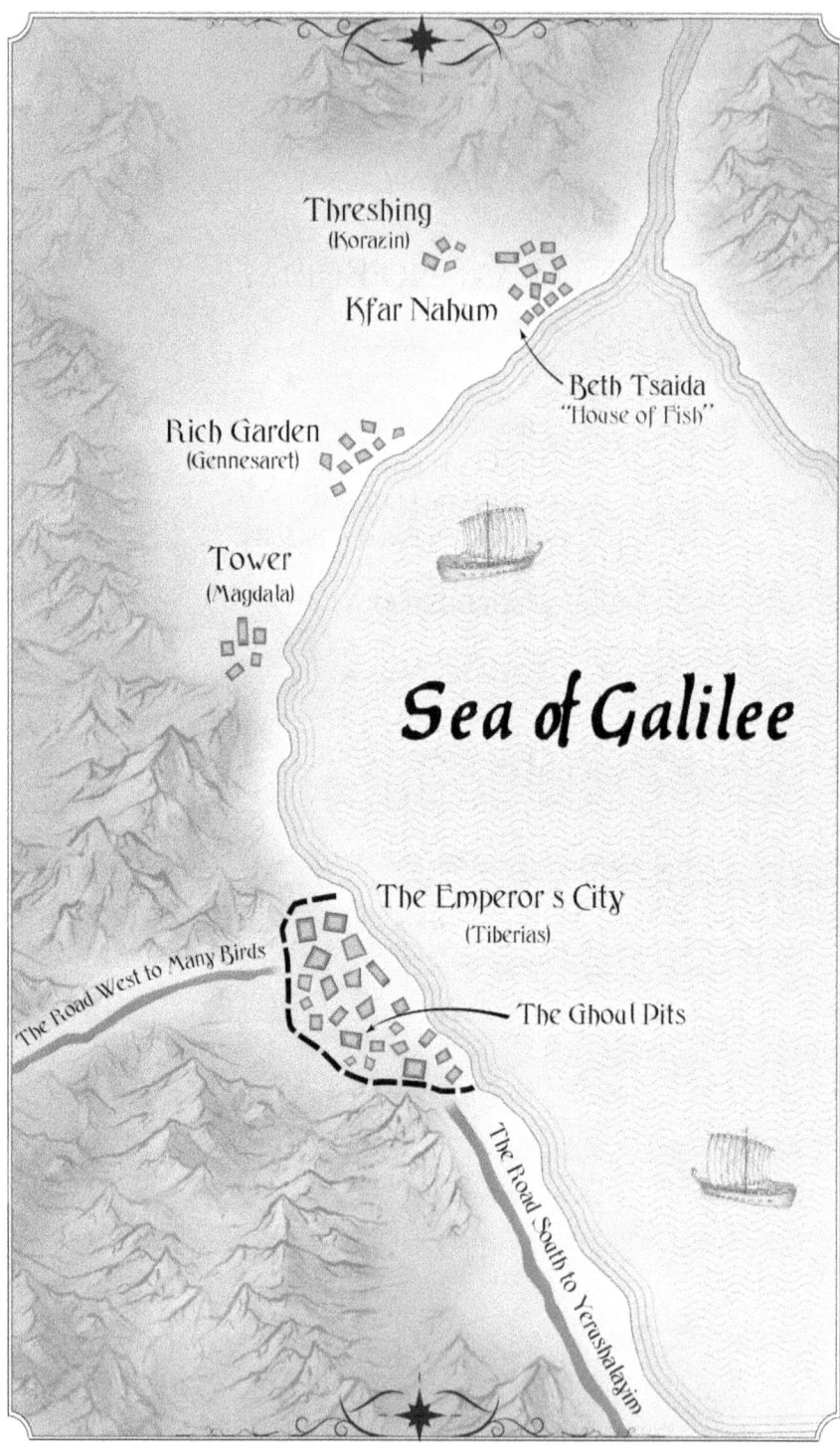

514

PART 1

AD 26—Present Day. Kfar Nahum,
in the Roman Province of Galilee.

OUR FATHERS' SEA

SHIMON TOOK precautions. He asked the town's nagar to reinforce the door of his house with strong pine. And every evening at sundown, Shimon gave his crippled brother a curt nod and made sure that his mother bolted the door behind him with heavy planks of wood; through the door, he could hear her breathing hard with the effort. Then he walked out through the storm-battered houses of the fishers and hurried down the grassy tideline to the boats, to join Yohanna and Yakob, his uncle's sons, in readying the boat that had been his father's for their night's long battle with the sea.

The fish they brought back, a few dancing in wide nets, were just enough to keep them all alive—never enough for them to buy another boat or gather any wealth. The sea had been plentiful once, so much so that the fathers had told them that their fathers had been able to walk across the water from one shore to the next in calm weather without getting more than the soles of their feet wet—the fish had been so thick, they had just walked on their backs. The sea had been that full of the blessings of God.

But Shimon knew, with an ache of grief and old guilt as he pulled the oars and they went out to sea—Shimon knew the dead had poisoned the water. In the old stories, the lurching dead had blighted farm and field. Men and women who had been strong and hale sickened and perished. Perhaps it was the same with the fish. Sometimes in his dreams, while he shivered in his threadbare blanket, he thought he heard the emptiness of the sea, a kind of silent cry, like the cry the womb makes in a young woman who longs for a child and has none. The sea, once so full, longed for fish.

And some nights, out on the sea, they would haul up one of their too-empty nets and feel some weight in it. Looking down they would see rising out of the deep one of the dead tangled in the net, its face lifted toward them, eyes pale and white like those of a dead fish. Already reaching a hand toward the surface, its jaw opening.

Shimon hadn't slept well in years.

Often, as he lay in his bedding in the morning hours while Rahel and his brother moved quietly about the house, he would wake, shaking, remembering. He recalled the eyes most. It was never the lurching walk or the low moaning from a dead throat that stirred him from his sleep; it was the eyes, for wherever Shimon hid in the dream country, those eyes were waiting there for him. He might be dreaming of having a great house of sunbaked clay, cool inside with many carpets—like the houses that men of the Law had, in Yerushalayim far away. He would dream of holding a great banquet there, and many men would come in clothes so fine that Shimon's eyes ached seeing them. But always, when Shimon looked up from his food, he found his banquet guests staring back at him with those dead eyes. Those terrible eyes, in all their faces.

Or he might be dreaming of a woman, her body soft and scented beneath him. He would slide into her as smoothly as he might slip into the sea, and feel her clasp him, feel her arms about him, holding him to her; feel her breasts and her thighs against his body, damp with sweat. Yet as he began to move in her, she would not moan or cry out, and he would glance down at her face and see her looking up at him with those same eyes. Those eyes that held no life.

And he'd wake, his sweat cold on his face and back. He'd bite his lip and lie without tears, gazing at the open sky over the atrium where he and his family slept in the summer—or at the ceiling over his head in his cramped little side room if it were winter. In those months, the cold light from the atrium revealed the stone slabs of the roof laid over stout wooden beams, but though that wall between him and the vast unanswerable sky was familiar, it brought him no comfort. Shelter for the body, never for the heart.

* * *

Tonight Yakob rowed them quietly out into the dusk, and Shimon and Yohanna stood in the boat casting the nets again, the ropes cold and wet in

Shimon's numb hands, a damp that he could feel even through his thick fishing gloves. The nets were woven flax and weighted, and one had to hurl them out over the water; it took a lot of strength and precision to cast one, and it could take two grown men to pull up a net if it was full—but the nets had not come up full in a long time.

The boat creaked beneath them; it was old. In his father's time, that boat would have been recognized anywhere on the Sea of Galilee. Now its sand-red paint was almost entirely gone; the boat had been skinned white by the water, like driftwood and sea wrack. Shimon and the others toiled on it like survivors scrambling for food in a ruin, as though they were three brothers who were the last remnant of their town. But the true brother of Shimon's own blood sat broken at home in a broken house, his absence a bitter core in Shimon's heart. Above the shore behind him, all the houses of Kfar Nahum were broken, each house a wounded body, burned and scarred and in some cases empty and boarded up, so many structures of memory and stone maimed years ago by men, living and dead, who had taken out their anguish, their rage, their grief and hopelessness on the bodies of others.

They knew their work, these three. Yohanna had the best eyes, and he watched the water. Yakob could endure at the oars the longest. And Shimon could sense the smallest shift in the wind; he knew when to let the sail fly or when to furl it up tight against the sudden rages of the *shedim* howling over the water.

"Maybe today," Yohanna said, as he always did at the casting of the nets. He was a man who liked to hope. Shimon might have resented that, but Yohanna's hands on the nets were strong, and in any case Shimon found it difficult to stir the ashes of his anger these nights. He felt emptied out, like his father's house. He swung one of the nets, feeling the pull of its weight in the sinews of his arm. As it came around he lifted it high and cast it out into the wet dark, letting the rope pay out through his gloved hands, the cold sound of the water swallowing it. Shimon began the count.

"Maybe today." Yohanna glanced at Shimon's face, and his own fell. He added in a low voice, "There are blessings left in this sea. We just haven't found them yet. We have to keep trying. Until the *navi* heals the land."

Shimon ignored Yohanna's optimism, as he always did, and Yakob changed the subject, as *he* always did. His hard eyes softened as he looked at his brother. "Tell us again about your navi," he said. Yohanna had been one of the town's self-chosen exiles, leaving two years past to seek out the wild caves in the cliffs above the Tumbling Water, where Yohanna ha Matbil, the baptist, whom some men called *navi*, or prophet, lived in defiance of the moaning *shedim*, forsaking town and city, living on locusts and camel's milk and leading men and women down into the water to wash away their evil.

Shimon's count reached twenty and he tightened his grasp on the rope, stopping its slide. He sat quickly on one of the boat's two benches—the one nearest the stern—and knotted the rope around one of the iron hooks set between his feet. The original hooks had long since needed replacing, and it had cost him severely. The iron came from Threshing, and the men and women of Threshing wanted nothing to do with those surviving families who wrestled their hunger in the emptied houses of Kfar Nahum.

Yohanna cast his own net and told his story as he knotted the rope. Shimon took up another net and swung it out into the night as he listened.

"He brings everyone up from the water with his own hands; he won't let any of his followers do that. He will look into the eyes of a man he's lifted from the river, and say things that I still hear in my heart though my mind doesn't understand. He would look in your eyes and say, *Prepare yourself, God is very near.* Or he would say, *We are all kin. All tossed together by God into this world.*"

"We are all kin," Yakob repeated quietly.

"I asked him about that," Yohanna said. "One night when the stars were out and all the baptized slept in their tents by the riverbank. I went to him and I said, *Rabboni, my teacher, my master.* I said, *Who are my kin?* And he just looked at me as though I should know the answer without asking. He is like that. He doesn't talk much, Yohanna ha Matbil—unlike me, though we have the same name. He hardly ever says anything, really, and so he teaches us all to listen."

"We are not all kin." Shimon's voice was gravelly, as he hadn't used it yet that night, and it startled him to find himself speaking now. "The Romans are not my kin. Those Greek-loving Hebrews in Threshing and Tower, they are not my kin." Something flickered inside him, then settled, and he sat back on the row bench, silent and heavy. The others didn't answer or challenge his silence, and after a few moments he ceased to be a man and became a part of the boat again.

* * *

Then there was only the silence and the sea and the starlight. A few times, the men pulled up the nets for a look, and the few small, lean musht they caught soon lay glistening in the bottom of the boat. Perhaps enough to feed the three of them and their families for one meal. When the nets were back down, they slit the fish open and gutted them and then wrapped them in sheaves of lake-weed that they kept in a bin behind Shimon's bench, a bin filled with water to keep them fresh. Shimon watched the wrapped fish for a while, numbly; then he lifted his eyes and watched the dark surface of the lake, that watery mirror of his own heart. There was no wind tonight; years before, when Shimon hadn't yet learned despair, he would have been thankful for that. The wind was to be feared; demons rode it, the *shedim* that wandered in the desert places until witches called them out of the dark or until the wind picked them up and swept them into the towns and the stone houses of the People. Sometimes one heard them howling and keening in the rocks high on the hill of tombs, and if a man did not live a good life and keep the words of the Law often on his lips, if he opened his mouth too often to speak blasphemies or untruths, the wind might blow a demon into his mouth. The demon would inhabit his body as a man inhabits a house, but would damage the house it dwelled in, casting the man to the earth in fits or tormenting his mind and making him shriek and curse at people who weren't there. Zebadyah the priest claimed that these same demons inhabited the corpses of the unburied dead and the unclean and half-eaten, that it was these *shedim* that drove those corpses stumbling to their feet and made them pursue and feed on their living kin.

So when there was a cold wind over the water—as there often was, chopping the surface of the sea and cutting even through his water-coat—Shimon shivered amid his numbness and his grief, and drew his coat more closely about his body, as though by keeping covered, he could keep the demons from slipping inside him. And when the night's catch brought up a few fish, he was always careful when he gutted them to take out the heart and wrap it in a bit of lake-weed, tucking it into his coat. Before sleeping for the day in the empty house that had been his father's, he would hand the heart to his mother, who lay it on the coals of the smaller firepit in their atrium, the one they didn't use for cooking. The smoke from the fish's heart would keep even the most malicious of the *shedim* away, for their fathers had taught that the fish were God's gift to the People, to make them strong and virile and prosperous.

But now it was rare to smell the heart-smoke of the fish, and Shimon feared that each wind brought more *shedim* into the town, and that even the water itself had become a house for the demons, a dark mirror of the air that was their usual home. Somewhere down under that dark, placid surface were many pale corpses, some buried perhaps in the sediment, some drifting in the water.

A soft glow on the far edge of the sea signaled the coming dawn, yet Shimon felt cold.

"Do you never think of what waits beneath our boat?" he asked suddenly.

The others turned to look at him.

After a few moments, Yohanna cleared his throat. "Fish, I hope. Somewhere." He was pale.

"I never stop thinking of it," Shimon said. He kept staring at that still, deceitful surface. "You think you can forget everything in this silence over the water. You think you can leave your dead beneath the waves. But there is no lasting burial."

* * *

They took up their oars and rowed slowly, letting the nets trail behind in the water, in no hurry to return to their surviving kin with news of another night lost. Shimon sat in the middle of his despair like a hard gray stone. But then he glanced up from his oar and saw a single white seabird, the morning's first. It skimmed low over the sea with a swiftness that was holy. His gaze followed the bird's long glide, and for a few moments the sight of it made his numbness almost pleasant, the way that the last slide into sleep is pleasant, when a man loses all feeling but that soft weight of drowsiness.

Even as the bird lifted into the sky, the sun burst over the water behind them like the sounding of a shofar, lighting the bird's wings and the water beneath it, and blazing against the white walls of Beth Tsaida, the fishers' houses by the tideline below Kfar Nahum town. Those were houses of stone built to withstand the strong winds from the sea. Houses built to last; only the people inhabiting them had not.

As if in answer to the sun's arrival, an eerie cry sounded over the water. A high, wavering cry, a wail. Shimon stiffened; for a moment he didn't know what creature was uttering that scream, though he thought there were words in it.

"What was that?" Yohanna gasped.

"A man," Yakob said, looking over his shoulder. "There's a man on the shore."

Shimon glanced where Yakob gestured, even as the cry died away, leaving his heart beating fast. They were close enough to the shore now that if Shimon had held up his arm and tried to cover the man with his hand, he would have needed to use nearly his entire palm.

He squinted against the sun's glare on the water. One of the boat people, maybe, though the man was standing with his feet in the sea. Why one of the vagrants would walk out into the breakers and risk the touch of the waterlogged dead, Shimon couldn't imagine. The man wore a wool robe the color of sand, though it was torn, dirtied. There were bruises on his face and arms. A vagrant, maybe one of those men with a demon that made him shriek in the night until the fishers of Kfar Nahum drove him away.

Yet that cry, that terrible cry.

Shimon could not slow the thumping of his heart. The oars slipped in and out of the water, and the boat moved smoothly toward the shore and the man.

The man on the shore lifted his hands to his mouth and called out again, and the cry carried loud and far. Yakob cursed and made the sign against the evil eye. That high wail as though he were the God of their fathers in the desert, calling the People to Har Sinai, the mountain that touched the clouds. Shimon made out one word in old Hebrew, strangely ululated: the word for *fish*.

"God, I wish he'd stop that," Yakob whispered, pale.

The very air seemed to quiver as the cry went on, and on. Then the boat lurched hard to the larboard, tilting, nearly tossing Shimon into the sea. He grasped the bench and his feet scrabbled against the side of the boat as the gunwale nearly touched the surface. The boat—they were tipping! With a bellow, Shimon threw himself across and up against the highside. Yakob and Yohanna did so, too, shouting over the cry from the shore.

"Did we strike something?"

"I don't know!"

"Right the boat!"

Shimon roared. He knew from the boat's tilt that the keel was coming dangerously near the surface, and he heard water lapping over the low gunwale as the boat fought for balance. Glancing down, he saw dark water coming over the gunwale and the nets trailing in the sea, and gasped.

There the nets were, some way below the surface, and he could see that they were full, in fact perilously full, of teeming, squirming fish. Musht and barbels and sardines caught in the tight weave of the nets. The fish were blue-silver and they flashed in the dawn, like pieces of living iron. Their thousand mouths opened and closed helplessly, their eyes dark and glassy as if with shock at their sudden birth and capture, as if tossed in one slippery instant from God's hand into the waiting nets.

"*Fish*," Yakob whispered. "*Fish*."

"*Fish*," Yohanna whispered.

Then Shimon was whispering it, too. The word fell from their mouths like a sigh of awe, like an invitation to wake from an evil dream. *Fish . . . fish . . .* Their sigh went out over the water until that word and the slosh of the waves against the boat and the slapping of the wet scales of fish against each other's bodies and against the straining nets became one sound, one hope.

FACES IN THE WATER

EVERY MAN older than a boy knows this, and likely every woman, too: You cast out your nets and catch some flash of new life. Then your dead rise from the waves of your past to wrest it from your hands.

The boat began to right itself, but only barely. Even as Shimon looked down into the water, he saw a pale corpse clinging to the bottom of the net and trying, clumsily, to climb it; its face tilted back, and its small, lifeless eyes gazed up at the water's surface and at Shimon above it. Shimon gazed back at those empty eyes for one terrible instant, his heart violent in his chest, his body cold with horror that this ruin of a human being, its insides perhaps crawling with *shedim*, might seize his flesh, might *eat* him.

Great strips of flesh trailed from the thing's cheek, where fish and the water itself had been at it. Shimon reached for one of the small spears stowed beneath his bench for incidents such as this, and he took the spear in his gloved hand and began thrusting it down into the water, cautiously but quickly, knowing he mustn't cut the net. Knowing also that the corpse must not come up *with* the net.

The face emerged from the water and its mouth opened as though to moan or hiss, but water poured out instead of sound; the corpse reached one maggot-white waterlogged arm toward him. With a wild cry, Shimon drove his spear into its face; his hook tore through the thing's scalp as easily as through a fish. In a moment it hung limp from Shimon's spear, its eyes still dead and unseeing.

Then it slid away and sank into the deep. Its face still gazing lifelessly up, it faded to a dim white form far beneath the water, and then could no longer be seen.

Shimon threw his weight back against the far gunwale, fearing the tilt of the boat. He was breathing hard. He felt a hand clap his shoulder, and Yakob's breath near his ear. "It's all right, Shimon. It's all right."

But his hands were clenched so tightly around the spear that he couldn't loosen them. He just kept staring at the surface of the sea. And then he saw them. Faint in the murk, clinging to the bottom of the nets, beneath the flashing silver of the fish, other pale figures. The corpses of the sea of Galilee.

In the next moment, Yakob and Yohanna glimpsed them, too.

"Holy God," Yohanna breathed.

"We've brought them up with the fish," Yakob whispered.

"Spears," Shimon cried hoarsely, his body so shaken with fear he felt that if he let go of the spear he held, he might retch and fall into the sea.

But then the boat tipped harder, tugged down by the weight of the dead crawling up the ropes from the nets. The mast swung down, dangerously near the surface. Yakob and Yohanna didn't spare a moment to grab spears; they threw themselves hard against the highside gunwale, fighting to balance the weight of the dead. Gazing down with his spear still clutched in his hands, Shimon saw the nets and the fish beneath him, and the dead breaking the water, reaching with their long gray fingers for the gunwale and the warm bodies above it. Their eyes pale stones glistening with seawater. Shimon stabbed down at them. But one grasped his fishing spear and pulled, nearly wrenching Shimon out of the boat and into the lethal water. Such strength. For just a moment the corpse's face was only an arm's length from his, with its dead eyes and torn flesh hanging loose from white bone. Its jaws opened, spewing water.

And then, in the dawn light on that dying sea, Shimon did something that he could never afterward truly believe he had done. Something in him roared awake, like a lion springing from a cave. So many nights he had failed to bring home fish for his family, failed though his father had been a boatman envied on every coast of the Sea of Galilee. So many mornings he had come home to see his brother's skin stretched too tight over his ribs, to hear their mother's voice shrill with the bitterness that hunger breeds in the heart. How often he had heard weeping by day in the house nearest his as he tried to sleep despite the growl of his belly, or seen beggars listless in the shade of derelict boats just above the tideline, their eyes vague with the nearness of death and their faces gray as the faces in the water. So many silent nights on the water, so many empty nets. But not this time. This time, nothing living or dead would keep him from bringing the fish home.

Shimon took up an oar and leapt on the gunwale and spun the wooden blade in his hands to give it momentum and force. He slammed the blunt wood into one of the pale faces. The corpse lost its hold on the net and was hurled aside into the waves, where it sank as swiftly from sight as a dream upon waking. Then, roaring as though furious at the dead and at the sea and the sky and Mighty God himself, Shimon spun the oar, slamming it into one face after another, dislodging the dead, in one case crushing the corpse's skull so that its body went limp as he sent it back to the sea.

The last of the dead grasped the gunwale with one hand and with the other, the haft of the oar, just above Shimon's own hand. Hissing. Shimon lifted the oar in both hands, drawing up the dead, water streaming from the corpse. Shimon caught a brief glimpse of its eyes near his, white gums drawn back from its teeth, water trickling out from a great gash in its cheek. All his nightmares made real. His memories given flesh. With a shout he swung the oar over the water away from the nets and shoved it out into the air; oar and corpse fell back, attacking the surface of the sea in a fierce splash. The corpse clung to the oar, but the waves bore it away from the boat, its dead eyes still watching Shimon. Still hungering. After a moment its wavering moan called out across the water.

Shimon fell back into the boat, his chest heaving. Yakob and Yohanna tried to haul up the nets, heaving on the ropes, hand over hand. Doubtless, if they could get the fish into the center of the boat, they could keep the craft from trying to pitch itself into the sea. But after a moment they gave up, faces pale with strain, and let the nets fall back into the water. They gave the ropes a little slack and tied new knots, letting the nets sink deep, and at last the boat righted itself, its slender mast swinging slowly back toward the sky.

Yakob collapsed onto the other row bench. "Can't haul up those nets," he gasped. "We'll go under. We have to drag them in nearer the sand."

"Only one oar." Shimon had caught his breath.

"Two," Yohanna said. "I stowed a spare beneath the bench before the last Sabbath."

"Then row," Shimon growled, forcing himself up and onto the bench.

The others grabbed up the oars and swung them out and began to row fiercely, rowing backward so that they could keep their eyes on the shore. Shimon sat with his hands empty, his face dark and brooding. He could hear the man on the shore calling to them, but didn't heed the words. He heeded only the low moan of that corpse being carried out on the tide, riding its oar back toward the empty heart of the sea. Its voice was like another he'd heard, fifteen years before. All those years his past had lurched after him, threatening to swallow him. Moaning for him. He had hidden his heart in cold numbness and now that numbness had broken open, revealing blood and fury inside. Even as the boat lurched on the water, each stroke of the oars bringing the fish-heavy craft near to foundering, Shimon kept his gaze fixed on the stranger on the shore. This man who had called the fish, and called the dead up with them.

---

15 Years Past. The Fall of Kfar Nahum.

THINGS DYING
AND BEING BORN

THE DEAD FEASTED in the town that night, devouring Roman and Hebrew alike. Before they came, Rome's mercenaries had set up their tents in a half-moon around the town's north, as though all the birds of prey around the Middle Sea had settled here, ravenous, with blades for talons. They all wore Roman armor but their features were those of an entire world: faces dark-skinned and white, black hair and golden, short men and giants. The conscripts of an Empire, come to punish the town that had hurled a Roman tax collector into a house filled with the dead. All day they had plundered Kfar Nahum, and with the fall of dark, they reveled, peeling the town and its people open like fruit to be enjoyed and devoured.

But they had not come alone.

Something more ravenous even than they had followed them down out of the dry hills, perhaps attracted from old battlefields where they'd stood silent and waiting by the loud clink and clank of strange armor. The moaning dead fell upon the tents and the houses, and the town filled with shrieks.

Soldiers who only moments before had been slaking their hungers with wine or rape were tugged beneath growling, grasping corpses even as they reached for their swords. The natives of Kfar Nahum were bewildered at this judgment that fell upon both oppressors and oppressed; some ran to grab up fishing hooks to use for spears; others ran for the shore and the boats and the safety of the dark waters of the Sea of Galilee, that freshwater lake of storms; others tried to get back to their houses.

Shimon bar Yonah was only thirteen, short, and as yet unacquainted with despair. He peered out through a chink in the window of his father's house, but could see only dark silhouettes against the fires the Romans had kindled at the edge of town to light their carousing earlier that night. He heard screams, heard the wavering moans of the dead. His urine ran hot down the inside of his leg, and the reek of it filled his nose. He was never afterward able to forget the shame of his terror in that moment.

The outer door slammed open, startling a cry from him, but when Shimon turned to see the man who came to stand at the entrance to his small room, dark in the doorway, his chest heaving, he was not one of the dead nor any Roman but his own father. Yonah, the man other fishermen in the village looked up to. A man who seemed a giant to his son, as perhaps all fathers do, a man who towered over him and could surely carry a boat out of the sea on his shoulders.

Yonah was clutching his left arm near the shoulder. He dropped to one knee and looked into his son's face. His voice was raw with pain. "Son, listen to me. Your mother—I hid her in the *kokhim*. The tomb of our family. The one place the Romans would not look. You must go there. Go there now. Run. Don't let the dead follow you. Go to your mother. Go *now*, son!"

He grasped Shimon's arm and thrust him toward the door. Shimon glanced back wildly at his father. In one dizzying instant, he saw blood seeping between his father's fingers where he clasped his left arm. Shimon hesitated; he felt the slow crawl of panic into his chest.

"I'll be behind you," Yonah cried. "Run, boy!"

And Shimon ran.

* * *

Shimon's heart was a wild, desperate thing in his chest; his side burned as he tore through the narrow streets of the town, ducking as screaming figures darted or fell past or tried to clutch at him. Dying men and women lay writhing in the dust behind him as he ran, and other shapes fell on them with snarls. Once, Shimon saw ahead of him, at the doorway of a house, a woman screaming in the street, her belly torn open. He saw her face—the town's midwife. A man with only one eye glanced up from the ravaged body with entrails clutched in his hands, and his eye was white and had no life in it.

Shimon screamed and veered to the left, ducking as two corpses in the street hissed and snatched at him; one caught hold of his sleeve at the wrist but the fabric tore and Shimon stumbled and ran on, with the corpses pursuing. Ahead he saw the door to the weaver's house, where the Roman mercenaries had herded all of the town's small children. An oil lamp still burned within, and Shimon had a brief glimpse of adult shapes bent over small, still bodies, large hands pulling entrails and red organs from their bellies. One of the feasting corpses glanced up and its eyes shone like cat's eyes in the light of the lamp. Shimon ran past, sobbing, but the corpses pursuing him ducked within the broken door and joined the feeding.

Everything after that was a confusion of snarls and moans and hands grasping for him, and a man in Roman armor lying in the street, his legs torn away, two of the dead bending over him, sucking greedily at his insides. His screams as he begged for help. Shimon covered his ears. He couldn't stop. He had to get out of the town and find his mother. He couldn't stop. Crying, he ran, and ran, and *ran*.

Then he was through the houses, and his small legs carried him up the rocky slopes of the hill west of the town. A wind was picking up, and he could hear the *shedim* screeching and howling among the stones and crags. He hurried for the refuge of the tombs, where no demons could enter and where the dead were always silent. The family *kokhim*, and those of the other fishing families of Kfar Nahum, were chambers dug out of the side of the hill. On shelves carved into their interior walls were laid the bodies of their ancestors. Once, centuries ago, the People had piled mere cairns of stone over their dead; now they gave them beds inside the earth and often left the tombs open to the air so that God could look in and see the dead, and remember them.

But these walking dead that had lurched into their town during the night, interrupting the carousal of the Roman legionaries, were not the dead of Kfar Nahum. Shimon didn't know where they had come from, only that their faces were unfamiliar and twisted in savage hunger. Perhaps they had come down, as a few dead did each year, from the great battlefields left neglected in wild places. He didn't know.

Behind him, the light of flames rushing before the wind. Parts of the town were dying in heat and fire and screams. His body went cold with panic as he panted and forced himself uphill toward those dark tombs. Suddenly, he heard a thin, faint cry—from ahead, not behind. An infant's cry. Shimon froze, listening. Then he bolted, running up the slope to the tomb of his family.

* * *

The *kokh* was open and dark, the dead inside silent on their shelves. Shimon leaned into the opening, the cool of the tomb on his face, and called out, "*Amma, amma*, mother, mother!" into the cool, dry night within.

"*Shimon?*"

"I'm here. Father sent me." He was shaking.

"Shimon—" Almost a moan, and Shimon caught his breath, fearing for her and fearing the dark. He stepped in, stumbled over loose pebbles, and caught himself on his hands, there at the very lip of the tomb's round chamber. Even as he picked himself up, his eyes adjusted and in the faint starlight and the dim glow of the town's burning he saw his mother lying on her back near the wall. Her body was flushed and damp with sweat; the distant glow from the fires in her eyes. She lay naked on a blanket, her legs parted, the knees lifted, and Shimon averted his eyes. She was clutching something small to her breast; he could hear suckling. The woman glanced up at Shimon, her face twisted in fear and exhaustion—her son stood there and not his father.

Shimon stood in the door, not knowing what to do. His face flushed as he watched the small life suckling at his mother.

"Your brother," Rahel said after a moment. She sounded hoarse and breathless, as though she had been weeping. "This is your brother."

* * *

Rahel bat Eleazar had given birth alone, without any midwife to assist her, and though she had been blessed with a clean birth and a living baby, she was left weak and shaken. Obeying the words she whispered there in the shadows of the tomb, Shimon took up a fold of the blanket she lay on and pressed it between her thighs to stanch the blood. Weakly she touched his hand with hers, pressing slightly, and Shimon held the cloth to her. He listened to the sounds his brother made. He listened to Rahel's breathing, heavy in the dark. And he listened to the cries and moans from the town below. Whatever entered his heart as he listened to these things, as he sat where no man or boy was ever permitted to sit, between the knees of his mother at the place of birth—whatever this moment did to his heart, there was always a quietness in him, for all his life afterward.

When his mother slept and Shimon was sure that no blood had soaked through the blanket, he left the cloth bunched up and pressed to her as best he could, then took up the waterskin his father had left there for her—it was empty now—and slipped out of the tomb. He knew his mother would thirst when she woke, and he knew there was a spring farther up the hill, where he and the other boys used to go and watch the moon rise over the sea. Standing on the slope, he glanced once at Kfar Nahum's stone houses and the dark murmur of the sea behind. Some of the fire had been put out, though it still raged near the synagogue. He could just see dark shapes against it. Somewhere a man was screaming, high-pitched and desperate, in Latin, words Shimon didn't know. He heard moaning still, but thought there was less of it.

Shivering, he turned his back and crept up the hill, bending low so that his silhouette would not be seen against the stars. Halfway to the water, he stopped—not because he had seen or heard anything, but because something had coursed through his body, cold and sharp, a shock of instinct that he could not have described or understood. He dropped and pressed his belly to the dirt, breathing in small gasps of fear.

A moment passed. Then another.

The man far below was still shrieking his incoherent Latin words.

Then, somewhere near, the slide of a foot over the soil. Shimon tensed.

Now a step. Then another slide, the sound of a foot dragged across the dirt. Shimon's heart set up a panic beat in his chest. He lay trembling.

A dark shape slouched by perhaps a stone's throw from where he lay, just a moving patch of night where no stars shone, a man's shape or a woman's, hunched forward, one arm hanging uselessly at its side. Shimon held his breath, and his heart was like all the shouting since the world began, ready to give him away. Yet the corpse didn't hear it; it just dragged that one foot behind it, swaying as it walked downhill. The reek of it reached Shimon and he gagged; he covered his mouth and nose and fought with himself to stay silent.

The screams in the town seemed faint now, drowned beneath the roar of blood in Shimon's ears, but he could still hear them. He could see again the midwife being eaten, the midwife who might have helped his mother. He could see again the blood on his father's hand. A mad urge seized him, to leap to his feet and shout and throw himself at that corpse, perhaps with a stone in his hand. To make that shambling, violent corpse *know* that this town it meant to consume had people in it, men and women like Shimon's father and mother, people who lived and loved and breathed. To smash the stone into its face, if that's what it took to make it see.

But he didn't leap up.

He held still. He clenched his fist about blades of the coarse grass, as though holding himself to the ground.

The corpse was moving down the slope now. It tilted its head back, drew in a long breath that Shimon could hear in the dark, and then it *moaned*. A low wail of need and demand that wrenched at him. It was the sound of a man whose tongue had been cut away, and then his mind, and then he had been left on the shore of the sea with no sight or sound of his wife and children and all his kin, but only the need to find them and clasp them, crushing them to his body with strong, stiff arms and consuming them in his need. That low moan of a man who didn't know where they might be found or how he might come to them again. Such profound and despairing need as Shimon had never heard in a human voice. He shivered in the grass.

The moan went on and on, far too long. Longer than a living man would utter any cry, long past when the lungs would burn, for the corpse voicing it felt no pain or anguish of the body. Or if it did, that was as the bite of a flea beside the pain of its solitude and hunger.

Then the moan fell and the corpse passed on down the hill. The sounds of its feet faded into the noise from the town and the chill breeze carrying the unbodied *shedim* through the grass. Its shape was distant now but dark against the glow of flame and easily seen.

Shimon lay breathing a while, recovering. He knew he had to be brave. Brave for his mother and her baby. All at once, he got up and ran forward at a crouch. He rushed; he had to get the water and get back into the tomb before any other corpse appeared on the hill. The momentary urge for battle had faded; after hearing that moan so near, he dreaded any further encounter with the dead.

And he wanted to be there when Rahel stirred. He could not let her wake alone in the dark.

PART 2

"I AM ALIVE"

RAHEL WAS ALREADY awake when Shimon returned; he heard her breath catch when his shape filled the opening to the tomb. Then heard her relax when he called, "Amma," softly. For a moment he hesitated, glanced over his shoulder at a night filled with stars and the sound of the sea and the glow of flame, the houses of his father's town burning far below at the edge of the water. Distant moaning, screams. Fewer now. Anything might be happening in the world outside the tomb. The Romans and the people of the town might be spearing the last of the dead, or the dead might be eating the last of the living. No way to know.

He felt vulnerable and exposed. He ducked into the tomb. Went to his mother and knelt by her, held the waterskin to her lips and listened as she drank. She did so in small swallows, and took a long time. Then her fingers touched his hand weakly, and he pulled the skin away, set it aside.

"Your father," she said hoarsely. "Where is he?"

"I don't know." He couldn't tell her. He couldn't tell her about the blood he'd seen on Yonah's hand, the raggedness of his father's breathing. His throat closed against the words. To speak it would be to make it real, to make his fears become truth.

Rahel shut her eyes tightly and clutched her infant closer to her, and a tiny, almost inaudible sound of misery came from her throat. Shimon closed his eyes, too, not wanting to see her pain, not knowing what to do.

After a while, Rahel whispered in the dark:

> *Though the fig tree does not flower,*
> *And no grapes are on the vines,*
> *The olives give no oil*

And the fields no barley
The flock does not come home to the fold
Nor the herd home from the field,
Yet I will cry out in joy.

Her voice trembled, yet she did not allow the silence of the tomb to swallow her song. The song of Habakkuk, a navi of their People in years past, one of those blessed or cursed with the gift of seeing things that usually only God saw. A song he'd made at a time of war.

I will cry out in joy,
I will take joy in my God.

God is my strength;
He makes my feet like the deer's;
He makes me walk in high places.

"How can you sing that?" Shimon said suddenly. "How can you?" His hands were shaking. "Everyone's dying. I saw— They're being torn *apart*."

Rahel looked at him in the dark. "Oh, Shimon, Shimon. I am alive, I am alive, I am alive, and my sons are alive."

And she began whispering the words again. Shimon turned his back, overwhelmed with the night's horror. He glanced up, saw the round openings in the tomb wall into which the ancestral dead had been slid feetfirst onto their shelves in the dark and the silence. There were corpses there, many. His father's father and his wife, and their parents, and theirs. And many of their brothers and sisters whose faces had been forgotten but whose names remained, chipped into the stone beneath their places of rest. He reached up to the lowest of these shelves, ran his fingers across the deep Hebrew letters, worn by time yet still readable if there were only enough light. His hand still shook a little at the memory of the corpse walking down the hill, at the memory of its cry of hunger, yet the silent dead on their shelves above him and all around him did not frighten him. Their silence and their presence was strangely comforting. Death had visited the People again and again over the long weeping of the centuries, yet the People lived.

"Would you like to hold him, Shimon?"

His mother was lifting the small baby in her hands, holding him out.

"It's all right," Rahel said, seeing him hesitate.

Swallowing, Shimon took the boy in his arms as gently as he might a sacred scroll, terribly aware of his brother's fragility. Yet as Shimon felt the small weight of his brother's body, the warmth of him, something blossomed open inside his heart. Settling the boy into the crook of his arm, he freed one hand and touched the child's face, first the tiny brow, then the soft cheeks, feeling his brother's warm vitality in the dark. His throat tightened and he wished to squeeze his brother to his chest, but he didn't for he feared hurting him. After the horrors he had seen this night, this warm body in his arms was a miracle, as though God had reached through the door of the cave and touched the world, in this one place, at this one moment.

He ran two fingers over the boy's hair, which was fine and sparse. Then he touched the boy's left arm, marveling at its smallness. He found the boy's hand and felt the small fingers close around his; he drew in his breath. That firm grip, and the soft glint of the eyes in the dark. Shimon wished his father was here, that he might hand him the baby and see the two of them together, but also he was glad that it was he who held the child and who got to look into the little boy's eyes. Those eyes were as bright with life as though they were God's eyes, looking out of that tiny face at a darkened world.

Solemnly, Shimon touched the boy's right arm, and gasped. That other arm was so thin, and the boy didn't move it at Shimon's touch. The arm hung limp at the baby's side.

"Amma," Shimon whispered in the dark.

She looked at him. Shimon saw her eyes and the faint glow of distant fire on one side of her face.

"He's broken," Shimon whispered.

"Hand him back to me, Shimon." No urgency or surprise in her voice.

Gently, his hands shaking from the fear that he would drop the boy or break him further, Shimon handed his brother back. Their mother held the baby to her breast, and Shimon looked away. A sense of crushing disappointment settled over him, a fierce pressure on his heart. To have a new life, a new hope offered in one moment and then torn away in the next, to find that his brother, like everything else this night, was maimed and broken—

"He is your brother," Rahel said quietly. The baby made no sound of suckling, just soft breathing; perhaps he was falling asleep, pressed to the warmth of his mother, his whole world her living flesh, unknowing of any dead outside or of any hunger but his own. "Whether he is broken or not, he is your brother. Shimon, never forget that."

Shimon didn't move; he just stared into the dark.

"Shimon?"

A moment later: "Shimon?"

He glanced at his mother. She had suffered this night. Though his insides burned with wrath, he leaned over her and pressed his lips to the baby's head, felt the softness of the infant's skin. He did not even hear the distant cries in the houses burning by the sea. Rahel turned the baby toward him, and after a hesitation Shimon felt for his brother's heartbeat. Found it, so much faster than his own, and in all the lethal night there was no other sound.

ZEBADYAH

DAWN FOUND the last men and women of Kfar Nahum laying the bodies of the dead outside the town in long rows, both Hebrew and Roman, and shrouding them in white linens. When the linens ran out, they used blankets, or coats, or whatever they could find. Most of the legionaries had perished, and those that hadn't had fled into the hills—that left many, many dead. The charred and broken houses of the town reeked of them.

A few of the living women took ashes that were still warm from the ruins of the houses and the Roman tents, and put the ashes in their hair. Then they knelt by the corpses and keened, as other women had done before them on many battlefields and in many burned cities throughout the long centuries of their time in this land. Zebadyah the priest ignored them at first, searching the dead for the face of his father. As he passed, men and women lowered their heads in weary reverence, but Zebadyah turned his gaze away from them. There was sand in his graying hair and his white robe had been torn and soiled by his flight when the Romans broke the door of his synagogue and by the long night hours he had waited hidden beneath one of the boats out above the tideline. There, with the boat's keel for his roof, Zebadyah had covered his ears against the screams of his people and the wailing of the dead in their hunger. He recalled, as in a nightmare, a whisper in his ear out of the air, when the Romans first began pulling people from their homes: *Go. Go quick. Hide.* And the same whisper as he hid beneath the boat: *Stay here.* Now shame smothered his heart.

His father Yesse had suffered during the night; one of the others among the grieving had told him of it, his voice shaken, as soon as Zebadyah had walked into town from the shore. In the hours of their drunkenness before the dead came lurching out of the hills, and while Zebadyah trembled beneath the boat, the mercenaries had stripped and beaten and mocked his father, for no better reason than that he was old and weak and Hebrew. The legionaries had dragged him from his house. This was a man with white hair and a long beard, who had served in his youth as a priest and who stood ready still to serve as one, if he should ever be called again to the *lev ha-olam*, the heart of the world, the Temple in distant Yerushalayim. Yesse had outlived two wives and had survived the deaths of three of his five sons, who had drowned in a storm at sea. He was revered by the town, and Zebadyah, the oldest of his two living heirs, brought fish for him and sat with him each evening as he ate. The drunken legionaries pulled this old man from his house and made him dance in the open ground before the synagogue, and then at swordpoint they forced him to strip away his garments and stand naked. He wept as they made crude jokes about his circumcision, as they asked him if he found he could still give pleasure to women, or whether he had lost some piece of his manhood and grown so white-haired searching to find it again. Perhaps they would have humiliated him further, but at that moment the moans had broken out, and the famished dead from the hills had fallen on them with their lethal hunger.

When Zebadyah found old Yesse at last, groaning in pain and grief where he sat against the side of a stone house near the edge of the town, the elder rebuked his son. "Tend to the People first," he rasped, "and let God tend to me, Zebadyah."

* * *

Zebadyah carried his father to the synagogue, feeling by instinct rather than conscious thought that it was the town's safest place, though he grieved to see the door broken from its hinges, blood smeared across the letters from the Law that his father's father had carved, with great labor, into the lintel and doorposts. He could hear the other survivors groaning within. The usually dim, cool interior was now lit with candles and stuffy from the smoke and the heat of the bodies smothered together beneath the low roof. The tiny flames shone strangely on the polished cedar of the cupboard against the east wall where the

Torah was kept. The menorah had been knocked over and lay flat on its table and the shofar that used to be beside it was missing, but at the time Zebadyah hardly noticed.

Yakob and Yohanna were already there, with Leah bat Natan and several other women, carrying waterskins among the suffering and the feverish, or pressing wet cloths to hot faces. When Zebadyah's sons saw him, they hurried to lay out bedding for Yesse.

"There are many here who are unclean, father," Yakob whispered as Zebadyah laid his father down. His eyes showed their whites. By unclean he meant *touched by the dead. Bitten.*

Zebadyah nodded wearily, whispering words of praise in his heart that his sons were both alive, however haggard they might look.

"Was grandfather bitten?"

"I am fine, boy." Yesse opened his eyes.

"He is fine," Zebadyah repeated numbly. He sat for a moment, just to catch his breath. Gray-eyed Yohanna, his face become overnight that of a man and not a boy, crouched beside Yesse and lowered the waterskin to his grandfather's parched lips.

Zebadyah heard a raised voice behind him and glanced over his shoulder. He saw Benayahu, the town's *nagar*, the woodworker, repairer of houses and boats, with his back to the synagogue wall. His face twisted in rage and horror. "Snatched her," he was crying. "Snatched her from my hands. My wife. They took her from my hands; they *ate* her!" Beside him stood a boy whose dirt-darkened face was streaked with pale rivers left by his tears, and the boy— who was not Benayahu's—held the *nagar*'s yearling daughter in his arms, asleep.

But Benayahu did not glance up at either the boy or his child. He had torn away the right sleeve of his tunic and he held the ragged, rolled-up cloth tightly to his upper arm. Zebadyah didn't know if the bandage covered a bite or a wound from a Roman blade, but at this moment he did not have the strength either to care or to fear.

The priest worked his mouth a moment, to get enough spit to speak clearly. He looked to his sons' gaunt faces. "Where are Yonah and Rahel? And their boy?"

"We haven't seen them, father," Yakob said.

Zebadyah squeezed his eyes shut.

If they were not here . . .

He forced his head up, looked around at the refugees of their town. More than forty lay on the clothes and blankets that had been tossed across the synagogue's stone floor for bedding, some of them shaking, some of them still. Some with horrible wounds, and their kin huddled over them, praying or giving them water or pressing wool against their limbs or their bellies to staunch the bleeding. Feverish faces in the candlelight—all these men and women waiting for death and for what nightmare might come after. A few of the unbitten stood solitary or sat against the wall, their heads down. None of them would ever sleep well again, ever trust the night again or the strength of their doors. A few looked his way, but Zebadyah lowered his eyes. He had hidden during the night while they suffered. He hadn't known the dead would come. He had hidden from the *living*. The Romans. But he hadn't been here—that was the accusation he believed he'd see if he faced them. He hadn't been here. He, their priest.

He realized Yakob was speaking to him. Perhaps had been for a while. His son's words rushed toward him from some distance like a flash flood down a river channel.

"—never got in the synagogue. It was Bar Nahemyah, father. He held the door against them during the night, and the corpses piled about his feet."

He glanced up at his son, whose face was drawn. He tried to understand. Bar Nahemyah—but he was only a youth, hardly older than Yohanna.

"Then he took some of the others and left. Yohanna and I stayed because people started bringing their wounded here, and they needed water and help."

"Have to find them," Zebadyah muttered, rising to his feet.

Yakob caught his arm to steady him, but he shrugged away his son's grip and the look he turned on his son must have been grim and desperate and near madness, for Yakob stepped back quickly.

"The old altar," Zebadyah rasped. "Past the grain caches, between the tanner's house and the ruin of the old wall. That one. Burn an *olah* there, while I find Yonah."

"We have no goats, no doves, father," Yakob said hesitantly. The altar hadn't been used since the days of the Makkaba; instead, Zebadyah went to Yerushalayim once a year to atone for the sins of the town, buying a goat to sacrifice from the market in the great city.

He muttered, "Perhaps God will accept a few fish. This one time."

He bent quickly to grip Yesse's shoulder and whisper, "My sons will look after you." Breathing raggedly, Yesse didn't open his eyes, and after a few beats of his heart Zebadyah left him and staggered toward the door of the synagogue.

* * *

He stumbled on through the death-reek of the town, seeking his brother Yonah. He stepped through the broken doors of houses and peered into emptied, unlit rooms with bloodstained walls. At the door of one house he heard low growls and he ducked away quickly, shaking.

He even strode out among the legionaries' tents beyond the north end of the town, but searching there he found at first only dead Romans and dead women and corpses whose heads had been split by Roman blades. Too many of the bodies were known to him. He saw Asher lying dead across the body of his wife, where he had perhaps died defending her from either the living or the dead. He saw Nahemyah's two sisters, their bellies torn open, entrails spilled messily about them where the dead had feasted. Their eyes glassy with death. But Zebadyah noticed one of the women's fingers twitching. He gasped and hurried by.

Nowhere did he see Yonah, or Yonah's wife or his son. Yet it was unthinkable to him that Yonah had perished. Yonah the ironhearted, Yonah the furious. He recalled the rage in his brother's eyes that autumn as he cast the tax collector the Romans had sent into a house at the edge of town, a house empty except for the corpse that had wandered inside and been trapped. The man had shrieked and pounded on the door from the dark interior, and Yonah had not flinched, though Zebadyah's own palms had gone slick with sweat. He tried to remember that tax collector's name, and in a moment it came to him: Matityahu, a Hebrew from the Greek city of Many Birds to the west.

Reaching the end of the Roman tents and finding still no sign of his kin, Zebadyah glanced back and was struck to the heart by the sight of his smoking town and the shore and the wide, wide sea. For a moment he couldn't breathe. When he was a boy, he used to stand on this shore beside his father, near this very place, once a week, welcoming the Sabbath Bride with song, with shouting and praise and the slapping of his hands against his thighs. The Bride would tread lightly over the water with the dusk from the eastern shore, hurrying toward them from God's house in the heavens to bring rest to God's People.

When he was a boy.

Now beside the beauty of the waves his town lay crumbled and reduced to charred stone, like a withered old corpse seated beside a lovely woman, a woman who has not yet consented to bury him, though she can no longer feed him bread or fish. Zebadyah closed his eyes and pressed a fist to his breast, as though he must hold in the anguish or it would burst him open. "What evil have we done, O God?" he moaned. "How have we broken your Law?" His voice gathered strength, as it had so many times as he prayed on the synagogue steps. "Lord and judge of the earth, for what do we stand judged? Was it our violence against Matityahu, who was Hebrew as we are? Was it that we took goods from the heathen traders, the pig-eaters, that we defiled our town? Was it for the Grief of Ezra? For what, Adonai?" He sank to his knees, the hard earth. "Why? Why have you made a wasteland of us?"

At that moment he heard a cry. A hoarse voice, a small voice, a child's, calling out for help. Zebadyah opened his eyes and looked to the tents.

There it was again.

Staggering to his feet, the priest followed the sound. After a moment, he stopped, called out: "Where are you?"

The cry that answered was inarticulate and without words, but it led Zebadyah to a great tent crimson as the insides of the eaten. The centurion's tent. It was cut open on one side, doubtless by the slash of the centurion's sword as he made his escape from the dead lurching through the tent's door.

Inside, Zebadyah found a corpse with a cloven head and heard gasping breath from beneath the centurion's overturned desk, a heavy thing of no wood the priest could recognize, one of those ostentations the Roman military brought with them on their galleys from other shores across the world.

Pinned beneath the desk was a boy of eight years, his eyes glassy in a gray face. Zebadyah knew the child, for he had circumcised him and given him the name his father Cheleph had chosen for him: *Yakob*, a name Zebadyah's own eldest son shared. But Zebadyah had not seen the boy's parents at the synagogue.

"Yakob," he breathed. He bent quickly to feel for the boy's pulse. It was fast but steady. "Oh, Yakob."

The boy's gaze wandered a moment, then met his.

Zebadyah felt weary as the land itself. "I am going to get you out of here." He drew in a quick breath and got his hands under the edge of the desk and pulled, prying it off the boy. It was much heavier than he'd expected. He strained against it, gasped a prayer, heaved again. A surge of strength surprised him; it had been years since he had set his hand to an oar or heaved up a net from the clinging water. But he would *not* leave this boy to die in a heathen tent. The boy made no move to wriggle out as Zebadyah raised the desk, but the priest pulled at it until he had the desk high enough to thrust it to the side with his hip and shove it away, thudding into the dirt.

Breathing hard, he bent over the boy again. Yakob bar Cheleph was naked but for a thin night-tunic, and he had soiled his legs during the night, for his underclothes were gone. With a bit of nausea, Zebadyah wondered suddenly if the boy had been raped by the centurion, and the desk thrown against him on purpose, in hopes that the dead would bend over it and feed on the boy while the Roman escaped. This had not happened, clearly; the corpses must have followed the centurion out. The desk had lain across the boy's hip, and he was bruised there, badly. Running his fingers quickly over the boy's hip, Zebadyah didn't feel any bones broken. Yet when he got his arms under the child and lifted him, the boy cried out and nearly fainted.

"Father," the boy gasped as Zebadyah regained his feet with the child in his arms, "father—"

"He's gone, boy," Zebadyah said. His voice hoarse. "He's gone."

The boy shook; even to be held must have been a torment, his body was so bruised. Zebadyah blinked, forbidding his tears, and held the boy gently to his chest. The boy's eyes were glazed with pain and shock, the need in them louder in Zebadyah's heart than the roar of his own shame. Zebadyah looked to the door of the tent, where a wind from the sea tugged at the canvas. At that moment, he made a vow, and he made it without sacrifice and without ritual. He made it as a man, not a priest—the first time he had ever approached the God of his fathers so nakedly. He vowed to raise the boy with his own two sons. Little could Zebadyah do to repair the shattered houses and shattered lives of his town—he had not even been there to protect his own father—but he could shelter this one small boy. Surely he could do that.

THE GRIEF OF EZRA

THE DEAD must be buried: that was the one most important condition of their Covenant with God. Generations before, the Makkaba had left so many fallen in empty places in the hills with their eyes open to the sky. Furious to drive out both the Greeks and those Hebrews who wished to be like the Greeks, the Makkaba had rushed from battlefield to battlefield, striking hard like the hammer after which he was named, not pausing either for burial or for tending the wounded. Kfar Nahum had paid the price of that neglect of the Law during the night. Many of their people now were bitten and feverish. Those few still on their feet would invite no new disaster. By midmorning, Zebadyah led some forty of the survivors of Kfar Nahum in carrying the dead up the slope to the tombs. All the dead, not only those who were Hebrew.

The tombs nearest the town were long since filled with their ancestors; farther up the hill were those of the living families, with some shelves occupied and some vacant and waiting. And highest on the hill, three new kokhim that had been dug in the past few years at Yonah bar Yesse's request, in anticipation of good harvests from the sea and growth for Kfar Nahum. "Who is born, dies," Yonah had said with a cold smile. "Will we have no houses waiting for them?"

Zebadyah and the others brought the hastily shrouded dead to these new and empty *kokhim* and there they set the Hebrew corpses on shelves, and in heaps against the wall they lay the corpses of the legionaries, some of them still in their armor. Though most of the tombs stood open to the air, that God might look in and see the dead and sing them to restful, unwaking sleep, each of the caves holding these dead would be sealed behind a great stone. These dead, whether Hebrew or Roman, would lie forever in the dark.

Zebadyah bent and took up a handful of dirt, dry and grainy, and rubbed it on his hands. He was grim. His father would live, but many down in the synagogue would not. And those who did—how would they live, after what had happened? Most of the town's women were dead, because most of them had been forced to the Roman tents before the dead came, and the dead had reached the tents first.

He glanced down the slope, found the winter-bared sycamore that stood by the entrance to his own family tomb. In it, his wife, taken by death while bearing his third child, the one who hadn't lived. The girl. This morning he felt no pang, staring down at her tomb. Only dull relief. She had been spared the brutality of the Romans and the coming of the dead. She had been spared this day.

Yakob bar Zebadyah stepped from one of the *kokhim* to get another body to bear within, saw where his father was looking, and walked over to stand beside him, his own face drawn with weariness and fear. He had left Yohanna in the synagogue tending Yesse and Bar Cheleph; of their kin, only he and his father were here on the hill.

"She was a good woman," Zebadyah said to him after a few moments. "She lived by the Law. Never a Greek garment in our house, never an uncleanness on her lips. I loved her."

They stood by each other, in silence.

Not heeding the priest and his son, the other men worked quickly, carrying bodies into the hill. They shelved the dead, then hurried back out into the pale sun, not pausing even to chisel or scratch the words of Ezra into the stone beneath the burial shelves, as was usually done: *For you God are holy and we who are flesh lie before you; who can stand before your face?*

A gust of wind across the hill, and Zebadyah stiffened against it, his lips closed tightly. Only when the wind died away did he speak. "God has withdrawn from us, Yakob." He gestured at Kfar Nahum below them by the bleak sea. "Look at the town. Our houses are built like Greek houses. Look at the women grieving, look at their dresses. Look at the decorative designs along the hem, designs that are not Hebrew." He thought of those he'd never see again, and of his brother, whose body he hadn't found. His heart grew small and cold. "God has turned his face. We were unworthy of his protection. The Grief of Ezra, my son."

Yakob only looked at his father with eyes that had seen too much suffering in one night to know or care how that suffering might be interpreted. But Zebadyah bent over one of the bodies, gripping beneath its arms to lift it, his anguish violent in his breast.

* * *

The Grief of Ezra.

That was what their People called the words of Ezra the Scribe, who centuries past had led the People home over the desert from their captivity beneath the walls of Shushan and the other cities among the mountain forests and wide plains of the east. Returning to the holy land after long exile, they had found their fathers' country ravaged by the hungry dead. They'd hastened to rebuild the long-crumbled wall about the great city, Yerushalayim, and those towers whose names their fathers had sung to them when they were young— names beautiful as the names of rivers: the tower of Meah, the tower of Chananel.

Every man toiling at the stones kept his spear beside him, where he could grasp it quickly if the dead lurched out of the olives on the mountain and came at them. When the dead came, hissing in the dark, many men who sealed the gaps in the wall with their bodies and their spears died, torn apart by hands that were without warmth, devoured by bodies in which there beat no heart. And as darkness ate the sky or as dawn bled into the heavens above the eastern ridge, more dead would stumble down from the high olive groves. Always more dead.

At sunset on the nineteenth day while the wall was still low and half-finished in some places, Ezra the Scribe stood before the People with his back to the stones and demanded of them that they stand and look out at the corpses. *Our land that God gave to our fathers is defiled,* he cried, *and you can smell the reek of it. Yet after all the evil that our fathers did, God has delivered us, patient as a father, and given us back our city. Yet even this day we do not keep his Law. Many of you have taken heathen daughters to your beds, and dress in the clothing of the east, and burn gifts of berries or small fruit to the gods who are not ours. And now we may be devoured. And this day, this night, will we still fail our God, until he turns his back again and no remnant of our People remains on the earth, and there is never again a return home? For God is holy and we are flesh before him.*

Then Ezra gave his fatal command, that the strange wives must be cast outside the wall and given no home within the city. *We must wall out what is unclean,* he shouted. *We must be clean and Hebrew again. Or this very night we will be eaten, and perish.*

Some of the men in the city refused, and some were slain. Ezra's speech had filled those at the walls with fear—the men who had gazed night and day into the eyes of the dead, men who'd taken up their spears and fought for the wall with their lives. At Ezra's word, many of these turned against their brothers in the city, tore their wives from their arms, and threw them over the low wall. Some of the women beat on the stones of the wall and screamed the names of their husbands. Others ran in search of crevasses in the rock or shrubs under which they might hide from the corpses that already lurched toward them.

While the dead ate, some of the men threw down their spears, set their backs to the wall, and covered their faces, shaking. Others toiled furiously at the stone and mortar, but did not look to the ground below. Ezra alone stood on the unfinished wall that night, watching by starlight and by the light of a torch he held as the screeching dead devoured the women. It was said afterward that he did not look away or blink or cover his ears against the screams and the cries for help. That he watched silently without tears as the women the men of his People had loved were caught and eaten, one after another, shrieking as they died.

Only when dawn came and there were at last no screams but only the moaning of the *shedim* through the mouths of the old dead and the new dead—the heathen wives risen in hunger, with horrible wounds that did not bleed—only then did Ezra come down from the now-finished wall. As he walked through the streets of Yerushalayim, such was the horror in his face that any who looked on him fell stricken to the ground, and died.

543

Ezra did not halt. Passing through the gates of their ancient city, he walked out alone into the wilderness above the Tumbling Water, speaking to no one. And he was never seen by the living again.

* * *

That was how Yesse his father had told the story.

Now, after the night of the dead, the Grief of Ezra held a new horror for Zebadyah.

"We must wall out what is unclean," he said quietly as he and his son carried another corpse into one of the crowded tombs. The reek was in their clothes now, in their hair. Though they both wore heavy fishing gloves and though the dead were shrouded to protect the living against any accidental touch, both men stank of rot. Zebadyah imagined that even if he were to swim in the sea, as the Greeks did, he would not be free of that smell. "We must wall out every heathen influence, every heathen word, every thing in our homes that was made by heathen hands and brought from outside, anything that may have tempted God to look away when the dead came last night. We must scrub every bit of rot from our doorsteps and our walls. We must bury and seal away these dead. We must be clean again. Until the *navi* comes. We must be Hebrew and faithful, so that God's gaze will be drawn to us again. To bless us, not to curse us. God gives and God takes away." He glanced at his son, whose face was pale with horror, and said, "Blessed be the name of our God."

"*Selah*," Yakob whispered. *Always.* His face was still gaunt with shock, his motions stiff as the two of them carried another body in. This one was a beardless mercenary in Roman gear, one of the heathen polluting their land. He had paid for that, and Kfar Nahum had paid with him.

After they threw the body down among the corpses in the chamber, Zebadyah put his arm around his son and drew him close, held him as Yakob shook with silent cries. Just held him. The others bringing in bodies stepped around them without speaking. At the sound of song, Zebadyah and his son stirred and stepped from the tomb into the chill air. The surviving women of the town—thirteen of them—had formed a line before the tombs and were singing the Words of Going that were as old as the People, words of lament for those who were lost and could not be recovered. That cold morning, their traditions and their memories were all they had left. No help had come from

Threshing beyond the hill or from Rich Garden or Tower south along the shore, though a few from Kfar Nahum had fled to those towns during the night.

After the women fell silent, Zebadyah lifted his own voice. His eyes were dry, his back stiff and straight. In his deep baritone, joined after a few moments by the other men, he sang the cries of Iyobh whom God had tested, words of grief that in the long years of exile and then return had become the words of their People, the essential song of a tribe whose first duty was to endure:

> Man that is born of woman is of few days, and full of trouble.
> He comes forth like a flower, he is cut down.
> Yet there is hope for a tree, if it be cut;
> At the scent of water it will bud, and bring forth boughs.
>
> But man dies, and wastes away;
> Yes, man gives up his breath.
>
> The waters wear away the stones:
> Washing away the things that grow out of the earth,
> All the hopes of man.

Then they closed the tombs.

* * *

Even as the last of the great stones slammed into place, as some of the People knelt in their grief and others turned their faces again toward the town below, a strange and unexpected sound rang out, echoing against the slope of the hill and out over the sea. A horn call clear and deep as the voice of God himself.

The men and women glanced at each other's faces in wonder.

The call of the shofar.

GOD WEEPING IN THE GRASSES

SHIMON BAR NAHEMYAH, the town's *other* Shimon, held the horn to his lips, the ram's horn he had taken from the synagogue. In his other hand, a heavy stone. His shoulders bore a fisher's thick storm-coat, snatched up from his house during the screaming cold night. Other young men stood to his left and his right, their faces pale and shining with cold sweat. Bar Nahemyah put all his breath and all his fury into the cry of the horn. He blew the *t'qiah*, the challenge that meant: *God is here! This place is his!* On how many battlefields of his ancestors and at the start of how many holy feasts had that same call gathered the People in strength?

Letting the horn fall to hang about his neck on its tough bullhide cord, Bar Nahemyah lifted the stone, his hands shaking in his cold fury. He and the other youths were a short walk up the shoreline from the last houses of Beth Tsaida, and before them, in a great pit into which each day's incoming tide poured cleansing water, was the town midden, the feasting place of gulls, where the poor left unwanted girl-babies before their eighth day and their naming, and where food that had been defiled and could not be eaten was left for the birds.

It was low tide, but there were no birds there now. Only the dead, both the quiet dead and the ravenous. The bodies of bruised, naked women lay across the heap, where the Roman revelers had tossed those who had collapsed during the repetitive rapes of the night. Three of the wakeful dead crouched over the women, tearing their flesh, their shoulders hunched, reminding Bar Nahemyah strangely of town elders gathered about the scroll of Torah, heads bent, peering into it for some sign of God's purpose.

There was an old man in the pit also, and though his face had been chewed away by the dead, Bar Nahemyah thought it was Asa the tanner. He was clothed and there were no bruises on his body from being beaten, no visible wounds except where the dead had been at his face, their groping fingers digging out his eyes and their teeth tearing away the soft meat of his cheeks. He had not been thrown there by the Romans. Doubtless he had taken refuge beneath the refuse, witnessed the women hurled into the pit over him, lain shaking with his eyes clenched shut, hoping the Romans would not notice him there. Devoured from within by his terror.

But though the Romans must have hurried away quickly, shunning the midden after tossing in those they'd used and killed, there were no places shunned by the dead. The dead knew neither fear nor shame nor disgust at any stench. Only hunger. Perhaps Asa had screamed when he heard the corpses hissing at him from above the midden pit, dark silhouettes against the stars. Screams that were utterly lost amid the death-cries of the town. Or perhaps he had lain silent and still while they fed on the dead or dying women, until one of the corpses found him, too.

Bar Nahemyah and the others had kept silent in their approach; until the call of the shofar the dead hadn't looked up as they lifted red flesh and entrails to their gaping mouths. Watching them, Bar Nahemyah had stood cold, as though he had swallowed the winter wind and given it a place to lie still and icy inside his chest. When he had left the synagogue with the shofar, he had not taken time to wash away the dried blood on his hands and arms from the two Romans he had killed during the night, nor the filth that had spattered across his coat as he drove a hammer into the heads of the groaning corpses that sought to surge through him into the synagogue.

He was fifteen and only recently a man. He had watched skulls burst apart beneath his hammer, had seen the meat and bone inside the human body. Had seen the girl who had given herself to him in an hour of gasping and heat on the night of their betrothal torn apart before his eyes, screaming for a few brief moments as the dead ripped out the insides of her belly, hollowing her until she lay still. He had seen all that. Now Bar Nahemyah was cold, everything in him cold. The shaking that had taken him after the violence had subsided before the rising of the sun, leaving behind only this heatless fury. No messenger or messiah of God had arrived during the night to halt the slaughter, no Makkaba riding from the cities of the south with vengeful, armed priests on dark horses behind. No miracle, no deliverance. There had been only the hammer held in his hand.

He had cast away the hammer in disgust and wrath once there were only bodies before the synagogue door, and he had not stopped to retrieve it as he strode out to check for other dead. Only after he came down to the shore had he realized his hands were empty; he'd stooped then to take up the stone he held now.

As the notes of the shofar faded, he lifted that stone and gazed down at the dead in the midden. "Heard that, did you?" he called to them.

The dead hissed and lurched to their feet, their jaws opening to reveal bloodied teeth.

"Don't get too close," Bar Nahemyah said to the others.

Then he hurled the stone.

For the briefest of moments it spun in the air like a ball in one of those games the pig-eating Greeks favored.

Then it smacked one of the corpses in the left shoulder. The corpse spun about and crumpled to its knee. The other two shambled past it. But even as Bar Nahemyah's companions threw their own rocks down at the dead, the first corpse looked over its shoulder at them and growled like a beast as it staggered to its feet.

Then the men were hurling stones down at the midden, to the cracking of bones and the growling of the dead. One of the corpses toppled and lay still, its head crushed in. The others lurched on up the shallow sides of the pit, reeking of death and offal and salt water. A stone crushed one's thigh—a corpse that, in life, must have been a girl nearly old enough to bear a child, her hair long and lank about her gray shoulders, one of her breasts chewed half away. Still she dragged herself across the shore with her hands, hissing and snarling.

Their bodies broke beneath the rocks, yet they kept coming.

And coming.

"Fall back," Bar Nahemyah snapped. "More stones."

The young men retreated at a stumbling run toward the grasses at the tideline, and along the way they lifted from the sand and shingle what they could: rocks smoothed and tossed landward by the sea, gnarled driftwood, shells of sea creatures blind and deep and strange as the world's beginning, anything that could be thrown at the dead to do damage.

Another corpse fell, a large-bellied man, most of whose face had been eaten away before he rose. The sharp edge of a broken shell lodged between his eyes like Dawid's slingstone, and he toppled backward and did not get up.

The last corpse still growled and lunged toward the living with uneven steps. It was the girl; she had risen up on one foot and was coming after them at a crouch, dragging her bad leg behind her. It was nearly on them now, and Bar Nahemyah's companions fell back into the grasses. Bar Nahemyah himself stood his ground.

"Be still, you unclean *tameh*," he cried, wrenching a long branch of driftwood free of the sand. Lifting it like a club, he waited for the corpse to stumble nearer. Its eyes were fixed on him, those gray, scratched eyes. Its jaw worked, opening and closing.

With a shout, Bar Nahemyah swung the branch, slamming it hard into the side of the corpse's head, knocking it to the sand. He leapt over the fallen girl, spearing the end of the branch toward its head even as it hissed and tried to get up. The side of its head gave, yet it spat, and the thing's hand clutched the end of Bar Nahemyah's coat. Then he was slamming the branch down against its head, again and again.

Until it was still.

Bar Nahemyah stood over the body, panting. The other young men drew back in mute horror at both the dead and the man who had fought. The corpse's fingers were still curled about the hem of Bar Nahemyah's coat. Bar Nahemyah roared, shouting all of his rage and impotent grief at the thing's dead face, and lifting one foot he drove the heel of his sandal against the clutching hand and broke its grip.

The hand fell back limp against the grit of the shore.

Bar Nahemyah gazed down at it for a long moment, breathing heavily. Then glanced up at the other pale-faced youths. At the midden and the stinking dead lying on the offal. Heard the sigh of the waves and behind him, at the tideline, the rush of the wind in the grasses like the sound of God weeping. He cast the branch aside into the sand. Though his lips moved, no words came. He swayed on his feet. Then he tilted to the left and vomited.

STANDING AT THE SHORE

BEFORE SUNUP, Shimon had walked to his father's house in Beth Tsaida, that long line of fishers' homes just above the tideline. He found the house empty and in disarray, its atrium open to the sky and silent but for a few of his mother's chickens, the small, enclosed rooms around the outer wall dark. No one was there. The ewer his mother used for water had been shattered, and there were streaks of blood across the atrium's dirt floor. For several long moments, Shimon stood staring at those dark stains, hardly breathing. All he could think of was the blood on his father's hand. Was this more of his blood, or had others entered the house and struggled during the long night's fight with the hungry dead?

But his father clearly was not here, whether this was his blood or not. And that meant this day was up to him.

Hastily, Shimon scooped up an armful of blankets and ran with them back up the hill to the tomb. He ignored the weeping he heard in the town and ignored the fear in his breast, knowing that if he stopped moving, that would be it. He would be too exhausted and too panicked to get up again.

When he reached the tomb, he wrapped Rahel and the maimed baby in blankets. He put his mother's arm about his shoulders and, supporting her weight, he helped her slowly down the hill. Rahel looked about with bloodshot eyes, her face paling with horror as she smelled the smoke and witnessed the ruin of their town, the crumbled houses, the bodies in the streets.

A few survivors were already moving, shrouding the corpses or simply walking in listless circles, their faces bloodied or tearstreaked. No one called out to Rahel and her sons; no one challenged them, not one.

* * *

His heart beating fast, Shimon lay his mother down on her bedding in the small winter room she'd shared with his father, and handed her the baby, that small, crippled baby, that shattered hope. He covered them both with blankets. Rahel was shaking, but her son didn't know if it was with cold or fear or grief or shock. He rubbed his hands together a moment, trying to think. Swallowed against his own fear. This was too big for him. They needed his father. Where was his father?

"Shimon," Rahel whispered. "There." She lifted a trembling hand, pointed.

He looked. It was his father's white *tallit*, the four-cornered prayer shawl he wore to the synagogue, still folded over its peg in the wall, miraculously undisturbed by whatever chaos had struck their small house.

"Bring that here, please."

When Shimon pressed the tallit into her hand, Rahel took the folded shawl and brought it to her lips, kissing the rough fabric. Glancing toward the roof, she whispered fiercely, "Adonai, find him, bring him home to us. Please. Let him be breathing. We need him. The boys and I. We need him. Bring him home."

Her voice wavered. She kissed the *tallit* again, her eyes shining. She sang softly:

> *Though the fig tree does not flower,*
> *And no grapes are on the vines . . .*

She closed her eyes, fell silent. After a moment, she ended her prayer as prayers were always ended in Kfar Nahum: "Bless us and keep us, O God. Until the *navi* comes."

* * *

At those words, Shimon straightened. He recalled the rough way his father had shoved him to the door, uncaring of his own safety. If God were watching, he would not bless him or his town for shaking in the dark. He heard the soft sounds of his crippled brother mouthing, reaching for a breast.

He went to the bin in the atrium beneath his mother's olive tree, took up a clay bowl from the stack beside it, and scooped some of the last of their grain from its bin. He brought the bowl back to his mother and saw the relief in her eyes. He realized from the way her hands shook as she accepted it how fatigued and hungry she actually was. He glanced about, made sure the waterskin was within her reach. Then he met her gaze.

"You are safe," he said. "I'll go find father."

Rahel nodded, her eyes closing. "The boats, my son. The boats. He would have gone to the boats. Gone out on the water, to get to some other shore where there were no dead. So he could circle into the hills and come back to us. See if his boat is here."

Shimon took his mother's hand quickly and kissed it, his eyes filling with tears that he blinked back. Then he turned and hurried to the door and flung it open, nearly ran across the packed dirt of the narrow street outside before stopping himself and turning to shut the door, putting his weight against it. Again he saw the blood on his father's hand. Breathing raggedly, he leaned a moment against the door, gathering his courage. Then he hurried through the battered houses and out to the wild grass. He saw the sea, open and vast with its horizon of far hills, and he ran for the line of boats, the long row of wide-beamed fishers moored above the tideline.

It took him only a moment to be sure. Some of the boats were missing. His father's boat, others. The tide had come and was now receding, and had washed away whatever track Yonah's boat had left in the sand when his father dragged it out to the water, a task that normally took two men. It was not a small boat, and his father never brought in small catches.

Swallowing, Shimon straightened and looked out over the waves. A few cranes glided low over the water, but he could see no dark shape of a boat out there, nothing but the blindness of the sun's fire on the sea.

A fear took him then, and he walked out onto the sand and planted his feet there among the shells and lake-weed the tide had left behind like memories the sea refused to carry. For no reason he could have given, Shimon was certain in his heart that if he went back to his mother now, he would never see his father again. That he must wait here, faithfully. Watching the sea. Awaiting the rock and pitch of the boat's return on the waves. His mother had water and grain. He had found her and brought her and his brother safely home; he'd done his father's command. Now his duty was here, at the edge of the sea.

* * *

Once, while he waited, he heard the call of a shofar and lifted his face. The call was very beautiful, and it carried over the water, and the hills across the Sea of Galilee gave it back. Shimon looked to the sea with fresh hope. Perhaps his father would hear the call and row toward it or run toward it along the shore if he was already on the land and not on the water. But there was still nothing on the sea, neither boat nor bird.

* * *

When Bar Nahemyah and other young men, ten or twelve, began bringing bodies down to the shore and laying them out in a long line on the sand, Shimon watched without speaking. The sight of the corpses was horrible, yet he neither flinched nor looked away; he felt detached, as though this were happening on some other shore and not here. He could see the rise and fall of their chests; these bodies still breathed. Their faces were flushed with fever, and they bore terrible wounds on their faces or their arms. Bites. Some had been torn open, and those were pale as though emptied out. Shimon bar Yonah knew some of them. There were old men and young, old women and young women, nearly a hundred. And among them, a few mercenaries, some dark-skinned, some olive, some white. Hired swords from every part of the Roman world, broken away from their brothers and then reassembled into a unit that could be put to the use of Empire, fighting for coin and glory rather than any bonds of blood or kin or covenant. Shimon did not understand how such a thing could be.

"*Shalom*, Bar Yonah. Will you aid me?" Bar Nahemyah called to him. He had the eyes of a man who did not remember sleep or rest, and so would not seek either. Gore had spattered his storm-coat.

"I have to wait for father," Shimon said, his voice distant. "He'll need me."

"All Kfar Nahum needs you, every man who still breathes." Bar Nahemyah's voice was low and intense. He swept out his arm, indicating the line of unconscious bodies. "By noon all of these will be dead, and some will have risen, and they will hunger. They will want to *eat* our People, what is left of our People, our kin. Look at them. Romans and heathen, and our own brothers, our own sisters gone from us. *Every one* of these will kill. But that is *not* going to happen. Let us have justice. I will see that these unclean monsters suffer for all time, for what they have done this night. For Ahava my beloved. For our fathers and our children dead."

But Shimon had turned his head back to the sea, whose waves were louder in his ears than Bar Nahemyah's impassioned words.

When he said nothing, the other man's eyes flashed hot with anger. "Your father understood justice," he cried. "He would have helped me."

Shimon felt no guilt. His whole heart was pulled by the emptiness of the sea, and he felt tugged beneath waves of dark terror. He gazed out desperately for some sight of his father's boat that he could cling to.

Bar Nahemyah's face hardened. He turned away.

There was the sound of Bar Nahemyah exhorting the other youths, a drone in Shimon's ears. Then cries as other young men came down to the shore. Yakob the priest's son was with them, and he exchanged harsh words with Bar Nahemyah. Heated voices. A fight broke out, men beating each other, some to protect their ill, others to seek vengeance for the eaten. For a few beats of the heart, men fought on the sand over the bodies of the dying. Still Shimon ignored them.

In the end, a few ran back to the town, led by the priest's son. The others turned the bodies onto their bellies and bound their ankles. They took cloths and filled these with stones from the shore, then knotted up the cloths and bound those to the ankles of the bitten. One after another they lifted the feverish bodies, one youth at the head and one at the feet, and carried them into the boats, piling them atop each other like fish. And when there were no more, the boats slipped from the shore, each with two youths at the oars, their eyes hot. Shimon felt a dull horror as he watched the boats grow smaller on the waves.

Those in the boats were not dead. They lived. They breathed . . . though none of them were awake or aware, and none would survive the morning.

553

Dimly, Shimon understood that Bar Nahemyah meant to toss them into the sea, that there would be no tombs on the hill for these. Yet the horror of it was something outside of him, like water beating against a rock; the horror *inside* of him, the memory of the blood on his father's hand, the frantic look in his father's eyes—that was far more personal and overwhelming.

Behind him, the priest's son came running back with Zebadyah his father panting behind him. Perhaps the priest had been searching again among the tents and ruins for survivors; it had taken Yakob a while to find him.

And now it was too late.

When Zebadyah reached the shore, he broke to his knees in the sand, his eyes wild. He screamed at the retreating boats: "No! Come back! Bar Nahemyah, come back! The dead must be buried! They must be buried! The Law! Come back!"

But no answer was called back over the water, and none of the boats turned its bow.

* * *

Shimon felt someone beside him, and though he didn't turn, he knew by the sound of the youth's breathing that Yakob was there.

"Amma is in the house," Shimon said. He kept his eyes on the water.

"Yohanna and I will bring her water," Yakob promised. He stood by Shimon a moment, seeming to understand why his friend was here, and whether because he could not think of something to say or because he knew that there wasn't anything to say, he spoke no word but only gripped Shimon's shoulder. Then he turned and went to help his father up from the sand. The strength seemed gone from Zebadyah's limbs; his face glistened with tears.

Numb inside, Shimon gazed always past the boats out across the empty sea, looking for one boat, one boat that had set out in the dark and not returned.

Somewhere out in the middle of the water, as the sun rose hot over the sea, the youths set aside their oars and stood, their legs spread wide for balance as the boats rocked. They lifted the bodies over the gunwales and slid them, one after the other, into the cool womb of the sea. The wrath Shimon had seen in the youths' eyes as they set out made the reason for their act clear. The young men knew the bodies would rise, and the memory of the dead devouring their village during the night was bitter in their minds and hot in their hearts. They needed someone to suffer for what had been done, for the kin who had been eaten, for the kin who were dying now. They needed to take an eye for an eye, a tooth for a tooth. They could not make the Romans suffer; the Romans were gone, eaten or fled. They could not make the dead who'd attacked suffer, for they had been destroyed during the night and the dawn that followed, by Roman swords or Hebrew fishing spears or by Bar Nahemyah's hammer and stone. But these bodies that lay now in their boats would become eaters, too. Unless speared through the brow or burned with fire, they would walk and moan for years, feeding on the People.

Or—dropped into the sea, their ankles bound, these new dead would writhe in the water, without food, without breath, their moans heard only by the fish. They could be made to suffer. The youths hoped this fiercely, and like the heathen tribes from whom their fathers had wrested the land many centuries before, they gave their dead to the sea. Not in reverence but in fury and a longing to forget. A punishment meted out, justice done, and the pain of that night would lie beneath the waves, never to be spoken of.

Afterward, as they beached the boats and walked back to the town, each of the young men spoke quietly to himself.

My father died in a storm at sea, one man whispered.

My brother perished in his boat, another said.

My wife was drowned.

My sisters were taken by the waves.

My friend, my beautiful friend, perished in a fishing accident.

It was easier that way.

All those whispers of fear and forgetting. Even a century later, travelers along that shore would claim that they could hear those whispers on the wind among the tombs.

* * *

But on the shore, Shimon still stood on the sand. He stood there throughout the day, unmoving, thinking neither of food nor rest. Just watching the sea. When the tide came up to his feet, he looked at the water's edge lapping his sandals and realized his throat was scorched with thirst. Crouching, he cupped his hands in the water and lifted some to his mouth, but he kept his eyes on the sea, like Gideon's men drinking while watching the far ridge for the coming of the dead in the old story.

Afterward he walked above the tideline where the boats were moored. After the violence of the previous night, many of these boats no longer had owners, and their nets lay in them unused and unnoticed like dry leaves. Shimon stood among the derelicts and watched the sun set on the water, a fire as though God had seen that the land was defiled and had decided to burn it away and start anew.

Then the sun was gone and it was dark and there were stars, and no moon rose. Yet, by starlight, Shimon could see one boat coming back, a dark, low shape on the water. No splash of the oars. Just drifting in on the tide. Yet Shimon knew whose boat it was. The youths' boats had all returned in the late morning after giving their cargo to the sea, and no fishers had set out with their nets this night. As the boat neared, Shimon could see that a single figure sat on the bench, its hands in its lap. A dark silhouette.

"Abba!" he called softly. "Father!"

The figure rose unsteadily to its feet, making the boat rock on the tide. Shimon heard its low moan of longing and hunger, loud over the water.

After a moment he covered his ears, his cheeks moist with tears or mist from the sea, but he could still hear it, he could still see that boat sliding in.

PART 3

AN EVENING VISITOR

RAHEL'S HUSBAND had been dead four nights when there came a knock at her door.

A knock at the door, a strong fist, but the knocking was too urgent, as though the man demanding entrance was uneasy, uncertain of himself. Rahel lifted her face from where she knelt in the atrium with her husband's *tallit* across her knees and the baby sleeping in his basket beside her, and for a moment she considered not answering.

Again the knocking, insistent.

She pressed the heels of her hands to her eyes, breathed deeply a moment, then folded the prayer shawl carefully and rose to her feet, the *tallit* still in her hand. She moved toward the door.

There were too few of them left to ignore each other.

That, and she couldn't quite escape the candle-flicker of hope in her heart. She had seen her husband's corpse, had confronted him on the sands. It couldn't be him at the door.

And yet.

She found that she was running. She leapt from the atrium into the antechamber at the old door, and quickly tugged at the bolt. Unlatching the door and letting it creak open, she found herself confronting the priest. Zebadyah's face was strained and pale—he hadn't slept in several nights, perhaps—but his eyes were hard with purpose.

"*Shalom*," he said.

"*Shalom*," Rahel whispered.

They stared at each other, one of those silences that are both uncomfortable to keep and uncomfortable to break. *Shalom* had always been their traditional greeting in Kfar Nahum, a wish for peace and a plea for peace. Not a Roman peace, not *pax* or order, the absence of conflict. No, Hebrew peace, wholeness, a community living and thriving together.

How empty that wish now seemed.

"Do you want to come in, Bar Yesse?" Rahel said at last. A week ago it would have been unthinkable to her to open her door to a man who was not her husband when no one else was home. But the pain in Zebadyah's eyes called to her, and he was at least a survival of her husband, in some small part. And the days were brutal on her heart, alone in her house with her children. The house was strange to her now, for it had too many empty and silent spaces.

Zebadyah's face became stern. "I have come to offer you my home."

"I don't understand."

"You were my brother's wife."

Her eyes burned and she blinked quickly. It would be unbearable, weeping when her door was open and her face visible to the street.

"Now you are alone and you have a son—"

"I have two sons." Rahel's throat tightened. Such had been her grief that she'd had little time to fear, either for herself or Koach. Now all the fears came rushing in.

"You were my brother's wife, now his widow. You have a son who is too young for the boats. When a man dies and his sons are not old enough to feed his house, the Law tells us his brother's duty is to take his wife and provide for her, and to take her gladly to his bed to give her more sons in his brother's name, so that his brother's line might not die out from our land. All my life I have kept the Law. I will not fail to keep it now." His voice turned gentle. "I had not planned to seek a second wife, but if I had, I could not have hoped to find one lovelier. My brother chose well."

"No," Rahel whispered. "This can't be."

Zebadyah's face darkened. "Don't make this harder than it is, woman. I grieve for him, too. But the winter is on us, and there isn't much time."

Rahel shook her head and began to swing the door shut, but Zebadyah blocked it with his hand and leaned into it, holding it open against her. She took a step back, but he followed, and then his hands were gripping her arms just below the shoulders, firmly. An echo of her husband's strength. She gazed up at his face with wide eyes. She felt small and caught—by him, by the Law, by her bereavement. As though it were not his hands that held her but God's, pitiless and demanding. God's hands that demanded that she live a certain way, fulfill commitments that were made before her grandmothers' grandmothers were born, and always without any sure promise from God beneath her feet, only shifting sand, pulled out from under her by the vanishing tide.

"I will treat you and Shimon well, and Cheleph's son also," he said quietly. "I loved Yonah. I will not let his widow starve alone in this house."

"What about the baby?" She just managed to get the words out.

Pain in his eyes. "You know what has to be done."

"No."

"We will talk about it later. Come to my house. There are witnesses there already. You will eat well tonight, and you will have a warm bed."

"Your bed," she choked.

He gave a small nod.

"And my son? Will you have someone just take him out to the midden, leave him there? To die?" Her voice rose, shrill.

He was quiet a moment and she tried to twist away, but he held her fast.

"We tried to follow only those parts of the Law that were easy. And look what happened. You have duties, Rahel, even as I do."

"Don't call me that." Her heart beat a panic drum against her breast.

"I am trying to help, woman! You are my responsibility—I am trying to help." He pulled her to him quickly and kissed her. She stiffened as his mouth covered hers. Warm and moist and so different from Yonah's. The kiss was rough yet there was something tentative in it, as though he were a man never completely sure of himself. For a heartbeat or two she permitted it, still in shock. Then her stomach turned and she shoved her hands against his chest, turning her head away. "No," she gasped.

"Rahel," Zebadyah said quietly.

"I was his, and I will die his," she said.

"*Rahel.*"

"You will call me Bat Eleazar. You have no right to my name." She tried to pull away but he held her. Her eyes went dark with fury. She was shaking, though she didn't know it. "I will wall my door against you and starve first." Her voice rose in pitch. The panic was not so much that he would touch her, but that he would take from her the memories of Yonah and of her life here, in this house. The thought of sleeping beneath his roof was almost worse than the thought of sleeping in his arms. She drew back into the shadow beneath the arch leading to the atrium. From his basket by the olive press, her infant began to cry.

"Please go," Rahel said.

Zebadyah glanced in the direction of the cries, and seeing the hard purpose in his face, Rahel went white. "This is your brother's son," she pleaded, her voice low and intense.

Zebadyah turned his face back to her. The gentleness was gone from him and his eyes had become hard as small stones. "Ezra cast even the wives, the heathen wives, over the wall," he said quietly. "What is unclean, what isn't whole—we must cast that out of our homes, out of our hearts."

Zebadyah thrust her to the side firmly and made to step by her, but she caught at his arm and threw her small body back between him and the atrium and her son.

His face darkened. "Step aside, woman," he growled.

"Get out!" she cried. "Get away from my son!"

He struck her.

Her vision white, she felt the wall against her back. Her head rang. She dug her fingers against the wall, desperate to stay upright. Panic in her heart like cattle breaking through long grass, trampling it, crushing everything in their way. Yonah had never, *never* struck her.

Her vision cleared.

Zebadyah stood silent, hesitating, as if startled by his own violence.

The baby's cries broke her panic. She screamed and leapt at him, but the priest caught her wrists and held her as she kicked at him, still with that look of dawning horror on his face.

"What is going on?"

A young man's shout.

The priest had left the outer door open. Shimon stood there, his face full of thunder—looking suddenly very like his father. Yakob, the priest's son, stood beside him on the doorstep, his face shocked.

"Shimon!" Rahel cried, almost faint with relief.

Zebadyah released her quickly, as though his hands burned. He looked at his son and nephew, and his face darkened slowly with shame. "Bar Yonah," he said, his voice a little hoarse, "I need to make sure your family is provided for."

Shimon's eyes were cold. They took everything in: the screaming baby in the atrium, the bruise developing over Rahel's cheekbone, the priest's slightly hunched stance. "They will be," he said quietly. "Your son and I have reached an agreement. I am taking my father's boat out tonight, to fish where he cannot. Yakob will help me, for a while." He glanced at Rahel. "I'll be able to feed us, mother. I am sure of it."

For a moment, no one moved. Rahel drew in a sobbing breath, looked at her son carefully, and at Yakob. She saw in their eyes that Shimon had known she would not accept the protection of Yakob's father. Shimon had *known* this. He had done this—taken on this responsibility—for her, and to honor his father. Knowing what it meant. Shimon's *bar 'onshin* had come and gone; in announcing his intent to feed the house of his father, he claimed that house and all within it. What was to be done with his brother, what was to be done with his father's widow—this was all up to him now, and to no other. Rahel's breast warmed with pride and gratitude. Shimon was his father's son. He was *her* son.

Rahel straightened, smoothed down her garments, grateful none of them were torn. She wanted to touch her face where it hurt and burned, but she did not. Her hands were shaking, and she clutched her skirt until they were still. She stood with dignity, and though her voice quivered, it was not weak. She faced the priest. "God will provide for my sons and for me, Bar Yesse."

He glanced back at her, his eyes full of so many things that he must have wanted to say and couldn't. Then he looked at her son, and Shimon met the priest's gaze with quiet resolve. It was as though a weathered old tree were facing a tall rock.

The priest looked away first. "It is your house, Bar Yonah," Zebadyah said quietly. His shoulders tensed. Then he stepped past him to the door, Yakob moving aside to let him past.

Rahel's heartbeat did not slow until the sound of the priest's footsteps, and then his son's after him, had faded in the street. Not until she held the baby in her arms, holding in tears that she would not shed where her son could see. Not until she felt the cool cloth against her cheek and Shimon's words soft by her ear, promising that he would care for her and for his crippled brother both, whatever might come. That she would never be hungry. That she would never need to go to the priest if she didn't wish it. That she was his mother and he loved her. And then she did cry, and it was a long time before she was done.

FIRE ON THE WATER

THE STONE STEPS leading to her roof were cold under her bare feet, but for once Rahel didn't mind that; the shock of sensation each time she set her foot carefully down—so carefully, because she was sore, and carrying her child in her arms—reminded her she was alive.

It was after dark now; the first panic of Zebadyah's visit had dulled, to be replaced with a throng of small, sharp fears, each of them nipping at her like wolves harrying deer. She felt that each step might send her body crashing to her knees in fatigue, yet her mind was fiercely wakeful. In any case, she couldn't bear finding a place to sleep in her open atrium or in the small winter rooms around the inner walls of her house. The house was too empty; the family they had once shared it with had not survived the night of the dead. Shimon had succeeded in scrubbing most of the blood out of the walls, but Rahel thought she could still smell it. And Shimon had also boarded up the outward-looking windows of their house, which made it worse. She understood why he had done it; many had died that night because the dead had climbed through open windows. Other houses throughout the town were boarding up, too. But in seasons past, she had often leaned out of those windows and talked with the town's other women as they passed by. Now those other women were gone, no one left to sit *shiva* with her and mourn with her for her husband, and even her windows were gone. This no longer felt like her home.

Only the rooftop felt the same.

Reaching it, she stood still for a few moments, just breathing. The wind from the sea was chill against her face, but she didn't fear the *shedim*. Let them come. What more could they take from her?

She gazed out at that sea, where she could see the white chop of the waves and a few dark shapes rocking on them: the boats moving out to gather the night's fish. They looked so few, so few. Only a week before, the boats had set out like a flock of great birds, fast over the water. Now she could count only ten. In one of them, with Yakob and young Yohanna, was her older son, setting out in his father's boat, on the sea without him for the first time. Tears burned her eyes. She blinked them back and made her way to the little bed of cushions Yonah had made for her during the early months of her pregnancy, knowing how much she loved the open air and the sky and the scent of the sea.

Her infant stirred slightly as she settled with a groan and a sharp ache where she had torn in birthing him, but she held him close and drew the shawl in which she'd wrapped him up over his head until he fell asleep again. She held him to her, kissing the top of his head with the softest brush of her lips, again and again. She smelled baby, and she smelled her husband, for the shawl she'd swaddled him in was Yonah's *tallit*. It was wrong, perhaps terribly wrong, to swaddle a baby in a prayer shawl, but the cloth carried Yonah's scent and her heart knew the shawl would protect her son, as Yonah himself would if he were here.

Her heart beat a little faster. She tried to think of whether Yonah would have lifted this child into his hands and accepted him as his own son, if he'd lived. She felt certain he would have. Yes, she was certain of it. The man who had held her after that storm on the sea would never have turned away any life that came from her body.

She glanced out at the sea again, its wind in her hair, and could not remember ever having felt so alone. "What do I do?" she whispered, pressing her nose to the *tallit*. "What do I do?"

But her husband was not there to answer her. There was only her, making decisions to stand between her children and the hungry grave. Shimon would bring home fish, and perhaps . . . perhaps he would not grow to resent her for not going to the priest's bed, for risking her children in the winter.

It was not too late, she knew. She could run from the house, up the street, knock on the door of Zebadyah's house, endure the staring eyes of the few other surviving women from the windows and rooftops of their own homes. She could give herself to him, undress for him, and whisper after he lay in her, "Please, feed my sons." Many women of her People had done so before.

But her belly twisted at the thought, and her face throbbed where her husband's brother had struck her. She clutched her baby closer, shivering.

She didn't know if Shimon would be able to bring enough food for the three of them. She didn't know if Zebadyah would be harsh with her, if she went to him, if he would often strike her. But she knew he would never feed *both* her sons. He would not take her second son into his house.

As though hearing her thoughts, the infant stirred and began to cry. She lifted him to her breast. Seeing the way he kneaded her flesh with only one hand while the other hung lifeless at his side, Rahel closed her eyes, forbidding herself tears. A feeling of warm sleep stole over her as often happened when the baby fed. For a while her fear for him pierced through it.

* * *

Yet somewhere between one breath and the next, she slipped into the dream country. And it was water, all water, dark waves covering all the world and nowhere any shore. It closed over her, taking away sound and light. Then she flailed about and found herself facing Yonah, her husband's face stern yet his eyes turning gentle when he saw her, as they always had.

She had wedded Yonah when she was fourteen, had wanted to believe he would be a shelter and a strong place for her in this uneasy world. Once, when she was still young, he had rowed her out onto the water, uncaring that the sea was for fishermen, not their wives. That one night, he had gone without nets or spear, just rowing out with his wife until they were far from shore and no other boats could be seen dark on the water. The waves rolled them with a motion that was soothing and sure. There he made love to her, while the stars moved slowly across the sky. She remembered the sound of his breathing, his face above hers, his touch. Afterward, a storm had fallen on the sea. He bound her to the row bench, then cast his coat over her, while she watched the surge and growl of the sea and the heavy dark of the sky with wide eyes. She watched her husband fight the waves, and the sea tossed them and spun them. Water came over the gunwale and tried to slam her from the boat, but her husband's ropes held her fast.

Then the sea was quiet, as suddenly as though the storm had been a candle snuffed out. The clouds broke open, revealing the moon. Yonah cut his wife loose from the bench even as she sobbed and gasped in great gulps of air no longer laden with water. She shivered with cold as he clutched her to him, tearing away his soaked tunic and then tearing away hers, so that her body and his were pressed naked to each other, and she could feel the fire in him and his heart loud against hers, as when they had made love. His rough hands rubbed life into her arms and back. She shook and clung to him and sobbed, and heard him sobbing in her ear, too.

The moon had set while they made love, before the tempest; but now there was a moon in the sky. The storm had lasted all of a day and it was now the next night, the Sabbath night, and as they warmed each other, Yonah started to murmur the words of a song in her ear, words he might sing to greet the Sabbath Bride as she came over the water.

Though the fig tree does not flower,
And no grapes are on the vines . . .

* * *

Rahel woke with a start, her infant asleep at her breast. She heard shouting in the distance. Blinking quickly, she looked about and her first impression was that the sea was on fire. But as her eyes focused, she realized that men had built a great blaze on the shore among the wrack left by the outgoing tide. She could see their shapes dark against the glow of it, and hear their voices, most of them indistinct but one calling louder than the rest and carrying to her on the sea wind.

Zebadyah.

He was reciting passages from the Grief of Ezra. Catching the words, she shivered and clutched her infant tightly. She watched with wide eyes as the men on the sands tossed items into the flames, and she heard the roar and rush of the fire as it fed. She couldn't see what they were burning, but she could guess.

The remains of the Roman tents. Any clothing of Greek weave or any ornaments from other towns that the Romans had looted from their homes, or any they had left. Anything that was not Hebrew. Anything that was unclean, or broken, or suspect. Anything that might tempt God to look away from the town when the dead lurched near.

They were cleansing Kfar Nahum.

Perhaps it was only that she had just risen out of the waters of sleep. Perhaps it was only the stress and anguish of the past few days. Whatever the reason, Rahel had a vivid, brutal vision of Zebadyah lifting her infant up and casting his small, wailing body into the flames.

She shivered. Pressing her lips to the baby's head, she whispered, "It's all right. It's all right."

But she could not look away from those flames, or from the dark silhouette of the priest standing so near them, nor shut her ears against Zebadyah's harsh, grieving cries. And she did not sleep again that night.

ONE OF OUR TRIBE

SHIMON'S FIRST NIGHTS at sea exhausted him. After he and Zebadyah's sons pulled the boat up to the tideline, gutted their fish by the predawn light, and stumbled back into the town with their catch, it was all he could do to embrace Yakob at the door of his house and offer a tired grunt of thanks—though if he'd been able to summon more words, he would have called him *brother*. Then he'd enter with a weary nod toward his mother and her infant, tumble into his bedding in the olive's shade in the atrium, and snore until long after the noon heat. He had been out on the sea with his father a few times, but it had never been like this—*his* hand casting the nets, and no midnight nap while his father fished. You didn't nap when you were one of the men in the boat, when it was your hand that must keep the tiller or the oars if a storm came up.

On one of these first mornings, he stepped through the heavy cedar door of his father's house and heard his infant brother shrieking. Not a hunger cry but a pain cry, a thin, desperate wailing that tore through Shimon's body, making his blood run cold. There was a hoarse note in the cries, as though the boy had been wailing for a while.

His heart sped up. Where was his mother? Was she all right? Why hadn't she come at her infant's cry? He burst through into the atrium, not even pausing to toss away his coat or peel off his gloves that reeked of fish and were slippery with oil.

And he stopped, shocked.

Rahel knelt on a rug she had unrolled across the atrium's dirt floor, a rug that had belonged to one of Yonah's kin, now dead. She was holding her baby tightly to her, her own eyes squeezed shut; she must not have heard Shimon come in, not over the baby's screams. A stone knife lay discarded by her left knee, and in the early dawn light blood shone on the blade. Her hands were bloody, too.

Shimon took it all in at a glance, and realized it was his brother's eighth day. The stone knife—stone, not iron—was used for circumcision. He didn't know where Rahel had found the knife or from where she'd taken it.

"Where's Zebadyah bar Yesse?" he asked hoarsely.

Rahel gave a start, glanced up at him, her eyes red from weeping.

Not knowing what else to do, Shimon came and sat by her. The baby's cries were deafening.

"He thinks my child is unclean." Rahel's voice quivered. "Do you think I'd trust him with a knife?"

Shimon knelt by her. Without speaking, he took his infant brother and held him, that small, squalling, misshapen thing that had brought such anxiety into their house. Rahel put her face in her hands, shaking silently, staining her face with blood.

The baby kept wailing. Shimon swallowed. For days he had tried not to look at his brother. Now he couldn't look away. Uncomfortably, he held him, uncertain of what to do. The boy's wound had been cleaned and bandaged.

After a few moments, Rahel drew a shuddering breath and rose unsteadily to her feet. She left, then came back with a cloth and pushed one corner of it, which she'd dampened, into the baby's small mouth. One hand pressed to her left breast as though it pained her. For a few moments the baby still shrieked; then his mouth closed around the cloth and he sucked at it vigorously, making small, muffled whimpers.

"He is Koach. Koach bar Yonah," she said.

"Koach?"

"Koach." Her face was wet with tears. Tears for her child's pain, tears for her own. Tears reddened by the blood on her face.

On the eighth day of a boy's life, he is circumcised and gifted with a name and a blessing that tell him what he will be. This was always a rite performed by the priest, but today, by the morning's light in her own house, Rahel had laid the boy on this rug and taken up the knife and had done it herself.

She had named him Koach.

The word for "strong."

Silently, Shimon and Rahel knelt beside each other, gazing down at that small, anguished face. A bent child, but the only child Rahel would ever have again. The three of them were the only family they had left.

Gently, Rahel drew her fingertips along the curve of the boy's cheek. "You will grow strong," she promised him. "Strong." Her voice low and fierce with that tone that only mothers use, the tone that over the cruel years of history has made even emperors kneel before those who birthed them, has made even kings seek the embrace of their mothers' arms.

Fourteen Years Later—AD 25.

BARABBA

THE MAN WAS Barabba the Outlaw, the Roman-killer, and he rode one morning out of the hills and out of the wilderness and walked his horse through the streets of Kfar Nahum as though he owned the town. His beard was dark and there were small twigs in it as though, like a prophet of old, he had neither time nor attention to spare it. His face was brown with dust. From the right side of his saddle hung two heads with their hair cut in the Roman style, and to the left side he'd roped three more heads, these torn with strips of flesh missing as though they'd been savaged by beasts. Each with a puncture wound in its brow. Their faces those of the unclean dead, the dead that hunger.

Men and women drew back into their doors as Barabba passed, not wanting to be near the unburied heads. Barabba himself was a forbidding figure, a giant on a black horse larger than any they had ever seen. It was as though God had turned a bear into a man and sent him into their narrow streets. Every town in the land had heard of this man, even ruined towns. In the dead-haunted hills above the Tumbling Water, this man and others like him, men who knew the use of curved blades and of poisons, waited in caves or lurked by the high pass called the Red Way. They set themselves against the living and the dead alike. *Bar Abba*, their leader called himself, "son of a father," to hide his kin and his home from the Romans. None knew where he had come from, but they said he had not seen his brothers, his sisters, his mother in long years. They said he had never been seen to weep. Or laugh. That he had once ridden his horse into a

Roman centurion's house and killed the man with a blow of his steed's hoof, then swept his wife and daughter up into the saddle—and that they had later been sold from the block in Yoppa, to be slaves in far provinces across the sea. They said that he had once left a Greek idolater flayed alive and hanging from the gates of Beth Anya as a warning to any who might defile the holy places of their People. That he had abducted a levite who had informed the Romans about his movements, and had taken the man up to a cave in the hills and forced him to eat a poisoned loaf.

In the cities of stone several days to the south, some hoped in him. Some feared him. But in Kfar Nahum's crumbling houses, he had been only a story. Until this day.

* * *

Barabba didn't speak until he had reached the open space before Kfar Nahum's synagogue, a massive basalt edifice. The synagogue was the only building in this town that was still well-kept; the others had fallen into a dilapidation and a weariness that conveyed the town's poverty as starkly as the gaunt faces and thin, brittle-looking arms of its inhabitants. But if Kfar Nahum's poverty affected Barabba, he revealed no sign of it. He looked at the faces of those who had gathered, but without pity.

Before the polished steps of the synagogue—polished only because aging Zebadyah made the washing of them his religious duty each day, a duty performed with his own hands and his own cloth and water he had carried up from the sea himself, for the only slave he had owned had died on that night he refused to remember—before those clean, white steps, Barabba sat his saddle and glowered at the crowd that was gathering, men and women who had slipped from their doors to follow his horse—at a safe distance—through the streets. In fact, by the time the hoofbeats fell still, most of the people who still lived and breathed in Kfar Nahum stood in that public space or filled the alleys that emptied into it. Their faces were pale; they couldn't look away from the corpse-heads that hung from the stranger's saddle, moving a little as the horse breathed.

Koach stood there with Rahel, apart from the others, occasionally lifting his one good hand to scratch at his cheek, at the first fuzz of beard on his young face. Shimon stood near, blinking in the sun, called from his rest after a night at sea by the hoofbeats and the shouts in the town. Yet Shimon stood with his back to his younger brother. Koach used to try to draw his attention, to help him clumsily with small tasks. Now he knew better.

Small and weighing less than a milk-goat, Koach was unobtrusive at his mother's side, yet he felt how the others standing in this open space looked away from him or past him, as though despite his size he were so obvious and so visible that it took great labor *not* to see him.

All but a few, like Bar Cheleph, who watched him in open hostility, his eyes hot with the capacity for violence; once, Koach had been set upon and beaten in the street. Vividly he recalled Bar Cheleph forcing his hand open, tearing a small carving from his fingers and tossing it into the grass. Vividly he recalled the blows falling on his back. To many of the ragged survivors in Kfar Nahum, Koach was an unwelcome reminder of the night of tombs, and all their grief. Of sorrows they'd rather bury and forget. *Hebel*, the men called him, "useless." Rahel had sewn his right sleeve longer than the left to help him conceal his deformed right hand, and she had padded the sleeve with wool to hide the thinness of his withered right arm, yet it made no difference.

He cast a resentful glance at that synagogue door, with its old Hebrew letters carved into the lintel and the doorposts—words of the Law. He was barred from entering; he should have stood before the men of Kfar Nahum and recited from the Torah, a year since. But the priest would not allow him his *bar 'onshin*.

Koach stared up at the stranger with sudden heat in his eyes. Barabba was so different from him—a strong man on a giant horse, with muscled arms and a scarred, cold face. No one would ever deny *him* anything; he would never be helpless or useless.

Barabba turned his horse slowly and made a disgusted sound in his throat. "I came here looking for men!" His voice was low but strangely clipped. His was not a Galilean accent, but it had none of the softness of the Greek in it either. "I came looking for men, but all your faces are pale and your mouths gape like fish. Tell me this is Kfar Nahum, the town of Yonah bar Yesse."

"This *is* the town of Yonah bar Yesse," a tired voice said from the door of the synagogue.

Zebadyah stood there, his *tallit* over his head, having just come from his prayers within. He stepped out and stood in the whiteness of the sun and the whiteness of the synagogue steps, the whiteness of a world long since drained of color.

"Good! This is what I've come to say." Barabba leaned a little from his saddle, addressing the priest, though all the others could see his face and hear his voice, which carried. "If there are true men of Yehuda tribe in this town, they are needed. Each year there are more dead in the hills, and they are in the cities now, too. And what's more—" His voice rose hot with hate. "There are Romans! Always more of those, too. They mock our ways, they starve us, they spit in the face of our God. Beth Anya would not pay their pig-tax, so the Romans broke the doors of their synagogue and burned their Torah. In our Yerushalayim they've hung Roman eagles of gold and silver on the walls of the Temple. Graven *images*, in the places where we *worship*! While you in the north sleep, Rome has come into our house like a thief, to take our bread and defile our women and hang their foul gods on our walls."

Koach heard the stirring of the men and women of Kfar Nahum, indrawn breaths and muttered curses. A few hands flickered in the sign against the evil eye. The corpse-heads at Barabba's saddle stared sightlessly.

"For two generations the Romans have done so with us," Zebadyah said quietly. "Why ride all the way here to tell us what we already know?"

"Because it is getting worse." Barabba stroked his horse's neck, then dropped his hand to his side. "I know your kind in the south, priest. Pharisees. Appeasers. Most of our People cower and shrink back from Romans who pass in the street, but you—the Romans own you already."

With a quick move of his wrist, he unhooked one of the heads—one of the unclean heads—from the right of his saddle and hurled it into the center of the square. It rolled a moment, then stopped with its dead eyes gazing up, as if to accuse God in his sky of crimes of violence that its lips had never been able to reveal in words—only in a long moan of anguish silenced by Barabba's knife.

Everyone drew back.

Koach swallowed against the tightness of his throat. The dead. The dead that were in the water, the dead that were in the past, the dead no one talked about.

But this severed head was here, and terribly close, and could not be ignored.

"Look at it." Barabba's voice was a whip crack in the dawn air. "*Look at it! Can you appease that?* When our People returned out of exile—the only one of the twelve tribes to come back, the only one true to our Covenant—we found our land crawling with these. Teeming like ants. Because the heathen have never cared for our land as we do. Have never cared for the dead as we do. But we took back our land, built walls against the dead, lit the sacred fire in a new Temple. We carried out the Law until no moan could be heard in our land. We did that, because we are a People whose faith cannot be bent and whose teeth cannot be drawn. We are a People of lions." He turned in his saddle, his gaze sweeping the crowd. "Well, that is how we have always been. Exile in Susa did not tame us. The Greeks did not beat us. And now, now, will you let the *Romans* take your teeth? The Romans are good at stilling the dead—that's what I hear the children of Israel say, wherever I ride. There have never been men with swords like those the Romans breed or hire. They may walk on us and ravish us and starve us, but they keep our land safe. That is what I hear. But our Roman masters, they take our teeth, our claws. Until we are sheep. And then what? What then? What happens one day when the Romans tire of us, or are busy defending some other shore? Will we sit about like a flock of sheep, waiting to be eaten by the dead?"

"God will send us a *navi* to deliver us," one of the younger men called out. "A messiah!" After a moment, Koach realized that was Bar Cheleph's voice.

"*Navi?*" Barabba turned his horse about and walked it toward Bar Cheleph, staring him down. "We make our own *navi*, our own messiah. God waits too long; let God affirm whom we anoint, or speak from heaven with his own voice if he dissents. Follow me, men of Kfar Nahum. We will make this land Hebrew again."

"What can you do?" That was Shimon bar Nahemyah's voice. He stepped forward to face Barabba. "The Romans are strong. What can you do, Barabba?"

"A strong man can still die with a knife in his back. Even a Roman." He leaned nearer. "There are many of us—in the south. Not so many in the north. But there, about the Mount of Olives, we harry the Romans wherever we find them. Another year, boy, and we will make the Romans *beg* to leave Israel."

They held each other's gazes, each measuring the other.

"What is your name?"

"Shimon bar Nahemyah."

"Ride with me, Bar Nahemyah. I see the shofar about your throat. It's time for the ram's horn to be heard in our cities again. I tire of the braying of Roman trumpets and the din of Roman drums."

Bar Nahemyah watched him a moment; the others watched him. Shimon frowned. Bar Nahemyah's yearning was naked in his face. In a moment, perhaps his old rage would return, that rage with which he had once faced the dead at the synagogue door. He still wore that night's shofar about his throat, having refused to relinquish it to the priest after the battle with the dead fourteen years before.

"You were hiding," he had accused Zebadyah in the days that followed, when they met at the door of the synagogue.

The priest had looked stricken. "It is not my sin that I am here to discuss," he said hoarsely, "but yours. The dead unburied, the dead you threw in the sea."

"The Romans came, and you hid. The dead came, and you hid. You weren't there at the synagogue. You didn't blow the shofar when it was needed," Bar Nahemyah had told the priest coldly. "*I* will carry the safety of this town, and do what needs to be done."

And he had left the synagogue steps that day and had never again stepped within it, not even for the Sabbath. Bar Nahemyah had no surviving kin, no wife, no children. It was said that Bar Nahemyah lived and ate alone in the atrium of his father's empty house, with only his bitterness and anger for company. And in Kfar Nahum, only he and Koach did not go to meet God with the other men.

The thought that he might leave the town struck Koach with sudden fear. Unlike his own brother Shimon, Shimon bar Nahemyah had never been ashamed to speak with him, had never looked away from him.

Bar Nahemyah never looked away from anyone.

It was he who had driven away Bar Cheleph and the other young men who had knocked Koach to the ground, that one hot morning. Often Bar Nahemyah would pace the unkept streets of Kfar Nahum, his eyes fierce, the lines of his body taut like a ship running before the storm. Years ago, some had left Kfar Nahum, fleeing to other towns along the shore, but any who encountered Bar Nahemyah as they slipped from their houses stopped, looked down, and quietly went back within their doors and unpacked. There was a fury in Bar Nahemyah's face that none could ignore. While he, *he*, remained in Kfar Nahum, who else would dare abandon it?

* * *

"I want to," Bar Nahemyah said at last. "I want to come with you. My heart demands it. But my head hears the screaming of our People in your smooth words."

"Maybe it is the Romans you hear screaming." Barabba's face darkened with anger, but his voice was steady.

"Maybe."

"Go with him!" Bar Cheleph cried out. His face bore that same fear that

Koach felt. As he always did, Bar Cheleph was lashing out before he could be hurt. "And others with you! We'll have fewer fish. And fewer mouths."

"Be quiet, son," Zebadyah said.

Bar Nahemyah was staring coldly at the corpse's head, where it lay defiling the earth near the priest's feet. "I trust my own hands and anything I hold in them," he said. "I do not trust you, Barabba. I've fought my fight. I am done."

"Go, stranger." Shimon bar Yonah lifted his head and faced the horseman, his voice bitter, his shoulders hunched as with remembered pain. "We are men who grieve, and this is all that is left of our home. We will not leave it for you or anyone else."

"Pray the Romans don't take it from you," Barabba snapped.

"We have little left for them," Shimon said. "If they want it, let them try. But you, leave us be, as you've been asked."

Koach stared at Shimon in wonder, never having heard his taciturn brother speak so many words at once.

Barabba wheeled his horse about in a cold fury. "Why are the rest of you silent?" he cried. "Rise up! I call you, rise up! What is wrong with you? Maybe you are all half Roman or Roman-lovers." Suddenly he caught sight of Koach, where he'd shrunk back against his mother's side. "There! That boy! What is wrong with his arm? Why haven't you cast him out? What kind of Hebrews are you?" His voice rose in a shout. "He is probably a Roman's child! A rape child!—"

"He is *not*!" Rahel shrieked, and her small hand thrust Koach behind her.

"The Outlaw is right!" Bar Cheleph cried. "God does not bless us or feed us. We are starving! We have let such a boy live!"

"Starving!" someone else shrieked. "We're starving!"

"Stone the boy!" He recognized Mordecai's voice.

"Stone the boy!" others shouted. "Stone the boy!"

It was as though all the griefs and terrors of fourteen years had been poured into a wineskin and sealed, and the wineskin had held them contained and out of sight. But over the years, the skin had grown brittle, and now Barabba with his words and his hurling of severed heads to their feet had dashed the skin against the earth, and everything this town had refused to look at was gushing out. It was gushing out ugly and sharp as vinegar. These angry faces no longer seemed those of men and women whom Koach knew. They stared at him with dead eyes and opening mouths, like the mouths of the dead.

Several stooped to lift stones from the side of the street. Koach took a step back, blanching, but the stones did not fly. Not yet. Shimon stood between

Koach and the crowd, his body tensed. Some of them wavered. Bar Nahemyah and Benayahu—the town's *nagar*, the woodworker and repairer of boats whose house stood by theirs—took their stand by Yonah's son. Zebadyah looked on in horror.

Rahel gripped Koach's good arm, her face rigid with fear. "If they throw," she whispered, "you run."

"Amma . . ." he whispered.

"You *run*, Koach. Your brother and I, they will not throw at *us*. They will *not*." There was a savage edge to her voice.

At that moment, Barabba wheeled his horse, and his long knife rang from its sheath. "I will take care of this for you," he shouted, and kicked his heels in. But even as his gelding sprang forward, Shimon tore the heavy fishing coat from his shoulders and flung it over the animal's head. The horse reared, hooves striking the air. Cursing, Barabba fought for balance.

"Run, Koach!" Rahel cried.

Koach stumbled back, then fled, the slap of his sandaled feet against the dry, packed earth before the synagogue. Someone grabbed for him and missed; others sprang out of his way. Glancing over his shoulder, Koach caught a glimpse of Barabba tearing the coat free and hurling it aside. A spray of red in the air as his knife took Benayahu across the face; the *nagar* had tried to grab at the bridle, and now fell back with a gurgled cry. Zebadyah was shouting, and there were screams, and Rahel stood before Barabba's horse.

Then a turn in the narrow streets hid the synagogue and the Outlaw from view, and Koach panted as he ran. More screams— terrible screams—but he didn't dare stop. Panic beat an overpowering drumbeat in his chest, and in his ears he heard his mother's voice: *Run, Koach, run. Run. Run.*

He ran. Gasping for breath, he leapt as far with each stride as he could, down the slope of the land toward the sea. He began ducking through the narrower spaces between houses. Behind him, hooves like battle-drums against the packed earth of Kfar Nahum's streets, and in his ears the rush and roar of his blood. Without thought, Koach ran to where the small houses were packed thickest, nearest the water where his mother and his brother and the surviving fishers lived. Barabba bellowed somewhere behind him, but he ran on, panting. He had the confused impression that if he could get to his mother's house, he might hide somewhere within. But already his sides burned, and he ran half hunched over.

Then he could see his mother's house ahead, that small stone structure, its walls whitened by the sea, and the hooves were louder behind him. He ran past the last few houses, and the door to the house ahead of him—the door of the last house before his mother's, the *nagar*'s door, in better repair than most—was thrown open. A girl stood there, one his own age, a girl with a strange face and a frightened look.

"Inside!" she cried. "Quickly!"

Koach had only half a breath in which to make up his mind. Home was before him, but he would be alone there, in an empty house, with a furious man and a blade coming for him. He could hear the hoofbeats behind, just around the corner. He didn't trust others in the town, none but his mother and perhaps Shimon his brother and perhaps Bar Nahemyah who was alone, as he was.

"Come on!" the girl cried.

Something in her eyes told him what he needed to know.

With a gasp he flung himself toward the girl and her door.

PART 4

THE CARPENTER'S DAUGHTER

THE GIRL caught Koach's hand—her fingers so warm around his—and pulled him up against her side and into the house; her other hand caught the latch of the door and swung it shut against the sound of hooves. Her eyes were wide in the soft dark. Koach could hear her breathing and his. He could also feel her body, the softness of it, pressed to him. It made places low in his body heat in a way that astonished him.

She put her lips to his ear and whispered, "Come on. I'll hide you."

She led him quickly across the atrium of her father's house, beneath the open sky. Koach looked at her in wonder. There were few young women in

Kfar Nahum, and few young men, but Koach did not remember having seen her before. There were finger-shaped bruises just below her sleeve, as though someone had gripped her arm hard enough to drag her across the atrium and fling her to the ground or into a room. But at that moment, with Barabba's hoofbeats still loud in his ears, Koach barely noticed them. She had a strange face. Her eyes were wide apart—too wide—but they were fierce with the fire of her heart, and for a moment he found it difficult to look away from them.

She did not look at him with the horror he was used to seeing in girls' eyes.

She pulled hard at his wrist. "Come on!"

Outside, the hoofbeats went still.

"God of Hosts," she whispered. She pulled him out of the atrium into one of the small rooms along the wall, drew him in, and let the great rug that served for a curtain fall closed across the door. Within, shards of light speared toward the floor from a window long boarded up against the dead, in lines as sharp as though a man had drawn them there. Koach could see motes of dust flashing into existence as they drifted into the light, and then fading out of existence again, each one lit up briefly with fire from the sun. Despite the terror in his heart, it startled him; it was so beautiful. As the girl stepped through the light and into the shadows behind it, Koach caught the briefest glimpse of hair the color of rich earth.

A clatter as his heel struck a pile of clay bowls.

"Hide!" the girl gasped, and her small hands shoved him down into a heap of bedding. She began reaching for blankets to pile over him.

"Why?" Koach panted. "Why are you helping me?"

A small scream, muffled against her closed lips. "Don't ask questions!" she whispered fiercely. "Hide!"

A horse's whicker at the door. Koach stiffened.

In another moment, there was a hard rap against the wood, as if something blunt had struck against it. The Outlaw's sword-hilt, perhaps.

Another rap.

Then two more.

In the moments that followed, Koach could hear his breathing like a wind over the sea. He hadn't known breathing could be so loud.

"Come out! If you're in there, boy, come out!" A pause. "That's how you want to die? Hiding? You come out, I'll let you run."

Shamed, Koach began to get up, only to feel the girl's hand pressing him back.

"Don't," she whispered.

He shook his head, tried to get up again. Her hands pinned his shoulders.

"No, he won't break the door." Her mouth barely made any sound, just the movement of her lips. "He won't. He won't defile another's house!"

There was a harder pounding at the door, and a great crack. The girl's face went white. Koach peered past her, through the tiny gap between the rug and the wall. He saw the outer door half fall to the side, the wood splintered about its rusted bronze hinge.

Barabba stood with his hand still on the ruined door, his expression lethal. For a moment, Koach's heart clamored in his ears; he was sure the Outlaw would kick the door the rest of the way open and come for him with knife or stone, tearing aside the rugs to reveal the inner rooms, until Koach was found.

Yet the girl had been right: even as the door broke, Barabba hesitated. To violate the sanctity of another man's house, a man of your own People, to stride in boldly as though you owned the house and all within, that would invite the wrath of holy God. That gave even Barabba pause.

The Outlaw's eyes burned. As Koach and the girl held their breath, Barabba visibly struggled with himself. Then he turned partly away with a snarl. "Hide, then, in the house of good men!" he called, his voice thick with a fury that had been building perhaps for years, like a storm piling hot above the sea.

"Hide, little rat! But it doesn't matter how deep you burrow. One day soon, when we've thrown the Romans into the sea, good men will rip you out of your hole, you and every heathen and every *hebel* and every unclean weakling, and drag you out to be stoned in the open before the eyes of God. Hide and shiver."

"He's right," Koach whispered, barely moving his lips. "I'm not just *hebel*; I'm a coward." He was shaking. Too well he remembered the pain from Bar Cheleph's fists. Barabba would be worse.

"Shh! He'll *hear* you!"

But he knew that he had to get up. Shimon his brother had stood before the Outlaw without fear in his face. Koach had not been permitted to stand before the other men in the synagogue; if he couldn't stand like them now, or if Barabba did burst in and this lovely girl who'd hidden him was hurt in his place...

Koach took one of the girl's hands in his, dislodging it from his shoulder. He opened his mouth to call out to the Roman-killer, who still stood furious in the door. The girl hissed in frustration, and then suddenly her small weight was pressed down on him and her lips found his and they were warm and soft, and his heart pounded in alarm. Any intent he might have had to call out or rise and stride to the door washed away like sand on the tide. After a moment, his lips parted around her upper lip and he kissed her. His one good hand still clasped her wrist captive, for he did not know whether to let go or to put his arm around her. It took his entire being just to manage the kiss. He did not even hear the Outlaw's boot strike the ruin of the door, or his steps retreating, or the whicker of his horse as he reined it about outside. Koach heard nothing but his own heart and her soft breathing through her nose as her own lips parted and the kiss became something new and different and overwhelming, something much more than just a frustrated girl silencing him the only way she could think of, something so warm and real and moist that it was painful.

"I'm sorry," he gasped when the kiss ended.

Silence thickened between them.

Then she whispered, "I'm not."

Startled, he looked into her eyes, which shone in the light from the window. There was a look in them he had never seen before. It scared him and excited him.

"What is your name?" he whispered.

"Tamar," she said. "Tamar bat Benayahu."

"Bat Benayahu," he whispered. He had no idea what to say, or how to say it. So instead he touched her face with his fingertips. "You are so graceful," he said.

She shook her head. "No. I know that's not true." She looked pale. "I'm not . . . not what you said. Graceful."

"You are."

Her eyes glistened. Her voice dropped to nearly a whisper. "He keeps me shut in here, mostly. Forbids me to step outside the door. Because I am ugly. Because . . ." She lowered her head so that her hair hid her face. "My father is ashamed that no one has asked for me."

"You are not ugly," Koach whispered. "You are beautiful."

She shook her head sharply.

He put his hands on her shoulders. "You are *beautiful*," he said again. "Beautiful as the moon on the sea and the shells on the shore."

"You are kind," she whispered, a catch in her voice. "I knew that. The last time father let me out, I saw you walking with your mother. My father says terrible things about you, and I know others do, too. I know that your arm is weak. But you are Yonah's son. They say that, too. And I—I've seen how you help her. Your mother. Her face—you can tell that she cries often. You're what she stays on her feet for. You're not *hebel*. You're kind."

She glanced up at him through her hair, and her eyes were wet. They caught at his heart.

"Is this what it's like to be kissed?" she whispered. "You press your lips to a boy's, and your heart falls out? And suddenly you're saying things you didn't mean to?"

"Yes," he whispered back. "Or . . . I don't know. I haven't kissed anyone before." For Koach, it wasn't like his heart spilling from him in a rush of words. It was more like all the words in the whole word getting stuck in your throat, and being unable to get any of them out.

Suddenly he remembered.

"Your father—your father is hurt," Koach gasped.

She gave him a wild look.

"I don't think he's hurt badly. But Barabba was striking at people by the synagogue."

She glanced at the broken door, and her eyes held terror and dread. "I have to find out what's happening."

He grabbed her arm, but she shook her head.

"Wait here. Quietly. I won't be here to hush you," she added, blushing.

"If I shout, will you kiss me again?"

"I might," she whispered after a moment.

Her face was a deep red now, and Koach felt a flash of anger at her father. How could he have told her she was ugly? He cupped his hand behind her neck and drew her face to his, quickly, before he could change his mind, and kissed her, open-mouthed and anxious.

When the kiss ended, she rushed to her feet and darted across the atrium, swift as a deer. Koach sat dazed.

Then she was gone.

* * *

Koach lay beneath the wool bedding, which smelled like Tamar—a scent of sawdust and wood and clear water and long-held fear that seeps into the skin so deeply that it becomes a scent, too. The warmth of her lips remained with him, new and bewildering, as though God had touched him and changed something inside him, forever. He didn't know *what* had changed. He only knew that he was not the same youth he had been an hour earlier.

He wanted to know her, know everything about her. Did she climb to her roof sometimes and gaze at the moon over the sea, as he did? Did she like to sing softly in the evening? Did she have a secret place, a place God had shared only with her, where she went to think? He wanted to listen to her talk of herself, as no one had ever done with him, and he wanted to kiss her again.

There was a shout at the broken door, and Koach tensed. He'd heard no hoofbeats. Wood creaked as the remains of the door were yanked open. Then steps and loud breathing. He peered out at the atrium from under the corner of his blanket. A thin, wiry man with a dark shock of beard was moving quickly from one room to the next, glancing through the inner doors. Benayahu. He held one hand clutched to his right eye, and there was blood seeping through his fingers. A gash opened his cheek below his hand and it gaped red and dark in the dim light. His mouth was curved in a snarl of rage, his face flushed; the way he moved, the aggression and violence latent in his body, made Koach hold his breath.

"Tamar!" her father roared. "Tamar!"

When there was no answer, he made a low feral sound—a sound Koach had never heard a man make before—and he stooped over a basket in the atrium and tore out a cloth, pressing it to his face. He swayed on his feet a moment. Then he glanced across the atrium at the small chamber where Koach lay. Koach drew the blanket entirely over his head, tried to make himself as small as possible beneath it, and lay very still.

Benayahu strode near, seized the rug over the door, and tore it aside, letting in a flood of sunlight. He stood there looking in, breathing hard.

Koach didn't move. He began to count silently.

He made it to four.

Then the *nagar*'s breath hissed out between his teeth. He let the rug fall back.

Benayahu strode to another room without speaking. Koach heard the flapping sound of another rug pulled aside. Then another. When Benayahu stepped back into the atrium, Koach shivered at his glimpse of his face. He had seen such a face before. He remembered the way Bar Cheleph had stood over him in the grasses, beating him. In a dull horror he remembered the bruises he'd seen on Tamar's arm. He swallowed and lay very still, hardly daring to breathe.

He remembered the small carving he'd made, a fish, torn from his hand, though he'd tried desperately to hold on to it. And the scent of the grasses, the way a few wild blades had brushed his face as he shielded his head with his good arm. The sharp, violent pain that came with each blow of Bar Cheleph's feet. The shouts of *"Hebel! Hebel! Hebel!"*

And that terrible moment when he wondered if he was going to die, if Bar Cheleph and the other young men were going to beat him to death there on the tideline.

Then Bar Cheleph's strangled yell.

The blows stopped.

Startled voices, then running feet. Running away from him.

Koach lay still. His back and left side were one dull burn of pain.

A hand on his shoulder made him tense. He was rolled onto his back. He found Bar Nahemyah's face above his, stern but concerned. The shofar hung about the man's neck, and the knuckles on his right hand were bloodied.

"On your feet, Bar Yonah," he said.

Koach just looked at him, dazed, trying to breathe.

"I said get up. Yonah would have been ashamed of you. He would have wanted you to fight."

Bar Nahemyah grasped Koach's arms and pulled him up until he was sitting. Then he took a closer look. "God of our fathers, your face is a mess," he muttered.

"Don't hit me anymore," Koach whispered. "Don't."

"No one is going to hit you. But put away your wood and your knife. This is a town of Yehuda tribe, not a settlement of pig-eating Greeks, worshippers of wood and stone."

"The fish—"

Bar Nahemyah glanced about, his lips in a thin line. "Bar Cheleph took it when he ran, I think."

Koach moaned softly. A terrible sense of loss.

"Be thankful. It can curse his house instead of yours. What were you thinking, making such a thing?"

"It was beautiful."

"So is a blade, or a woman's body. But there are times when it is evil to hold one."

Koach didn't understand. He groaned when Bar Nahemyah lifted him to his feet.

"Damn," Bar Nahemyah whispered. "You can't stand, can you?"

Koach tried, but the world seemed to tip; Bar Nahemyah caught him and lifted the boy into his arms with a grunt. "I'd better take you to your mother," he said grimly, carrying the youth as he began walking through the grass toward the houses, his body lean and wiry against Koach's. "If your brother finds you here, like this, he may kill Bar Cheleph. He is Yonah's son."

Rahel had already been awake when Koach returned to his brother's house. She'd listened with fierce eyes as he told her what had happened and hissed through her teeth at his bruises. Then she swept him into her arms and crushed him to her. "My son! Oh my son. My son, my son."

She cleaned his face with a damp cloth and lay him in his bedding, and for a while she sat beside him singing to him softly, though her eyes burned dark with fury.

* * *

The ruined outer door shut with a crack, and then Benayahu was gone. Koach let out his breath. Now that the danger was past, he thought of Tamar. The bruise he'd seen on her arm.

He wished he had some way to warn her that her father knew she was gone from the house and was searching for her. His own body felt sore with remembered blows, and he thought: *Tamar and I are the same.*

Except that he had been beaten *once*, while she lived under her father's roof and might be beaten many times. Bitterness twined about his heart like a thorny weed, and the hurt of it was far more cruel than anything he had felt before.

People often think that violence, though it causes pain, is something that can be shrugged away, or healed, or walked away from afterward. But it isn't. The violence of a man's fists on a boy's body, or of a man's sex forced into a woman's body or a girl's, doesn't just inflict pain. It tears away another person's security, their ownership of their own body, their faith in their ability to direct and protect themselves. However briefly, they become another's property, another person's thing to beat or destroy, and when it is done, it is a long work, a fierce work, to convince themselves entirely that they are their own again.

* * *

"He's gone."

Koach opened his eyes blearily. Tamar's face was inches from his, her breath soft and warm on his cheeks. It was pleasant.

582

She straightened, smiling, and he rose to his elbow. His eyes were dry with sleep. The exhaustion and adrenaline of this morning had been too much for him.

"He's gone, Koach," she said again.

"Is my mother all right?" The words rushed from him.

She nodded. "She's hurt, but others are helping her." She saw his face and added quickly: "Not badly hurt. The horse—its hoof struck her hip. The priest says the bone is broken but he thinks she will heal. Seeing her struck—a mother of Israel—it made everyone furious. When Barabba rode back to the synagogue and saw it, even he looked ashamed. Then everyone started lifting stones; they were going to kill him, Koach. They were going to try."

"What happened?" he breathed.

Her eyes were bright. "They made him go away. Out along the north track, toward Threshing. He was yelling and screaming over his shoulder. I've never seen anyone look so angry, not even—" She blanched.

"Not even your father," Koach said softly.

She gave a tight nod.

Koach reached out to her with his left hand, gripped her arm just below the bruise, but he let her go quickly when he saw her wince. She looked at him.

"He shouldn't do that to you." His voice hoarse with emotion.

They sat silently for a while. Then she whispered, "I have to get you out of here. Before my father comes."

"He came while you were gone."

She flinched.

"Come to my mother's house," Koach said suddenly. "What?"

Her eyes widened. "But—I am my father's. I'm not betrothed to your brother, or . . . or you. I'd be stoned. Father would think I was in your bed, or Shimon's."

"You hid me," Koach said quickly. "I want to hide you, from whoever would hurt you. I want to keep you safe."

He couldn't believe the words that were rushing from his heart to his lips, but neither could he stop them. The urge to protect her, to do *something*, rushed through him like wind and fire.

"I— You have to go." She tugged the blankets from him, and Koach got carefully to his feet. Tamar grasped him by his sleeve and led him quickly through the atrium, glancing at him over her shoulder.

Koach stopped by the outer door. "Wait—"

Her eyes were round and dark.

"Thank you," Koach said after a moment. "For hiding me."

He could hear the beating of his heart.

"Go," she whispered. And unlatched the door. "Go."

He leaned in quickly and brushed his lips over her eyelid, everything in him suddenly tender. He heard her breath catch. Then the battered door creaked open, and her hand between his shoulder blades pushed him through. He stumbled out, caught himself. The door rattled shut behind. He stood blinking in the sun in the empty street, and in the direction of the synagogue there were many voices shouting.

For a moment he stood dazed. He stared at the cracks in Benayahu's door, reluctant to leave. Everything in him was a rush of feeling and want and hope and fear. Then he recalled the danger to Tamar if she was caught with him, and he turned and ran the few steps to his mother's door.

WHERE GOD TOUCHED THE WORLD

TAMAR HAD spoken the truth. The Outlaw had returned to the synagogue to find grim and furious faces. By then, Rahel had been carried to the steps, her face white with pain. Another fisher's wife knelt by her, pressing a warm cloth to Rahel's hip and talking with her softly, Rahel's dress drawn up about her waist. Shimon and Zebadyah stood with their backs to her, facing the oncoming hooves, and men and youths of their town stood beside them.

No one remembered later who hurled the first rock, but the stone was a large one and it smacked against Barabba's left shoulder, nearly knocking him from his horse. Then there were many stones, the men and women before the synagogue stooping swiftly and then straightening to hurl the rocks with cries of rage. Barabba wheeled his horse in a circle, screaming curses on the town, calling them Roman-lovers and hiders of the misbegotten and unclean. The air filled with stones, hurled wildly. One struck the back of Bar Nahemyah's head, and as he stumbled, stunned, Barabba rode at him in a rush. Leaning out, the Roman-killer caught him as he fell and hauled him up over his saddle.

"One recruit, at least, I'll take from this ruined town!" Barabba shouted. He drove his knees into his horse's sides. The steed screamed as rocks struck its flanks.

"Stop!" Zebadyah yelled to the others. "Stop! You'll hit our own!"

Then the horse was galloping down the streets with screaming men and women rushing after, but Barabba was quickly out of their reach and riding hard along the shore like a leaf before a storm wind, with Bar Nahemyah stretched dazed and unmoving across his saddle, taken from them swiftly and without farewell.

When Koach heard of that, he said nothing for an hour. It was as though his brother had been torn from him.

* * *

Shimon carried Rahel back to his house, lifting her in his arms as though she were a child. He lay her in her bedding beneath the olive in the atrium and gave her wine to dull the pain. He shouted for Koach to bring water, and Koach carried it to him in a small bowl—because he could not manage a ewer with only one hand. Rahel was no longer pale; she was flushed with wine, but she looked so frail where she lay, her face twisted in pain, that Koach stumbled in shock, dropping the bowl and spilling the water. Shimon turned on him with a look of rage. "You're useless!" he roared. "Get out of here."

Koach left the atrium with what dignity he could, blinking back hot tears. He had seen the whites around his brother's eyes, knew it was fear and worry for his family that fed his brother's anger, but the words hurt deeply nonetheless. He sought out one of the rooms along the outer wall of his mother's house. Not the room in which he slept during the cold winter, but a quiet, unused room where he hid his secrets.

He sat with his back to the wall and shut his eyes. He could still feel Tamar's kiss warm on his lips. After a while, he turned and slid out the loose stone at the bottom of the wall at his back, the one that concealed his secret place. It took a lot of work to slide the stone out one-handed, but he was practiced at it.

In the small, concealed space, he kept his carving knife. In another corner of the room lay pieces of driftwood like a pile of kindling, some as small as his thumb, others nearly the length of his arm. He took up one of the pieces now, a scrap the size of his hand. The wood had been cedar once, perhaps a tree on some mountain slope in White Cedars to the north, washed down the Tumbling Water to their sea. Koach clasped the wood securely between his knees and stared at it for a while, searching for the beauty in the heart of the driftwood. Then he found it, and began working the knife with his left hand, carving, cutting away the pieces that weren't needed, working slowly, calming the beating of his heart. Losing himself in it. Ceasing for a few moments to think of Barabba and his rearing, terrifying horse, or of the girl with earth-dark hair who had hidden him and kissed him.

The carving was Koach's secret, and it was his commerce, too. His creations might be unclean—in fact, in the Law, the Second of the Ten declared, *You shall carve no image in wood or stone*—but they were also beautiful. He had learned that, the evening Bar Cheleph had beaten him to the earth and taken from his hands the first carving Koach had ever made—a small, simple replica of a fish. He had seen Bar Cheleph's eyes. Not just his hate but his desire for the object Koach held. The people of Kfar Nahum were a severe people, but they were also people of the sea. And that meant they were lovers of beauty, though compared to their Greek neighbors in other towns of the Galilee, they loved it quietly.

Seeing that, Koach had not cast aside his knife after carving that little, forbidden fish. He had kept making things. He carved little boats. In time, the boats even had oars and nets, delicate traceries of wood that took him days to complete.

And because Koach lived most of his hours alone in the house with his mother, he listened. Whenever he heard his mother lamenting for some lack, he would slip away quietly when she wasn't looking, a wood-carving stowed within the long coat he wore. He would go to knock softly on one of his neighbors' doors. He did this usually in the late evening, after the fishers went down to the sea, and a fisherman's wife would open the door at his knock.

After the Romans' raid on the village and the fires that had scorched the town, the houses of Beth Tsaida were sparsely furnished and sparsely decorated, and even what pottery the village had was simple and unadorned. Koach's wood-carvings were unique in all the town, its one bit of beauty. It was not difficult to barter them for things his mother needed—salt, or oil for her lamp, or a bowl of dates or figs. Not difficult . . . as long as he chose carefully which fishermen's wives to approach. And as long as he bore with patience the way they avoided any accidental touch, any brush of their fingers against his. The way they avoided looking at his right arm. They took the carving as often as not, and handed him the little pouch of salt or the spare needle or the thimble of fine thread, but they did not look him in the eyes. They did not speak his name. In fact, they rarely spoke to him at all.

He never went to Zebadyah's door. And there were other doors he avoided, too. Doors where he would be greeted with a kick. Or where not even a love of beauty could turn the house's occupants from a strict observance of the Law.

Yet Koach felt little shame as he whittled at the driftwood he held between his knees. In a cruel world, a boy or a man must find beauty where he can, or hunt after it until he does. Or else the hard edges of life will gut him as a man guts a fish, and toss him wriggling to die in the sand.

* * *

The day passed. Long ago, when Koach was small, the atrium would have been loud with his mother's chickens, but those hens had long since been eaten or bartered away. Now the house was quiet. A few times Koach heard Rahel cry out in pain, and he peeked around the door of the small room. His mother still lay beneath the olive tree, her face white. Shimon, tall as a bear, brought her a fresh wineskin. Another time, there was a knock at the door. Koach heard the door open, a murmur of words, then heard it slam shut. A few moments later, he heard his brother and his mother talking in low voices. He could make out most of what was said.

"Who was it?"

"The *nagar*."

"How is he?"

"He'll keep his eye."

"God. Oh, God."

"It's all right. It's all right."

Shimon sounded numb again, the way he usually sounded. The rage that had leapt up like fire taking a cedar was gone, and he stood in his ashes.

Silence fell over the house.

Koach slipped the half-carved wood and the knife back into their place in the wall. Then he settled back, his lids heavy. The carving had brought him quiet without bringing him peace: he couldn't recall ever having felt so fatigued, so overwhelmed. All of it was too much. The horseman's fury, the fear for his mother, the unexpected, impossible warmth of Tamar's lips against his own, the dread of her father's barely restrained violence, the screams in the town, the dead eyes of the townspeople as they lifted rocks from the dirt; the hoofbeats, hoofbeats in his ears, in the earth beneath his feet, hooves louder and louder, riding him down, riding him down, riding him . . .

He woke to the slam of the door in the early dusk: his brother leaving to fish. It took him a moment to breathe evenly again. As his heartbeat settled he stirred, and realized there was a pillow beneath his head, a small, sewn square stuffed with crow's feathers. It was his mother's pillow; she must have come while he slept, despite her pain, and tucked it beneath his head. He hugged it to his cheek with his good arm, overwhelmed with a sudden tenderness toward her. It was a feeling he hadn't experienced before— not a boy's clear-hearted awe but a man's love for his mother, his acknowledgment of her sacrifices and her truth.

After a few moments, he stepped softly from the room and found his mother beneath the olive, asleep with her mouth open, her face still flushed. He watched her breathe for a few moments, his heart in turmoil. She had been hurt today, because of him. Because he was useless. Because he was *hebel*.

Though he couldn't have said why, he walked quietly to the stone steps in the opposite wall that led up to the rooftop. The stones were cool beneath his feet; he hadn't spared a moment to put on sandals. Once up there, he glanced first to Benayahu's house. The *nagar*'s house was separated from his mother's only by the narrowest of alleys, and its roof was lower, so that he could see into a part of the atrium and into the small rooms on the far side of the house if the rugs that covered the doors of those rooms were drawn aside. The few he could see into now were empty.

He sighed and turned toward the sea. There was a breeze against his face, but only a light one. Boats were setting out on the water. His brother was out there, he knew. And Yakob the priest's son and many others. All young men of Beth Tsaida who'd had their *bar 'onshin* in the synagogue and had learned to handle the oar and the net. All but he.

"I want to be of use." A whispered prayer. "To my family. To Tamar. To someone." It had always seemed to him as though the night he was born God had turned his back on him and on the town, had walked away across the water and never looked back and never returned. Now God seemed far away, hardly relevant. But who else was there to talk to?

Suddenly he heard footsteps approaching, a man's steps, heavy though muffled and slow, as if he were trying to be silent. The man came through the narrow clutter of fishermen's houses until he passed by Benayahu's. Koach slipped to the edge of the roof, lay down on his belly, and peered over it, his heart racing.

The man was Zebadyah bar Yesse.

The priest stopped before Rahel's door, close enough that Koach could have spat on him. The boy covered his mouth and nose with his hand to hide the sound of his breathing.

The priest stood before the door for a while. Then he called out Rahel's name in a low voice that he clearly hoped wouldn't carry.

There was no answer.

"Bat Eleazar," Zebadyah called again, just above a whisper, and he gave the door a tentative rap with his hand, just enough that someone inside might hear it.

"Bat Eleazar . . . Rahel, come to your door. Please. We need to talk about your son. And we need to do so now, while others sleep. Please."

The door rattled quietly and then swung half open. The pale oval of Rahel's face appeared in the dark. Her eyes were dilated and black.

"I am grateful for what you did today, *kohen*," she said. "But I know you are no friend of my son's." There was a quality to her voice that made Koach realize, with a start, that his mother had been weeping.

For a moment, heat flickered in Zebadyah's eyes. Then he sighed. "I am tired," he said. "That man left those heads on our soil. Yakob has taken them up the hill to bury, but Bar Cheleph and I have been all day washing the uncleanness from our earth." His gaze was direct. "I stood by your sons because we cannot allow our town to be trampled ever again by outsiders." He nearly spat the word. "But we must talk. You know what your son has been doing." His voice sank to a whisper. "Those . . . those *images*."

"It is the only thing that makes him happy," Rahel said. "The only thing that makes him feel useful."

Koach blinked back moisture from his eyes.

"It has to stop," the priest said. "It has to . . . Look, I do not think as Barabba does, not any longer. Your son is a good boy, and you love him; I can see that . . ."

"Then let my son have his *bar 'onshin!*"

"I *can't!*" Zebadyah cried. "I am thinking only of what is best for the town."

A soft hiss of breath. "*I* am thinking of what is best for my son."

The priest glanced about quickly, as though concerned that the rising of his voice might have drawn listeners. "Take him, then," he said, his voice trembling with the effort of holding back what he felt. "You, Shimon, your crippled boy. Take him from the town. I will send goods with you, what I can. You can go to Rich Garden or Threshing." His face clenched in pain, as though it were a great sacrifice to wrench these words from his heart. "Find some new home. But the boy cannot stay here."

"He is Yonah's son." Her voice fierce.

"I know!" Zebadyah cried, with a sharp gesture of his hands. Rahel shrank back into the doorway. A few faces peered through the windows of nearby houses. "I know! Do you think I do what I do lightly? You damned, unreasonable . . . *woman*! Is your son more important than every life in this town? Would you imperil us all with your grief, your pride? He cannot stay here; I have overlooked him for too long because I loved my brother, because I love you." He nearly shouted the last, and then stopped abruptly, as if shocked at what he'd said.

An uncomfortable silence. The woman at her door, the priest outside it.

Zebadyah breathed, "I am sorry."

"I am your brother's wife," Rahel said coldly. "Not yours. And you have no authority within the walls of this house."

Zebadyah's voice was muted now, pleading. "Bat Eleazar, just listen to me."

"I am done listening."

"He is broken, unclean, and he carves images in defiance of everything we believe in, everything we are. He has to go. It is God's Law."

"If God had had a mother, his Law might have been less cruel."

"Blasphemy," Zebadyah gasped, drawing back a step, a hand raised as though her words were something physical that he could ward away. "I can't . . . I can't hear this!"

"Then don't." Rahel's voice was sharp and it began to carry; Koach could see doors of nearby houses cracked open. His mother's voice was fire; Koach was certain that if she had addressed *him* in that tone, he would have withered like a vine in the sun's heat.

"This is my husband's house," Rahel hissed. "My husband's. The first man of this town. The man who stood against the Romans when you would not. A man who gave his *life*. So that my son could be born in a Hebrew town. And how *dare* you come to his door and talk to me of God? My husband knew God. Do you? Was it God who told you to hide shaking by the boats? The night they beat and crippled your father, the night my husband *died*, was it God who told you to bow and scrape before our heathen masters? Was it?"

Zebadyah went pale. Utterly pale. "Remember yourself, woman," he rasped. But she shut the door on him.

For a few moments Zebadyah stood very still. "I paid for my sins," he whispered at last. "I pay for them every night. Every night until I die."

Then it seemed to occur to him that he was speaking merely to a door of wood, and not to Rahel or to her dead husband. He turned and walked away with his head bowed. A few faces watched the priest from nearby doors. Zebadyah strode by without looking at them. Then the doors shut again, closing each family once more within the hungry gloom of its own house.

Koach was breathing hard, as though he had run to the *kokhim* and back. He just lay there on the roof, trying to take in all he had heard. No one had ever spoken to him of his father's death, or been willing to. His mother looked sad when he was mentioned. Shimon's face just went cold and hard. Koach only knew his father's name because everyone in town spoke it reverently when they addressed his brother. *Bar Yonah,* they said, *Bar Yonah,* as though Yonah had been some hero out of old stories, whose death had left a hole not only in Koach's life, but in Kfar Nahum itself. Koach tried to imagine him, a man he'd never seen, standing with a fishing spear in his hand, or an oar, or a knife, as Roman soldiers or the lurching dead came at him.

Koach suddenly wanted to run down the steps into the atrium to his mother and demand stories from her. Stories of Yonah that might tell him who his father had been, and who *he* might be. But sounds from the *nagar*'s house broke the moment, snapping his thoughts like kindling. He froze, listening: the murmur of a voice in anger and a faint sound like a sob.

He got to his feet and returned to the edge of the roof facing that house, and looked down into it. The rug over one of the far rooms had been drawn aside, and there was a light, a small candle burning on a table. Tamar was sitting on the floor beside it, hugging herself and rocking back and forth. Her head was down, her hair covering her face, but Koach could see that she was shaking and that she was naked to the waist. He blushed hotly for just a moment, but the tingling in his loins disappeared as quickly as it came, for everything about the way Tamar held her body spoke of terrible pain. Koach had the impulse to leave the roof and go unbar the door of his house, slip out into the street, and run to Benayahu's door and knock and call out to her, make sure she was all right. But just at that moment, a dark shape cut off the candlelight, and he knew that a man was standing between the candle and the door. His voice was raised harshly, but his words were muffled by the room he stood in, and Koach couldn't be sure what was said. After a moment there was movement against the light and a quiet crack, as of a hand striking flesh, and a small, strangled sob. Koach sucked in his breath. He was beating her, and the crack of his hand sounded again. And again. And *again.* Koach's hand became a fist.

The shadow moved, and he glimpsed the man grasping Tamar's hair, holding her still as he hit her. But at that moment her gaze flicked up in pain, and she saw him.

They saw each other. From the rooftop to the small room.

Had Koach been able to think past the shock and the fury in his heart, he might have expected to see anger in the girl's eyes, or shame. Shame that he would see her like this. But Koach didn't see those things in her eyes. Only recognition. Then her eyes glistened in the light of the candle, as though filling with tears that she had forbid herself until that moment.

And her face relaxed. Like letting go of a burden too heavy for her. Like glancing down and seeing warm bedding before you when you are tired. Like relief.

Relief that one other person knew she was suffering, and cared.

He took a step back, but her gaze held him. A silent demand in her eyes: *Don't go. Don't leave me alone.*

So he stayed.

Something in him died and something else was born, something dark and furious, as he watched the blows fall on this young and beautiful woman. He did not turn his head; he would not betray her. He witnessed all of it. And when Benayahu had left his daughter sobbing on her bedding, Koach longed to go to her, to tend her bruises with a damp cloth or to hold her. But he didn't know how. He could not call out to his mother. Rahel was not a man; she could not interfere in the doings in Benayahu's house. There was no one to go to, no one who would listen to a one-armed boy, or care. His brother, maybe, a strong man, could leap from this roof to the other. But Koach was not his brother. If he tried that leap, he would only break his body on the stones between their houses. He might go down to Benayahu's door, but why should the *nagar* open up his house to him?

He did the only thing he could: he waited with her while she cried, though a gulf of air separated them. Finally she lifted her face from the bedding, and the misery in her eyes smote his heart. Quickly she brought her blanket up to her face and dried her tears. Then Tamar rose and slipped from her room, disappearing from his sight.

Koach stood still on the rooftop. He felt emptied of all feeling. He counted the beats of his heart. Somewhere around two hundred, he saw Tamar emerge onto her own rooftop, stepping onto it from unseen stone steps. At first she didn't look at him. She just stood there with her head down, in her blanket, the moon on her hair. As lovely as Batsheva must have looked to Dawid the king. Like Dawid, Koach had seen her naked, but unlike Dawid, the sight moved him to a desire to protect her, not possess her. He had seen her bruised and now, as she lifted her head and their gazes met, he saw her heart in her eyes. Her solitude and pain.

Neither of them looked away.

Neither dared call out, for fear of alerting Benayahu or breaking the intimacy and peril of this moment.

They stood like that a long time, seeing so much hurt in each other's hearts.

Finally, he mouthed the words in his heart, keeping them silent but exaggerating the movements of his mouth, to be certain she would know what he said:

I want to help.

I know, she mouthed back. Then: *You didn't leave me. That is help.*

A shake of his head. *I will help.*

They considered each other. Then she did something he did not expect. She let the blanket slip from her shoulders, let it settle to her feet, gently as feathers. For a moment, she held her arms across her breasts, then let them fall to her sides. She lifted her chin, though her face burned. She let him see her, all of her, her beauty and her bruises. This gift of herself. Her father might strip her or beat her, but he could not take this from her: her right to open her heart and her body to one whose heart called to hers. Koach held his breath. All his life, he would remember this moment. His first sight of her. The memory would be holy to him. As though her rooftop were the place where God touched the world and created beauty.

His loins stirred for her, yet his face was wet.

Whether he wept for her, for himself, or for them both, he couldn't have said. His hand trembled as he lifted his fingers to the clasp of his own tunic. He kept himself fully clothed at most times, even in his mother's house; he couldn't bear the way others looked at him when his deformity was visible. But he could not hide it now, could not conceal it when this young woman had unclothed all of her bruises, risked everything to be seen by one other.

He kept his movements slow, his heart loud with his fear. It took some work, with only his one hand and not his mother's to aid him. But at last his clothes were in a heap beside him, and he stood naked on the roof, the air cool on his skin. There was mercifully no wind to chill him or carry to his ears the voices of the *shedim*. He stood as straight as he could; his phallus had stiffened and grown so that it stood hard, as he had found it lately in the mornings when he woke, but for once it did not embarrass him.

He wanted to give her what she had given him: a sight of all of him. Even, no longer concealed in its long sleeve, his withered arm and deformed right hand, the hand that could never touch her face or bring her pleasure or work to feed her. Never having felt so naked, he looked to her eyes anxiously. Saw them tearful. But she was also smiling.

He felt warm through every part of his body. Whatever the days ahead brought—whether hunger or ill dreams or riders out of the south with heads tied to their saddles, or stones hurled at him, or dead lurching up from the waves—whatever the days brought, for the first time he was certain he would not face those days alone.

One Year Later. AD 26—Present Day.

THE STRANGER

SHIMON'S BOAT approached the shore, riding low in the water and almost tipping into the sea from the weight of its nets. Even as the fishers breathed in the fecund scent of kelp and dead shellfish, the stranger came wading out toward them, the lake water about his knees, his eyes wild. "Your nets!" the man cried, an edge to his words, a hill-country accent Shimon couldn't place. "Your nets!"

Shimon stared at him as he heaved at the oar, uneasy. The man's clothes were strange—not a tunic and cloak but a long robe of brown wool. His arms and legs were smeared with dirt, as though he truly had walked here out of the deserts in the south. His hair was lank about his bruised face. His right arm bore bruises also, as though he had tried to shield himself from blows. With him came the reek of a man who had spent long days without a roof or clean water.

Even as they heard the scraping welcome of the shingle against the keel, the stranger took the gunwale in his hands. "So many!" he gasped, gesturing at the nets, staring wide-eyed at the fish. His face was wild with shock. "So many!

And they're . . . they're *beautiful!* I didn't know this would happen, I just cried out, I cried out, I cried out!" His gaze shot to Shimon's face, and in his eyes there was sudden joy, like a man who has walked all his life in the dark and for the first time sees firelight burning away the shadows. Shimon just stared back, the others silent behind him in the boat, startled at this raving man.

"Don't you understand? I *heard* you!" the man cried. "I could hear all of you, all last night, all of you moaning . . . your hunger, I couldn't bear it, couldn't bear it, couldn't. . . and I heard the father, I heard the father weeping for you, and don't you see, don't you *see*, he must have heard *me*, he must have heard me, too, he must have heard me, the father heard *me!*" His hands tightened at the gunwale, as though he were going to pull himself into the boat, his voice rising. His eyes shone with tears. "Do you understand! Do you understand! It was too great to bear, the hunger and the father's cries and the screaming and the screaming and the screaming"— his voice was now a wild shriek of joy, so that Shimon leaned back away from the man—"and I cried out and *he heard me!*"

The stranger's eyes rolled back and he pitched to the side, crashing into the water.

Shimon swore and cast his oar aside, leaping to his feet. He sprang over the gunwale as Yakob and Yohanna looked on, their eyes wide. He felt the water about his shins, the cold shock of it against his toes, and pebbles shifting beneath his sandaled feet. The boat scraped past him and he plunged his arms into the water, groping. Shimon found the man and hauled him up. The stranger's head lolled back and his mouth fell open.

"We'll get the boat up!" Yohanna cried behind him.

Shimon didn't answer. He slapped the man's cheek to rouse him.

Yohanna and Yakob leapt from the boat, the familiar sound of their sandaled feet sinking into the sand. Their hands gripped the gunwale and they began sliding the boat up the shingle. Though large, the boats of Kfar Nahum were lightly built; yet it was a great labor dragging the craft up toward the tideline.

After a moment, Shimon dragged the man out of the sea and lay him on the sand. Life came back to the stranger's eyes, and he gasped, "Water."

Shimon got to his feet and ran to the boat, exchanging a bewildered look with Yakob. Reaching in, he snatched up one of their waterskins, then ran back to where the stranger lay.

He held the waterskin to the man's lips, saw his throat move in great gulps. Then the stranger choked a little, and Shimon lifted the waterskin and set it aside. Even as he did, the man's hand grasped his wrist with a fierce strength. His eyes were intense. For a moment the stranger fought for breath. Then he gasped: "Cephas!"

Shimon didn't understand. Cephas was the Aramaic word for *rock*.

"Cephas," the man said, swallowing, getting more moisture into his voice. His gaze held Shimon's with an insistent, desperate demand. "Somewhere I have to be. Something I have to do."

Shimon shook his head. He didn't know whether that was a question or how to answer.

"Cephas, Cephas." The man fell back, his eyes turning toward the sky. "Something, something I have to do. I knew it, I knew it so clearly, so clearly only a moment ago. Like my father had spoken it right into my ear. Right *into my ear*, Cephas. When the fish came, I knew what it was, this thing I have to do. For just a moment, a breath, I knew it, Cephas. I knew it." He seemed to be fighting to catch his breath. "Now it's gone, gone, like . . . like leaves blown into the desert."

"Who are you?" Shimon gasped.

But the man closed his eyes and his grip on Shimon's hand weakened. Then his chest rose and fell as though he were asleep. Shimon slipped his wrist from the man's grip and stood, a little shakily. He gazed down at the man's battered body in its ragged brown robe. If Shimon had not heard the man's eerie cries, calling the fish, he would have thought him one of the boat people, the beggars and outcasts wandering up and down the shoreline of the Galilee who had become stuck here at their shore, too sick or too weak to move on. They often slept under the derelict boats just above the tide's reach. Shimon glanced uneasily up at those boats where they lay rotting in the tall grasses, but there was no sound or sign of movement. Yet there were always beggars there.

His hands shook. Had this man's cries—his eerie calling for fish over the water—filled the nets? The man's words were like raving. Like the words of a witch who had called the *shedim* into his body to inhabit it. The body was a house: What was living in this man's house?

Yet the nets had been empty, and now they were not.

"Yohanna!" he called.

In a moment, the son of Zebadyah was at his side. "Who is he, Shimon?"

Shimon only stepped back, making the sign against the evil eye.

"Wait." Yohanna gave the man a closer look and drew in a breath. "I know this man."

Shimon looked to him quickly, but Yohanna only frowned. "I don't know who he is. But I've seen him. I'm certain of that. I have seen this man before."

"He must be one of the boat people, one of the unclean," Yakob called behind them. Glancing over his shoulder, Shimon saw the boat half up the shingle with Yakob trying to pull it up alone, the veins standing out against his forehead. The nets were still in the water. Cursing, Shimon sprinted for the boat and lent his own arms, gripping the hooks beneath the gunwale and lifting the boat as he dragged it. In a moment, Yohanna was with them, leaving the stranger behind on the sand.

"He's not one of the boat people," Yohanna gasped, as they pulled the boat up the sand.

"He *looks* like one of the boat people," Yakob grunted.

"Didn't you see his robe? Fine wool. Pattern at the hem. Not rags. Not boat people. Essene, I think."

"Essene," Yakob wondered. "What is an Essene doing here?"

"I don't know."

"But his face—he's Galilean. He's one of us. Not from Kfar Nahum, but he's from here."

"I know."

Shimon took a steadying breath and turned his back on the stranger with the bruised arms and face. "Talk later," he said. "Nets won't wait."

* * *

A few moments of struggle, and they had the boat up into the tall grass above the tideline. Yakob took the prow, guiding the boat into place in the line of fishing vessels. Those still in use were at the end of the line nearest the town; those farther down were long derelict, decaying and spattered with gull feces, wooden corpses of themselves waiting for time to eat away their last timbers.

Then they ran back for the nets. Shimon glanced at the man lying in the sand, but he didn't have time to stand about wondering. They needed to be quick, for the oncoming tide was tugging at the nets, and the flashing silver of the fish, tails wriggling against the nets, was drawing down out of the sky white birds, swooping low.

They ran down the sand, which was wet and packed beneath the slap of their sandals. They took up the casting ropes and strained to pull up the nets, fearing the nets would break and spill this miracle catch back into the sea, the way a broken body spills back into the dark the life God once breathed into it.

Shimon sucked in air through his nose and breathed out through his mouth, pulling hard on the ropes on each inhale. He kept his eyes on the water and the wild flopping of the fish, fearing that they might yet haul another corpse out with the catch. His forehead was clammy with sweat.

Then two hands grasped the rope beside his and pulled, and the net came half out of the water. Shimon glanced to the side; the stranger stood there. The sea had washed most of the smell of the hills from him; water still trickled from his hair, making dark streaks down his robe. He returned Shimon's look, then heaved at the rope again.

"What are you?" Shimon panted. He wanted to pull away from this strange beggar man, but he didn't want to let go of the rope. The nets were heavy. He could not remember them ever being so heavy.

"A friend," the man said. He was calmer now, though his voice was strained.

"You've been in the desert." Shimon glanced at the man's brown robe.

"I have," he said.

"Are you an Essene?"

He shook his head. Not one of the desert hermits, then, who lived in their small communities hiding in caves from the dead and teaching their bodies to endure any hardship, that they might draw nearer to God.

"You're tattered and bruised." Shimon's voice was thick with his distrust of outsiders. "Are you unclean?"

The question appeared to startle him. "No," he said, and heaved at the rope. "No, I don't . . . I don't think so. Not unclean."

"I don't know what you are, who you are, but you called the fish," Shimon said, struggling to understand. "What *are* you? I *heard* you call them."

The man's eyes were dark and he stared past Shimon and over the water, intently, at some far other place. His voice changed, going quiet and intense, burning with terrible clarity. "Something is happening, Cephas. And whatever is happening, it will be like sword and like fire and like bread in the mouths of a thousand, thousand children, and nothing will ever, ever be the same way again."

Shimon stared at him, uneasy.

The stranger's attention returned to the rope they were straining at. "I cried out, and they came," he gasped. "Barbels, musht. No catfish, nothing unclean to throw back. How many will they feed?"

"The town," Shimon said. Hoarse. "The entire town. For two weeks, maybe three." He heaved at the net, and suddenly it broke open, spilling fish over the sand, flopping and wet.

The stranger gasped.

Shimon caught his breath also. There, where the water met the land, where the net had broken open at their pull, their last heave had pulled a white corpse half up onto the sand. Its hand was caught in the netting, with the fish flopping about it as though in panic at the unclean touch. The corpse itself was still, a gash in its brow where Shimon's fishing spear had caught it.

"No," the stranger whispered, his face white with horror, as though the appearance of the corpse was some intimate betrayal. "No."

CEPHAS

THE THING'S JAW was open in gaping, eternal hunger, its eyes sightless. Gazing down at it now, Shimon felt none of the rage that had surged in him, hot and violent, when he'd defended his nets on the sea. Only dread, cold in his belly. One thing to encounter the dead out on the sea, or in the dark waters of the dream country. Quite another to see one wash up on his shore.

It seemed to him that if he were to take his eyes from the corpse for even a moment, its hands might twitch and it might lurch again to its feet.

But it didn't move.

The corpse just lay there on the shingle like a stain of blood on a garment, one that could never be cleansed, never be entirely hidden or forgotten.

"El Shaddai," Shimon whispered, stepping back. There had always been one or two that would walk out of the waves and feed on the vagrants under the boats until they were discovered and stoned. But there had been three already this year.

And then this.

He tore his gaze from the dead thing and looked out at the cold waves, at that sea older than humanity that could hold so many dead concealed within it. The dread in his belly hardened, like a heavy stone to crush him to his knees.

The stranger was pale. "That . . . that's what you were beating at, with spear and oar, when you stood in your boat."

"Didn't you hear them moan?" Shimon said.

"I heard them moan," the stranger said. "Every moment I'm awake, I hear them moan." He let the rope fall from his hands and walked down to crouch beside the corpse.

Torn between watching the raving stranger and watching the corpse, Shimon stepped near and took the net itself in his hands, his muscles bunching, pulling it away from the hungry tide. For an instant the corpse dragged over the sand. The stranger gripped the tattered remnants of its tunic in his hand as though to pull it from the net, but the water-drenched garment peeled away from the corpse like an old blister, leaving the stranger crouching with it in his hand and the corpse dragging nakedly after Shimon, the sand sloughing some of its skin away as though its skin were only a second and equally decayed garment.

The stranger's face was so full of pain that Shimon had to look away. He kicked the corpse's hand a few times, knocking it loose from the net. Then he left the stranger and the corpse there, pulling the net with him, leaking fish. The corpse would have to be buried, in accordance with the Law—under earth or hard rock, so the uncleanness of it wouldn't spread to blight the plants that grow in the open air. But that could wait until the fish were brought in. It would have to.

* * *

Soon the other nets were half up the shore. Shimon, Yakob, and Yohanna ran back to gather up the spilled fish in their arms and carry those up, too, before the tide could take them. They had to work fast. There were other boats approaching the shore but still a ways out. Yakob ran to their own boat up above the tideline, snatched out an oar and an armful of the sheaves of lake-weed for binding the fish, then ran back. He tossed the sheaves into the sand at the others' feet, then veered and ran down the shore to a great white rock that was always above the tide and could be seen from some distance out. He leapt up on the rock and waved the oar, shouting at the far boats. Out on the water, men stood up against the rock and sway of their craft and called back to him, their voices thin in the dawn.

Yohanna and Shimon opened the unbroken nets, and the fish rivered out onto the sand in a flood of flashing scales. Still breathing hard, Shimon clapped Yohanna's shoulder. "Get help from the town. Bring bins, baskets, anything you have."

"What about him?" Yohanna nodded to the man still crouching at the water with that garment in his hand.

"Never mind him. Don't you see the gulls? Be quick!" Overhead, the sky was filling already with white birds, swooping down in wheeling circles, screaming their hunger. Shimon's blood roared in his ears. No time, no time.

"There won't be much help. We came back earlier than most," Yohanna said.

"Then bring the women!" Shimon roared. "We are *not* losing these fish! Not to the dead. Not to the sea. And not to the birds. Get me some hands!"

Yohanna nodded, clapped Shimon's shoulder in return, and then sprinted for the tideline grass and the low, crumbling houses beyond. He was the fastest runner in Kfar Nahum, a man with long legs as though he had Greek blood, but even if he had been short and slow, Shimon would not have left the nets himself.

Swiftly, Shimon crouched beside one of the opened nets and began wrapping the fish in sheaves of lake-weed. Even as he worked, the fish slick and wriggling in his hands, the air about him filled with beating wings and hoarse shrieks, and the gulls descended on him like the host of God. Some dove at Shimon's face and he beat them off with an arm; others settled on the nets or on the spill of fish on the sand, digging in with their sharp beaks. Then Yakob leapt in front of him and swung his oar about, slamming the hard wooden blade against the birds. There was a grate of other boats on the shingle, and then running feet, and other men sprang over the fish with oars in their hands.

A man knelt by him; Shimon glanced to his side and saw the stranger, his eyes still haunted. His dousing in the sea had washed away his stink but it could not wash away his bruises or his desert-tangled hair. Shimon shrank back. The stranger looked so much like one of the under-the-boat beggars, only he *moved* nothing like them. He took up a fish and wrapped it swiftly. His man's hands were free of rope burns and the straight scars that came of cuts from a slipped fish knife, but they were calloused and rough. He was a man who worked with his hands, then. Only not with fish. His feet were raw and scarred and bare, as though he had walked long on this shore or in the hills without sandals.

He looked . . . unclean.

The stranger reached for a second fish, and Shimon's breath hissed in through his teeth.

The stranger stopped. Hurt flashed in his eyes, but he concealed it quickly.

His own movements quick, tense, Shimon knotted a bit of cord about a sheaf of fish, baring his teeth against the storm of feathers about him.

"I'd like to help," the stranger said.

Shimon ignored him. The stranger watched as he bound a few more musht. The scent of the fish maddened Shimon's belly; he yearned to abandon the nets and gather up one armful of musht, just one, and run with them over the sand and through the grasses to the stone fishers' houses, to his mother and brother whom he'd often left ravenous, as his father never, ever had. He longed to cry out at the door for Rahel to light the firepit in the atrium. Or he might not even gather up that armful, might not even leave the shore; he might lift the fish raw to his teeth, even as he crouched here near the water.

The stranger reached again for a fish—with his bruised, unclean hands—and Shimon turned on him, his eyes fierce. "Stranger," he said.

The man crouched, very still. Watching him.

"Your accent," Shimon said roughly. "Are you half Greek? From Many Birds?"

"Natzeret. Both my parents are Hebrew."

Natzeret was a small town high on the hill on the road west, above the Greek colony city that the Hebrews called Tzippori, or Many Birds, because of the brightly feathered creatures that the Greeks had brought from many parts of the world to sing among the town's well-watered trees and marble pillars.

"Those bruises on your face, your arms . . . ?"

"Stoning," the stranger said.

"What?" Shimon shot him a look of horror. "What were you stoned for?" His voice was little more than a gasp. This man might be a killer, or a seducer of men's wives, a blasphemer, or a witch.

"I . . . I don't know." The stranger's eyes were full of raw pain and bewilderment.

That was hardly reassuring.

"I'm . . ." The man glanced down at the fish. "I'm having trouble, trouble remembering. There are all these rooms, these rooms in my mind. Some have people in them, people I've known, people I grew up with . . . mother, father, brothers, priests, and weavers. Children running and laughing and singing. And others are empty and cold, as though whoever was there packed and left and is not there anymore. And there is one roo—" He took a breath. "There is one room with a rug hung over the door, and that room burns with light and I can't see in." The man looked away. "Maybe that's where my . . . my missing memories are, Cephas."

Shimon swallowed. That was not the answer he'd expected. No sin confessed or evaded . . . only these mad words that made little sense.

The man gazed fixedly at nothing. Perhaps he was walking through that house in his mind, checking the empty rooms.

"The gulls," the stranger said. "And the tide. You don't have much time. May I help you?"

Shimon tossed three more fish into a sheaf, bound it, and muttered, "Why do you call me that?"

"Call you what?"

Shimon met his gaze, boldly, intending to stare him down. But the stranger's own gaze was intense, and for just a moment, Shimon thought he was gazing into a mirror, a dark mirror, where he saw the inside of his heart and the inside of his gut reflected, and everything he regretted and everything he'd given up. The stranger's gaze was direct and unguarded and piercing, uncaring that they were strangers and might share no kin, uncaring that they might be different.

It rattled him.

"Cephas," he muttered, trying to recover. "You keep calling me Cephas."

The stranger just looked at him.

"I am Shimon bar Yonah." The anger rose in his voice. "Everyone here knows my name and my father's. He was the greatest fisher on this sea. I am Shimon his son."

"I am Yeshua bar Yosef," he said, "and I *know* you. You are Cephas, the rock. We have met before. Or . . ." The man looked just past him, his eyes going cold and clear, as though he were gazing far out over the wooded ridges and high peaks of Ramat ha-Golan. ". . . Or we *will* meet. I know this," he whispered. "How do I know this? It's your voice, isn't it? I heard your voice . . . when I was in the desert. I am certain of it. It was your voice."

Shimon watched Yeshua out of the corner of his eye. The desert. If this ragged man had spent long nights out there, alone, in the wilderness of the Essenes, where the wind screamed almost without cease and the *shedim* moaned in their hundreds on neglected battlefields, what uncleanness might he have brought back with him or within him?

Yet, whatever his misgivings, the tide was coming in. The shrieking gulls were swooping low now in numbers that might be too much for Yakob's swinging of the oar to keep back. Shimon needed help, and quickly. "Fine," he said. "Whoever you are, help."

The stranger nodded and bent quickly to the work.

* * *

Other boats slid up onto the shingle, escaping the night hunger of the sea. Men leapt out, Mordecai and Natan El and others, bringing armfuls of lake-weed to use in wrapping the fish. Some ran to stand sentinel with Yakob, oars lifted in challenge to the screaming gulls. One—Natan El—began searching the shoreline for stones large enough for a cairn, to bury the corpse they'd dragged up. The water had destroyed the thing's face, and it was impossible to tell who that corpse had been, whose kin. No tomb for the waterlogged dead, only a pile of rock. Other such cairns stood at places along the shore, sun-bleached and stained with the leavings of gulls.

Some of the fishers joined Shimon and the stranger at their work, not speaking but gazing about at the heaps of fish with wild eyes. A few cast wary glances at the corpse where it lay lifeless on the sand and lifted their fingers in the sign against the evil eye.

Then, with a shout, Yohanna came running down toward the shore from the stone houses. Others ran beside him, women and old men carrying empty baskets. Glancing up, Shimon saw his mother Rahel, and Bar Cheleph with his bad hip. And, running behind, his gray hair wild in a gust of wind, Zebadyah the *kohen*, Kfar Nahum's priest.

"What has happened?" the *kohen* cried out against the wind. "What has happened?"

"Fish!" Yakob shouted, and swung his oar against a bird that had swept too low; the gull wheeled quickly out of the way. "Fish!"

"Fish!" Bar Cheleph cried.

"My son!" Rahel cried, and her eyes glistened. "Oh, my son!"

Yeshua looked up at her, and for a moment a sad smile transfigured his face.

Soon the sand and shingle was littered with baskets and lids and rolls of cloth and bits of cord, and half the town crouched with the sea lapping at their feet, working swiftly to gut the fish and bind them or basket them. Several women, their eyes shining, began carrying baskets and sheaves of musht in a line up the shore toward the stone houses. Bar Cheleph—whose limp seemed to be bothering him—hung back. Perhaps because Shimon glared at him. The younger man had beaten Shimon's brother once, and Shimon hadn't forgotten it. Yet his anger was not as strong as his guilt, for when he gazed at Koach with his useless arm, he saw what Bar Cheleph saw: a body twisted and unclean, a broken oar on a boat that needed all its oars. But Koach was his mother's last child, the last she would ever have. And no one would lift their hand against anyone his mother loved, not while he stood near.

Bar Cheleph moved down the shore a little way, gathering up bits of wood and other drift as if for a fire. As if he meant to begin roasting some of the fish *right here*. On the shore, this very morning. That changed Shimon's mood quick as a sea wind.

There hadn't been a fire for cooking fish on the shore since he had been a boy. Since before that night . . . He swallowed back some of the saliva filling his mouth, wiped sweat from his brow with the back of his hand. He felt suddenly faint.

The priest stood on the shore looking about with startled eyes. His gaze moved over the sand as though he were looking for the footprints of God, looking for some reason why this blessing had been visited on ruined Kfar Nahum so unexpectedly.

Then his gaze settled on the stranger. Yeshua had risen to his feet and stood over one of the baskets, lifting wrapped fish quickly into it.

"Who are you?" Zebadyah said bluntly, without any note of welcome.

"He is the one I told you of, abba," Yohanna said. "He says he called the fish."

"He has a mouth. He can speak." He raised his voice. "Who are you and who are your kin, beggar?"

Yeshua glanced up, his face still drawn with memory of pain. He opened his mouth as though to answer, but at that moment there was a cry from farther down the shore.

"Look! Look!"

They all swung about to look.

Some way to the south, a man was walking up the shore, coming toward them. That was strange, both because few walked beside the sea—most took their boats to move from one town to another—and because hardly anyone ever, *ever* came to Kfar Nahum.

But he did not walk like one of the boat people. He strode along that shore like one accustomed to long travel and unafraid of it, though not unwearied by it.

"Who *is* that?" Shimon murmured.

Yeshua straightened from the basket, and his shoulders lifted as though whatever pain he had brought with him was abruptly gone. He stood tall and still. His eyes had that intense, elsewhere gaze again, as though he were staring intently past them all at something only he could see. "I remember this," he whispered. "Father, I remember this. When the father needs a thing done, he calls us together, all of us, all those he needs." He shook his head slightly, as though in wonder. Then he cupped his hands to either side of his mouth and called out: "*Shalom!*"

The distant walker lifted his hand in response, and it was clear that he carried some object in it. He brought it to his face, and suddenly a loud blast rang out against the hills. A horn call, deep and resonant. Shimon could feel the call even in his bones.

"My God," he whispered.

Yakob and Yohanna both gazed at the far traveler without speaking, their faces struck with wonder.

Zebadyah scowled. "It can't be," he muttered.

After more than a year following the Roman-killer through the streets of the cities of their People and into wild places in the hills, Bar Nahemyah had come back.

PART 5

THE CARVED MAN

THE NEWCOMER strode with purpose up the shore. Yet his eyes held not just the fatigue of a man who has walked through the night along the sands, but the weariness of a man who has walked a year and found no place to rest in all that time. His shofar was still slung about his neck; he wore a tattered but heavy cloak, and his clothing was simple and plain though of southern weaving. His beard had grown long; his hair he wore in a braid down his back. Girded about his waist was a cracked leather scabbard the length of his forearm, from which protruded a hilt of polished bone. He carried a waterskin over his shoulder but no pack; he was lean, his face weathered, bitten by the wind and by the stress of things he wished he hadn't seen. He slowed his stride as he reached the men and women standing on the shingle, then stood with his hand lifted in greeting.

Zebadyah spoke first. "Dead have been coming up from the sea. What makes you think you are welcome here, Bar Nahemyah? You who gave our dead no burial?"

Bar Nahemyah's face tightened. He glanced past the priest. "*Shalom*, Bar Yonah."

"*Shalom*," Shimon said hoarsely.

Silence. Bar Nahemyah heard only the gulls' cries and the beating of the oars against feathered bodies. Men stood with fish in their right hands and baskets in their left. All eyes on this man who had saved their town and then destroyed it. This man who'd felled the corpses at the very door of the synagogue, saving the town's last men and women, and then filled the sea with their dead and dying. And who had, a year ago, been taken from them. And who hadn't come back. Like all the town's fathers, like God and Yonah and so many, Bar Nahemyah had abandoned them.

Here, facing his town . . . Bar Nahemyah felt unsettled. He didn't let it show in his face. But even as he and his town watched each other, the wind gusted and tore his cloak aside, baring his left arm. The men at the nets gasped. Zebadyah cried out. Bar Nahemyah braced himself but made no effort to conceal his arm. What they saw there had been dearly bought.

"What have you done?" the priest moaned. "Bar Nahemyah, what have you done?"

Nearly twenty fine scars, white against Bar Nahemyah's sundarkened skin, had been cut in parallel lines between his left shoulder and his elbow. They were too fine and too close a pattern to be wounds from a battle; anyone looking knew that they were a deliberate scarring of his flesh.

"You've defiled your body," Zebadyah said, his eyes dismayed.

"No." He let his voice ring with cold purpose. "This is a covenant. My body was marked when I was eight days old. That was a covenant with God. This is a covenant with the unclean dead. Nineteen of them I have put in the earth since leaving Kfar Nahum, and nineteen marks I bear in my flesh, to remember." His voice fell. "Though I don't think I could ever forget. I have seen Herod's ghoul pits."

The other men's faces went white.

Even in Kfar Nahum, it was known how the old Herod, that desert king hired by Rome to rule over an enslaved People, had grown old and mad. They had heard how he'd slain even his own kin. How he had filled the Roman baths in his palace with the dead, and thrown first his wife and then his own young daughter into the water to be devoured. How he'd sat on the steps of the baths, watching with tears on his face as his daughter was eaten. How at her shrieks, all the blossoms in Herod's gardens had withered. How he had sealed off the baths afterward with so many layers of stone that the wailing of the dead could no longer be heard. How he'd then sat in his bed reeking, unbathed, for the better part of a month, and anyone who came to him with reminders of affairs of state, he'd had put to death.

When Herod had been a young man, he had built great cities of marble on the coast, cities of Greek design and Roman public spirit, cities to rival any in the world. Caesar's City, and Yoppa rebuilt, and a new Temple in Yerushalayim, far greater in size and beauty than the Temple of the ancients, though this one had been built with unclean hands. The young Herod had sat in his gardens and sang poetry and made love to his wife beneath the stars. The older Herod had slaughtered all the children in Bet Lechem on a whim, and given his family to the dead to devour, because he believed they were plotting to poison or knife him in his sleep. When the moaning *shedim* creep into a man's ears and his mouth and into his heart, no one is safe.

Herod had been entombed for years, and his son, the new king, Herod Antipas, hid from nightmares of the brutalities he remembered, devoting the dark hours of his nights instead to endless revelry, to feasting and wine and the dancing of naked young women before his seat of white marble. But Antipas's bitterminded wife found the memory of Herod's bath useful; she'd had Greek stonemasons wall up the baths in Antipas's house, though she bid them open up the roofs to the sky. Corpses had been tossed in, and Herod's wife often had dissidents lowered down to them on long ropes.

Bar Nahemyah had seen a man, one of Barabba's, lowered into the stink and the dark, kicking his legs and screaming as the corpses below reached for him with long, grasping fingers.

He had seen *her* watching, standing at the edge of the wall. Herod's wife. Had seen the slight curving of her lip, and her eyes shining in the dusk.

He had turned away and covered his ears against the shrieks.

* * *

"I have seen," Bar Nahemyah repeated.

Zebadyah's voice was quieter now, less of a shout, yet thick with dread. "What deeds have you done since Barabba took you? Who have you killed, that you have fled back to us for refuge? Were you pursued? Have you led the Romans upon us?"

"Pursued, yes." His voice was cold. "But I lost them near the Hittim. I have no yearning to witness another night of fire and fear in my own town. No one has followed me, *kohen*." His gaze flicked back to Shimon, who had a desperate look in his face. "Yet the day . . . the last day, when we must rise with knives against Rome's living and its dead or die the slow death ourselves, that day is near. And I do ask you for your help."

"We have none to give," Shimon said.

"We have nothing to do with Barabba's knifemen, or with you," Zebadyah said.

"That isn't for you to say." Bar Nahemyah touched his fingertips to the ram's horn. "I still hold the shofar." The accusation was in his eyes: *coward.* Zebadyah's own eyes went dark with rage. But inside, Bar Nahemyah quailed. He had come back to his own town, his own place, and in their eyes—even in Shimon's eyes—he saw that he had come back like Barabba: stranger, killer, one outside the Law.

Turning away from the aging priest, he approached the gathered people on the shore and saw for the first time what they were gathered *about.* He sucked in a breath at the sight of that once human corpse the nets had brought up, weeds tangled about its legs. It had been dragged far above the advancing tide, with a mound of stones stacked beside it ready for burial. Near it stood a strange man with lank hair and a bruised face, his eyes watery but intense. He wore a brown robe that clung, soaked, to his body, as though he had walked up out of the sea. And all around him, the nets, *the nets,* the fish on the sand thick as pebbles in the hills.

For a moment he forgot his desperate journey and his dread at the corpse. He walked toward the fish, his mouth open. He couldn't understand it. Couldn't believe it. There were so many.

"The fish," he whispered.

"They've come back," Shimon said hoarsely. "Our fathers' fish have come back."

The pang of guilt and hope was sharp as a knife's twist in Bar Nahemyah's belly. "But the fish were gone. They were dead."

"Nothing's ever really dead," the strange man with the bruised face called out. He stared not at Bar Nahemyah or at the fish but up the shore at the derelict boats by the tall grasses at the tideline. "Not dead, not *really* dead, unless we let it be. I think that is so."

"I am Shimon bar Nahemyah. I do not know you. Who are you?"

"Everything comes back up," the stranger said. "Everything rises, everything rises, sun and rain and sun again, and all our dead, all our dead . . ." His voice fell until it was too quiet to hear.

"The town is beset," Zebadyah cried, "by madmen and heathen!"

"This isn't madness," Bar Nahemyah breathed. "It's prophecy. He's seeing visions." His heart beat a little faster—for he had heard something like this before, had heard holy ones in Yerushalayim city, men whom God had touched. He'd heard them talk in such a way on the Temple steps, while the alley stones behind echoed with the moans of the dead and with the hard footsteps of men in Roman armor. And now here, on this northern shore, he found a miracle of fish spilled across the sand out of some story of his fathers, and man who spoke like a *navi*. Hope lit like a heathen corpse-fire in Bar Nahemyah's heart, burning away decay and despair from his year in Barabba's caves.

"There are no more prophets," Zebadyah said, his tone bitter.

"Ha Matbil is a prophet," Yohanna said quickly.

"No!" The priest's eyes were fierce. "Enough with your Ha Matbil! El Shaddai preserve me, I have no use for sons or kin who follow killers or witches into the desert and leave the rest of us to mourn alone."

"I did not follow Barabba," Bar Nahemyah said quietly, not taking his gaze from the stranger. "I was taken."

"But you did not come back!" Shimon cried.

"Those," the stranger said suddenly, before Bar Nahemyah could reply, "those, those by the boats, who are they? Who are they?"

The stranger took a few slow steps up the sand toward the boats. Bar Nahemyah saw that a few men had emerged from those broken shelters and stood in the tall grasses, gazing down the shore at the fish, some of which still flopped on the sand. The men were ragged and gaunt, their faces gray from illness and lack of food.

"Scavengers, Yeshua bar Yosef," Shimon muttered.

"I don't understand," the stranger, Yeshua, said.

"They are boat people," Bar Nahemyah said. The sight of them there, a terrible reminder of the land's ruin, made Bar Nahemyah feel even more weary . . . and old.

"Other people's poor," Shimon said impatiently. "Other towns'. They come to us hungry like the dead, when there is already so little to eat."

"No," Yeshua whispered. He bent to lift a basket of fish and he nearly fell, but he caught himself, still muttering. "No one goes hungry, no one goes hungry, no one goes hungry, not this day, not this day, not this . . ." One arm around the basket, he took a step toward the old hulls.

"What are you doing?" Shimon cried.

At that moment several of the gulls swooped low, for Yakob and the others, listening, had let their oars fall still. One of the screaming birds flew at Yeshua's head while the others swooped at the basket he held. Yeshua's eyes went hot with anger and he shot his hand out against the bird and shouted, "Enough! *Enough!*"

A rush of heat nearly tumbled Bar Nahemyah from his feet, as though a fire had roared into existence. The gulls tumbled back, screaming and beating their wings, as though knocked aside by a hot wind. Yeshua straightened, one arm about the basket, the other outstretched and emitting heat. His eyes were fierce. His hair lifted, but not with the wind.

Another gull swooped low but veered away from his hand. Then *all* of them veered away, and in a moment they were gone across the water, wailing, gliding away on their white wings low over the waves.

There was silence on the sand.

Bar Nahemyah fell back, as though winded by what he had just witnessed. He stared at the stranger, at his wild eyes and his outstretched hand. The others stared also, standing as still as Lot's wife, translated from flesh to pillars of salt by something they should not have been allowed to see.

SITTING SHIVA

SHIMON BAR YONAH stared over the water after the gulls, his face still warm from that rush of heat. Hardly breathing, he glanced back at the stranger. Yeshua lowered his hand, and then his head, his hair falling over his eyes, lank and damp with lake water. He was panting, his hands clutching the basket now as though it might somehow keep him standing.

Zebadyah recovered himself first. "Witchcraft," he gasped. "This is witchcraft! The man has a demon. *Shedim.* Bar Yonah! Yohanna! Get away from him!" He stepped back. "Stones! Sons of Kfar Nahum, sons of Beth Tsaida, bring stones!"

"Wait!" Bar Nahemyah cried.

Yeshua began laughing, a quiet, desperate laughter that carried in the stillness left by the departing gulls. Zebadyah looked on in horror. "Stones," Yeshua said, shaking his head. "Stones. So I haven't left Natzeret after all. Stone me, stone me then. Suffer me not to live." Without looking at the priest, he turned and walked toward the derelict boats.

But the stranger still carried the basket of fish. *Shimon's* fish, fish to feed his town and kin. "What are you doing?" Shimon called after him, his heart beating in sudden alarm. When the stranger didn't answer, he cursed. "Yakob, Yohanna, get the rest of these fish up from the tide!"

He strode after the man from Natzeret, stumbling a little, the wind suddenly fierce at his back, threatening to knock him over onto his belly. He heard Rahel call out his name, and the priest also. He did not stop. The grasses at the tideline bent in waves before the sea wind. Behind him, a rush of talk and shouting as those on the shore demanded to know what was going on, who this stranger was, whether possessed or prophetic. He ignored them. He ignored them all, a sudden fire in his heart. No. This stranger was not going to invite *boat people* to eat his fish. Fish from his sea, his father's sea.

Bar Nahemyah ran up alongside him, and the town's two Shimons went striding up from the sea together, one with a shofar about his neck, the other with fishing gloves tucked into his coat.

"Who is he, this man?" Bar Nahemyah said quickly. "He who speaks like a holy one? He sent those gulls away as easily as a boy might throw a rock."

"I don't care who he is. I don't trust him." Shimon lifted his voice. "Bar Yosef! Those fish came into shore in my boat, my nets. Whatever wonder has been done here, these fish are to feed *my* family!"

But Yeshua didn't turn. Didn't answer. He just walked along the line of the boats with that basket. He seemed to have forgotten that he held it. He looked at the boat people, and his face grew haggard with grief. Shimon hurried after, his alarm louder within him. He tried not to look at the people by the boats, tried just to barrel after the stranger, but the horrors there were such that he could not keep his eyes averted. Nor could Bar Nahemyah.

There were men and women both among the splintering and rotting boats, some lying beneath them, some sitting against the sides of the old hulls. Few were entirely clothed. One woman lay on her back, her eyes lifeless though her breasts rose and fell with her breathing. Her cheeks were hollowed; her rags had been torn from her hips, leaving her legs naked and bruised. They lay apart, where probably one of the other vagrants, or many, had thrust them open; she had not closed them. Perhaps she had not moved for hours.

Shimon and Bar Nahemyah hurried past.

By the next boat, a naked man sat by a pile of broken bones, bones too long to be those of a gull or a crane or a goat of the hills. He lacked the gray look of the other boat people, his face flushed with color as though freshly fed, and his eyes glinted as he noticed Shimon. Shimon's body went cold; there was something in that man's eyes that he had never seen in a man's eyes before, and it made him fear. A fear of the gut, a fear of the hunted.

To those who slept and breathed and died beneath the boats, more emaciated even than he and his mother and brother, any flesh might be food, anything with meat and bone might be sustenance.

Yeshua bar Yosef stopped walking at last and, setting the basket down by his feet, he knelt by two women who sat listlessly against the hull of an overturned boat. One's face was drained of life, her eyes sunken, her breathing ragged. The other—barely more than a girl—watched the first. Her eyes were moist. She held a sharp rock in her hand, dried blood at its tip. She lifted it warily.

"Don't be afraid, *talitha*," Yeshua said softly.

Talitha. Aramaic for "little girl." As a man might call his daughter or his child-sister. The word and the tenderness in it struck Shimon. Why was he claiming kinship with her?

"I will not hurt her," Yeshua said. "I will not . . . not do that. I only want to help."

The girl just watched him silently.

The dying woman beside her stank of urine and sweat; Shimon and Bar Nahemyah hung back. But the stranger knelt by her as though he had no fear that she might touch him. The girl beside her took her hand and gripped it fiercely, and the woman lifted her head slightly and looked at Yeshua. Her face was so covered in grime that it was impossible to tell whether she was old or young, but the shape of her nose and the hue of her skin were Greek, not Hebrew, though the young woman beside her was one of the People. Shimon gazed at the dying woman in dread. She seemed barely human to him. There were footsteps soft in the grasses around them, and glancing up, he saw boat people standing on the other side of the derelict, staring at the basket of fish with desperate eyes. Bar Nahemyah curled his fingers around the hilt of his knife, and the gaunt men approached no nearer.

Yeshua reached for the woman. Her companion's breath hissed softly, but the girl did not move. Only watched him.

"Don't *touch* her, Bar Yosef!" Shimon cried.

"Why?" Yeshua's shoulders quivered. His eyes were dark again with that anger with which he had hurled the gulls out over the sea. "Because everyone else refuses to?"

He parted the woman's rags, baring her breasts and her ribs, which stood out in stark violence against her skin. Shimon drew back another step, and Bar Nahemyah closed his eyes as though against a sudden rush of memories.

"Oh," Yeshua whispered.

"We starve and die." The woman's voice was dry and slow, as though she rarely used it. Her eyes seemed out of focus. "They've been . . . eating the bodies. And the dead come up from the water. We are forgotten."

"You are not," Yeshua said, his voice hoarse with emotion. He covered her again with her rags. She made no move to help him or hinder him, as though her body were no longer a part of her, no longer her concern. Her hands lay beside her like wrinkled, dead things. The young woman who sat with her took her right hand and squeezed it, her face pale. She hadn't put down the sharp rock.

Yeshua watched the dying woman a moment, then seated himself beside her, not touching her, just sitting with her.

Beside Shimon, Bar Nahemyah whispered, "Bar Yonah, the women of our People all look that way, in the alleys of Yerushalayim, the city of our fathers. So many women leaning against walls, breathing, barely alive. Starving. Our own People. They look just like her. And they will go on looking that way until we shove the Romans into the sea."

"We've shoved enough into the sea," Shimon said bitterly, thinking of that terrible, beached corpse. He bent slowly and lifted the basket of fish. He could take it back down to the shore, get away from these starving beggars. The other boat people watched him. Yet he hesitated. Beside him, Bar Nahemyah stepped back and leaned against another boat. Shimon gazed at the woman, unable to look away. She was covered in her rags now, but the sight of her ribs seemed burned into his mind. It was his own nightmare: that the sea might one year yield no fish at all, until his mother and his useless brother were only skin stretched over bone, like this woman.

"Bar Yosef," he whispered.

Yeshua did not look up.

"Bar Yosef, she is not of the People."

No answer.

"Are you going to just sit there?"

Yeshua took a slow breath. "I am in pain, Cephas."

Shimon looked at him, startled.

"Great pain. Not just these . . ." He touched a bruise on his arm and winced. "This," he said, lifting his fingers to his right ear. "It doesn't matter if I wake or if I sleep. Always, always I hear screaming. You and your fathers and your sons yet unborn, all of you screaming, all of you . . . hurting. Sometimes it is so bad I can only stand, stand completely still, like a . . . like a rock, Cephas, like a rock, for hours and hours and hours." His hands began to shake. "And I don't know why, why none of you hear it, why not one of you hears it, why only I, only I am alone, I and the father and the father weeping in the desert. In the . . . She is screaming, this woman here, screaming, both of them, and no one hears. No one hears," he whispered. "If I can comfort just her, just one of you, just *one*, maybe it will stop, maybe the screaming will finally stop."

"She's only a boat woman," Shimon said. His voice subdued.

"What does it matter," Yeshua said wearily. "The father made her and I heard him, I heard him, Cephas, weeping in the desert, and you cannot tell me, you cannot, that he doesn't care. You cannot tell me that." He lifted his face, and his eyes were bloodshot. "I have hungered and thirsted out in the desert, and I have been driven by stones, and I have been alone. So alone. No one should ever, ever be alone, Cephas. She doesn't have to die alone."

Yeshua lowered his head. All around him, Shimon could hear the boat people whispering, "Fish, fish . . ." Shimon clenched his teeth. But Yeshua said nothing more. He was sitting *shiva* with that woman. Sitting in silence, mourning her own death with her.

The woman's breath rasped. Shimon realized she didn't have long, and this *shiva* would be short. He shook his head and stepped away, taking the basket with him. He would not stay to watch her die—that would be too much like his nightmares—and he would leave this man to his madness. There were fish to gut, to fry, to eat and store. A long day. Yet as he walked back down the line of boats with the gaze of the boat people on his back, guilt sat heavy in his chest.

Why should he feel that? These were not his kin.

When he'd been a child and the fish were plentiful and the boat people less near to starvation, some of the fishers had made a custom of tossing a few glistening musht out of their boats onto the sand as they came in to shore. Seeing the beggars fight over the few small fish, some of the fishers had laughed. Still others tossed none at all, but fended the vagrants away from their nets, with the blunt ends of fishing spears if need be.

His father had been one of those.

Shimon's belly growled, and he glanced down at the fish, some of them still opening and closing their mouths. Some of them motionless. The scent of them. His hunger woke like a beast within him. He shuddered; perhaps the whole town was turning into boat people.

He reached the last of the derelicts and leaned against it, breathing hard. He closed his eyes a moment but opened them immediately because in that brief darkness, he'd seen dead faces rising from the water again, dead fingers reaching to grasp him.

Shimon gave the boat a hard kick, needing some way to assuage the storm within him. The long-disused hull gave a little before his foot, and there was a startled cry from under the boat.

Shimon froze.

"Who is that?" he shouted.

This time there was no cry, no sound even of soft breathing. No one slipped out through the tight gap between the gunwale of the tipped boat and the ground.

"Come out!" Shimon dropped the basket to the grass at his feet. "I know it's you."

Again, no answer.

Shimon took the gunwale in his hands and lifted, gasping at the strain. For a moment the boat didn't move, but then he managed to heave it slowly up and tip it, letting it fall back onto its keel with a crash that brought cries from a few of the boat people behind him.

The young man beneath the boat . . . was Koach.

SHIMON'S BROTHER

KOACH HAD BEGUN to dream of horses.

Even now there was a bulge in the left side of his shirt, where his mother had sewn for him that hidden inner pocket. He had concealed a wood-carving there, small enough to hold in his palm. A horse, strong and sleek as Barabba's, carved of cedar. He had dreamed sometimes of Barabba's stern face and the flashing hooves of his steed, but he had also dreamed of the scene Tamar had told him of: Barabba riding furiously from their town, his horse faster than wind or bird. A horse might carry him away from here, he and Tamar together, to some place that did not hate them.

Often, he rode horses in his dreams.

* * *

He had taken to visiting the boats on the shore where they were harbored by day. He studied how they were made, and learned which ones were damaged, which ones had fittings that had cracked or were under strain. He spent weeks at this, climbing beneath the overturned boats and reaching up and learning with his fingers. He went early and returned early, feeling his mother's eyes on him as he left the house and fearful of being caught by the town's other youths, now that Bar Nahemyah had been swept away from the town.

He began carving fittings for boats, leaving them, one at a time, on the doorstep of the *nagar*'s shop attached to Benayahu's house. He did this many times. One day, as he approached the door, Benayahu opened it and gave Koach a hard look, then glanced at the fitting Koach held.

"You have a skilled hand."

Koach sucked in his breath and tensed to run, fearing the man's anger at his presumption and his gift, already feeling the blows to come. Benayahu stood in the door a moment more, his silence full with thought. Then he turned and went inside, leaving the door open. An invitation, or a reprieve. Koach wondered which. He gathered what courage he could, then strode to the door and ducked into the shop, into a dim interior rich with the smell of cedar curing.

Benayahu was there, smoothing a long plank by the flickering light of an oil lamp. The shop had a window but it was boarded up so tightly that barely even a chink of sun made it through. He was a man who had lost too much to the dead.

He didn't look up to acknowledge Koach, but with his foot he slid a block of wood and a knife across the floor toward him.

For several beats of his heart, Koach was all but overwhelmed with an urge to take Benayahu's hammer in his one hand and drive it into the man's brow, such was his fury at this man who left bruises on Tamar's body. The man had turned his back to Koach, bent over his work.

Koach forced himself to breathe calmly. He was here to be near Tamar, to find some way to help her. Striking her father and getting himself stoned would not help. His face hard, Koach sat on the floor. He set the block between his knees and got to work.

* * *

From that day, Koach had assisted Benayahu with his carpentry. He had found a use at last, a wall to build between himself and the name Hebel. And he was good at it. He didn't know how many fishermen in the town realized it, but within the year his craftsmanship had appeared on half the boats on their shore.

Benayahu was a strange man, silent and moody like Koach's own brother, his eyes often dark with guilt and violence barely restrained. He rarely said a word, just gestured to show what he wanted Koach to do. Sometimes he took a tool out of Koach's hand, without touching him, and showed Koach how to use it correctly. There was no affection in his face at those times, only a cold determination. The man had no son, and no other apprentices in his shop. Except for his daughter, he lived alone, and he must have lived with the certainty that when he died, his skill would die with him.

Sometimes, after he put his tools away, the aging *nagar* went to stand by one wall of the shop, where thick Hebrew letters had been carved into the stone. It was a name, a woman's. The *nagar* would just stare at the letters. Then he would turn and pass through the inner door into his house, leaving Koach in the shop. The lock would slide shut with a hard, bronze clack. Koach would stand there, his hand clenched, shaking with helpless anger. Because those were the evenings that ended with Tamar being beaten.

* * *

At first, Koach tried to think of some way to speak with Benayahu about his daughter, but he could not find that way. He had also hoped for a chance to speak with Tamar herself, but he caught few glimpses of her by day. The door between the shop and the house was kept shut, and Benayahu did not invite him in. Nor did the man leave his shop; each day he brought a waterskin in with him before Koach even arrived. Once, only once, Koach glanced up to see the door open the smallest crack, and Tamar peering in at him. In the next moment, Benayahu struck the side of his head. Tamar's eyes widened and she shut the door swiftly.

"Look at my daughter again and I'll throw you in the sea with the dead, *hebel* boy," the *nagar* said, his voice quiet and cold. Those were almost the only words he had spoken to Koach since the first day.

Koach lowered his head, nodded. He unclenched his left hand, rage hot in his heart. His face ringing.

* * *

The beatings had become worse, so that some nights Tamar did not come to the rooftop but only lay shaking in her bedding in the atrium, where Koach could barely see her.

They could not shout to each other from rooftop to rooftop, but over the nights of that year, they made for each other a secret language of signs and gestures, and with movements of their hands they sang silently to each other of love and need. His need to be useful to one other person, to be *loved* by one other. Her need to be free of her father's house. A hand pressed to the breast meant: *My heart. You touch my heart.* A flapping motion with one hand meant: *How I wish we might fly away like birds.* Fingers pressed to the lips meant: *I wish you could kiss me.*

Having found no way to speak to her father, Koach began to dream, by night and by day, of carrying her away from that house, as Samson or some mighty one of centuries past would have done. But he was not Samson, nor mighty; his very name was a lie.

By day in the shop, he'd glance down at the fittings he was carving, his thoughts feverishly intense. He lacked strength, but he had skill. The *nagar* had seen that; others might also. There were Greek towns across the sea where there was no Law and no priest. He didn't know how the Greeks would look on a cripple, but surely they needed skilled woodworkers. If Tamar would fly away with him, perhaps there was some place, somewhere he could carry her to.

At last, a night came when he stood on his roof, shrugged the concealing wool from his shoulders, and, gazing across at her body, beautiful as the curve of the moon, and at her eyes that were so strangely calm after her pain, he decided he would tell her what he intended to do.

They would meet by the boats, but they would go on foot, the long walk around the shore. He couldn't row a boat, and the town had no horses.

THE BOAT PEOPLE

THE BOAT TIPPED and the sky opened hot and blue above him. Koach blinked up at his brother's face.

"What are you doing here?" There was nothing polite in Shimon's voice, and something in Koach hardened when he saw the contempt and frustration in his brother's face.

Koach was lying in the sand beneath the boat, wrapped in a heavy water-coat that had been their father's. Rahel had woven Shimon his own coat for the cold nights on the sea and had given this one to Koach, the only protection he had from his dead father. But it was too large for him, and often he felt small and childlike in it.

Koach rose, an ungainly move that involved pushing himself up with his good, left arm and then hopping to his feet.

"I'll go home." He couldn't keep the bitterness from his voice.

"Why are you out here?" Shimon said again.

"I was waiting." He didn't meet Shimon's eyes, concealing the wound in his heart.

He had slipped down to the boats after dark, after his brother had gone out to sea and his mother had given herself to sleep. He had waited, and *waited*, until the day crept beneath the gunwale of the overturned boat and it was too late to slip quietly back. Then he could only lie there while gulls called somewhere above the wooden roof of the boat's keel, their lonely, forlorn cries giving voice to the fears of his heart. And when the shore had echoed with the startled shouts of the town's men, he had lain still and silent beneath the boat, touched by no curiosity.

She hadn't come to him.

Perhaps she'd realized that the young man she'd been dreaming with could never cast a net for her, never catch fish, never bring home food for the fire.

Now he'd been discovered, and his face was dark with shame. A boy with no *bar 'onshin*, no betrothed, with dreams he hadn't earned. A boy who had thought, for one year of longing and desperation, that he could be a man.

"Waiting for what?" Shimon demanded, towering over him, as he always did.

The look Koach turned on him was resentful. "What do you care?" Koach cried.

"*You.*" Shimon started to step away but then turned back, every line in his body tense.

"Bar Yonah," a quiet voice said, and with a shock, Koach recognized Bar Nahemyah—Bar Nahemyah who'd been gone so long— walking toward them through the boats.

"Stay out of this," Shimon said. To Koach he said, his voice quiet and cold, "Every night I risk my life and my neck for you, to feed you, and I cannot even keep you safe in my own house! Get out of here. You shouldn't be here. *Raca*—you have never been anything but a dead weight, something I have to look after, house, clothe, protect—and you give *nothing* back. There's no place for you here, among the boats. Run home."

Koach couldn't bear to see any more of that old disappointment in his brother's eyes. As he backed away, he saw the stranger rise to his feet, a few boats down, a look of pain in his bruised face. Slouched against the hull behind him sat a woman as gray as a corpse and a young woman beside her, her shoulders shaking. Koach stared at the girl; she was weeping without sound, the way Tamar did.

"You're always ashamed of me," Koach said. He didn't look at his brother. He just blinked quickly and then walked away from them all. He heard his brother call his name.

"Give him a moment, Bar Yonah." Bar Nahemyah's voice.

Koach walked on unchallenged until he was a little way up into the tall tideline grasses, pale blades that brushed his cheeks in the chill wind.

He was not crying.

He didn't cry anymore.

This moisture on his face was only drops of the sea carried to him by the wind.

Only that.

For a while he gazed bleakly at the cracking, battered houses ahead. He could walk up there now, to Benayahu's shop, as on any other day. He could pretend nothing had happened, draw his shame about him like a coat, growing smaller and smaller inside it. Or he could stand at the door of the house and call for her. But that would shame and endanger her, and himself. And what could she say, what could she tell him that he didn't already know?

The voices behind him grew louder, more heated. "Your brother," the stranger was shouting. "That was your brother, your brother, your own brother. And you call him *hebel* and *raca*? How can you . . . how can you do that? My own brothers . . . my own . . ." His voice choked, and it took him a moment to speak again. "What is *wrong* with you? Do you even know how blessed, how blessed you are, that you *have* a brother, you have kin in your own house, your own roof, people who sit with you to eat . . ."

Koach glanced over his shoulder, saw the stranger gesture wildly toward the shore. Following the gesture, Koach realized for the first time what was happening there. He walked back through the grasses, aghast. All those fish. All those nets spilled open on the sand. All those *people*, the fishers' wives and their older kin and even a few from Kfar Nahum itself, men who worked in small shops and not in boats. All of them gathering up the fish. Koach stared down at that crowd of baskets and bins, speechless.

"None of you stand *near* each other," the stranger was shouting as Koach approached, "not even brothers! And all your boats . . . all your boats on the water, none of them calling out to the others. Just silence, that silence over the water . . ."

Koach listened. The aloneness in the stranger's voice was familiar to him.

"If you were one of us," Shimon said, "you'd understand—"

"I *want* to understand!"

"—but you aren't one of us."

"I know!" the stranger cried. "I am unhomed! They threw me out. I came back from the desert and told them what I'd heard, *what I'd heard*, what I still hear, what I keep hearing, and what woke me weeping in the night, the truth, the truth, I told them the truth, and they threw me out." The stranger's voice was quiet and nearly choked with pain, yet his words carried. "And I ran, Cephas. I ran. All the way here. And I am exhausted and I am hungry and I am afraid . . ."

He was interrupted by a loud, prolonged rasp, something unlike any other sound Koach had ever heard. An alarming sound. He turned to look. It was the woman with the gray face, the woman sitting against the cracked and beaten hull. Her breast fell once more and then did not rise. Koach saw the light leave her eyes. One moment her eyes were those of a living woman. The next, they were empty. It was like looking to see your reflection in a bowl that has no water in it, no mirror.

She was gone.

The wind in the grass.

The stranger gazed at her body with horror. "No," he whispered.

Even Shimon seemed shaken, as though the *malakh ha-mavet*, the angel of death, had brushed his shoulder as it passed.

"No." The stranger went pale. "I told her she didn't need to die alone."

Shimon murmured, "Yeshua bar Yosef . . ."

"No," Yeshua cried. "No! All of you screaming and screaming and screaming *and none of you hearing*! Do not *talk* to me, Cephas! Just do something about it! Please!"

The stranger bent and lifted the basket of fish from the sand, and thrust it into Shimon's arms. The broad-shouldered fisherman staggered back until he caught his balance.

"*Help* me," the stranger pleaded.

"Bar Yosef, our own families starve."

"No, no one will . . . no one will starve, no one. There will be so *many* fish." He sounded as though tears might come. "*Please*, Cephas. Feed these women and these men, Hebrew or Greek or whatever you see, just *feed them*. Please."

The man backed away, his face still stricken with horror. Then he turned and all but ran through the grasses, away from the boats, his pace desperate, the wind tearing at his hair.

"Wait!" Bar Nahemyah called. He ran after the stranger.

Shimon stood shaken, staring after them, still holding the basket. As though the woman's death rasp was still too loud in his ears, in his heart. Koach could see the horrified recognition in his brother's eyes: The boat people weren't supposed to be like *that*. Like people. Like men and women who might weep for each other and then die hungry and alone.

Shimon exhaled slowly. "You and I, we will talk later," he muttered, then walked slowly away down the line of boats, the basket in his hands, with some of the boat people shuffling after him or stumbling to their feet as he neared them.

* * *

With his brother gone, Koach only felt empty. He was *hebel* again, useless as a bit of a driftwood washed up among these grasses.

Numbly, he approached the two women, one alive, one dead. The younger woman glanced up at his approach with grieving, tired eyes. A sharpened rock slipped from her hand to the sandy dirt, as though she simply didn't care anymore. Her face was wet with tears, but her crying was silent and she barely trembled with it. After a moment, she leaned her head on the dead woman's shoulder.

Here was yet another person who was entirely alone, with none to comfort her in her suffering. Another outcast, like himself. Like Tamar.

Without thinking about it, he shrugged off his father's coat. One-handed, he draped it clumsily about the woman's shoulders, then patted it down. His brother would likely be furious at this use of the coat, but Koach didn't care. He took the woman's arm and tried to lift her to her feet. After a moment, she stood, letting him help her. Some of her hair fell across her face, dirty and tangled. She kept her eyes lowered.

"What's your name?" Koach asked softly.

She shook her head weakly.

He frowned. "I am Koach bar Yonah."

She touched her fingertips to her throat in response. The sound she made was caught somewhere between a grunt and an exhalation.

"You can't speak," Koach whispered. He felt a small thrill of fear. Zebadyah the priest taught that when a man or a woman could not speak, it was because the *shedim* had slipped down their throat into their body, and they could only moan, or make no sound at all, like the dead that walked. But this young woman did not seem that way to Koach. She seemed small, and frightened, and so stricken with hunger and grief that she could hardly stand. And she had remained by her dying friend, so she loved.

Koach tried to think of some comfort for her. He glanced down at the corpse. "The priest will make sure there's a cairn for her. He won't leave her unburied . . ." He trailed off; the woman was still keeping her face hidden, and he realized that it must be terrible for her that her grief was this naked. He considered leaving her there, but his cheeks darkened with shame. He had left Tamar in her father's home for a year, not knowing what to do, and she was still trapped there. He couldn't leave this woman alone in her anguish, too.

He glanced down the shore, and caught his breath. For a moment he just stood with the woman beside him, staring down at all the people from the town and all the fish being gathered into baskets. Some men were dragging boats up toward him, and a few were settling logs of driftwood over small, improvised firepits far above the incoming tide. Bar Cheleph sat at the nearest fire, but Koach didn't even shiver at the sight of the man who'd once beaten him into the grass. He was too swept away by the sight of all those fish and all those people. A gust of wind brought the scent to him, and hunger groaned violent in his belly. He saw the stranger his brother had been talking with striding out now along the shore with Bar Nahemyah following him. He saw his mother walking among the firepits, pausing to speak with the town's other women. He saw Yesse, the priest's crippled father, seated by the nets, lifting fish in his hands and shaking his head. Yesse was *hebel*, too, but was allowed to be, because he was old and had served his tribe for many years. Someone must have carried him out to the sands.

Koach's eyes stung with moisture. His own grief seemed suddenly small. The fish had come back.

"Come on," he said, gripping the woman's arm. He could feel the warmth of her body through the sleeve of his father's coat. "I'll get you to a fire."

The woman cast him a quick glance before lowering her face again. Her eyes, shining with tears, were Hebrew.

Koach helped her down from the grasses onto the shore, her steps small and uncertain. Sand fleas darted from beneath their feet. She was shaking.

"It will be all right," Koach whispered. "It will be all right."

* * *

Afterward, Shimon could never explain how he came to be walking among the derelict boats with a basket of fish. Yeshua bar Yosef had spoken with such anguish and anger that there had seemed no choice but to respond. Now Shimon moved with quick steps along the boats, tossing fish into the sand. Everything inside him rushed about, as though the stranger had let the wind into his body the way a man might let wind into a house.

He heard the priest's rough voice.

"What are you doing, Bar Yonah?"

Zebadyah stepped between him and the ncxt buat, pointing a gnarled finger at the basket of fish. His eyes were cold. "These," he said, "do not eat with us. They do not grieve with us. They mutter Greek prayers by our sea; they take our food. Sometimes they come up in the night and reach into unboarded windows, or tap at our doors. You know this. What are you *doing?*"

The windows of the house of Shimon's heart clacked shut, and rage boiled within like trapped summer heat. At this moment, he saw no kinship to his father in the priest's face. Zebadyah bar Yesse seemed old, shrunken, his fingers crooked and curled as though he were fighting to grasp sand. And this man, this weak, frightened man, who had once dared to strike his mother, now dared tell him how he should manage his nets.

"I am Shimon bar Yonah," he said. "I do what I please. This is my father's town. That is my father's boat. These are my father's fish." His voice hardened. "You . . . are not my father. Get out of my way."

Zebadyah's face flushed as though he'd been struck. He took a step back. "Shimon . . ."

"Get out of my way, old man," he said.

"Ezra," Zebadyah said hoarsely. "Remember Ezra. I tremble, Bar Yonah. There are fish, but all this can be taken away in a few beats of the heart. The waters wear away the stones. You are Yonah's son, and the town will look to *you*. Do not listen to that witch!"

Shimon shoved by the priest and walked on, ignoring everything but the blood in his ears and the rage in his heart. Finally, he threw the basket into the sand by one of the vagrants in disgust and turned away as the emaciated man reached into the basket with terribly thin hands. Shimon stumbled to the last boat in the line, a boat with its hull stove in and no one sheltering beneath it. He sat down against it, closing his eyes. He could hear his own heartbeat. He breathed raggedly. The sun was growing hotter in the sky, and the insides of his eyelids were red and bright.

After a while he smelled fried musht and felt a cool cloth pressed to his head. "I brought you a musht." It was Yohanna's voice.

He opened his eyes against a blaze of light and then shaded them with his hand, wincing. He could hear the smacking of lips and the moans of the boat people all around him, as the fish both filled and tormented their long-empty bellies. Yohanna was crouching beside him. He handed Shimon the cloth, then passed him a sheaf that had one musht in it.

Yohanna smiled faintly. "They're cooking these, down by the water."

Shimon took it, felt the heat against his hand through the lake-weed. The fish must have just been lifted from the coals and wrapped moments before. His belly snarled within him as all of his hunger woke. He lifted the fish to his mouth, tore into the hot flesh with his teeth. It burned his lips.

He didn't talk until he'd finished the fish, and Yohanna just crouched nearby, watching his face.

"I spoke harshly to your father," Shimon said.

"I know." Yohanna took a slow breath. "He can be a hard man to speak with."

Shimon grunted.

After a silence, he said, "That man. What is wrong with him? He treats the boat people like they are his kin."

Yohanna's eyes widened. "Kin," he whispered. "'We are all kin.' God of Hosts, Shimon. That's where I've seen him. I *knew* I'd seen him."

He frowned. "What are you talking about?"

"The stranger. I saw him once. With Ha Matbil."

SCREAMING IN THE DESERT

YESHUA PACED the edge of the tide, heading up the shore away from the nets and the people gathered about them. His shoulders were tense, his eyes dark. The wind tugged his hair across his bruised face. The bruises did not bother Bar Nahemyah; he'd seen enough men stoned in the south to know that a man finds rocks hurled at him not when he offends God but when he offends other men.

Yeshua had a long, restless stride, and Bar Nahemyah had to strain to keep pace with the man.

"I let her die alone. I shouldn't have let her die like that. How could I let her die like that?" Yeshua stopped to look out over the water, but his tone was as restless and haunted as his stride had been. "I heard this town's hunger in the night, I heard it. I heard all of you. Night and day and night again in the desert. And the father . . . I heard the father weeping, weeping for you." He glanced at his hands, his face raw with grief. "I cried out, and the fish . . . but for what? You are still screaming."

Visions. The man was having visions. Bar Nahemyah trembled. Since the night of Ahava's death, the night he'd held his beloved's body shattered and bloodied in his arms, Bar Nahemyah's yearning for a navi, a messiah to save their ravened land, had hardened into cold steel within him. Now that steel was desperate and strong. The yearning for one who would be another Makkaba, riding against those who wounded their People, but who would be a *navi* also, one who saw visions in the desert or struck water from a rock. Some God-sent mighty one out of the stories of his fathers.

Barabba had not been that man.

"The fish and the birds heed you," Bar Nahemyah called to Yeshua. "You are the *navi*, aren't you?"

The stranger turned. "You think I'm a prophet, Zebadyah thinks I'm a witch." Bar Nahemyah forced himself not to look away from the intensity in his gaze. "You should worry less about what I am," Yeshua said, "and more about what I will do." He glanced back toward the nets. "What can't I remember?" He paused. For a few heartbeats, there was only the sigh of the water and the distant calls of the banished gulls. "Those corpses in the water. I can hear them even now. How did they get there?"

"The Romans—"

"The Romans." Yeshua's face tightened. "The Romans! The Romans didn't starve those women by the boats. The Romans didn't throw those dead in the sea and forget them."

"No." Guilt settled cold and heavy in his belly. "I did that."

Yeshua stopped and looked at him. Bar Nahemyah found his voice suddenly hoarse. "Help me make amends, *navi*. Israel is unclean. I would cut the rot out of its body. Barabba would cut off the whole limb, but that cannot be the way. You . . . you *care*. For every one of our People, even those under the boats. I saw that." Quietly, he knelt in the sand.

"No." Yeshua's voice was choked. "You mistake me for the Makkaba, or for your Outlaw. I don't know what I am. I don't know, I don't know, but I am not that."

Bar Nahemyah lifted his head, and he felt the first twinge of doubt. But he was on his knees, the hope in him too sharp to permit any turning back. "Place your hand on my head, *navi*. I will be the first to follow you. Say one word, but one word, and I will lift this shofar to my lips and sound a blast that every Roman in our land will hear. Don't you have eyes to see? Ears to hear? You said you have heard the screaming of our People!"

"I have heard." The pain in his eyes was terrible to see. "I hear them even now. Even now. The part of me that grew up a child in my father's house suffers exile. The part of me that walked out of the desert suffers the exile of all men and women, living and dead." He paused. "I have to get through the door. Where I have to go, what I have to do, it is on the other side of that door. That burning door. That burning, burning, burning . . ."

Bar Nahemyah gasped.

Yeshua's hands and face appeared to blaze with light. Bar Nahemyah felt the heat of it on his own skin, as though he were in the presence of mighty Eliya himself, who had burned the heathen priests from the land and summoned chariots of flame. His hands shook.

Then the heat and the light were gone.

Yeshua lowered himself to the sand and sat with his arms about his knees, his face stricken. "Can't step through," he whispered.

Bar Nahemyah was shocked to see tears on the man's face.

"Please," he said. "I know you are hearing what God hears. That is what the *navi* does. And it terrifies you, and it *should*. I understand your anguish. The things I have seen, *navi*. Things that make me want to cut out my eyes. I have seen Roman eagles on the walls of the Temple, on the walls of the *lev ha-olam*, the heart of the world. Children sitting with their backs to its gate with their ribs showing. I have seen Herod Antipas's hired dogs arrest craftsmen who couldn't pay their last coin to Caesar, and have them tossed into pits of the dead to be eaten. I saw a woman crawl to Barabba's feet and die there in the dust after pleading with him to free our land. She died . . ." He swallowed. "She died from bleeding to death, *navi*. She died because those desert men the Romans hire to do their killing when they've wearied of it had cut away her breasts. They cut out her sheath, then her tongue. And when she begged for help, she could do so only with her eyes.

"That was a Hebrew woman. That was one of my tribe. I saw her and others, strong men and weak, die begging God to send a *navi*, a messiah. I saw—" Bar Nahemyah choked a little. His voice went hoarse. "The earth is drenched in the blood of our People. *Our* People, ground into the dirt by Roman heels. Our wounded, screaming People."

Yeshua looked up at him wearily. "If you think to add more screaming, you are no son of Abraham nor of our father who watches us from above. You are someone else's son, not his." An edge of anger in his voice. "This land has always been taken in violence, but it has . . . it has never been held so. Our fathers did not hold and keep this land safe by violence against either the living or the dead, but by the Law."

"The Law!" Bar Nahemyah cried. He would *not* let this man hide, like Zebadyah, behind the Law. "The Law says a man may take an eye for an eye!"

"What will you do, Kana," Yeshua said slowly, "when you and the Romans have no eyes left?"

Kana.

Bar Nahemyah stopped, watching the man, holding the name in his mind.

"Kana," he breathed. The Hebrew word for *zealous*. "Kana. I will take that name."

"I think it is your name already," Yeshua said. "But put away this thirst for death, put it away, please; death will find us all soon enough."

"I don't understand you," Kana cried. "Are you a coward? Do you want us, all of us, all Hebrew men, to stand with our knives sheathed while Romans walk by and strike us across our faces, knock us to the dirt and take what they will? And you . . . you who hear . . . whatever it is you hear . . . you who speak with a voice of . . . of prophecy . . . what will you do? With your baskets of fish? What, will you feed men in the morning who will be dead by evening?"

"I . . . I don't know what the dusk will bring." Yeshua brushed the bruises on his arm with his fingertips. "I don't know. Only the father knows that."

THE SILENT WOMAN

WITH THE WOMAN from the boats leaning hard on him, Koach approached the small fire Bar Cheleph had kindled in the sand near the tideline. He had dragged driftwood and weeds and grasses to toss into it, and now sat solitary on a log and dug out a few hot coals with a stick to make a smaller firepit, one for cooking. A basket of fish waited in the sand by his hip.

When Koach seated the silent woman across the firepit from him, Bar Cheleph said without looking up: "I made this fire, Hebel.

Find another." "You can't hit me, Bar Cheleph." There was no quiver in his voice. "Not here, where my brother and kin can see."

Bar Cheleph bared his teeth at Koach, but said nothing. He began laying the fish across the coals.

At the scent of the fish roasting, oils bubbling out from the slit in their gullets, Koach's mouth watered. The silent woman, too, stared at the fish.

"You hide behind Shimon bar Yonah as though you are his woman," Bar Cheleph said in a low voice.

Koach bit back his anger and took up a small stick, stabbing one of the fish. Letting out his breath slowly, he turned and lifted the fish to the woman's lips. Her eyes, still reddened from weeping, glanced at him gratefully as she bit in. Koach found the sight sensual, and disquieting: her head leaning forward, her small teeth cutting into the fish, her gaze lifted to his. He was suddenly aware of the woman's body beneath his father's coat, her curves. He swallowed.

She stared back at him a long moment before lowering her eyes. He took a breath. Shaken, he understood. Bereft of her last companion, hungry and alone, she was offering herself for the assurance of food. In the next moment she must have glimpsed his awareness of this, for her eyes dilated briefly—with fear, not with desire.

"You don't have to do that," he said, his throat dry. "The fish is a gift."

The fear in her eyes grew. Perhaps she had never been offered a gift before. Not being able to offer something herself, not knowing what he might want in return, or whether it would be something she had to give—this had to be terrifying to her.

Koach saw all that in her eyes, in one of those flashes of insight that very young men sometimes have.

"No," he said again. "I just want to see you eat."

Bar Cheleph grunted. "Take her up the shore and rut with her, Hebel. Might be the only woman you ever get. That is"—he smiled, his eyes cold—"if you *can* rut."

On any other day, Koach would have fallen silent and hung his head. But not this day. He rose to his feet, his good fist clenched at his side. All the fury and helplessness of the past year—of his whole life—rushed up at once, like a wave of the sea driving a boat before it. "My hand makes fittings," he shouted. "Fittings for the boats! So that they can get out on the water. So that the town won't starve. I am *useful*! What do *your* hands do?"

For a moment, Bar Cheleph kept his eyes on the coals. His face tightened, and Koach knew his words had cut deep, too. Bar Cheleph worked hard at mending nets, always worked hard at them, because his right hip didn't work the way it should, not since that Roman officer had thrown a hard cedar desk onto him in his rushed escape from the dead. Bar Cheleph could not stand easily in a boat, and he did not go out with his adopted brothers and Shimon to wrestle with the sea. Yet his arms were thick with muscle, and he had succeeded in not being *hebel*. Barely.

Now Bar Cheleph looked up, and his eyes were hot with hate. For a moment Koach was sure he meant to stand and strike him. He tensed. Then there was a footstep behind him, and a new voice, a sharp voice: "Will you always trouble my sons, Bar Cheleph?"

Koach glanced up as Bar Cheleph whirled.

Rahel stood behind him, leaning on a stick she'd plucked up from the sand, her eyes cold as winter.

Bar Cheleph's face darkened, even as Koach felt a rush of shame. Was he so *hebel* that he needed his mother to protect him?

"You've made the fire," Rahel said. "They need you at the nets, do they not?"

Bar Cheleph hesitated, grunted, "They do," and got unsteadily to his feet. He gave Rahel another dark look, then slid past her and hobbled down the shore. Rahel made a small noise in her throat and seated herself on the log where the priest's foster son had sat a moment before.

For a while they were silent. Rahel, her son looking down at the coals, and the unknown woman timidly biting at her fish. At last, his mother said, "Why do you share food with her?"

"She's hungry."

Rahel's eyes were cold and keen. "And what about Bat Benayahu?"

Koach's breath caught.

"I am your mother. Do you really think I sleep deeply enough that my son can slip out to the boats without me knowing it?"

Koach took a moment to breathe. Then said, "I meant to give her my pledge."

"I approve. Though Benayahu might not." Rahel turned to the silent woman. "Go. Now."

The woman started to shrink back, but Koach caught her arm in a fierce grip. "No. Stay, please."

"Son!"

"I offered her food and water, and that is father's coat."

Rahel's lips pressed together. "That hospitality was your brother's to give, not yours."

Koach looked aside at the silent woman as she nibbled on that fish. The fire was warm on his back and its warmth got inside him. He wished suddenly that he could know her name. His thoughts were loud within him: *I have fed her, protected her.*

I provided for someone.

For a woman.

For another person. Even a boat person.

To her, to this woman, I am not hebel.

Keeping her eyes averted from Rahel—as though to show that she offered no challenge to her protector's mother—the woman finished her fish, dropped the bones into the fire, and licked her fingers, as though years of hunger had taught her to waste not even the oils.

A shell of resolution hardened over Koach's heart, like ice over water. He felt the wooden horse, solid and reassuring, against his side: a thing he had made, a thing that was more than just a dream of some magnificent steed that would carry him and a woman he loved far from this place. At that moment he decided he would bring the carving to Tamar. He would find some moment when the *nagar* was away and bring this gift to her door. He would ask her why she hadn't come, and find his answer in her eyes.

"I am a man in our house also," he told his mother. "Always you are protecting me, telling me when to hide within the house, when not to step outside our door. I can't row. I can't help with the nets or the casting. But I can carve fittings, I can cook a fish, I can do *something*."

A long silence.

"You are like your father, little Koach." There was no accusation in his mother's voice, only sorrow. Koach glanced at her, and for just a moment, there was a woman in her face he didn't know— not his mother, with her stern hold on the life and future of her family, with her determination and the hard steel of her love for him—but a woman vulnerable and alone, a woman who did not unclothe her heart for anyone. This woman gazed out of Rahel's eyes for the briefest of moments, then was veiled again.

"So much like him," Rahel said, and there was pride and grief in her voice. "More than your brother. He is more like *my* father." She smiled faintly. "I wish you could have known your father. Yonah was a man who did as he pleased. But he also had two strong arms, and the love of all the fishers of Kfar Nahum." She bit her lip slightly, as though struggling to hold back words. Then she said, simply, "She is a stranger. Be careful, my son."

Rahel stood slowly, favoring her left hip. She glanced over Koach's head and her eyes widened. Koach saw the glow of reflected flames in her eyes.

"No," she whispered. "Oh, Bar Yesse, no."

Koach looked quickly over his shoulder. He could see dark smoke roiling over the grasses of the tideline, the dull red flicker of flames in the midday sun.

One of the overturned boats was burning, one of the relics of their fathers. A gust of wind blew the dark smoke toward the town itself. Against it stood a figure in white, a torch in his hand, the air wavering around him in the heat.

Then he heard the roar of his brother's voice, and men and women were leaping up from the cookfires and the nets with loud voices. Koach found himself on his feet, but Rahel was quicker; she was already running across the sand.

WALL OF FIRE

BURN THE SHELTERS under which the boat people took refuge, and they would have nowhere to sleep, nowhere to stay. The unclean and the heathen would have to leave. No longer would they lie like fish on the shore, like so many meals, an invitation to the dead. They might try to take shelter in the emptied, boarded-up houses of Kfar Nahum, but squatters had been driven out before.

With smoke billowing dark all about him and scratching his throat, Zebadyah strode from one boat to the next, setting fire to each in turn. One of the boat people, only one, came at him. It was a wizened man who might have been only twenty, though his face was gnarled as tree bark and his hair gone white from suffering. The man was yelling; Zebadyah thrust his improvised torch in his face, and the man stumbled back, shielding his eyes.

The others just watched the fire from either side of it, standing still as cairns, their faces gray. The sight of them—so many hungering strangers, so many lurkers about his town—chilled Zebadyah. They looked to him like the dead.

The priest had never really stopped reliving that night. Even in the light of day, he often heard and saw those dead about him, felt the clamminess of his palms and the outbreak of cold sweat on his brow. So many times he'd had to stop and stand, breathe for a few minutes, persuade himself that he stood in the cool of his synagogue, his hand still poised over the scroll of Torah. He would gaze down at the scroll and its letters and breathe, and realize that night was long past.

Now he fired another boat, roaring out a song in desert Hebrew, a song of Dawid from centuries past. Never again would he stand by as strangers swarmed into his town, leaving his people starving, dying.

"Stop!" His brother's son was pelting up the shore toward him, a few others behind him. "These are our father's boats!"

"Our town will not become a midden for beggars and heathen!" Zebadyah shouted. "Yonah would not want that."

And, turning, he put another wind-bleached hull to the torch.

"No!" Shimon cried.

Yonah's son threw himself at the priest, his hand shoving hard against Zebadyah's shoulder, nearly knocking him to the grasses. In panic and fury, Zebadyah thrust the torch at Shimon's face. As Shimon staggered back, his hands over his eyes, the priest heard a cry behind him. As Zebadyah turned, Yohanna his son seized the torch just above his grip.

"You," Zebadyah gasped, the sight of his younger son like a physical pain above his heart. Shoving the pain back, he backhanded Yohanna, hard, across his face.

His son sprawled into the sand.

"Craven boy!" Zebadyah stood over him, livid. All the pain of the years tore its way out of him, making his voice savage. "You abandoned our town! You went out to live with unwashed heathen and bandits of the desert! No son of mine! *No son of mine!*"

While Yohanna still lay dazed, Zebadyah stepped away from the boats, out onto the sand where all could see him. He looked out at all their pale faces, his torch held high, cracking and spitting. "Remember the Grief of Ezra! Remember Ezra standing at the wall! Remember. We have no wall of stone or brick to keep out the unclean, either living or dead. But by the Law of El-Shaddai, Mighty God, we will make a wall of fire."

They stared back at him, some grim, some fearful, some bewildered. Yohanna rose slowly to his feet, a bruise already darkening his right temple.

Zebadyah's own eyes were hard. In the silence he could hear, loud as thunder, the cracking of wood beneath the devouring fire. The crackle of his torch. The quiet, dry sound of one of the boat people weeping. The sigh of the tide and the hiss of wind in the grass. Shimon slid to his knees in the sand, his eyes still covered. He moaned in pain. Zebadyah felt a stab of regret that was then eaten away by his anger: that *Yonah's* son, his *brother's* son, should shelter these vagrants and eaters of flesh.

"Bar Yesse . . ."

He stopped.

That was *her* voice.

Rahel bat Eleazar's voice.

"Bar Yesse . . ." She walked toward him across the shore, approaching from the cookfires. He did not answer her. He gave the next boat to the hungry flames.

She stepped past her kneeling son, her fingertips touching Shimon's shoulder briefly. "Bar Yesse," she called, "these boats are all that's left of so many we've buried and so many we couldn't. Bar Yesse . . . *Zebadyah*, please."

He watched the fire lick its way up the hull.

"Please, Zebadyah," she repeated softly.

He had never heard her say his name before.

When he faced her, her eyes held sorrow, sorrow deep as the sea, and even . . . empathy. For him. Looking in the eyes of this woman he'd wanted, this woman his brother had left behind, his shame deepened. The torch he held seemed suddenly repulsive and out of place.

"Zebadyah," she said. She bit her lip. "He would not have wanted this."

No one else on the shore spoke.

He hadn't noticed before how much she had aged, how many lines there were about her eyes, not until this moment—but she was all the more beautiful. The wind caught her hair and blew it across her face like a dark veil, and he could not bear her beauty.

"Bat Eleazar," he whispered.

When he spoke up, there was a note of pleading in his voice. "Everything is broken and unclean. Sons. Walls. Our whole land. Everything is broken."

She only gazed back at him. With those eyes.

The torch fell from his fingers and the sand half-smothered its flames.

He heard Yakob step near, felt his son's arm around his shoulders. "Come, abba," Yakob said against the crack and roar of the flames behind them, "come, let us get some fish. There are fish roasting, abba." His voice was soft, and Zebadyah's heart shrank within him as he recognized it—it was the same tone he used with crippled Yesse, when his own father was being difficult.

Worse still was the pity in Rahel's eyes.

"I am old, son," Zebadyah murmured. "I've grown old, as the Law is old."

He looked away from Rahel's face, his eyes dry though his heart was full of weeping. He let his oldest son lead him down the shore. All around him, men sprang into action, as though awakened abruptly from sleep, and ran to scoop water from the sea to fight the flames, but he didn't spare them a glance.

* * *

Shimon kept his palms pressed to his eyes, gasping for air. That had *hurt*. God, but that had *hurt*. But the sharp flecks of burning at his eyes did not hurt as much as the sound of fire eating the boats.

More than just old wood was burning.

He wanted to leap to his feet, take up a waterskin or fill his coat with sand that he could hurl over the flames to silence them. But even as he lowered his hands and blinked against the pain, he saw that it was too late. The wood burned quickly, and some of the boats already were mere piles of charred drift. He stared at them, numbly.

A hand gripped his shoulder. "Cephas," a quiet voice said, behind him.

And the sound of that voice was like a torch touched to the dry pine of his heart. This was all Yeshua's fault. He had come and upended *everything*. When had strangers ever brought good to their town? Matityahu the tax collector, who had trailed a Roman legion behind him. The swordsmen the Romans hired. The Outlaw on his dark horse. All of them had brought evil and dismay. Now there was this vagrant from the hills who brought up the quick and the dead.

"If you are of God and not a beggar or a witch, you who call up fish," he said without turning, his voice shaking with anger, "why were you not here ten years ago, fifteen?" His words became a shout. "Why heal us only after we're broken, feed us only after we've starved? Prophet or messiah, where were you *then*?"

The hand squeezed his shoulder. "I don't know. I don't know, I don't know. I don't know how to answer you. I can't see the road I have to walk, the road ahead or the road behind. It is dark and it is dark . . ." Yeshua's voice was thick. "The road is dark, and I don't know what I am. Or what to tell you. I am sorry."

The anger flowed from Shimon like water, leaving only weakness behind, and sobbing. He shook, on his knees in the sand, with the sea at his back and the boats of his People burning before him. He let the stranger hold his shoulder, and he just shook and wept. The pent-up fury and despair of fifteen years rushed through him like a school of fish with sharp teeth, chewing at him as they passed through and over him, leaving him gasping in wordless pleas against the violence of a world in which fathers sought to devour their children or in which some children were born wrong and some children starved.

"I am sorry, Cephas," the stranger kept whispering, over and over. "I am sorry."

* * *

Shimon might have wept there for an hour, or a month, or a year, or a year of years, for all he knew. But suddenly there were cries up by the houses of Beth Tsaida, and then shouts from the men at the nets and the fires, and the slap of running feet against the wet sand. Shimon looked away from the boats at last and saw men and women standing against the cookfires, their faces terrified.

A newcomer was running from the direction of Beth Tsaida, and he was Natan El, one of the younger fishers, only a little older than Shimon himself. The man stumbled, caught himself with one hand splayed against the sand, and got back to his feet. Then he was bolting down the shore toward them, his legs pumping. "The dead!" he cried. "The dead!"

Shimon felt all the warmth leave his body.

"It's Benayahu!" Natan El cried. "Benayahu the *nagar*! I saw him running north past the midden, bleeding from his hip. He said he saw the dead! In his house! His house! In the town! He saw the dead in his house! The dead!"

PART 6

KOACH'S BATTLE

KOACH DIDN'T HESITATE. He cast the last fish from the coals to the feet of the silent woman who was gazing at him with wide, terrified eyes, and he sprang to his feet. Natan El was still scrambling down the sand toward them, screaming about the dead in Benayahu's house.

The *dead*.

There was shouting all along the shore, Zebadyah demanding to know what was going on, whether Natan El had actually seen the dead. Yakob was already striding north along the shore, stooping as he went to lift a large shell from the sea wrack left by the previous tide. The shell had been broken, and it had a jagged edge. "We have to find Benayahu!" he cried. Other men sprinted to catch up with him. To them it was already clear what had happened: Bleeding from his hip, Benayahu had fled Kfar Nahum, fled to the hills perhaps, so that he would not be boarded up within his house for the seven days of uncleanness while the town waited to see if he would die and then rise, moaning, to his feet.

But Koach realized something else.

The dead were in Benayahu's house.

In *Tamar's* house.

Koach cried out her name and broke into a run. The silent woman gasped as he left her by the fire. He'd forgotten her, forgotten Bar Cheleph and Bar

Nahemyah, the stranger, even the great sheaves of fish, forgotten his grief beneath the boat, forgotten everything but the way Tamar's shoulders had trembled as her father beat her, and the hot shame in his chest as he watched and could not help. Everything but the warmth of her lips pressing his.

He ran.

* * *

Koach found the door of the *nagar*'s house ajar. He touched it with his fingertips, his heart pounding, and felt the grain of the wood. He pushed slightly. Its hinge was well-oiled, unlike the door to his mother's house, and it swung open as silently as thoughts in the mind of God.

Some instinct older than speech or fire warned Koach not to call out. He slipped through the door. The atrium was empty, as was Benayahu's room across it, but Tamar's room was concealed by a heavy rug drawn over the entrance. The stillness of the house pressed on him, urging silence and slow movement. Hearing the roar of his own blood in his ears, Koach stepped across the atrium beneath a pale sky, leaving the door open behind him. As he neared Tamar's room, his breath seemed loud to him, and he held his hand over his lips. He could see that room in his mind so clearly: the little heap of bedding, a bundle of clothing in the corner, a small pot, a table for an oil lamp. The shadow of Benayahu against the small light. The rise and fall of his arm. Tamar's silent shaking, her silent tears.

He hesitated, then drew aside the rug.

The air behind it was warm and heavy with the scent of recent death. He could see her silhouette against the dim light. She stood on her bedding, with her back to Koach and her face to the boarded-up window, her hair lank and unwashed about her shoulders. Koach stood very still, his belly heaving at the smell. He clamped his jaw shut against the nausea.

Tamar was breathing, but far too slowly, as though she were asleep. He could see her shoulders rise and fall. She was holding her hands behind her at the small of her back—no, they were tied. Coarse fishing rope, the kind used for netting, wound savagely about her wrists. In the dimness, Koach could make out the dark line of it cutting into her skin.

Koach could neither step through nor let the rug fall and walk away. He could not move. His heart beat so fast from his run into the town—like that day Barabba had hunted him and Tamar had pulled him into her father's house, onto that very bedding where she now stood, stinking like fish left to rot on the shore. Koach kept looking at her wrists. He should step forward; he should unbind her. He should hear her whispering to thank him for coming to help her, at last, after the years of being beaten and broken with none to step between her and her father. He should help her now.

But his mind could not grasp the strangeness of this scene. This girl who had kissed him, tied in her own house. Reeking.

He heard a soft footstep behind him, at the outer door. A hoarse whisper: "*Koach?*"

His mother's voice.

The corpse standing on the bedding turned its head slowly, its eyes glinting in the dark. It hissed.

Gasping, Koach lurched backward, tripped on the edge of the rug, and fell, tearing the rug aside, letting in a flood of sunlight. Even as the floor knocked the breath from him, he caught a nightmare glimpse of Tamar's body stumbling toward him, one foot caught in linens, her arms trapped behind her, the dull sheen of her eyes.

Rahel screamed. Her cry held not only fear for her son but anguish, as from some night of grief years past yet horribly present.

The next moments were confused, like things witnessed during a fever. For an instant the dead girl was on top of him, her breath cold as winter on his throat. Her teeth snapped near his skin, her body shaking with a low growl. Then the weight of her was gone and he was rolling to the side and there was another scream from his mother, a scream that cut into his heart.

Koach scrambled to his feet and saw his mother and the girl grappling. They rolled on the floor and his mother was on top of her and drove the heel of her hand down against the corpse's chin, driving her head back. The neck didn't break, and the corpse lunged up, snapping its teeth at her, its jaws closing on her hair. Rahel gasped and fell back, pulling the corpse with her; there was a flash of metal in the sun, a knife in Rahel's hand, pulled from somewhere within her clothes. She pressed her arm to the corpse's throat, keeping it at bay while she sawed swiftly through her hair near the scalp above her right ear. It bit toward her hand and she jerked back, dropping the knife. It rattled across the floor.

Breathing in quick gasps, Rahel scooted backward away from the growling dead, kicking wildly as it lunged at her. Then Koach grasped his mother's arm. With a strength that startled him, he pulled her to her feet, his body hot with adrenaline. For an instant her gaze met his, her eyes wide. Then they *ran*.

They rushed into the atrium, with the corpse right behind them.

"Tamar, *please!*" Koach cried, glancing over his shoulder.

She was stumbling after them, snarling, her arms bound behind her, her hair wild about her face, her eyes glazed with death.

Mother and son ran to the outer door. Koach gasped her name under his breath, over and over again: *"Tamar, Tamar, Tamar—"*

They burst through the door out into the street, and turning, Koach saw the girl staggering after them, lurching across the threshold, her jaw distended in a snarl of hunger.

Rahel stumbled, and Koach tore his hand from her grasp.

"Koach!"

"No," he gasped.

He couldn't leave Tamar like that.

Even as he faced her, he heard running footsteps, a few shouts. Men from the shore, and a few women. Bar Cheleph was there, and Yohanna. Their faces were pale.

The dead girl turned its head, taking in all the living, and then lurched toward them. But it stumbled and sprawled on its face.

The townspeople formed a wide semicircle, keeping back while the corpse thrashed in the dirt. It lifted its head and its jaws gaped open, a low groan of hunger.

"Tamar," Koach whispered.

She had torn her dress in her fall, and Koach could see glimpses of her body. He recalled those nights on the rooftop, gazing at each other. His belly heaved and he twisted to the side, falling to his knees and retching into the dirt outside her father's house.

He knelt there, vomiting up everything he could and then vomiting up empty air, uncaring if the body of his love reached him or not, everything coming apart inside him. An arm around him and a murmur in his ear told him Rahel was with him, but he didn't turn to her. He just shook and shook and spewed out his insides.

A sandaled foot stepped past him. Koach glanced up in a haze, saw Bar Cheleph limping toward the corpse where it twisted in the dirt, having rolled onto its back. Bar Cheleph held a hooked fishing spear in his hand, perhaps taken from one of the fishers gathered silently about them. Anger had contorted his face. It was as if, seeing this dead girl bound in the dirt, helpless to seize and devour, he saw a moment at last where he might release his rage. His fury at his parents' deaths, at his town's, at all that had been taken from his

People by the living and the dead. He lifted his foot and drove it into the corpse's face with a feral cry and a cracking of bone beneath his sandaled heel.

"These things!" he shouted. "They eat up everything, everything we have, everyone we love." The crowd watched him and the dead girl, mute in their horror or in their catharsis. Their eyes glazed with a particular kind of lust, a need to see violence done. Koach got to his feet, breathing hard, just as Bar Cheleph bent over the corpse and drove the spear down through its breast. The dead girl spat and hissed, one side of her face crushed in, her wrists trapped beneath her, her body twisting and writhing in the dirt. Her head jerked up and her jaws snapped, but the fisherman was out of her reach.

Bar Cheleph stared down at her face, his own contorted. He twisted the spear in her body, his weight on it holding her pinned to the ground.

"Stop!" Koach cried.

Without thinking, he threw himself at Bar Cheleph, slamming his small weight into the man's side and grabbing the spear with his hand to wrest it from him and pull it free of Tamar's corpse. Bar Cheleph gasped as the breath was driven from him. He backhanded Koach savagely, knocking the boy to his knees. A sigh from the gathered men and women, as though they were witnessing violence committed in a drama, as the Greeks do.

"Leave him alone!" Rahel cried, and struggled against two women who held her back.

It took Koach a moment for his vision to clear. Then he saw Bar Cheleph looming over him, his face cold. The corpse spat and twisted on the ground, trying to get at either of them.

"Get back to your mother, Hebel," Bar Cheleph snarled.

But now Koach's body was hot with his own anger, and he was wild with his own grief, which was no less than Bar Cheleph's. Koach glanced at the dead girl's face and his eyes were dry. *Hebel.* Useless. He had not been able to help this lovely girl who had kissed him, this girl who had protected him from the Outlaw, this girl who had been kind to him. He had not saved her from her father's blows. Nor from this.

Bar Cheleph turned his back to the boy, wrenched free the spear, and drove it in again. The corpse uttered no sound of pain, only frustrated, animal hunger. It threw its small body from one side to the other, but could not free itself of the spear, nor lift its arms to catch at the warm, enticing life above it. Whether it could hear the drumbeat of a living heart or the ocean sound of Bar Cheleph's blood or the wind of his breathing—whatever it sensed that made it yearn for meat and flesh—it could not reach him. The girl's lips gaped wide and it *screeched*, a sound that cut into all who were listening like the crack of a Roman whip. And the screech went on and on, a primal demand for life and food, a demand that could never be satisfied.

That screech wrenched Koach into motion. Maybe he had been *hebel*, but he could not allow himself to be useless to her now. Groping with his hand in the dirt, he found a jagged stone a little larger than his hand.

Koach got shakily to his feet. Bar Cheleph ignored him; he was merely the useless, unclean boy that he had beaten aside. The man's whole attention was on the screeching corpse. Koach looked down through a blur of moisture at the stone he held, something heavy and solid and final.

He had to do this.

There was no one else.

"Forgive me," he whispered.

Koach bent quickly over the corpse, startling a shout from Bar Cheleph. Tamar's body lunged at him, her jaw gaping. With a cry, Koach drove the stone down into her head. He screamed her name once, then fell silent but for a small, choked sound.

WOUNDS FROM THE DEAD

SILENCE IN the street.

"My son," Rahel whispered.

But Koach didn't answer. He just crouched over the body of the young woman he'd loved, the woman who had touched him so often in his dreams as he lay in the quiet hours in his bedding. He squeezed his eyes shut and breathed raggedly. The stone fell from his limp hand, a soft thud into the dirt.

No one spoke. No one moved. Rahel swayed a moment on her feet as though feeling faint, but she didn't approach. Bar Cheleph took a few unsteady steps away, looking on, wild-eyed.

Koach opened his eyes and, against all Law and custom, he pressed his hand to the dead girl's cheek. Her skin was cold. So cold.

His chest clenched in on itself. Pain, a new pain. He had known fear and rejection and grief, but this was a new loss. She was someone he had loved, someone whose heart had mattered to him, someone he had yearned to protect. Gone, torn from her life as savagely and quickly as a fish might be ripped from the sea.

"Tamar," he whispered.

There wasn't much left of her face; he had destroyed her with that blow from the rock. His hands began to shake.

She hadn't forsaken him.

She had never intended to miss their tryst.

While he had been reviling her bitterly in his heart, she had been in that room, dying. He leaned back on his heels and just breathed. Just breathed. Then he took from his pocket the carving he'd made for Tamar, the wooden horse.

He turned it over and over in his hands, feeling the smooth length of its limbs, the intricate carving of its mane, the small roundness of its eyes.

She was dead.

She had tried to *eat* him.

But more than that, she was *gone*. The *shedim* within her corpse had eaten her heart and her soul, leaving only hunger behind, only that.

Koach didn't know how long he sat there, turning that carving in his hands as though it were the only thing real left in the world, the only thing that wouldn't fade away and die. But at last he tucked the carving gently into the bodice of Tamar's nightdress, giving it to her as he'd meant to. Then he rose to his feet, while others around him murmured. He stepped up through Benayahu's door and into his atrium, hardly aware of his own movements. He found the small knife his mother had lost and brought it back to the body. No one took a step toward the corpse; no one bothered Koach as he knelt by Tamar and turned her gently to her side. Then he sawed at her bonds, one-handed. She must have been bound by her father, who had then fled his fevered daughter and his house when she stopped breathing.

Or even *before* she stopped breathing.

But no, there was blood on her mouth; she had risen and bitten him. But how had *she* been bitten? How? Her father had kept her so tightly locked away. Had she started down toward the boats to meet her lover, then been set upon by some corpse out of the sea? Run home then in terror, bleeding? Or had something crawled into their house? Had she eaten a fish that had nibbled at a corpse? Could such a thing make the fish unclean, and the one that ate it unclean? If so, why wasn't the whole town defiled? How had this *happened*?

The cords snapped with a quiet, rasping sound, and Koach set down the knife, his hand trembling. He lay Tamar on her back again and rose to his feet, breathing hard. She had been *bound*. That man—that man who had beaten Tamar, night upon night upon night—he had just tied her like a slave and *left* her here. Clear in his heart he recalled all the times Tamar had walked painfully to the roof after a severe beating. He recalled his own fantasies of killing her father, of driving a fish hook through his breast, of taking a boat and slipping out to the sea by night with her, to seek some far town on the other shore, some place where he would not be shunned for his withered arm, some place where a cripple might find a way to feed and shelter the woman he desired. He recalled the beatings he had seen, how he had seen them—and done nothing. Now it was too late.

There was a bellow, and without turning he knew that his brother was forcing his way through the onlookers. "Koach!" Shimon cried hoarsely. "Koach!"

Koach didn't answer. His fist was clenched at his side, his other hand limp and useless. He felt Rahel's hand on his shoulder, but he shrugged it away.

"Koach!" Shimon shouted again. Then a grunt as he shoved someone out of his path. "Let me by!"

Koach glanced back then and saw his brother break free of the press, all those faces drawn with horror. Bar Cheleph had faded back into the crowd; Koach caught a glimpse of his face, flushed as though with shame.

Shimon stopped; the two brothers faced each other. The rage in Koach's breast went out like a candle at a breath of the *shedim*, a gust of wind in the night. He looked from his brother's face to Tamar's, her lips still pulled back as for a snarl or a screech; her fingers still half-curled into claws, her chest completely still. Koach unclenched his own fist, and fatigue settled over him like heavy mud. His hand began to shake.

"I am not strong enough to carry her to the tombs," he said.

* * *

Shimon glanced at the rock that had fallen from his brother's hand and then at Koach's face. This was his younger brother, the feeble one, whose very birth had failed the hopes of his family. Yet what he saw now in Koach's eyes struck him to the heart. This was no boy looking back at him with tears in his eyes; this was a young man. In his face Shimon saw graven both the stubborn strength of his father and the ferocity of his mother, to defend his own. A hot pool of regret settled in his belly—regret for his words earlier, by the boats.

Grimly, Shimon shrugged the heavy water-coat from his shoulders and lay it on the ground beside the girl's corpse. Then he took the fishing gloves from his belt and put them on. He took hold of the body and rolled it into the coat. "I will take her," he said, wrapping the coat about her like a shroud. He pulled the hood over her face, shutting away that feral grimace, that bloodstained mouth.

His brother watched him silently as he lifted the girl into his arms. She was light, as though he held only a few coats. Neither of them said anything. What was there to say?

A hand gripped his shoulder. "I will help, Bar Yonah." That was Bar Nahemyah, his gaze fixed on the dead girl.

"No need, Bar Nahemyah."

"Call me Kana," the man said softly. "It is a long walk—"

He fell still at Shimon's look.

Shimon turned toward the crowd, who stood between him and the walk out of this town to the tombs of his People. He could feel Koach's gaze on his back. The sun overhead seemed too cold. After a moment, those gathered parted to let him pass, standing aside, staring at him as though they were witnessing some holy rite. Bar Cheleph leaned back against the wall of the house opposite Benayahu's, his face lowered. As Shimon passed his mother, whose face was flushed as from exertion, she lifted her voice softly and began to sing the Words of Going, the most ancient of songs, the keening lament for the dead. The sound made Shimon's eyes burn; he could never hear it without recalling the singing on the hill the morning after most of Kfar Nahum died. The grief of the town's women, carried to him on the air as he cared for his mother and infant brother, as he ran down to the sea to watch for his father's boat.

Having passed through the crowd, Shimon looked back. He saw his brother still standing alone where the body had lain, with that haunted look in his face. Then Shimon could not hold back his fury. The last of the day's numbness broke, and all the anger of a fatherless son poured out, and in that moment he knew the breach in the wall of his numb grief could never be repaired, never be shored up again. Though his heart was naked and torn with pain, he faced the men and women of his village. His gaze swept them all, and some of them ducked back as though he had struck at them. Bar Cheleph didn't look up.

"The Romans," he said in a voice cold as the tomb, "say we are a small people. Would you prove them right? Do we defile our dead? This is not worthy of our fathers. It is not worthy of our town. It is not worthy of our People. You are small men, and you shame me." His face quivered with emotion; then he got it under control. "My brother, who you call *hebel*, he is the only one today who is *koach*, the only one whose heart and will are strong." Shimon spat in the dirt before their feet and glanced at Bar Cheleph, who didn't look up. "I am ashamed of you," he said.

Bar Cheleph's shoulders tensed.

Then Shimon turned and carried that dead girl from his town.

* * *

Koach lowered himself to his knees and touched his forehead to the earth, oblivious to his brother's receding footsteps and to the whispers around him. "God," he murmured, "let me sleep and find that this is only the dream country." His shoulders shook, but he did not weep. He heard his mother's voice fall silent. He heard some walk by him and depart. He paid none of them any mind, just pressed his face to the dirt. It was like something deep inside him was lost and he couldn't find it, didn't know what it was, didn't know where to start searching.

He heard Bar Cheleph, his voice anxious. "Bat Eleazar, I meant no offense to your son."

By which he meant Shimon.

Koach didn't hear his mother's reply. He whispered, "You killed her."

Stillness.

"You killed her," Koach said. Louder. Lifting his face from the dirt.

Bar Cheleph looked shaken. "She was already dead, Hebel."

"You *killed* her." His voice a hoarse whisper. "You never even saw she was hurting. That she needed help." His chest went hot. "You all killed her."

Bar Cheleph drew back, as though wishing to flee. Yohanna, who stood near, took his arm and murmured something in his ear. Around them, a few other faces went ugly. Koach braced himself, every line in his body taut and furious, but before either words or blows could fall on him, he heard a low gasp.

"Koach—"

Turning, he saw his mother swaying on her feet. Her face had gone gray, her eyes a little glazed. She held her right hand pressed to her left arm just below the shoulder, and with a shock Koach saw that her sleeve had darkened beneath her grip.

"Koach . . . I don't . . . I don't . . . ."

Her voice was faint.

Then her eyes rolled back, and with a slow, terrible kind of grace, she slumped to the ground as though between one heartbeat and the next her body had been emptied of her spirit.

WHAT HAPPENED AT RAHEL'S HOUSE

KOACH WAS by her side at once. He pressed his left hand to her brow, and paled. She was burning.

"No," Koach whispered.

Slowly, as his heart beat brutally within his chest, he drew Rahel's sleeve up her arm. The underside of the sleeve, between wrist and elbow, had gone dark with blood.

Then he found it: a bite in her arm, just above the elbow. Flesh had been torn out of her arm, and only the thickness of the wool sleeve she'd pressed to the wound had prevented it from spilling her life's blood already to the earth at her feet. Now that she had fainted, it ran down her arm in a rush like red water, darkening the soil beneath her. With a cry, Koach pressed the sleeve quickly against the wound again, holding it there with his one hand. His eyes burned; she had concealed the bite from her sons, had not wanted them to know she was about to die.

About to die.

His legs gave out beneath him; he found himself sitting by her, everything a blur to him but the wound on her arm and the pressure he held against it. Tamar, Rahel. The waters wear away even the stones, and nothing is left.

Yohanna crouched by him. His voice came from a great distance. "*—have to get her inside. Make her comfortable. Let me help, Bar Yonah.*"

He glanced up at the older man's face, saw the pity in his eyes, but it was like looking at a reflection in the water rather than at something real.

"*She needs you to be strong, Koach. Strong.*"

Strong. His name, Koach. The word for *strong*.

He heard his breathing, loud in his ears. "Yes," he whispered. "Inside."

Yohanna placed his arms around Rahel and lifted her, his face strained; Koach got his arm around Rahel's legs and did what he could to help carry her;

people gave way as the two carried Rahel awkwardly toward the door of her house, so near Benayahu's. At the doorstep, Koach set her legs down and fumbled a moment with the latch on the door, then swung it open, putting his shoulder against the heavy wood. Yohanna carried Rahel through, and Koach followed, his heart pounding, panic rising dark and shrieking in his mind.

As he caught the door with his good hand and began to swing it closed again, he found Bar Cheleph on the doorstep.

"I'll help," Bar Cheleph said quietly, his face dark with shame.

Koach shut the door in his face.

* * *

Yohanna carried Rahel into the atrium while Koach ran and gathered up blankets from her room. He made a small bed by the olive tree, then left Yohanna to lay his mother there and hurried for water from her ewer. When he came back, he found Yohanna pacing. Rahel lay with her eyes closed, her fingers moving restlessly over her blanket. Small whimpers came from her throat, each of them like a shock of ice to Koach's heart.

"She's going to die," he whispered. "She's going to die."

"I have to get the *navi*," Yohanna said, his face pale. He bolted toward the door.

Koach heard his steps. Heard the door sway open, heard it slam shut. He sank to his knees by his mother, a bowl of water in his hand. Some beast was clawing its way up his chest, tearing him. An old beast, the helplessness. He was *hebel* again. His mother was dying, dying the worst of deaths—the one where the body staggered, lurching, to its feet once it no longer breathed. His eyes blurred. His brother wasn't here; there was only him. And he could do nothing.

He took her right shoulder and shook her gently. "Amma," he moaned, "amma."

Her breathing was shallow. Her eyes opened at his call, making him gasp, but they didn't focus; they seemed to stare past him, at the open sky.

"My son," she rasped.

He fumbled, found her hand, clutched it fiercely. His throat was dry. "I am here, amma. I'm here."

"My son, your father would have loved you." She began to shake, as though she were terribly cold, though her face shone now with sweat. "I kept you too safe. I was so . . . afraid . . . for you. He would have seen how strong you were. He would have been proud of you."

"Amma," he whispered, pleading.

"*Tzelem elohim*, my son. Your face is God's face; you are his likeness. What does your arm matter. Your face is . . . so beautiful. Tell Shimon . . ."

She fell silent.

"What? What do I tell him?"

But she didn't say anything more. Her breathing was even shallower. Koach watched the tiny rising and falling of her chest, cold with fear.

* * *

He didn't know how long he sat there watching her die. He didn't care. In all the town only Rahel and Tamar had spoken to him as to one who might be respected and loved. And perhaps Bar Nahemyah. Now he would be alone. He'd thought he was alone before. Now he would truly be alone. What hopes he'd kept secret had been crushed; what people he'd leaned on had been torn from him.

Breathing against the tightness in his chest, Koach tucked Rahel's blanket about her. That took some doing with only one hand, and for a moment he glanced down at his lifeless arm and hate seared through him, self-hate, hot as a furnace. He struck his chest with his left hand, because the pain of that small blow distracted him and jarred him back to the present, to the things that needed to be done. He got up, went to the little room that was Rahel's during the winter, took down his father's *tallit* from its peg, and brought it back to her. He lay it folded beside her, then took her right hand and curled her fingers around its edge. His father could not be here, at his mother's last breath. There was only his son, only one of his sons, the worthless one. His father's shawl was the only small comfort he knew how to provide.

A heavy knock at the outer door startled him.

But he didn't rise until the knock came again, and Yohanna's voice called: "Bar Yonah! Bar Yonah!"

Numb, he went to the door and opened it. Yohanna stood at his doorstep, and with him stood the bruised, haggard beggar-man he'd seen on the shore, the man who was as alone as he.

Yeshua looked past him, toward the atrium. He looked exhausted, his eyes bleary.

"Will you let us enter?" Yohanna said softly.

Koach hesitated. Once you invited someone over the threshold, they were no longer a stranger. They were your guest, as fully under the protection and provision of your roof as your own kin. You were bound to them, and they to you.

But he had strength neither to argue nor to shut the door. He could hear his mother's ragged breathing in the atrium behind him, and that quiet, desperate sound to him was as loud as shakings in the earth. He nodded tensely.

Yeshua stepped by him, without a word. Yohanna followed, gripped Koach's good shoulder, then shut the door for him.

As if in a dream, Koach followed the other men into the atrium. The stranger seated himself by Rahel—gently, as though she were sleeping and he didn't want to wake her. He just sat by her in silence, as Koach had moments before. There was sorrow in his face.

Seeing that, the heat of Koach's fury returned. His mother would not live long. He understood what was coming, as much as any young man could. He didn't want anyone else here, certainly not any stranger to their town. Why had he opened the door?

"Why did you bring him here?"

"He is the *navi*," Yohanna said softly.

For a moment, the word stirred Koach despite his fear. A word of hope from remembered stories. Rahel's stories. Always when the dead had risen to devour the People, there had been a *navi*, one anointed to counsel and preserve their tribe. Elisa, who had called the very *malakhim* of heaven down in chariots of flame to scorch the unclean dead from the earth. Yirmiyahu, who had faced a corrupt king and begged him to shatter the gates that locked in the living with the dead. Daniyyel, who had prayed an entire night unharmed in a cave of walking corpses.

But how could this man, in his ragged brown robe, with those bruises on his face . . . how could he be the *navi*? Koach peered at those livid marks on his skin, and his throat tightened. They were so much like Tamar's bruises. This man had been beaten, like her. He was a man someone had failed to defend.

"I know him now," Yohanna said. "I've seen him before. I couldn't remember where at first. It was last summer, with Yohanna ha Matbil in the wilderness about the Tumbling Water. I was there." He was quiet a moment, and when he spoke, he did so quietly, as though fearing to disturb either Rahel or the stranger. "We light few lamps and we live in the dark and we try to sleep, Bar Yonah. We don't want to remember. Your brother seems content to sit in the silence, to sit *shiva* until his last breath, but this silence grew too heavy for me. So I left. To live with Ha Matbil beneath the open sky. I was there on the Night of Five Hundred *Mikvot*, when so many were immersed in the river to be cleansed. Nothing I've said about that night is an untruth. People's faces shone as they rose from the water. Men, women. And the moon was full and the stars as bright as they were for Moshe in the desert. And I heard the singing, I *heard* it. The *malakhim*, the angels of God, calling to each other in the dark, from one hill to the next. Like something important was happening in the land, a blessing, at last. That night we did not hear the moaning of the dead but the singing of angels."

He fell silent for a moment, but Koach didn't say anything. He was barely listening. He watched the rise and fall of his mother's breathing. In his heart, he stood in a dry, bleak place, where Yohanna's words were little more than the wind in the stones.

"At sunset before the song in the night," Yohanna said slowly, "a man came walking down to the shore. Ha Matbil immersed him in the water. And after, as the man walked from the east bank out into the ravines, Ha Matbil pointed him out to me and to the other men who were with us, and he said—I remember it—*There is the* olah, *the lamb of our God, who takes away the evil and the uncleanness from the world. A navi has come like one Israel has never seen, and I am not worthy even to tie his sandal-string.*

"That's what brought the hundreds. It was a mighty sign, Bar Yonah. That night they came to the water. So many. Hundreds. All of them kneeling before Ha Matbil, confessing all they had done and all they had seen and not stopped, every uncleanness they had witnessed or made happen in our land. And Ha Matbil gave them to the water and brought them up again. To each one of them he said, *The time of God is near. Be ready. It is near.* And oh, Bar Yonah, what we heard. What we *heard*. Ha Matbil, he looked at the hills, at the singers none of us could see. He saw what would come—like a *navi*. And he said, *It is near.*" Yohanna looked rapt. "Your brother thinks this man from Natzeret has one of the *shedim* eating him from within. But I think he is of God."

"This." Yeshua spoke suddenly, though he did not lift his gaze from the rise and fall of Rahel's breathing. "This. This is what the father wanted me to see. What he whispered in my ear, out in the wind, in the rocks, in the wind in the rocks. It has to be, it has to be. This. This is what I have to do. This . . ." His voice trailed off. Yohanna stared at him intently.

"She's dying," Koach choked.

"She is dying," Yeshua said. "And I am dying, and you are dying, and those women and men out by the boats are dying. We are all dying, dying, dying . . ."

The stranger traced his fingertips over Rahel's arm, over the torn edge of her skin. She didn't stir. "But not today. No more dying today."

With fingers as gentle as though he were touching a lover, Yeshua opened Rahel's right eye and gazed into it a moment. Her eye was very round and very dark, but she gave no sign that she was aware of him. Koach tensed—that a stranger should touch his mother!—yet he found himself waiting, waiting for he didn't know what. Breathless.

Yeshua's voice was soft and distracted, as though he were talking to himself, or to someone who sat right beside him, someone only he could see. Koach held himself back, tense.

"My mother . . . she told me once that our father did not promise a life without pain," Yeshua murmured, closing Rahel's eye. His words were slow and spoken with terrible clarity. "Not without pain. Only that he would weep with us. Only that his heart would break. Only that he would take each moment of suffering, each death, each, and hold it in his hands, and . . . and bring from it something, something even more beautiful than what was lost. A forest of cedar grows from a field of ash, and each seed, every seed must fall to the earth, fall and fall and crack open and die before it can become a barley plant." He touched Rahel's hair, stroked it a moment. His gaze never left her face.

He began singing softly, words in the dialect of old desert Hebrew, and after a while he hummed them, as though he needed his mind elsewhere and could no longer spare any of it to make articulate words. He moved his fingers carefully over Rahel's arm and hummed that quiet desert melody, one Koach had never heard before—though hearing it, he could imagine men and women of his People singing it or playing it on flutes as they stood at the doors of their tents, long before they came to this land.

Koach watched like a man gazing over the brink of a cliff, his heart thunderous inside him.

Then Rahel sighed softly and closed her eyes, and the stranger moved his fingers back and forth over the inflamed bite, kneading her torn skin as though shaping clay with his hands. The bite closed, and then, a moment later, it was gone. Simply gone. The olive skin of her arm was smooth and unbroken as though it had never suffered so much as the press of a thumb.

THE SCENTED FIRE

RAHEL DREW in a shuddering breath, and her eyes opened. For a moment they remained glazed as with fever, and then they cleared. Her eyes focused first on Yeshua, and a light came into them as though she had stepped out of the desert to find her door open and a banquet in her home, with friends waiting for her whom she'd thought long dead. Koach had never seen such a look in her eyes.

"At last," Rahel whispered.

Yeshua didn't speak. There was a sheen of sweat on his face, as though he were the one who had wakened from fever. He lifted his fingers from her arm and sat back, his breathing ragged.

The word "amma" caught in Koach's throat; he sat staring at his mother. What he had just seen could not be; he didn't dare move, didn't dare find out if what he'd seen was real or if he was only sitting in the dream country, deceived in thinking himself awake.

Then Rahel's gaze flicked toward him, and she breathed his name.

Koach let out a cry and flung himself down at her side, putting his good arm around her. "Amma!" he cried. "Amma!"

"My son, my son," she wept.

Yeshua and Yohanna were forgotten. Koach wept openly against her shoulder, enveloped in the scent of his mother's hair and the sharper scent of the blood that was drying on her clothes.

"What happened?" she rasped. "What . . . I was . . . burning up. I was bitten, unclean. Son, what has happened?"

He squeezed his eyes shut and just held her.

"Ah, Rahel." Yeshua's voice. "Rahel, Rahel."

The stranger stood unsteadily. In a moment Yohanna was at his side, offering an arm for him to lean on, but Yeshua pressed his hand against Yohanna's chest and then stepped away on his own. His face had gone white and his eyes were wild like a man staring into the great emptiness of the desert, an emptiness that perhaps not even God could fill, an emptiness that devoured all things, all peoples.

"I need air," he whispered. And he moved out across the atrium, almost stumbling on the way. Yohanna hurried after.

Rahel was shaking. "I was dying," she breathed.

"You're all right, amma. You're all right." She drew in quick breaths.

"Yes. Yes, I am." She lifted herself onto her elbows. "We have a guest, son. Help me up. We need to get him food and water. Help me."

* * *

Yeshua sank against the wall of the atrium, breathing shallowly. Quickly Yohanna swept up one of the blankets from Rahel's bedding, and drew it about the stranger's shoulders. His voice was a low murmur. "*Rabboni*, it will be all right. Just breathe."

Yeshua coughed. "Water."

Yohanna brought him some in a clay bowl from the ewer at one corner of the atrium. Yeshua's hands shook when he took the bowl, but he drank deeply. A little water trickled from the corner of his mouth, making Yohanna acutely aware of his own thirst.

Yeshua lowered the bowl from his lips; the water sloshed in the bowl, cupped between his calloused hands. "I should've . . . should've asked for . . . for wine, not water."

"You healed my kinswoman, and my friend's mother," Yohanna said softly. "I will bring you all the wine in Kfar Nahum if you ask it."

Yeshua glanced down at his hands. "Healed," he whispered. "How, how did I do that?"

"You sang," Yohanna whispered back.

"I asked," Yeshua said. "I could hear her, hear her hurting, hear her dying. I could hear it so *loudly*. And I asked, I asked, I called out . . . Like with the fish. Like with the gulls. Like with . . ." He groaned. "For just a moment I *remembered*. I remembered *everything*. Everything. All of it, all of it from the desert. Every word, every . . ." His eyes glistened. "What I'm to do, and why, and what I *am*. And now it's gone, all of it gone. Why can't I hold on to it, Yohanna, why?" He squeezed his eyes shut. "All those nights, those nights with my back to a rock, a rock in the desert. All the screams in my ears. And it's hard, so hard, to recall anything else but that moaning, that moaning that won't stop, that will never, ever stop . . ." He swallowed. "Help me, Yohanna. Help me up. Help me stand."

Yohanna reached for his arm, gripped it, and lifted him to his feet. Something nagged at the edge of his mind. Then, as he steadied Yeshua with a hand at his shoulder, the thought burst in on him with a suddenness like a crack in the mast. He gasped.

"I will be back." Releasing the *navi*'s arm, he ran for the door. "I will be back!"

He flung open the door, burst through, and slammed it behind him. In the street, he shoved aside Bar Cheleph and another young man who were laying planks of heavy wood beside Rahel bat Eleazar's doorstep. He hardly noticed them; he broke into a run, and he ran faster than he had ever run in his life, faster even than on the night of the dead when so many young men and women he knew had died. He ran and his heart beat with a hope that was so violent it was like panic.

* * *

Yeshua leaned against the wall of the atrium, drinking his water, his eyes dark with thought. Having almost forgotten he was there, Koach helped his mother kindle flame above the coals in the cookpit in the atrium. There was another pit near it, a smaller one, long unused, but Rahel kindled it also, and took a small pouch of spices and herbs and sprinkled them over the coals, and their redolence filled the air. Koach had not smelled that in . . . nearly a year. The scented fire. The coals on which you would lay a fish's heart to keep the *shedim* away.

"I hope it will," Koach whispered, watching the little flames. He should have been the one to carry Tamar to a tomb. It should have been him. But he couldn't have carried her with one arm. He should have gone with Shimon, at least.

"I hope it will too, son." Rahel didn't need to ask what he meant. The scented fire seemed to them small and fragile, but perhaps it meant no one else would be eaten.

"I thought we'd have to bury you, too," Koach whispered, blinking quickly. He looked to the stranger, Yeshua, a surge of gratitude and confusion in his heart.

"Don't tell Shimon," Rahel said. "Your brother has worries enough." She closed the pouch and set it aside. "The Sabbath is coming," she whispered. "This evening. If my sons can rest, really rest, with full bellies . . ." She smiled faintly. "That, I ask for. I feel . . . so weak. Like I might fall over."

Koach said nothing. He was thinking. For the first time since that cry on the shore—"The dead! The dead!"—he was thinking.

Something had fed on Tamar, but hadn't eaten anyone else. It had found her on her way to the shore to meet him, and either she'd . . . *stopped* . . . it, or after wounding her it had pursued someone else, following them away from the town. And the attack must have happened some way up the shore from Koach's own hiding place beneath the boat, because he'd heard no cry from her, nor any moan from the corpse.

He tried to make sense of that.

The corpse might have been missing part of its throat, might have been unable to voice one of the low wails of the dead.

But he should have heard *her*.

Surely he would have heard her scream for help.

Perhaps Tamar had needed to take the long way through the stone houses, to avoid watchful eyes. Or there might be some other reason she had not been near.

Or perhaps she *had* been.

Perhaps the thing had seized her, torn into her before she even knew it was there, and perhaps she—who had learned how to suffer beatings in silence—had swallowed her own cry, to keep him from running out to her.

That thought was more than he could bear.

"There are still dead out there," Koach said.

Rahel's hands paused in their work, but only for an instant. Then she whispered, as though to herself or to God, "I ask only for rest for my sons. And for me."

The dying wasn't over yet.

Koach thought he knew why the corpse that had killed his beloved was not in the town, nor on the shore. Tamar had led it away, in silence, led it away from her lover and her town, before finding some way to slip back unseen by it. And when she had, the fever had already been on her, the fever that would burn her away, leaving her body empty for one of the hungry *shedim* to make its home in. She hadn't come to him to say goodbye. She had run to her father's house, perhaps with dawn already in the sky, to die there.

To protect him.

To protect their town.

She had been the strong one.

Rahel looked at him, and her face softened. "It is all right, my son," she said. "Sometimes you have to weep."

657

He lifted his hand to his face. His cheeks were wet.

"How do you bear it?" he whispered.

Memory flickered in her eyes. "You just do."

"Does it get better?"

"No. It doesn't." She reached for a small basket lined with cloth, something to place fish in. "But you get stronger. The burden is not less heavy, but you are more able to carry it."

Koach's face crumpled, "I want her back, amma."

Her face crumpled, too. She held out her arms and he threw himself into them, as he had many times when he was a small boy.

"I know," she whispered into his hair, holding him tight. "I know."

* * *

A heavy slam of wood against wood interrupted them. Koach gave a start and sprang to his feet.

The door. It was the door.

He exchanged a fearful glance with his mother. Her eyes hardened.

Koach ran to the door and pulled it clumsily open. A plank of rough-hewn pine barred the way at the height of his shoulders, and two men—Natan El and Mordecai—held it in place while Bar Cheleph swung his hammer.

He was *nailing* it to the doorposts!

"What?" Koach gasped.

Bar Cheleph's eyes were wide with fear. "Get back, Hebel. All within are unclean. You'll die, and rise," he said. "But we won't let you break loose to devour the town."

The men let go of the board and reached for another.

Heart racing, Koach glanced past the men. The street outside had emptied. A few people watched from the doorways of other houses, eyes showing their whites. He caught sight of the silent woman, standing in the shade cast by the nearest wall of Benayahu's house. She had pressed herself to the wall as though to make herself unseen or unnoticed. Her face was white with terror.

"No one's unclean within," Koach said. His throat tightened. "My mother lives."

"Not for long." The board clacked into place beneath the other, and Bar Cheleph set an iron nail at one end and drove the hammer against it. The sound was fierce and brutal and loud, the board driven against the doorpost and the doorpost driven against the stone wall of the house. Bar Cheleph kept swinging the hammer, rhythmic blows as though the house were being beaten. Koach shrank back, a wild image in his head of the house boarded up for the ritual seven days, he and his mother and Yeshua dying of thirst within, unless they found a way to leap, unseen, from the roof.

Koach drew himself up, his voice high with fear. "This is my brother's house—"

"And when he returns, he'll understand. Seven days to separate the unclean from the living. Then he can go inside and sort out the living and the dead, the clean and the bitten."

"Don't!"

"Get *back*, Hebel." Bar Cheleph lifted the hammer, the whites of his eyes showing. "We *saw* the dead girl touch you, saw you touch her cold flesh. I grieve for your mother, we all will. But she is dead. Or will be in moments. We all saw the wound." He glanced over his shoulder at those who stood at their doors. "Help us! Quickly. Before she rises!"

Mordecai lifted a third board, and he and Bar Cheleph slammed it into place below the others, at waist height. Koach shivered; he was looking now at a wall, a wall of hard wood with chinks of light between the planks.

He ran back into the house's interior, into the open atrium. Rahel was nowhere to be seen. Koach ran to the stranger, who still leaned against the wall with a nearly emptied bowl of water in his hands and one of Rahel's blankets about his shoulders.

"Bar Yosef," he cried.

The man didn't look up. His eyes stared into some other place.

"Bar Yosef . . . *navi* . . . they're boarding up the door. Help me stop them. Please!"

Still he didn't look up.

Koach bit back a shout of frustration. If only he were not *hebel*, if he were a man like any other, *he* would be carrying his lover's body up the hill and Shimon would be here to stop Bar Cheleph. "I have only one arm. *Help* me!"

"They aren't boarding up the door. They've stopped." Yeshua frowned. "Or they will stop. In a moment . . . Can't you hear them, Koach? The dead, all the dead."

Koach felt a chill. But he couldn't think about that now. He looked about the atrium desperately, and then rushed to his secret room. He ducked inside and knelt by the cold wall, his fingers scrabbling at the loose stone. There. He felt the hilt cold in his palm. His carving knife, small but freshly whetted and sharp.

He stepped out of the small room and hesitated, his heart wild in his chest. That hilt in his palm.

Yeshua watched him, his face troubled, but said nothing.

Ice in his heart. "I'll do what I have to," Koach whispered.

Suddenly the rug over the door to Rahel's room was drawn aside, and she stepped out into the atrium and walked with swift purpose toward the outer door. No trace of her earlier struggle, her fever, or her torn and soiled garments remained. Her hair was combed and bound back as though she were preparing to host guests in her home. She wore her cleanest, least tattered gown, one green like the grass by the sea. No kohl for her eyes or adornments for her ears and throat, for she was Hebrew, not Greek. Yet she stood tall and regal. Bar Yonah's wife, once a power in the town in her own right.

Koach fell in at her side, his knuckles white about the knife.

"I am not dead, Bar Cheleph," she called out in a cool, clear voice.

Bar Cheleph looked in over the boards and his eyes widened. "Get back," he said.

"It's all right," Rahel said. "I have no fever. I am well. There is no need to board up my door, or to do any violence to my house. Let it stand as it stood when my husband lived in it."

"Bat Eleazar," Bar Cheleph whispered.

She met his gaze, then drew her sleeve up her arm to the shoulder. "Whatever this stranger from the inland hills might be," Rahel said, "he has washed away my fever as I might wash away dirt from this gown. I am well."

Mordecai gasped and stumbled back.

Bar Cheleph only stared at Rahel's arm, at the smooth skin where a wound had been. The muscles of his throat moved.

"Tear down the boards," he said hoarsely.

When neither of the other men moved, he gasped, "Tear down the boards. Now. As you love my father, move!"

There was a great wrenching of wood and the cry of nails being torn free of the doorposts, and then the men cast the planks aside and the door was again an open space. Koach took a slow breath, let it out. Then he slipped the knife quietly into the pocket inside his tunic. He hadn't needed it. He shivered. If he'd used it to carve flesh, he didn't think he would ever again have been able to use it for carving wood.

But he had nearly lost his mother today. He would not lose her again. For a moment, just a moment, he understood his brother. Understood his brooding, his brief storms of temper. Understood the strain he felt, protecting their family.

Bar Cheleph's shoulders were tense. He kept his gaze lowered. Her face stern, Rahel turned and walked back into her atrium.

Before he could either follow or shut the door, Koach was startled by a cry in the street. He saw Yohanna striding down from the direction of the synagogue and his father's house. In his arms he carried a lean figure in a white robe. His face was strikingly like Yohanna's, only folded up into wrinkles, his hair and beard the clean white of foam on the night sea.

He was Yesse.

The priest's father.

Behind them came a great crowd of people—men and women, fishers carrying baskets, and even a few boat people at the back, their faces slack with fatigue and grief and the awareness of the heavy tread of despair stalking the street behind them.

"*Navi!*" Yohanna cried. "*Navi!*"

They turned and saw Yeshua standing in the middle of the atrium, his hair hanging about his face, lank and sweaty, half concealing the darkness of his eyes.

"Little time," he said. "Little . . . little time. The dead. . . I can . . . can hear . . . All of them, all of them coming."

YESSE

"WATCH THE shore." Yeshua's voice was as calm as though he were mentioning the color of the sky. "They are coming."

Bar Cheleph cast a wild glance at his adopted brother and grandfather, and then turned and bolted from the doorstep, racing down the narrow street. The others looked on with wide eyes. Koach swallowed, realizing suddenly what the man's words might mean—if he were indeed the *navi*, if he indeed could see the things God could see.

Yohanna didn't seem even to have heard. He simply carried his grandfather over the threshold, his gaze on the stranger's face. "Help him, Bar Yosef," he said. "Help him."

Yeshua was staring after Bar Cheleph, and he didn't answer. Rahel glanced from his face to Yohanna's. "Bar Zebadyah," she said softly, "will you lay your grandfather by the olive?"

He nodded quickly, and carried him past. Rahel joined him, laying out blankets by the tree.

"I need to be there," Yeshua murmured. "I need to be there, there at the heart of it . . . but for what . . . what do I need to do, what do I need to do . . ." He let out a groan of frustration and lowered his head. For the briefest moment, his hands seemed to *burn*, as though he were holding them before a hot fire and the light was shining through his flesh. Koach's eyes widened.

"*Navi*," Rahel called.

Yeshua was breathing hard, as though he'd been straining against a locked door. The light faded, and he glanced up. His face beaded with sweat, as it had been after he had healed Koach's mother. He walked slowly toward the olive in the atrium, where Yohanna had lain his grandfather gently down. Koach followed. Unnoticed behind him, the people in the street who had followed Yohanna began to step through the door, their faces troubled or awed.

Yeshua knelt by the old man, gazing at the ruin of the elder's leg, twisted on that night of destruction long past. Rahel sat beside him, while Yohanna stood anxiously by. Yesse gazed back at the stranger with a question in his eyes.

"Help him, *navi*," Yohanna said.

"I am already tired," Yeshua said softly. "Already tired."

"You are *Eliya*," Yohanna said fiercely. "You are the *navi*. You are the one who takes away the uncleanness from the earth. Ha Matbil said it."

"The door is too hot," Yeshua murmured. "And even if I can, even if I can step through, what I will see, whatever I will do, whatever power this is the father has put in my hands, I cannot heal the whole land, Yohanna, not the whole land . . ." He swallowed, and his voice dropped, and he hung his head. "Yet what else, what else? Listen to the screaming until I am mad? Until it drives me back into the rocks? Into the sand and the wind and the wind and the desert? I cannot do that. I cannot."

The atrium was filling now with men and women. Rahel cast them a troubled glance but kept her attention on the stranger who had called her back to life with a song and a touch. The others, and Koach with them, looked on silently, waiting, as they had waited to see God's touch on their town for years, but now their waiting had a sharpness to it, an immediacy. Yesse's eyes bore that same look. It wasn't hope. It wasn't exactly hope. Only the demand for an ending.

"Who wounded you?" Yeshua asked without lifting his head.

"It doesn't matter." Yesse's was an old voice, rough and full of memory. "He no longer breathes." Yesse wet his lower lip with his tongue. "You spoke of the dead, the unclean lurching dead. There was a corpse on the shore. I saw it with my own eyes."

"More coming," Yeshua whispered. "I hear them."

"Is it true, what my grandson tells me?" Yesse gripped Yohanna's hand with bony fingers. "That God has sent a *navi* into the land? When have we needed one more?"

"When have we . . . you have said it," Yeshua said softly. His shoulders straightened. Then he said, quiet and clear, "I was raised the *nagar*'s son, his son, in Natzeret on the hill. I take things that are broken and broken apart and I join them, I join them together again." Suddenly Yeshua reached for the old man's other hand and gripped it tightly. His gaze met the old man's, and his eyes burned with sudden, dark intensity. "This is the truth, the truth, the truth I heard in the desert: All the world is broken and broken and broken apart. But nothing is broken that cannot be remade. Nothing is ill that cannot be healed, nothing captive that cannot be freed. Do you believe this, do you believe it?"

"I do," the old grandfather whispered, held by his gaze. "Yes, I do. Today I saw nets full of fish. I believe you."

"Then I can believe it also. Stand, old father," he whispered. "Stand. Your faith . . . it has made you well."

Yesse stared at him, his hands shaking. A strange look passed over his face. His right leg shifted slightly. He glanced at his calf, and his eyes were wild. Yohanna let go of his grandfather's hand and stood, almost falling over.

Yeshua rose more slowly, bending over the old man, still clasping his other hand; Yesse clung to his fingers. After a moment, Yesse got stiffly to his feet beside the stranger.

Those watching gasped, an almost sexual sound.

Yesse's eyes were wide, his hair adrift about his face. "I . . . I . . ." He glanced about wildly.

"Yes." Yohanna's voice was choked. "You are standing. You're standing, grandfather."

Yesse stumbled—as though his legs were numb from sitting too long—and Yohanna leapt forward, catching his arm, but Yesse shoved him away with a furious and wiry strength. "No," he said. His grandson stepped back, and Yesse recovered his balance. He took another step. This one was stronger.

Yesse kept his gaze on his feet. Then he laughed, a short bark. He glanced up at Yeshua with watery eyes. "You *are* the *navi*," he breathed. "The *navi* who will save Israel. All my life I have waited for you. All my life."

Yeshua's eyes were guarded, as though he were holding up his last shield against the yearning in Yesse's eyes. "I want only to sit by a fire, by a fire, and eat fried fish and talk," he said. "Or work with the wood, the cedar and terebinth in my father's shop. Only I can't stop the screams. I can't, I can't stop my ears."

* * *

The house of Rahel bat Eleazar filled with people and with activity. Men lay baskets of fish about the olive tree, and others threw fish over the coals. Rahel herself crouched with a knife—a spare from her supplies, not the one she had used against the dead—and she slit open one of the fish and pulled out its heart. This she set on the scented fire, and then leaned back and closed her eyes a moment, breathing in the redolence of it and, with it, the hope of safety for her house.

The silent woman—the woman from the boats—slipped into the house last, her face pale and so thin. But Koach only looked away. He cast aside his small knife and stepped out through the door. He needed to breathe a moment, and the atrium was too full of people; he didn't dare slip through them to his secret place. It would be like revealing that place to the whole town. So instead he leaned against the doorpost, his back itching from dried sweat. He felt something against his shoulder and stepped away from the post, saw a hole in the wood amid a corona of splinters, where one of the iron nails had been torn out.

Koach touched it with his finger, felt the sharpness of the splintered wood. Heard again Bar Cheleph's cry, *Board up the house! Board up the house!*

"He is afraid," he whispered.

For years, Bar Cheleph had seemed a giant to him: a fierce and brutal man with heavy fists. But Koach was not so much shorter than Bar Cheleph now. And he had seen Bar Cheleph's eyes. The man was only afraid. Terrified. Trying to live in a world that had tried to eat him.

The thought troubled Koach. He glanced back toward the street. And so he was just in time to see Zebadyah round the corner, hobbling toward him at a pace quicker than most men stride. Yakob was behind him, a net slung over one shoulder, his eyes anxious.

But *Zebadyah's* eyes . . .

The old priest had a desperate look, as though he were staring over the edge of a sea-cliff a mere breath before plunging in a long fall toward the deep. He all but ran to the doorstep, his hair wild about his face, bringing with him the heavy scent of wood smoke from the burning of the boats. Before Koach could step out of the way or say a word, Zebadyah grasped his weak arm and with strength like a bear threw him to the side. The priest rushed into the house as Koach struck the ground with his hip, cried out in pain, and rolled into the street.

PART 7

KANA

HALFWAY UP the hill, Tamar's body—which at first had felt as light as a bundle of dry twigs—became heavy in Shimon's arms. The sun overhead burned hot, and sweat slickened his face; Shimon clenched his teeth and kept placing one foot before the other. Though he longed to stop and rest, he did not want to hold that defiled, coat-swathed body cooling in his arms even a moment longer than he had to. He wanted to be done with it. And—

And he could see, so clearly, the grief in his brother's eyes, the anguish as Koach gazed up at him and asked him to perform this duty that he could not. His brother, who had never asked him for help before. His brother, who always asked *to* help. His brother, whom he had always rebuffed, knowing he would be useless at the nets, at the oar, at the hauling of the boat down to the sea.

That look in Koach's eyes haunted Shimon. Tore at his freshly opened heart. Though he placed each step with care over the rocky ground, Shimon shut his eyes a few moments against the sun, shut his eyes against the turmoil in his heart. The sea wind blew at his back.

So he did not see anyone approaching, and no scent forewarned him. The first warning he had was the weight of a body slamming into his right side, carrying with it the sickly sweet smell of rot.

His eyes flew open; he cried out as earth and sky tilted. Tamar was knocked from his arms. Shimon had a confused glimpse of her hitting the ground, her limp body rolling free of the coat. Then the earth slammed into his back, a jagged rock cutting his shoulder. Everything above him went dark; the silhouette of a human head blocked out the sun. Hands clutched at his face and shoulder, the fingers so cold. Shimon shouted and kicked, his own hands scrabbling at the thing's wrists. The creature's weight fell on him. It snarled. Shimon stared up into the dull sheen of its eyes, like unpolished iron.

Shimon had a terrible flash of memory; he was on his back in the sand with his father's corpse looming over him. Then he pushed the memory away with a shout and drove his knee into the corpse's gut. It didn't even notice. It hissed just above his face, its breath on his cheek cold as the sea. He drove the heel of his left hand hard against its brow, his right hand peeling its fingers away from his face.

The corpse bit into his sleeve and worried at his arm like a wolf, trying to tear away the wool and get at the warm, vulnerable skin beneath. Shimon cried out and kneed the corpse in the groin. It just kept tearing at the cloth with its teeth, growling. Panic ran cold through Shimon, like ice water pumped from his heart out to every part of his body, freezing him more with each heartbeat. All the world constricted to that face, those dull, empty eyes, the snarls from its throat. It was stronger than him, and it was going to eat him. Only a thick woolen sleeve held away his death. He was shaking.

Shimon had a momentary sense of someone looming over him and the corpse. A large hand gripped the corpse's shoulder and pulled the creature off him. Shimon had just time to draw in a shocked breath before glimpsing a flash of bright metal, the curved tip of a knife catching the corpse beneath its chin and then sliding smoothly up until the hilt of white bone pressed against the thing's chin, sheathing the knife in its head. The knife tip emerged from the creature's brow. The corpse jerked once and then went limp.

The man who had stilled it rolled it aside, and the body lay in the grasses, unmoving. Bar Nahemyah—Kana—stood bending over it. With a grunt, he set his sandaled foot against the creature's collarbone and then gripped the hilt and wrenched his knife free of the dead flesh. As Shimon scrambled back, kicking himself away from the corpse, and got unsteadily to his feet, Kana wiped the blade clean on the tattered remains of the corpse's garments. Shimon watched the blade; it was easier to look at that than to look at the dead.

"That's a Roman knife," he breathed.

The curved blade was nearly the length of Shimon's forearm between the elbow and the wrist.

"They call it the sica," Kana said quietly, stepping away from the corpse. "You catch the bottom of the jaw with the point—or you catch the bottom edge of the helmet, if you are stabbing a Roman—and you set your palm against the hilt and shove hard. Drive it up through the jaw and into the face. All the way to the scalp. One swift strike, and the corpse falls still. Then you do the next. And the next."

Shimon gazed at him in horror. The name he'd heard Bar Nahemyah claim—the name *Kana*, the zealot—rang in his mind, a name of knives and dread.

Kana began cleaning the blade on a tuft of grass. "The *kanna'im* have taken to carrying these. The fighting priests. You can't imagine it, Shimon. What Yerushalayim is like now. The poverty. The stink in the alleys. The dead. The Romans keep them down. Sometimes. The other times, *we* do." His voice went hoarse, as though he were holding back some great torrent of feeling. "We are the People, Shimon. The people of Yehuda tribe, the last of the Hebrews. The other tribes are dead. On all the earth, only we know the Law and the Covenant. Only we can keep this land, our land, free of the dead. The Romans bring hunger and slavery, and finally a weary death for us all." Straightening, Kana gazed down at the corpse.

"I said I didn't want your help," Shimon said. "Why did you follow me here?"

"I needed to talk with you." Kana's eyes were intent. "It is coming, Shimon. A dark time. You could help stop it."

"Your killers in the hills don't need me," Shimon muttered.

"*I* need you. This town respected your father. Revered your father. Your father, who stood against both Rome and the corpses that walk."

"My father is dead."

"But you live. And whether you like it or not, Shimon, Israel needs you. All men who are still true to the Covenant in their hearts wait for you. You could lead the fishing towns of Galilee to rise up. You could do it. They know your father's name."

But as Kana spoke, Shimon gazed at Tamar's body where it lay in a fumble of limbs like a crumpled spider. The stink of that corpse was worse now. One hand lay bent, and something had fallen from the sleeve. The object drew Shimon's gaze: a small wooden horse, no larger than a clay cup, an object you could hold in your hand. The intricacy of its mane, the small eyes and mouth, the lines of its flanks—this was something his brother had made.

Shimon crouched beside the dead girl. He picked up the horse carefully, ignoring Kana's frown. The small wood-carving felt cool in his hand; with an inward shiver he realized it had been nestled against the cold flesh of the dead. Yet he did not drop it or hurl it away. He held it, looked at it—the first time he had really *looked* at one of this brother's secretive carvings. He suddenly felt . . . heavy. Old. The burden of his People, his Law, his God, his heritage a weight on his shoulders. He didn't want to worry about the Law; he didn't want to revere his God or the traditions of the father who had betrayed him by being so long absent. He didn't want to fight each night for scraps from the sea to keep his family alive, fighting alongside other men's brothers because his own was too weak. He certainly didn't want to seek trouble with the Romans, or even to acknowledge that they existed on days other than those on which Zebadyah collected what few goods the town had to send to the tax collectors in the Emperor's City. He wanted only to sit in his boat, cast the nets and pull them up, and be silent like the water.

But he had made Koach a promise.

He would keep that promise.

"My brother is strange," he said. "But he is my brother." He turned on Kana. His voice heated. "What you've said, Barabba has said all this before. And right after he said it, he rode down my brother in the street. My *brother*, Bar Nahemyah. He tried to drive a spear through my brother's body. So you tell me, 'Kana.' What place will there be for Koach, for my kin and my blood, in this new uprising of yours?"

Kana was silent, his face cold with remembered pain.

"I have devoted every night of my manhood to the netting of fish, to the boat, to bringing home food for my family. And you would have me throw them away? It is more important to see that my kin eat than it is to hate the Romans."

"The Romans hate you, brother."

"Let them."

"Your father hated them."

"My father is *dead*," Shimon nearly shouted. "I am going to his tomb. He is *dead*, and we here in Kfar Nahum are all fatherless sons. Get out of my way, Kana."

Shimon rolled Tamar's corpse gently back into the coat and lifted her from the earth. He made to stride past the other man. Kana stepped out of the way but said quietly, "You can't sleep forever, Cephas."

Shimon stopped.

"Someday the Romans will want more taxes than Zebadyah bar Yesse can send. Someday, there will be nothing left, not even what you have now."

"What did you say?"

Kana looked at him strangely. "I said—"

If Shimon had not been carrying a corpse, he would have shoved Kana violently in the chest. Rage surged hot and wild like the sea inside him. "I am *Shimon*. God of our fathers, what do you all want from me?"

He began striding up the hill. He could see the *kokh*, the tomb in which his many dead kin slept the long sleep. Kana called after him: "Cephas is the *rock*. We want you to be your father's son, the man our People need. The man you were born to be!"

His Father's Tomb

ONCE HE reached the tomb Shimon did his work quickly, for that place forced memories on him that he did not want. He lifted the girl's shrouded body and slid her feetfirst into the empty shelf to the left of his father's. The sunlight in the entrance to the *kokh* was pale, but the dimness of the tomb was not creepy or unnerving, only quiet. This was a place where the wind did not enter, a place where no *shedim* shrieked or whispered or demanded entrance to the human mind and body. Shimon slid the girl into the hole in the wall, onto the long stone shelf inside the hill, until only her hair was visible.

In this very tomb, Shimon's brother had been born; here, Shimon as a youth had held and comforted his mother as she bled from the birth. Everything that defined their family was here. The birth. Their father's body. And now this girl Tamar had a place on these cold stone shelves. Shimon gazed down at her hair. In the synagogue, Zebadyah had said once that God spoke a word, a secret word, into the ear of each child at the moment of its birth. And that this word, which each of them forgot as children but remembered when they had grown into men and women—though perhaps they had to spend many nights listening for it before they heard it again, spoken anew—this word was God's hope for their lives. Shimon wondered what word had been spoken into this girl's ear. Surely that word, that hope, had not been that she would be beaten by her father or devoured by the dead. Shimon thought the word must have been his brother's name. If the dead had not come to Kfar Nahum that night, if their father had not died, if the town had not been destroyed, if the corpses had not been dumped into the sea, if Koach had been born with two strong arms like a man, then he and this girl would have been together. Shimon had heard it in his brother's voice.

But whatever word God had spoken into Tamar's ear, she would never hear again. And whatever word he had spoken into Koach's ear, hearing it now would only bring his brother the sharp misery of joys glimpsed and gone.

* * *

All his heart a growl of grief, Shimon stepped toward the door of the tomb. Hesitating, he glanced at the shelf in the wall on which his father lay. He wrestled with himself, part of him longing to go to the shelf and pull his father's body free of it and see his face. He imagined unwrapping the burial linens, imagined hesitating before peeling free the final layer, fearful of seeing those eyes open but unliving, fearful of hearing again that terrible moan. But no, the face within would be still and shriveled tightly to the bone, preserved like the mummies of Kemet, though not so well. His father's eyes would be closed. The Greek pig-eaters placed coins on the eyes of their dead, to pay the boatman to ferry their souls over the last river; the Hebrews brought to their dead only spices and song. At his father's burial, Shimon had had neither. He had stood shaking and silent while his mother sang the Words of Going, the memory of his father's lurching over the shore still fresh and vicious in his heart.

Shimon stared helplessly at that shelf. Out of some chasm in his heart, rage welled up, hot as fever, until he shook with it. Rage at his father for leaving him standing on that shore, leaving him alone to care for his mother and his infant sibling. Rage at that other father in heaven who had turned his back when the Romans descended on their town. When the dead came down from the hills. When the dead devoured or blighted the fish beneath the sea. His father who had left them all like children outside the walls of a house, to eat what scraps they could find. Rage at both his fathers, who had proven too weak or too disinterested to help. And neither of them had been there to tell him that he was man enough to handle what would come, or to teach him how to.

And, finally, rage at the newcomer, the fish-caller who spoke so glibly and easily of fathers, and who thought that filling the nets could erase the pain and death-cries of a People as easily as an incoming wave might erase footsteps in the sand.

Shimon turned and strode from the tomb, breathing hard. Outside, the day was aging fast and God's sky was empty but for a crane winging slowly northeast toward the high ridges of Ramat ha-Golan. A slight breeze stirred the grasses on the hill, but Shimon did not fear it. He gazed down at the town at the sea's edge and saw it suddenly as he had never seen it before: a cluster of ill-organized stone houses about a tall synagogue, but with no wall, no shelter from the wind or from strangers out of the hills. Vulnerable to the dead and the living alike. Zebadyah was right. They should cast this man out. And Kana too. They should wall everything out, forever. They had lost too much. Let them cling to what little they had left, though it be only rags, though it be only empty nets. When had anyone outside the small atriums of their houses ever cared for them? The Romans preyed on them—though now from a distance. Barabba would prey on them, in his own way. Threshing and Rich Garden and Tower pretended they did not exist. Maybe they *didn't* exist; maybe the apparent survivors of Kfar Nahum were only ghosts, *shedim* without bodies, but too recently dead to realize it.

GREATER THINGS THAN THESE

"RAHEL!" ZEBADYAH cried. "Rahel!" Forgetting in his panic that her name was not his to use or to call, he sprang through the door, hardly noticing that he'd hurled Koach aside. There was only the terrible thought of Bat Eleazar—of Rahel, oh Rahel—lying cold as stone in her house, as cold as his own dead wife so many long years before. His breath heaved; he had run through the ruined outskirts and past the tanner's shop and through the square of the synagogue, where some sat with baskets and were gutting fish, unaware of any shadow of the dead. Rahel, Rahel, beautiful Rahel. He had wanted only to keep her safe, to honor his lost brother, to . . . to hold her. To think that she might be gone. Worse, that she might come *back*. That she might rise to rend those about her with her teeth and nails. No. Not Rahel. Not her. God of our fathers, not her.

He rushed into her atrium and stopped short, for he could see Rahel bat Eleazar bending over a cookfire and prodding fish on the coals, calm and focused, as though she had never known pain. The air was rich with the smell of fried musht, mingled with the herbs from the scented fire. Rahel glanced up at him, and her eyes were full of life. So full of life.

"You are alive," he whispered. "Alive."

"Of course I am alive," she said, and straightened. There were others around them, other people in the atrium, but Zebadyah hardly noticed. He could see nothing but her face. She should have been shaken with fever, or dead, or . . . or worse.

After Yakob had led off his search party for Benayahu, Zebadyah had gone out to the old altar, the all but abandoned altar. There he had thrown himself to the ground and wet the soil with his tears, praying for a consolation that did not come. Natan El had found him there and had gasped out a story of Rahel bat Eleazar bitten by the dead. Zebadyah had found himself on his feet and running, running into the town.

And now she stood before him as full of life as when she had been young and he had been young, as when he had first seen her laughing as she walked alongside his brother. She was alive, she was alive. With a hoarse cry of joy, joy that wrenched everything in him, he leapt forward and seized her arms and pulled her to him, crushing her, his mouth finding hers, the heat and softness of her against him. So, so alive.

She stiffened. Then her hands beat at his shoulders, and he let her go. He took a step back and nearly fell, dizzied. She stood staring at him, a few strands of hair across her face, her cheeks flushed, her eyes wide with alarm. "Bar Yesse!" she gasped.

"Get away from her!"

The shout came from the door. The whelp, Hebel, stood there, his eyes cold with fury—looking so strangely, in that moment, like Zebadyah's brother Yonah. But the priest felt neither unease nor anger. He was too overwhelmed. He opened his mouth to apologize to Rahel, but only laughter came out. And then he fell on his rump and sat there in the middle of her house, laughing, his eyes squeezed shut, as though he were a small boy again.

"Zebadyah." That was an old voice, a rasping voice. "I don't think I have heard you laugh in a long time."

Zebadyah looked up. For the first time, he took note of the others in the house. The men and women preparing for a meal. The boat people, crouched back against one wall as though to communicate that they were no threat. The witch from Natzeret. And beside him—standing beside him—his father. Yesse.

Standing.

"Abba," Zebadyah whispered. "Abba."

Yesse walked slowly over and knelt beside Zebadyah, putting his arms around his son, pressing his lips to his hair. Zebadyah wanted to weep, but could not; so many mornings he had crouched beside his reclining father, holding him, comforting him, and always he had longed to be the one comforted, the one guided, the one fathered. Always he had felt his aloneness and his inadequacy, his guilt for hiding beneath the boats while his father was maimed.

Now his father was back. Consoling him. Lending him his strength.

It was as though the sky had fallen into the sea and the sea had become the sky. He was spinning, falling. He clutched at his father's arm. "Abba," he moaned, "help me to my feet."

A moment later, they were standing together. He faced his father, looking into those eyes old and gray as the voices of cranes over the water. His hand trembled where he held his father's arm. He tried to say with his eyes the words he had never voiced to Yesse, words of regret for that night.

I'm sorry.

The skin around Yesse's eyes crinkled. *I know.*

Drawing in a slow, shuddering breath, Zebadyah glanced about him, saw the pale and hungry faces of those gathered in the house: fishermen and a few of their wives, and boat people, and the bruised face of the stranger from Natzeret. This house was now filled with just such an assembly as he'd feared: a mingling of the clean and unclean, a collapse in the order he'd so carefully shored up against storm and wind, and no wall of fire or stone to hold it back.

Yet—

"I should thank you," he said, and found it difficult to swallow. He didn't know whether to laugh or weep or rage. Perhaps he was asleep and didn't know it; perhaps he was lost in the dream country. The world had stopped making sense.

Yeshua's face shone with sweat. "You will see greater things than these," he said. His voice was sad.

Zebadyah gazed at his face, trying to understand. His father's hand was strong on his shoulder. He choked back fresh tears, a tightness in his throat, and rubbed his eyes with the back of his hand. This sudden joy in him was running out at his eyes. Prophet or madman, he didn't know, couldn't know. But he had his father back. He turned his head at a sound and saw, through bleary eyes, Hebel still standing by the door, the boy's face white with wrath.

* * *

Koach didn't even notice the people gathered behind him on the doorstep. He felt he could tear down a wall, even one-handed, even weak, he was so angry. When the priest turned his face toward him and Koach saw his eyes wet with tears, it was too much. The priest *dared* affront his mother. That hateful old man who had denied him his *bar 'onshin*, whose son had beaten him in the street—he *dared*. He would *not* feel sympathy for this man.

"This is my brother's house," Koach said, his voice loud in the atrium. "And you are an uninvited guest."

Yesse frowned, and Zebadyah flushed—though whether with anger or embarrassment, Koach didn't know.

"Koach!" His mother rose to her feet. Her face was flushed, too, but her eyes flashed. Her tone cut through Koach's anger like a boat's keel through water, parting it.

"Bar Yesse," Rahel said, her voice cool though her face betrayed how shaken she was, "has done me no lasting harm. If I were to see my own father here, and strong, I would be wild with joy, as well. He is the *kohen* of our village and deserves your respect."

"How can you say that?" Koach cried. "He hates us."

"Koach!"

"He does! He always has. He acts as though he is the father of this house, but he is not!"

His mother straightened, and there was such fire in her eyes that he fell silent.

"Koach," she said, her voice sharp, "we have all said hateful things, and many of us have *done* hateful things. Because we are hungry, and we are tired, and none of us have slept well in many years. But there are fish, and we are sitting to eat. And we have this chance to make things right again." She glanced down, and for a moment her hands trembled as though she were fighting to hold in some tempest of emotion. Koach suddenly burned with shame, though he couldn't have said why.

"Help me make things right," she said.

"Amma," Koach whispered.

Rahel turned to Zebadyah, her tone tightly controlled. "Bar Yesse, I would ask you to atone for the insult to me by accepting my sons' hospitality and sitting at our fire for a while with your father."

Koach bit his lip, hard, to keep from opening his mouth and letting out the harsh words in his heart. He certainly didn't intend any hospitality to the priest—or to *any* of these people. His mother needed rest, and he . . . he needed time to breathe, privacy, a chance to retreat to his secret place and think. His hand itched to hold his carving knife. Finding beauty within the wood, he would find also some way to cope with the strangeness and the horrors and the joy of this day.

Rahel said, "Will you sit at my sons' fire, you and all these others, Zebadyah bar Yesse? It has been a long time since Kfar Nahum sat together."

Zebadyah stood as though struck—so long this house had been barred against him. But Yesse took his arm and drew him to the cushions that lay about the olive tree. "My son accepts, and so do I, Bat Eleazar. I have missed my grandson's house, and my daughter-in-law's cooking." And Yesse sat, seeming a little sore from age, but otherwise as able as any other man, as though his hip had never been twisted, his dignity never assaulted by Romans or the dead.

Rahel took charge, as though she were a queen in a palace of Shushan and not a fisher's wife. She knew all the names of those who had stepped into her house, all but the boat people, and she demanded theirs. Then she recruited helpers and seated others, and soon more fish were roasting, and a few women were helping her grind bread while others poured water for the ritual washing to the elbows before a meal. With a start, Koach realized the silent woman was among them, still clothed in his father's coat, its hem sweeping along the ground at her feet. She had already washed her hands and arms, for they were clean, and she sat down to grind bread as though she were any other woman of Kfar Nahum, dipping her finger into the meal and lifting some to her mouth as she worked. Rahel gave her a cool look but let her be; when there is an entire community to feed, a woman doesn't turn down help. Mordecai's sister and Natan El's wife carried platters and bowls around the circle that the seated guests formed. Yeshua stood alone, to the side, and for the moment none bothered him. The scent of food demanded the attention of those who'd been starving far more than any miracle of healing could. Zebadyah sat by his father, his face dappled by shadows and sun through the leaves of the olive, and his eyes were dazed. Yesse gripped his son's shoulder and leaned in to speak into his ear.

The bustle had sprung up so swiftly, Koach was left standing by the door. His stomach snarled at the scent of fish, but he ignored it. He couldn't join them at the meal, couldn't bear to be around so many people, his heart naked to their eyes. Breathing raggedly, he leaned back against the wall and lifted his hand to his face; he could smell death on his skin. Tamar's death.

Abruptly, he realized he wasn't alone. Yeshua was leaning on the wall beside him.

"Why don't you eat?" Koach said. "You are a guest."

"Eat," the man whispered. His eyes were a little glassy in a face that shone with sweat. "How can I eat?"

Koach wet his lips, not understanding. The man unnerved him, and the grief was so sharp in Koach's chest that he wanted no company. But this man had helped his mother, had . . . healed her. Brought her back. He blinked quickly against the moistening of his eyes.

"Your hands are shaking," he said.

Yeshua lifted his hands to look at them; his fingers were trembling. He was very pale. "There's a door, Koach," he whispered. "A door. I'm doing too much. Too much, too fast. Not ready, not ready for it yet, whatever is coming. I have to . . . have to be able to stand in that door, see what he sees, first."

"What are you talking about?"

"But how can I stand there?" His voice low. "I heard him, *heard* him weeping in the desert. Like all the world weeping, such terrible cries. Tore at my heart." He shut his eyes, the shaking in his hands worse. "How can I stand in that door, in that light, stand to see what makes him weep? Isn't the moaning in my ears enough? How can I bear any more? I can't, I can't bear it."

His shoulders shook and, startled, Koach realized Yeshua was sobbing. The man let no tears leak from under his eyelids. He let no sound break from his lips. He just shook. Koach stood awkwardly, unsure what to do. He was accustomed to his mother's comfort and to the indifference or hostility of others to his own pain, but he was not used to standing by another.

Except Tamar.

Except her.

The stranger drew in a ragged breath. "I am grateful to you," he said, opening his eyes.

Koach shook his head.

"You are the only one here, Koach, the only one who has made no demand on me. None. Though I hear your screams, too, and they are loud, they are loud. But the others. Prophet. Witch. Heal my grandfather. Heal Israel. Bury the Romans. You . . . you make me a guest in your brother's house. You didn't even bring me your arm, though you saw a lame man stand on his feet."

Koach went still. He had been so furious—at the priest, at Bar Cheleph, at the town and himself for letting Tamar suffer and die—and in such panic and then delirious relief over his mother, that he had not even considered that the stranger might . . . might straighten and strengthen his arm. He stared at the man in shock.

Koach glanced down at his right arm, concealed in its thick woolen sleeve. No, not concealed. He could never conceal it. Instinctively, he glanced at the people eating. Some of them kept looking up from their fish and watching Yeshua and himself by the door. Others were talking together in low voices. He listened to their talk for a moment, caught bits of it:

. . . *a lame man healed* . . .

. . . *the fish, and the fish* . . .

. . . *and Bat Eleazar. Signs, these are signs* . . .

. . . *signs* . . .

. . . *he's the* navi . . .

. . . *he must be the* navi . . .

. . . *no, he's a witch. You heard how he babbles, and he* . . .

. . . *said the dead are coming, the dead are coming. A vision* . . .

. . . *end of our town, this is our last meal* . . .

. . . *over there with Hebel? Why is he with Hebel* . . .

"Could you . . . ?" Koach whispered.

"I think so," Yeshua murmured. He was staring at those feasting, too. "But I know why . . . why you didn't ask. You have a worse injury. I know that injury. It is mine also."

"Your bruises," Koach whispered. He understood. Though this man had two arms, not one, somehow he had suffered as Koach had.

"I haven't eaten with my kin in . . . in some time," Yeshua said. "I tried to. After the desert, after that. I came back, slept one night in my mother's house, only one night before her neighbors lifted stones to throw." He looked down. "I miss that town, Natzeret. It is a small town, Koach, so small. Much smaller than this one. It is . . ." He swallowed. "It is lovely. There are olive trees and one press that still works, and in the morning, in the beautiful morning, I wake and I hear . . . the press creaking. And when the night . . . when it's night, I fall asleep to my father's hammer, tapping, tapping in his shop by the house. I miss that. Sometimes I am sleeping, in the lee of some ridge, and I wake, suddenly, quickly, so that the world tilts as though I've been spinning too fast, too fast, like a small child, all the stars wheeling around me like the gulls. And I hear it. That tapping. It sounds so real. I miss it. I miss it, Koach. He made beautiful things. I miss hearing him work. Miss helping him. I miss the old midwife's scowls and the way the weaver's children play stones in front of the well." He rubbed his hand quickly across his eyes. "Ah. I think I *will* eat." He indicated the gathering people with a small motion of his head. "You mustn't hate them, Koach. The priest, the others."

Koach met Yeshua's gaze, and then it seemed to him that this stranger who had healed his mother was gazing not only at him but *into* him. As though everything he had ever hidden, every secret place, every word he'd signed to Tamar, every time he had tossed in his bed, every time he had dreamed of taking her far across the sea to some new place—as though everything, everything, was laid bare before this man.

"They hate *me*," Koach said.

"No." Yeshua gave a vehement shake of his head. "No, they don't. They do not hate *you*. Because they . . . they have *never* seen you. They look at you and see only what they fear, only that." Yeshua's face twisted in pain; he closed his eyes and put his forehead to Koach's own, an uninvited yet comforting touch, as though they had a shared history. The stranger whispered a word in Hebrew too softly for Koach to hear. Then he said, "They do not hate *you*."

"I'm scared," Koach whispered back, startling himself. But now he'd spoken and the words could not be taken back. Tamar was dead. His mother had almost died. His brother loathed him. There might be no one who would really see him, ever again.

"We are all scared," Yeshua whispered. "Every one of us. Maybe even the father in the desert. We could all lose so much, so much."

Hearing a footstep, Koach lifted his head and found the silent woman standing before them, still in his father's coat, which enveloped her small body like a winter blanket. She held out a bowl of water cupped between her hands. Her eyes lifted for a single instant; Koach saw the flash of them before she lowered them again. As Yeshua looked on silently, Koach took the bowl unsteadily in his left hand, felt the smooth clay against his fingers and palm.

"Thank you," he said.

The water was cool and clear in his mouth.

The young woman offered the bowl next to Yeshua, who took it and drank in slow gulps, watching her over the rim. His eyes were not unkind. She blushed, which surprised Koach, who had seen her perform a small seduction at that cookfire on the shore earlier without any reddening of her face.

As though flustered, the woman turned back to Koach. She made a small sound in her throat, and from within the long coat, she brought out an article of wood and placed it in Koach's hand, lifting her fingers quickly so that her hand would not brush his.

He searched her face a moment, and then glanced down. It was a wooden horse, warm from her touch. Rougher than the one he'd carved over many weeks for Tamar. He'd made this one to practice. He must have left it in one of the long pouches sewn inside the coat.

His chest constricted. "Thank you," he whispered again.

Knowing the carving to be his, she must have meant its return to comfort him. Yet it made him think of Tamar. He dropped the carving carefully back into her palm. "But you keep it. Someone should have it."

"Cast it away," Zebadyah called. "Or throw it into the fire." The priest had turned where he sat, his back to the other guests, legs crossed, hands on his knees. His beard tumbled down his chest. He had begun to recover from his shock, but his eyes were anxious. Yesse beside him chewed gingerly on a bite of fish, watchful.

Koach bit back the words he wanted to say. "It's a gift to her."

Yeshua set down the clay bowl. "May I see it?" he asked.

The silent woman took a quick step back. For the second time, it occurred to Koach that this might be the first day since she was a small girl that she had been given a gift. In the past few hours she had been given a coat, fish to eat, and a wood-carving, a small thing of large beauty for one whose life held none—with nothing expected in return. It might break her to give it back. He wished he could understand the emotions, wild and dark, that he saw in her eyes. He wished that she could speak.

"It's all right," he whispered.

Yeshua held out his hand, with that quiet intensity in his eyes.

The woman's eyes were wet, and she hesitated. Then she placed the carving in the stranger's hand and jerked her fingers back quickly, fear in her eyes. Perhaps she'd been beaten in the past for an unwanted touch.

Yeshua lifted the wooden horse, looked at it closely. Then he walked away along the wall of the atrium, as though he'd forgotten them. Koach watched him, bewildered. He was so *strange*.

Zebadyah rose to his feet, but Rahel murmured without looking up, "He, too, is my guest, Bar Yesse." "We are open to the sky," Zebadyah said, his tone urgent. "What we do here, God can see. You, stranger. You have given me back my father, and I don't know what you are, if you are a *navi* or a witch, if it is prophecy and vision that make you shake like a twig, or *shedim* from the lord of flies. But that is an idol you hold in your hand, one touched by a heathen slut—"

"She is no heathen," Koach said sharply. "And—"

"She has spoken no word of Aramaic, no word of Hebrew."

"She *doesn't* speak. At all." The fury from before came back up, scorching. "Can't you see she is suffering and alone?"

Zebadyah reddened. "How dare you speak. You who made that *thing* of wood. You who insult my brother's memory—"

"Bar Yesse!" Rahel cried.

"Son," Yesse said.

"I will not see our town distracted by small gods!" Zebadyah's voice rose, thick with contempt. "Gods you can hold in your hand, rather than a God who can't be held, who will not come at our call, for we come at his. That!" He threw his hand out toward the stranger and the wooden horse he held. "That is an evil, a distraction you shape with your hand. A crack in the wall, while the dead press against the stones. That is not safe; it is not *useful.*"

Yeshua turned on the priest, his eyes hot, the wooden horse clutched in his hand, his voice loud and quick. "The father who made you may not find *you* useful—or you—or you—" He took them all in with a sweep of his hand. "Of what *use* are any of you to the Holy One who shaped the earth and filled the seas? But I have been in the desert and I . . . I believe this: There has never been a day when the father has not found you beautiful."

There was silence. Even Koach was taken aback at the hardness in the stranger's voice.

Yeshua turned the horse over a few times in his hand, peering down at it. His face was troubled.

"I think it is possible," he murmured, "to keep every letter of the written Law yet fail to live a lawful life. And maybe it is possible to yearn, even to yearn for the father's heart and yet . . . yet miss him entirely."

"Bar Yosef . . ." Zebadyah began.

"Sit, my son," Yesse said behind him. "Eat. Our town has been unclean a long time, and the cleansing of it can wait until after we eat. Tonight we are guests in Bar Yonah's house. I'll hear no shouting in my grandson's house."

Zebadyah kept silent, his face drawn with old pain. But he did not sit.

Yeshua walked back to the young woman and pressed the wooden horse into her hands; she took it and backed away.

"Bury it in the sand, if you will," he said. "You do not need it. You do not need it, *talitha.*"

* * *

As Yeshua stepped away from the woman, his face went white. For a terrible moment he stood completely still. Then, with a hoarse cry, he clutched at his ears, at his head.

"Bar Yosef?" Koach cried.

Others leapt to their feet, staring in horror or confusion. Rahel stood, too, her face lined with worry. Their shadows appeared long before their feet, with the approaching Sabbath.

It was a long moment before Yeshua spoke. When he did his voice was thick. "Just stop . . . just stop screaming . . . stop . . ."

"Witch," Zebadyah whispered. Yesse took his son's hand, squeezing his fingers.

Rahel was at the stranger's side in a moment, her fingers all but touching his shoulder, though he was neither husband nor kin to her.

"Water! Get him water, amma!" Koach said to her.

Yeshua stretched out one hand as though to push them all away. "No," he gasped. "I am all right . . . It is just sometimes . . . sometimes too much . . ."

His gaze fixed on the young woman who still held that woodcarving.

"You are the loudest," he said. "The screaming in your heart . . . without pause. What . . . what hurt you so?" He drew in air, his chest heaving. Then he staggered toward the silent woman. The whites of her eyes showed, as though in a moment she might turn and run from the house.

There was a desperate look in Yeshua's eyes.

"Don't hurt her!" Koach cried.

"It *might* hurt, *talitha*," Yeshua said. "It might. You lost this, and it may hurt, coming back."

Talitha, he'd called her again.

Little girl, little daughter.

He reached for her, and she stood, trembling, as he touched her hair. Koach stood tensed, unsure what to do. Rahel's eyes were watchful. All their eyes were watchful.

Stepping near to the young woman, Yeshua bent his head and did a shocking thing. He pressed his lips to the woman's throat, gently.

The touch was intimate and familiar and unsettling. Not because he appeared to *want* her, but because he was treating her as the very closest of his kin, as though anyone who looked up into his face with such naked need might *be* his kin. No one spoke. All of them—those seated at their meal, those standing—all of them just watched the stranger, this man who stepped over their People's traditions and their boundaries as simply and without regret as though these were only lines drawn in the sand.

Yeshua straightened and looked at the woman's eyes a moment; she gazed up at him in shock. Her lips parted; she released a sound like a sigh, like something leaving the body. She began to tremble.

Koach saw her take a breath. He went still, seized with sudden, fierce premonition.

She was shaking.

She sang a high, wavering note.

Her eyes shone with tears.

"It's all right," Yeshua said softly. His own eyes shone. "It's all right. The Sabbath Bride, she is here, even just outside the door. Will you welcome her in for us, *talitha?*"

She lifted her voice higher, and her eyes filled with tears. Other eyes moistened around her. She began to weep as she sang, and she laughed helplessly.

"Come!" Yeshua cried, spinning to face the others, his arms out, his hair wild about his face. "Have the waters worn away your hearts and your lives like Iyobh's stones? Does she need to sing alone?" He took the girl's hand and lifted it high, and he held out his right hand to Rahel, who stood nearest. "Take my hand," he said softly, and with wondering eyes, she did. "Everyone, please. Sing."

He lifted his voice in Hebrew, strong Hebrew words out of a desert so deep in their past. Then Rahel began to sing, too, her voice thin at first, then stronger. Old Yesse stepped near, staring at the young woman; Rahel reached for his hand, and without even seeming to notice, he took her small fingers in a firm grip that belied his age. And as if that one touch poured water from a cistern, they all began to sing, some taking hands, some not. The song was an ancient psalm and one they had heard recited in the synagogue, though without music. Dawid himself might once have stood at the entrance to the Cave of Adullam and sang that psalm to the morning air in that voice of his that had charmed the land's women and its men and even the six-winged angels of heaven.

The house sang. In ten, twelve, fifteen voices, they sang their love of the Shabbat Bride who brought with her a covenant of rest and peace between God and all living things for whom even the drawing of breath is a labor.

Then something happened that had never happened before in Kfar Nahum or in any village of Israel. Those who were seated because their bodies gave them pain rose shakily to their feet. Sinews reknit themselves. Limbs straightened and strengthened. One beggar's murky eyes cleared and gazed for the first time on a world of color and shape. The healing passed by touch from one person to the next, swift as a whisper, and the room filled with heat. Each face lit with a glow like that of flames on a winter night. The hair of the men and women crowded into the house rose as in a lightning storm, and wind swept against their faces. They heard the walls creak with the pressure of God's presence, the *shekinah* that had fallen on their fathers' tents in the desert, now filling this small house until the stone out of which it was made groaned. Then the heat rolled through the door and out into the street, and dust billowed in the sudden wind.

The townspeople and the boat people looked on each other in wonder, hearing each other's voices. Most of them hadn't sung in years.

Not in this silent town where even the synagogue knew neither music nor laughter.

Not in this place of grief.

Not in the house-shaped tombs of Beth Tsaida by the sea.

* * *

One of them didn't sing.

Koach took up a clay pestle, small and heavy, that his mother had dropped by the firepit, and then retreated to the doorstep. There he stood and gazed out at the dust blowing in the street. He was shaken. Singing and joy and that heat in the house were as alien as the fish flopping in their hundreds on the sand. He clutched his weak arm. The dust gusted up from the street as though stirred by the footsteps of the Sabbath Bride.

Whatever had killed Tamar was out there still, prowling the shore or the wild slopes like a roaring lion, looking for someone to devour. Likely the sound of song and feast loud over the shore would bring it back, summoning that lurching corpse like a guest arriving late.

Koach glanced down at his right hand, the hand that was thin and dead. He tried to make it into a fist. His fingers didn't even twitch.

His eyes stung.

What if that arm were to be healed? That would not make him a man, not make him whole. He had been denied his *bar 'onshin*. He had been barred from the synagogue. He had been struck, spat upon, thrown to the dirt.

You have a worse injury, Yeshua had told him.

The other young men—Yakob, Bar Cheleph, Bar Nahemyah, Yohanna— they were not in his mother's house feasting with the old and the women and the beggars. They were probably all on the shore, watching for the dead or searching for signs of Benayahu.

Even while he sat idle here.

He had only one arm, but he had two eyes; he could watch. He could shout. He could do his part. He drew in a breath. It was for boys to mope and men to act, he told himself. He'd had no *bar 'onshin*, but at least he could do his best to be like a man. Anything less would shame the woman he'd loved, who was dead. He thought of Shimon entombing Tamar, doing her the honor he could not, and his face burned.

The surge of heat and power within the house behind him faded, but he still heard many voices singing, his mother's among them, pure and beautiful as he'd rarely heard it before. He didn't know what was happening, what was changing within this town. He didn't know what was changing in him. But he knew what he had to do.

He might step inside again, find his carving knife. But no, no, he would not go to watch for the dead with that in his hand. He was a youth who carved things of beauty and fittings for boats; his blade would remain a craftsman's tool, not a zealot's knife. His grip tightened instead about the pestle his mother had used for grinding meal.

Koach took a breath. This was a thing he had to do. But he would wait for his brother's return; he wouldn't leave his mother alone in a house crowded with others.

So he watched the dust move with the wind's breath, and listened for the approach of his brother's feet.

PART 8

RAHEL'S STORY

IT WAS almost dusk before Shimon staggered back into the town. Even as he reached the outskirts, he heard the singing of women. He stopped, astonished. Listened. Strained his ears as though his ears were cups to fill with all that music. He drew in a ragged breath. How long—how long since he had heard music like that? The Sabbath Bride was walking across the water into the town, following the last footsteps of the setting sun, and for the first time since Shimon was a boy, the town was welcoming her.

The singing stopped about the time that Shimon reached his house. The door was open, but Koach stood at it like a doorkeeper, with a pestle clutched in one hand, and their gazes met. There was a question in Koach's eyes.

Shimon found he couldn't speak, so he only nodded.

He saw the relief and sorrow in his brother's eyes and was startled, for it was not the sorrow of a boy he saw, but a man's grief. Whoever this youth was, he was not *hebel*. Suddenly Shimon wondered if his brother had grown to manhood while he slept between the nights' battles with the sea. The thought shamed him. But there was also a warm flicker of pride for his brother, something he hadn't felt before.

"I have to go," Koach said quietly.

"Go?"

He lifted the pestle, and his eyes glinted with a hardness that Shimon had seen before only in the eyes of the fishers.

"Something's still out there. Zebadyah's sons have gone already to watch. They'll need help."

Shimon stood very still. He could hear voices within the house, but not their words.

"Be careful," he said at last. There was nothing paternal in his tone. It was just one brother's advice to another.

Koach gave him a grateful look, and then inclined his head respectfully. "You also," he said. He stepped past Shimon and began walking quickly around toward the back of the house and the stretch of shore behind it.

Shimon watched his brother go. He gripped his shoulder a moment; it burned where the rock had cut him. Maybe that corpse up on the hill had been the only one they had to worry about. But he didn't think so. From Koach's tone, he knew Benayahu had not been found. And there might be others. Sometimes, it was not just one corpse you dragged up in your nets. There might be three or four. Since his thirteenth year he'd known that any winter might be the town's last. Nothing was certain, nothing was safe.

He stepped inside his house, turned, and shut and barred the door by long habit. And stopped. Startled. There were new scents in the air. Fish roasted for food, and the sharper scent of spices. His mother must have placed a fish over the spirit fire to keep the shedim from the house. He hadn't smelled *that* in . . . so long. For the first time, it really sank in that there were *fish*. There was food. There were hearts to lay on the coals to keep the *shedim* away. And maybe, just maybe, everything was going to be all right.

He blinked, his throat tight, and stepped through to the atrium.

The beggar-stranger from Natzeret stood with his back to the olive tree. Perhaps twenty men and women of the town—and perhaps ten boat people— sat around him, their faces upturned, listening. Some of them, Shimon knew, had been broken in body. One had been blind. And that young woman had been mute, the one who appeared to be wearing his father's coat—his *father's* coat, but Shimon was too overwhelmed, too bewildered, for the coals of anger in his chest to flicker into fresh heat. He just stared. Those who had been broken now sat hale and whole, and he knew the singing he'd heard had come from this house.

Facing the others, Yeshua was drawn and pale as after great labor. He was talking in a low murmur; Shimon couldn't make out the words. The stranger looked completely intent on those sitting near him, and didn't glance up as Shimon looked on, bewildered.

This man stood in his house, in his *house*, with more than two dozen unexpected guests. He looked about for Rahel, but couldn't see her; she was not among the seated guests. She was not at the firepit, though there was evidence of a meal. A *vast* meal.

His belly growled so fiercely that some of the guests glanced up at him.

There had been a feast here, a feast of strangers. He stood outside their circle, unsure how to act, everything in him a wash of confusion and fatigue.

686

He glanced about, saw that the rug was drawn across the door to Rahel's small room along the outer wall of the house. Had she gone to bed, with so many strangers in the house? Nothing here made any sense.

* * *

Too weary and his emotions in too great a turmoil to deal with the strange *navi* or the people pressed all about him, or even to throw them from his house, Shimon went to find his mother. Stepping into her room, he let the rug over the door fall back behind him to block out the sight and some of the noise from their atrium. There was a little light, very faint, from between the slats of the boarded-up window, and by it Shimon saw that Rahel lay in her bedding with her small hands clasped at her breast, her fingers curled around a tattered shawl. His father's *tallit*. Shimon's throat tightened. In this dim light, though he had seen them many times before, his mother's hands looked suddenly wrinkled and aged.

"Amma," he whispered.

She glanced up, and he saw that she had been crying. A day ago, when he had been numb, it might have wearied him rather than distressed him. Now he ached for her, and hurried to sit beside her, setting his hand on her shoulder.

"Amma, what is it?"

She just shook her head.

"Amma—"

"All our people," she whispered.

His face hardened. "I will get them out of the house, amma. And that . . . that man from Natzeret. I'll throw him to the dirt."

"No." She smiled up at him and took his hand in hers. They *looked* frail, but her grip was strong. "It's not that, my Shimon. It's only that I didn't know. I didn't know our town was so broken, so many of us ruined. How bad it had become. Your father—" Her voice caught. "He would have wept to see this, Shimon. He *believed* in Kfar Nahum. He believed not even the Romans, not even the dead out of the hills, could do this to us. Could *ever* do this to us."

"What happened, amma?" Shimon took a breath. "There are people out there who were ill, a few who were maimed. Now they . . . What happened?"

Her gaze strayed to her arm. Shimon followed that glance, but saw nothing there. Just her olive skin.

687

"The dead are coming back up," she said.

"Yes." His own voice caught.

"They're coming for *him*. Have you seen his eyes, my son? He burns with life. So much that it spills out of him and touches the rest of us. It's like fire, and the *shedim* are moths, Shimon. He's drawing them out of the sea, just by being here."

"Then we have to get rid of him." Shimon's voice was cold, colder than he would have thought possible. He thought of the stones he could lift from the street outside. Thought of the bruises that purpled the man's face and arms. Perhaps this was why he had been driven out into the desert, so that the dead might follow him where he went and leave the living alone.

"No," Rahel said. "I have no fever."

"Amma?"

"I have no fever, Shimon. I thought—at first I thought it might come back. But it didn't."

He sat back on his heels. "What *happened?*"

Fever? *Something* had happened. And Rahel was—different. Lost in thought. Lying here in her bedding as though utterly exhausted. That wasn't like her. And Koach—he was different, too. His insides went cold with dread.

"It's not important," Rahel whispered. "He's what's important. He's anointed, Shimon. Our *navi*, our messiah, our anointed one. I have to tell Zebadyah bar Yesse tomorrow; he has been so afraid. I have to tell him. This stranger—he *is* the one we've waited for." She closed her eyes. "Fifteen years. I've waited fifteen years."

Shimon kept silent. He sensed that she needed to speak, needed badly to speak.

"I prayed, Shimon. That night your father died. As I held little Koach in my arms. I begged God, in the silence of my heart, I begged him to send the anointed one, that I would see him with my own eyes. I told God, *My boys need me. And everything out there is burning and dying. I can hear it. I can smell it. Let me see Kfar Nahum healed before I die. Let me see my two sons together and strong.*" Her eyes glistened. "When I opened my eyes this day and saw him there, I knew. I *knew*. I had suffered enough, enough even for El-Shaddai Our God. He had chosen to answer my prayer, little Shimon. He would not let me die until I saw that man. With my own eyes."

"Amma," he murmured, but said nothing else.

She squeezed his hand. "You can break a family or a People even as you can break an arm or a clay bowl. Everything had broken that winter. When the

Romans came. They broke the doors of the synagogue. They took . . . whatever they wanted, Shimon, whatever they wanted. To fill the tax debt. They broke us." A hiss in her voice. "They took some of the boats, all the food, all the fine clothes. They hurt our girls. Yonah your father . . . he hid me." Her eyes softened. "He was so brave, your father. He hid me out in the *kokhim*, among the dead. The one place the Romans didn't think to look for anything of value, and the one place no one else in Kfar Nahum thought to hide anything. I was so scared, Shimon. It was dark, and all about me the bodies and bones of our dead. Yonah brought food and water when he could, but I had to ration it so carefully. He couldn't always come, and he didn't trust anyone else to. We were all afraid, everyone.

"Most of the time I sat huddled against the wall of the bone chamber, just praying. My belly was so full with your brother. I didn't want to move or do anything but sleep. And I was hungry, so hungry." Her voice trembled. "I was terrified that something would go wrong. That I would lose the baby. I did rise once, and I explored the tomb with my hands, because I couldn't bear not knowing what was there. There was the great chamber, and the tunnels leading out from it, and the shelves where our dead are slid into the living rock. I touched a few of them, Shimon. I . . . I had to. I had to know they were still."

He touched her hair gently. "It's all right, amma. It is long past."

"Long past." She smiled weakly. "Nothing stays buried, my little one. Maybe nothing stays broken, either. I hope that's so."

Her little one. It had been years since she had called him that.

She hadn't called him that since Koach was born.

Since before his father died.

Shimon blinked and swallowed against a tightness in his throat.

"I heard them carousing. The shouts, the screams. I could hear it all, all the pain of the women I knew, the men. And I couldn't do anything." Her hands shook. "I couldn't even cry for them, Shimon, because my labor took me, and all I could do was breathe, just *breathe*, between the pangs. Breathe and hear. Such horrible screams." She closed her eyes. "Even the moaning of the dead wasn't worse than that." She drew in a breath. "For all I knew, Yonah was dying while I fought to push Koach out of my body. Oh, Shimon, I wanted to die. And I wanted to live. I cursed your father, biting my lip to hold in the screams. He wasn't there with me. I hated him, for a few brief moments." She shook her head. "I didn't know if he lived, or if you did, or if I would live, only that I had to *push* that baby out into the world. Even if there was nothing left out there, nothing but the dead. They moaned all around the tomb, and my heart—I have never felt fear like that. Or rage. Or—"

Her hands trembled.

"And then I had two sons," she whispered, and fell silent.

* * *

All his adult life, Shimon had stood with his back to the memory of that winter. That memory had stalked him at every waking hour, until its cold fingers touched his very shoulder, and when he lay down to sleep it sprang on him like a lion on a gazelle. Now, in his mind, he turned and looked into the cold eyes of his pursuer.

He remembered waiting on the shore, unable either to shout or to flee as the boat came in. With its scrape against the sand, his father's body had staggered into the gunwale and toppled over to lie half in the water, half on the moist land. Shimon had stared in fascinated terror at this human shape that looked so much like Yonah, the fisher, who in the last year had taught him to carve an oar, to gut a fish, to tack a boat against the wind.

He remembered his father's face turning to him, the eyes lifeless, the low hiss in the dark. Remembered scrambling away over the sand and loose shingle, stumbling, getting back up, falling again. Remembered kicking up sand, frantic to regain his feet, the corpse bending over him, dried blood on its hand. His father's blood.

And he remembered his mother's scream, a cry raw with fury and pain and grief, as she leapt between Shimon and his father.

Then Rahel had stood painfully straight, her tunic dark at her thighs with the blood of the day after childbirth, her hair sweaty across her face. Both hands whitened about the haft of a fishing spear. The iron point had gone through his dead father's eye and into his skull and there it was sheathed. His father's limbs hung limp. He no longer moved or moaned, but the spear held him up, so that he appeared to be standing there beside his wife, gazing at her with those eyes that had looked out, unseeing, on the water and that had looked across the sand, unseeing, at his child.

With a low wail, Rahel wrenched the hook free; it left his father's body with a quiet squelching sound not unlike the spilling of innards from a fish's belly. Yonah's body toppled to the sand and he lay still. The wound was dark in his brow, a wound that didn't bleed. Rahel stood over him, breathing hard, the fishing spear held at her side. The hand that gripped it shook violently.

A wind came in off the sea, and her hair blew across her face, hiding her anguish from her son. Shimon felt the chill of the wind on his brow, which was damp with sweat.

"Abba," he gasped, "abba."

"No," Rahel whispered. She swayed on her feet.

Leaping up, Shimon caught her as she fell, a woman weak from horror and loss of blood from her labor; even as Shimon threw his arms about her and held her tightly, the spear slipped from her limp hand and sheathed its point in the sand.

* * *

That moment, and others, flashed through Shimon's heart like a school of fish. Rahel between him and the corpse of his father. Or leaping before Barabba's horse. Even Koach his brother, standing over the body of his beloved, that blunt rock in his hand. For so long Shimon had thought his entire life was but the last rattle in a corpse's throat—a last fight for air that was without meaning or hope of victory. His failure to bring in fish enough to feed his kin had always shamed him; now his days of despair shamed him more. While he'd sat in his grief and his gloom, his mother, who'd once given birth in a tomb even as the *shedim* moaned on every side, had stood constant, had never stopped hoping and believing in her sons. The waters may wear away the stones, but no matter how the waves crash against the shore, some hearts can never be worn away, can never be crumbled, can never be pounded into sand.

"How did you do it?" he asked suddenly. "When father came back. How did you do it, amma? How did you find the courage?"

Her face showed her pain. "I did it," she said slowly, "because I loved him. I loved him, Shimon. Most wives do not love their husbands, because most husbands do not love their wives. But I loved your father. I loved him from the moment he appeared at my father's door with a net of fish and a plea in his eyes, asking for me." She smiled faintly, her eyes wet. "I loved him, so I had to."

"Amma," Shimon whispered.

She reached up and grasped his hand again, tightly. Her eyes sought his. "Your father would be proud of you, Shimon. Never doubt it."

He choked. "I love you, amma."

"And I you, Shimon." Her face was tight with weariness. "Will you sing to me the way you did when you were a boy? After your father had kissed me, while he was gathering up his things for the boat, you would come sit by me and sing me to sleep. Do you remember?"

"I remember," Shimon said hoarsely.

"I am going to try to sleep." A faint smile. "I don't care how many people are here. You and Koach can care for them a while. Sing me to sleep, my Shimon."

Shimon drew up her wool blanket and tucked it around her chin. Long ago it had been dyed blue, but its color had faded away with time, like so many other things. Behind him, Shimon could no longer hear the *navi* and others speaking; it was quiet out in the atrium. Outside the house, his brother and the priest's sons might be watching for the dead, but he could not hear their footsteps or their fear. For the moment, there was nothing in the world but mother and son. Rahel squeezed his hand and he returned her grip, and sang in a low murmur, for her. A song he'd heard her sing once in a tomb, far away, on the other side of time.

Though the fig tree does not flower,
And no grapes are on the vines,
The olives give no oil
And the fields no barley
The flock does not come home to the fold
Nor the herd home from the field,
Yet I will cry out in joy.

God is my strength;
He makes my feet like the deer's;
He makes me walk in high places.

THE LIGHT SHINES IN THE DARK

LEAVING HIS MOTHER sleeping, Shimon stepped out into the atrium. The house was nearly empty again. The people who had gathered there were gone, and Koach hadn't returned. Yeshua sat alone by the cold firepit, holding a small lamp in his hands; there was a little flame—he must've lit it before dark fell, before the Sabbath Bride settled down for her night's rest—and the scent of rancid oil mixed with the lingering smell of roasted fish in a way that did uncomfortable things to Shimon's stomach, though it also made him aware that he hadn't eaten since the morning. The town had feasted, yet he had not.

He crouched across the firepit from Yeshua, giving him a wary look. Two fish still lay on the coals. Shimon snatched one up in his bare hands; it had cooled long before, but when he lifted it to his teeth and bit, the oil and flavor of the fish ran into his mouth, and his hunger roared in his belly. He tore at it in urgent bites. A small sound made him glance up, and he noticed the beggar woman—the one Koach had helped—leaning against the olive tree, in its shadow.

Shimon cast the bones of the fish down over the coals; he would clean out the pit in the morning. He considered Yeshua. Madman or *navi*, was this man a blessing or a threat to the town? His mother trusted the stranger and thought him a holy one—*the* holy one, the *navi*. The bruises on the man's face were dark in the lamplight, his face thin. Shimon wondered whether this stranger in his house had eaten much, either.

"There were . . ." Shimon glanced around. "People."

"Gone home for the Sabbath," Yeshua said quietly. "All of them. Or to what shelters they could find or that those who feasted here would . . . would offer. All gone. I am alone." Anguish in his face, he didn't look up from the light. "Still alone. I'll always be alone, won't I, even if I feed a house, even if I feed a town, even if the lame walk and the mute sing. I am still alone. I am still standing in the desert, listening to the screams."

Shimon grunted. Earlier in the day, the stranger had been almost *furious* with energy. He had moved with a hastiness and an urgency that was entirely alien to the slow, exhausted men and women of Kfar Nahum. But now a hush had fallen over him; he looked faint. Worn. Shimon realized, startled, that there were wrinkles about Yeshua's eyes that had not been there in the morning. Now he looked more like the men Shimon knew. Even his voice, the way he talked, had changed. He no longer sounded frantic, desperate, dangerous.

Only sorrowful.

"You have the hospitality of this house." Shimon's voice was gruff. He would honor his mother's wishes and her hope.

"I would . . . I would like that," Yeshua said, a flicker of gratitude in his eyes. He stared at the small flame.

"Well," Shimon muttered. "I will bring some bedding out here."

"My mother lights a lamp," Yeshua said, as though he hadn't heard. "A small lamp, much like this one, a *lot* like this one, every night. *Every* night. Though oil is costly in Natzeret." He glanced at the fish bones on the cold coals, such grief in his face that Shimon had to look away. "I suppose it is here, too."

The flame wavered; the stranger glanced at it and then stilled the shaking of his hands. He took a breath, then set the lamp carefully to the side. "They are so loud. I hear them, Cephas. I hear them whether I rise or whether I lie down. I hear them always. Every hour, every day."

"Hear who?" Shimon peered cautiously at the man's face, but his eyes held a cold, clear intelligence. There was no madness there. Only thought and pain.

"The cries," Yeshua answered. "Their moans of hunger."

Shimon's breath caught. "The dead?"

"The living," Yeshua said sharply. Then he pressed a hand to his eyes. "The dead. Both." His voice was calm, though thick with fatigue—as though his raving had been a thicket he'd broken through and now he was in the open again, but sweaty and weary from his work. "All of you eating alone, and not together. So many closed doors, so many windows shut. So many of you dying alone in your lonely houses." He sighed. "Kana is wrong. Zebadyah is wrong, too. We can't avoid our past, its violence. Can't deny it, not ever. The screams in our desert. Nor even atone for them." His eyes were distant. "Only forgive."

Suddenly, a scream pierced the air. Shimon gasped. Yeshua's face hardened. Outside, a few doors slammed; wooden slats rattled shut over one window.

The murmur of the sea, the sigh of water on the sand.

Then they heard it.

Low, wavering moans. Distant yet loud in the stillness.

"You did this," Shimon said, his insides numb and cold. "You brought the dead back up."

"Yes." Yeshua's voice was quiet and sad. "And the fish also. But by this time tomorrow it will be over, I think."

Shimon stood. "We have to bar the door," he breathed.

"No." Yeshua's face hardened, and he stood, too. "Let others hide. You and I, we will do the father's work."

Shimon turned on him in horror. "Don't you hear?" Hardly daring to speak above a whisper. "The *dead* are coming."

Those strange eyes of Yeshua's were bright and fierce in the light of the lamp. "No matter how the door burns, Cephas, I have to step through it in the end. I can't flinch back from it anymore. Whatever the father wishes me to do, the weeping father, it's time I did it." He gripped Shimon's arm. A hard, tight grip. A workman's grip. A *nagar*'s grip.

His voice was clear and calm.

"Don't be afraid, Cephas."

When Yeshua stepped past him to the door, Shimon followed, still meaning to bar it. But instead, Yeshua took hold of the door and threw it wide. Shimon could see the shadow-shape of the house that leaned just across the narrow street from his own.

Then he sucked in his breath, for in a stab of cold dread, he remembered.

Yakob and Yohanna. And Koach.

His brother was out there.

A Pestle, a Menorah, a Shofar, a Sica, and the Heat of a Sun

Bar Cheleph saw them first, and when the others—Koach, Yakob, Yohanna—turned their heads, it was as though Bar Cheleph's shriek had split the night open and let the *shedim* tumble out of nightmares into the real world, the world of time and suffering. The corpses stumbled up the shoreline toward them, lurching, their arms lifted, their moans muted by the surge and song of the sea, but no less terrible. There were perhaps ten or twelve of them, their eyes glinting in the faint light off the water. A few boat people, having lost their shelters, had erected hasty windbreaks of driftwood draped with lake-weed and had huddled behind them against the cold of night. Now they leapt to their feet and sprang, shouting, across the sands, fleeing the oncoming ghouls. The same wind that had brought the Sabbath Bride to Beth Tsaida with the dusk swept up, bringing to Koach's face this time the reek of the dead.

"God," Bar Cheleph gasped, "oh God."

Yakob and Yohanna went very still.

But Koach's face hardened, and his grip whitened around the pestle he'd taken from his mother's house.

The dead came trailing sea wrack and weeds from their arms. Sometimes the town saw straggler corpses from the hills, but these dead had risen from the sea, somewhere north along the shore. Benayahu was not among them.

"So many," Yakob breathed. "Why? Why now?"

"It doesn't matter," Koach said. "We have to stop them."

"No," Bar Cheleph whispered. "No." He glanced wildly at the faces of his companions, then broke and ran across the grasses.

He fled *toward* the houses of Beth Tsaida.

"You fool!" Yakob cried, his voice loud over the sand.

Three of the corpses turned their heads, their attention caught by Bar Cheleph's scrambling run, their mouths gaping. That *moan*, that sound without words or thought that made the blood move cold and sluggish like mud in the hills. The three lurched away from the group and slouched up toward the tideline, following Bar Cheleph. Koach's breath hissed out through his teeth. Bar Cheleph would lead them *right* into the houses of the fishers. To his *mother's* house.

Koach whispered a prayer, a bitter, desperate prayer, under his breath—*If you are a father, El Shaddai, El Shaddai, if you are what the stranger says you are, help us*—and then he ran along the grasses, leaving the others behind, pursuing the dead who pursued Bar Cheleph, though he felt out of breath, felt as though he might faint. He called out Bar Cheleph's name, but the other man didn't stop. Nor did the dead turn from their chase of him; they could not run, yet Koach closed the distance only slowly. He felt the fear, the fear eating his mind, trying to make him into a small, shivering animal who might drop into the tidal grasses to quiver and hide. It was more overpowering than when he'd faced Tamar, for then his fear had been crushed under a weight of grief. Now he could think only of cold fingers grasping, cold teeth biting into his arm or his throat or his belly.

He shoved back the terror, kept staggering toward the houses of Beth Tsaida.

* * *

The rest of the dead lurched after the boat people, who stumbled up the sand toward the priest's sons. Earlier Yakob had led a small search party north along the shore, searching for Benayahu and finding blood in the grasses but no sign of where the man had gone. He'd thought—for a moment—that he heard a moan in the hills, distant, barely audible. He had shivered and started back, his heart full of dark thoughts and darker fears. Now his fears were enfleshed.

"Shit," Yakob breathed. "Shit!"

He ran toward the boat people, gesturing wildly with his arms. "You! All of you! Follow me!"

They turned to him, their eyes fearful, desperate.

"Come *on*!" he shouted.

Yakob thought quickly. He could lead the boat people down the shore, away from the town, trailing the dead behind—then circle up into the hills, in the hope of losing the dead in the wild. Some of the boat people would falter and collapse, some would be eaten. But his brothers, his father, his grandfather, they would be safe.

He *could* do that.

Instead, he got his shoulder under one of the haggard women even as she stumbled. Half carrying her, he began walking up toward the houses of Kfar Nahum, toward whatever sanctuary the broken town could offer.

A moment's choice, a moment's decision.

His brother fell in alongside him, his face twisted with fear. Yakob met his gaze. "We are all kin," he said.

Yohanna nodded, pale.

The woman coughed faintly. Others ran past. Yakob refused to glance back at the moaning dead. "It's all right," he murmured to the woman. "Just come with me. It's all right . . . Yohanna, run. Run ahead. Warn father."

"And leave you to face this alone?" Yohanna choked.

"Hurry, brother. God will keep me."

Yohanna whispered, "God had better."

The wailing behind them drew nearer. The boat woman began whimpering almost too quietly to hear. Yakob gave his brother a strained smile . . . or something he meant to be a smile. He clapped Yohanna on the shoulder. "Go!"

* * *

Once again, Koach ran through the stone houses and decayed shelters of his people, with lives at stake. The stone pestle was cold in his palm. The sound of his breathing was loud in his ears, and sweat stung his eyes. He was not made for running, had done little of it. But there wasn't far to go.

Bar Cheleph had already strained his hip throughout the day, and Koach caught up with him as he was panting past the houses of the fishers. As they ran near, Natan El threw open his door, and he and his young wife stood at their doorstep across from Rahel's house, gazing out with horror in their faces. They could see Bar Cheleph stumble and catch himself; they could hear the moans of the dead, coming up from the shore behind their house. In another moment, the door across the narrow street swung open, and Rahel looked out, her face haggard, newly wrenched from sleep. Her face went white as she gazed out; even as Koach closed the distance with Bar Cheleph, calling out his name, the three corpses lunged from around the corner of Natan El's house, right in front of Bar Cheleph. One grappled him, its gray hands seizing his arms, its weight bearing him beneath it to the ground. The second staggered across the street toward Rahel. The third lurched past, toward Natan El's door. A shrill scream—from Natan El, not from his wife; he sprang back, and his wife swung shut the door even as the corpse reached it, slamming it against one groping arm. The door rattled hard, the corpse hurling itself against the wood. Across the street, the other corpse threw itself against Rahel's door.

Koach let out a cry and sprang on the nearest corpse from behind, swinging his pestle. But the creature turned, hearing him, and its hand caught Koach's arm just above the elbow, a grip fierce and strong. Koach felt himself pulled from his feet toward the thing's mouth; its head snapped at his arm, the teeth closing on the thick wool his mother had woven for him. He felt the pressure of its bite and screamed, kicking wildly, thrashing in the thing's grasp. Those horrible, dead eyes looked at his for an instant as it worried his arm like a wild dog. Nothing in its face but hunger.

Then the door wrenched open. There was a sickening crunch of bone and a spatter of necrotic flesh as an iron shaft was driven into the thing's cheek. The corpse didn't release Koach's arm, but it turned, pulling Koach with it, its jaw still grinding, trying to dig into Koach's flesh through the wool sleeve. Koach fought to bend his hand and the pestle toward its head, but he had only one arm, and the creature held it. He caught a glimpse of Natan El's wife, Bat Abner, in the door, her face a grimace of terror. Both hands whitened around the haft of her husband's fishing hook. She was tugging at it wildly, trying to free it of the corpse's face, to thrust or swing it a second time, but the hook had caught on the creature's jaw and she couldn't free it. The ghastly face tore at Koach's arm and it growled against the wool. The scent of its decay was too much; Koach vomited, the fish of his brother's catch surging up his throat and out of his mouth in a hot, steaming rush, fouling his chin, his clothes.

Helpless.

Again.

Always.

No.

Vomiting, shaking, furious, Koach swung his body, lifting his left leg and slamming his sandaled foot against the corpse's groin. It didn't feel the pain, but the impact drove it back, even as Bat Abner's pull on the spear tugged hard in the other direction. The iron hook tore the creature's jaws free from Koach's arm, tearing the sleeve with it. Koach's arm slithered free of the thing's grip, unsleeved, and he fell, smacking his chest hard against the stone doorstep. Ignoring the stab of pain, Koach rolled hard. He'd dropped the pestle; it fell near him and he scrambled to it, lifted it in his hand, and turned to see the corpse biting wildly at the hook as its cold hands reached for Bat Abner. It shoved itself through her door, thrusting her back, the two of them, the living and the dead, separated by only the length of that small spear of iron. Shouting wildly, Koach surged to his feet and rushed the corpse, swinging the pestle; the hard stone drove in the back of the thing's head. He heard it spit and snarl, and he swung the pestle again, again, crushing in the creature's skull, until its legs crumbled and it hung, a silent, limp weight on the end of Bat Abner's spear.

* * *

Less than three paces away, Bar Cheleph struggled for his life. The thing he wrestled had been corpulent in life, and its dead flesh was massive and held him crushed to the grit of the street. The rage he'd felt when he speared Bat Benayahu's corpse had deserted him, leaving only stabbing, wild terror and hot shame, hot urine wet on his thighs. His fingers gripped the thing's face, holding its jaws back from his throat, and he panted and wept. The corpse's eye gave beneath Bar Cheleph's fingers, but the thing didn't shriek, didn't rear back, just kept biting at the air above his collarbone.

Then the corpse's jaw slackened and gray matter sprayed outward from the back of its head; its grip on Bar Cheleph's shoulders loosed. Glancing up, Bar Cheleph saw standing over him Koach, a clay pestle clutched in his left hand, the end of the pestle dark with gore. Gasping, Bar Cheleph just shivered beneath the corpse, staring up at his rescuer in shock.

The youth who stood over him was grim-eyed and fierce. And not in the least *hebel*. Yakob bar Cheleph did not know this boy.

Koach cast the pestle aside; bending, he wrapped his hand in the hem of his wool tunic and gripped the corpse's arm through the fabric, his fingers protected from the touch of skin against unclean skin; a heave, and the corpse was rolled aside. Bar Cheleph scooted out from beneath it, kicking. Then he stopped, his chest heaving.

Koach freed his hand of the wool and offered it.

Bar Cheleph swallowed. "But I . . . I tormented you."

"I forgive you." The youth's voice was quiet. "Now help me. One of them is at my mother's door, and I need more than one hand. Help me."

Bar Cheleph gazed up at him helplessly. Then he took Koach's hand and felt himself pulled to his feet. He marveled at the strength in the youth's left arm.

"My brother," he gasped.

Koach's eyes went cold, but he nodded. "Brother."

* * *

There was a moan behind them, and then a sharp crack. Turning, Koach gasped. The other corpse had stood facing his mother's door, its back to him, but now it swayed to the left and fell. Rahel stood at her open door, her hair wild about her shoulders, her husband's *tallit* drawn over her like a woman's shawl. Her face was gray, and she held tightly in both hands a shard of pottery longer than her hand, its broken point dark with gore. Other shards lay shattered about her feet, and there was a dark puncture in the head of the corpse. That sound they'd heard . . . Behind her in the doorway, the woman who had been mute gazed out with wide eyes.

Rahel glanced up from the corpse, and though she had no words, there were a thousand in her eyes, and memory dark as the sea—unburied memory of a night of the dead.

"Amma," Koach breathed.

Bar Cheleph, still panting, bowed his head slightly in respect. "Bat Eleazar," he murmured.

"My son. Kinsman." Her eyes flashed in the dark. She let the gory shard fall from her hand; it rang against the stone beneath her feet. She bent and spat on the corpse, then straightened, her face flushed. "Help me get this thing off my doorstep."

* * *

The boat people fled like deer between the old houses of Kfar Nahum, the empty houses that sat quiet as desert stones farther in from the shore, their doors and windows long since boarded up against squatters living or dead. Yakob was near the rear now, carrying that ragged woman who could hardly stand, let alone flee. The dead followed, lurching against the houses and scraping along the stone walls, but ignoring the structures, intent on the fugitives from the shore.

The vagrants broke out into the open space before the synagogue, its white basalt luminous in the rising moon. For a moment they stopped, their eyes round in the dark, glancing about, uncertain where else to run. Even as the first dead lurched into the space after them, the door to the synagogue was flung open, and a man in the white robes of a priest burst out onto the polished steps, a great menorah held in his hand, its eight candles new-kindled. His eyes burned as with fever. In an instant, a single beat of the heart, he took it all in: the pursuing dead, the sickly stench of them. The sobbing, stumbling boat people. His son Yakob half carrying one of them, risking his body and blood for these heathen and half-heathen poor.

Yohanna stepped out beside him, his face tight with fear.

"Go, son," Zebadyah said gruffly. "Warn the weaver and the other houses. All you can."

Yohanna gave a shaky nod. Then he sprinted; in a moment, he was gone.

Zebadyah wanted to slam the door of the synagogue against the boat people, but the old guilt coursed hot through his veins. He could not let others die before him, as he had long ago. The dead were within the town; whatever walls of fire or stone or will Zebadyah might have erected, it was too late. There was no time to sort out who were his kin, to protect, and who were not. And his oldest, by his act of carrying that woman and bringing all of them here, had already committed his house to sheltering these men and women. There was no wall here, and he was not Ezra.

He lifted the menorah high. "Into the synagogue!" he shouted. "All of you!"

His cry broke the stupor that had fallen on the boat people as sharply as a branch might crack beneath the blow of a man's heel. The vagrants rushed past him, stumbling up the steps and through the door, into the holy place at the heart of the town from which they'd so long been banned. Last, Yakob brought in the woman and laid her on the floor below the cabinet that held the scroll of Torah. Even as he glanced up from her, his eyes full of the intent to join his father, Zebadyah swung the door shut.

Zebadyah ran from the synagogue steps out into the open, wielding the light and hope of his People, like the knife-wielding *kanna'im* in the south, the grieving priests. Alone in that open space before the steps, he took his stand, thrusting the fiery menorah into the faces of the pursuing dead, their eyes glowing in the flames. His ears were full of the shrieks and moans of that other night, that terrible night, that night he had never woken from. Again he heard the whisper in his heart, *Run, little priest. Run. You are not Ezra or Moshe or Aharon. You cannot face this. You will be eaten.* That quiet whisper of the *shedim* waiting to take his heart and hollow it out and live inside its cold shell.

"Not this time," he growled.

The dead shied back before the stabbing flames, but only barely; and now the corpses closed in on either side. There were nine of them, their jaws snapping as they tried to press in on flame and priest. Though Zebadyah darted to the left and to the right, one man with a stick of candles, even a holy one, could not hold them all. He fell back but stopped when he heard the door of the synagogue thrown open behind him. Clenching his teeth, he swung the menorah in an arc of flame. Grasping hands, the growls of the dead—

"Father!"

Yakob at the door.

Run, little priest, run. You will be eaten, eaten, eaten—

To silence the drumbeat of his heart and the knife-sharp cutting of that whisper into his spirit, Zebadyah raised his voice in a desert scream of desert song, words invoking the strength and refuge of a desert God, ancient and severe, in whose presence all unclean things, whether mortal or immortal, withered like grass:

His arms are mighty,
He shatters the foe!

He is my tent
My refuge,
My rock and fortress . . .

He trains my hands for battle,
And my fingers for war!

He drove the menorah into a corpse's face. It spat and hissed as it fell back, and then cold hands, so cold, grasped his extended right arm, and suddenly he was on his back gazing up at the stars in their sky and the dark shapes of the dead bending over him. Fingers dug into his flesh, into his arm, his shoulder. Then the touch of a cold face and the pain of teeth, more violent and sharp than he could have imagined or feared, peeling away his skin, tearing away a part of him, a part of his *body*. This was his death, his death . . . In a scream of agony Zebadyah cried out the life-prayer and death-prayer of his People, hoping that God, however distant, would hear his words: *Sh'ma Yisrael adonai eloheinu . . .*

* * *

Kana blew a long call on the shofar, desperate and loud. Then he dropped it from his lips and leapt into the crowd of dead at the synagogue steps, his sica flashing in the dark. He saw the priest tugged beneath the corpses and he howled in his rage, as he had once heard Barabba howl on the dusty pass of Adummim, the Red Way, the Way of Blood, when a pack of dead lurching out of the rocks took one of his most trusted warriors. Tonight Zebadyah had not hidden beneath any boat on the shore, leaving Shimon bar Nahemyah to stand in his place at the door of the synagogue. Instead, tonight the priest had stood in Kana's place, while Kana paced brooding on the slope of the hill of tombs. Hearing the moans, he had unsheathed his sica and run into the town, run fast until his sides burned. And yet he was too late.

As he drove his knife under the chin and up into the skull of one of the growling dead, he heard a cry from his left.

"Father! Abba! *Abba!*"

He knew the voice; without sparing a glance, he shouted, "Get him out of there!"

Another of the dead grasped at him; Kana caught the corpse's arm in a hard grip and pulled it in close—a wild glimpse of teeth—and he drove the knife in, then pulled it free just as swiftly, slamming his hip into the corpse to shove it aside and out of the way. Even as it fell, he had chosen his next target; he grasped the thing's arm to pull it near, but the soggy remnant of its sleeve came away in his hand, and he staggered back from the force of his pull. The thing turned on him, hissing. Its hands gripped Kana's shoulders, a grip fierce and cold, cold even through his cloak. With a shout, he drove the sica up through its chin and saw the thing's face go slack.

Others behind grasped at his shoulders, his hair. He dropped, had a confused glimpse of unsandaled feet all around him, pale and heavy with stench, as he let himself fall to the ground to roll away and back to his knees. A hop up to his feet, and Kana crouched with his sica ready. The corpses lunged at him, bending to grasp him, and then he was whirling and ducking and slicing in the dance of the fennec, the fox in the desert, the dance Barabba—damn his heart—had taught him in caves far from the sea, in ravines where the dry dust still carried the footprints of dead that had passed through years before. Fingers cold and damp brushed his shoulders, his arms, even his face, but none found a grip. He moved as quickly as the wind, for none know where the wind has come from or where it will go, they only feel the strength and the swiftness of its passing. On this wind there was a blade, with a bite sharper than winter or hunger itself. And when Kana slid the point and then the curved, cruel length into unclean flesh, he shouted, a hoarse bark like the fennec. Exultant, fierce, the cry at the kill, for he was alive and another was not. He danced, and another was still.

Memories crowded upon him as he spun and cut. That day of ambush on the high Adummim last summer; the sweat and heat of his long night's battle at the synagogue door fifteen years ago; the scream of Ahava, his beloved, dying as the teeth of the dead tore at her; his encounter with a dead child in the alleys of Yerushalayim, its empty eyes and wild hiss, a tattered doll still clutched in its hand. Kana shoved the memories away, hard; he had no time for them. Every bone, every beat of his heart, every breath had to be focused on this moment, on the slide and shriek of his Roman knife, on the lurching, groping movements of the enemy he faced. On killing.

* * *

The call of the shofar rang in Shimon's ears, a blast of sound like the roar of some beast, except deeper and clearer than any beast's cry in all the world.

Following its call, Shimon stumbled into the space before the synagogue, gasping for breath. Yeshua was there already, walking toward the knot of dead about Kana, and for an instant, Shimon stopped, breathless, seeing the other Hebrew dance among the dead, seeing his face and the efficiency of his movements, as though he were a Roman trained to kill. In that moment Shimon glimpsed what it must have been like in the wilds about Yerushalayim with Barabba the Outlaw. He wondered if this was what Yehuda tribe would become, in this generation or the next, or the one after. Caught between the Romans and the dead, both intent on devouring the People. Driven to the sica and the fever of killing, until they visited distant fishing villages and taught even the youths there to kill—as Barabba had sought to do.

Then Shimon saw Yakob pulling his father free of the corpses, and he let out a cry. Stooping, he took up a small stone from the street and ran at the dead.

But Yeshua was there before him. He walked into the dead, and his face and figure shone as though Shimon were gazing at a sun; he put his hand up before his eyes to shield them from the harsh light. Bars of fire flared across his vision. There was pressure against his chest, and he stumbled back with a shout.

Then the light was gone, and he was blinking against a blaze of color, his heart pounding. He made out Yakob drawing the priest up onto the steps, and Kana crouched with his knife in his right hand and his face red as though baked by the sun's heat.

And Yeshua.

The stranger stood with his arms out, the dead silent and still on the earth about his feet. Not one of them moved or twitched. Not one of them rose to its feet. Not one moaned in that hunger, cold and empty as the dark between the stars.

A BILLION STARS

SHIMON'S HEART was a storm on the sea. All these years, the dead had been his nightmare, his horror. And this man—this stranger he'd feared and hated—had just *walked* into the corpses and they had withered before the heat of his presence like leaves in a drought. All that he feared and all that he had known was as nothing to this man. Shimon fell to his knees on the hard earth.

"*Rabboni*," he whispered. *Rabboni*: My teacher, my master.

"On your feet, Cephas," Yeshua said quietly, without looking at him.

Everything in him shaken, Shimon rose and followed Yeshua toward the synagogue steps, where Yakob held his father's head in his lap. Kana stood near, his head bowed, his sica held at his side, the blade dark with gore.

The priest's shoulder and part of his neck had been torn open like cloth, and ragged strings of sinew and muscle had been pulled out of him. Shimon saw the glint of white bone. Blood had pulsed out over Zebadyah's chest and belly, dark and slick, running over his skin like olive oil. Yakob had stripped to his loincloth and was pressing the woolen tunic he'd worn to his father's wound.

"Zebadyah," Yeshua whispered, sitting down beside Yakob.

"He's dying." Yakob's voice was choked.

Zebadyah opened his eyes. "Yakob," he gasped.

"I am here, abba."

"Is Bat Eleazar safe?"

Yakob cast a glance at the navi and Shimon, and these were not the calm eyes of the fisherman Shimon knew. There was panic there. Shimon only nodded, his heart wrenched with pain for his friend.

"She is safe, father."

The priest's eyes glazed. "Tell her. Tell her that I love her still. As I did when I first saw her. That no man . . . that no man has ever been so jealous of a . . . a brother. That I hope her sons live long and good lives. Tell her that I am . . . that I am sorry."

Yakob's face crumpled.

Yeshua crouched beside him, his own face twisted in sorrow. As Shimon stood near, the stranger set his hand on Zebadyah's chest, as though blessing him. "You are not what I thought you were," Yeshua said softly. "*Shalom, kohen* of Israel. Whatever it is, this thing that burns in your memory, your shame, it is melted away like water."

Shimon stared at Yeshua. The stranger did not speak as he had earlier that day. His voice carried a quiet, clear authority.

Zebadyah's face tightened. "Only God can forgive or forget . . . evils," he panted. "Take your . . . hand . . . from my chest, Bar Yosef."

"Abba," Yakob whispered, pleading. "This man might heal you. He healed grandfather."

"No, Yakob. *No*. Not worth . . . I will die clean. If I must face . . . face our God at last, I will do it clean. I do not know whether this man's healing . . . whether it is a sign from El Shaddai, or some witchcraft . . . but I know that he has come . . . he has come to our town and the *shedim* have . . . have come up with him." He gripped his son's hand; his own shook. "I have made mistakes, terrible mistakes," he rasped. "But I have lived to keep my town clean . . . and . . . and faithful and *safe*, and I will die so."

The light had gone from Yeshua's face. His eyes were troubled. "So be it," he said softly. He rose slowly to his feet.

Yakob pulled Zebadyah close against his breast, his father's blood running over his hands.

"Keep our People faithful," Zebadyah whispered. "And safe. Follow no stranger. For me, Yakob. Ezra. Remember . . . Ezra. . . . Until the true *navi* comes."

Then he shuddered, and his face went slack. His chest rose and fell, shallow, for a few moments. Then stilled.

* * *

Shimon stood silent. Yakob's face was wet with tears. He clutched his father's body to his chest.

Kana crouched beside him, his sica still unsheathed in his hand. "Do you want me to do it?" The words came out gruffly.

Yakob shook his head quickly, and squeezed his eyes shut, his breath shuddering.

"I understand." Kana took Yakob's hand in his and opened his fingers gently. Then he pressed the hilt of the sica into Yakob's hand. "It's cleanest if you place the point beneath the chin and thrust up," he said quietly.

The look Yakob turned on him was a stab to Kana's heart. A look as though Yakob were gazing at a Roman, at a killer of his kin, at a man utterly strange and alien to their People. Swallowing, Kana closed the other man's fingers around the hilt and stood, turning away, leaving father and son alone. Staring down at the silent dead, he traced his thumb over the thin cuts on his arm, his lips moving. Counting.

"You were right," Yeshua said to Shimon. "I came to you too late. I hesitated at the door, and it . . . it is all wrong."

* * *

After that the night went thick and sluggish; they each moved as if in the midst of a fever. Yakob sat with his father's head cooling in his lap. After a while he took his hands from his father's face and was careful not to touch the skin that had lost its warmth, lest he be unclean. His pain was written on his face as dark and irrevocable as the words of God on the scroll of Torah.

When Yohanna returned to the synagogue after warning all those in Kfar Nahum to shut their doors and not open them, no matter what they might hear, he found his brother and his father like that. He stood over them, stricken.

Yakob lifted his head. "I waited for you, brother."

Yakob's tears had been silent, but Yohanna let out a long, low wail, as though something had been ripped out of his heart and he could not believe it.

As Yohanna wept, he and his brother lifted their father from the steps and carried him away into the dark. An empty shelf waited beside their mother's in a tomb on the hill.

* * *

Shimon walked to his house, found Rahel and Koach there, and embraced each of them fiercely. Then he took up a small shovel from the stack of tools he kept by the outer door and left without a word.

He began to carry the dead out behind the town—not to the old midden, but to a stretch of dirt near it, where he dug fiercely at the hard earth. To his surprise, some of the boat people, using rags torn from their own bodies for gloves, helped carry the corpses out to this fresh grave, helped him lay the bodies within it. The vagrants' eyes shone faintly in the starlight. Then, when the dead lay in the ground in a silent heap, they shoved the dirt back in over them and packed it down. They gathered stones, the heaviest they could find, and covered the grave, as the Hebrews had done long ago when their people had only just left the desert and were still uncattled and living in tents. They made a cairn over all those dead, a cairn taller than a man, perhaps the largest that had ever been made in the land, or the largest that ever would.

When the last of the rocks had been set atop the cairn, Shimon leaned his back against it, breathing hard, and several of the boat people leaned against it, too. He listened to the waves. After a few moments, gruffly, he asked their names. Obed, Philippos, and Xanthippos. One Hebrew, two who were Greek.

He would remember their names.

* * *

When the moon came up high over the water, Kana found the *navi* standing near the edge of the sea, gazing at the water, troubled. Kana was so weary he could barely stand; he had been checking to make sure no dead had broken into any of the abandoned and empty houses to remain a lurking threat that might fall upon the living later. He'd found none, but it had been dark and uneasy work.

Yeshua kept his gaze on the sea. He spoke softly as Kana approached. "I've been thinking about what you said. About the Romans. When they walk by and strike you across your face."

"It doesn't matter," Kana said bitterly.

"Kana, there . . . there may be . . . a way to face a man, an enemy, living or dead, without a knife in your hand. There may be. When a Roman strikes you across your face, turn your other cheek."

"My other . . . ?"

Kana's eyes widened.

When a Roman struck a Hebrew across the face, he did so with his left hand, and always with the back of the hand. To turn the other cheek to him . . . that would be a challenge; the Roman would have to strike with his right hand, or at least with his open palm. To do so would be to acknowledge that he was striking an equal. Then the Roman would owe a debt of honor to the man he'd struck, the man who was *not* his inferior and who had as much right to strike him and yet had chosen not to.

For one dizzying moment, Kana stared out over the waves in the dark and glimpsed what such a resistance could do.

What if a hundred, five hundred, a *thousand* were to behave so? The rulers of the land could not feed them *all* to the dead in the ghoul pits. The Romans needed men to work, women to warm their beds. If every man and woman in every town were simply to turn the cheek, or to do any of a dozen such acts, acts that involved neither cowering nor lashing out, but simply *insisting* that they and the Roman facing them were akin . . . could such a thing work? Or would the Romans not burn this land to ash, to keep such an insurrection from spreading across their world?

"God," he whispered, a prayer that was one word, one gasp.

"Don't you have eyes to see?" Yeshua said, his face sad. "Ears to hear?"

Kana's own words, turned toward him. Their original meaning had been peeled away, like that dying woman's rags by the boat, to reveal stark ribs and emaciation beneath, something that could not be unseen or avoided or forgotten. It seemed to him suddenly that he had lived his life fleeing from one violence to the next. He remembered the pale corpses dropped into the water like so many stones. He remembered the heat of the dust on the Red Way. And more than that, he recalled a girl sleeping, a Roman girl in a Roman bed. Recalled his own hand shaking in the dark, his palm slick with sweat about the hilt of his knife as he stood over her.

For a moment, he could only breathe.

"We are all screaming," Yeshua said. "We are all suffering. We are all kin. We must . . . we must gaze in our enemies' eyes and . . . and see our kin gazing back at us."

Kana didn't answer. He tossed his sica into the sand. It was all too much. Too much, too much. He bowed his head and struggled to shut his memories away.

He lifted his head when he heard footsteps in the sand. Koach was coming down the shore toward them, a ragged figure with one sleeve torn away and his other arm limp at his side. He stopped a few feet from Kana.

"You're back," he said tonelessly.

"I'm back," Kana said.

Koach glanced at Yeshua, then at the cairn. The boy had changed. He was still short and his right arm was still useless, but he *stood* differently. There was a hardness in his face that was not cruelty. Kana tried to recall where he had seen such a face before. He only knew that whatever man young Koach was growing into, he'd be a man others could trust. And Koach was not likely, Kana thought, ever again to need his protection against others in the town.

"Is it true?" Koach said after a moment. "Bar Yesse is dead?"

Kana's lips became a thin line. "It's true."

Koach gazed at the cairn a moment, then at the stone houses behind, and something flickered in those hard eyes.

"Then I will grieve for him," he said.

* * *

For a while the three of them stood together in a world without any speech but the crashing voice of the sea. Koach watched the shimmer of moon on the water and gazed at the horizon where sea and sky faded into endless dark. He thought of his fantasy of rowing Tamar, one-handed, over that sea in a boat. Of finding some far village that would not mind a cripple and a fatherless woman making a home beside them. A child's fantasy. He could not have given her that. He had not given her freedom. Only a release from her pain.

His thoughts were broken by a distant moan. Glancing up, he could see the corpse approaching over the shingle from the north, dragging one leg behind it. In the moonlight he could see that its bad leg was bare of cloth; it had been torn savagely just above the knee, as by an animal. Near the hip was a great gash, straight and sharp, as though the man had tried to cut his bitten leg away before he died, but had failed to complete the task—fainting perhaps from horror, or loss of blood, or the onset of the fever that brings the walking death. Koach sucked in his breath. A footstep warned him a moment before Shimon stood beside him; the boat people stayed by the cairn, watching.

Watching it approach.

Koach knew this corpse.

It was Benayahu.

* * *

Koach felt a sickness of fear moving like cold, sluggish water through his body, yet flame burned on the surface. The corpse's face was Benayahu's face. The same cheekbones, the same fleshy lips, the same scar by his eye. This man he'd hated, this man in whose shop he'd worked.

This man who'd beaten Tamar.

Part of him wanted to run out to that corpse and deliver some blow, some swift vengeance for the woman he'd lost.

And part of him wanted to bend over and be sick in the grass.

The *reek* of it.

Koach stooped to take up the sica Kana had thrown to the ground; one needed two hands to wield it as Kana did, but only one to stab with it.

"No, Koach, no." Yeshua pressed a hand to Koach's chest, stopping him. His eyes seemed very dark, pools that might swallow up stars, or pools out of which stars could be born. Before Koach or Kana or any of the others could argue, Yeshua stepped out over the sand to stand in Benayahu's way.

He put out his hand and the corpse halted as though pressed to a wall of stone. Its mouth opened and closed soundlessly. The air shimmered with heat.

"This is what I had to remember," Yeshua called to the others. "I am sure of it, almost sure. We must see the living and the dead as our father sees them, even if that sight burns us away like . . . like candles, because nothing else, nothing, will ever suffice. Our father, he sees all of us who are here and all of our children unborn and all of our fathers and their fathers and *their* fathers, all one People, in every moment that has been written or will be written, and we must leave not one behind and starving, not one of our People living or dead, not . . . not if we can do otherwise."

The corpse took no step forward, but it interrupted Yeshua with a low, quavering moan—such an agony of hunger. Koach barely held back from covering his ears. He stared at this corpse of the man who had been his enemy, though perhaps that man had never known it.

The sica was half-sheathed in the sand, yet Koach did not touch its hilt, and Kana did not reach for it, not yet.

"What are you going to do?" Kana called.

That haunted, desert look returned to Yeshua's eyes. "Try and find the man who was starving, the man the father lost."

The corpse leaned forward as though into a high wind. Its jaw worked as though it were chewing open-mouthed. It hissed at the living.

Yeshua straightened, his voice thickening with grief. "Benayahu, I see you. I know what you have done. I know what you did to your daughter. I can hear them all now, all the voices, all the words that before were lost in the moaning." His eyes shone with unshed tears. "I hear her, and I hear you. I hear Koach there behind me, and Kana, and Cephas, and all of them, all of them, and it hurts. It hurts." He sucked in a breath, and took another step toward the corpse. "And I know that somewhere in that rotting flesh you wear, somewhere deep, even now, your self-hatred and despair eats at you. I hear it loud as wind, as locusts in the crops. You can devour a hundred of your kin, a thousand, to fill that emptiness that not even your beating of your daughter could fill. And it will never be enough. I tell you the truth. Benayahu, it will *never* be enough."

The corpse growled, its eyes staring sightlessly ahead, and tried to slouch forward a step.

"No," Yeshua said. Koach could hear the tears in his voice, and even his mother's voice had never sounded like that, never sounded that hoarse with sorrow, that raw with pain. "It doesn't have to be like this," Yeshua said, pleading. "There's a choice. Everything we do is a choice. Everything. I *know* this. I hear us all, all, in my . . . in my *head*," he choked. "How could I not know this? I will not let you walk into that town, Benayahu. Nor any other corpse that may come. I promise. I promise. Not one. I can send you away." The heat made the air ripple like water, and the corpse staggered back one step.

They all did. Koach held a hand before his face.

"You can turn around," Yeshua said, his voice quivering. "You can walk away in that corpse you wear. No one will drive a blade into your head. I promise it. But you will not feed again on your kin. Not ever. If you leave, you will walk this earth always, hungering, thirsting, unsatisfied, in a misery whose origin you cannot even remember, until that body has crumbled away at last and is only soil, only that, only the dust it was in the beginning. And yet . . . and yet you will *still* suffer, famished, in an eternity without sleep, though no other will ever do you harm. If that is what you choose, Benayahu, my kin." Yeshua turned his hand, presenting the palm to the corpse, as though to invite it near. The heat abated, though the night was still warm, too warm for the shore of the sea. "Or let it go. All of it: the hunger, that body you wear, your fear and bitterness. Let it go." His voice dropped to nearly a whisper. "I hear your pain. And it is *my* pain. I am standing in the door, Benayahu, and I am burning, I am burning." Tears on his face. "The door of my father's house. And it hurts. God, it hurts. Take my hand. I'll help. I'll help you step through. We can't flinch away. Our father in heaven still loves you, Benayahu. He still finds you beautiful . . . as the day he made you. You think he won't welcome you, but he will, he will. Do you know what is on the other side of this door? His house . . . his *house* has so many . . . so many rooms, Benayahu. I wouldn't say this if I didn't see it. I see it. I see what he sees, and I am weeping, weeping like him." He touched his face. "These are his tears. That house where there is finally, finally no. . . no screaming. So many rooms. One even for you. And you can't even imagine it. It's that beautiful. So beautiful."

The corpse's head swiveled from Yeshua to the others. It *screeched*, making Koach start, his heart violent in his chest. He found himself staring at Benayahu's bloodied teeth in terrible fascination. All day Koach had grieved; now he was intensely grateful that Tamar was not walking the shore in just such a reeking corpse as this. Trapped like this, hungering like this, her mouth full of blood. He felt ill, unsteady on his feet.

"No," Yeshua said. "You look at me, Benayahu. At me. And choose. Please. Everyone chooses. Please."

The corpse faced Yeshua, and stood still. Something very strange began to happen. When he lay in his bedding later that night, Koach would not be entirely sure he had really seen it, had not imagined it. The life, the spirit, the person that Benayahu had been—all of that came back into the corpse's eyes. It came the way a great fish rises from the deep, murky and indistinct at first, and then gradually nearer until it was clear as a flash of sunlight on scales. Koach looked away swiftly, for all of Benayahu was in the corpse's eyes—all that he had ever loved or feared or craved, every moment of pain or regret. Koach didn't want to see that much of the man he'd hated, or that much of *any* man, all in one shattering instant. He kept his eyes averted.

Yeshua's face and hands began to burn with light, the way the sea does when it reflects the sun's fire. As Moseh's face must have when he lowered his hands from his eyes and gazed upon God at Har Sinai. As though all this shore was covered with God, with the fire of his presence, and only Yeshua could see it. The rest of them saw it reflected on his skin, and felt it in the heat that now scorched hot as the desert in the month of the lion. In a moment, all the sweat had been burned away from Koach's face, leaving behind only the taste of salt on his lips.

Yeshua's hand trembled as he held it out. "Please, Benayahu."

Benayahu staggered toward him, dragging one foot. His jaw slack. He reached for Yeshua, and his fingers, tentative as an old man's, touched the stranger's palm. The corpse's eyes filled with regret and pain so fierce, it hurt to look at them.

The corpse let out a slow sigh, a last exhalation like the world coming undone. Then its eyes emptied. Its knees gave way, and Yeshua caught the dead man in his arms and held him, the weight carrying him to his knees. He lay the body down on the wet sand.

Without knowing why, Koach found himself by Yeshua's shoulder. He stood over the corpse, the last of Tamar's kin. But he also remembered the misery in this corpse's eyes. And the way the nagar had stood staring at his wife's name on the wall of his shop. His hate was doused, for the pain in the man's eyes had been such that it could only inspire sorrow and regret, a regret deeper than the sea. Slowly, his throat tight, Koach leaned over the body. With his left hand he closed Benayahu's eyes.

"I'm sorry, Tamar," he whispered. "I didn't help you, and now you are gone, and your father, too. I'm sorry."

Beside him, the light faded from Yeshua's face as quickly as it had come. He fell to the side, but Koach caught him against his hip, breaking the fall. In a moment Shimon and Kana were there, helping him lower Yeshua gently to the sand.

Silent tears. Yeshua blinked them back. "Abba," he whispered. "The door is open. And the light, the light, the light . . ."

"*Navi,* are you all right?" Shimon asked hoarsely. He and Koach exchanged a wide-eyed glance.

"I looked into his eyes," Yeshua whispered, the tears running from the corners of his eyes down to his temples, tracing a path in the day's dirt and sweat on his face. "And he looked into mine. And I could see, oh I could see. Myself, reflected in his eyes. I remembered." The smallest shake of his head, his eyes glassy with pain and wonder. "I could breathe out a billion stars. All that life and beauty. Everything so beautiful—and so fragile. Everything dying and being born. And the sky, always getting bigger, always bigger. Too small to hold all the things I love. Cephas, I remembered." His hands were shaking, and Shimon caught one, squeezed it. Kana took the other, and cushioned Yeshua's head on his arm.

"It's slipping away now," Yeshua breathed. "All the suns and all the worlds and all their peoples. A moment ago, I could see them. See all of them. For just a moment—" He closed his eyes, but the tears still escaped him. His hands still shook as the men of Kfar Nahum held him.

"It's gone," he whispered. "I am Yeshua bar Yosef, a son of man, the *nagar,* of Natzeret on the hill."

PART 9

SIGN OF THE FISH

THE NIGHT WAS aging and Shimon staggered when he reached the doorstep of his own house; he hadn't slept since the day before this past one. Through bleary, bloodshot eyes, he peered down at the object that awaited him on the stone step, small and white in the starlight. He took it up in his hand; when he saw what he held, a shiver ran through his entire body and his entire heart. He didn't know how long he crouched there, holding the object, but his legs felt stiff when at last he lowered himself and sat on the step.

It was a fish carved from driftwood. A tail but no fins. A small, empty eye, just a circle carved into the wood. A simple thing carved by a child. Shimon held the small, precious thing in his hands and his cheeks were wet with tears. Glancing up, he found through the blur of his vision Bar Cheleph leaning against the house across the street, watching him.

"I took that from him, Bar Yonah," he said. "Years back." His eyes were dark with memory, his voice slow as though burdened with sleep. "He called me brother, tonight. That is his."

Shimon stared at him, mutely.

Bar Cheleph folded his hands uneasily behind his back. "I troubled your house. I regret it."

Shimon closed his hand around the small fish and rose, turning to his door.

"I'll watch your house tonight," Bar Cheleph called out quickly.

Shimon stopped, his fingertips just brushing the wood of his door.

"More dead might come. I'll keep watch."

Without turning, Shimon said, "You want to atone for striking my brother. He may forgive you; I don't. I don't need your atonement, Bar Cheleph." And he opened his door and stepped within, shutting it behind him.

WHERE THE WAVES EAT THE WORLD

SLOWLY, HOLDING her breath, Rahel walked out onto the sand, hearing bits of driftwood and the bones of fish crack beneath her naked feet. The world gray with the approaching dawn. Her husband's old prayer shawl was rough against her arm where she had tucked it into her sleeve. She kept her gaze on the man ahead of her, a man whose clothes were tattered, his face and arms dark with bruises. She had come down to the water to mourn a dead priest and a long-dead husband, and to be alone with the sea, but she found Yeshua there before her.

He stood where the land ended with the breakers wetting his feet, his arms extended, his hair tangled from a night walking in the wind without sleep, and without comb or basin to wash in. Though her sons had returned to the house in the late hours, and Yakob with them, as though he were unwilling to go back to a house now bereft of his father—Yeshua had not. All through the hours of the dark, he had been out here. Glancing to the left and the right, Rahel saw a few others here on the shore. Kana sat with his back to the cairn. Bar Cheleph stood leaning on an oar, a little way down the shore from Yeshua; Yohanna was at his side, a hand on his shoulder, his lips moving with words too quiet for Rahel to hear. Yesse sat cross-legged on the sand a few strides from them, his face desolate.

Even as Rahel drew near, Yeshua began calling out in high, quavering wails as if he were God calling some new world into being. The old desert God of their fathers. The God Rahel had always revered and resented and feared. Yeshua's arms were lifted as though he were prepared to part the sea as Moseh the Lawgiver had done. Then she gasped. Forms were rising from the water at his call, shapes of men dark against the morning in the east, at least ten or twelve. Corpses streamed water from their lank hair and the rotted remnants of their clothing as they staggered out of the waves, strands of seaweed caught about their limbs and trailing behind. Their arms rose from the sea, reaching for the man they saw before them.

"Amma!" A cry behind her. Glancing back, she saw Shimon, his hair wild about his face, his eyes bloodshot from anguish and lack of sleep. Behind him, Yakob, looking scarcely better after the dark hours mourning his father. Both of them were in the dirtied garments they had worn the night before last, out at sea, when they had pulled up the nets full of fish. Some distance behind, slower, Koach stepped through the tideline grasses. All her boys, and Zebadyah's. One of them must have wakened to find her gone from the house; she had strained to lift the bar over the door but had done it quietly enough, and had stepped out softly, her grief so deep that she had forgotten her sandals. But after the deaths of the past day and night, an unexplained absence might well be an occasion for panic.

"Amma!" Shimon called. "Get back!"

Yakob called out, "*Rabboni! Rabboni!*"

The man from Natzeret let out another piercing cry. The dead were walking out of the waves now, their mouths opening to moan, water pouring out from between their dead teeth. Rahel's heart pounded with anger more than with fear—always, these dead rose to take from her those she cherished—and she might have approached nearer, either to stand by the strange *navi* or to scream her grief at the restless dead, but at that moment her sons reached her. Shimon's hand settled heavily on her shoulder.

Yeshua stepped out into the water and took the first corpse by the arm, gazing into its eyes and whispering something none of those on the shore could hear. Then Rahel saw what her sons had seen the night before. She saw the rush of life back into the eyes of the dead, its last, exhaled breath, and then its fall back into the water. That was a shock to Rahel's spirit greater than the rising of the corpses had been—that a man could whisper some word that would give rest so complete and final. She gazed at Yeshua in wonder, as he strode knee-deep along the surf, gripping each of the corpses, one after the next, as though they were his brothers and he was welcoming them home after a night of casting the nets. One seized his throat in its long fingers and pulled him near to bite, but he simply placed the heel of his hand against its head and pushed, holding it back long enough to catch and hold its gaze.

"Amma?" Shimon reached her side, breathless. "Are you all right?"

Rahel couldn't look away from the falling of the dead. "I dreamed this," she whispered. "Last night. A figure, all in white. White fire. Corpses falling like old leaves. I couldn't see his face."

"His robes are brown," Shimon said.

"Yet it was he in my dream."

"Amma!" Koach reached them, panting.

"I am all right, Koach, Shimon."

The corpses lay still as dead fish in the surf. And Yeshua stood there, water to his thighs, gazing down at them. If only all of this had been a dream—not only this night but all the nights previous, all the past fifteen years. All the moaning of the dead. Yet as Koach stepped close, she smiled faintly. No. She would not give up the past fifteen years with her sons. Not though her husband and his brother had been torn out of her life, if not out of her heart.

"He needs us," Rahel said quietly. "Come on."

* * *

Yeshua knelt a moment by a fallen corpse that lay half out of the surf, then lowered his hand to its face, closing its eyes. Those eyelids must have long since gone stiff and cold, yet at his touch they slid closed as easily as though the corpse had died only a moment before. The thought of that touch, that unclean flesh, made Shimon shiver; yet the corpse, now that it lay still, with its eyes closed rather than staring in endless hunger, seemed . . . *clean*. Like one who had lain down the burdens of the night and given himself to sleep, and who might wake before sundown to cook fish over the coals and ready the boat again. It was strange, so strange. He repressed an urge to approach the corpse, to kneel by Yeshua and gaze at it, see if it was truly at rest.

"I must get out on that water," Yeshua said.

"What?" Shimon gasped.

"There will be too many to face on the sand, too many, too many, yet they must come up. They must all come up." Yeshua's voice was cold and calm. His face might have been one of Koach's wood carvings. "I must get out there, Cephas."

"On the water? It's the Sabbath."

"The Sabbath was made for man, not man for the Sabbath."

Shimon swallowed. "There's dark weather coming."

"The darkest." Yeshua's eyes were hard. "And when the dead come up with it, I must be there to meet them. Will you row me out?"

Shimon hesitated, glancing at the bodies at the water's edge. Yeshua stepped near, lowering his voice so that only Shimon could hear. "Years ago, something reached into your town and tore out its heart. The *shedim* have roamed that hollow space it left, and their moans have filled your ears. And you hear it, I know you do, in your mind, even now, even as I do. But we can end it. We can *end it*. You've shivered in the wind . . . too long. Let your faith be as a rock, Cephas, to shield you. Let it be as the Ramat ha-Golan, like mountains that can . . . that can challenge the sky. I tell you, I tell you, on such a rock as that I will build a new town, and a gathering to live in it such as this land has never seen. And not even the shrieking wind of Sheol will prevail against it."

Yeshua's words stirred him; a hard glint came to Shimon's eyes. Whatever revelation had come to the stranger with the light and the heat as he faced the corpses, it had burned away much of his uncertainty, his dread. Yeshua's face was still bruised, his words still rapid and breathless, but he spoke with a fierce confidence and a demand for help to which there could be only one answer.

Shimon glanced at his father's boat. "I will take you out there," he said.

Yeshua gripped Shimon's arm below the shoulder and squeezed so hard it hurt.

"We can end it," he said again.

Then he let go and strode back down to the water's edge.

"Come on," Shimon muttered, and ran down the shore toward that other line of boats, those still seaworthy. Yakob stood, hesitating a moment, staring after Yeshua. Then he ran after Shimon, shells and other sea debris cracking beneath his sandals.

* * *

Rahel watched Yeshua walk down the line of the sea. He was different this morning, Yeshua. Harder, colder. All his formidable energy channeled into one fierce purpose, as though every breath he took before launching out on that sea was a breath taken at high cost.

Rahel stared at the bodies of the dead. With the fingers of her right hand she reached into her left sleeve and touched the old, woolen shawl she had tucked away there. Yonah's *tallit*. It brought her a smile of both remembered happiness and remembered grief. All those years ago, she had grieved alone. Most of the women she could have called friend or sister had died that night, violated and beaten by the Roman mercenaries and then eaten by the dead. Having none to turn to for comfort, Rahel had taken to carrying her husband's *tallit* with her while she cooked and while she slept, while she nursed her crippled child. It was all she had left of him besides their children, and for a while, the cloth still carried his scent. It was many months before she could bring herself to wash it, and she did so only after the scent was too faint for her to detect it and after she had forgotten what that scent had been like. She had waited until her infant was sleeping and Shimon was gone from the house, then had wept as she washed the shawl in her basin, scrubbing it until the water was browned with the months of oil and dirt, then wringing it out and scrubbing it again. When it was clean and beautiful (though less so to her eyes than it had been), she had draped it over its peg to dry, and then sat for most of a Roman hour by the basin, staring at the dirtied water. In her heart she had felt that the last of her husband's scent and the last of him was in that water, and she could not bring herself to pour it out. She thought of asking Shimon to spill that water out over the sand or over the sea when she could not see it done. But she had decided at last that it had to be her, and, asking Shimon to watch the baby after he came home, Rahel had carried the basin down to the sea.

Now she gazed on the bodies of the dead, wondering who they were, and whether men or women in Kfar Nahum had grieved at their death. Their faces had been eaten away by time and the sea and the hunger of fish. She couldn't even tell if they had been Hebrew. One of them might even have been a woman she had laughed with by the cistern. She couldn't know.

The back of her neck warned her she was being watched, and a glance behind showed her Koach's waif, the young woman who had been silent and then had sung. She was picking her way carefully through the grasses. The sight startled Rahel, and she realized suddenly that the girl must have slept the night in her house. She should have been angered, but strangely she felt only pity and a sense of kinship, though this bewildered her. She and that girl—they had both been touched by the *navi*. Both of them had been given back something lost, something resigned. Both of them had been, by that act, torn away from their old lives. Now they stood in the empty place, the place of waiting, where the waves eat the world and yet the world remains. She didn't know what was going to happen.

* * *

While Yesse stood some way up the tideline and watched, his face drawn with grief, the men drew Shimon's boat toward the water, the scrape of it against the shingle an oddly comforting sound, an ancient sound, one the People had heard night after night upon this shore for generations—the sound of their men leaving behind land and bed and security and setting out on the fragile surface of a terrible deep. The boat slid quickly, its bow toward the surf, for Yeshua lent a hand, and Bar Cheleph did also, though Shimon gave him a look of furious warning, a look that said as clearly as a shout: *Get your hands off my father's boat.*

Rahel reached the boat just as the men brought it down to the surf. She took the gunwale in her hands and sprang in, almost as though she were a young girl again. She winced when her feet struck the bottom of the boat, jarring her hip.

Shimon gasped and motioned for the others to stop. They let go of the gunwale and stared at Rahel.

"Amma! What are you doing?"

"Going with you," she said, her teeth clenched against the pain. She seated herself between the oar benches, using one of the nets for a cushion, her back to the hard wood of the hull.

"No, you are not."

Rahel met his gaze, her own as hard as winter. "What began with a spear through your father's brow—I want to see it ended."

Leaning against the gunwale, Shimon exchanged uncertain looks with the other men. Yeshua was staring intently at the sea, seeming hardly to have heard. Then Bar Cheleph spoke, his brow damp with sweat. "I am coming, too."

"*You*," Shimon said, "are not welcome in my father's boat."

Bar Cheleph smiled faintly. "I am the adopted brother of Yakob and Yohanna. I would have been casting the nets with you long before, if I had any bravery at all. But . . ." He looked down. "I had dreams. The same dream, each night. I'm out on the water, and we're casting the nets, and in the dream I always bring *them* up."

Shimon gave him a startled look. He knew such dreams all too well.

Bar Cheleph whispered, "I never knew if my father and mother were among those who were tossed in."

Kana looked away. Yeshua stood gazing at the waves.

Shimon hesitated, the incoming sea nearly reaching his toes. "You are blessed," he said after a moment. "Never to have seen your father risen, like that."

"Not knowing is worse." Bar Cheleph looked out over the chop of the water. "Not knowing if he found rest. Or if he is hungering."

"He found rest." Shimon's tone was harsh. "Fathers don't pursue their children across the sand to eat them. Whatever is down there, it is not him. Nor your mother either."

Yakob nodded to Bar Cheleph, his face drawn. "I put your father in a tomb last night, and mine. Our father had two Yakobs. Never forget that."

Bar Cheleph's eyes moistened. He whispered a word of gratitude, so quiet it almost couldn't be heard.

"I always disappointed him," Yohanna said softly.

Yakob gripped his brother's arm.

Shimon looked away to let the two brothers have that moment to grieve. "Let's get the boat out," he said gruffly.

"One moment." Bar Cheleph walked to where Yeshua stood behind the stern and knelt.

"Before we embark," Bar Cheleph pleaded, "baptize me, *Rabboni*. I . . . I have done evil. My own kinsfolk loathe the sight of me. Immerse me. Please. Make me clean. Then I can follow you even against the dead. I will go where you go, eat where you eat. I will not be parted from you. I promise it. El Shaddai witness it!"

"Do not promise." Yeshua's face went stern, as cold and hard as the face of a mountain. "Do not promise me," Yeshua said, "and do not promise God. Do you think God who promised the stars they would burn each night will wait on your promises? Or that the father who has written his promises into stone itself will trust the vows of men and women, who break them? Say only yes or no. Do not promise. Only do."

Bar Cheleph swallowed.

Shimon listened with disquiet. The Yeshua he had known the previous day had worried him because he seemed a vagrant and because his raving questioned everything that kept Shimon's town and his family secure. But this Yeshua, the one who had faced the dead, worried him even more. This Yeshua called for a boat, and received one. This Yeshua dismissed the Sabbath and spoke of God as though he had something to say about him. This Yeshua seemed more the *navi*. The prophets of their past had raised and buried kings, called fire from the sky, and torn apart cities with a word. What might this one do?

Yeshua stepped away from Bar Cheleph and gripped the gunwale as though to leap into the boat.

"Please," Bar Cheleph cried.

Yeshua stopped, his face stricken, as though some defense he had erected that night against the screaming in his mind was shivering. For a moment he stood at the gunwale. Then he turned back. He placed his hand beneath Bar Cheleph's chin and lifted his face. Something flickered in his eyes. "You are loved," he said, his voice quiet and firm, "you are, and the way you were hurt, it does not change that. It never has. It never will. What hurt you have done to others, the father has forgiven. He has forgiven it. Hurt no one else."

Bar Cheleph gave a small nod, though that yearning had not left his eyes. Yeshua turned again and leapt into the boat and seated himself against the gunwale—leaving the benches, as Rahel had, for those who would be rowing. After a moment, Bar Cheleph followed, with a grimace of pain much like Rahel's. Yohanna climbed into the boat as well. Kana sprang in, too, a gust of wind pulling his cloak aside to reveal that he carried, once again, the sica at his hip. But his face was pensive.

Then they had the bow in the water, and Shimon got behind the stern while Yakob pushed from the starboard, and Koach came running, splashing into the water, with the beggar woman wading in beside him. They reached the gunwale opposite Yakob, and Shimon looked at them in shock. Bar Cheleph rose and stood over the gunwale.

"She is coming, too," Koach said. "It's important to her."

Bar Cheleph didn't say a word. He just reached down, let Koach take hold of his arm just below the elbow, and lifted the smaller man into the boat. Then he and Koach turned and lifted the woman in, water running from her coat and from the ragged remnants of her dress beneath it. She stepped toward the stern, tripping over the nets, but Koach caught her arm and helped her down onto the short bench at the stern. Then he shrugged his thick-sleeved outer garment off over one shoulder and used his left hand to tug it off the other. He threw it into the bottom of the boat as though it repulsed him, this garment his mother had made to conceal his arm. In just his tunic, with his withered arm naked, bare for anyone to see, he sat beside the strange woman. His face had set in hard, determined lines as though he had carved it from driftwood, as he had carved so many other things.

Staring at Koach's right arm, Bar Cheleph muttered, "Didn't he heal you?"

"He did."

And that was all Koach said.

Shimon cast a pensive glance at his mother. "A storm is coming. I can't take all my kin out there. And what use are women in a boat?"

"I have been in this boat before," Rahel said quietly.

Shimon frowned, not understanding. Then he glanced at the sky. Definitely a storm. Worry clenched in his gut.

Yeshua watched his face from where he sat near the bow, but he didn't speak.

Yohanna slid one of the oars into the oarlock and held the oar blade up above the shallow water. "It is written," he said softly, "that when the anointed *navi* comes to deliver the remnant of Yehuda tribe, his coming will make hills into valleys and valleys into hills. That what was wilderness will be as a straight road. Ha Matbil spoke of this often." He gave Koach a thoughtful look. "Perhaps his coming will also make women into fishers and brothers whose bodies are broken into boatmen. We are only men. Who are we to argue with what God has written?"

That talk did nothing to settle Shimon's unease. But Yohanna had always been like this—speaking more like a priest's son than a fisherman. "We are all fools," Shimon muttered.

The hardness in Yeshua's face broke, for the first time, into a wry smile. "You speak the truth."

Still Shimon hesitated.

Yakob exchanged a glance with him, a dry look, as though to say, *We are a long row from where we were last night, aren't we?*

And Shimon's eyes answered back, *We are, and I am not sure how we have ended up here, or where "here" is.*

Every night for fifteen years—except for the Sabbath and that one winter when Shimon had taken ill—he and Yakob had slid the boat carefully down into the sea. Just the two of them—and in the last year Yohanna, after he'd tired of eating locusts and wild honey with Ha Matbil by the Tumbling Water.

Now the boat was full of people. Bewildered, Shimon glanced up the tideline toward Yesse, whose white hair streamed behind him in the rising gusts of wind. But if the elder did not approve of this break with tradition and Law and all good sense, he gave no sign. He only watched. Shimon blew out his breath, recalled Yeshua staring into the eyes of the dead, the wonders Yeshua had done before collapsing into his arms. With a mutter beneath his breath, he gave the craft a great shove, and Yakob with him, heaving with their feet planted in the sand, and they ran the boat down onto the water until the next wave surge lifted it and the water was cold about their knees, and then each of them gripped opposite sides at the stern and pulled themselves in.

ONE MORE PROMISE TO KEEP

BEING OUT ON the water is an isolating experience. The world is gone, the land barely visible, if at all. There are only the people in your boat, only the sound of your own breath and the lonely cries of gulls or the loud calling of cranes echoing over the water. The sky is wider and deeper than any sky over any town or village on the earth, and you glance up at it cautiously, knowing that at any moment it might crack open and unleash the wrath of God over your small, bouncing craft.

The sky was heavy. Shimon found that he and the others spoke in hushed voices beneath it. Even Yeshua's voice was soft. "I feel that I could sleep until Pesach," the *navi* murmured. "I have never been so weary, so weary. All of you, I see your eyes, I see them; you are too scared to rest. Don't be. Whatever . . . whatever happens on this sea, don't be afraid."

"I have lived most of my life afraid," Kana said, after relieving Yakob at the oar. "But I am not afraid today. I am here because I have seen *your* eyes. I know you have seen what I've seen. More than that. You've seen things I haven't. Things that would break my mind if I did see them."

Yeshua was silent for a bit. He leaned against the side of the boat, his head against the gunwale, and though he could not have been comfortable there, his eyes were lidded as though he might fall asleep in another breath. His face was still pale. "We are the same age, Kana," he said at last. "And we have both seen too many things. Too many."

"That is the truth," Kana said grimly.

"A dark time *is* coming," Yeshua said, and Kana breathed in sharply, hearing the echo of his own words. "But the father can take that time and make . . . make of it something different. Have faith in that." More softly, Yeshua added, "As *I* must."

"Where are we going, *Rabboni?*" Yakob asked.

"Out there," he said, with a nod toward the middle of the sea.

"Yes, but when do we stop? We can't row all morning, not with that storm coming."

"We will know when to stop," Yeshua said. "For now, keep rowing, keep rowing, and wait. You will need to wait . . . often, if you come with me."

"Come with you?" Shimon said, his throat tight. "With you, where? We haven't said we're coming with you."

Rahel smiled faintly, as if at some memory of his father, but said nothing.

Yeshua smiled too, a different smile, as though he wanted to laugh but was too fatigued. He opened his eyes slightly. "All your life you have fished for barbels and musht, Cephas, all your life. Come with me, and we will fish together for the hearts of men."

Shimon heaved at the oar, and wrestled again with the strangeness of this man. He remembered the man gasping for air, after . . . after what he did with Benayahu. After those words about stars and memory, the night before. *I am spent,* Yeshua had whispered, gazing past Shimon's head at the night sky. *I have to go, have to go. Just for a while. Into the hills, to some quiet place, some place where the screams are not so loud, not so loud as this. There are so many, Cephas, so many, so many. The cries, the cries I hear. I need to be away. Just the father and the stones and the wind.* Yeshua had sucked in a breath, and his body had trembled as though with fever or great pain. Yet Shimon had no longer feared that there were *shedim* in him, that he might be unclean or a witch.

But not yet, the man from Natzeret had whispered. *Not yet. One more promise to keep.*

Shimon stared at him now, in the boat. Yeshua's face had settled into hard lines, as though he'd set his body against some great boulder and was bracing himself to push. One more promise to keep. Shimon didn't know what Yeshua meant to do, but he knew what promise was meant.

But because the riddle of this man could not be answered, Shimon turned to one that could. Kana was watching the sea, and he didn't look up when

Shimon spoke. "Why did you come back, Bar Nahemyah?" His voice was rough. "It wasn't to recruit me, or others, not really. You were running. Hiding. Why? And why did it take you a year to return?"

Kana's face went tight with pain.

The others hushed, listening.

"The way you fought," Yakob said after a moment. "The way you moved with that knife. I've never seen anything like that."

"One of the things I spent that year doing." A bite in his voice.

"You almost saved my father." Nearly a whisper.

"Almost." Kana lowered his head.

Shimon had heard the memory beneath Kana's words, and knew the memory to be a bad one. He frowned. He had always thought Bar Nahemyah had thrown in with Barabba, that he had never come back because he had chosen not to. That, and the dead rising from the water in ever greater numbers in the year since— dead that Kana had dropped into this sea—had done little to endear his memory to Yonah's oldest son. Now Shimon wondered.

"Why *didn't* you come back?" he asked, more softly.

Kana's face darkened with shame. "At first, Barabba kept me bound in a cave, and men came—" He paused, then glanced at the young woman in the stern huddled beneath Koach's water-coat, the coat that had been Yonah's. Kana stared at her for a long moment, and then, as if deciding suddenly that if a woman who had seen horrors could bring herself to sing, then he could at least speak, he went on. "Men with blood on their hands," he said. "Not that you could see it, but you could smell it. They came to the cave and spoke with me, one night and then another and another. Told me what Barabba was doing in the land. Not his plans, but their effect. And stories of what Rome was doing. In the long days in the cool of that cave, bound and naked, I craved their return, their words. I can't explain it to you." His right hand trembled; he stilled it, and his face became distant, the secrets of his heart buried deep, drifting like restless corpses far below the reflective surface of his eyes.

"They took everything from me. My coat, my strength. I was thirsty and weak and shaking when the nights came. But they left me with the shofar, at least." His fingers touched the ram's horn where it hung at his breast. "And then, when I thought I would live the rest of my life in that hole in the rock, Barabba came to me. He looked bigger, somehow. He said, *I need men who will blow the shofar even in the streets of Yerushalayim itself. The dead and the Romans alike will devour us all, if I haven't such men.*" Kana was silent a moment, and then he glanced not at any of his kin but at Yeshua, the stranger. "He took me there. To Yerushalayim. Showed me how our People suffered. Not in Kfar Nahum, not in Natzeret, not in any ruined village of our land, but there, in the very heart of the land God promised us, where people rot where they stand and the moaning fills every street and our people die between the cold stares of the priests and the Roman walls." His voice went hard and cold. "You don't know what it is like. You can't know. What it's like in Yerushalayim."

"I know," Yeshua said, his eyes unfocused as though he were listening to distant voices.

And then Kana's control crumpled.

The *anguish* in his face. Shimon swallowed. He wondered if his own face had looked that way, sometimes.

"You don't have to tell us any more," Shimon said. "You are home." He took a hard pull at the oar.

"Home." Kana gave a small laugh, hardly more than a breath. "I haven't been home in fifteen years. Since that night. I am an outsider, in my own town."

"We've all been that," Shimon murmured. Kana nodded, took a breath. "I fought for him for a while. After what I'd seen. Because I *had* seen, and I couldn't look away. I couldn't just run back here or steal some Roman's horse. Not after what I'd seen. So I stood before Barabba in the hills and he put the sica in my hands. The very knife he'd used to cut my bonds. And I made the first of these." He brushed his hand over the cuts on his arm, his face still raw with emotion. "I fought with him. Killed. But—" He struggled a moment. "There was a . . . a woman, and her husband, their daughter. Roman. The man was some petty official under Pontius Pilate. It was . . . a test. So Barabba would know if each of us could do what had to be done, if we were in truth to rise against Rome and drive the Romans back to the sea. There were four of us; we went into that city. I haven't seen the other three since, because I left that night and kept moving until I reached this shore." He met Shimon's eyes, and Shimon wanted to look away from the pain there, but he couldn't. "That family, that Roman family, was given into my hand. I was to kill them. In the night, as they slept. With the sica I carried. All three, Barabba said, and any slaves in the house." He wiped the back of his hand across his eyes. When he continued, his voice was hoarse. "I thought I could do it, Shimon. I thought: They were Roman. I could do it. I was in their house, I was standing over their daughter's bed. The sica in my hand. And I . . . I couldn't. She was young. I just kept thinking of the dead I'd seen. And Ahava, my betrothed. I hadn't thought of her in so long. Do you remember her, Shimon?"

He nodded, though he had rarely spoken with her as a boy. She had been tall for a girl, he remembered that, and she used to sneeze tiny sneezes that sounded like laughter.

"Now I see her, every night. Every time I close my eyes." Kana looked away, his voice unsteady. "I couldn't do it. We can be torn from our lives so easily. Can be left grasping and moaning for what we've lost. All my life I have loathed and feared the dead, and now I don't."

"*I* fear the dead," Bar Cheleph muttered.

Kana said, "I pity them."

For a moment there was only the splash of the oars, the chop of the waves against the boat, the duck and roll of their path out onto the uneasy sea.

As he heaved hard on the oar, Shimon glanced at the *navi*. His eyes widened.

The stranger rested in the crook of the prow, his shoulders against either gunwale. His head was bowed almost between his knees, as though he was at the end of his strength after facing the living and the dead. Heedless of the roughness of the sea.

He was asleep.

SKY FULL OF DARK

IT WAS DAY but the sky darkened, clouds piling onto and over each other, the wind whipping the waves into white fury, until the boat ducked and spun. The storm came on quickly, relentless, as though whatever *shedim* shrieked over the sea meant to crush this fragile boat carrying Israel's *navi* out over the water.

The boat tossed and heaved, and the hue of Bar Cheleph's face went green, though the pitching of their craft did not wake Yeshua. The silent woman drew her coat over herself, looking very small in the stern, a bundle someone had tossed there and forgotten. Koach, who had listened pensively to Kana's story, went to sit by her, his good hand resting on her shoulder.

Rahel, who had been out on the water only once in her life, stood straight on her bench at the stern, her face cold and controlled; if she felt ill, she revealed no sign of it. At last, she reached grimly for the rope that waited, coiled, beneath her bench. She took it up in her hands and, bending, she reached for the silent woman's ankle. The woman gasped and drew back.

Koach touched her shoulder. "It's all right," he said softly by her ear.

"You're thinking the boat may sink." Rahel gave the younger woman a stern look. "If the boat sinks on this sea, none of us will see the shore."

The girl gazed at the chop and surge of the waves, and shivered. Koach squeezed her shoulder, and she gave a small nod. Rahel's lips compressed into a thin line; she bent again, took a firm hold on the younger woman's ankle, tied a loop around it. The other end she fastened to one of the iron hooks set in the bottom of the boat, hooks meant to secure items against a storm.

"Bat Eleazar is right," Yakob said. He took up another coil, and began cutting lengths and passing rope to each of those in the boat.

Rahel fastened a harness of rope about her own waist, and then Koach's. For a moment he sat quietly while her small, sure hands knotted the rope. His face burned. It was embarrassing to be seen cared for in this way; though she had helped him dress each morning, that had been in the privacy of their house, before no other eyes. Yet it would be more humiliating by far to be seen fumbling one-handed with the rope himself, laboring with careful attention at a task that any of the other men in the boat would have found simple. He especially didn't want the woman in his father's coat to see that.

With a pang of sorrow, he recalled standing naked on the rooftop, with Tamar's gaze on his body, his every weakness visible to her. He blinked quickly to make the world less moist and blurry. Maybe he would never again feel so safe with any woman. Or maybe he would. He didn't know.

"Are you all right, son?" Rahel whispered.

"No," he said. He took her hand, stilling its work at the rope. "No more hiding. I'll do this, mother." His name must be a lie no longer.

Rahel searched his face. Then her eyes filled with both pain and pride. Biting her lip, she nodded slightly and backed away.

While Koach wrestled awkwardly with knotting the rope, Rahel took up one of the curved wooden blades that the fishers used for bailing from its place in the bottom of the boat, holding it ready in her hand. Kana relieved Yakob at the oar, and Yohanna tried to relieve Shimon, but Shimon gave a firm shake of his head and heaved at the oar, his shoulders tensed. His face was set, as though he were hunting something over that water and would not give up the chase, not though the day ended and the world grew dark.

But in fact it was not yet noon.

The beggar woman looked away from the growl of the sea, and after a moment she pressed her fingertips to Koach's tunic, at his shoulder. He glanced at her, his face twisted in the effort it took not to cry.

"Miriam," she whispered.

He looked at her. The others did also.

It became very quiet in the boat.

"Miriam." She was pale, her face twisted in anxiety, and she held his gaze, her hand at his arm, as though they were siblings or lovers. Her eyes shone with her reawakened desire to speak, to be known.

"Miriam," Koach repeated.

"My name. It's . . . my name. Miriam bat Elisa. From Tower. From Magdala."

Koach stared at her a moment. She had been silent so long; now the giving of her name seemed a gift of great trust. "Don't be afraid," he said.

Miriam's eyes were serious. "I *am* afraid." Her voice was halting, betraying how unaccustomed she was to making words rather than hearing them. "Father. Mother. They were eaten. In our house in Magdala. When I lost my words." She moved her hands as she spoke, touching her belly when she said *eaten* and placing her fingers at her throat when speaking of her long silence. Her eyes moistened as she searched Koach's face, then the others' faces, though whether she was pleading for empathy or forgiveness or only an acknowledgment of kinship, they could not have said— only that her eyes demanded some response. Seeing their own faces reflected in her eyes, they each saw the smallness of how they had treated her and others like her.

Koach took her hand and gripped it. After a moment, he felt her fingers curl around his and grip back.

"Need to be here," she said, her voice so soft it was almost lost in the cry of the wind. Her hair blew about her face. "Need to see. Need to . . . not be afraid."

"Shimon bar Yonah," Kana interrupted. He was staring up at the wild growl of the sky.

"I know," Shimon said, loudly over the wind.

A moment before, the wind had been only the first roar of a gale; now it was tempest, now it was the sky ready to tear their boat apart. The waves became walls that rose and crashed, and the boat pitched violently.

The others roped themselves quickly to the iron hooks. Yakob and Yohanna secured the mast and its small sail; Shimon slid the oars under the benches by the fishing spears. He should have tied them down also; they would be no use in this storm, which could only be ridden out, not argued with. But

STANT LITORE

Koach saw the whites of his brother's eyes and knew his brother did not want to be without spear or oar, something he could lift in his hands.

"He still sleeps," Rahel shouted.

Koach looked and saw that it was true; the man from Natzeret's face, which had been pale, was now ashen, and his bruises were dark shadows—as though this was not sleep but the first touch of death. Koach shuddered.

Then the storm buried the last of the light out of the sky, as though a lamp had been covered with earth, and Yeshua was only a silhouette. They all were. What light remained was ghostly, showing the white edges of the waves. Koach's hand tightened about Miriam's fingers. She squeezed his hand again. Yet he didn't know if she meant to seek comfort or to give it. He felt her pressed to his left side, and he wished that he might put his arm about her, but he would not let go of her hand.

"Don't be afraid," he kept whispering. "Don't be afraid. Don't be afraid."

"They're coming," Shimon shouted.

The water frothed—not just from the storm but from what was coming up *with* the storm. Koach gazed over the gunwale into the crashing dark, a small noise of fear in his throat. The sea was full of faces, and there was moaning in his ears that was not wind.

SILENCE OVER THE WATER

THE DEAD WERE rising—not just one, not just a few.

All.

They surged and fell back, white as foam on the waves. Already some of the corpses were driven against the boat, their hands beating the hull as the waterborne dead had beat at the sides of the Ark in the old story.

The sky was dark like the ending of the world, and the air and the sea were black. There was only the dull sheen of their eyes and their silhouettes against the water. And the moaning, a sound that merged with the wind to become the wailing of all the *shedim* that had ever hunted in the lonely places of a broken land.

732

Koach and all the others and their entire town were but a tiny boat, a chip of wood on the wild thunder of the sea, and so many pale hands out of the past were grasping that fragile chip to drag it beneath the waters. These were the old dead, thrown into the sea fifteen years before. The cords about their wrists had parted long since, and their bodies were bloated with water. Some were without eyes or face, sea-eaten. The waterlogged flesh peeled back from their fingertips even as they grasped the gunwale. Their weight began to pull the boat down, down, into the dark, the water sloshing over the side. More of the white dead climbed over those first corpses, clambering over their backs to get at the warm life in the boat. The reek of them was stronger than the smell of the sea, covering that ancient scent the way slick, sickly oil covers the surface of the water. Miriam screamed, shrill and piercing over the moans of the dead, and Koach found he was screaming with her. He had only one hand, only one; he let hers go and snatched up the cold metal of a fishing spear to defend her, and himself, and his kin.

A horn call rang out, clear and deep, a challenge to sky and sea and everything within them. Those few notes, music raised in defiance of the dead like the voice of all the living deepened and strengthened. The sound woke the others from their horror.

Kana let the shofar fall from his lips. Then they were all on their feet, taking up hook, oar, or net, whatever they could grab. One of the dead, fat as though it had swallowed the sea, came up over those clutching at the gunwale and slipped into the boat, sliding into the bottom on its belly like a swollen fish, spewing water from its mouth. Shrieking, Rahel threw a net over it. Koach leapt onto its back and drove a fish hook, one-handed, down into the back of its skull. Vaguely, Koach recalled Yeshua's words about the dead, but in this darkness on the sea with the dead surging into the boat, he had no faith in his ability or anyone else's to stare the dead in the eyes. His insides were cold and weak with panic. As the corpse beneath him went still, he caught glimpses in the dark, all around him: Yakob and Yohanna thrusting the points of the other two fish hooks into the shoulders and faces of the dead with little effect. Kana with his sica, the pale sheen of it, driving it up through a corpse's chin, and then another, implacable as the *malakh ha-mavet*, the angel of death. Each of the corpses jerking once, then going still. Rahel beside him, with a knife out, slashing across the fingers of the dead, cutting away their grip on the boat, so that the dead slid back, pulled down by the grasping hands of those surging up behind them. Water rushed in over the stern. Then the boat righted itself, barely. Miriam took up one of the heavy nets, and Shimon lent his strength; they cast it out over the dead, entangling several.

Lightning, sharp against the eyes, revealed for one frantic heartbeat all the dead in the water, all of them climbing over each other toward the boat, all of them surging on the wildness of the waves. Koach saw one of the dead half over the other gunwale, its hands gripping Bar Cheleph's storm coat. Even as Bar Cheleph struggled, flailing, to shrug away the garment, another corpse climbed up over the first, its fingers gripping the first corpse's face, digging into its left cheek and its right eye, hissing as it fought for purchase. Koach screeched like one of the dead himself. Stepping to the side of that man who had once assailed him and beaten him to the grass, he brought the fish hook down and sliced neatly through one of the dead wrists clutching Bar Cheleph's coat, half severing it. The fingers slackened, and Bar Cheleph pulled his coat free of the thing's other hand and fell across the boat, shouting wordlessly, his eyes white. But the corpse grabbed Koach's spear with its good hand and moaned. The weight of the corpse behind it pulled it back, and both slid down into that water teeming with pale bodies, pulling Koach over the side.

With a cry, Koach released the spear, but too late, he'd been pulled right over the gunwale toward all those faces beneath him, all those faces white as rotting fish, their mouths gaping. The rope harness about his chest went taut; their fingers brushed his arm, his hair, and he screamed. Then something pulled him back, something had his belt and he was yanked fiercely back into the boat. Then Bar Cheleph's arm was around him. Koach screamed and screamed, kicking wildly as the dead came up over the gunwale after him. A flash of lightning, and there, stark against the shadows, a corpse with only one eye, its belly balanced on the brink of the boat, its legs in the water, its hands reaching for him.

The blade of an oar smacked into its face, hard, the sound of the blow lost in thunder that cracked the roof of the sky. Shimon stood there, bellowing against wind and storm, sudden rain lashing his face and hair.

* * *

That thunder had been right above Shimon's head, so loud it must have cracked open the world and all the water would now pour out. And it had cracked open time, for Shimon stood with his oar raised, gripped in gloved hands, the rain sharp against his face, and before that oar came swinging down, he stood in a single moment that held an eternity of thought and terror. Then a flash of lightning, the whole world light and dark; as Shimon brought the oar down, his heart wild in his chest, for an instant he could see the others in the boat, all their terrified faces, all of them about to die together. The woman from Tower, weeping as she bent to haul up another net, with Yohanna stooping to aid her in Shimon's place; Rahel driving her knife into a corpse's brow even as it clutched at her left breast like some nightmarish lover, seeking some hold to pull her toward its teeth; Yakob swinging the point of his spear hard against the grasping hands, breaking fingers; Kana wrestling with one corpse that had grappled his knife arm, then tossing the knife deftly to his left hand and sliding it up beneath the corpse's chin and through its head as though it were made of butter and not flesh and bone. Bar Cheleph falling back into the bottom of the boat, clutching Koach to him with one arm, Koach's rope tangled about his legs. And Yeshua, still, silent, seated in the bow, his face stark like a skull's in that flash of wild light.

All of them about to die.

And in that moment, in all their faces, Shimon saw himself, saw the horror that had eaten away all his life and left him only a husk. Between one beat of the heart and the next, he saw himself, and forgave.

He forgave Zebadyah the priest for hiding beneath his boat.

He forgave Kana his rage and his tossing of the dead into the sea.

He forgave his father for dying, for leaving him to raise his brother alone and to fish on the sea without guidance or aid.

He forgave himself.

For every moment he'd wakened shivering from the dream country. Every morning he'd brought home not enough fish. Every night he'd sunk like a stone beneath the water of his anger, his helplessness.

Because neither the priest nor the zealot nor his father nor he nor all the town together were enough to put their dead to rest. To hold in his heart the bitterness of so much wrath, and not forgive—it was as though a puddle of water were to hate itself for drying beneath the sun's heat in the month of the lion, the month of desert. The pool of water was not sufficient to withstand the sun that would devour it, and he was not sufficient to withstand the rising tide of the town's dead, of so much unforgotten history and pain and hunger.

In the next moment he might die, or not. But he could no longer hate himself, or his brother, or his people.

* * *

Shimon dropped the oar and flung himself to the floor of the boat beside Yeshua. He grabbed the man's shoulders and shook him, screaming, *"Rabboni! Rabboni!"*

None of them were sufficient.

But he had seen the stranger from Natzeret call a dead man back into his body and give him rest. If they had any hope, any chance of burying the dead, that chance was with Yeshua.

"Rabboni, my master, wake, or we perish!" Shimon cried. "Please!" He screamed his plea, desperate for the need of one small man on a small boat to sound louder than wind or water or the shrieking past. How was it that God heard prayer? Or that any human being heard another's cry for help or for love, when each day, every hour, every moment our minds are deluged by the cries of everyone around us and the cries of those in our memory, the thousand cries screaming within us?

"Please!"

Yeshua opened his eyes and blinked back water from his lids.

"Master!" Shimon shouted. "How can you sleep! The dead! The storm!"

Yeshua swept his lank and soaked hair out of his eyes, then reached for Shimon's hand; Shimon took it, and Yeshua surged to his feet. He looked out into the storm, his eyes dark against the night, though whether with fury or grief, Shimon couldn't tell. He released Yeshua's hand. There was a shriek, and a moving shadow that must have been Miriam throwing a net over one of the dead that was clambering into the boat. Yeshua stepped past her. Wood cracked behind him, and a spar swung loose from the mast toward his head; he lowered his head without glancing back, and it swung by. He placed one foot firmly against the gunwale, standing even amid the pitch and heave of the boat in the storm, even as the dead grasped at his ankles, his shins. His hair flew about his face, dark in the wind. Shimon gazed up at him in wonder and dismay.

Screams from others in the boat.

Then the sun's heat was all around him and passing through him, and this time there was no light but only heat, heat, *heat,* as though the world might burn away and leave nothing but flakes of ash beneath the cold stars. Shimon cried out and heard the others' cries and the wailing of the dead and the howl and crack of the storm. He saw the empty eyes of the dead all about him glinting in the dark, their hands reaching for him. And pressing on his body and his heart . . . the weight, the *kavod,* surely the same glory that the *kohannim* taught filled the Temple at times and made its pillars creak. The unbearable weight of God, the lightest press of whose fingertip might crush the land.

Shimon cried out, falling back.

Yeshua spoke, and his voice was soft as wind in the grass, soft as sunlight on still water. Yet Shimon could hear it in his very heart, hear it above all the noise of the world's wreck.

"*Shalom*," Yeshua said. "*Shabbat shalom.* Be at peace."

* * *

Zebadyah the priest had taught that the land had always had history, even before there *was* land. God had not made the world from nothing, as idle thinkers among the Greeks taught, but from the turmoil and wrack of the *tohu vavohu*, the whirling chaos, the dark materials that were without form or shape, the great waste of the sea upon which no light shone and in which drifted the debris and detritus of uncounted things that had not yet been shaped into anything living or beautiful. Sundered pieces that made up no whole, drift that clashed and crashed in the dark.

And because peace, because any bringing together, any settling of history's chaos into a new and meaningful story begins with words spoken and words heard, in the beginning God had whispered a few words into the rush of that primeval sea. And there was land amid the waters, and light.

* * *

The sky broke into pieces. Spears of sun pierced the clouds and fell into the cold sea, each of them doused in the water with a hiss so quiet only the *malakhim* could have heard them. For one wild moment, the eyes of the dead shone in the sudden light, so many sightless eyes, so many empty faces on the dark waves. All their mouths were open, their jaws slack. Shimon found that he was weeping, and he didn't know why. Only that, in this light, with the heat and the weight of Yeshua's power pressing him back against the opposite gunwale, all those staring faces were no longer a thing of terror but of sorrow. His face was wet with his tears.

Then all the eyes filled. He was looking out at so many of his dead rocking on the sea. The midwife he'd seen eaten on that night of the dead, she was there. And the eyes of young mercenaries who had rallied to Rome for coin or glory from far ends of the earth, and the eyes of young men and old men, and of women who had known men and women who hadn't, and of those who had borne children and those who had recently been children. All of them were there, all of their dead. Their spirits looked out of their white faces for one last instant, all those souls peering out as if in second birth. Harrowed from the dark waters, the dark fields of the sea.

Bar Cheleph whispered, barely more than a breath, "They aren't there. Amma, abba. They aren't there. Oh God, they aren't there."

The eyes closed—one pair, then another—and the dead slipped back into the water. All of them falling back into the crash of the waves. The last to go were the ones clinging to the gunwale, but their grip slackened and then they slid away, too. Shimon saw one hand remain for a moment, ghoulish and pale. Then it was gone.

All of them, gone.

The wind stilled, the rocking of the boat slowed. A quiet creaking where the broken spar still swung from the mast. Then even that went still. The Sea of Galilee went quiet as a pool in the rocks. Shimon glanced over the side, his hands shaking. The water was clear as the first water ever made. He could see far beneath the boat. Not to the bottom, but for just a moment, he thought he could glimpse the pale shapes of the sinking dead. Then nothing.

Silence over the water.

"*Shalom*," Yeshua whispered again. "My peace I give to you. Not as the world gives do I give. My peace I give to you."

Peace.

Gazing out over that still water, Shimon realized for the first time that a hunger for peace could raven the body and gnaw the heart almost as sharply as a hunger for fish could chew at the belly. That hunger could waste you away, day after day after day, until you were thin and empty as a corpse, though you still walked and moaned, grasping for something you needed, though you didn't know what it was.

Peace was more than stillness. More than sleep. More than numbness, more than the absence of conflict.

Peace was consolation and wholeness. Peace was two men breaking bread together, forgiving an old quarrel. Peace was a mother holding her infant up to its father for the first time, or a mother opening her eyes to greet her child after long illness. Peace was two lovers in each other's arms after a long, good night. Peace was an open door and a wall torn down. Peace was a *cephas*, a rock lashed by the waves yet unmoved. A rock people could stand on.

Kfar Nahum had starved for peace. *He* had starved for peace. He looked at his brother's face and saw the same shock of recognition there. His mother sank down to the bench and put her face in her hands. Yohanna and Yakob—their eyes were wet. Kana was gazing at the water as though he were looking at the face of God. The girl Miriam stared at Yeshua where he stood, her face bathed in awe. Bar Cheleph was looking at the others' faces, even as Shimon was, and their gazes met.

How strange, that they were all in this one boat. The son of the town's most renowned fisherman, his crippled brother, and the man who'd beaten him. Two women, one of them an outcast. A priest's sons and a trained killer and a stranger who could call up out of the water the living and the dead. All here, on this little bit of wood on the surface of the sea. *Shalom.*

* * *

Yeshua stood still while the boat rocked on water older and deeper than the dreams and the yearnings and the breathing of human beings.

His voice was soft above the waves, and sad as rain before dawn.

"So little faith," he said. "We have so little faith."

He turned to them then. His face burned briefly, and glancing at his eyes was like looking into the sun. Yet Yeshua's hands shook, and after a moment he sat slowly against the gunwale, tucked his knees against his chest, and closed his eyes. The light went out. His chest rose and fell.

The men in the boat and Rahel and Miriam of Magdala watched him sleep, their faces awed and troubled. Silent, but their silence no longer that of the fishers on the lifeless sea. And beneath their boat, the dead drifted at last in that same silence. All of them still beneath the irrevocable weight of a glory that could not be understood or named, only witnessed. So many bodies carried beneath the waves on currents no men knew, drifting to final sites of sea-burial marked and noted by none living, and whether God might remember them where they lay or whether their souls had gone to great rooms in God's house, none could tell. Unless perhaps that one man resting now against the gunwale, that man of sorrows whose eyes burned with a fire that consumed his memory to ash and whose coming had tumbled the houses of their town and all their lives into an architecture new and unpredicted. Yet perhaps not even he could tell, not even he.

AFTERWORD: THEY FACED THE DEAD

YOU'VE MET THEM before, or you think you have. You have seen their faces in stained glass, or in prints of da Vinci's *Last Supper*. You've heard their names recited in children's nursery rhymes or in your fathers' prayers—Jesus of Nazareth and his companions, who in the first century AD changed forever the way our world confronts the recurring threat of our restless and ravenous dead.

Yet if you who read this are to remember those who stood against the walking corpses—if you are to do more than remember, if you are to know what they knew, grieve as they grieved, burn with fury at what angered them, or smile at what warmed their hearts—then you must know them by their own names, not our English ones. And you must meet them in their own boat, the wood of the oars cold even through your gloves. Or on the shore with the fierce wind off the sea in your face. They are:

In Hebrew or Aramaic	In English
Shimon/Cephas	Simon/Peter
Koach	Andrew
Yohanna	John
Yakob	James
Shimon bar Nahemyah/Kana	Simon/The Zealot
Yakob bar Cheleph	James, son of Alphaeus
Miriam of Magdala	Mary Magdalene
Yeshua	Jesus

There they are, the first of them. And this is the first of their stories.

***

Koach

Entire libraries have been written about Simon Peter, but relatively little in recent centuries about his fierce brother. Yet the apostle Andrew has often been a figure of fascination. Today he is held to be the patron saint of nations as diverse as Scotland, where he brings victory in battle against overwhelming numbers; Malta, where he is associated with a rich harvest of fish; and Russia, where he is recognized for farsight and prophecy. The third century devoted an apocryphal text entirely to him: *The Acts of Andrew*. Other texts describe him, late in life, traveling among the nomadic tribes north of the Black Sea, teaching them the sharing of bread, and leading them to stand against the dead that in the later part of the first century lurched out of the Caucasus in great numbers. Overshadowed in history's eyes by his brother Simon Peter, Andrew yet possessed courage and compassion every inch as deep as his older brother's heady mix of loyalty and guilt. And he, no less than his brother, changed the world.

No Hebrew or Aramaic name is remembered for the apostle we know as Andrew; "Andrew" is from the Greek, and it means strong or manly. It means vigor. In reconstructing the events of AD 26, I have chosen to use the Hebrew word for strength and vigor—*koach* (the first syllable rhymes with the archer's *bow*, the second with the Scottish *loch*)—as Andrew's original name, speculating that the Greek recorders may later have translated it.

Koach was of course a physically weak man, and the vigor that others saw in him was a strength of the heart. The Hebrews regarded physical illness and weakness as a sign of evil, a blighting of the People; the Greeks and the Romans saw it as the outward sign of an inner malformity of the soul. Yet even in these cultures, the man Koach was able to achieve such stature through the strength of his heart—for he did not believe that the condition of his body was an impediment to his mission—that even the Greeks who loved beauty and feared its opposite consented to call him Andreas, the Manly. In this story we encounter him as still hardly more than a youth, though even then, he was a formidable youth.

The only irremovable impediments are those we shore up within our own hearts.

I WILL HOLD MY DEATH CLOSE

———————

BASED LOOSELY ON
THE EVENTS OF JUDGES 11

CIRCA 1120 BC

———————

*for the millions of young women
whose names no one remembers*

1

I HAVE FOUND WATER, the remains of the creek that cut this ravine out of the earth, but there are dead already here. I have never seen so many. Shaking, I stumble back. The sacrificial tunic I wear is torn and darkened with dust, my feet are sore, and my throat is desert. Yet I dare not go near that water.

They stand with the creek halfway to their knees, the reek of them sickly sweet over the scent of cool water, and I want to retch. Rags hang from their shoulders. Some of them are naked, with chunks of flesh torn out of their bodies, as though my father's god tried to undo his work, ripping them apart, only to be called away, leaving his destruction unfinished.

They are lurching up out of the water; I can hear the splash of their feet. They sway like trees in wind. Their mouths gape in low moans, and the sound of them makes me weak. All their eyes are watching me. I have had men and women stare at me before, but this is different. Once a wolf watched me from a stand of terebinths and I could see the hunger in its eyes, and I ran for mother's tent, but this is different. The eyes of these dead are empty, completely empty, and they will seize me in their cold hands and drag me to their mouths and into their eyes, and I will fall into that emptiness forever.

Turning, I run, the earth hard and dry under my feet. My sides burn and I can hear myself weeping in ragged sobs.

***

They are behind me. Further back now, but I can't run like this for long, and they don't stop. I am running back uphill the way I came, and it is hard, and now there are dead ahead of me, too, three of them; they must have followed me down the defile during the night. I stumble to a stop, panting for air. The cliffs are sharp against the sky, and I want to call for my father, but I don't. I don't have the breath. Either he is there watching me and he will save me, or he won't. His stone knife waits for me, but maybe he will let these dead have me; then he won't have to cut me, and he can sleep without dreaming each night of my blood welling out over his hand. I glance behind me, so many corpses shuffling up the defile. I glance before me, the three of them getting nearer. Their hands reaching through empty air, reaching for me. I am sobbing out words of prayer to Yah and to my grandmother's gods who have no names. I don't want to be afraid; I want to face them like mother did. Even when the dead came for her, she stood and faced them, with a stick from the fire in her hand. That is the kind of woman I want to be.

***

The rock is cold in my hand, this tiny shard of the earth that one god or another shaped with his hand long before my mother or her mother or her grandmother were born. I used to take up rocks from the river by father's camp and turn them over and over in my hands for hours. Those beautiful stones, each of them a story of the place they rolled downstream from. But now I hold this one in my hand, and I can think only of its sharp edge and of how small it is, the only thing I can hold between my body and death.

The first time I swing the rock against one of the advancing corpses, my own scream startles me. My shriek does not startle the corpse; it walks right into the blow, the rock slicing through its gray skin just above its left eye. The corpse twitches and then falls to the side; my stone is stuck in its brow, and the weight of it pulls the rock from my hand. I bend and try to pull the rock out, but almost immediately I have to scramble back, because the other corpses are lurching in, their jaws opening and closing like the mouths of fish. Someone is screaming, again and again, and it might be me. Something trips me and I fall back, my hands in front of my face. One of them bends over me, its hand grasps my wrist. So cold. No life in it at all, no warmth, nothing that hears a young woman screaming and feels any pity or kinship. I am gazing through the fingers of my other hand at eyes that do not care if I live or die.

And that saves me. Because it makes me angry that they want to kill me without even caring to know my name or whether I am afraid or whether I am ready to die. It makes me furious, my blood suddenly loud in my ears. I bring one foot up and kick the ghoul hard in the face. The corpse doesn't wince or cry out or stagger back, but its head jerks to the left, and its lower jaw snaps loose. Even as I bring my knee up and slam my foot against its face again, there is a hissing in the air nearby, then another, as though small gods are flying past faster than the wind, their breath expelled in screams that are nearly silent as they rush by me. My heart has no time to wonder at it; I keep kicking wildly at the corpse's face, flesh crumpling and splitting away from my heel, its bony hand still tight around my wrist. I am screaming and screaming and finally its face breaks open and it falls back and its cold fingers fall away from my skin.

***

More of the dead lie still, some with long shafts protruding from their heads, but I haven't a moment to think about that, because several others are coming at me. I stumble to my feet, screaming my mother's name, her name, again, and again. It is all I have. I would scream a god's name, begging for his help, but what god do I really know? Yah, god of wind and fire, of hard Law written in stone, god of the phallus and the altar and the knife my father has sworn to cut me with? That god wishes to eat me, as these corpses would. My grandmother's gods, then? She was Canaanite. I wish I knew how to call to hers. I would like to pray to a god who is a woman.

***

But maybe the gods are not women and are not men either. Maybe they are like the stone of these cliffs, bleak and harsh and unforgiving, and you can't climb up to reach their blessings because the cliff face is too sheer and your fingers bleed when you try.

Or maybe the gods are dead. Everything else is.

***

It doesn't matter. What could I give to any god to make her listen to me, to make her care whether my heart keeps beating?

I can make no vow as my father did, offer nothing; I own no daughters of my own, no cattle, no tents. I am only a woman and have only my own blood and my own body. I can make no vow. I face these corpses alone, without any god, and I am screaming. My hands scrabble but find only dirt; I throw handfuls of it at the faces of the dead to blind their eyes, to make them gasp in pain and collapse to their knees; but they do not. They don't even blink. Their eyes are full of dust, and still they stumble after me. The nearest of them is terrible, naked above the waist and most of its chest hollowed out, broken ribs and emptiness inside them. One breast hangs slack above the gash. Its arm swings toward me, and I duck and dodge to the side, and then they are pressing me back against the wall of the ravine. My skin is alive with the terror of their touch, their teeth. I hold my hands before my face; in a moment I will be dead, and everything in me is cold with panic. My anger has failed me.

Their breath on my arms, dry and cold like winter night.

There is another hissing in the air near me, then another.

The corpse before me falls, toppling like a tree before the ax. Panting, I gaze about with wide eyes.

All about me, the dead are still, their heads impaled and pinned to the dry earth with javelins. A small forest of javelins has grown here while I fought.

A man is walking down the ravine toward me. The world tilts dizzily and everything blurs, but I know from his walk that he is my father.

2

MY EYES OPEN. It is dusk. Father is sitting beside me and there is firelight on his face and I can hear the cracking laughter of the small fire he has made. He is still clad in the dark, boiled leather of a raider; the last few years, I have rarely seen him in anything else. He does not take off his armor even when he stands at the altar. He wore that same armor when he stood on the high rock and made his vow to the sky, a promise, a bartering of sacrifice for victory, before lifting his javelins and springing down to do battle with the dead that were devouring us in our tents. From his belt hang two heavy gloves, so that he can handle bodies without the risk of uncleanness. A pleated skirt protects his thighs and greaves of bronze protect his legs; he took those from a caravan in return for his protection from the roaming dead. A collar of leather is fitted about his throat, as though he is a slave, but I know he wears it because he is afraid of leaving any soft place on his body open to the ghouls' teeth. My mother showed it to me once while she oiled his armor, and I saw that the inside had been worn soft as a baby's skin.

My father's armor looks no different than it did a day ago, when he sent me into the hills to meet with the god in the empty places, when he told me he would need time to pray and that I would, too. But now he has come for me.

He looks the same. Except for his hair. It is grayer than I remember it.

He has laid the stone knife across his thighs, and my breath catches when I see it. At his hip sits a bundle of javelins, bound with cord like a sheaf of barley. Their points are darkened; he hasn't wasted water to wash the dead from the wood. He has dragged the corpses into a heap, a stone's throw from our fire, to be buried beneath rocks later; to leave them uncovered would be to invite more unclean dead. I can smell them, and I shiver.

I try to sit up but find my wrists bound behind me. After struggling a moment, I bite my lip and lie still. My hands are numb. And I didn't know I could be this thirsty. The heat of it. It's as if there is a fire in my throat. There is a waterskin slung across my father's chest, and I stare at it; it is all I can do to stay still and silent. He has drunk deeply of it; the leather pouch is nearly flat against his tunic. But there is water in it, I know there is. Cool, dark water, undefiled by the feet of the dead. I want to cry.

My father feeds a little wood to the fire. Watching me without speaking. I long for him to say something, anything. Perhaps he will tell me why he has bound me or why he made the vow he did, that terrible promise, bartering his own daughter for a god's favor. Perhaps he will tell me why his face is so cold when he looks at me. Why it has always been so, even when I was small and he was tall as a mountain.

But I know why.

"Please say something, father," I whisper.

He doesn't speak.

"Please."

Still, that silence.

"Say *something*! . . . Tell me a story."

When I was small, my father could pretend I was his son, not the daughter he never wanted. He used to sit me on his knee and talk with me for hours, until the stars were out and sparks from the fire were racing up the wind like deer to meet them, and I was covering my yawns with my hand so that he would not see them and send me away to sleep. Father would talk with me about his battles or tell me a story about how he talked one of the elders in Gilead into giving him a better price on a brace of corpse-heads. Or if he'd had a little wine and his face was flushed, he'd talk about his youth in that long-ago winter when the dead first wandered into the land in vast, moaning herds. He'd tell me how Gideon led the three hundred against the unclean corpses beneath the Hill of Moreh; how Devora the prophetess brought flame and sword into all the grain fields of the land, burning out the dead, until the sky was dark with ash; how Lappidoth her husband took the tents of Shiloh and moved them into the high hills like a flock of birds alighting and settling again, veering away as at the approach of wolves. Those were the stories my father told, men's stories of fighting and battle. I mostly remember the warmth of his arm around me, and the scratch of his beard against my forehead and cheek, and the way his voice and the heat from the fire and the distant noises of the night, jackals' cries and a solitary owl, became all one murmur and glow of feeling, all one thing.

He stopped holding me like that long before my tenth year. I began to bargain for every touch, every kind word, bringing him meals or pouring wine for him or throwing a temper in the morning before he rode out with his men. I was beaten for it a few times, and I began to hate him, but I loved him, too. I didn't understand at first why he pulled away, and I certainly didn't forgive him for it.

Now I never will.

***

"Your mother had hair dark like a river, hair like laughter at night," my father says at last. He is stirring the fire with a stick, and his eyes are full of the flames. I listen very quietly, as though I might hear between his words some way to save myself. Yet it is hard not to scream in frustration. Why is he telling me the color of her hair? I know the color of her hair.

"I was so afraid of her." The corner of his lip twitches. "I have never feared anything else as much. Until this day."

He is silent again.

Alarm at his silence grips my heart, and my irritation flickers and is gone. My mother was someone we both shared. I don't think he can kill me if he is thinking of her. That is what I hope. But I know him for a cold man who can do terrible things. He hunts the dead. He brings their scalps, swinging from his saddle, to Gilead, and brings home to us grain and beer and clothes. He and his raiders keep the dead from the fields, and in return the town keeps us supplied, and well. Mother used to wear a gown as green as well-watered leaves; I used to feel the hem between my fingertips, behind her, when she wasn't looking.

"Tell me about mother," I plead.

But he only watches the fire.

***

I don't know how much time has crawled by. He is still staring at that fire, and everywhere around us it is dark. I am afraid of him and of the unsheathed knife, which seems to burn in the firelight. And I am afraid of the dead that might see the light and come lurching toward us. Something will be done to me here, and I have no say in it. I want only to close my eyes and pretend that none of this is happening. Instead, I keep thinking of mother. How she screamed and hit at the dead with her stick. Though she raged at them, they still ate her. Nothing she did mattered. They tore her to the ground and *ate* her.

Nothing I can do matters.

There is no choice I can make, no defiance I can offer.

I am food. Either for the dead or for my father's god.

Thinking these things, I feel something dying inside me. Like leather drying and cracking in the sun.

I didn't give up at the creek. I fought. I survived until my father's javelins flitted through the air.

But whose javelins will save me now? If I struggle, twisting in these ropes, what will happen? I'll feel even more trapped; the panic that is crouching behind me in the dark will seize me, and I will scream and will never really be myself again, only a frightened animal to be laid across the altar. That is the one thing I cannot let happen. I can't die that way. I can't.

***

752

I have to urinate; the pressure of it inside me is hurtful. I press my thighs tightly together, struggling to think.

"Tell me about your god," I whisper. I want to understand this god who would devour me.

"He is a hungry god," my father mutters, and he tosses the charred stick onto the flaming coals. "And this is a hungry land, dead and dry. I tire of it. Our fathers should never have come here."

A tiny hope in my heart, like a moth spreading its wings in the dark. "Maybe we could leave." I wet my lips with my tongue; they are cracking. "We could go far away."

Mother suggested this to him once as they lay together on their bedding. I heard them whispering.

"I made a vow." His voice is hard.

The wings snap shut, and the moth stiffens and becomes a cold rock of anger in my heart. "What if *I* make a vow?" It is all too much, it is all too unjust. "What if I vow to your god that I will die an old woman in a tent? Or give myself to an altar in twenty years or thirty, after bearing children first to serve him?"

My father glances at me, and I see bitter amusement in his eyes.

"You are just a girl," he mutters.

My own eyes fill with tears. This is what my mother tried to tell me in all her songs: that from the day we start to breathe, what matters to us can be taken from us, is taken from us, will be taken from us, until we are bound shivering beneath a knife or until we lie choking in the dust, wrinkled and old, and the men who have been inside us or who have come out of us have left us alone, at last, in the dark. This is why she was always afraid. Yet she never shrank back.

When I lived with mother in our tent, I was a child. Now I am a woman. Not because I bled or because my breasts are swelling, but because I can look at my own death.

***

"Did you love my mother?" I whisper.

Father sits very still.

"Did you love her?" My cry is the loudest thing in the world. Louder than the fire or the dark or the distant moaning.

"As the wheat loves the dawn," he murmurs. He keeps his eyes averted.

"I am all that is left of her. Will you really watch this dry ground drink my life, or give me to flames to eat?"

His jaw tightens. "I keep my vows." He glances up, and his eyes glint in the fire. "You thirst," he says suddenly.

I try to work a little saliva in my mouth, and I nod.

He stands and unslings the waterskin from his shoulder. I can hear the voice of water splashing within it as he walks toward me. I almost cry out. Crouching, he takes my chin roughly in his hand; with his other, he opens the skin and presses the aperture to my lips. The touch of the leather is soft and warm. I suck in air desperately for a moment before I get water, cool, wonderful water, filling my mouth. I choke and splutter.

"Slowly." His voice and his hold on my chin are both rough, as though he is angry with me. But whatever fear or fury I might feel is washed away before the water like sand. Swallow after swallow. I never knew water could taste like that.

He takes it away too soon, closes the skin, and slings it back over his shoulder, rising to his feet. I make some quiet sound of pleading, some whimper or animal noise, and I am too thirsty and too tired to be ashamed of it.

As my father turns from me, he stiffens. I am staring past his ankles, and I can see that he left the knife by the coals. I think of how easily it could cut the cord about my wrists. But then my father is sweeping up a javelin from the earth, and I am watching him and not the knife, because he is striding from the fire and something hisses at him in the dark. There are eyes there, glinting with the flames. There are dead.

Several have come. They lurch into the firelight, and my father stands ready for them. He moves so fast. I have never seen anyone move so fast. It is terrifying. The edge of the javelin cuts the air like a bird's wing. He drives it through one's face; he hooks his foot behind another corpse's knee and pulls sharply, toppling it to the earth as he would any living person. It moans at him from the ground, but already he has ripped the metal point free of the first corpse and he is spinning the javelin in the air and slamming the cold, killing metal down into the head of the second. Its moan falls silent without any gasp of pain—just a silence as sudden as the darkening of a torch plunged into water.

There is a third, and it has lurched past my father and the other two. It comes right at me, its arms lifted, with a low growl. I kick wildly, pushing myself back away from the fire that is between us, even as it stumbles right into the coals. Its leg goes up in flame. For a few beats of my heart, it stands in the fire, and the flames, hungrier even than the dead, lick their way up its body, devouring, as though the dry corpse is tinder and straw. Then a sudden, gore-darkened point appears between its eyes, and its jaw goes slack. My father behind it wrenches the corpse from the fire and hurls it aside to the earth, on the point of his spear. He pulls the shaft free and stands over the burning body, his chest heaving. I glimpse my father's face in the firelight and it is terrible. As though he has seen so much death that he has almost forgotten that there is anything else to look at, anything else that he might see.

I am shaking, though I try to stop. My throat has closed tight. I cannot even scream.

My father's voice is low and hoarse. "Cairns should not wait for morning."

Piling stones above the dead, as our Hebrew ancestors have always done, crushes them to the earth, holds them in place where they can become fixed, recognizable, monumented parts of our land that nourishes us. The cairns keep the corpses from wandering, from tearing apart the tents and booths of the People. From devouring. The Ten are carved into stone tablets in far Shiloh, and stone keeps the dead in place. Stone is what our People trust the most.

My father stumbles away into the dark. He goes to gather stones for the cairns.

I lie by the fire, sobbing. I can't seem to stop. Something is broken inside me. Something is broken. My thighs go warm with my urine.

***

Mother used to sing to me while the stars came out, as they are out now. She would sit at the door of her tent and hold me, and her voice was like river and like sunset. I no longer recall what she looked like, but I remember her voice. She sings to me about sorrow and dying and falling in love and being loved and losing the one you love. When I was a little girl, I didn't understand her songs, only the beauty of her voice and the warm nearness of her. But now her words come to me, and the earth is cold under my back, the sun's heat already gone from it, and I think I understand her songs now.

I will never kiss a young man, or an old one. I will never have a man inside me. The god and I will never grow a baby together. That is what her songs are telling me. The things your heart wants are like full, ripe grapes for your thirsty throat, but they are just out of reach and maybe they will always be.

***

I lie soiled, the tunic clinging, damp, to my legs. My arms and shoulders ache with pain. Yet I am hardly aware of that. Quiet has come to my heart after the tears, and I am thinking. When my father returns from raising the cairns, my eyes are dry. Part of me wants to struggle again, but I don't. I lift my head a little, one side of my face covered in dust. I wish I could wash it from my skin.

He crouches by the coals and sets his fingertips on the stone blade. He doesn't look at me; if he is aware that I have wet myself, he shows no sign of it. I stare at the flames, thinking for the first time not of the knife but of what will come after: my father will lay me across dry tinder, and once I have bled, my body will be burned, and wherever his god lives in the sky, he will breathe in the smoke and the scent of me, and be fed. Strangely, I feel no dread now, only a deep quiet. The dance of the few small flames among the coals fascinates me; I can't look away from it. Though my body hurts as though I've been beaten, there is a fullness in my breast, and I realize that this moment by this fire, and even my father's silence, is a gift. My mother died with so many words still on her lips—things she might have said to me, or to her god, or to my father. Things she never had the chance to say. But I have that chance. I can say the things that need to be said. Because he is not speaking, and he is not lifting the knife. And because I am a woman, not a child. Because he is giving me this last gift, this moment to speak. He might command me to silence, but I might not obey him. He might beat me until I do. But he is not doing any of these things. Maybe he is thinking of mother, too. Maybe he is remembering that she never said farewell to him. I don't know. But I am grateful for this moment.

I work a little spit in my mouth and speak.

"You wanted a son." Despite my efforts, my voice is little more than a hoarse whisper.

His eyes moisten, and seeing that, my voice breaks.

"I hope you find another wife," I tell him, "and that she gives you one."

I don't know why I must die. He brought me water and watched over me, and kept the dead away. Yet he can't be dissuaded, because he always does— has always done—what he feels he has to do.

"I love you, father."

It is the first time in years that I have said those words.

I can't be sure, but I think they are true.

I don't know why they should be true. It has been long since he has held me or even spoken my name; he does not say it or acknowledge it now. But his eyes are no longer cold. And he is my father. And whether the words I say are true or not, or only partly true, I need to say them. Otherwise I will have wasted the gift of this moment. They are the right words to say. It is a way of saying farewell.

I glance once at his face, then at the flames. Shivering, I close my eyes.

"I am ready to die," I whisper.

***

A wind rustles the grasses on the cliffs above us. After a while, I hear him get up. Then a furtive step. And another.

I keep my eyes closed for a long time.

My body goes hot with anger. How can he do this to me? I have said my farewell. Maybe his only farewell will be the slide of that knife across my throat. But he is not giving me even that. He is prolonging this, and it is cruel. I regret telling him that I love him. He is cold and cruel, and his god is cold and cruel, as well.

"Father?"

There is no answer.

Opening my eyes, I find I am alone and surrounded by the cairns of the silent dead.

He is gone.

I lie there, bound, just breathing. Fighting down panic. Did he step away a moment for prayer, or is he really leaving me here? Bound, like this? To starve or be eaten? Maybe he has struck some new and perverse bargain with his god—he will sacrifice me, but not by his own hand. Instead he will leave me for the wandering dead—bound, helpless, powerless to choose the moment of my own death.

I draw in another shuddering breath. That is what I wanted, I realize. To choose the moment that I would die. That's why I fought the corpses, why I gave father my farewell, why I told him when I was ready. And now he has taken even this from me.

I scream, making the cliffs echo with my cry.

But only once.

3

THE ROCKS HERE ARE BROKEN and sharp-edged, as though Yah has been pounding on the hill with his foot, year after year, trying to shatter it. My father has not come back, and the fire he made is only coals. The stars are also coals, without warmth. I am shivering. I can't tell whether the sounds on the slope above are wind or the moaning dead.

My death is my own to make.

This thought is clear and cold in my mind, like ice on water.

Sawing the ropes against a jagged stone makes my hands sting with pain, and my blood is warm and sticky where it flows down over my fingers. It takes a long time, but finally the ropes snap free, and I bring my hands in front of me, clutching one wrist numbly with the other. My hands hurt with returning life, so that I have to bite my sleeve to keep from screaming. My breath comes ragged.

If the dead are what I hear moaning on the hill, they are loud and close. My father has forgotten me. He is gone. I would be numb with the pain of it, but my heart is thunder inside me, and my fear is ripping at me the way summer hail tears holes through green leaves.

I don't want to die. So I must be stronger than my fear, faster than my terror.

Though my hands still hurt, I walk quickly to one of the cairns, where my father has leaned a javelin against the stones. I can see that the bronze point is broken, as though chipped against a bone, but it still looks sharp. My father should not have left it. There are others, several, with the points thrust into the dirt between the cairns so that they stand like thin, leafless trees. Briefly I wonder if my father *meant* to leave them for me, like this, or if he left these here for some other purpose known only to his own heart or to his god. The wooden shafts are slender, and I can carry two in my right hand and leave my left hand free. I don't know how to throw them as my father did, so that they strike where I wish, but I can stab with them. That is what I will do.

***

They are coming. There are four of them, moving downhill toward the water behind me. I can't see them, but I can hear the shuffling of their feet. I can smell them. I wait in a crouch with the javelins, and I can hear my own blood. The night is sharp. I hold my death close; it is my own, and these unsteady corpses will not take it from me.

They are nearer.

I try to count, to calm my heartbeat, but it doesn't work; the rising numbers make me anxious. So I start to recite the names of the god silently, without moving my lips. Though I don't know which names I can trust, or whether all these names belong to a god who wants me dead, they are all beautiful.

Yah.

Elohim.

El Shaddai.

El Olam.

Yah Yireh.

Yah Nissi.

Adonai.

These are the names of the god, but I don't know if that god is harsh like my father or kind like my mother. Though my mother called out the same names my father did, she sang about a god who is a giver of life, a god of the womb. That kind of god would give me breath, hold me while I weep, then pull me to my feet and tell me to stand as my mother did. A stick in my hand.

The shambling footsteps are near, and I can see the dead silhouetted against the dark and the faint, faint glint of their eyes. I leap to my feet and plunge one of the javelins up and forward with a shout. My arm is strong and fast, and there is little resistance as the javelin spears through a corpse's face in the dark. Even as the other closes with me, the first falls to the side. Wood cracks like a bone breaking, and I am holding in my right hand only a splintered haft, while the rest remains in the corpse at my feet; I cast aside the haft with a cry. Now I hold only one. These are my father's tools; of course they would be of two minds about protecting me.

Cold fingers grasp my shoulder. I lunge aside, and the corpse comes with me; my heartbeat is wild. I thrust the length of the javelin crosswise between me and the corpse's throat. The thing's teeth snap in the air, so near my face. That winter, winter breath. Tears on my face. I cry when I am scared. But then, I have seen even my father do that, once. Frantically, under my breath I gasp the names, and the recitation is all that holds me together, a wall of words raised like hard stones against the wind of panic. El Olam. Yah Nissi. Yah Yireh. Yah Yireh, Yah Yireh. I can't find any other names, any other words, everything is gone from my mind; there is only the clack of those teeth, a finger's width from my skin, and the burn in my arm as I fight against its weight, fight to hold it at bay with that slender length of terebinth wood. I recite that last name over and over: Yah Yireh, Yah Yireh.

Then we are on the earth. I must have stumbled. Shoving my knee into the corpse's belly, I throw my weight to the side and roll up onto it, and then my fingers are in its eyes. I have let go of the javelin; I am just digging my hands into its face, as though I am kneading dough with my mother. And I keep doing it, my heart pounding, pounding. And then it is still.

So still.

I have survived again.

I glide along the knife's edge of my fear, the exhilaration of being alive, *still* alive, lifting me the way the god's unseen hands lift a bird into the sky. The small sound of my tears hitting the dead flesh beneath me. The rasping of my breath in my throat. Taking up the javelin quickly, I get to my feet. Still panting, Yah, Yah, Yah. Yes, yes. Yes. I live. Yes. Yes.

I am panting, here in the empty night. I don't know if there are other dead nearby. The air is still. At the warmth trickling over my wrist, I glance down. I can't see, but suddenly I feel my nails biting into my palm, where I hold the one javelin I retain deathly tight. With a low moan, I open my hand. The pain is sharp, but it is also good, because I am alive. Drawing in quick, shuddering breaths, I step around the corpses. I should cover them with stones, as my father would, but I fear staying here. I will leave them behind, the way we leave all our dead behind in the end. I will walk out alone into the dark, not knowing what my feet will find, or what will find me.

4

I REEK, AND I HATE IT. I found a tuft of wild grass in the dry dust, tore it up and scrubbed my legs until I bled a little, but though I am drier, I smell like urine and the dead. The smell is in the white tunic; it is even in my hair. I would cut away my hair if I could. I want to smell like me again.

Though my hands shake with fear, I am walking uphill now. Not toward the creek behind. The dead are by that stream; I know that now. If I want to escape them, if I want to live, I must climb up these hills, up toward the roof of the world. There is water there, too; rain falls and collects in small pools in the rock on the high slopes, and if I walk north, toward White Cedars, if I go far north, there will be trees, and maybe I can find honey to eat. That will be dangerous, too, because I will have to break into it with a stick or with my hands, and the bees will hurt me when I run, with honeycomb in my hands, to flee them. I will have to find some place to hide from the bees before I attempt it. Maybe I can find cool mud, or . . . maybe there will be food other than honey. Berries, if any grow that high, or bird's eggs, or maybe I could catch a small animal. That would be better than honey, and safer than bees.

But I don't know what to expect. I have never been in these hills.

I whisper old stories to myself as I walk, every story my father told about ancestors of ours who fought in the Ramat ha-Golan. I am searching for anything that could help me. Anything that was said about the places to the north, the places uphill.

Because I am going to live, to the last moment I can.

My mother died, and she might live only in me. Who else will remember her name?

Who will remember mine?

My father might have other children, but they will be with other wives, women I don't know. My name is mine alone to carry. I may die of cold once I am up higher, or worse, I may die of thirst and the terrible drying of my body—but I will *not* be eaten. I am walking uphill, toward the sky where my father's god lives. And if, when I get up there, where there is nothing but empty air between me and the stars, if I hear his god calling, I will call back, and I will demand that he answer me. That he tell me why he wants me to die.

If I die, I will choose the moment of it.

I do not want to die.

***

I have tried a few times now to climb out of this ravine, but in some places the rock is sheer, and in others it crumbles under my weight. I am frustrated, and it is so hard to keep the panic from my mind. Every time I hear a moan behind me, back toward the water, every time some small desert mouse skitters among the loose pebbles beneath some dried bush ahead of me, I startle like a rabbit and nearly bolt. I cannot do that. I cannot. My mother would not startle like that. I have to just breathe slowly and walk, keep walking, and not stop, not ever.

There must be a way out of this ravine.

There must.

***

Has my father left the ravine? Is he somewhere ahead of me or somewhere behind? That uncertainty is what makes me jump at each sound, more than the thought of the dead and their teeth. He took his knife with him; men don't leave their knives out for the weather. He might come back. He might still lay me bound across an altar of warm rock and cut me open. My eyes moisten, but I blink back the tears furiously. I must not think of my father. He left me bound in the night by the cairns, as though I were dead already, awaiting my turn for burial. If he had meant to go through with sacrificing me, surely he would have made his altar and then waited by me for the dawn, to fulfill his vow. I asked him to. I told him I was ready. And he walked away. He is not coming back.

***

Wind has come up, and the noises it makes in the rocks are frightening. Worse, it has torn clouds out of some secret place in the sky, and they have taken away the stars. It is so dark, I can't see the ground. It's not always easy to tell where the moaning comes from. It has to be behind me. I hope it is behind me.

Mother told me once about the winter when she was younger than I and she got lost in a wood. She told me how her heart threw itself against her breast like a wild thing, but she also told me how she sang softly, under her breath, and how the song warmed her and calmed her until she found the edge of the wood and saw the smoke of her father's camp and ran, laughing, from the trees toward its fires. But I don't dare sing. Something that doesn't live might hear me.

***

I have found it. I knew there had to be a way out. And there is. I might have missed it in the dark, but the ravine has narrowed, and I have started running my fingers along the near wall and running the haft of the javelin quietly along the far wall as I walk.

And here it is: a narrow dip in the rock, and a few steps up it becomes almost a tunnel, with just a tiny gap of air above my head. Some of the rock is worn smooth; water must come down here, singing and splashing, in wetter months. Now it is dry, but the footholds are still difficult. I have to use one hand to help bear my weight and steady me as I move carefully upward. At one point I have to press the javelin into the crook of my shoulder and hold it there, awkwardly, with my head tilted to the side, so that I can use both my hands. The ascent becomes steeper, and I press my belly to the rock. After days of dry earth, this smooth rock is unsettling; it is as though I am squirming my way up the gullet of some giant animal. Vertigo makes me clench my eyes shut. I cling to the rock, breathing hard, until I can convince myself that I am not falling upward.

Then I climb. My breathing is too loud between these walls of stone.

But then the rock around me opens up, and there is sky again. Even as I step out of the ravine, the clouds part above me—at last!—and there is starlight. I stand and breathe, feeling the cold air fill my body. Though I am exhausted, I have never felt so awake. I am like a deer, alert to every sound, every scent in the air. I listen. I watch. I am silhouetted against the stars, but nothing moans or lurches toward me.

There are dry grasses beneath my feet, and as the wind picks up, it hisses in the blades. I gaze down at them, then at my feet, which I see are cracked and bleeding. I came barefoot to this high land, a sacrifice for a god whose hunger is wide as the sky. But it is the rocks and now the grasses that have been drinking from me. I feel no faintness at the sight of my blood or the bruises on my feet and ankles. I have seen so much this day, I do not think I will ever feel faint at anything again.

Glancing up, I find the star that mother called North. And that tells me that I am on the wrong side of the ravine, the southern side. Only a few trees are up here, lonely things, but I can see where there are more, across the ravine and in the distance, where there must be water. I might be able to leap across here; the walls of the ravine are close together, but it is a frightening gap at my feet, and in the dark beneath is cold death and thirst and the lurching corpses. I must find some place where it is narrower.

I begin to run, ignoring the soreness of my feet. I run along the edge of the defile, using the starlight. This ravine cannot be forever; there will be a better way across.

***

In this desolation, far from my father's tents and my father's stories, I think that maybe the god *is* a woman, beset as I am by the dark and by the day's heat. I do not know my father's god, whose meal I would have been. I think my mother's god is running beside me in the dark, like a deer, and we flee the hunger of the earth together, and it is men, living or dead, who would devour us.

5

BY THE STARLIGHT I see that the two corpses ahead of me are desiccated. Dried up, like bodies left in the desert. Even the stench is gone. The eyes, too, eaten by birds. I approach and crouch near them, with my javelin held across my thighs. I don't feel sick looking at these, only sad. These were people. They were a man and a woman; I only know this because the man's phallus lies crooked and dry across his hip, a flaccid, withered length like the husk shed by a serpent. I saw the men dancing, drunk, at the fire once, outside the tents. They were stiff and frightening. But this man is dead, and his spear is only a limp stretch of skin, after all.

The other has the wide hips of a mother. Were these two man and wife, or man and slave, or brother and sister fleeing, as I am fleeing? Like me, lost in the dark? If they were walking toward the heights, as I am, they never made it there. I still can.

I suck in a breath and rise to my feet, but suddenly one of the corpses stirs, the dry sound of its hand scraping across the grit. I nearly drop the javelin, stumbling back so quickly.

The corpse crawls on its hands toward me, dragging its legs behind it. With a cry I jab my javelin at its head, but it grasps the wood just above the bronze point and wrenches the weapon forward, and me with it; I scream as I lose my footing and fall to my knees. The thing grips my arm and pulls me down and it is on top of me, so strong. Its long teeth snap by my ear. Its breath is so *cold*, its burn on my skin like the first touch of frostbite. I am screaming and screaming, and kicking. Panic has eaten my mind. I slam my arm against its throat, trying to push it up and off me. Its hand grips my face. I scrabble at the rocks and dust, trying to find my javelin, but I can't, it isn't there. I can't see, I can't breathe, my heart is loud and this is it, I am going to die.

But I have squirmed aside just a little, and I have my hip beneath it and I lunge, and we are rolling. Its cold fingers catch at my tunic, but my struggle and my climb among the rocks has torn the cloth, and I tear loose, leaving my garment behind in the corpse's grip. I scramble away on my hands and knees, with the hiss of its breath behind me. My hand strikes the javelin, and I grasp it, then leap to my feet and run and *run*. The air is cold on my body, but I don't feel it. My blood is rushing everywhere inside me, and there is only the slap of the dry earth against my feet and the snarling thing pursuing me. Then the ravine opens beneath me, and I hurl my javelin across the gap, hear it clatter against the rocks even as I spring, leaping across the empty dark with a shriek.

The ground strikes my belly, and my legs kick at empty air. I clutch at loose soil. Falling. But my foot finds a root, a root! I put my weight on it and thrust myself upward, even as I hear the wood creak as though about to break, and I throw my breast up onto the cliff. My left hand finds a tussock of weeds, and I pull myself up, groaning, my lungs burning. I get my legs up and roll onto my back, and I am sobbing, shaking. The night above me has been shot through with stars, as though warriors have hurled spears through the tent of night and left those shining holes behind. I clutch the earth with my fingers, afraid I might fall off into that dark cloth of sky. I can hear the corpse shambling along the far edge of the ravine, and I can hear its shuddering moan. I shut my eyes tightly and just breathe, just breathe.

I have lost my breath, my tunic, everything but the javelin nearby. I am naked in the dark. But I am alive.

Fierce joy in my heart. I am alive.

Men, living and dead, are often stronger than we. But not always smarter, or faster.

I am alive. And undevoured.

The corpse on the far brink moans again, and that long, lonely wail fills the night. My eyes open again on the stars.

I will not fear that moan.

Let men, living or dead, moan as they will. They cannot ever truly have us, truly devour us. My death remains my own to choose.

Great gulps of air. I fill my body with air.

Maybe if I can just breathe in enough, I will lift from the earth like a bird. All those stars—I would like to fly through them into whatever bright world lies outside this tent in which we and the god are trapped. Maybe outside, there is no hunger.

My face is still wet from my tears when I stand and look about. The land before me is wide, and I walk out into it, moving quickly, leaving the cry of that corpse and all my dead behind.

6

I HAVE REACHED the roof of the world. No one told me it would be this beautiful. The trees here are stunted but dark with needles, and the wind blows my hair back, stings my eyes, and raises goosebumps on my arms and breasts. I wear no white for sacrifice; no man has clothed me for his purpose or his god's; I stand naked and my own. I smell water. And the stars, and the stars.

There are no dead here, and this javelin I carry is only dead wood that I have brought with me out of a memory. This wind has carried away my death. With a single breath, a sigh as I gazed out at these dark plateaus, my death leapt from me into the air. I throw my head back and shout my name, and give it to the wind, too. Let that wind take it, too, far away, where no one will remember it. They will think me dead at my father's bloody hands. Let them. My father took that life from me, but he also set me free into these hills. I still breathe. I still walk on this wind, between earth and sky. If my father's god or my mother's is up here among these stars, let that god fly with me. If not, I will fly alone. This is not one of my father's stories, not a story of my tribe. I do not know what this story will be, but I am the one telling it. That girl who had a name and a tribe, a mother and a father, and a tent in which to sleep, she is slain and dead.

Only I remain.

JUDGES 11:40

FOR GENERATIONS after the dead were cleansed from those hills, the young women of that tribe would walk up into the dry and thirsty places after the coming of their first blood, in memory of Yeptha's daughter. Though they could not remember her name, the young women used her story to understand their own predicament, the predicament of being young women.

They wandered the ravines for four days and four nights, neither bathing nor changing their clothes. Before returning to the tents, each woman would face the inevitable truth of her own death and learn to hold it close. Each would weep for Yeptha's daughter; she would weep for the changes in her own body and for the suffering she knew she would face as a woman in a land where either the dead or the living might devour her. She and all her sisters would weep until the land echoed with their cries, and their cries were such that neither the world, nor men, nor mighty Yah could find any silence in which to hide from their voices.

BY A SLENDER THREAD

AN EXCLUSIVE EXCERPT

———————

THE ZOMBIE BIBLE - BOOK 6
COMING IN 2017

———————

STANT LITORE

MATER ROMAE

THE DEAD WOULD be here in moments; Regina could hear them moaning as they lurched through the labyrinth of alleys behind, wailing with a hunger that could devour her city, or the world.

She strode through the door of the insula before her and into the narrow atrium, the interior garden open to the sky. Peered up at five stories of darkened rooms. Brutus Secundus followed her, clad in his guardsman's boiled leather, his face tight with fear. Brigitte stepped in, too, towering over him; she had to stoop to pass under the door.

"Mother." Brutus' voice was almost a whisper.

"I heard a child. Find her."

"Mother, we can't delay."

"I heard her crying from the street. We're not leaving anyone behind. Find her. Please, Brutus."

He swallowed. "Brigitte, fourth and fifth story. Mother and I will take the lower three. Let's go."

Brigitte bowed slightly. Though her thick brows gave her an eternally fierce look, Regina could see the whites of her eyes. She was scared, too.

They were all scared. They'd been scared for days. They were scared when they went to sleep and when they woke up. Regina drew her coat tighter about her. The coat had been Polycarp's, and he had *not* been scared.

She let Brutus lead the way from one door to the next. No answer came to his fist heavy against the wood, and neither of them dared call out. Regina could hear the hard footfalls of Brigitte climbing the interior stair. She found her breathing fast and shallow, tried to calm it. That moaning. If only the dead would be silent. If only they were silent, she thought she could bear it easier. All of it.

A child's cry. Second story. Something smothered the cry, like a hand covering a mouth. Evil memories shrieked in the dark in the back of Regina's mind, and she slammed an old door shut on them. Her heart went hard and cold. She'd expected to find a lost child in this old building, not a captive one.

She and Brutus exchanged a look. The slither of steel against leather; she stopped his hand before he could pull his *gladius* free. Shook her head. He drew in a breath, nodded.

You didn't draw a blade unless you meant to kill. And Regina didn't mean to kill. Not ever.

They hurried to the stair.

***

Brutus swung the door open with a creak, revealing a cramped interior apartment with a low bed. A narrow window let in what little, dim light had been trapped in the tiny crack of space between this insula and the one across. Below the window, against the wall, sat a man with graying hair cut in the Syrian fashion, his face crumpled into a nest of wrinkles and deathly pale, one of his eyes milky. He held a girl of maybe nine winters on his lap, a gnarled hand over her mouth, a cold blade across her throat. Her eyes were wide with terror; his own were red from weeping, his cheeks damp.

"You're not the dead." His voice creaked like the door. "You're living."

"Put down the knife, father," Regina said. She put a hand to Brutus' chest, and he stood still, by her side.

"I won't let them have her!" His face twisted in anguish, his voice lifting— dangerously loud, with those corpses no more than a street or two away. "Do you hear me! I won't. Get back." He dug in a little with the knife, and a little blood welled around the edge. The girl shook with sobs that were eerily silent.

A great pit opened beneath Regina's heart. She understood. This man was no slaver and no purchaser of slaves. The girl was his daughter, a child born to him late in life. She could see this in his eyes, clearly as another might see the shape of the man's face or the cut of his clothes.

"You don't have to do this," she said softly, crouching so that their eyes were the same height. "I promise, if you let her go, I will keep her safe."

"Promises." The man's voice sharp and bitter as the knife. The trembling of his child. "All my life, these promises. Give me this coin, I'll heal your brother's fever. Come to Rome, they'll be work. Kiss me, I will never leave you. *Promises.* To Hades with your promises. You can all rot, for all I care. Rome can rot. But they won't have my child, my only one. I keep *my* promises, I do. With cold steel, I keep them."

Regina spoke quietly in Aramaic. *"I am of the Brothers and the Sisters of the Fish. You must know of the gathering in Antioch. Whatever you have heard about us, you must know that we keep our word. That we speak no untruth, though we die."* A little guilt twisted in her belly. She *had* spoken untruths. Necessary ones.

He looked at her in shock, to hear his own language, not the hard march-step of Latin but a language that whispered and gusted like the wind in the hills of their birthland. He responded in kind, some of the edge gone from his voice. *"You're from the old land."*

"Yes."

"I can't." Fresh tears. *"I can't let them have her. All the gods forgive me, I can't."*

His knife hand shook. There was a little more blood, dark and slick. The girl let out a tiny, whimpered sound under his hand. A sound that tore at Regina's heart. *"You let her go,"* she cried. *"This is* not *how you protect her!"* In horror, she realized she might not be able to save this child. Not if she couildn't reach through this man's madness and grief. Brutus and Brigitte both looked on, their eyes tense. Brutus' hand at his blade.

Regina pressed her hands together as though praying to the Roman gods. And in her heart she *was* praying, frantically, though to no deities of Rome. Her palms moist with sweat. As the old man's shoulders trembled with his sobs, Regina realized her own face now was wet, her throat tight. "I am Regina Romae," she said, her voice clear and passionate, "and I am anointed mother of the gathering in Rome. And I swear to you, I will not let your child die."

He gazed into her eyes, held by her. By her tears. Perhaps no one had ever wept for him before, or not since he was a small boy. His face opened. With a cry, he took his hand from the girl's mouth and thrust her to her feet, then shoved her toward them roughly. Regina lunged and caught the child, drew her close, felt her trembling. The back of the girl's night-dress was covered in blood.

"Go!" the man said. "Take her. Don't let her see."

Regina heard Brutus curse. To her horror, she saw where the tunic had been torn loose from the man's belly, and where beneath it the skin had been torn open, a wound made by reaching, grasping, *digging* fingers. It had been hidden by the girl's body. That was why the man had been so pale. Now the blood pulsed freely onto the man's lap and thighs. He lifted the knife, pointed its tip toward his heart.

"Papa!" the girl cried.

"I can help you," Regina whispered. "I know a doctor, back at the Safe House. I can help you."

"Wound is mortal." The man's teeth clenched. "Now get out. Don't you hear the dead? I don't want to be here when they come, and neither do you. And I don't want her to see where I go. So get out. And you keep your promise, woman of my homeland. You keep it. You be the first woman in my life who has."

She glanced away from the wild desperation in his eyes. She handed the girl to Brigitte. The girl kicked her legs, cried for her Papa.

"Get her out of here," Regina said. "Brutus, go with her. I'll be right behind."

"I haven't left your side in two weeks, Mother, and I'm not going to now," Brutus said quietly.

Brigitte cast an anxious glance at him.

Regina shook her head. "Wait for us at the door, Brigitte."

"What are you doing?" the man rasped.

"Staying with you," Regina said, crouching, "man of my homeland."

The man's lip trembled. He watched over her shoulder as Brigitte lumbered from the room, then the corner of his lip twitched upward in a caricature of a smile. "Your kindness unmans me," he whispered, "and I hope you prove true to it, 'Mother.' But I'm not one to let you watch me die while the dead close in nearer and nearer my child. Be good to her. The gods be with you." And as suddenly as a scream, and before Regina could stop him or speak, he drove the blade into his own breast. He jerked once, then went still.

READ *BY A SLENDER THREAD*
IN 2017

———————

FOLLOW THE AUTHOR
AT WWW.PATREON.COM/STANTLITORE

ABOUT THE AUTHOR

STANT LITORE doesn't consider his writing a vocation; he considers it an act of survival. As a youth, he witnessed the 1992 outbreak in the rural Pacific Northwest firsthand, as he glanced up from the feeding bins one dawn to see four dead staggering toward him across the pasture, dark shapes in the morning fog. With little time to think or react, he took a machete from the barn wall and hurried to defend his father's livestock; the experience left him shaken. After that, community was never an easy thing for him. The country people he grew up with looked askance at his later choice of college degree and his eventual graduate research on the history of humanity's encounters with the undead, and the citizens of his college community were sometimes uneasy at the machete and rosary he carried with him at all times, and at his grim look. He did not laugh much, though on those occasions when he did the laughter came from him in wild guffaws that seemed likely to break him apart. As he became book-learned, to his own surprise he found an intense love of ancient languages, a fierce admiration for his ancestors, and a deepening religious bent. On weekends, he went rock-climbing in the cliffs without rope or harness, his fingers clinging to the mountain, in a furious need to accustom himself to the nearness of death and teach his body to meet it. A rainstorm took him once on the cliffs and he slid thirty-five feet and hit a ledge without breaking a single bone, and concluded that he was either blessed or reserved in particular for a fate far worse. He married a girl his parents considered a heathen woman, but whose eyes made him smile. She persuaded him to come down from the cliffs, and he persuaded her to wear a small covenant ring on her hand, spending what coin he had to make it one that would shine in starlight and whisper to her heart how much he prized her. Desiring to live in a place with fewer trees (though he misses the forested slopes of his youth), a place where you can scan the horizon for miles and see what is coming for you while it is still well away, he settled in Colorado with his wife and two daughters, and they live there now. The mountains nearby call to him with promises of refuge. Driven again and again to history with an intensity that burns his mind, he corresponds in his thick script for several hours each evening with scholars and archaeologists and even a few national leaders or thugs wearing national leaders' clothes who hoard bits of forgotten past in far countries. He tells stories of his spiritual ancestors to any who will come by to listen, and he labors to set those stories to paper. Sometimes he lies awake beside his sleeping wife and listens in the night for any moan in the hills, but there is only her breathing, soft and full, and a mystery of beauty beside him. He keeps his machete sharp but hopes not to use it.

zombiebible@gmail.com
@thezombiebible
www.stantlitore.com
www.facebook.com/stant.litore

ACKNOWLEDGMENTS

STORIES ARE OUR FIRES lit against the dark; we warm ourselves beside them. A great many people gathered with me to help kindle these stories. My thanks are due, now and always, to my dear friends Ever Saskya, Tim Grade, Roxanne Herbert, and J. R. West for their moral support; to my editors past and present—Andrew Hallam, Jeff Vandermeer, Clarence Haynes, Juliet Ulman, Alex Carr, and Jason Kirk—for their patience, wisdom, and red pens; to the many, many writers who advised me or comforted me or challenged me over the years it took to write these five volumes; to all the fans who wrote me letters or emails to tell me how much these stories meant to them; to my Patreon members, who helped fund the newer, independent release of the series (including this book you hold in your hands); to Roberto Calas for his cover design and to Lauren K. Cannon for her beautiful cover art that brought my characters to life; and, most especially, to my wife Jessica and my daughters River and Inara, without whose love and laughter none of these books would ever be written. May all of you find some warmth in these pages; I am so grateful to you all. Εἰρήνη ὑμῖν.